The Concerned Father's Club

By Que Kelley

Acknowledgements:

I happily dedicate this manuscript to my patient and understanding wife, Shavon, and my three sons, who I love greatly. May God always *bless*, *guide*, and *keep* us *all* under his amazing grace and mercy.

Repay no one evil for evil, but give thought to do what is honorable in the sight of all. If possible, so far as it depends on you, live peaceably with all. Beloved, never avenge yourselves, but leave it to the wrath of God, for it is written, "Vengeance is mine, I will repay, says the Lord." To the contrary, "if your enemy is hungry, feed him; if he is thirsty, give him something to drink; for by so doing you will heap burning coals on his head." Do not be overcome by evil, but overcome evil with good.
—Romans 12:17-21

"If an injury has to be done to a man it should be so severe that his vengeance need not be feared"
—Niccolo Machiavelli

An eye for eye only ends up making the whole world blind.
— Mahatma Gandhi

If you prick us do we not bleed? If you tickle us do we not laugh? If you poison us do we not die? And if you wrong us shall we not revenge?
—William Shakespeare

"Only a fool would fight the rain."
—Que Kelley

The Concerned Father's Club

By: Que Kelley

PROLOGUE:

Present day…

Somewhere at an undisclosed private estate, quietly sits a middle-aged man in a plush half lit room in a deep train of thought. The office where the man usually conducted his business seemed a bit colder than usual to him these days. An overwhelming sensation of dread flowed over his brain, like the cascading rush of a pack of angry bulls, contemplating what was next to come. Under different circumstances, the gentleman would not have had any lingering feelings of remorse, or a sense of responsibility for his or anyone else's actions regarding his business. After spending many years building his powerful empire through all means of intimidations, bribes, extortions, and blackmail, none of that paled in comparison to his current state of mind, or brought him a comforting thought. Maybe, just maybe, he went too far this time, the man pondered. After all, how much was too much, in regards to attaining all the money and power one man could ever want, and at what cost? How much blood must be shed, or on a man's hands for him to say enough was enough? This self made man and proud owner of a broken soul, amassed substantial amounts of both, but at a cost he was not prepared to pay. The gentleman knew that his latest scheme had the chance of imploding in his face, like a cannonball barreling through an old castle wall. For the very first time of his long and dangerous life, the man felt a sense of responsibility for his past actions. He regretted how some of those actions led to the deadly consequences of both his family and other undeserving families. It was time for him to really do something meaningful for someone other than himself, he thought. No more of him standing around behind a desk and barking at underlings, assistants, whores, mongrels, etc…he has got to correct his mistakes "once and for all." He rationalized.

As the troubled man's eyes peered through his sizable, but alluring office window, his pre-occupied mind barely even notices the rain that has picked up steam outside. The raindrops slam up against his window pane, as if they were like wandering woodpeckers rapping against the glass, and from the background came a faint knock from his office door. The brooding man broke his daze long enough to answer as if annoyed, "Not NOW Oscar…" The man said ferociously. There was a pause at the door. "But, sir…" A voice at the door began. "I don't want to be disturbed right now!" He commanded once more from his gigantic desk. "Yes, I know that, sir…but you did ASK me to alert you once "HE" arrived!" The voice from the door said. "Come in..." The man said painstakingly from his chair. "Thank you, sir." The voice at the door said. Finally, the door slowly crept open to reveal a man's head as he stuck it inside to see if the coast was clear. He then waited for his approval before he made his first step, "I'm sorry Oscar, I'm just tired…bring them here." The man at the desk said. A looming dark figure in a black suit entered the room, "Here are the files you requested me to appropriate, sir." Oscar said, "Uh, do you want me to…" But before the person named Oscar could finish his question, he is halted by a wounded "No." The brooding man said. "Harlan, about this…plan…of yours…" Oscar asked, before his employer's fierce gaze caused him to stop talking mid sentence, "Okay, if THIS is what you REALLY want, sir." Oscar swallowed. Oscar then quickly fled the room and gently closed the door behind him.

Harlan sat there quietly to allow his private thoughts to digest. The folders his assistant "Oscar" brought him were his one shot at salvation. It was the final piece to a five thousand piece puzzle, the "Pandora's box," he was more than willing to reopen. He knew that once he reached out to the men in the allotted files that it would signal the beginning of the end to his own life, but he feared loose ends more than he feared his own death. Lives have been stolen that were not meant to be and it was after all, in his mind, a fair trade. An eye for an eye is what they used to say back in his day.

The rain started to pour down even harder outside, banging diligently against the glass as if it were under attack from a hundred angry Apache spears. Thunder severely pounded the evening sky so loudly that one might assume it was the rapture of Jesus Christ. Harlan removed his smudged eyeglasses and rubbed his exhausted eyes violently, as though they were on fire, while pondering in silence his next course of action. What he would ask of these men may condemn them all to hell or, possibly get them killed, but the trade off would be well worth the risks, Harlan concurred. No longer was it a question of what these distraught men had to live for anymore, but what did any of them have left to lose? He wondered. Their lives were pretty much done for the very minute the price of doing his business became involved, Harlan concluded. They would ask him questions, but he would only offer answers when the time was appropriate and besides, it made no sense in passing out the dessert before serving the main course, Harlan fiendishly agreed. Harlan reached for his stereo remote control; clicked on the play button, and music instantly filled the Venetian decorated room. It was the sound of Mozart: "Piano Concerto No. 21." It was one of his mother's favorites. His mother Agatha loved classical music, so it was only fitting that she made him take it up. However, playing for the New York symphony orchestra never panned out for him. Orchestrating organized crime seemed more fascinating to him anyway and he eventually took up importing as his "career choice." Since the beginning of his time as an independent importer, Harlan harnessed the fine art of profit making and mastered moving other people's "goods." Nothing pleased him more than the power that his money and influence brought him. While he always enjoyed the quiet comfort of being the somewhat, "man behind the music," it was FAR past time that he finally faced some, Harlan believed. Innocent lives have been lost that "he" was indirectly responsible for taking and he believed that there was only one way he could provide the justice they never received. In doing so, lines will need to be crossed and their sins will need to be paid for. Harlan knew that the only way that the wages of sin get atoned for is with a fountain of blood. They will use their prey's dead bones as their pound of flesh they use to barter with God to take their souls up to heaven. Harlan reaches for his cell phone and dials with a curious smile on his face. Perhaps it is due to the joy of a new beginning that he does so, or quite frankly the relief to a new end. Either way, a reckoning is coming and it will be moving with the same exacting and vengeful swiftness of a mighty wave like from Exodus. Harlan will do what he does best and will do everything in his power to make good on the things he made go wrong. This will be his final grand symphony, and within their chaos, he will create his finest and deadliest orchestra…

* * * * * * *

Chapter 1:

Jovan "Big Camp" Campbell

Downtown Houston, Texas: A few years ago....

Like clockwork, from Monday through Friday, most drivers in the city usually wasted the first part of their mornings "car fencing" through the unforgivable traffic to get to their various destinations amongst the looming shadows of the three-hundred, or so high rise buildings located downtown. Every pedestrian starting off each of their aggravating work day, forcing one another to endure the constant lane jumping from the few slackers who have apparently hit the snooze button one time too many. Not to mention, enduring unexpected road construction, along with unforgivable waiting periods while police sorted out vehicular accidents that usually lead to some elephant sized migraines for most. The city's Metro buses hogged most of the rugged driving lanes, and if you drove to close too one, the greater the chance of you being "pan-caked" on some putrid curve. Since last hosting Super Bowl XXXVIII back in 2004, majority of the city's landscaping endured a drastic do- over to compensate the massive spectacle, all the while, leaving some hopeful of adding yet another sports stadium to occupy the already crowded city. Houston's downtown area was already home to the Houston Rockets and Houston Astros respectively, and would eventually become home to the universally loved Houston Dynamo as well. Due to the city's growing notoriety, from both a sports and nightlife standpoint, the surrounding communities had to become a reflection of Houston's flourishing prosperity. New shiny condominiums and homes were being erected around the surrounding area for those who could afford it, or who just wanted to be a part of the party ambience.

During the business week though, the vast vagrant population usually campaigned for change and food scraps on each corner, despite being greeted by the working class citizens with a writhing humidity that rivaled the untamed Houston weather. Since 2005 a great number of the city's homeless had been comprised of displaced Hurricane Katrina evacuees, who were still without a place to live and no place to go. Saturday afternoons, on the other hand, was where the contrast often lied. Although the languishing weather remained unchanged (often feeling as if God had exhaled his morning breath onto you) the Saturday afternoon traffic had been pretty much non-existent. Even though homelessness was both rampant and commonplace in the streets of downtown Houston, vagrancy was not appreciated much by the police, especially during games and concerts. While the night scene may have been the envy of the entire state, the daytime was clearly reserved for those with families. In downtown Houston, there were no shortages of affordable eateries for any decent family looking for a delectable southern meal, or a simple change of scenery. One family in particular could not have expected the life altering events that were awaiting them around the corner though, after arriving at a local downtown McDonald's fast food restaurant.....

"Kay' baby, who's the best daddy in the world?" Jovan Campbell asked his now three- year- old daughter Latavia, "You are daddy!!!" She responded gleefully. The sound of her gentle sweet little voice was like soothing music to his ears, "So where's daddy sugar?" Jovan asked pouted. His daughter was sitting down and trying to enjoy her food, "D-a-a-a-d-d-y…I gave you SUGAR already!!!" Latavia groaned. Jovan laughed uncontrollably inside the usually stoic McDonald's, where many friends and family were gathered to celebrate his daughter Latavia's third birthday. It still amazed him, that even till this day, his only daughter hated being kissed or hugged on. When it came to giving out affection, young Latavia had been wonderfully stubborn her entire short life, which was a trend he had prayed would continue well into her "40's." Although he kept it far into the back of his mind, Jovan fretted the day when she would become a full grown woman and invite some "fool" over for him to meet and probably could never appreciate her enough in his eyes. He also realized that that "harsh reality" was yet still very, VERY far away, at least far enough away for him to stock up on enough gun ammunition, Jovan figured. Jovan took pride in never allowing the possible future to dictate what was happening around him in the present. Everyone who had seen him play saw in him the same potential to play professional football like his father once had, but ever since Latavia came into his life the only thing Jovan Campbell sees when looking into a mirror was her dad. When he kneeled down to hug her, Latavia stared at her youthful father's giant hands with the same hesitancy of a mailman worrying about a vicious dog in yard, "Oka-a-ay!" Latavia said defeated. Latavia got down out of her chair stuck out her dainty little arms and whipped her head to the side, as if she were bracing herself for a shot at the doctor's office. Jovan gave her a big loud kiss on her cotton ball like cheek. Regardless, of her resenting open affection, young Latavia still loved her father greatly. Suddenly Jovan could hear someone trying to clear their voice as if they were about to make a public address to the nation, "And what about your momma, girl?" a voice bellowed from behind him. He knew who the voice belonged to without even bothering to look back, "As usual….You're late Tasha." Jovan said dryly, looking down at his new Fossil watch. Little Latavia opened her squinted eyes and screamed happily, "Mommy!!!" His daughter nearly knocked him over despite him being six-two and weighing two hundred and forty- five pounds. Tasha Greenwood, who was not much taller than her young daughter, squeezed the diminutive Latavia and managed to sneak a quick kiss on her cheek, "No kisses!" Latavia squealed, and swiped off her face. Tasha could only shake her head at her cute little vanilla colored princess after putting her back down. It was clear to Tasha that Jovan was in his feelings and also tried to ignore her for being late to the party, "Why don't you turn yo' big butt around, SO I can tell you WHY I'm late, boy!" Tasha demanded. Contrary to her height and size, the sawed-off Tasha Greenwood was not only attractive and intelligent, but also highly volatile when she needed to be. Despite her high skin tone and model like features, it was no secret that she took no shit off her superstar "baby-daddy," which was a virtue he greatly admired. He could never put a finger on it, but something about her country tone always seemed to cause a spark in him, like the unsuspecting sensation one gets from drinking a glass of zesty flavored wine too fast. His ego would never allow him to tell her how much he got off on pushing his proud girlfriend's buttons and constantly fighting the urge to keep things quiet between them, "Well?" Tasha asked, with her hands on her hips. He responded by shrugging his shoulders nonchalantly, but then took a deep breath anyway, as if he was about to prepare for a high dive into a swimming pool and turned to face her, "I'm listening?" Jovan said discerningly. If there was one thing Jovan Campbell knew about his child's mother, was that she did not mind getting "ignorant" in any public place, "BOY, I sent you a text explainin' that I couldn't leave my post until I was properly relieved and my co-worker, Jonathan, had a flat tire on his way to work. Did you even bother checkin' your damn cell?" Tasha asked emphatically. She knew how single minded Jovan could be at times and waited eagerly to hear his response, "Yo, why you always got to be so loud? A-a-and…yeah, yeah I checked it!" Jovan said stuttering. The "other" thing he also knew about Tasha Greenwood was that she was not anyone's fool. Tasha reached out to give him a fake hug, but instead cleverly snatched his cell phone off his hip, after he raised his arms high enough. Her tactic caught him by surprise, "Say girl!? What'chu doi…" He protested. Tasha went through Jovan's cell phone call log and felt a large sense of gratification after what she had found, "Just what I thought…you ain't checked shit!" Tasha yelled with satisfaction. Jovan's mother Patricia Campbell was sitting nearby and could not help herself from chuckling in the background while her son was digging a massive hole for himself, "Boy, I'm glad you don't play football the same way your ass lie!" Patricia joked, while shaking her head. Jovan scrunched up his face, "Come on momma…" Jovan pouted. He knew he was not being completely honest, and felt a tad bit embarrassed after trying to put his girlfriend on the spot in front of the family. Deep down he knew she would have had a good excuse for not being at their baby's birthday party, especially after being the one who booked it in the first place, Jovan thought. Although the young collegian had been in love with her from the first day they met, his pride was still as strong as rebar encased in concrete, "Nah man, I-I did check it….I-I jus (Jovan snatched his cell phone back from her hands and paused)…alright, maybe I didn't check my cell… But, yo' lil' ass still could've called! Damn man, you got Indian in your family don't you? You could have blown a nigga' a smoke signal, or suthin!?" Jovan shouted. Tasha stood silently for a brief moment and simply shook her head in disapproval of him, "O-o-o-o, you lucky I love yo' big ass, or I'd just pistol whip yo' big butt, all "up" in this Mickie D's!" Tasha quipped. The way Tasha

Greenwood and Jovan Campbell portrayed themselves (often in public) could have easily been mistaken as a "War of the Roses" type relationship. But, this simply was just not the case. Even though the young couple never married, their passion for one another was only rivaled by their tendency to get on each other's nerves. Petite Tasha Greenwood had always been a feisty smart young black woman that came from a family of modest means. She was the youngest of her two meddling sisters, Latonya (the oldest) and Teresa, and the only one of them with a child out of wedlock. Regardless, of her sisters looking down on her for that minor transgression, Tasha's mother, Georgia Mae Greenwood, gave her all the support she ever needed. Tasha looked up to her proud mother, who she watched raise three bad ass kids on her own, while holding down two full-time jobs. Despite their surroundings as children, Georgia Greenwood never allowed her family to hurt for anything. Living in a somewhat poor neighborhood came with some disadvantages and Georgia often found herself at odds against degenerate hustlers, crooks, and pimps just to keep her daughters virtue clean and minds educated. Jovan and Tasha were each other's first love. Most would agree that those days were much quieter back then. Unfortunately Tasha had gotten pregnant with Latavia while she was still a teen in high school, but despite the momentary setback, Tasha garnered enough courage to return to school and still managed to graduate on time. Tasha eventually got a job working as a security guard at Sharpstown Mall and took online courses to earn herself a degree in business management. All-American pro prospect Jovan Campbell on the other hand, had different plans. Jovan had been a standout middle linebacker back since high school and earned himself an athletic football scholarship to University of Houston. Jovan had become a once in a generation phenom at his position and had been receiving national attention since his freshman and sophomore years. It had long been Jovan's hope and dream to one day get drafted to the NFL, and maybe play for the Rams like his dad, LJ, once did. Unfortunately, his father was not good enough to get drafted due to infrequent injuries and substance abuse questions. One of the main rumors around town was that Jovan's father had been a superb athlete and drug addict, who on one tragic night, stole drugs from the wrong drug dealer and was found shot dead at some motel up in California. Jovan worked diligently to escape the sordid stains left from his notorious father's shame filled shadow. He did not allow himself to envision living life as precariously as his father once did, and pushed himself every day (until vomiting on most of those days) to separate himself from his father's legacy of infamy. Jovan never partied and spent most his free time running hundred yard wind sprints in the triple digit Texas heat, to the point of his heart feeling combustion. While his friends would head home for the holidays, Jovan stayed on campus torturing his body endlessly with weight training and swimming. Between a hectic class schedule and all of his football training, Jovan still managed to find just enough time to keep a solid relationship with Tasha, with whom he promised to make a better life for one day. In spite of that promise, their bickering had started to wear thin with Jovan's mother Patricia, "Are you two finished?" barked Patricia Campbell. They both immediately stopped talking after hearing the sound of Patricia's elevated tone, "You two REALLY need to get a grip on yourselves! It's your baby's birthday and the both of you acting like bees trapped inside a damn pickle jar without holes on the top of it! You even got these "white folks" looking at us crazy!" Patricia whispered. During their heated exchange, neither of them bothered to notice the odd silence their quarrelling was causing. They began apologizing to their family members and the surrounding customers inside the McDonald's restaurant. After things died down between them, Jovan started to go on another rant, "It wasn't me anyway, it's her crazy ass, always popping off at me…. always got to get the last word…" Jovan professed. Patricia ran her hands through her hair to compose herself, "Child…" Patricia interrupted, and stood to her feet. In fear of aggravating his mother any further, Jovan decided to yield, "Okay, momma, dang! You ain't gotta' go all Ester Rolle on a nigga…" Jovan quietly submitted. Tasha stuck her tongue out at him and grinned sadistically until her mother Georgia caught her and popped her on the back of her hand from her seat, "Ow…momma?" Tasha winced, and rubbed her sore hand. Latavia was watching and giggling at her parent's immature antics from afar in the arms of her aunt Latonya, who was Tasha's oldest sister. Georgia did not need to speak, as her eye squinting and disapproving finger was always enough to get her daughter's attention, "Okay!" Tasha said. Jovan considered his mother's plea and decided to make things up to his impressionable daughter, "Come here La La..." Jovan said sullenly. Jovan took a seat and put Latavia on his lap and deeply sighed, "Look baby, all daddy just wanna say is… is that your momma is really, REALLY sorry about fussing at daddy on your birthd…!"

Jovan playfully began. He noticed out the corner of his eye that Tasha was staring at him while patting her pistol. Jovan mumbled under his breath and shook his head, "Ahem, what daddy really MEANT was…we are BOTH (looking at Tasha for her approval) both sorry, for fighting on your birthday." Jovan confessed. Latavia then put both her little soft hands on his cheeks and looked him directly into his face, "Daddy, I know you got issues!" Latavia said matter-of-factly. Everyone in hearing distance laughed hysterically. Jovan was caught by surprise at her candor, "I got is….where'd you hear that!?" Jovan asked frantically. Latavia pointed her finger at her mother Tasha, who quickly found a seat and drink next to Georgia and who also was conveniently staring out the window, "Momma!!!" Latavia said modestly. Tasha bit into a hamburger that she did not seem to possess a second ago, and continued pretend as if she were not aware of Jovan and Latavia's conversation. Jovan could not find fault in his disgustingly adorable daughter's honesty and could not help himself from laughing out loud. After their moment ended, a McDonald's worker waved to him in the background to signal that the play ground was finished being set up. In the play area, where they were keeping the birthday gifts, looked like a scene out of "A Miracle on 34th Street," Jovan thought. Jovan felt blessed to be surrounded by so many loving faces, and vowed to return the love as soon as he got selected in next year's NFL draft. He picked up his daughter and asked everyone to follow him into the playing area to gather together to sing to her happy birthday. When they all finished singing, everyone surrounded her with plenty of loving hand claps, "Now, are you ready to see what daddy got you?" Jovan asked excitedly. Latavia sprang to her feet like a bouncing baby kangaroo, "Yes, daddy!!!" Latavia screamed ecstatically. They walked hand and hand toward the mountainous pile of endless birthday presents, "Here you go baby girl…open it and see what daddy got for you." Jovan asked, and turned toward his smiling proud mother Patricia. Leave it up to little Patricia Campbell to straighten out big ole' Jovan Campbell, which was not an easy feat considering she done it all on her own. She could only sigh as she gazed at the man-child who nearly ate her out of house and home, but could also had the incredible knack for knocking a quarterback's lights completely out. Patricia felt so much amazement as she looked upon her almost fully grown son who had reminded her so her late husband LJ. Besides her son's height they shared the same Campbell handsome chiseled good looks: broad shoulders, thick legs and more muscles sprouting out of their arms and chest like carrots standing out in a garden patch. She often wondered what her long deceased love would have to say about their superstar son. It also really saddened her that LJ could not be alive to see his only grandchild, but no one else worked harder at trying to keep that man together than she ever did, Patricia painfully recollected.

<u>The quick rise and fall of LJ Campbell</u>

Unsurprisingly for Patricia though, handling her late husband's escapades during the 90's did not come as easy to her, as playing linebacker came to her gifted son Jovan in the 2000's. The talented London Jermelle Campbell, or "LJ" that he preferred to be called by, had played the role of both the saint and the sinner. Both he and Patricia were high school sweethearts, very much like their son Jovan and Tasha were. There was no mistaking from where Jovan's incredible gift for athletics came from, as London himself was a former all-around standout athlete at Jackson McKinley High. While LJ's immaculate reputation among his teachers went unblemished as an honor roll student, the same could not be said for his promiscuous nature around the ladies. Patricia was not scared off by all the accusations that LJ was labeled, by most of the girls at school, as an undercover weed smoking whore. Despite hearing all the wild rumors and innuendos, Patricia still took a huge gamble with her heart, and gladly gave it to LJ. Though the longer they went on dating, the more writing would go up on the girl's bathroom walls about his dick size, or about whom he fucked on the days he skipped school. She still remembered enduring all the various headaches and crying nights over the suspected abortions his football coaches helped him hide during high school. But LJ convinced her that they were all telling lies and promised her that she was the "only one he ever loved," and by her senior year their relationship appeared to have gotten reasonably better. He stopped giving her any more reasons not to trust him and she was elated after he accepted a full football scholarship to Texas Southern University, while Patricia graduated summa cum Laude and received an academic scholarship to the same university. She was starting to see growth in his maturity and believed his high school antics were simply a passing fad, but little did she realize that it would only be the tip of the iceberg. Their freshmen year went by without incident and by the start of their sophomore year LJ was finally the starting tailback for the football team. Spending time together was beginning to become increasingly difficult between all LJ's football practices, games, and classes, as well as Patricia's own commitments. During each passing semester, they were starting to grow more and more apart and it did not take long for gossip to start up. There was even a rumor his position coach helped pay for another abortion, but LJ denied it of course. LJ partied hard and studied even less. Back in high school, marijuana was his drug of choice, but soon found a new love in snorting cocaine. It was not long that she would begin catching him red-handed in his dorm room strung out with other naked women, sometimes more than one. Patricia shuddered at the memory of both the emotional and physical abuse she endured as LJ struggled through his many mood swings, alcoholism, infidelities, and lies. But regardless of what he put her through, LJ always found a way to get back into her good graces. The young couple had many ups and downs, but things had really made a bad turn for the worst during their junior year. The incident occurred during the university's Homecoming game and LJ Campbell was having the game of his life. An opposing player dove at his leg just as LJ reached out to score his fifth touchdown. LJ made the six points at the high cost of blowing out three knee ligaments and crippling any chances of getting selected to play professionally. After losing the rest of his football season due to that terrible injury, LJ's drug dependency had become much worse. The combination of taking too many pain killers and many cocaine binges started to warp his mental sensibilities to think rationally. He had also become highly distrustful of everyone, including Patricia, and his paranoia caused him to get suspended from the team. Through it all, Patricia never gave up hope for him, nor did his coaches. When their senior year arrived, LJ's drug habit had seemed more like an aberration of the past and was a new man. LJ was no longer skipping his classes, and both he and Patricia had gotten to a better place in their on-again and off-again relationship. He even proposed to her prior to that following year's NFL draft. LJ pledged to finally do right by her and vowed to buy them the biggest house his first contract could afford. The ring he gave her was bought with money given to him under the table from by a former alumnus of the school, who was exuberantly happy about him scoring those five touchdowns against their rival during that frightful Homecoming game. Even till this day, did Patricia find difficulty in looking down at the radiant heart shaped 1-carat engagement ring. Regrettably, it would end up being the only meaningful piece of real jewelry he would ever be able to buy for her, only costing him a knee to get it, LJ sometimes said. Amazing as that moment felt, it turned out to be both the best and saddest days of her young life. LJ's knee was never quite the same, but he continued to play hard afterwards. When the NFL draft came, LJ waited what felt like an eternity for him to get a single phone call from a team, but one never came. The entire draft was over and that brought LJ to tears. This was the first time Patricia had ever seen him cry and she remembered feeling as helpless as a lost child marooned on a deserted island. Football was not her world, but it certainly was LJ's. Despite not getting selected through the draft, LJ did manage to get some tryouts during the pre-seasons and was always travelling. They eventually got married and he worked part-time as a warehouse selector to help her pay on the small apartment they shared on the southeast side of town. LJ had been clean for a little while, until that fateful year when he had to fly to Los Angeles for a game. It was his first big break and the team had numerous injuries at their tailback position. LJ was having the best camp he ever had professionally and was ultimately called on to be the team's starter. Patricia had a relative who lived on the West Coast that LJ was often staying with, and unfortunately who was the first person who brought her the news of LJ's death. He had been apparently celebrating his promotion on the team at a rink-a-dink-night club, and later on that night, left the club with a small group of people he did not even know. Apparently, LJ had partied hard that night with some local drug dealers who slipped a Mickey into his drink, then severely beat and robbed him at gun point. A woman LJ left the club with turned out to be a prostitute, which did not really surprise Patricia when she was told. What did surprise her was the news that the prostitute's throat was so severely torn open that it was barely left attached to the body. LJ's fingers were also cut off on one hand and suffered many gunshot wounds to his face at close range. Hearing the news of her husband's murder left her devastated, as LJ never lived long enough for her to tell him that she had become being pregnant with Jovan.

Latavia's birthday party….

Jovan began to worry about his mother Patricia, who he caught wiping tears from her eyes. He could always tell when his mother's mind was someplace else or, thinking about his father, "Momma? You ok?" Jovan asked softly. Patricia had been so caught up by the thought of her hurt filled past that she jumped at the sound of her son's voice, "Oh!?! Oh, yeah baby. Momma was just, I-I was just thinking, baby…I just wished your daddy was still around to see you, and his grandbaby, that's all. I know I probably haven't told you enough of how proud I am of you, and Tasha too." Patricia said pleased. Tasha was surprised to hear such flattery when she came and sat down near them. Tasha never fully understood where she and Jovan's mother stood at times, but she highly respected her nevertheless. Jovan told her that his mom "just wanted what was best for him" and that "some women would try to get pregnant by him," because he was so great at football, Tasha recollected. Patricia reached out and took them both by the hand, "When I look at the two of you together… it just brings back memories of me and your father. He would be so proud of how you turned out, Jovan. Not only about all the football stuff you doing baby, but with you being there for your daughter, and taking care of your responsibilities. That shows great character son." Patricia said proudly. Jovan gazed at his mother as if she had shot him in the forehead by a pellet gun. He was not used to receiving many accolades from his mother, who often tried to keep his head from swelling up by challenging him to "always do better." But, it was public knowledge how Patricia Campbell notoriously rode his ass like a pinecone stuck to a wood peckers ass, "Well… I had a great teacher." He replied. Patricia and Jovan embraced each other as if he was flying off to some unknown planet far, far away. Not wanting to be left out of the fold, little Latavia ran up to join in the private hugging session. They all go on to enjoy the sweets of the day, clearly unaware of the unfathomable events yet to come. Unimaginable events that would create an enormous crater into the hearts and souls of any caring parent alive…

Across town: The freeway…

…The Houston police department is heavily engaged in a deadly police chase that shortly began on the southwest side of town, leaving a flurry of demolished automobiles in their wake alongside the freeway. At least twenty police units are in hot pursuit of the bold assailants, while they unleash carnage in the city streets. During their kamikaze like race it was revealed over the police blotter that three fugitives dressed as window washers, robbed a Bank of America and have already killed twelve innocent bystanders in the process, while wounding four others. It turned out to be a botched robbery, after one of the perpetrators managed to get shot by one of the bank's security guards. The three men on the run are gang members Eddie "EJ" Jones, Taleek "Lil Leek" Wilson, and Jacory "Big Cory" Jackson, all of which, have been frequent residents of the Houston downtown judicial system. Eddie Jones had always been slight in build, but despite his skinny disposition, was known around his neighborhood as being both intolerably ignorant and highly trigger happy. Like any other hoodlum from the street, Eddie grew up dirt poor and rough on Houston's north side, and with those painful experiences, helped him harness the ability to bring misery to others. His mother Adina Bartee, who was a local prostitute on welfare with eight children, never finished high school. Their family, all eight brothers and sisters, lived in a two bedroom shack deep in the crevices of Houston's hardnosed 5th Ward area. While he was growing up, EJ was forced to share a bed with some of his younger brothers and sisters who had not been potty trained and were susceptible to bed wetting. They faithfully pissed the bed so much that the smell saturated the walls of the house, which was not very hard to do, considering it was never clean to begin with. Their floors stayed littered with dirty clothing, used diapers, empty soda cans, and any other imaginable thing possible. Eddie's mother barely could afford cab fare to the local laundry mat, so she often had to clean their clothes outside in an old aluminum tub. The walls inside the home were all cracked and busted open as if it had been hit by an earthquake. There was never any money for new clothing for school either, and so the children had no choice but to rummage through their neighbors heavy haul boxes for what they needed. When she hooked on the streets, Adina occasionally got arrested and sometimes would get extorted out of her money by wannabe pimps, or even the police, after they caught her. Most of the time, Adina could avoid being incarcerated by offering a free fuck or, giving them a courtesy blowjob. She was willing to do whatever it took to keep from going to jail. Seemed like every other night, Eddie was at his mother's mercy when she would stumble through the front door reeking of alcohol, cigarette smoke, and funky sex. Her lipstick would be smeared across her sweaty dark toned face as if she were a stand-in for the Joker in a Batman movie. Her clothing, what little she did wear, would be filthy and had clear evidence of dried sperm trails all over her. Eddie could always tell when his mother was high from the perspiration that saturated her swanky semen soaked clothing. Whenever her money ran low, Eddie was the object of her hateful rage, which appeared to be all the time. Because she had to drop out of school to have him, Adina constantly blamed Eddie for her mistakes and would bludgeon him badly with her fists for it. Sometimes he had to miss some time away from school to heal. He eventually got older though, and a lot taller, and when he did, Eddie began hitting back on his mom, as well as the other kids in the neighborhood. By the time he entered junior high school Eddie Jones had already joined his first gang and killed his fair share of innocent children in more than one drive by shooting. Eddie met Taleek on one of his many visits to the juvie hall. Though Taleek was from a different side of town, their circumstances were still similar in some ways. Both Eddie and Taleek grew up stealing cars and sticking people up for their personal belongings and would celebrate by getting totally wasted afterwards. Even though EJ "loved" his liquor, it was not matched by the love Taleek appeared to have for crack cocaine. Taleek would get so high that it would even worry the "never scared" Eddie Jones. It was no secret that they both had it rough as children, but whatever happened in Taleek's past was obviously still troubling him, Eddie figured. And whatever "the IT" was that Taleek was trying to forget, must not have been worth bringing up in the place, so Eddie never bothered to ask, which was alright with him. He knew what hell felt like and the last thing Eddie felt he needed was someone else's shit unloaded on him. Let the truth be told, Eddie Jones knew his parents were not shit either…

The heartbreaking origin of Taleek Wilson

At the current stage of his young life, Taleek Wilson carried an "I don't give a fuck" attitude, about any and everything, but for a very good reason. His white stepdad, Kurt, had been molesting and torturing him ever since his mother had married him. Taleek was just around five or 6 years- old when the molestations began. Brenda, his mother, had always been eerily reluctant to go to Kurt about the allegations Taleek would make against him, which often make things worse on him. It all started out with his stepdad sneaking up into his bed late at night, where he would began rubbing and touching him in places he knew he had "NO" business doing. When Taleek became older, he once tried to contact his uncaring grandfather, but to no avail, and was on the receiving end of a vicious beating from his mother for doing so. On one occasion Kurt caught wind of Taleek's plan to alert his middle school principal, after overhearing him talking about it over the phone with a friend from school. His stepdad did not appreciate being ratted on and decided to withdraw him out of school early one afternoon. He drove his innocent stepson to the back of a secluded park before Taleek could notify his principal of his stepdad's vileness. When his stepfather was convinced that no one else was in the vicinity, he smacked Taleek hard in the face, as if he were a professional tennis player serving off to an opponent at a tennis match, "Is this how you repay me, after taking in your ungrateful little ass?" He yelled. Taleek had been in shock from the amount of force behind Kurt's hand and his mouth had begun to bleed profusely from landing against the car's dashboard. Kurt went into his suit pocket and pulled out an alcohol flask and took a drink from it. "Come over here…and open that goddamned ungrateful mouth of yours!" Kurt demanded angrily. When Taleek hesitated, the grown man punched him in his ribcage, causing Taleek to cry out, "Shut your fucking…ungrateful…mouth, you little black bitch!" Kurt screamed. Taleek was scared to death of his stepdad and believed he was crazy enough to actually kill him if he did not do what he wanted. Kurt was bigger and older than he was, and for all Taleek knew, if he did not do what was asked, Kurt could just kill him and leave his dead body in the woods and claim he just ran away. Taleek had no other choice but to give in to the deranged stepfather's demands. Kurt grabbed Taleek from the back of his little head forcefully to perform oral sex on him. It greatly pleased Kurt that his sinister act was causing young Taleek to cry voraciously as he gagged and partially vomited in his lap from him forcing Taleek's head down over his crotch. After his stepdad climaxed, he then threatened to kill him and his mother if he ever told anyone what happened. It did not matter either way, because Taleek had no one he could turn to. No matter how much he bathed, no matter how much he scrubbed, Taleek could never clean the stench of his evil stepdad's touch all over him.

Taleek's mother, Brenda Fontenot grew up living a very privileged and aristocratic lifestyle. Her father Terrance Fontenot III, was a successful business owner who inherited his dad's glass business, while her alcoholic mother Geraldine Fontenot, was a socialite who was on her third husband. The couple spent most of their nights entertaining other socialites by hosting parties and gatherings. Terrance Fontenot took family stability very seriously and had often invited a who's who of guests to their extravagant home. It was not unusual for Brenda to see the mayor of Houston or prestigious types like U.S. Congressman Sheila Jackson Lee, or the Reverend Jesse Jackson at those events. Brenda's father would make it his business to make sure his gifted daughter was on display, by making her sing or play classical music she learned on the piano. All that came to a screeching halt on the day she met Herman Patrick Wilson. Herman was a scruffy looking, hard working young black man, who was a college student and also worked part-time as a busboy at her father's galas. The two of them had seemingly fallen for one another, but because they came from different backgrounds Brenda's father never approved of their relationship. As a final result, Brenda received an ultimatum, either end their relationship or be cut off from her trust fund. Brenda was accustomed to living a certain lifestyle and could not imagine living a life without having the finer things in life. She claimed she loved Herman, but deep down Brenda did not want to give up her lavish lifestyle. Brenda was not really sure about giving up the spa treatments, the manicures, body messages, grand restaurants, hair salons, shopping sprees at the Galleria Mall, and her own expense account; these were the things that really made her happy most of all. Unfortunately her decision to call off her romance came a week too late. After breaking off the relationship, she found out that she was pregnant with Herman's child. In frustration, Herman left without saying goodbye, never fully saying where he was going. Her father felt ashamed and disgraced by the pregnancy and would frequently verbally abuse her, "What good are you to me now? To us!?! To this family!?! Is this how you fucking repay me after all I've given you?!" He scolded. For days he tormented her throughout their household, screaming and yelling his displeasure to her usually drunken mother. When Brenda's father could no longer live with the idea of her having a child out of wedlock, he put her out on the street to fend for herself. He called the pregnancy an "irreparable and deliberate infraction against his good name."

Due to her own ineptitude for survival, Brenda constantly struggled with her finances to find a good job and support her and Taleek. She went from someone who normally dined at the finest restaurants Houston had to offer, to waiting at the end of the welfare line for her monthly food stamps. Brenda managed to catch a break a month after getting evicted from her trashy one bedroom apartment, when she came across an old acquaintance, Linda Albertson, who she once attended high school with. Linda was not the typical white girl from the valley. She did not "come from money" and spent most of her life around blacks and Brenda even once dubbed Linda the nickname "Ebony Cream." Linda's parents, Ted and Alice, were former 60's hippies and knew a thing or two about oppression. They understood Brenda's plight all too well, as they both came from nothing and knew what it was like to have to struggle in a cold cruel world. It was this very thing that made Brenda's family so well-respected in such a predominately black community. Brenda eventually got a job working with Linda as a cashier at a local Target department store. Though they were more than welcomed to stay, Brenda and Taleek would eventually move out of Linda's house, soon after she met Kurt Kimble. Kurt was a self made millionaire stockbroker and accountant. Despite his meager looks and the fact he was not black, Kurt still lived the type of lifestyle that Brenda starved and yearned for, ever since she got put out on the street by her dad. The both of them had not known each other a full month before they up and married. She had met him while waiting for her bus ride after work one evening, and he pulled over in his new 2001 Jaguar to talk to her. The odd couple only dated for a little while before her and Taleek moved into his lavish three storied home in The Westland's Cove, a gated community property on the Westside of Houston. Ever since he first laid eyes on him, Taleek had been leery of Kurt. When the molestations first began, Taleek tried to warn his mother that Kurt had been touching him while he slept. She rewarded him with spite and pity trips for being forced out the luxury of her father's home after giving birth to him. As long as Kurt continued to make her happy, Brenda chose to ignore Taleek's cries and the molestations would carry on for years. As a teenager though, his behavior at school had changed dramatically. Taleek was acting out in class and repeatedly gotten into fights with both teachers and students. He once put another student in the hospital for calling him a "faggot," by bludgeoning him in the head with a very large history book. When Taleek acted out though, Kurt had his own "special way" of disciplining him. Kurt would wait until they were alone and would drag the young man down into his dark and dank smelling cellar. Once in there, Taleek would endure unimaginable horrors. Taleek had been raped and tortured on a constant basis by Kurt. He suffered so, that on most days it became a chore just for him to sit. Kurt also invited his demented fraternal brother Konnor over to his house and they both would get their kicks out of passing young Taleek around, as if he were the "piece of trash" they claimed him to be. Konnor Kimble was very much like his scraggly looking brother, except he was well-endowed and Kurt was not. He was always the roughest on him physically and sexually. Konnor made it his business to hurt young Taleek, either by humiliating him, drugging him, dressing him as a woman and cursing him savagely during intercourse.

This went on and on until one day, when Kurt was not home, Taleek found a 9 millimeter pistol while rummaging through Kurt's drawer. Instead of finding enough money to finally escape the hell that was his life, Taleek found what he believed was a better way out. Taleek marveled at first sight of the shiny chrome pistol and cautiously took it out the drawer and laid the gun down on the bed. He then realized it was in the same bed his mother shared with his abuser every night. Taleek had reached the lowest point of his own humanity and could not bare living another day as someone else's toilet. No more would he take another day of abuse or the nightmares that made a home in his sleep. He contemplated killing himself in the beginning and started to put the muzzle of the pistol inside his mouth. After all, he thought, who would miss him? Taleek had been worn down from of all of Kurt and his brother's cruelty and his mother's neglect he sustained over the years. They all treated him like shit and it felt terrible always having nowhere to go, or no one to turn to for help, Taleek contemplated. Soon as Taleek finally decided to pull the trigger, he heard Kurt and Brenda coming through the front door downstairs. Kurt had taken Brenda out for her usual weekend splurge. It was her blood money. A payment for letting Kurt do whatever he wanted to him, and for the son she no longer cared about, Taleek thought angrily. Suddenly, Taleek had an epiphany and decided to put his suicidal thoughts on hold, and quietly tipped out the bedroom.

Later on that Saturday evening, Taleek hid Kurt's pistol down in the cellar, in hopes to use it the next time Kurt wanted to "make him pay" again. Taleek had stayed awake the whole night plotting against them. The following Monday, Taleek intentionally started a fight at school by punching out his math teacher, and like clockwork Kurt had been the one notified. Whenever Taleek got suspended from school or detained by area truancy officers, Kurt made sure to invite his brother Konnor over to perform some sick form of corporal punishment. Even though it sickened him to listen, Taleek still managed a satisfactory grin to himself when hearing Kurt bragging to his brother Konnor on his cell phone, about who was going to make Taleek scream the most. Everything was happening according to Taleek's plan. Brenda was not home as usual, when they pulled into the driveway and the two brothers were high fiving themselves gleefully as the three of them made it downstairs into the dark and dank cellar. This was the only time in Taleek's life that he ever looked forward to coming down into the dark cavern. He normally would force his mind to go elsewhere and think about the good things that did make him happy whenever they ravaged him. But that was the past and it was Taleek's turn to finally be the one in control. In the back of his mind, Taleek knew that the both of them could not resist the temptation of playing out their sickest fantasies and believed he could use that temptation against them. As soon as they all made it to the bottom of the cellar, Taleek felt an overriding surge of confidence cascading from deep within him, causing him to boldly lash out, "So what you two bitches ready to do?" Taleek asked defiantly. The Kimble brothers looked at each in stunning fascination and complete confusion, "Don't just stand there breathing over each other, bring it on you two miserable faggots?!" Taleek commanded, while rubbing himself. The brothers searched the other's face to see if what they were being told by the young man was part of their imagination, or fact. Either way, they both were overcome with the same urge of excitement that the other was feeling, unaware of Taleek's hidden intentions to do with the pistol he hid in the chestnut colored desk they normally sexually assaulted him against. Taleek had started to undress and mock them even further, "I know what you motherfuckers really want." Taleek said coyly. He picked up one of the toys they would usually use on him and licked across it as if it were a lollypop. In order to get Kurt and Konnor's guard down, Taleek knew he would have to challenge them by being boastful and unpredictable. Taleek smiled and turned his back to them, pulling down his clothes, unfortunately during the Kimble brother's excitement, they had not noticed Taleek actually bending over to grab the stolen 9 millimeter pistol from Kurt's bedroom drawer. Taleek pointed the glistening pistol at both Kimble brothers, "Neither one of you sick motherfuckers move!" Taleek ordered. Kurt immediately froze in his step, "Where did you find…why you ungrateful little mother…you know, since you DO have it, whatcha' gonna' do with it?" Kurt boasted. Both he and Konnor were inching closer towards Taleek and began patronizing him, "Hey T, everything's cool man! You don't really want to hurt us, now do you? Why don't you just put the gun down? So we can make things, you know, right between us!?!" Konnor asked sinisterly. "Yeah, man…put the gun down before you get yourself hurt, or something! All we ever wanted to do was just love on you…" Kurt said dastardly. Taleek was so disgusted at the very sound of the two lying men's voices, that he started to cry, "I said, don't move motherfucker's…I mean it!" Taleek hollered. But, the two men continued to inch closer and closer, while tormenting the young man in the process, "Yeah, man, that's all we ever wanted to do was try to make you fe-e-e-el good!(Konnor giggled) Just let us bro's work it out with you, put the gun down ma…" Konnor pleaded. When Taleek looked into the soulless eyes of his onetime tormentors, he could see both emptiness and coldness across their evil faces. Taleek knew that he had come too far to turn back now, if he did, God only knew what they would do to him then, Taleek worried. He had never shot a gun before and worried if the safety was still on. When they got close enough they both tried to rush him, but then two loud shots rang out. Kurt hit the ground dead first, while Konnor was busy grabbing his bleeding testicles. His sobs were like that of a newborn child begging for his mother's milk. Taleek picked up one of the wigs Konnor made him wear before and dropped it on Konnor's head, "Who's the bitch now?" Taleek asked, and began smiling.

Brenda got home earlier than usual from all her shopping and spa treatments she normally partook during the day. She barely noticed that both Kurt and Konnor's vehicles were in the driveway after pulling up. As soon as she put her house keys inside the locks, she heard gunfire coming from inside the house. The gunshot startled her enough to cause her to drop her shopping bags. Brenda then hurried herself through the front door and yelled out to her husband, "Kurt? Baby, are you okay? Where are you? Konnor…? Are you guys alright?" Brenda roared through the house. The house was eerily quiet and Brenda felt a shiver race down the small of her back when a voice finally called out to her, "We're all down here…why don't you come join us!" The voice said from the downstairs cellar. Brenda tiptoed her way through the lavish home as if she were a cat burglar prowling up to a large safe. While she stood atop the cellar steps, she peered down into the dark void, forcing herself to deal with her fear and racing heart. Brenda swallowed hard before she called out again, "Kurt what's going on? I thought I heard gunshots!" Brenda asked. After a long pause, the voice from the cellar spoke again, "Everything's cool now mom, we're all here downstairs...waiting on you." Taleek said gleefully. Once Brenda realized the voice from the cellar belonged to her wayward son, she stormed down the steps, cursing him in a fit of agitation. What she saw next caused her body to freeze at the bottom of the cellar steps. She gasped at the sight of both her husband and brother-in-law's motionless and heavily bloodied body lying on the floor. The gun Taleek used to kill both his manic stepfather and his twisted brother with was now pointed at her shocked face. Taleek was wearing a red wig with lipstick smeared over his mouth like a circus clown. Brenda could feel herself going into cardiac arrest while gazing into her son's crazed filled eyes, "Taleek…why?" Brenda asked despondently. Taleek marveled at his mother's audacity to pose such a question and fought the temptation to laugh at her. He always believed his mother had known from the very beginning what Kurt had been doing to him, but instead of confronting Kurt, she chose to sell her soul just to shop at Neiman Markus or, dine at the Cheesecake Factory every weekend, He thought. As Taleek drew closer to his mother's head with the 9 millimeter, he had seen enough confirmation of guilt in her expression that he needed to do what would come next, “So, you DID know…ready for your turn bitch?” Taleek said. Brenda shed one parting tear down her right cheek, “Taleek, I’m sor…” Brenda tried to say, before Taleek fired a single shot into his mother’s forehead. The bullet caused the back of her head to explode brain particles across the staircase and left her forehead smoking. Her body dropped to the floor like a sailboat dropping its anchor into the middle of the Pacific Ocean. Taleek managed to drop the gun and spent the next hour staring into the unblinking eyes of his dead mother until the police arrived.

Though charges were never filed against Taleek into the murders of both Kurt and Konnor Kimble, the judge who presided his case, still felt obligated to hold the death of his mother against him. Taleek’s defense attorney could only prove that he was a victim of rape and molestation by the Kimble brothers, but did not have enough proof to prove his mother was either aware, or involved. The judge ordered him to serve a two to five years sentence of solitary confinement at a juvenile detention center, under the private care of a psychiatrist, plus five years probation upon release. Taleek had been unfazed by the judge’s proposal. What was done was done, Taleek felt. He believed what he did was a justifiable way of slaying his demons, or curing his nightmares. But instead, all it did was made room for new ones. Since Taleek’s grandfather never wanted anything to do with him or his mother, and with his Aunt Linda possessing a family of her own (and was practically afraid of him) civil services eventually placed Taleek in foster care after his release from juvenile hall. In the end, Taleek ended up being essentially raised by the very same system that had evidently failed him...

The police chase…

…Taleek and his motley crew of would be bank robbers, continued to press their way through the busy city streets and freeways, while evading the police at whatever cost. Big Cory was their getaway driver, and had took a bullet in the arm, causing him to smash into other oncoming cars on the road, “Why wasn’t yo’ sorry ass looking out for the guard fool? Now my arm all fucked up and shit!” Big Cory screamed. “Nigga’ just drive!!!" Taleek hollered, as he open fired on the police cars that were busy chasing behind them. When he looked through the rearview mirror, Big Corey noticed Taleek's spotty aim, "Can you at least shoot straight nigga?" Big Cory asked. Big Cory had been driving erratically and swerved constantly to avoid them getting killed, "Can you at least drive straight nigga!" Taleek fired back. "Fuck man, they gainin' on us!" Eddie screamed, from the backseat. Big Cory rolled his eyes, "You two nigga's shut the fuck up and hold on!" Big Cory yelled. He was doing everything he could to get away from the police. Many of the off ramps were either tied up with too many cars exiting, or by other HPD officers in the vicinity blocking the path. In a panic move, Big Cory made a drastic turn into oncoming traffic that were forcing oncoming cars to slam against the walls of the freeway, "You drivin' on the wrong side of the fucking road again, nigga! You gonna' kill us all before we can even spend one Goddamn dime!" Eddie yelled. Big Cory turned his head and gave Eddie a cold stare, "Shut yo' bitch ass up, fool...before I shut 'chu up!" Big Cory commanded. The only thing Big Cory knew for certain was that he was not going to go out quietly, and that he had over one million reasons not to. They had made off with what their inside connect claimed would be close to two million in cash, making him more enthusiastic to stay alive to spend it. His body was so high off both marijuana and adrenaline that Big Cory had not realized he was in shock from the bullet wound. Sweat squeezed from his pores like water through a sponge. The Houston police department refused to give up on the hunt and chased them unmercifully throughout two counties. Both sides of the used 2010 Dodge Charger they were driving was riddled with so many bullet holes, that it could pass as a giant metal pin cushion. Running from the cops did not bother "Big Cory" though. He had been running from the law for almost, what seemed like to him, his entire life. In one more last desperate attempt to shake the police Big Cory decided to get back off the freeway, "I think I know a shortcut to the hideout, but I'm gonna' need yo' help Taleek!" Big Cory pleaded. Big Cory's plan was supposed to be a simple one: They were to case the bank from inside out, find some disguises, pay some "homeless guy" a few bucks to go in and distract the security guards, and while the security guards escort the "homeless guy" outside the bank, they bust out their disguise's and bumrush the tellers. The only thing Big Jacory Jackson had not planned on was for his trigger happy cousin Eddie Jones to blast the teller in the face with his pump shotgun. He knew the only way he could even pull off the robbery in the first place, would be with the help of his crazy ass little cousin EJ, cause after all, he did front him the guns through one of his gang connections, Jacory considered. However, having Taleek as a stickup partner was not his idea, but since it was EJ's homeboy, Jacory figured to do him a solid since Eddie was blood. Regrettably, getting shot in the arm was not part of Big Cory's plan either. Prior to hooking up with Eddie and Taleek, Jacory had already done a couple robbery jobs with a few crews, but he never had the pleasure of planning one. After seeing the type of money the other crews he worked with brought in, Jacory believed the risks were well worth taking, especially with a much smaller group, which meant a bigger split for each of them. Eddie noticed the blood hemorrhaging from Big Cory's arm and made Jacory drink some whiskey to dull the pain. It was not a big secret what was coming up next for him, as it was the type of thing a person who grew up conditioned to their lifestyle was accustomed to. Jacory took a big swig of the whiskey a few times, "Okay cuz, I'm ready…Taleek man, grab the wheel, fool!" Jacory hollered. EJ had been heating up a switchblade in the backseat in order to cartelize his big cousin's gunshot wound. Eddie does not speak a word to Jacory as he started to burn his skin to stop the bleeding. Jacory bit down hard onto the belt Eddie gave him off his own person. His skin was searing from the pain. He screamed in great agony and forced himself to take his mind off the sizzling knife. Flashes of his long lost childhood past began to pop into his head. Slowly did the long forgotten images funnel to the forefront of his cerebral cortex, to the first time he started out jacking people in the hood, "Yo', you good cuz?" Eddie asked concerned. The more EJ spoke, the more Jacory's mind took him further back in time, way back when. Back then, during a time before he was getting shot at…before he started jacking people for their loot…before he ripped people off on the street…before he raped that girl… before… Jacory looked back at his little cousin, "Yeah, man…my shit's cool. Hang on lil' nigga, I think we're almost there!" Jacory said, "Both you fool's hold on! We almost…."

// Back in the day…//

….. "We almost there Cory!" screamed a young out of breath Eddie Jones. Staggering not far behind little EJ was young portly Jacory Jackson, "Are they still behind us?" Jacory asked panting. Out of fear, Eddie did not want to risk looking back over his shoulder, "Don't worry bout' them, just keep runnin' nigga!" Eddie screamed. They were being chased by a large group of local teenagers who were trying to corral them for a big cash reward, promised by a Vietnamese store owner. Wheezing in and out of breath, Jacory figured they would not make it back to Eddie's place (whose house was the closest) without getting caught by the mob of children who were stalking them. But what the eager teenagers and his cousin Eddie did not suspect, was that Jacory had some "friends" nearby too and could not wait to see their faces after he introduced them. As children, Jacory and Eddie used to steal all the time from their neighborhood corner store, especially whenever they had no money. But since either child never actually had any, they primarily stole for the pure pleasure of it, which was just another day in the life of skinny "little" Eddie Jones and "Fat Jack" Jacory Jackson. There was not a day that passed that the two local hardheads were not being chased after for doing something they knew they were not supposed to. Pudgy Jacory was almost as poor as his bony little cousin EJ, but neither ever allowed being broke to stop them from taking whatever they wanted. His mother Adonna Bartee was Eddie Jones' mother, Adina, fraternal twin. Much like his curvy aunt Adina, Addona too had a shit load of babies as well, six to be exact. But unlike her sister's children, most of Adonna's kids were either locked up or murdered. Out of the three baby daddy's she's procured over the years, the only boyfriend who tried to stick around was Jacory's dad Jacob. When Jacory was three, his father was shot to death in front of the hole-in-the-wall café he was doing security for, after denying entry to some drunk under age kid. Jacory really did not get to know most of his other older siblings, but could hardly stand the one mean older sister who was still living with them. Like her sister, Adonna was a hustler, but only her hustle was selling crack cocaine. It pissed Jacory off that his mother still worked part-time as a waitress at the same establishment that got his dad killed. Since their mother Adonna was barely home, Jacory's big sister Diana, usually had different guys coming over all the time, and would kick Jacory out of the house, until they were done fucking her. Without any real parental supervision, Jacory had no choice but to run the streets. Eddie looked up to his big cousin, who lived but a few blocks away, even despite the amount of mayhem that he always found himself into by hanging around him. Despite believing that both their lives were shit, the two 5th Ward bred delinquents still had each other. As time went on, the store owner had become fed up with the two little thieves and decided to take matters into his own hands. At first, he offered free products to anyone who offered any information on his suspected shoplifters. The owner was an old Vietnamese man named Tran, whose facial hair made him look like a karate grand master. Tran had been doing business at the corner store called "Trans Mini Market" for over twenty-five years in Houston's 5th ward area. As the owner, he was often not a big fan of people hanging around the front of his store, let alone "the dark kind," and either him, or his son Han, would always follow his pigment challenged customers around if they looked suspicious. Nevertheless, all the children in the neighborhood knew Jacory and Eddie loved stealing from Tran's store and often bragged to anyone willing to hear about it. But after coming up short hundreds of dollars worth of candy and sodas from his store over the years, Tran had finally reached his limits. Figuring since some of the neighborhood kids were dirt poor, he came up with the bright idea of turning them against the duo by offering a two-hundred dollar reward to who ever caught them. Due to their penchant for starting shit everywhere their feet trotted, both Eddie and Jacory were already disliked by many of the kids in the neighborhood. School was not any different, as they did everything from ganging up on scared kids and hassling them for their lunch money, shooting dice, breaking into other people's lockers, etc…you name it, they did it, until finally, some of the older kids who were not afraid of the duo had decided to team-up on them to split Tran's two-hundred dollar reward. The group was led by a tall narrow-headed teenaged kid named Marlon Manuel, who never liked Jacory anyway, because he was never scared of him like the other kids at school. Marlon convinced his friends to gang up on them at a play ground Eddie and Jacory regularly hung out at near their school. They both had seen through Marlon's friendly façade, after trying to approach them to "ask a favor," with seven other suspiciously big kids by his side. Jacory was not going to go quietly and was very strong for his age, so he quickly picked up a half broken brick off the ground and flung it at

Marlon, hitting him square in his chest, sending him to his knees. They then began chasing them endlessly throughout their broken down neighborhood, until Jacory finally ordered little Eddie to cut through an old woman's front yard and over her back fence. After Marlon and his crew pursued them over the tall wooden fence, Jacory was then brandishing a shiny pearl grip snub nosed nickel plated 38. He found the gun in a ditch a week prior to their ambush, on his way home from skipping school and decided to hide it underneath an abandoned crack house for safe keeping. Without hesitation, Jacory began firing the weapon feverishly at the unsuspecting group, causing them to flee for their lives. Of course, no one was killed (that day) but Marlon and his boys were so afraid that Jacory was still going to try. Fearing for his life, Marlon wasted no time crying to his father about the incident, which landed young "Fat Jack" some major time in juvenile hall.

Jacory was always stout as a youth, but when he became old enough for juvenile hall, his body started to look more and more like Lou Ferrigno from the old Incredible Hulk TV Show. It was more than obvious that Jacory did not spend his days and nights faithfully reading Daniel Steel novels. He came back to his neighborhood an even bigger menace, literally and figuratively, than before he left. If you were a dope pusher he did not know on his street corner, chances were, you were getting knocked out for your dope and dope money. Should he lose his money in a dice game, then you were getting a beat down for the money you won "and" the money "he" lost. Everyone in the hood began taking notice of his size and reputation, and was afraid to retaliate. They began calling him "Big Cory," especially after cleaning the clock of one of the neighborhood's most dangerous and notorious thug's at the time, "Big Bo Manley." Eventually, Big Cory was ordered by the courts to return back to high school, where an old elementary friend convinced him to try his hand at baseball. Despite his rawness in the sport, Big Cory and his coaches discovered he was a natural for the game, earning him a free ride to Colorado State A&M in the process. Attending college opened his eyes to a new world he never felt existed outside of his usual life in the grime and actually considered making the most of his opportunities. But, even though Jacory had left the hood, the hood unfortunately, never had really left him. Barely a year had passed, before he began intimidating his fellow collegians and teammates alike for their grant and student loan money, despite receiving a monthly stipend from the university. Rumors about his volatile behavior off campus started to escalate after a couple reported off-campus shootings and physical assaults he was allegedly involved in. Upon getting named in a point shaving scandal, for the sake of their program, the school's Alumni were pressuring his coaches to revoke his scholarship, which did not seem to bother Jacory. College life just was not fast enough for his ambitions and aspirations to become the next Tony Montana, or Nicky Barnes anyway, so he dropped out on his own. As Jacory was making his way back home, "Skinny" Eddie was making his back to jail for drug possession, leaving Big Cory without his main man to run the streets with. It would not be long before Big Cory ran into an old former baseball teammate from high school named Orlando Scott, who was "then" into stealing cars. The curly haired and stocky framed Orlando Scott was a half-black and Hispanic kid from Corpus Christie, who transferred to Jacory's high school a year prior to their graduation, after a terrible altercation he was a part of (at his former high school) led to the death of another student. Jacory was ready to make a serious come-up in the dope game and remembered how good he and Scott got along back in their playing days and decided to partner up with him. But since Big Cory and Orlando lacked the capitol yet to purchase a large quantity of drugs, they sought out to do "other" criminal endeavors to find some. To get the ball rolling for their business venture, the new duo started out doing a few car-jackings together and then moved on to doing some smash and grab jobs across town. After dabbling in a little gun running, the tandem had collected enough money to make a move to buy some kilos from a major drug distributer. They invested in a shack and day and night they hit the block from sun up till sun down until finally achieving their ghetto super star status. Jacory and Orlando were coming up incredibly fast in the dope game. They both owned two chromed out expensive luxury cars and eventually made enough cash to hire their own street workers. When time went on they formed partnerships at night clubs, which opened the door to access of plenty of beautiful women, and also bought a large 4,500 square foot condominium together in a high rise on the south side of Houston.

Their partnership was going strong for a while, at least up until the day Orlando brought home his brand new girlfriend, Alicia Masterson. Alicia had that shit brick house build on her that most brothers from the hood often went for. She stood around five foot eight, without high heels on, and kept her red hair cut in a tight fade in the back with curly bangs in the front. The only problem was Jacory, along with a "slew" of his former friends and teammates used to fuck her back in college. It had been a while since he last remembered seeing her, which was when he and a couple of his other homeboys from the school's football team ran a train on her back in his old dorm room. She was the first girl to ever ask him to attempt doing anal on her, while loving it at the same time. Alicia also loved giving head too (and very fond of swallowing afterwards) just as much as Jacory loved receiving it. Alicia was one of the campus's top freaks and would allegedly fuck anyone with an athletic scholarship. Regardless, of his and Alicia's past, he knew going forth as Orlando's business partner could lead into a conflict of interest, if it ever got out he already slept with her. On the other hand, Jacory was not positively sure if he could keep a straight face around the couple, since he was the only one aware of her past reputation, all while Orlando was busy trying to make her a house wife. Nevertheless, to keep from jeopardizing his and Orlando's partnership, both he and Alicia privately agreed to never bring up their previous "history." But as fate would soon have it, Orlando had a last minute family emergency he needed to attend to late one evening. Alicia had just come through the door, after finishing her shift as a resource manager at a temp agency she was working for, and did not bother to argue with her boyfriend when he insisted that she stay home and rest. Alicia waited patiently by his bedroom window until being completely sure he was gone, before she made her next move. Jacory pre-occupied with playing video games in the living room when she decided to pounce on him, like a ravenous octopus gobbling an unsuspecting prawn. Alicia always liked having experimentally wild and kinky sex, especially with Jacory. She also had no qualms ever telling him that he had the biggest dick she had ever seen, and he KNEW she had "seen" plenty. That night, Jacory initially was caught off guard by her deceitful actions, but was hardly shocked by her devious confession, "Mmmmm, baby…ain't you glad that nigga finally gone! You know I am." Alicia said relieved. Alicia began kissing all over his face and then quickly made her way down to her knees in front of him and squeezed the front of his pants as hard as she could, causing him to drop his game controller. Jacory immediately sprung up from the sofa in protest, "Bitch you out of line, that nigga' love yo' hoe ass!" Jacory yelled, wiping off her loud colored lipstick from his face. Alicia smirked and began to rub her vibrant nipples, "See, that's what I'm missin'…a real nigga who ain't afraid to talk dirty to me! So…..you gonna quit bullshit'n (bending over onto the coffee table to show off her loud pink lace under wear)….or you gonna fuck me?" Alicia kindly asked. As long as he had known her, the high yellow complected Alicia Masterson never showed any signs of pride, or self esteem issues, but was the type of female who just always knew what she wanted. Having been promiscuous probably her entire life, he suspected that if asked, she could not honestly remember who broke her virginity first, which was more than alright with him.

Later on that same evening, Orlando arrived home earlier than he had previously expected. He spotted an old woman selling flowers in the middle of the street after pulling up at a traffic light a few blocks away. Orlando felt bad for running out on his sexy new goddess and decided to surprise her by splurging on two dozen red stemmed roses. As Orlando drove closer to the home, he could not help but notice that none of the lights on their floor were on. Figuring that Big Cory might have taken Alicia out for a quick bite to eat, Orlando dismissed any notions to worry. After he parked his silver BMW in the garage, to his dismay was Jacory's navy blue SUV still parked in its usual space. Then he remembered the new honey on the third floor Jacory liked fooling around with sometimes, and that maybe Alicia was at home still taking a nap, Orlando guessed. While going up the elevator, all Orlando could think about was how happy Alicia might be with her new bouquet of flowers. Filled with suspense, Orlando opened the front door quietly, just in case she may have been napping on the living room sofa. Although the living room television was on, no one was there watching it. He began worry and when he started to look around had noticed some of her clothing on the floor. Then he heard a loud moan, then another, and another. It was coming from Jacory's room. Orlando did not have to be a MIT graduate to know when his girl was getting the lights fucked out of her. He then busted through the door, "How could you, bitch?" Orlando hollered. Alicia was tied up by her wrists on the bed with Jacory's dick hanging out her, "Look man, she came on to me…" Jacory tried to explain, but before Jacory could finish his sentence, Alicia yelled rape and Orlando went for his gun and fired at Jacory. Having no other choice but to defend himself, Jacory dove onto the floor where his glock was stashed in his nightstand. Orlando ran to the side of the bed where Jacory was and as soon as he did,

Orlando was struck in the neck by a bullet. Orlando immediately dropped his gun to grab his gushing throat and Jacory fired once again into his chest. The impact of the gunshot sent Orlando spinning around like a blindfolded child prepping to hit a piñata at a birthday party. Jacory shot Orlando in self defense, but since his gun was unregistered and marijuana found in their house, he still had to serve a light sentence. It was during that stint in jail that Jacory met his overtly cautious and calculating cellmate Alvin Berry, who inspired him to go into bank robbing. Alvin promised him a spot on his crew after he got out jail, which was paying around ten to fifteen-five thousand dollars a piece, depending on the job. After paying all his attorney fees, Jacory was broke and thought long and hard about Berry's generous offer. And soon as he was released from jail on good behavior, he eagerly hooked up with Alvin and his crew. Alvin usually did bank jobs with no less than five or six experienced guys at a time. Jacory never really trusted Alvin's people and felt underappreciated when it came time to getting paid his share of the take. Since Jacory was the lowest on the totem pole, his cut was always the smallest, which finally led him to branch out and do his own thing with people he trusted.

However, this latest handpicked crew had not exactly panned out the way he had first envisioned them too. Kelvin Foster, who was supposed to be his original choice as his getaway driver, got arrested for purse snatching on his way to meeting up with them before the "actual" robbery. Even though he looked the part, Eddie's friend Taleek Wilson still had a severe drug dependency that affected his focus when it came to following instructions. Then there was his cousin Eddie, who was always going to be his first choice when it came to picking someone to do some dirt with. The only drawback that came with working with his slender-sized cousin that bothered Jacory was Eddie's severe temperament issues. In hindsight, Jacory would not have ever picked such a sloppy bunch to do a bank job with, and greatly regretted it afterward. If they did manage to get away from the cops who were chasing them, Jacory had the right mind to shoot them both in the head. Despite Eddie being his family, at the end of the day, business was still business and even family sometimes can become a huge liability…

Back at Latavia's birthday party….

Jovan and the rest of the family quietly gathered around to watch his precious little girl unwrap the gift he bought for her. Once she obliterated the pretty golden wrapping her birthday present came in, the surprised look on her face was enough to explain her feeling. Before he could even ask her what she had thought of her gift, Latavia's sweet tender face was already glowing brightly. He always felt a sense of euphoric warmth each time he managed to get her to smile, and it also reaffirmed how they, as her parents, made the best choice in keeping her. Jovan recollected a time when both their parents felt it pertinent that Tasha abort the pregnancy, but despite the understandable fears that came with their youth, they overcame the temptation to go through with it. Much like Tasha, Latavia had her mother's radiant light- brown colored skin and long platted wavy hair that had a coarse sheen to it. Latavia's baby fat made her cheeks appear as if they were stuffed with a half a pound of chocolate candy. Patricia would agree that Latavia got her tomboyish traits from Jovan and he would often tell people that she was mean enough to play football. Latavia's face had a certain glow to it, not like a lighthouse caught in a midnight fog, but the kind that would stand out like the glare from a rising sun. He finally bought her the baby bear she had been wanting ever since she first saw it on television. Jovan truly loved his daughter with a special kind of grateful endearment and would move heaven and Earth to keep her satisfied. Whenever she had a cold, he would be there at her side to wipe her nose and feed her soup. If she needed someone to play with, he always stopped in the middle of whatever he was doing and played with her. Every time he got dog tired during football games, he would picture Latavia's face to gain his strength back to remind him what he was playing for. There was absolutely nothing he would not do for his baby girl. If Jovan had it his way, nothing or no one would ever be allowed to harm her, but deep down Jovan knew that life was not about what we always wanted. Jovan was aware of the evils of the world and that bad things sometimes happen to good people some of the time. Although he was not always present for church on Sundays, Jovan still believed that and if God wanted you out of here, then you could "kiss yo' ass goodbye," He figured. When he was much younger, he remembered once asking his mother if she was mad at God for taking his dad away, and her reply was, " Jovie, It doesn't matter how much you may have loved this person or that one, when it's your time to go, you have to let go and let God…." Jovan tried his best to live by that type of outlook on life, by choosing not to waste his days (not unless it's a on a day Tasha wanted him to do something for her that he did not want to do) Jovan jokingly pondered. Latavia smiled at her youthfully strong father, and it was as if she could read his mind, she grabbed him by the face, "I know what'cha thinkin' and it's okay daddy! I promise not to ever lose this one!" Latavia promised. He looked her in pretty golden face, "You swear?" He asked reassuringly. Latavia stepped out of her stubborn comfort zone and kissed him on the cheek. Jovan was stunned as though he were a dizzy gazelle tripping over a lion's paw. He picked up his loving daughter, (much to her chagrin) and returned the favor, rather she liked it, or not, he was not about to care. She was his only child and had promised Tasha that he would love the both of them with everything he had, even if it killed him. But, the funny thing about life is though, no matter how hard you may love something, or someone, you may never really know what you are sometimes asking for in return….

The getaway car…

…"Nigga, I thought this was supposed to be a shortcut? The God damn cops are still hot on our asses!" Eddie shouted. Jacory was trying to resist not shooting Eddie in the face himself in frustration, "Just keep blastin' at them niggas, fool!" Jacory screamed. He looked over to the passenger seat and realized Taleek was napping, "Taleek!!! Yo' nigga…wake the fuck up!" Big Cory screeched, "This supposed to be yo' side of town fool, what's the quickest way back to the freeway?" Jacory asked. Taleek had been getting high unknowingly the entire time they were being chased by the police. Half the time he barely even knew what was going on inside the car, but he did manage to look up long enough to point in one direction. "Man, head that way……dis 'ain't really my hood, though." Taleek said lethargically. "Ole,' USELESS ass nigga..." Jacory yelled in disgust.

Long goodbyes

In the parking lot, Jovan and Tasha's family are packing things up and saying all their final goodbyes. He barely makes it out the restaurant doors before Latavia makes an inquiry about next year's plans, "Can we please have my next birthday party at Chucky Cheese's daddy…please daddy, pretty pl-e-e-e-a-a-a-s-s-e!!!" Latavia begged adorably. Jovan looked down at his hopeful looking Latavia. She had an irresistible twinkle in her pretty little eyes that sometimes made it hard for him to resist, "Maybe, La La…." Tasha quickly intervened. Tasha knew that her boyfriend large heart was simply putty in their daughter's spoiled hands, and Chucky Cheese was no joke price wise, Tasha pondered. Jovan could not wait to see the day when things would be better for them financially. He had been approached many times by various agents, going as far back as McKinley High, but his mother shot those plans down and wanted him to concentrate more on his studies. Either way, Jovan was not a big fan of breaking NCAA rules anyway. He could not help but wander though; if accepting a little money under the table from some rich alumni was good enough for his dad to buy his mother a wedding ring, how much could it REALLY hurt to take a little bit for a Chucky Cheese party?" Jovan often wondered. The reality was that Jovan "was not" his dad and that he worked his ass off too hard to start back peddling in his judgment now, Jovan thought. If he was going to get the money for his little princess, then he knew would have just to figure something else out, "Man, whoever it was that said "those who never learn from the past are sure to fail it….I bet NEVER had to answer to a pushy little three-year-old!" Jovan said aloud.

The getaway car…..

…The chase that had begun halfway from Richmond, Texas had made its way as far as downtown, "Go up…two mo' blocks, Cory!" Taleek mumbled. In shock, the bulky Jacory stared at the drugged out Taleek and was in complete awe, "O-o-oh, now you conscious motherfucka'? You believe this shit?" Jacory snorted, "EJ, I swear to God nigga, this is "THE" last motha'fuckin' job I do wit' you bitches!" Jacory shouted. A stray bullet from one of the policemen chasing them finds its way to Eddie's shoulder cavity, causing him instant agony, "Shit nigga…I'm hit!" Eddie cried out. Jacory turned around and shook his head at him, "Man up nigga, I got plugged too fool." Jacory yelled.

Across the street, not far from the McDonald's restaurant…

"I loaded up all the gift bags in the car, Tasha!" Jovan said panting. Tasha rolled her eyes at her well built boyfriend, "Good, now He-Man… let me see you go back across the street and get my baby back from yo' momma!?" Tasha quipped. Jovan stood there for a few moments contemplating if it was worth wasting his time gratifying Tasha with a smart comeback. Instead of entertaining his sassy future fiancé he had choose to take the high road and just did what she asked. Tasha smiled sinfully at her beloved boyfriend. Jovan back over to the McDonalds parking lot, "Okay momma, you got to let her go home now..." Jovan kindly demanded. Patricia ignored his request and waved him off, "Tell TASHA, "I said" to quit hogging my grandbaby! She hardly brings her by the house lately and when she does, it's only for a little while! And YOU can also tell her that "I said," don't make me wait until I'm rolling around in a wheelchair when she finally brings her back!" Patricia pouted. Not wanting to exacerbate the situation any further, Jovan just played the role of devil's advocate and humored his sensitive mother, "I will see what I can do momma, but we gotta' go!" Jovan insisted. Though frustrated her son made her, Patricia caved in, "Oh, alright…La La, why don't you give your G-Momma' some of that good ole sugar?" Patricia asked. Latavia reached out to her grandmother and gave her a peck on the cheek, "He-e-e-y!?!" Jovan jealously protested,

"How come grandma gets all the sugar and I get all the salt?" Jovan asked. Patricia laughed at Jovan's whining and gave Latavia one last hug, that looked tighter than a koala grabbing on a eucalyptus tree. Jovan grew impatient and began looking down at his watch to expedite things, "Okay, okay, momma'! Latavia is just going home, not going off to Spellman College!" Jovan groaned. As they both walk hand in hand across the barren street, Latavia realized she was missing her new baby bear. "There, you happy now?" He asked sarcastically and handed Tasha Latavia's chubby hand, "Very." Tasha said seductively. Tasha grabbed the six-foot-two inch Jovan Campbell by the back of his head and unleashed on him a very long endearing kiss. Tasha knew full well how to use her emphatic charms on him and also knew he would do his best to act indifferent, "Oh…now I get a kiss from you?" Jovan nonchalantly asked. She then grabbed a hold of his growing crotch and gives it a firm squeeze. "Yeah…and if you stop trippin', you might get to use this when we get home!" Tasha teased. Jovan moaned uncontrollably and almost stumbled over her, "Damn girl, why you gotta' go tease a nigga' like that?" Jovan asked excitedly. Tasha simply smiled and began to act innocently and squeezed his crotch harder, "Like what?" Tasha said coyly, and rubbed him across his broad chiseled chest at the same time. "Get me all worked up then…you KNOW this is the shit that got us into trouble the first ti…" Jovan began just as his mother cried out to him, "JOVAN!!!!!!!!!!!!!!!!!!" Patricia screamed from behind him, along with the sound of a loud screeching from a car.

All time stops

In the blink of an eye, life as Jovan Campbell knew it was completely over, as he watched the roaring Dodge Charger maul poor Latavia's small fragile body at 90 miles per hour. Her tender flesh and brittle bones laid rendered beyond disbelief and had brought panic and mortification to anyone who had a front seat to the unspeakable madness of it all. As the people stood around hollering and screaming, time in Jovan's young mind seemed to be standing still. He could no longer feel his heart beating from within his thick chest and found it hard to breath. Tasha Greenwood fell to her knees in horror as pieces of the child that she proudly spent thirty-three hours in labor to give birth to, were splashed across the warm city streets. Distraught family members who were still near Patricia managed to catch her in mid-air, as she fainted from the suffering images of her brutalized granddaughter. Jovan could not at first find the strength to move. His thought processes were also slowing down and was struggling to rationalize if what he was seeing had actually happened. Subconsciously, he could hear the sirens bellowing loudly in the background, but his spirit felt as if it left his body. Then suddenly he could slowly feel something dark boiling up inside him, deep within the pits of his tight stomach. Jovan began to vomit profusely as his insides started to whirl inside him like spokes on a tire. The police cars were storming down the streets causing him even more confusion and anguish. When his attention went and locked onto the bloody road, he saw pieces of Latavia's dismembered body sprawled across the street, like some animals dead carcass. His trance was broken by the frantic sound of his girlfriend Tasha, who balled up on the ground and was crying and praying. Onlookers also fought to find air to breath at the sight of the horrific act. Jovan looked over his shoulder and saw the stolen getaway car smashed against a telephone pole and was surrounded by the Houston police. After hitting Latavia in the middle of the street, Jacory incidentally lost control of the wheel, causing them to crash. Due to his body being thrown from the car, Taleek Wilson died instantaneously from the impact of the crash. Taleek Wilson finally found the peace he sought from the very ground his mangled corpse quietly laid. Eddie "EJ" Jones, who had been sitting in the back seat, was also in critical condition. The brutish Jacory Jackson was the only survivor intact and was yelling hysterically from the vehicle and threatening to shoot himself if the police did not back away. Though some of them would not admit it aloud, Jacory believed that the Houston police department was probably more inclined to wish that he would kindly blow his brains out after everything he had done up to this point. Jovan was still trying to work things out in his head and all the noise was not helping his mental state. The shock he felt was so strong that he had not realized he was shaking in the middle of the street. When the ambulance finally arrived Jovan barely even reacted to getting out of the way of it. As it passed by, there was something peculiar lying in the corner of street that caught his eye. Whatever the shiny object was, it gleamed abundantly off the sun's rays and seemed to put him under some hypnotic trance, drawing him nearer to it. Once he was on top of the bizarre looking object, Jovan could not wrap his head around what he believed he was actually seeing. He leaned in closer toward the round glittering red object and it appeared to be a half torn doll that looked just like the one he bought Latavia, Jovan thought. What Jovan saw next caused him to lose all his sanity. Jovan's eyes bulged from out his eye sockets, as if they were being pumped with helium. His mouth salivated for anything moist he could find on his dried lips and his stomach boiled hotter than a Crockpot left on its high settings for too long. The scream he made is so ferociously loud and disturbing that everyone in the vicinity had no choice but to stop what they were doing to look around. Jovan looked back down at the ripped up bloodied baby bear with its glittering gem stone eyes and to the tiny bloodied hand that was still attached to it. The hand, in which he finally came to terms with, once belonged to his sweet innocent, barely three year old daughter, and the revelation of it sent Jovan into a steaming fit of rage. His fists start to clench tighter than a pair of vice grip pliers. Tears streaked down his dark skinned face, almost to the point of blinding him as he stomped toward the direction of the crashed Charger.

The police were still trying to talk Jacory down, but Jacory refused to not go out on his own terms. Jacory's head was riddled with blood from the crash, as he continued to threaten to kill himself in the front seat of the ruined Charger, "Back the fuck up, you goddamn pigs! Back the fuck up or, watch me blow my God damn brains out! You motha fuckas' get back, I swear I'm gonna do it!" Jacory hysterically screamed. With everyone's attention so focused on Jacory, no one paid the fuming Jovan Campbell any attention when he ran up to the car. The driver's door was barely hanging by its hinges until Jovan reached out and ripped it the rest of the way. As an All-America linebacker for the University of Houston, Jovan possessed a six hundred seventy five pound bench press and a thousand pound squat (which made him the strongest player on the whole team) not to mention the 4.25 jailbreak speed (that also made him the fastest). Despite the pleading from the HPD officers, Jovan yanked the gun away from Big Cory and began to beat him uncontrollably in his face with it. He bludgeoned the defenseless Jacory Jackson's head to the point his blood was smeared totally across the inside of the windshield. The officers threatened to shoot Jovan, but he would not listen, until family members intervened. Though they initially hesitated after it was further explained what the men in the Charger had previously done to his daughter, the HPD officers finally decided to coral Jovan, before someone's TV crew came through in a helicopter to film Jacory's death. Jovan had been beating Jacory senseless for almost a full minute before the officers could get a hold of him. Grabbing and containing him though, was easier said than done. It almost took ten to eleven policemen to get him under control, "He don't deserve to breathe! Let....GO of me...he doesn't deserve to live!" Jovan frantically shouted. Jacory was beaten so badly that his left eye ball hung from out his head. "Look at her! Look over there you son of a bitch!" Jovan moaned. The officers pried Jacory's bloodied body up from the car. With his left eye now deformed from the beating he suffered at the hands of the college football standout, he only could manage to peek in the direction of Latavia's remains using his other one, "Y-Y-Y-o-o...I-I-I'm s-s-so...(spitting out blood) I-I-m-m sorre-e...m-m-man, I-I'm s-s-so...!" Jacory said, and passed out. Jovan managed to wrangle himself to his feet with his hands cuffed behind him, "You what!?! You sorry!?! Motherfucka' look at her! You butchered my baby!" Jovan shouted and started to sob deliriously, "Can't you see? Jovan moaned. "My baby's in...in PIECES you son of a bitch! Do you hear me? You destroyed her...Oh, God! You destroyed...my baby's life! You destroyed MY life!!! Ya'll LET me go!!! Let me go God damn it!!! I said...let me go-o-o-o!?!" Jovan screamed for what seemed like an eternity.

Her name was Latavia Nicole Campbell, and she had just turned three years old.

Chapter 2:

Reverend Thomas Templeton Jr.

In the beginning…

…The outspoken and highly revered, Reverend Thomas Ezekiel Templeton Jr., was born a preacher's kid down in southern Georgia, in the small and sunny community of Fitzgerald in Ben Hill County. The city of Fitzgerald was founded by Southern confederates from the United States Civil War around the early 1900's and stored its cherished history among the many monuments and museums that are filtered along its beautiful Georgian landscape. The populace was never in danger of breaking any population records with a number barely reaching under 8,000 people at the time of his youth. Despite its modest size and antebellum architecture, the city had no shortage of things to keep a then young Thomas Jr.'s busy mind occupied. Back then, Ben Hill or the "Hill," was known by true southerners as home to some of the best deep fried chicken steaks and sweet potato pies this side of Georgia. It was not too long ago that the now seasoned Rev. Thomas Jr. frequented the once mighty Jelly Bean Skating Rink, which had been one of the staples of the community for years, and also where he was not known to be the nimblest of roller skaters amongst his peers. Thomas Jr. was the eldest of three children and was raised under his father's excessively strict standards. While as a child, Thomas Jr. may have been reared by his father's primary credo of living "Christ like," his mannish side sometimes got the best of him. In his heyday, it did not matter to him if the girl was "thick as a thesaurus, or as slim as Virginia," he oftentimes quoted to his friends. Growing up in those days, Thomas Jr. never lacked for confidence and after discovering his "manhood," he could not wait long enough to discreetly spread himself around. During his teenage years, one of his favorite pastimes was hanging out at the local skating rink on a Saturday night. When he was not too busy embarrassing himself (from busting his ass all over the skating rink floor) the mischievous Thomas Jr. would partake in a little "ass busting" of his own away from it. The future "reverend to be" knew he acted like a true heathen away from home and was taught better, but he always knew his flesh was weak, and often struggled to control his lustful urges from an early age. Those were the fledging days of his pubescent adolescence and over time, soon discovered that he had to put away his childish things and search for new horizons. Since his father's church commitments were so great at the time of his youth, the family spent most of their spare time at church, which caused him to lose interest in religion and inadvertently created the desire to leave home. But things soon changed during his college days after meeting his future wife Lucinda. After falling madly in love with her, the whole experience opened his eyes, and Thomas Jr. regained his passion for the Lord. By his mid-thirties, a then matured Thomas Jr. heard God's calling and started preaching at the very same church he spent years avoiding. Although he knew it made his father feel proud, by seeing them sharing the same pulpit, Thomas Jr. never envisioned himself as a preacher or family man. But nevertheless, he made it through twenty five blissful years of marriage and took up where his late father left off upon his death. On some occasions, he found himself lounging back in his father's church office (like he was doing now) and pretending to be smoking on his dad's old wooden oak pipe and often reminiscing on how things "used to be" around Ben Hill. Back then, things were a lot more laid back and everyone was not in such a big hurry to go nowhere. Despite witnessing the carnage that being raised around the Civil Rights Movement may have wrought him as a kid, not all of his childhood experiences were all bad, Thomas Jr. reflected.

Around that time, the population was twice as small as it was today and the people were a little more humble too, Thomas Jr. thought. The young people of his generation had more pride and enough respect for others, and themselves, not allowing their pants to hang down to their ankles in public, unlike how they do in today's world, Thomas Jr. remembered. The thought of the direction of his people often troubled him as he believed that they may have been lost. His father and mother fought for things that were now being taken for granted like sitting in the front of the bus or getting a better education. Regardless, of all the high racial provocation between the whites and blacks throughout the years, the black community still struggled with diversity among some of its own sects. He remembered a day, when a person needed something your neighbors would not hesitate to help you get it, if they did not already have it to give. Time had also played a major role on most of the local landscaping by causing once recognizable areas to change with the times. The old Ben Hill he grew up in endured a series of makeovers, like anything from adding a recreational center here, a hip hop recording studio there, a few more nice new hotels here, and an exotic strip club there. Even the old Green Briar Mall he often hung out in had suffered through its countless face-lifts. A lot had changed over the years for the grizzled Thomas Jr., but he still had fond memories to fall back on to help him get through his day. Memories of how he would sneak out late at night after his parents were asleep, and head out to parties his father did not allow him to go to, or maybe catch a late movie at the local drive in, or maybe do a little dry humping with whoever was his flavor of the week. Although he hated being gone all day on Sundays as a child, being the son of a famous preacher did have its perks, He felt. Thomas Jr.'s parents were major affiliates of the NAACP, which made Thomas Jr. and his family both a target and very popular around their community. Both of his parents were constantly receiving really nice gifts at church for their bravery and achievements during the struggle of the segregation period. His much accomplished and heralded father, Reverend Thomas Sr., hardly ever had to pay for a meal in town. Whenever Thomas Senior took the family out to a local restaurant, someone who may have recognized them always covered the bill. On the days they did not eat out, the Templeton family was always welcomed to dine at a church member's home. If Thomas Jr. needed extra money to buy some comic books, new clothes, or etc… he always had the option of cutting a neighbors grass, babysit for them, or wash their cars. The harder his father fought for equality for his people, the more the community stood up to take care of them.

The Fearless Thomas Senior

Life at home was not always easy for Thomas Jr., as his late father was the non tolerant and greatly revered Reverend Thomas Ezekiel Templeton Sr. Though Thomas Jr.'s father had been known for being a humble and educated public speaker, at home he was also a very stern and intimidating man (all 6'4 230 pounds of him) and to say the least, was not putting up with any of little Thomas' bullshit. Thomas Sr. was well respected around town and the people in the "Hill" dubbed his dad "the next Martin Luther King Jr.," whom he eventually crossed paths with at a peace rally in western Kentucky long ago, where Thomas Sr. spoke at a protest of the murders of a black teenage boy and his little sister. The two children, William (11) and Sandra (9) Whitfield were walking home from school one late afternoon and during the long trek home, they became hungry. Upon their usual four mile hike, they would notice a beautiful vineyard along the trail. Unfortunately, the garden had belonged to an ornery farmer named Kenneth "Cuss" Zacharias, who was white and was somewhat of a public figure in town. He was not as overtly racist as his other colleagues in his community, but he was not going to put up with anyone stealing from him either. On that fateful day, the poor children grew increasingly famished and neither had any money to buy a snack from the store (if there was one to stop at during the long walk home). Not realizing that Zacharias had been home, William, who was the older of the two, began to pull carrots from out the garden for him and his baby sister to snack on. Nevertheless, it was well-known around town that the highly volatile and paranoid Zacharias drove around town with an old Winchester rifle on his person. On that day, he had spotted the children through his kitchen window and mistook them for common thieves. Without asking any questions, the old man ran outside and fired on the two from behind with a double-barrel shotgun that he often kept in his kitchen. The force of the buck shots had burrowed deep within their tender small backs, causing their skin to appear as if they were struck by miniature meteorites in which left them demolished. William's sister, Sandra Whitfield's, body was the worst to view, as her young head had been half blown off. Due to the massive trauma little Sandra Whitfield endured, the family had to have a closed casket funeral for her.

Despite this heinous act, Kenneth Zacharias was not charged for their murders and was initially set free. Since the children had been trespassing on private property, Zacharias got away with murder because of the minor technicality. It also did not hurt his chances that Zacharias' brother Zed (who had ties to the KKK) was a town deputy. Ultimately, the incident sent ripples throughout every black community in America, eventually causing a sect to form by the father of the children, Albert Whitfield. Initially, the frustrated group made plans to kill the unsuspecting Kenneth Zacharias and his racist brother, but Thomas Sr. had caught wind of the gaffe and was able to convince the father to choose a more "diplomatic" solution to get justice for his lost children. Instead of violence, he offered to spearhead one of the largest rallies ever seen in that region of Kentucky. Thomas Sr. formed an association called F.F.A.V. ("Fearless Fathers, Against Violence") and led a strong and stringent crowd of three hundred fathers up to city hall. The police were in awe of the unexpected sea of male ebony bodies that had enveloped the middling building like a group of disturbed hornets around a jubilant hive. His mandate had been crystal clear that day, "We ain't going anywhere, till there is justice served for the souls of both young William and Sandra Whitfield!" Thomas Sr. had demanded, until they were finally allowed to appear in front of a Supreme Court judge. He had spoken so emphatically to the courts that day to have Zacharias' case retried, that it even brought well devout racists to tears. Grudgingly, the Whitfield case had been reopened and Kenneth "Cuss" Zacharias was eventually sentenced to spend the rest of his natural born life behind bars. It was not long before Dr. King had caught wind of "Thundering" Thomas Templeton Sr. and was so impressed by his speech on the radio that Dr. King invited him to join his private staff as an advisor. Not long after joining Dr. King's staff, Thomas Sr. had quickly emerged as one of his most reliable consultants. He became instrumental in helping orchestrate many marches held all over other southern states that struggled for human rights in America, as well as the march on Washington, DC, where he co-wrote the famous "I Have a Dream" speech. With his position well-solidified in the NAACP, Thomas Sr. was asked to speak at a rally held in downtown Birmingham, Alabama after the tragic church bombing now known as "The 16th Street Church Bombing" after the deaths of four innocent black girls. But despite all his progresses, Thomas Sr.' darkest hour had come on an average looking sunny day, merely moments after he and Dr. King spent time joking around earlier in his motel room in Memphis, Tennessee. Soon after he left Dr. King to retrieve his bible from the car, gunshots rang out and then his good friend Dr. King was dead. Upon Dr. King's death, Thomas Sr. became a man obsessed with crusading on behalf of "all" minorities in America, therefore, making his father's already incredible shoes that much harder for Thomas Jr.' to fill. His dual duties, both as a preacher and civil activist, began to keep him away from home even more, but neither Thomas Jr. nor the family ever complained. Thomas Jr. had always cherished and respected his distinguished father and never once stopped cheering him on throughout the many years his father spent making a real difference for his people. He frequently stared at the immaculate oil painting that hung in his office of his late father and sometimes wished he could talk with him, at least for just one last time. Though Thomas Jr. believed that his father's spirit was in heaven, part of him yearned to know if he still approved of the man he turned out to be. After all, he never led any important marches on City Hall, let alone, spoke out of any injustices at any rallies for a good cause. He was just a simple preacher who inherited his father's position by default. In any case, Thomas Jr. did his best to live up to his father's memory in hopes that he was somehow appeased. This was but a tiny portion of the weight that Thomas Sr.'s enormous footsteps left him to bear and also, that kept him on his knees every night. Much like his father, the ill-fated Thomas Jr. made sure that he always gave his all during every sermon. In his free time, he prayed over the sickly at the hospitals and traveled to the prisons and did the same for the inmates. He even insisted on instituting special programs at the church to provide resources for people seeking employment training, basic computer skills, and daycare for single mothers who could not afford it. But sadly, it would soon prove highly disastrous for the middle-aged preacher that his latest good deed he does for humanity's sake, returns to him featuring a very fatal and frightful reward…

Over two years ago, prior to the present…

(Late Sunday evening at New Mount Greater Faith Baptist Church in Ben Hill…) "Congratulations Reverend!" said Sister Betty Lawrence, who was one of the church's hardest working elders. The woman savagely hugged the much taller Thomas Jr. with the equal vengeance of a car compactor. Thomas Jr. did not mind her enthusiasm as Sister Betty had always enjoyed his sermons and was also the main person who comforted his mother after Thomas Senior passed away. Sister Lawrence was a rather stout sized black woman and Thomas Jr. could barely squeeze out a "Thank you!" It was rumored that before she became "Big Betty" she fell into a sewer main as a small child, which in her present condition was hard for him to imagine. He never had the nerve to bring it up to her face, but would snicker to himself at the thought. It was the end of another usually long service and some of the congregation stayed around long enough to wish Reverend Thomas Jr. and his wife Lucinda a final farewell before they left out of town. The ministry leaders had gotten together months in advance to plan a surprise "wedding anniversary" evening service for the reverend and his wife. The other members had privately donated enough money to send them on a seven day Carnival cruise to Jamaica as an anniversary present. Almost everyone in church knew about the secret and they even created an imaginary fund to confuse Thomas Jr. to do it. That was the way it always was at New Mount Greater Faith Baptist Church. If the community had needs, then the church always managed to find a way to meet those needs. The church itself was built by his father Thomas Sr. and also, with the help of some of the remaining elders back in the mid 50's, who did their best to make sure that the church withstood the tests of time. In its illustrious past it has also survived countless close calls from various firebombing attempts by the KKK and other radical groups that hated minorities. What the building itself (which was made with fire red brick with white pinecone wood trimming) lacked in virtue of size of the other mega churches that existed today, made up for it in its praises each Sunday. When he was still alive, Thomas Sr. would preach to near death and would have to be packed to his office after every Easter sermon. Sister Lawrence stood in awe of her god son "I shole' hate your daddy ain't here to see how his lil' protege' turned out….but baby, my faith already tellin'me, that he's up there in heaven right now, with God and just smiling away at you." Sister Lawrence confirmed. Thomas Jr. pondered the thought for a full second. It had appeared as if in that second, his mind went to a special place in time before he could acknowledge her back, "I appreciate that Sister Lawrence. I know how much my father meant to this congregation, let alone to the rest of Atlanta. Thomas Jr. had only been preaching in his father's place at church for a short while. His father had died due to a terrible bout with pancreatic cancer and did not live long enough to see him ordained as the church's primary. It was very painful for Thomas Jr. to watch his father, who had been his hero, wither away like a lifeless orchid. Here was the man that had lead demonstrations, been beaten down by the police, organized worldwide peace rally's, been advisor to Martin Luther King Jr. been a devoted husband, and father of three who had offered so much to the world and was allowed to fade away before his time, Thomas thought.

The noise in the background broke his train of thought and Thomas Jr. turned his attention to the remaining members of his going away party, "Excuse me everyone! My wife…ahem…my wife and I, just want to say thank you again for blessing us with this wonderful and thoughtful gift! It has been both an honor and blessing, for us to receive this kind of appreciation of service from the members of God's church. Again, we can't say it enough…. So now, no thanks to you all, we only now have an hour and a half to get home, get packed, and get our antennas on a plane!" Rev. Thomas Jr. quipped. The tickets were scheduled for them to leave the following day, but would need them to fly out of Atlanta to Miami tonight. Knowing their reverend though, if given the time, would have probably talked them out of taking the cruise in the first place. They all laugh hysterically at his Katt William's impression from the "Friday After Next" movie, and finally allowed him and his family to leave for home. Make no mistake, Thomas Jr. loved his church, but the neighborhood was not what it used to be and that was partly why he had not lived there in years. On the long ride home the Templeton family, which consisted of his wife Lucinda and his two teenage fraternal twins, daughter Mia and son Markus, began a discussion of all the "do's and the don'ts" to follow while the adults were away, and also reminding them to mind their grandmother. "Markus, I don't want to hear about you sneaking any of your little fast assed girlfriends over while we're out of town!" Lucinda scowled. Markus tried his best to fight off the grin that already conquered his young handsome face. Lucinda had long known her son had taken his charm and good looks from his father and knew he would not waste any expense to have one climbing through his bedroom window the first chance he would get. "I mean it young man!" Lucinda repeated in earnest. Seeing that his mother was not in any playful mood, Markus Templeton straightened his halfcocked smile, "Don't worry bout' it momma, I won't sneak anybody over…besides, grandma may be older but she don't be missin' jack bro!" Markus complained. Hearing his son's familiar compliant made Thomas Jr. chuckle and decided to chime in, "I can definitely testify to that!" Thomas Jr. agreed. Thomas Jr.' mother had volunteered to watch over them, since she was no longer as active as she once was before Thomas Senior died. His mother Grace Templeton had always been a very gentle and soft spoken woman. It was never hard for him to see some of the virtues that his father had to have seen in his beautiful mother. Over the years, her skin's complexion hardly changed from the smooth caramel color it still was today. Thomas Jr. still remembered how pretty and sophisticated she looked in her old pictures from the Civil Rights era. She dressed rather conservatively in those days and wore her hair up then. These days, she still dressed conservatively, but wore her hair down exposing her gorgeously silky brown and silvery waves. His dad told him once that her wavy hair could have knocked over the USS John F. Kennedy air craft carrier. She had worked as a secretary at the post office when his father met Grace. For her, it was hardly love at first sight. His mother claimed Thomas Sr. had been harassing her by showing up at her desk job everyday with flowers and candy. Grace's snobbish boss did not like black men hanging around her desk and had threatened to fire her if she did not do something about it, so she quit, and had not once looked back since. They eventually got married and had three kids. Raising three black children through the 60's and 70's was not all tough for his mother Grace who was raised by her militant father, who fought in both WWII and the Korean War. Although she kept the foundation at home in order whenever Thomas Sr. would leave on business trips, part of her could not help but be in fear for his life on the road. It was not difficult to look back at all the times his mother spent crying alone in her room after getting death threats towards her husband. The toll it took on her was rough, but Thomas Jr. made it a priority to keep his mother in good spirits whenever it looked as if she would come apart. Since his father was now gone forever, he still felt obligated to do the same.

"Mia? Are you feeling ok, hun? You haven't said "one word" since the church announced our trip tonight." Lucinda asked puzzled. Mia glanced over at her mother, as if her face foretold the dark events that were to come. The soft spoken seventeen year old Mia Templeton had always carried herself as a kind and care free spirit, much like her mother Lucinda, while her twin brother Markus was the brash and bold one. "Mia?" Lucinda asked again, while turning around in her front seat. "I just…" Mia struggled to find her words, as if they were loose change in between a car seat, "I just have a bad feeling…." Mia explained. Everyone in the vehicle got quiet and offered her their complete attention. "Why do you think that, baby?" asked Thomas Jr. His sister's cryptic warning left Markus mystified and tapped her on the leg, "Yeah, Mia WHY would go a say a stupid thing like that?" Markus asked sarcastically. Her son's tone did not sit well with her and immediately put him in check, "Hush your mouth Markus!" Lucinda commanded. Markus smacked his mouth and rolled his eyes out his back window. "Don't be rolling your eyes at me boy or you'll be feeling for them on the floor!" Lucinda threatened. She composed herself and turned her attention back to Mia. "Now honey, where is this all coming from?" Lucinda asked concerned. Mia huffed out loudly, as if she had been held down under water for the last ten minutes, "How can you and dad, just up and leave?" Mia shouted. The worry in her shrieking voice caused them to stare at each other both frantic and confused. Markus smacked his lips once again and chuckled mockingly, "What chu' worried bout' Mia, the boat flipping over or sumthin'?" Markus asked. "Markus…" Lucinda said perturbed. Markus continued to poke fun at his sister's expense, "Don't worry lil' sis, mom and dad are swim champs, remember! They could probably swim to Jamaica if they wanted to!" Markus punned. His mother whipped her head over her shoulder with lightning speed, "Markus!" Lucinda snapped. Thomas Jr. could merely shake his head at his spoiled son's foolish remark. Though Markus's crude attempt at flattery was mildly appreciated, memories of his old glory days as a swimmer began to resurface his brain, like a nonintrusive periscope in the ocean from an inconspicuous submarine. He recollected all the good times he shared with his friends and the wild dorm room parties they crashed, all the loose women he chased, until luckily meeting Lucinda.

When he first met Lucinda "Lucy" Landry she started out as just another one of his latest conquest. They were both on Hampton University's Men and Women's swim team respectively and were also gold medalists. As sought after as Thomas Jr. was by all the ladies on campus, Lucinda surely did not make it easy for him. She played hard to get whenever he sought to take her out to dinner. In his mind, at least in the little mind down below his belt, believed she was worth pursuing. Back in the day, she too could have also had any man she wanted on campus, being on the swim team kept what was already an awesome looking body in perfect shape. Thomas Jr. had eventually found out that his "future wife to be" was more than just another pretty black woman with a great looking ass. Unlike some of the other women on campus, Lucinda was not too impressed about how he looked, or how great she thought his famous dad was (at least she never let on during that time anyway) If anything, she impressed "him" with her willingness to be upfront about everything and also her superior book smarts. Here it was 25 years later they were still looking at each other as those same young swimmers back in college. Lucinda's frame had hardly changed much, even after giving birth to the twins, and "that" he always was appreciative of. Although she was much older Lucinda Templeton was still that cool and calm type of black woman who always thought before speaking her mind. "Now honey, (Lucinda spoke with a calculated tone) I know that you're probably only worried because it's short notice, and also after…. (Lucinda needed a brief moment to contemplate her next words carefully)….your ordeal, but your father and I didn't ask to take this trip. It was a gift honey. A wonderful blessing from the members of our church," Lucinda explained. Mia eyes shifted towards her window as though she were looking to find something that was lost. "You know, your father and I put off celebrating our wedding anniversary for awhile now, and with everything this family's been through since the last ye…." Lucinda said before getting interrupted abruptly. "WHAT I BEEN THROUGH, MOM!!! That's exactly my point!" Mia asserted. "Now that's not fair Mia…" said a wounded Lucinda. "Seriously?" Markus balked. He threw his phone down into his lap in disgust, "Man, Mia…you really need to let what happened go and start moving on wit' yo' life, dang!" Markus insisted. Thomas Jr., who was now gazing at Markus through the rear view mirror, "That'll be more than enough, Mark." Thomas Jr. ordered. Markus was the one between the two who always had to get the last word in regardless of the situation. "But for real dad, you and mom really do deserve a br…" Markus pleaded again. "I said… that will be all, son." Thomas Jr. repeated sternly. Thomas Jr. was not as big as his late father was, but he was certainly every bit the disciplinarian he used to be. "Look Mia…What happened to you… wasn't right. But no matter "how" ignorant your brother may act… (Markus smacked his lips like he often did when displeased) he is right about one thing… You "DO" have to start living your life, honey, and be thankful God blessed you…blessed US, through a very ugly situation! But all that MESS is behind us now, and it's been a while since your father and I have been able to celebrate our anniversary ALONE together! Not to mention, all the trouble the people at church went through just to make this trip possible, and you know people POE'!" Lucinda joked. Mia tried to fight off the grin that barely pierced through her pretty brown and frowning face. Since the first day she was born, Lucinda Templeton seemed to always know how to barter a smile from her little girl, especially whenever she was upset about something, "Is that a smile I see? Aw-w-w… look, Thomas…is that our big baby girl showing off all those pretty pearly white teeth we paid for!" Lucinda quipped. Markus rolled his eyes and put his earphones on in contempt. Mia began to laugh even harder. Seeing Mia finally happy also put a smile on her own worried face, "You see? Now, doesn't that make you feel better? Now….about your grandmother…you know she's crazier than me, so….!" Lucinda explained. Lucinda's criticism of his mother caused her husband to snap, "Hey now!?!" Thomas Jr. interrupted. She was fully aware of her husband's feelings about his mother's well-being, so Lucinda felt compelled to poke fun at the sensitive reverend, "What I meant was…you know she doesn't "have it all" and it's only rightly so that you take FULL advantage of the time she has "left"….especially with her being a national pastime and all and besides, you never know…" Lucinda concluded mockingly. Lucinda's off-based comment was causing him to take his eyes off the road, "Know what? I don't know WHAT'CHU talking about…" Thomas Jr.' voice went up a few octaves (when normally his monotone was that of Rod Serling of The Twilight Zone) His shrieking tone made everyone in the car snicker underneath their breaths, with the exception of Thomas Jr. who was becoming slightly agitated, "Ain't shit....I mean, ain't JACK happenin' to MY damn momma! My momma gonna' live forever!" Thomas Jr. pouted. His protest only added fuel to the fire causing his family to laugh uncontrollably. Feeling sore about , "I don't know what the hell ya'll laughin' at… .man, all ya'll bout' to make me lose my Christianity up in here!!!" Thomas Jr. retorted. Their laughter was getting so out of control and infectious, that even he had to join in, regardless that the joke was at his own expense.

Meanwhile, as they were getting closer to their new two story town home in the North Atlanta uptown district, Thomas Jr. noticed that the gas meter was running low and decided to stop at a local gas station. He took great care while parallel parking his wife's SUV to the nearest gas pump. Lucinda seemed to love her car more than she loved him at times and was not in the mood to hear any of his wife's lip service, Thomas Jr. thought. On an average late Sunday evening, Thomas Jr. usually would be driving home alone in his own four year old Lexus, but due to the rising gas prices, both he and Lucinda agreed that driving together was more affordable. When he stepped out of the SUV he could hear every bone in his leg joints pop in harmony from sitting in church all day, and for a split second, his mind went numb at the site of the high gas prices at the grungy looking gas station, "Goddamn….I mean, uh…don't nobody get out, I'll be right back." Thomas Jr. instructed. He had always tried his best to live as a righteous man, but for that moment it had taken everything in him not to curse. Lucinda simply shook her head at her eccentric husband and resumed reading her Essence Magazine. After he went inside to pay for the gas, the lowly looking attendant working the register took his money (without so much as a glance at him) and had the audacity to shoo him out the line to get back to the movie he was too busy watching. The attitude of the gas attendant made him mumble underneath his breath in terminology that only he and the Lord knew. It was not that long ago that he did not mind doing a little swearing here and there, he recalled while he pumped his gas. Thomas Jr. was a Hampton University graduate who ultimately became its athletic director. Before his marriage to Lucinda, and his ordination to Christian ministry, he had lived a life of pure uncontrollable promiscuity. Going all the way back to grade school, little Thomas Jr. was always ahead of his age and his reputation at every school level was the same among his teachers, "very smart and bright young man...when his mind was not focused on the pretty girls in class." When he was younger, Thomas Senior would scold him in the presence of his mom after these accusations, but would be high fiving him when she was not looking. As a man of God, Thomas Sr. never approved of any wild or deviant behavior from any of his children, but his fatherly side approved of any healthy interest in girls from his sons (although his brother Terry on the other hand, was a different story) Thomas Jr. was not much older than his younger brother Terry, but his sister Candice was the baby of the group, who in time, studied law at Spellman. Although she was mentally tough like their father, Candice was just as blessed on the outside, thanks to their mother's beautiful genetics. Even as a little child, Candice could always litigate her way out of an ass whooping, Thomas Jr. often complained. After graduating law school, Candice soon married her college sweetheart Herbert McElroy, who was an accomplished piano player who also taught classical music at Georgia Tech. Herbert was a rather quirky, tall, slender, and well dressed looking black man, who favored little Richard more than a music composer who taught Ludwig Beethoven. He really impressed Thomas Senior after he discovered Herbert had previously recorded with Motown. Whenever Herbert and Candice stopped by, both he and Senior would break into songs by the mighty Temptation's. They would sing "My Girl" at least sixty-three times it felt like, Thomas Jr. remembered. Though they lived happily together for a short while, Candice died before she could ever have any children of her own. She had suffered from a terrible bout of pneumonia and her death tragically affected everyone in the family. Herbert, who was a person who abstained from alcohol, had begun to drink more than he composed, and in his sorrow, resigned from his job at Georgia Tech. Their mother, Grace, was so heartbroken by Candice's death, that she could no longer bring herself to travel with Thomas Sr. anymore. Not long after, Thomas Jr. left his career as Hampton's athletic director, began preaching fulltime in his father's place at New Mount Greater Faith.

The exile of Terry Templeton

Many, many, years ago…

Terry had always been rebellious toward his father, especially when it came to him liking the other boys at school. This type of abnormal behavior was not acceptable under the roof of New Mount Greater Faith Baptist Church, nor appreciated in the Templeton household. During his tumultuous childhood, Terry Templeton encountered countless beatings from his father behind his androgynous ways. So much so, that Grace once suggested he change his name to that of "Zebra." Thomas Senior occasionally found himself screaming at his problematic son ever since he was just a little boy, but it did not matter how hard, or how much he prayed, yelled or, beat on him, Terry Templeton still refused to change his effeminate ways. As his church's reverend and leader, Thomas Sr. could not afford the backlash his family might have endured for harboring a disobedient and homosexual son. Although being disobedient in the eyes of Thomas Senior was considered disrespectful, that alone was at least tolerable, but the scandal of raising a gay kid (in his era) might have tarnished his credibility and respectability as a shepherd of God. The more Terry matured, the more Thomas Senior worried about his secret getting out to the congregation and forbade him to have any male friends, but for all his posturing Thomas Senior's "worry" would soon come to an end. It happened around Terry's seventeenth birthday that he and Thomas Senior would have a terrible argument that would change their lives forever. On one fateful Sunday, Terry had complained to his father that he had not been feeling well and that he might have had a stomach virus. Thomas Sr. had been skeptical of his plight, but gave the peculiar Terry Templeton the benefit of doubt. Denying his instincts, Senior allowed Terry to stay home from church anyway, which was a rarity in the Templeton household. Back then, only death, sickness, or an act of God could get you a day off from church, but Thomas Senior was still nobody's fool. Terry always knew that the family normally did not come home until the late afternoon, but what he had not figured was the sudden surprise return of Thomas Senior. The rushing Thomas Senior had barely got halfway to the church when he told his wife he forgot his glasses and bible at home. The first thing that caught his attention upon entering the front door was that Terry was no longer lying down on the couch where they left him. Instead of calling out to find Terry, Thomas Senior made everyone wait outside while he searched around the house. After realizing that Terry was obviously not downstairs, Thomas Senior slowly crept up the stairway like a lurching hyena after a meaty bone. Each step he took was careful and quiet, as if he were a starving mountain lion stalking elk. The closer Thomas Senior had gotten to the top of the second floor of their house, the more he could hear the sound of voices. After finally reaching the top of the stairs Thomas Senior made his way towards Terry's room, which was further down the upstairs hallway. With the door already cracked opened, Thomas Sr. could now make out the voices that were coming from out of Terry's room. One of the voices belonged to eighteen-year-old Harvey Henry. He was both Terry's classmate and new neighbor, who had just moved in across the street with his family. Thomas Sr. also could hear Terry's voice as well, but his words seemed muffled by the sounds a person would make as if he were trying out a new delicacy. Harvey began to groan as if he had been relieving himself from a hard day's work from a twenty hour shift. "Deeper…" said a moaning Harvey. By this time, Grace had gotten out of the car and entered the house. Grace called out to Thomas Senior, but when she did not see neither he, nor Terry, her female intuition compelled her to quickly go upstairs. She tiptoed her way up the stairs like a petite alley cat after a naïve mouse. Once she reached the top of the stairway, she could see her husband in the hallway facing Terry's bedroom. Grace started to call out again, but the frozen posture of her devout husband made her not do so. In all the years she had been married to Thomas Senior she had never seen his face turn so pale, "Thomas?" Grace called. When Senior did not immediately respond, she scurried to see what it was that had his attention so transfixed. Terry's door was open just enough for them to see Terry on his knees on the floor half naked and with her new neighbor's son Harvey standing in front of him the same. What she had seen caused her legs to go wobbly due to the distasteful sight of what she was witnessing. The obviously experienced Terry Templeton had been giving Harvey Henry a very loud and very sloppy blowjob. "I've "BEEN" waiting a long time for a piece of this, ever since I first met you!" Terry said thrilled. Thomas Sr.'s ice cold trance was broken upon hearing his son speaking like a Saturday night slut on the Boulevard. Grace began sobbing and was trying to cover her mouth to control herself. She could not believe how Harvey merely stood their exasperated as their son Terry is swallowing another young man's penis. "Damn Terry….you got me almost passing out…" Harvey said in ecstasy. "I can't wait to get in that tight little"… Harvey's words are stifled by Thomas Senior's ferocious and horrified tone, "Get the hell out of my Goddamn house…you little son of bitch!!!" Thomas Senior commanded. Thomas Senior had not only HEARD, but had "SEEN" more than enough from his sacrilegious child. Harvey fell backwards from trying to conceal his genitalia. When he got to his feet, Harvey quickly scooped his clothes off the wooden floor, dashed in between Thomas Sr. and Grace and ran out the house half dressed. Candice and Thomas Jr. who were still outside, looked puzzled by the stumbling Harvey Henry as he tripped over and over again to get away from their house. They both laughed and jumped out the backseat of their father's car and ran back into the house. Terry could only feel shame and confusion as he looked into his father's scowling face, "Get off your knees boy..." Thomas Senior ordered. At first Terry hesitated, but eventually did like his father asked. But soon as he did rise to his feet, Thomas Senior slapped Terry across his face and sent him tumbling back to the hard wooden floor. "Now, get back up, get dressed, and come downstairs." Thomas Sr. said solemnly. Grace could only shake her head in tears as she followed her wounded husband down the hall. When Terry came downstairs everyone was waiting on the sofa in the living room. Thomas Jr. and Candice had been outside the entire while, did not need a degree in Aerodynamics to figure out what had just happened, after already noticing Harvey's half naked ass running out their house. Thomas Senior had had enough of his son's homosexual antics and promptly showed him the door. Grace tried to compel Thomas Sr. to change his mind, seeing that Terry was only seventeen at the time, but there was no going back. "He's man enough to have sex with other young men in my house… well then, now he can go "fuck" them at their house! But the one place he won't be doing it anymore is in my Goddamn house!" Thomas Senior growled. The entire room went opera silent. None of the children had ever heard their father swear at them before and it would be the last time he would have too. Terry left and was not heard from in years. His mother was fortunate enough to get a call from him once after he heard about Candice's death, but he neither called nor showed up for their father's funeral.

Maybe Terry did not show up out of respect, but if that were true that would have been silly thinking, Thomas Jr. always believed. It was their dad for crying out loud. Yeah, their father found out he was gay and kicked him out, but that was no excuse for Terry to alienate himself from the rest of us, Thomas Jr. thought, while he waited at the stoplight. Thomas Sr. had never once brought up the incident, at least not until he was on his death bed, Thomas Jr. recollected. All his adult life, Thomas Senior had been a very physically strong man who loved to build things with his own hands, but due to all the medical complications he suffered during chemotherapy, his former imposing body had become a drastically frail one. On his dying bed he managed to ask Thomas Jr. to do him one last favor, "Tell Terry…dad said…"h-hello"… a-a-and… t-that… I…I… was wrong...a-and…that d-daddy, d-daddy n-n-never, s-s-topped l…" Thomas Senior said, just before the machine that was keeping him alive buzzed loudly, as if it was the final quarter of an NBA game. Thomas Senior had been actually sorry for keeping his children apart all these years. The thought of that revelation brought tears to his eyes. Just as she yawned Lucinda took notice and grabbed her husband's hand. "Are we alright?" Lucinda whispered. That was his favorite thing he loved to hear his wonderful wife to ask. Thomas Jr. gave her a quaint smile, "Yeah baby. We alright! I love you Lu" Thomas Jr. said assuredly. The light turned green and he pulled off. Thomas Jr. still missed his little brother and sister.

Sonny Korne Pays a Visit

The Templeton home…

…It was not until well after ten that the Templeton's made it home. Thomas's mother Grace had a spare key and had already been at their home waiting for everyone to return. She had been sitting at the dining room table working on a cross word puzzle. Grace never really cared for Lucinda's choices of furniture. With age came arthritis and Grace always struggled getting out of her daughter-in-law's flashy leather sofas, especially just to go pee. Elder Deacon Stanley Golightly, who had been a friend of the family for years, already told Grace about the planned surprise trip. Grace always jumped at the chance to spend more time with her only grand babies. Whenever she looked at her granddaughter Mia she could not help but be reminded of her own late daughter Candice. Sometimes, Grace would tell Mia of that fact and they would share cries together over old stories about her. She would compare how both Mia and Candice shared liking the same things, loving the same foods, or about how beautiful they both were. She would also explain to Mia about how devastated she was after Candice's sudden death. Mia's fraternal twin Mark reminded Grace of both Thomas Jr. and Terry. It had been many years since she had last spoken to her youngest son. It was hard on her to see him put out the house at such a young age, but Terry was so wild and stubborn and always had a mind of his own. In those days, homosexuality was not viewed as normal behavior, or as open as it is in today's world, but with Thomas Senior being a reverend, she already knew it was inevitable he would one day be forced to leave home. Grace had long suspected something was different about Terry, even when he was just a little boy. Terry always volunteered to brush Grace's hair and no matter how much her husband fussed at Terry for walking feminine, the worst it seemed his walk had gotten. Her life is a lot quieter these days, and she did not get around like she once did back in her heyday. She knew she had led a full life and did not mind not living in her husband's spotlight anymore. Grace had spent most of her adult life on the go with her famous late husband. They both spent more time away from home than they actually spent in their own house. When Grace would find herself under the weather, she would always think back to those good times she shared with her colorful husband. One thought in particular, often tickled her to death. Thomas Senior had been travelling around the world nonstop at the time and complained of jetlag and told her, "When I get reincarnated, I'm going to ask God to let me come back as a bold eagle." Thomas Senior said. When she asked him why, and he said with a straight face, "Because, a bird's ass doesn't have to hurt everywhere they fly, and my ass feels flat as a greasy hamburger stuck underneath a steel spatula!" He said. The thought of that moment always sent her into hysterics. Despite his spiritual nature and beneath his infamous "always serious" facade, Thomas Sr. had a real comedic side to him as well, much like Thomas Jr., who was unlocking the front door, "Hey momma!" Thomas Jr. greeted, as the whole family filed in behind him. Mia is the first to greet her grandmother with a kiss on the cheek, "Hey grandma!!!" Mia said softly, as if she were avoiding waking up a sleeping infant. Grace held onto Mia's hand firmly, "Hello

Mimi…child, would you just look at you!" Grace said happily. "Every time I see you baby, you're looking more and more like my sweet Candy!" Grace complemented. Mia could not help but to blush, as she had seen pictures of how amazing her late aunt once looked. "Hello Mrs. Templeton…" Lucinda said coyly. It would sometimes bug Lucinda whenever her mother-in-law would show up. She hated how Grace would leave every light on in the living room, but would be sitting in another room adjacent to it, all for the sake of solving her shitty little crossword puzzles and avoid sitting in the very furniture she picked out. "You know…you don't always have to relegate yourself to the corner of the dining room table every time you come over Mrs. Templeton…" Lucinda said, as they shared a brief hug and an air kiss on the cheek. "Naw baby… I'm alright JUST where I'm at, and besides…you would've had a mess to clean up had I sat down over there. Sitting in those things, are like being trapped at the bottom of the underground rail road." Graced quipped. Lucinda rolled her eyes and stomped away. "Trust her Lu….she was there!" Thomas Jr. said jokingly. Grace put down her crossword puzzle and sat in attention, "Now, you hush it boy! I ain't too old to put you over my knees and give you a good ole ass whoopin'!" Grace urged. Thomas Jr. stopped flipping through his mail and tossed it all into the air and ran over to his mother and pretended to try and get into her lap, "Oh please, oh please mamma, would you for old time's sake?" Thomas taunted, as he kissed her repeatedly. Grace began to blush and started shooing him away, "Oh, stop that nonsense child! And don't you need to go pack?" Grace asked. Thomas Jr. had always known how to push his mom's buttons and sadistically loved to get under her skin. She popped him good on his shoulder to get his attention, "Ok, ok, I can take a hint...hey Markus?" Thomas Jr. called out. Markus had not been home less than five seconds and already popped his headset in his ears, Thomas Jr. realized, "Markus!!" Thomas Jr. yelled again. His father's booming voice startled the preoccupied Markus forcing him to drop his phone case on the floor, "Whuh?!? Aw-w man…dad look what you made me do? "You could've warned a brother…" Markus cried. Thomas Jr. simply lets out a tired sigh. "Look son, I know you don't care if by the time you turn thirty that you won't be able to still hear the sound of your own farts, but in the meantime do your dad a favor and take that crap out of yo' ears and go over there and speak to your grandmother, and would you please take out the damn trash!" Thomas Jr. insisted. A confused Markus watched his father huff his way up the stairwell. "Sorry bout' that dad!" Markus said apologetically. Thomas Jr. let out a disinterested moan. "Man, I can't ever catch a break…hey grandmamma'." Markus said in a patronizing tone. "Hello to you too, Markus…now get your little narrow ass over here and give your grandmamma' some sugar boy!" Grace directed. He wasted no time hugging his regal, but ornery grandmother, "Sorry Momma G, it's been a long day, you know? Sorry for trippin'…" Markus regrettably said. "It's alright baby, when you get granny's age, you gonna be doin' a WHOLE lot of trippin' yourself!" Grace kindly admitted. They both laugh out loud and embrace each other as if they had just won the Georgia lotto. Unknowingly, Mia had been staring at both her fraternal twin and their nuturing grandmother from the kitchen. A part of her wanted to share her true feelings about her parents impending trip, but Mia did not know how without sending her grandmother into a massive panic attack. Grace Templeton was always a woman of reason and who also believed in intuition and foresight. Mia knew that if she disclosed ANY anxiety's regarding her son's safety, Grace might have forced her father to call the whole thing off, so Mia decided to remain silent and allowed her grandmother's mind to feel at ease. After everything that Mia had already been through over a year ago, after meeting Sam Korne….after the rape…. it still caused her not to trust her feelings enough to allow them to ruin the only chance her parents had had at what peace of mind they could muster for one whole week away. Regardless of what had transpired, how could she possibly be selfish enough to ask them to stay? Mia worried. Suddenly, a cold rush of fear shot down her spine like a set of wet marbles and made her immediately take off up the stairs. "Mia?", "Is everything alright?" Grace asked alarmed. "Yes grandma everything's fine!" Mia said, without bothering to look back. Her granddaughter's odd behavior caused Grace to seek answers from Markus, who only offered a shrug, "I don't know Momma G… she been actin' kooky all night, maybe it's her time of the month?" Markus joked. "Well if it is, then it's no business of yours! And speaking of business, why don't YOU go on do what your father asked now, and take out that trash, boy!" Grace said displeased. "Yes ma' am." Markus huffed. "My lord….I don't know WHAT they gonna' do with that boy?!?" Grace muttered to herself.

Several minutes had passed and Grace began to worry what it was that was taking her grandson Markus so long to return. He was only asked to take out the trash, but where he had to go should not had taken fifteen minutes for her grandson to return, Grace contemplated. Both Lucinda and her son Thomas Jr. had been upstairs packing their suit cases for their getaway anniversary cruise and did not want to alarm them prematurely. Knowing her grandson Markus, he probably found somebody's baby momma to flirt with at the bus stop across the street, she thought disgusted. Grace was no fool, and knew Markus was a pussy hound just like his father Thomas Jr. was at his age, and worried about him catching one of those new diseases, or worse.

The nauseating thought of it made her roll her eyes, and then at that moment, the front door bell rings. When it immediately rings again, Grace could not help but feel slightly startled by the person's impatience. After the doorbell rang back to back, it was more than enough to get Thomas Jr.'s attention to come charging to the top of the staircase, "Who in the…?" Thomas Jr. shouted. Grace waved Thomas Jr. off to settle him down, "Your child probably…He might've left his key in his room again instead of with him to the dumpster! Go finish packing child, I got this." Grace said. Her dismissive tone causes Thomas Jr. to frown, "Yeah, my child…But YO' grandbaby!" Thomas Jr. quipped. His mother was not amused with his candor either and shared her displeasure, "Alright boy…" Grace fired back. Thomas Jr. laughed off his mother's empty threat and decided to come downstairs to check the door. "I think I can still open a door child. Let me handle this, ya'll gonna' miss your luggage check-in at the airport!" said Grace. The doorbell rang again and the sound of the doorbell began to agitate her, "Hold on Markus! I will send him on up to help you bring that shit back down." Grace promised. Thomas Jr. marveled at the way he could still raise the ire of his mother, who was always known for her fabulous mystique and superior elegance. But despite her vaunted regality, it never really took much work to push his mother's buttons, Thomas Jr. fondly recalled. For as long as he could remember, Grace Templeton never took shit off anyone. Because she was not born a male, her crazy war torn Veteran father always pushed her beyond her limits, both physically and emotionally as a child. She was never allowed to date and studied mostly in her spare time, when she was not too busy playing the organ for her church. Her father's oppressive childhood discipline also made her an effective activist as well, which led Thomas Jr. to believe was the reasoning for her being much harder on him than his father ever was, "Alright momma." Thomas Jr. agreed, and walked back toward his room. Grace was smiling proudly at her over protective son, as he turned and jogged back up the stairs. She found it hard at times to be around her fully grown son, who reminded her so much of her lost love. Despite their different backgrounds and ideals, it was easy for her to pick out the many similarities that they did share, like their love for music and for the people. Thomas Jr. and his father never wanted people to feel like they were alone in any given situation, no matter how bleak their situation might have been. No matter how disparaging a person circumstance might have been, Thomas Senior refused to give up on anyone, which was the primary attraction to her heroic husband. Grace scrambled to the front door to answer it, but something inside her made her take pause before doing so. The doorbell rang three more times, as if the person on the other side may have been furious, causing her to jump in a panic once again. As Grace gazed into the narrow peep hole, she could see Markus with his favorite Atlanta Braves hat and bouncing up and down like he had to take the world's biggest piss, "Hold on a minute boy, and have you lost "ALL" your damn mind?" Grace shouted. Once Grace finally unlocked the front door, too late did she realize that the figure who stood there was not in fact her grandson at all. Whoever the person was, had obviously stolen Markus's clothes and was not even black, but a white man. The man gave Grace a grisly looking grin and punched her hard in the mouth, sending her flailing to the floor. Her own blood filled her mouth like the mad gushing water off a geyser at Yellowstone Park. Shock and fear overcame her to the point where she could not find the will to scream for help. She tried her best to crawl away towards the steps, but to her, it felt as if she were swimming through a very deep and wide marsh, than just a common floor. Two more white men filled the room and the man wearing Markus's things admired her ability to take his punch, "Clevis… could you please go and grab that black bitch?" He calmly asked. The taller of the two men, seized Grace by the back of her hair, causing her to shriek out in pain. He was a giant of a man, who sported a large variety of Ku Klux Klan tattoos across his neck and who also resembled the actor who played the Jethro character from the Beverly Hillbillies, "Pardon me bitch." He said coldly. The man named Clevis then dragged Grace back to the man who was wearing Markus's clothes, "Now that ain't how you supposed to treat your uninvited guests, now is it?!?" He sinisterly asked, and punched Grace again, knocking her unconscious. Thomas Jr. heard the loud commotion and darted toward the steps and called out to her, "Momma!?!" Thomas Jr. frantically called. He heard the steps of an approaching large shadow that could not have belonged to his smaller mother, "Naw nigger preacher…I ain't cho' momma!" The man said menacingly. Extreme fright scattered down the back of Thomas Jr. like rain racing down a rusty rooftop. He turned and noticed Lucinda had quietly made her way to his side. Lucinda had the house phone in her hand, but the man heard her dialing from downstairs, "Tell that fine bitch of yours that she can stop trying to call the cops, the lines been…disconnected. We wouldn't want anybody spoiling our "family reunion" now, do we?" He said condescendingly. Thomas Jr. swallowed hard and gestured to Lucinda to put down the telephone, "Where's my mother and my son Markus!?!" Thomas Jr. nervously asked. Thomas Jr. noticed that the shadow was drawing nearer the more the man down stairs spoke, "Well now, that all depends preacher man…why don't you two just come on down from there, and grab holda' that sweet ass daughter on the way wit' cha'! After all, what's a party without…party favors!?!" The man from the shadow said eerily. A chill went up Thomas Jr.' spine after realizing that the man in the shadow could have already known them prior to breaking-in and that they were not some random target, "I won't let you near my daughter, so you can forget it." Thomas Jr. said boldly. The imposter who wore Markus' clothing pulled out a gun and walked away for a few seconds. Thomas Jr. could now hear his mother below crying and screaming. He then returned with Grace, with whom he was dragging. "You still want to negotiate?" He barked sarcastically.

Thomas Jr. pondered the invader's threat for a moment before responding, "Well?" The man asked. Of course, his decision was not a simple one. How could a man possibly weigh the lives of his mother, wife, daughter, and son in such a predicament? Thomas Jr. fretted. Thomas Jr. knew what he had to do, but just could not find the strength to use the words. Mia had been in her bedroom ease dropping from behind her bedroom door. She opened the door with her eyes fixated on her father's eyes, "I don't want anyone else hurt daddy, let's just go." Mia said softly. Thomas Jr. tried to play out different scenarios in which he could get help or, keep his family out of harm's way, but every idea that came to mind might have resulted in getting everyone killed, "Ok." Thomas Jr. agreed grimly. Mia grabbed her father's hand, while Lucinda was already gripping the circulation from out of the other one, and they all made their trek quietly down the stairwell. Thomas Jr. could almost hear the sound of his own heart beat as the rest of the family slowly descended upon their captor, "Mr. Korne, p-p-please…l-let m-my family go!?!" Mia kindly asked. A befuddled Thomas Jr. and Lucinda looked at one another in complete bewilderment, "Mia…who is that and what's this all about?" Lucinda whispered. It only took Thomas Jr.'s mind an instant to process the identity of his captor. The memory invaded his mind, as though it was an unwelcomed tsunami seeking to regurgitate over a hot Californian beach, "God no…." Thomas Jr. muttered. Of all the people in the world who could have forced their way into his home why did it have to be him? Thomas Jr. dreaded. The man took off Markus's Atlanta Braves cap to reveal himself as none other than Sonny Korne, who was the father of the young man who was imprisoned for the attempted rape of his daughter Mia, "Not yet darlin'...but I promise you, I will free you….hell, I'm gonna' free you all." Sonny said, with a vile snicker.

During every excruciating passing moment, Thomas Jr. and the rest of his family struggled to hold themselves together, as their entire world was being flipped upside down in the mere blink of an eye. Thomas Jr. and Lucinda had gone from celebrating their 25th marriage anniversary with his church's congregation, to being home invaded by the father of Sam Korne. The last time Thomas Jr. saw Sonny Korne, was when the judge sentenced his son, Sam, to serve 15 years in federal prison. Sonny had vowed to get "even" with the Templeton family, as it was with the help of Mia's "own" testimony that helped put Samuel away. It had been over a least a year or, so since Mia Templeton had went out to that frat party at Georgia University. She was not enrolled in college yet, but nevertheless, had enough connections to get inside a college party anyway. Mia met Sam through a mutual friend named Jackie Allsberry, who attended the same university, and who described Mia in court, as a star struck fan and claimed how "She wanted to have his children!" When he was in high school, Samuel or, "Sam the Man" Korne was the do-it-all "Mr. Everything" athlete across town at Drummond High in Irwin County. The school always had a nasty reputation for being racist towards its minority students, but after Mia met Sam, she did not seem to get that impression. Mia would explain on the witness stand, that Sam began the night acting like the "perfect gentleman." She would go on to say that Sam was not like the other white boys she was accustomed to meeting at her school at Martin L. King High. When he spoke, his slang actually fit in the right situation, and did not come off sounding contrived, Mia claimed. Samuel wore his hair cut low with a high top fade, just like the other black boys she was accustomed to seeing and even sported a goatee, "I thought he had a smooth Jon B vibe to him. He was making me feel special the whole time….like I was the only one in the universe." Mia explained. Mia admitted that she was "obviously physically attracted to him" and expressed to the court that it had "nothing to do with what he did on the football field or, the basketball courts." Mia told the jury. She claimed that it was not the fame that impressed her or the fact him being well built, but from the amount of tenderness and attentiveness he showed her. It made her feel safe…at least, in the beginning.

"Sam the Man"

Mia did not really care for drinking alcohol much, but she was overly thrilled after being invited to "The Biggest College Homecoming Party" of the year!" Jackie said. Although Mia only knew a few, out of the hundreds of faces at the massive celebration, she tried her best not to look out of place. To help her fit in, Mia's "then friend" Jackie Allsberry offered her a drink to relax at the party. It would eventually be proven during the court proceedings, that both the portly Jackie Allsberry and Samuel Korne had a previous "romantic relationship." The court prosecutor also would prove how Samuel "influenced" her to drop ecstasy into Mia's cup, to make her become more susceptible to any deviant behavior he had planned. Mia was not used to going out to many big university parties and usually hung out with her "own" in the Peachtree district. Despite her impulses, she tried to live a certain kind of way, due to her dad being a preacher and somewhat of a public figure. Mia would state in court, how the more she "drank from the cup, the more she had trouble getting in control of her bearings." When she tried to get some fresh air to clear her head, Samuel had managed to convince her to go back with him to his dorm room. Of course, Sam flatly denied any improprieties on his part, stating that Mia was more than willing to go back to his dorm room for some privacy. Though there was little truth to what he insinuated, "It did not excuse him for trying to take things that far!" Mia argued to the defense. She was still a virgin and the closest she came to being otherwise was from her gynecology visits. Even with Mia's mind tripping off the ecstasy she ingested, she still managed to be aware enough to realize what was beginning to happen. In Mia's confusion, she tried to leave his dorm room, but at this vantage point, young Sam "The Man" Korne lost control. Since Sam was such a charismatic star athlete, he was not used to receiving rejection from most females on most campuses, let alone being rejected by a black high school girl. Things got really rough and as she tried to escape his manic rage; Mia's face was slammed hard against the dorm room wall, rendering her dazed and confused. Mia later testified that he had then threw her down on his bed and gagged her with what tasted to her like a pair of dirty socks. He had been drinking rigorously and began cursing and spitting on her for rejecting him. She cried out for help when Samuel had bitten her on the shoulder like a rabid pit bull and warned her that if she tried to scream for help, he would bite her nose off. He then tied her hands behind her back with a red bandana and pulled her pants down. Mia who was visually upset at the time, had began to cry at this point during testimony, and went on to explain that Sam had tried to force himself inside her, but his roommate and teammate Anthony McCall and his girlfriend, had just come through the door. She met Anthony earlier during the party, who himself admitted could tell Mia was too young to go to the university. When Anthony saw what was happening he grabbed Sam and pulled him off her with a choke hold. Lilah, his girlfriend, untied Mia and told her to go home. Listening to his daughter's awful testimony made Thomas Jr.' stomach and head feel as if they were both being boiled in hot motor oil. He tried his very best not to jump off the bench he sat in from the galley to strangle Sam Korne for what he had done to his sweet Mia. If Lucinda was not there by his side, he might have tried anyway. Thomas Jr. also remembered how furious he was, after Mia came home that night. Contrary to his Christian teachings, and beliefs on restraint and leaving things for God to handle, Thomas Jr. wanted to kill that boy badly and might have, had Lucinda not talked him out of it.

Despite what Samuel Korne put his daughter through, Thomas Jr. had been proud of her to find the courage to tell her story. Mia already had a hard enough time dealing with the grime that an assault left on people, especially after the added media pressure and public backlash became another creature of its own to deal with. After all, Samuel Korne was a popular blue collar All-American quarterback and pro basketball prospect at a major university, who also had a spotless reputation around campus. It was going to be an uphill battle for the court prosecutor to prove that a white student athlete of his caliber, who signed autographs for sick children in hospitals, and worked in his spare time passing out hot meals at churches, could EVER be accused of such a heinous act, not to mention, who shared a room with his black teammate. Nevertheless, Thomas Jr. stuck by his daughter and his family, to make sure that she would be the last of his many victims. Anthony refused to testify against Sam out of fear of losing his athletic scholarship and his girlfriend Lilah, who was receiving threatening phone calls. The prosecutor managed to convict him anyway, despite him having very few material witnesses. There were other victims who ultimately came forward and one even had videotaped it with her cell phone. Samuel got 15 years federal time for his transgressions and the last thing Thomas Jr. heard about Sam's father Sonny Korne, was that he drank himself into a stupor and left town. But here he was alive in the flesh and holding him and his family at gun point…

The Templeton's home….

"You still haven't told me where my son is!?" Thomas Jr. demanded. Sonny Korne had spent the past several minutes holding a shiny Glock 9mm to his head, while brandishing a half-cocked smile. Any admirer of his former one-time future prospect son could look into the devilish sneer of Sonny Korne to see where the family looks came from, Thomas Jr. thought disgustingly. His piercing baby blue eyes were every bit as bloodshot as they were the last time Thomas Jr. laid eyes on the fanatical father. It was if someone pressure washed his eyeballs at a car wash, until they finally bled from out the sockets, "He's being well taken care of…." Sonny said unpleasantly. Sonny's other scruffy headed and skinny sidekick was not much older than Markus and laid waste to their once beautiful kitchen, Thomas Jr. witnessed. All their most expensive crystals, as well as his mother's antique dishes that once adorned their immaculate kitchen, had been smashed into bits and pieces. The stainless steel refrigerator, which they always kept full of fresh smelling fruits and the finest deli cuisine, were being ripped inside out, "…..Oh, and by the way….hope you don't mind us…."redecorating" the place a little bit….!" Sonny jeered. "Hey Sonny, I found some!!!" the man in the kitchen yelled. "Ah-h-h!" Sonny said appeased. "Well…bring it over, Pete! What kind of hosts could ya'll be without offering your guests a drink?" Sonny asked in a condescending tone. The man named Pete hustled to the living room holding two bottles of vintage wine. Thomas Jr. and Lucinda had glimpsed at each other in utter disappointment, as they made previous plans to use the wine to commemorate their anniversary. He handed over one of the bottles to their largest partner, Clevis. Clevis had been standing behind Lucinda and Mia the entire time while the younger one; Pete, rummaged through their now ruined kitchen and dining room for booze. "Thanks." Clevis scowled. The normally reserved Thomas Jr. was becoming agitated by the fiend's constant disrespect, "Some guest!?! You kidnap my son, bust into our home, assault my mother, and hold all of us at gun point. Just what is it that you hope to achieve from hurting me or, my family?" Thomas Jr. asked angrily. Sonny punched the proud reverend across his jaw. "So…the good reverend, preaching nigger, does have balls after all!? Well now, let me tell you…"Tommy" just WHAT the fuck I DO plan to achieve…." An overly pleased Sonny replied. He looked at Pete and Clevis and nodded his head and then the two men grabbed Lucinda and Mia and began to bond their hands behind their backs with industrialized zip ties. Thomas Jr. instinctively lunged at the men, but got cold cocked in the back of the head with the butt of Sonny's gun. Blood spewed from the giant gash that now resided in the back of the Thomas Jr.' blistered head. He breathed heavily, as he tried to gather himself on the floor. The two men grabbed him and started to bind Thomas Jr.' hands behind him as well. Sonny pulled out a cell phone and gave Thomas Jr. an uncomfortable wink. After he was finished dialing the phone number, the living room got so quiet, that the person who answered on the other line could be heard saying "hello" from the other side of the room, "Bring the little black fucker in." Sonny ordered. A full minute passed before a sudden loud and rapid knock came from the backdoor. Clevis rushed over and unlocked it with the comparable eagerness of an obsessed fan getting to meet his favorite star backstage at a concert, thus allowing a fourth assailant to enter (who was also carrying a bludgeoned Markus Templeton) The man was obviously a brother of the man named "Clevis," Thomas Jr. figured. He had the same build as he did, and sported the same KKK prison tattoos, but only he was a blond, "Oh, Thomas! Look what they did to our baby?!?" Lucinda cried out. Mia could not find the words or, strength to speak and could only cry out her feelings. "Drop his sorry black ass over here, Revis!" Sonny insisted. Thomas Jr. and his family watched in complete horror and astonishment, as the new stranger carried in and dropped their precious son onto the living room floor like an old bag of potatoes. Markus was unconscious and his hands were bound behind his back and with his mouth tapped shut. His face was clearly swollen from the attackers beating on him, Thomas Jr. noticed. "Sweet Jesus…." Thomas Jr. thought. Seeing his child handled in such a vicious and vile fashioned infuriated the proud reverend, "Just what the hell do you want!?!" Thomas Jr. screamed. Sonny turned his head with the speed of a lashing bullwhip, "Why, ain't it obvious by now reverend? We ALL here to do to you, the same FUCKING thing, you did to MY son Sammy, when you all judged him, and took away his whole life you black som' bitch!" Sonny protested. "My kid had a bright future. All he ever wanted to do was play ball, it didn't matter if in was in NBA or, the goddamn NFL, and maybe even buy his daddy a new Cadillac!" Sonny replied and struck Thomas Jr. again, this time in the stomach. He could feel all the air careen from out his gullet from the force of Sonny's sucker punch, "But, no…your precious little "chocolate drop" over here, made sure that that couldn't ever happen!" Sonny said regrettably.

Thomas Jr. was having trouble keeping his emotions intact, as he was forced to listen to the mad ravings of the lunatic who held them all captive. Tied up and outnumbered, Thomas Jr. knew he was at a clear disadvantage, so the only thing he could think to try was appeal to the fatherly side of the delirious Sonny Korne. If he could sympathize with him, maybe he could at least bargain for the lives of his children, Thomas Jr. hoped. "Mr. Korne, please, as a Christian man, and as a fellow father, I'm asking you…I'm begging you, to please….let my children g…" Thomas Jr. began, before getting kicked in the face before he could finish his sentence. The force of the man's boot hit Thomas Jr. with such a searing pain that he slightly lost consciousness. "No!!! Lucinda and Mia winced in unison. "Fellow father….how DARE you, mother fucker?" said the infuriated Sonny Korne. He walked over to a cowering Mia and grabbed her by the chin. Mia winced loudly, as the madman started to squeeze her, "Tell him cunt, tell him our little secret!" Sonny insisted. Thomas Jr. and Lucinda looked upon Mia in bewilderment, "Secret? Mia, what is this man talking about?" Lucinda asked. Sonny, who was still squeezing Mia by the chin, turned her blood rushed face toward his, "Glad you didn't spoil the surprise darlin', but it's alright now, Go on… tell em'. Sonny insisted. Her words begin to spew and crumble from out her mouth with the urgency of a volcanic lava flow, "Mr. Korne…s-s- said that…s-s-aid that if I told anyone… t-t-told anyone he was coming for me…he would take his rifle… and k-k-kill us all…one b-b-by one." Mia said. "Mia… no." Lucinda muttered. Sonny leans in and kisses her cheek, "…And I keep my promises too darlin'!" Sonny confirmed. He let go of her face and walked back over toward Thomas Jr. and knelt down in front of him, "Let me tell you sumthin' …you know, father to father…my son…my kid's dead, you fucking asshole…killed while trying to take a shower. He'd been beaten and raped by a group of niggers, much like yourselves…" Sonny said dryly. When Thomas Jr. caught his breath and looked into Sonny's Korne's cold blooded eyes, he could feel his ice cold stare piercing through the very layers of his soul, "When my boy first went in…I couldn't even keep my food down. I started drinking all the time and my wife couldn't deal with it no more, so the bitch left me…high and dry! My son was all I had left, and I couldn't even protect him. Oh no, not from those hypercritical ass raping coon fucks!" Sonny yelled angrily. Thomas Jr. could not believe the nerve of the eccentric Sonny Korne and growled back at him like an enraged grizzly bear, "So all this is our fault?" Thomas Jr. screamed in his defense. His fearlessness lasted only a few seconds, until Sonny leaned in closer, "No mother fucker, not OUR…just YOUR fault! When my Sammy tried and tried to apologize for what he done, it was YOU who wouldn't let things go! It was YOU that wouldn't let that bitch of a daughter even speak to my boy! He didn't… He didn't have to go, to jail. Not even once did you consider my boy's future!" Sonny yelled. Thomas Jr. knew he was debating with a deranged psychopath, but the preacher in him could not allow the entire truth to be withheld, "His future? So what you're trying to imply, is that "my daughter" has no worth? Why? All because you're "BOY" could slam a damn basketball, or throw a football really good? He tried to rape my daughter you maniac!" Thomas Jr. hollered. "That little whore of a daughter of yours led my boy on…that don't give her the right to go back and change her mind at the very last damn minute! She was the one who wanted to go back to his room, just what the hell did the little bitch EXPECT to happen!?! But now…now "all" that is just blood flowing under a broke dick bridge. My boy's dead… so it's about time for some fucking payback motherfucker!" Sonny confirmed. His profane outburst caused Lucinda to pray, as she recognized that same blood thirsty look in the eyes of her own husband during Sonny Korne's son's trial. Clevis became irritated by her mumbling and slapped Lucinda harshly across the mouth, "Shut up, you black bitch!" Clevis ordered. A rush of fright almost stopped Mia's heart seeing her mother smash into the floor, "Momma!?!" Mia hollered. The constant shouting woke Grace, who had been previously knocked out earlier by the same twisted man. Grace was from the Civil Rights era and was used to abuse, and in her anger, managed to get up to her feet and hit Clevis over the head with a fire place poker. "Get out, you damn demons!!!" Grace yelled infuriated. When Clevis dropped his gun Grace reached down for it, but was hit over her head with the wine bottle from Pete's hand. "Ha-Ha- Ha, man, I like this bitch! Let me do her first! Yo' Cleve, you cool bro?" Revis chuckled. The bloodied Clevis, who grew up a proud and adamant southern racist, loved getting hit too. Clevis stood up, with blood trickling down the side of his squared jaw line, "Naw…this bitch is all mine." Clevis said calmly. Thomas Jr. had lost both religion and his mind once his mother had been struck over the head with the thick wine bottle, "Momma?!? Why'd you have to go and do that? She's just an old lady you bastard!!" Thomas Jr. pleaded. Sonny was amazed by the misplaced boldness in the helpless preacher's words and appeared to have had an epiphany and decided to offer him a choice, "You want to save your momma, nigger? Then you're going to have to do "us" a FAVOR... Hey, Clevis…why don't you come over here a sec." Sonny kindly asked. Thomas Jr. could see that Sonny was out for blood and knew he was also out of options to save any one. The vicious beating he received at the hands of the vile Sonny Korne left him weak and disoriented. Clevis walked over to them and had a wide smirk on his face. "Now, my Aryan friend here, doesn't really LIKE your kind, 'BUT" as an exception for me, would be willing to let you suck his dick to save your momma..." Sonny plainly asked. "It's either that or, he's gonna' finish what he started with her jaw. Revolted and disrespected by the very thought of the idea, Thomas Jr. emphatically retorted, "You must be out of your God damn minds….hell no. I'm a child of God and a leader of his flock." Thomas Jr. said boldly. Sonny froze momentarily and began to stare Thomas Jr. eye to eye with the same repulsive disgust people get after they incidentally step in dog manure in their own front yard. He looked up at Clevis and pointed to where Grace was laying. The large man scurried over to her unconscious body and picked her up off the floor by the hair, along with the fire place poker rod she previously smashed him in the head with. Both Mia and Lucinda were in tears and could not bare to watch, as the large psychopath held the fire poker high above her tender head. "Well then, kiss this old bitch goodbye…!" Clevis said, and started to whale on the poor frail woman savagely. Thomas Jr. cried out in protest, but it fell on deaf and heartless ears. The blood splattered from off the top of her head like a yard sprinkler and adorned the living room wall with the coarseness and manners of a drive thru carwash. The mother who spent nearly seventeen hours in labor to bare her first born Thomas Jr., ten hours with her second Terry, and fourteen with her youngest baby, Candice who would be waiting for her on the other-side. Thomas Jr. could only sob, as he watched a man three times his mother's size, beat her senselessly right in front of him and his family, and could not do a thing about it to save her. His mother was the only one he had left from his childhood, his brother Terry was a runaway, and Candice died way before her time. Had he been alive to see him, Thomas Senior would have been really disappointed in him, Thomas Jr. pondered disappointedly. "How could I've been so stupid….to send my "only" son out into the night…to do such a meaningless task, only to endanger him as well as the rest of his family, Thomas Jr. regretted. "Oh, mama…" Thomas Jr. said aloud to himself. The Reverend Thomas Templeton Jr. did the only thing a man of God in his position could think to do in such a horrible situation, he prayed. He did so quietly to his self, as if the very words he had spoken were so delicate and fragile, that if said any louder might have been stolen away by thieves. Clevis dropped the bloody poker and the cold and clanging sound it made when it landed on the floor startled shivering reverend. Pete was sneering proudly from ear to ear like a wide-eyed starving jackal. It was painfully obvious to Thomas Jr. that the men who were holding them hostage were no strangers to extreme violent acts and feared they still may want even more blood. Clevis's entire hands were saturated with the now deceased Grace Templeton's blood. He breathed heavily, as if he might have smoked too much during the middle of a morning jog. Mia's fear level was beyond petrified and flinched uncontrollably as Revis came and stood quietly behind her. She could sense his lustful gaze upon her and causing her to feel terribly uncomfortable. Guilt had begun to permeate throughout the youthful mind of the shocked Mia Templeton. The sounds of her own mother's uncontainable sobs and seeing Grace's motionless feet from behind the sofa sent her further into madness. She would no longer be able to laugh at how much Grace hated her mother's furniture choices or, about how much Grace complained about not seeing her grandchildren enough. Lucinda was also struggling emotionally and could no longer hold onto her faith as her fear seemed to be strangling her after every breath. In her own mind, Lucinda was begging God for mercy on her family and most of all, for her husband. She knew that had the circumstances been different, Thomas Jr. would have done all that he could to save them, so it was left up to God to determine the outcome. Lucinda sought God's mercy, but on this night, mercy would not come for anyone. For reasons of his own, God seemed to have chosen to only act as a mere spectator for this particular night and for reasons unknown, were seemingly being greatly punished, Lucinda dreaded.

"The offer still stands asshole, so what's it gonna' be this time?" Sonny asked. Thomas Jr. was sulking on the living room floor and could not find the strength to lift his own head to speak, "As a reverend….I have to f-f-forgive you for murdering my mother, s-so you are forgiven you! B-B-hut, as a man…you can ALL go to hell!!! I will not stoop to your disgusting level. Get thee behind me Satan!" Thomas Jr. passionately implored. Sonny and Clevis laughed at the hysterically appearing reverend and immediately grabbed his weary body from off the floor and pinned him across the arm of one of the living room sofas. "We thought you'd never asked! Let me let you in on a little secret, coon; you niggers ain't the only one's packing! Pete…the lube!" Sonny asked happily. Pete went into his over-sized leather jacket pocket and tossed a small jar of Vaseline to Sonny. Sonny snatched down Thomas Jr. pants, and Clevis anxiously stripped down his own blue jean pants. Sonny gave the Vaseline to Clevis and he opened the jar and smeared it onto his obviously thick erection. Revis snatched Mia up by the waist and slammed her hard onto the dining room table, causing the wind to be taken out of her body. Lucinda tried her best to protest to an enraged Pete, but he quickly silenced her by punching her ferociously in the mouth, "Keep that shit down bitch!" Pete ordered. Lucinda's lips seemed to explode after contact from the young man's hard charging fist. Sonny grabbed Thomas Jr. by the throat and spit into his face, "Where's your black God now mother fucker? You took something from me, so now, I taking "everything" from you! Go on Clevis, tear him up…tear his ass up right in front of his wife and daughter!" Sonny screamed. The grinning Clevis grabbed the proud preacher from behind his waist and plowed unmercifully into his anus with his massive cock. Thomas Jr. tried his best to squirm away from the country strong Clevis, but to no avail was immensely overpowered. Clevis's eyes roll to the back of his head, as he penetrated him over and over and over again. Thomas Jr. had never been in such agony in his whole entire life and Clevis granted him no mercy. Sonny was in ecstasy, laughing and teasing Thomas Jr. while he was being raped by the large white man. "Go on preacher man, cry it up! Pop his black cherry Cleevo! Hey boy how yo' ass feeling? Ha-ha-ha!!!" Sonny quipped, while laughing hysterically. Lucinda was crying frantically over her husband being humiliated in front of them. The more she watched the large man pound into Thomas Jr. the more her temper had forced its way back to her now coarse throat, "You God damn bastards, I hope you all burn forever in hell for this!" Lucinda said viciously. Sonny Korne had had more than he could stand from the mouths of the Templeton women, "Hey Reve, why don't you and Pete show these ladies a good ole' time?" Sonny insisted. While Mia was being pinned down, Revis shoved his fingers underneath her skirt and shoved them hard into her vagina, causing her to scream. She cursed the vile man and he then shoved his other hand into her mouth to quiet her. Mia bit into his hand and Revis began to beat her with his fists until she laid there defenseless. Lucinda had her shirt ripped clean off her body by the twenty something-year-old Pete, "Wow rev, you sho' know how to pick' em! Got me a fine looking black milf this time! Thanks dude!" Pete thanked. Lucinda was numb with anger and pleaded with the young man to stop, but the young man could not be bargained with, "Hey baby, relax…I may be younger than you, but trust me, I know what I'm doing! Pete said sadistically. Although ailing from being roughly penetrated, Thomas Jr. refused to give up on his family, "L-L-Leave t-t-them alone, you son a-a-a bi…" Thomas Jr. yelled. The more Thomas Jr. tried to fight for his family the harder the overpowering Clevis slammed his manhood deeper inside him. Sonny punched Thomas Jr. with his pistol seemingly in unison as Clevis finally climaxed. Clevis, now drenched in sweat, shoved the exhausted reverend on the floor and blew him a kiss, "Thanks sugar!" Clevis said. "Careful Cleve…you know what they "all say" ….once you go black!" Sonny joked.

Thomas Jr. had endured both physical and psychological damage at the hands of a bruising homosexual maniac and was helpless to defend himself from it. He could not think clearly due to the pain and mental trauma he was experiencing and could not focus long enough to notice the screams that rung out from his wife and daughter, as they were being ravaged by the four men. They took turns abusing them in every twisted and unimaginable way, torturing them one on one, two on one, and even four on one. The men drank merrily and celebrated their despicable savagery, while Lucinda and Mia had been torn vaginally and anally Ad nauseam. Their lives no longer the same and forever changed in the span of a few hours. Mia's young virtue had been ripped from her, as though it were an unsuspecting present at the mercy of an eagerly awaiting child at Christmas. She could no longer feel her body below her waistline and feared that she may even contract a disease, let alone be impregnated by any of her four rapists. Sonny's goons had left her on the dining room floor a shivering mess, but she could still muster enough strength to look over at the lifeless arm of her mother that hung from it. Lucinda had finally succumbed to her fatal wounds. She had been strangled and beaten to death during forced intercourse with Pete and Sonny. Mia tried her best to cry, but the strain of doing so, caused her to faint. What had happened to them made Thomas Jr. believe he was caught inside some bizarre and gruesome nightmare he simply could not wake up from. The pain and humiliation he endured was so unfathomable, that he had almost convinced himself for a brief moment that in no way was it all real. He tried to force himself to accept that he simply imagined his mother's gruesome beating or that his son was being subjugated by white thugs. His mind could not let go of the facts that were staring right in front of his face. It was not supposed to happen to them, they devoted their entire lives to the church, the exhausted reverend thought. God could not have possibly allowed any of this to happen to him, to his family or, had he merely run out of grace and mercy? Thomas Jr. wondered pitifully. Had everything that he had done up to this point not been good enough to merit his family a pass on such a crippling and humiliating ordeal? Why me God? Have I not been humble enough? Haven't my family?" Thomas Jr. pondered. Each of the distraught reverend's head scratching questions caused both his adrenaline and blood pressure to wake him from his blinding concussion. Thomas Jr. had been brutally pistol whipped and was not fully himself mentally. His vision, as well his other senses were slowly returning to him. He had seen his bloodied wife of twenty-five beautiful years, lying on her stomach, unmoving and half naked. Thomas Jr. would be helpless to stop the onslaught of tears that ripped their way down his withered face. He could tell that the light that ounce burned so bright around his lovely wife had been snuffed out and extinguished like the flame on a scented candle. Thomas Jr. looked over to the floor and saw three of the men standing over Mia, who also was motionless. "What had he missed? What have they done to them? Maybe they were still okay?!?" The horrified reverend worried. The thought had never occurred to him that his motionless wife was already dead.

Thomas Jr. was overwhelmed with so much sorrow, so much grief, and so much confusion, that everything around him was too unmercifully difficult for his seasoned mind to process, "Lu?" "B-baby…baby please…w-wake up…" Thomas Jr. called out. Pete, Clevis, and Revis were rolling their eyes at the sight of the wounded preacher, while he pleaded aimlessly for his wife to open her eyes. He turned to his inanimate daughter, "Mia, darling…p-please…M-M-Mia, get up for daddy." Thomas Jr. cried. His heart was completely broken at the revelation that his family was now forever lost. Gone was the sweet joy he once shared with his life partner and the fruits she bared during her role as an incredible mother. The always appreciative reverend was there to watch his babies first steps, their first day of school, or anything else of greater importance they all shared as a family and prayed for them. Unknowingly, Markus was still unconscious, so Thomas Jr. believed him dead too. Where was God's mercy? Thomas Jr. began to ask himself. For the second time in his short career as a reverend, Thomas Jr. had doubt. Doubt in his faith, doubt in his role as a reverend, doubt he will even survive his present ordeal. With his hands still bonded together behind him, he managed to crawl closer to Lucinda to will her to speak, “Lu, honey, I know you can hear me…” Thomas Jr. whispered. “Save yourself the trouble nigger…Lucy has left the building! Man, I gotta’ tell ya,’ that sho’ was some fine piece of ass, reverend…after all, you should know!” Pete said. The three men were mocking him by high fiving each other and cracking jokes, all at the expense of his dead family. “And as for this silly bitch… (Pete looking down at the unconscious Mia) Pussy was “too” tight and gave lousy head, so…she gets the boot!” Pete screamed and kicked her in the side. Pete and the men began to stomp Mia over and over until the life she once had was extinguished. No more will the destroyed preacher be seeing her pretty smile shining from the front row of the church. She reminded him so much of his sweet little sister Candice and prayed she would be there to greet her. Was his family cursed? The feverish reverend wondered. Either way, Thomas Jr. had seen more than enough and willed himself to his feet, and charged all three of the men. The three men were completely caught off guard, and Pete hit the wall while Clevis and Revis went flying to the floor. Although Thomas Jr. was not the biggest man in the world, but all the years spent as a world class swimmer still granted him powerful leg drive and hit them with the force of a delusional rhinoceros. Thomas Jr. had new life and sprung back up to his feet with a lion’s quickness. When Pete recovered, he immediately struck Thomas Jr. in the jaw, but rage and hate had consumed Thomas Jr. so, that the punch had not fazed him and when Pete swung again and missed, he was head butted in the mouth hard, knocking out his front teeth. The brother’s Revis and Clevis, were scrambling to their feet, but not before Clevis received a deadly kick into his groin area. Revis could not get control of the raving mad preacher and was more than glad when Sonny blindsided the crazed reverend, “Dammit’ Sonny, what took you so damn long?” Revis asked. “Watch who you talking too boy, I’m running the fuckin’ show! Besides, that piece of shit you call a truck needed to be moved off the street, but it wouldn’t fuckin’start. I hope you don’t mind me breaking open your car window to borrow your jumping cables Tommy!?” Sonny asked. “Go to fucking Hell!” screamed Thomas Jr. Sonny had been ecstatic that he had finally broken the good Reverend Thomas Jr. He had won, and nothing pleased the white supremacist more than to see Thomas Jr. give up all he was and all he had before seeing him dead. A low moan came from behind Sonny. Thomas Jr. could see that his son did survive the malicious beating he took at their hands, but hoped that the insane Sonny Korne had not realized it. Marcus began to mumble loud enough a second time, but unfortunately Sonny turned his attention to the young Markus Templeton, "Okay boys… get your shit…time for us to go…but before we go, I want you to see this first mother fucker!" Sonny said. Sonny went into his coat pocket and pulled out the Glock and aimed it at Markus' body. Thomas Jr. screamed for mercy for his son, but the remorseless Sonny Korne put his foot on Markus' fragile chest and smiled at Thomas Jr., while he shot the young teenager once in his chest then again in his head. This was the end and Thomas Jr. knew it. There were no more words that he could say on this lowly and frightful night. The rest of Sonny's crew had grabbed all their belongings and headed out the back door. Just as Clevis ran out he turned to Thomas Jr., "I'm gonna' miss you sugar! Thanks for your "oh so warm" hospitality!" He said sarcastically while rubbing his crouch. Thomas Jr. began to dry heave at Cleve's words. Sonny snickered at Thomas Jr., as if he were a finished masterpiece he had spent months painting. He wanted revenge on the Templeton family and had finally tasted the fruits of his twisted labors.

Sonny had originally planned to shoot his daughter in the head from afar (right in front of him with his rifle) but his sadistic side would not allow Thomas Jr. the satisfaction of not knowing who killed her. "No," He thought at the time. After his son had been sentenced, the Reverend Thomas Jr. had more than one child to lose and what better way for any father to suffer, than by taking everything he had up close and personal, Sonny rationalized. "Look at me." Sonny instructed. The weary Thomas Jr. was beyond drained. Despite it all, he had hoped that maybe God would have at least spared Markus's life. Markus had absolutely nothing to do with any of this madness, He thought. Sonny Korne succeeded in taking just what he set out to take from him. "What was the point of even living now?" Thomas Jr. thought hopelessly. How could he possibly move on…as a man, let alone as a so-called preacher? His manhood had been ripped from him along with his entire family, but where was the mercy God promised?" He questioned. In the mist of his helplessness, Thomas Jr. had failed to do the "one thing" he promised his late father he would never do. Before his father's health failed him years ago, Thomas Jr. made an oath to never lose his faith under "any" adversity or, disparity life through his way. It seemed like a simple promise to make at the time, considering that that it was virtually impossible for him to foresee his imminent future, Thomas Jr. knew. But what he did know for certain, was that he was about to die, so how much was that promise worth about now? Thomas wondered. All his anger, all his self doubting, and all the mind numbing confusion that got built up, was now transforming his thought processes into self loathing and a total disregard for his own life. While his body racked with pain across the cold living room floor, a defiant Thomas Jr. stared back into the menacing eyes of the towering Sonny Korne, "Now do you see nigger? Now do you see what it's like to have your heart torn right outta' you....after someone takes somethin' away from you that cha' loved? Well...if ya' didn't....I'm kinda' guess'in that you do now." Sonny said. Sonny had the 9 mm pointed at Thomas Jr.' head and cocked the chamber. When Sonny Korne looked into Thomas Jr. face it was obvious to him that he was a defeated man who was ready to die. He had hoped to see the once proud reverend beg for his own life, but Thomas Jr. would not give him the satisfaction and said nothing. When Thomas Jr. seen Sonny's hesitating, he cleared his throat one final time. His throat made him feel, as if he was swallowing an entire pigeon. "What, you gonna' pray for me now, preacher man?" Sonny asked sarcastically. Not one time did the handgun tremble in Sonny Korne's rugged palm, as he held it firm and steady, like an experienced golfer teeing off on his last hole.

"Your black God don't exist here mother fucker!" Sonny concluded. Thomas Jr. shook his head in more defiance, "No...I'm done praying, for your sorry Aryan ass. Not even GOD can help a pathetic piece of shit like you...or your son. Hope one day... you get to burn in hell, right along with him." Thomas Jr. said audaciously. Thomas Jr.'s frosty remarks struck a deep cord within Sonny Korne's cruel soul, like they were loose shrapnel exploding from a well hidden land mine. Immediately, blood began to permeate his capturer's smug white round face, as he was being over taken by a violent rage, "You first motherfucker!!!" Sonny shouted. Thomas Jr. had closed his eyes while Sonny open fired on him at close range. He emptied what was left in his gun clip into the face and body of Thomas Jr. His body huffed and puffed, as if he was throwing the bullets instead of using his gun. Clevis stuck his head through the opened back door, "Yo' Sonny, time to roll! I think I hear sirens!" Clevis warned. Sonny Korne looked at the dying reverend one last time, "Come on!" Clevis yelled again. He spit on Thomas Jr.'s carpet and put his gun away in his coat pocket, "Alright. Fuck it." Sonny Korne said, and ran out the back door. The fading Reverend Thomas Templeton Jr. always did whatever he thought was his best in life. Throughout his adolescent years, the humble Thomas Jr. hardly gave his parents any trouble or, reason to mistrust him. After spending the majority of his life at church, Thomas Jr. eventually forsaken his worldly desires and followed his heart to do something that he believed he could never do, which was preaching the gospel. He buckled down and got married and even was very faithful to the love of his life, Lucinda. Thomas Jr. was always a great provider for her and their children, Markus and Mia. They all led, what had seemed to be, a very happy and fruitful existence. With all that said and done, Thomas Jr. could not understand what they could have done so wrong to deserve such a merciless indignity? Didn't he deserve better for all his efforts? Wasn't he being an effective enough preacher? These were the lingering questions that burned into his slipping conscious as he slowly began to bleed out. He struggled every millisecond to find air to breathe, but he could no longer hold on to the life that was snatched away like a thief in the night. His blood had flooded the same mouth that once was used to preach engaging sermons. Thomas Jr. eyelids were too heavy for him to keep open. His body went numb and ice cold from the bullet holes that filled his damaged body. Before he had ever taken on the role of a preacher, he used to believe they were untouchable, that nothing "ever happened to real preachers." It was his own father that taught him at an early age that, "God always took care of his own." The air that was occupying his lungs mere minutes ago, was no longer allowing him freedom to breathe. His chest felt as if it were being sat on by a baby elephant. This was it for Reverend Thomas E. Templeton Jr. and the last thought that ran across his dying mind before he blacked out, "If God does exist… he's got a lot of fucking explaining to do!" Thomas Jr. thought, before his weathered eyes finally shut. The room is eerily silent and the air is thick and musty. The promising family, who previously adorned the two story home through many special holidays, birthdays, and other grand achievements, was now written out of existence. Their lives were being erased like some pesky stray pencil marks made on a test paper. Many questions will be left unanswered and most people will begin to wonder; "If such gruesome acts could happen to a kind, respectable, God fearing preacher and his family, then what will keep it from happening to them? Yes, what indeed…

Chapter 3:

Lieutenant "Crazy" Kale Keegan

Des, Moines, Iowa: Just a couple years ago….

The night terrors that were troubling First Lieutenant Kale Keegan had been getting much worse lately, after each return home from active duty. Night after night, thoughts of his most God-awful and most despicable deeds done to protect the American way of life would become re-imagined repetitiously, like some daily exercise routine. Despite the many horrors that his subconscious was willing to drudge up, it was never enough to detract him from the call of duty. Most people who were intimately aware of his violent nature would unanimously agree about how much he really enjoyed what he did for a living. It was not until recently that his over-indulgence for war had gotten the better of him. His team's latest mission to Afghanistan ended in such a complete failure, that it almost cost him the life of someone very dear to him. The terrible consequences of that final mission sent Kale's tormented mind over the edge and himself struggling to get any rest for the night. Like every other night, Kale tossed and turned like a wounded animal in the King-sized bed he shared with his wife, Rita, to whom he frightened out of her sleep. Even with her back turned to him, she could already smell the strong putrid stench and dampness of perspiration that adorned their red satin bed sheets, which made his side of the wet mattress, resemble a musty kitty pool. On most occasions, Kale's dreams played out in his head like an over exaggerated 1980's action flick, which were also shown in the same "first person perspective" as a person at home watching normal television. The ear-piercing and gut-wrenching sounds from his screaming enemies were also intensified, as well as the massive amounts of bloodshed his murderous weapons manufactured. Every night, he found himself wandering about some foreign country's derelict region or, long forgotten warzone and being the primary contributor of a high body count. But on this particular night, his mind decided to play things back a little differently than usual. The guilt that he carried was both too fresh and too heavy for his mind to either forgive or, forget. When it came to disposing terrorists and the like, he never hesitated to dispatch lethal force for the sake of liberty, but never had he been forced to do such a heartless act to a fellow soldier, let alone his best friend. Even though Dave forgave him for what he done, Kale had not forgiven himself for being so careless. His team would have to take their mandatory psyche evals once a month which usually amounted to squat in Kale's eyes. But it did not matter how much therapy he received from the various military psychologists, the results remained the same. His last couple tours to Afghanistan had finally taken their toll on his psyche and triggered his brain to see the ghosts of all the men, women, and even children, who also died at the hands of his unit. In some cases, he would try to converse with his victims in hopes of a reprieve, but every time he tried, they would appear to be mocking his sad disposition. As of late, his wife, Rita, had been taking great pains to calming her estranged husband. Kale's dreams were so strong and believable to him, that she had to avoid grabbing him during one of his "fits" for her own protection. His combat training seemed to have a nasty habit of kicking in whenever anyone tried. Whenever Kale would have one of his night terrors, his shrieking would upset the kids, especially Kyle who was just an infant, leaving Rita up for hours at a time consoling him back to sleep. Often times, her husband's terrible sleeping habits could be tolerated, but as of late, Kale had been talking more and more with the demons, who awaited him in his sleep. Rita had overheard some of her friends discussing their husbands suffering from the same symptoms as Kale, once they returned home permanently from active duty. They called it a "post-traumatic stress disorder," which was something Rita had never heard of before. Either way, she could clearly see that whatever Kale was involved with overseas was changing him inside out and possibly a danger to their marriage. It had worried her that his eating habits had changed and was not eating properly anymore, if at all. There were moments when he would zone out on her during important discussions concerning the kids, who she knew he loved. Kale, who was a devout sexual maniac, was hardly touching her after youngest son Kyle's birth. Their relationship would seem to strain after leaving on special missions days and sometimes weeks, at a time. But not long enough for her to fall out of love with him. The only good she believed that ever came out of Kale playing "soldier boy" was how it kept his libido rock hard and his tanned frame chiseled. Rita had been a workout "fanatic" herself, prior to bearing their children and often worried about him losing interest in her after having the pregnancies. In her heart, Rita knew Kale would go through a brick wall for his superiors, but it did not seem fair to her, that he had to sacrifice pieces of himself to justify another man's cause. Kale was now twisting the bed sheets with his fists, as though he was breaking someone else's neck. He started to mumble louder as well, which normally meant it was time for Rita to try and wake him up, before he gave everyone in the house a heart attack from his screaming. Getting him to break out of his sleep had become as deadly as petting a rattlesnake for the diminutive Rita. She one time made the terrible mistake of touching him during the middle of a nightmare and he scooped her up by the throat and slammed her on the bed. On another occasion, he seemingly, out of nowhere, managed to brandish his trusty Swiss Army knife and pressed it against her delicate throat. Rita vowed never to make that stupid mistake ever again. The only thing that seemed to work to wake him up without incident was to call out to him gently. She spoke out to her young adult husband with the endearment of a school librarian. After she got him to finally wake, Rita already had his tea, with a tinge of Glenlivet Scotch mixed in, on the nightstand waiting on him. Tea seemed to somber his flailing mind after spending half the night in purgatory. When he laid his sky blue tortured eyes onto Rita's, he could tell from her weary expression that he had flipped out on her again. Without uttering one word he offered her an apologetic smile and reached over for his tea. Rita was hoping she could last the next night rather than the next five years of her husband's violent sleeping behavior. Back when Rita was bartending some years ago, she never could have fathomed the thought settling down with children so soon, let alone married to someone in the Armed Forces, but Rita liked good looking men in uniform, even though she did not prefer serving them at times. Although she felt they were great tippers, (thanks to having a strict bodybuilding regime and naturally beautiful Latino good looks), she did not care for their incessant drunken come-ons and hellraising at closing time. Meeting Kale Keegan seemed to change her outlook on dating military men as well. She never dated a white boy before either, but due to the circumstances of the night they met, caused her to immediately fall in love with him. Rita did not mind dating outside her race, but feared how her family might have reacted had she been the first to break their family's blood line. Making time for a relationship was not part of Rita's or, her parent's plan, especially with her on pace to graduate with a culinary degree at Polk County Tech in Des Moines, Iowa. Rita's dream was to one day be a top gourmet chef and someday, cook in her own restaurant. Since growing up as a little girl down in El Paso, Texas, Rita always enjoyed working daily with her parents in the food truck they owned. It was called "Los Famous Taqueria" and Rita learned how to cook from her mother Margarita, whom she was named after. When Rita lost her older brother Felipe to gang violence, her parents did everything possible to help her find a scholarship that would allow her a way out of their poor neighborhood and to a better life. Her parents already lost one child, but refused to lose another, so after she graduated from Betty T. Ross High, they sent her packing way up north, far away from the barrios of El Paso. Rita needed to make extra money to live off campus, so a friend of hers, Tina West, who worked as a waitress at Jay Buck's Tavern, helped her get work as a part time bartender, where she was an instant hit. She was a drop dead beauty with a sweet southern down home hospitality, witty banter, and was notorious for fucking anyone up with her fabulous mixed drinks. After all, Rita did have plenty of practice back home from some of the best teachers. Her family was rather large and loved to party hard at their yearly reunions. It was a craft she picked up by her father Rodrigo who once upon a time, was a young bartender himself. Back in El Paso, Rita would often test her knowledge on both her father and big brother Felipe over the weekends, where they would drink each other senselessly until the other was passed out. During high school, she hit the school books harder than the other neighborhood kids and did not have time to hang out and party. While her friends were too busy having babies Rita was too busy making the honor roll. She qualified for a large grant and received recognition for her high GPA an enrolled at Polk County Tech. It brought Rita great joy to have made her parents proud and it seemed like the world would be her oyster…at least, till Kale Keegan stormed into her life like a bat out of hell.

The night Kale and Rita met

The unassuming looking Kale Keegan and Rita Ramirez first met under excruciating circumstances, while their friends would later call it fate, her parents would call it an act of God. Rita had just finished working her evening shift at Jay Buck's Tavern during the frightful night in question. Her shift started out like any other typical Saturday night which was usually slow, but eventually the crowd picked up steam around midnight. As a community mainstay, Jay Buck's Tavern mainly catered to the political city's college kids and thirty-something year-old crowd. Most Saturday nights, the atmosphere was usually hyped up when house and rap DJ Mike Mixer was in the house. The thirty-eight hundred square foot restaurant /club were known for serving pretty decent steaks during the daytime, but even better drink specials late at night. Jay Buck's staff was always appreciated by its many valuable customers and Rita loved working the patio bar outside with her fellow bar mate, Anthony. Like every year, the Iowa Tech students had the establishment filled to capacity, especially during its homecoming weekend. On that particular night, the Iowa Tech students were celebrating their annual football victory over Iowa State College. Rita never expected to make much money off the college kids she normally served. Some of her customers did not even have jobs, and for the people who did have jobs, saved their hard earned money for paying their school tuition instead of bar tabs. Things were complicated enough when she had to compete with the club's more mobile and dainty shot girl's dangling their fifty cent Jello shots and fake tits everywhere. Then there were the greedy promoters, who constantly demanded complimentary drinks to some way look important, but nevertheless, she knew how to hustle and always took care of her regulars with a smile. The Tavern was its usual busy self and after an hour before closing time, a small contingent of men dressed in United States Army fatigues entered through the patio and club doors. Normally a dress code would be enforced, but it must have been hard on the door guy to turn away men who fought for their freedom to "party like a rock star" every week, Rita guessed. When the five men made their way through the patio, Rita could already tell that there was something a off about them. She was a little caught off guard after the blonde headed soldier, who was leading the pack, pointed towards her direction. Her side of the bar station was already getting slammed, but the men did not seem to mind and waited patiently for their turn for service. When it was their turn to order their drinks, Rita could tell by their dilated eyes and slurred speech that they were already too drunk to be served. Rita was an experienced bartender who did not need a medical degree to spot a drunk. Her first thought was to refuse to serve them, but they begged her again and again, claiming to have been celebrating their friend's birthday before they had to be deployed back to Germany. Rita, against her better judgment, decided to only serve them one round of shots, if they promised to take a cab home right after. They happily agreed and spent the rest of the night harassing her about how sexy she was to not have a boyfriend, and etc.... Rita was used to the same old lingo and as long as they were tipping her twenties and ten dollar bills, she did not mind it, not one damn bit.

Closing time…

At the end of the night, Rita made sure that the Tavern bouncers escorted them to the cab she ordered for them, that had been already awaiting them at the front of the building. After collecting her pay check, Rita kissed everyone goodbye and left for home. The shots that she previously took at work were quickly wearing off, as she could feel the cool night air cutting through her pretty light complexion, like razors through hot melted chocolate. She scurried to her car that had been parked up the block. Normally, Rita would have asked security to watch over her while she walked to her car, but the tavern security left before she clocked out and had no choice but to go alone. When she made her way to her red beat-up 2000 Mitsubishi Mirage, she could hear whispered voices and the scuffling sounds of footsteps rushing up behind her. Rita became nervous and her car keys fell out her hand as she fumbled to find the right one. When she bent down to pick them up, Rita was grabbed from behind. It had been the same group of Army soldiers from the patio bar. They obviously got out of the cab somewhere close by, and had been waiting to ambush her after work. "What's the rush, momma?" said the blonde headed soldier, who sported a skinny blonde Mohawk. Rita could feel her heart beating like a basketball in her throat, but tried her best to remain calm. She rubbed her chest as if she were about to have a stroke, "Oh, it's just you guys! I forgot my cell phone in the car and I was worried that my boyfriend had been trying to reach me all night!" Rita said worriedly. She was afraid and thought to say anything that would make the men give her some space to possibly make a run for it back to the Tavern. "Thought you didn't have a boyfriend? Tsk, tsk, tsk…now, Rita? That is yo' name now, isn't it? You wouldn't happen to be leading on a "devout" red bloodied soldier of the United States Army now, would ja'?" The soldier in the blonde Mohawk kindly asked. His slurred southern drawl had sent ice sickles down her spine. What was making matters worse was the unexpected cold weather, "Look, sir…" Rita began, before he interrupted. "Chip." He said. Rita looked at him sideways after he corrected her, "Look…Chip!?! It's getting very late, and I got classes in the morning…." Rita carefully explained. "On a Sunday?" Chip asked sarcastically. "Now that's two lies. What ARE we going to DO…. about you… and that sweet looking mouth… of yours honey?" Chip said sluggishly. The chuckling from the rest of the men was more than she could stand. Rita screamed for help, but one of them held her mouth closed with their hands, "That ain't gonna' be necessary, baby!" The man who held her from behind said. The soldiers were clearly too drunk to be reasoned with and all Rita could do was hope someone was watching or, was calling the cops. "Hey, baby chill out, now. The night's still young…we just want you to have a good ole' time!" Chip said sincerely. Rita was drug around the side of a building by the drunken soldiers who had called themselves "admirers" of hers. Rita bit down on the man's hand and she let out a scream that would put any Friday the 13th victim to shame. That night, Kale had just so happened to be across the street from the Tavern and was working on David's little brother car. David's younger brother, Daniel, had partied at The Frequency, which was an after hour's club down the street. Daniel and his friends had just dropped him back off at Jay's parking lot and realized he stupidly left his lights on the entire time he was gone. When Daniel could not reach his older brother David, he knew to call his best friend Kale. Kale had always dealt with insomnia anyway and Daniel knew he would be the only person up that hour, and was willing to come give his car a boost. No one who Daniel knew was more proficient at the use of profanity than Kale Keegan, who was wearing his pudgy ears out for bugging him in the middle of the night and also lecturing about leaving his lights on. He knew that that was just Kale's big brotherly way of expressing his worrying about him. Kale never had siblings and despite Daniel being black, treated him like a blood brother. "Hey dude, did you hear that!" Daniel asked, while tapping Kale. Kale had a perplexed look on his face, and stood up from under the hood of Daniel's car. Rita could be heard yelling for dear life around the corner. "Dude, there it goes again! It's either that or, I'm too fucked up and hearing things, but it sure sounded like a chicks voice!" Daniel said briskly. Without even speaking a word, Kale snatched his large jumper cables off the dusty silver Ford F150 he was using to jump Daniel's car and stormed around the building to the sounds of Rita and the five soldier's voices. Kale sneaked up behind one of the men and choked him to sleep. Before the others could react Kale was already on top of another one using the jumper cable like a lasso and choking him at will. The two other soldiers who were left standing, tried to surround the hundred and seventy five pound cowboy appearing Kale, but little did they realize that he was not as average as he seemed.

Kale's general father was every bit the fanatical and paranoid military man he was at the Pentagon, as he was at home. He made it a "priority" to ride his son's ass hard and after Kale would screw up, he would straighten him out in the backyard with his old boxing gloves, which seemed to be a common practice in the Keegan household. Despite all the crazy shit Kale would find himself caught up in, his dad always seen familiar, but untapped potential in his wayward son. He believed he only lacked discipline, and tried his best to use all Kale's anger and natural instincts to his advantage, in hopes of him one day joining him in the military. All it ever seemed to really accomplish was making his son even more dangerous. Chip was the only one left of his crew and was still trying to force his drunken mouth onto Rita's face. "Come on Rita darlin', give ole Chip some of that ole' spicy Latina sugar!" Chip said forcibly. Kale cleared his throat, "Excuse me, hoss?" Kale said politely. Chip sat up and ran his hand through his spiked blonde hair, but had not taken his eyes off Rita, "Aw, wait your turn Milt…" Chip said annoyingly. His attention had been focused so much on Rita that Chip mistook Kale's voice for one of his own unconscious friends. "Now…I know yo' mamma taught yew' better." Kale said again mockingly. "Didn't yo' mamma' teach you how to stay out of grown man's busi…" Chip began, but was dismayed by the sight of his friends laid out on the cold concrete after finally turning around. "What in "THE" hell?" Chip asked bewildered. He then tried to coyly pull out his hidden Army knife. But soon as he does Rita saw what he was up to, "H-He has a knife!" Rita yelled. Little did she know, that Kale was not anybody's fool, and had seen Chip going for his government issued knife, but did not want to chance getting Rita hurt by charging at him. Chip had quickly covered her mouth with his hand, "Who's asking you bitch? Can't believe you picked now to start tellin' the truth! You know what? I think I liked it better bitch when you were calling me sir!" Chip drunkenly balked. He stole a kiss from the flustered and helpless Rita. The 6' 2 Chip had disregarded the diminutive Kale, despite the fact that all his fellow cohorts were all spread out across the ground. Chip's overly intoxicated ego was convincing him that his friends either passed out from too much booze or, that dumb luck played a huge part of his friends being taken out by a half pint. This clueless theory allowed the delusional Chip to muster enough courage to stand his ground. "Well good fer' him, lil' peach! I tell yew' what hoss, why don't yew' jus' git' off that "ole' gal" there and come over here, and show me just how grown yew' think yew' really are…" Kale said steadily. Chip was not known by his fellow comrades to be the brightest light bulb shining in the stadium, but even he was intelligent enough to recognize a sarcastic threat when he heard one. He swung the fairly large knife erratically at the smaller Kale, assuming that his blade, which shimmered off the moonlight, was going to intimidate him. "Look what I got for ya', HOSS!" Chip said dastardly. "Well…how romantic of ya'…Ya' big stud!" Kale said, and unapologetically broke Chip down with a barrage of combat moves of his own. Kale moved with unmatched speed, experience, and savage ferocity that went unrivaled by any of the seasoned soldiers. When one of dismantled soldiers came to his senses, he immediately recognized just who this common "civilian" was, who just whipped the five of them as if they were simple fifth graders picking on Shaquille O'Neil. "Oh shit, it's the general's son!" He muttered. Rita had been in awe during the entirety of the fight. Kale was no more than 5'9 and a hundred pounds soaking wet, yet in still, turned her five assailants into Swiss cheese. She did not know what to make of her apparent hero at first. The clothing he wore was torn and dirty, and made him appear more homeless than heroic. She also could not help but notice the old beat up straw western hat, which covered most of his face and had a Florida University Gator logo on the front of it. Though Rita had been grateful for him intervening during her attempted sexual assault, but she wondered where he came from and also how was he able to handle himself so well. During that point of that time, Kale had not yet been the avid weightlifter he was after dating Rita. He was not too small of a man, but certainly did not appear as the type who could cause the same amount of damage from a Jason Stratham movie either, Rita pondered. The soldier that recognized Kale's identity was gathering up the others, "Hey man that's Keegan's kid! He said. "Keegan who?" another of the soldiers asked. "GENERAL Keegan, fool!" He yelled. Kale helped Rita up to her feet and stood in between her and the four men. They were all quiet at first, they then began to trample each other making apologizes for their devious actions and begged Kale not to notify his well-documented unmerciful father. "Leave all yah' wallets on the ground, and apologize to this nice ole' gal…" Kale authorized. Rita still could not make anything of him or, the situation she was in. "It'll be totally up ta' her on turning yew' dummies in, what chu' wanna do lil peach?" Kale asked in mannerable tone. He left the decision to call the police up to her. "Who is this man that commands this much respect and could handle himself so?" Rita worried. "I SHOULD call the cops!?!" Rita shouted hesitantly. The four men dropped their defeated heads in unison, as if they were preparing for a firing squad, "But, I won't… as long as you all promise to stay far away from me, my bar, and this neighborhood, forever." Rita warned. Chip was still groggy, but had heard everything from the ground. He staggered over to them and dropped his wallet on the ground as well, "That's a promise. I'm sorry for takin' thangs too far ma'am, and being drunk ain't an excuse!" Chip said, and turned toward Kale, "Please sir, we won't be back." Chip promised. Kale looked into the proud man's eyes. He appeared to be at least eight years older than he was, Rita surmised. "Super!" Kale said matter-of-factly. "Cause' if you DO come back here, well….I do have yer' all names and addresses now, and trust me, you guys won't have to worry about my daddy….cause I'm gonna' personally cut off yer' cocks with a hatchet and hang'em on this ole' gal's wall." Kale vowed. Rita was now feeling a Florence Nightingale effect, and believed she was on the verge of having an orgasm. She had no doubt that her new protector would not keep his word either. "Now yawl run along, and don't ever come back, ya' hear!?!" Kale commanded. On cue the fumbling soldiers thank him and scatted up the street like a group of field house mice.

"Are you okay?" Kale asked tenderly. He finally removed his hat so she could finally get to see the face of her "Kung-Fu Lone Ranger." When Rita looked into his face, she could not help but not be taken aback by his odd looking appearance. She thought his face favored a younger version of the late actor Anthony Perkins, back when he played in the movie "Psycho," but only with long kinky dark blonde hair. Rita could also see poorly healed scars over his right eye and chin. It was obvious he had been in his fair share of bar room brawls. Despite being put off by Kale's creepy resemblance to the actor, Rita did believe his light blue colored eyes made him look honest and that the scars on his young face also made him appear very mysterious. There was something else about him that was driving her crazy, only she could not really get a handle on what it was yet, "Yeah, I'm good." Rita shrugged. She was also being careful not to show interest. Exasperation began to saturate her mind and body. Kale put his cowboy hat back on and knocked the dust off the front of his jeans, "Well, guess my jobs done....yew' can go on ahead and have ya' self' a good night, Miss." Kale said cockily, and began to walk away. Suddenly, a funny thought had just occurred to her, and as soon as he began to make his quick getaway, his damsel in distress had some issues to clear up with her shining knight, "Old gal!?!" She loudly snapped. Surprised, Kale turned around innocently at Rita and had the same guilty look of a child with his hands caught in a cookie jar, "Ma'am?" Kale asked confused. With everything happening around her it was easy for her to overlook that thick southern Florida twang Kale spoke with. Kale stood with his chest firmly erect and had a funny looking smirk like Harrison Ford seemed to go to when trying to look cute. Rita's gratitude had quickly shifted towards borderline hostility when she remembered it was with his mellowing baritone that he insulted her, "Old gal....that's what you called me! You make me sound like I was some kinda' ugly horse or cow, or something. I outta' hit you." Rita suggested, and lunged at him. Kale could not understand what her deal was, but the more he tried to justify himself, the more awkward she made him feel, "Uh, n-now jus' waitaminute....I, ahem, didn't mean "nothing" by that, lil' peach..." Kale tried to explain to no avail. She then threw her hands up in disbelief, "And what is that?" Rita asked agitated. It was now clear to him, that his damsel in distress may have been simply over reacting to his southern play on words, but thought she looked cute all riled up anyway and decided to egg her on, "What….peach? Look, all I was try'na….?" Kale repeated in a condescending tone before getting cutoff. "Yes, that!!" Rita loudly confirmed. Kale quietly chuckled to himself, as the sexy Latina ripped into him while they were still standing in the middle of a dark alley. Rita was not actually angry with Kale, but his innocent and helpful bad boy demeanor was confusing her, and while turning her on at the same time. There he stood, all cocky and satisfied with himself, as if he just saved some stranded and helpless kitten from out of a tree, Rita thought. She also could not help feel disappointed that Kale did not seem to find her attractive, as most men often did, and it really bothered her that he seemed to be in a big rush to leave her. Although she was quite satisfied by the job of her "hero," Rita still had questions for the intriguing Kale, who she had back-peddling against an unsuspecting wall, "So…what's your name anyway, cowboy? And how do you know how to fight like that…from the Power Ranger Academy!?!" Rita quipped. Kale gave her a smirk, "Names Kale, lil'pea….u-uh, ma'am, or Rita, was it? Uh, look… I know yer' a little upset and all, but it's kinda' late, can't I jus' walk ya back to your ca…." Kale lobbied, before getting interrupted mid sentence. "Just stop it!!! Jesus…" Rita pleaded. Rita's heart was pounding rapidly inside her bountiful chest and her stomach ached with fire and passion. Without warning Rita grabbed the speechless Kale by his worn flannel shirt, "Could you just shut up?" Rita said erotically, and kissed him intensely on his smooth lips. The kiss lasted for a few seconds before she stopped. Her lips were full and felt extremely soft, like sheer velvet being laid across the young man's mouth, which sent sweet sensations deep within his masculine loins. Kale never felt a kiss so seductive before and was trying his best to fight off a stampeding erection. She loved kissing him and could her own knees buckle before she stopped, "Thank you, Mr. Kale….and yes, my name is Rita. I thought we should at LEAST get each other's first names out of the way before we started using pet names on each other…hoss." Rita jibed. He tipped his hat back to her, like how the men often did in old TV westerns, "Touche." Kale happily replied. His adrenaline was running so sky high during the brawl with the Army guys to realize just how gorgeous Rita actually was. It was obvious to him to see why they went after her and why she was definitely worth fighting a hundred men for, He believed. To top it all off, he could not believe she kissed him in such a way, Kale blushed. In his mind, he knew holding and kissing her felt both natural and good to him, "VERY GOOD TO HIM," and knew in his heart that he did not want to lose that. He reached out his hand to her and she immediately took it and gladly kissed him once again. The two seemed to melt into the other like wax underneath a fiery sun, while enjoying every bit of their sweet and sensual moment. "Oh, no…" Kale said. "What is it?" Rita asked. Kale smacked his forehead, "Daniel?!" Kale said nervously. "Tell me Daniel's not a boyfriend….?" Rita quipped, just as the stoutly built Daniel staggered from around the corner, "Hey, bro…you gonna' gimme a f-fucking ride or w-what?" Daniel griped. Kale and Rita snickered at the drunken Daniel standing there looking clueless, "Man you really gotta' (hiccup) get a bro home! I'm starting to see real life-sized G.I.Joes running around corners and shit….hey man, who's this!?!" Daniel asked intrigued and started patting hi hair. A smiling Kale Keegan did not take his eyes off her when he made his introductions, "Daniel, meet our new friend, Rita. Rita, meet my "little" big brother, Daniel." Kale jokingly replied. Rita reached out and gently grabbed Kale's chin, "That "all" you wanna' be, hoss?" Rita asked seductively. Kale grinned back at her, "Well now, that all depends on yew' ma'am!" Kale confirmed. "Tell you what cowboy….you keep playing your cards right, and maybe someday soon momma' might show you what a real "peach" tastes like…" Rita vowed flirtatiously. "Man, tell me she gotta a sista or, a cousin….hell, I'll even date her goddamn cat!" Daniel punned. Kale and his new found love Rita simply laughed in one another's arms and the rest, as they say, was history.

How Kale met David

Kale Keegan and David Lewis have been friends since they first met in high school. Of course, that little clue would be lost on anyone who did not already know them, though. They would often disagree over the smallest basic things, which made them come off sounding like characters from a bad buddy cop movie. Though the two made the perfect odd couple, there was never anything in the world that one would not do for the other. Back in high school, David was the large black, take no nonsense, straight A' varsity letterman, who aspired to excel in every sport and was also an accomplished artist. While the more brooding, hostile, and highly intolerant Kale Keegan was a world class bad boy/Army brat trouble maker, who excelled at excessive compulsive behavior. Initially, the friendship got off to a rocky start in the beginning, though. Like every year, during the end of both the football and basketball seasons, the more talented David Lewis usually played soccer as a way to keep himself in shape. The team was holding tryouts after school and those who lasted throughout tryouts received the opportunity to scrimmage against the varsity for a roster spot. Kale was not quite the imposing sportsman David was, but what Kale lacked in athletic prowess and bulk, he more than made up for with ample violent aggression. Kale qualified for the scrimmage game, where both he and David would eventually square off against each other. Since Kale was new to the school, he was unaware of David's competitive nature or, his innate ability at being a terrible sore loser. It did not matter if he competed in a simple gift wrapping contest or, a cross dressing competition David had to win it all. During the scrimmage, Kale's speed had gotten the better of him and in turn, provoked David to illegally hit him in frustration. But, what the highly competitive David Lewis was unaware was Kale's own hidden agenda for playing the sport in the first place. As always, Kale's emotions got the better of him and wasted no time showing David "exactly" what those intentions were. On every play, Kale made it his business to zero in on David with either an elbow to his face or, blindsiding him with a low shoulder tackle, as if he were creating a highlight real for NFL Sunday Night Football. Kale's intensity impressed the varsity coaches and earned him starting spot on the team. After being embarrassed on the soccer field, David decided to take things to another level and attacked Kale in the gym locker room. Despite being severely over matched by David's towering height and size, Kale still had his dad's special forces training to lean on. Things did not go as planned for the prideful David as he first assumed. For every swing David failed to connect, Kale made him pay dearly, until David had enough. In an act to save face, David ultimately quit the team. Not long, after Kale received word of David quitting the team, he later paid him a visit to his mom's apartment complex in hopes of changing his mind. He lived in a middle class neighborhood located on the Westside of Des Moines, where it still bred its fair share of knuckleheads. Kale recognized David's little brother Daniel, who was being harassed by some wannabe thugs near their apartment's swimming pool. Daniel was a well documented shit talker who could not fight his way out of a paper bag. The teens were wailing on him unmercifully while pinning him down to the ground. Kale overheard them yelling and screaming at Daniel about how sick they were of David always bailing out his" obese shit talking brother," or, how they felt it was finally past time to make his "fat ass pay." They began stomping on Daniel, until the brazen Kale Keegan rushed in and was handling the situation handedly with his martial arts training. One of the thugs managed to get a lucky shot with a beer bottle and hit Kale over his eye. Even though Kale's vision started to blur from the cut over his eye, he did not need 20/20 vision to see who was coming next. Once they began to pound on Kale, from out of nowhere, David made a stunning tackle as he smashed all three of them to the hard ground. David pounced on them with the reckless abandon of an enraged gorilla. Kale's vision cleared up long enough to help David finish off the rest of Daniel's attackers. When they got the best of them, they all retreated to their homes. "So much for being hard…" David said. He glanced over at Kale, "What chu' doing here anyway, fool? Man, don't you know where you at?" David huffed. Kale was knocking the dirt off his blue jeans and picked up his hat from the ground, "I'm here to talk yah' into coming back to tha' team. I know we got off on the wrong foot, but all that's history now! Tha' team really needs yah back." Kale said. Just as he was starting to walk away David froze in midstep, "Let me get this straight…first you make me look bad on the field, then you practically whooped my ass in front of everybody, and now you expect me to listen to you, just because you bothered to come to my crib? Man…I knew you were crazy, but now, I know you just plain stupid! Let's go Danny." David said, and began to walk off once again. The pudgy and rattled Daniel ran over to his brother's side, "Naw man, you were the one in the wrong." Daniel concluded. Kale was every bit as surprised at David's little brother's response as he was, "Huh?!? Stay outta' this Dan…now come on." David ordered. Daniel stood his ground and refused to budge, "No, I won't and you can kick my ass for it later! Look man, what my big bro really means is….THANK YOU." Daniel said. David had a look of both disgust and bewilderment on his face, "The fuck I am!?!" David yelled displeased. In all his years he knew him, Daniel Lewis never stood up to his big brother a day in his life, but something got into him today that gave him the courage to stand up for himself, "You're full of shit bro!" Daniel shouted. He had been surprised at this new side of his younger sibling and did not know rather to pat him on the back or, beat him half to death. "I'm sorry bro, but you're wrong, and I saw what you did to…hey, what's your name man?" Daniel kindly asked. Kale was enjoying the drama between the two brothers that he forgot why he was there in the first place, "Huh, oh…it's Keegan. Kale Keegan." Kale said. "I saw what you did to "Kale" on the field. It's the same old story bro. Even when you lose at playing me at Madden, you hate to lose, and you try to bully people that don't let you win! Then when Kale wouldn't take any of your shit, he gave you a taste of your own medicine, so you lashed out as usual, and got your ass whooped for it!" Daniel confirmed with authority. Never had his little brother ever spoken to him in such a way, but his words cut deep as they were true and David could not look his little brother in the eyes. The truth wounded him and he knew in his heart that everything was actually his own fault. "Damn lil' bro, I didn't know you had THAT much heart!?" David said proudly. "I guess something had to rub off from being around you, big bro." Daniel said. David put his arm around his stout little brother's shoulder and squeezed him close. He turned his attention back to his brother's savior, "Thanks man for…you know, for helping my lil' brother Danny out. How'd you find us anyway?" David asked intrigued. Kale rolled his eyes as if he just remembered an unpleasant memory, "There's a chick who works as an assistant in the attendance office that digs me. She gave me your address." Kale said. "Go ahead player! Soon you'll be rockin' that thick chicken!" David said pleased. Kale frowned, "Yeah, but it's kinda' hard rockin' a 300 pound chicken, if ya' get whut I mean!?!" Kale said displeased. David had paused with his head down a few moments to figure out who the lucky girl Kale had been referring to. It only took a second before David figured it out and whipped it back up at Kale in disbelief, "Aw-w-w-w man! Not "Big Cross-eyed Shelby," who helps Mrs. Porter during her lunch break?" David asked. "That's the one. I promised her a date this Saturday night." Kale said reluctantly. David and Daniel burst out into laughter and tears. "Jesus man, you must've really wanted me to come back to make a date with her big ass! Man, I'm flattered!" David said. Although they were poking fun at him, Kale could not help but to join them in their laughter. “So? How about it? I have no more dignity left in me!” Kale said. David did not waste a second to respond, “Okay man, I’m down.” David said. “Ya’ mean it?” Kale asked, once more. David put his hand out in front of Kale to shake his hand, “You had my brother’s back and mine, so now my brother with another color….I got yours!” David promised. Ever since Kale and David shook hands, they hardly left each other’s sight. Kale never forgave his father for creating the gaping hole in his heart after pulling the plug too soon on his mother. Since doing so, Kale felt as if his father had checked out on him too, since he hardly spent time with him afterwards. In a small way, both David and Daniel’s presence filled the gap left after his mom’s untimely death and his father’s abandonment. Being around the kindred David Lewis allowed Kale the chance to unload his inner most repressed feelings and vice versa. They became inseparable and formed what he believed was an unbreakable bond. Kale was now allowed to feel for someone once again.

The General

Kale’s father was a take no shit, spit, and polish Army general, who’s large influence had been used to covering his son’s ass on more occasions he was willing to admit to. After Kale lost his mother, Karen to a bout with Leukemia, he rebelled against his dad. They originally came from Tampa Bay, Florida, but moved around a lot after her burial. General Patrick R. Keegan was a person who did not share his feelings much, maybe because his job did not allow him to show weakness, especially in front of his impressionistic son. He often buried himself into his military duties, which caused them to travel a lot. On other occasions, his son more than wore out his welcome and often needed a change of scenery. Kale did not really seem to fit in anywhere after Karen passed and really did not become his old self until transferring to John L. Tucker in Polk County in Des Moines, Iowa. His father ran strategic logistics and training missions while in Johnston at Camp Dodge, while Kale lived mostly unsupervised in their rented home in Polk, which suited Kale just fine. The two Keegan's personalities had often clashed after Kale's father Patrick, lost his wife. Karen Keegan was every bit the beautiful care free spirit her son was and lived everyday of her short life to the fullest. She had fought with her sickness for months before finally succumbing to it. The wedge that had been driven between them began when his general father agreed to save her life by agreeing to try some new radical experimental cancer treatment that had not been sanctioned by the FDA yet. Karen's Leukemia subsided after showing promising results from the treatments, but she died a week later due to unsuspected complications from the aggressive formula. Kale held his dad responsible after over hearing him talking with the doctor who advised the tricky surgery. He thought his father should have at least asked his opinion in the matter, though Kale did not personally feel his mom's precious life was worth the risk. His mother was heavily sedated before the attempted operation, so she never got a vote either. After she was buried, trouble seemed to follow him everywhere they moved, largely from Kale never receiving proper counseling. In Ohio, Kale once stabbed a student for what he claimed to be disrespectful comments made about his dead mother. When they moved to San Diego, California, Kale nearly beat a gym teacher to death with a basketball after being threatened to receive a paddling for not dressing properly for class, then there was Indiana, where he pulled a childish prank on the principal, which ended up blowing up his BMW. Although the school never actually proved he did it, Kale was the primary suspect nonetheless. His wild child antics only kept the wide emotional rift that separated him and his father in a black void. It was not until they moved to Des Moines that Kale's attitude had gotten better. He started meeting new friends like David Lewis, with whom Patrick was really impressed with. Patrick admired David's savvy in the classroom, just as much as he marveled at his wondrous athleticism in sports. They had a common interest for the Armed Forces, which prompted the usually impassive general to grant him his blessing when David shared with him his thoughts of enlisting. He was not too impressed by Daniel, David's little "big" brother, who he thought could afford to miss a meal or two. David and Daniel's father Darrell R. Lewis, was an Army reserve that died in an earthquake while stationed in China, while their mother Tamera worked as a case worker for CPS (Child Protective Services). Tamara Thibodeaux-Lewis was a thickly built black woman with a dark complexion who was very religious. She seemed to have a second sight or, gift for clairvoyance as Tamara Lewis could see things in people that others did not. Her fortune teller mother raised her near the swamps of Baton Rouge, Louisiana where she may have picked up a thing or, two. Tamara loved her sons very much and sheltered them when they were little boys. Kale and Tamera's first meeting went awkward after David introduced him. He was borrowing his dad's car to take David and Daniel out to see a movie and just as he was about to knock on the door, she was already opening it. Tamera Lewis was looking at him in an odd way. She just stood frozen as she batted her large and pretty eyelashes very slowly, as if she had two butterflies perched over her eyelids. It was her way of "inspecting your soul!" David would often say. But, before they left Tamara Lewis grabbed Kale's hand and warned him, "Don't give your inner demons so much power over you, child. I can tell that part of you have already begun to rot…don't let that part take my son with you." Tamara Lewis said. David told Kale to not mind his mother, as it was just her way of intimidating his new friends. Regardless of what David said, the lonely woman's words haunted him for a while.

After graduating from high school, Kale had yet to decide what to do with the rest of his life. It was already a miracle that he managed to be incident free for two years. He already knew that his best friend David was joining the Army, but doing something that drastic with his own life did not sit well with him. Kale was not exactly the "following orders type" and preferably did not care for the same organization that turned the man he once respected into the cold hearted bastard who gave up on his wife. Just as Kale and Patrick were beginning to get past their personal issues, a middle aged woman pulled up into the driveway in a blue Mustang convertible. She got out and was wearing a bright red dress and who was coming by to pay his dad a visit. It was during a warm Friday afternoon and Kale was outside washing his father's car. Patrick introduced her as lance corporal Amy Foster. It was obvious that his dad was dating her and before Patrick could explain himself, Kale jumped into his dad's car a sped away. The story was, he drove the car for hours trying to blow off steam. It was too soon for him to start seeing some other woman in his mother's place, so he found himself drinking his woes away at a small pub on the outskirts of town. The slender brunette waitress who served him there was not having a great day either and never bothered to check his ID. Kale and his waitress,

Sophia Walters, had hit it off well and they drank whiskey shots for the next couple of hours. After her shift had come and gone, they made plans for a nightcap at the Hudson Powell Motel. Kale escorted his new and "much older" associate to his dad's Nissan outside. Unknown to them, a menacing figure awaited them hidden in the shadows. The man revealed himself as Andrew Walters, the waitress's estranged husband. An argument ensued among them and Andrew pulled out a .38 caliber weapon. Andrew's cousin, Norton, worked as the pub's bar back and called him over to intercede Kale and Sophia's midnight rendezvous. Witnesses on the night in question claimed that Kale struck the man in self defense, then his gun came loose from him and they struggled for possession of the weapon. A second later the gun goes off and Kale is the one still left standing. This was the night that changed the young Kale Keegan forever. He knew that he was guilty of making boneheaded mistakes in the past, but never saw murder coming in his questionable future. The police booked him and took him down to the Polk County Sheriff's Department. Within hours Kale had been released on bail by his unsurprised, but highly disappointed father. Kale was facing possible manslaughter charges, so Patrick made a call the next day to Des Moines Supreme Court Justice Joseph P. Williams, to collect on a favor that was owed to the gritty general. Judge Williams served under General Keegan as an ex-infantry man in the Armed Forces and agreed to help out an old friend. Kale pleaded self defense and was eventually acquitted on all charges. Patrick finally convinced his son that he was not trying to replace his mother and how it was finally time they both moved on with their lives. Kale agreed, and told his father that he needed another change of scenery and his father suggested that he join the army.

Several years later, Lieutenant Kale Keegan, along with handpicked Sergeant David Lee Lewis, lead an elite special ops unit that call themselves the "Razor Hawks," who prided themselves over their kamikaze style and reputation for getting the job done quickly and bloody. General Keegan oversaw the majority of their missions and watched as his highly decorated son, excelled through the Army ranks. Kale gained the moniker "Crazy Kale" for his penchant of wild displays of courage and balls to stand up to the higher ranking officers whenever his teammate's integrity were ever threatened. A "natural born killer" was another name being floated around and has kept the Pentagon, as well as other private government agencies intrigued with his future prospects. Rita on the other hand, was seeing things a little differently when it came to her marriage prospects. She was fighting for her husband's piece of mind and believed that Kale's superiors did not care about his mental and physical stability. They never had the joy of washing their bed sheets on a regular basis, because her husband could not control breaking into cold sweats every night. Neither did they have to explain to her children about why daddy cried whenever he saw things that were not really there. How much of her husband's blood (literally and figuratively) must be spilled, or sacrificed before there was nothing left for her and the kids? Rita often wondered. These were the burning questions that haunted Rita while she watched her poor husband drift back into his deep sleep. She hoped that he does not dream for the rest of the night, that no other ghosts decide to come by and pay her flailing husband an unwanted visit. Rita found it unfair that she did not know how to protect her lover who always made sure she felt safe and secure. Her greatest fear was to one day get that ring at the door, only to have two officers standing where her husband should be and to give her that "how sorry we are that her husband did not make it" speech. Rita rolls back over onto her side of the bed and prays for a dream of her own. In the dream, that she inspires to have will be one about her husband who tells her over and over again how much he loved her and the kids. He would also get a phone call from his superiors and then he would simply say…"No more." She closed her eyelids hard and quickly got busy sleeping…

Morning time at the Keegan's….

…It was nine thirty a.m. Saturday morning and Rita rose to an unusually quiet house. Her eldest son, Reese, apparently was still asleep or, else he would have stormed their bedroom by now. Reese was born a pure blooded hyper child like his mother who looked up to his father like he was a superhero. The headache she woke up with made her head feel as if it were being held under a hot pressing iron. The body heat that generated off her sleep deprived husband last night forced her to leave the ceiling fan on high, therefore causing her to wake up with one of the meanest sinus headaches ever. Though she loved her son greatly, these were one of those precious times Rita appreciated her enthusiastic son not being in her presence. She wiped the muck from the corners her eyes and mouth and peered over to Kale's side of the bed and was not really surprised to see him not lying there. On most occasions, when he returned home from his covert missions, Kale often served her breakfast in bed in the mornings. She loved that fact that Kale was a country boy who could throw down both in the bed, as well as in the kitchen. He would serve Rita fluffy golden brown freshly baked biscuits, a couple of garlic seasoned scrambled eggs, fresh grounded coffee, steaming pan sausages that could be smelled from across the street, lightly buttered toast with raspberry jam, and diced cantaloupes with sugar dipped strawberries on the side. Kale achieving this would be a miracle of course, Rita thought. He arrived from the airport late Friday evening and went straight to bed, not to mention, that he tossed and turned and screamed throughout the night. She thought of how sweet it was of him to go out of his way, after spending weeks fighting God knows who, to still remember to do her favorite ritual. Her infant son Kyle began to whimper in his cradle and so Rita jumped out of bed to give him his feeding bottle. Just as Rita began to make her way toward little Kyle's crib, she tripped over Kale who had been asleep on the floor, "What the fu…" Rita said startled. Kale immediately snapped out of his slumber and was breathing harder than Alfred Hitchcock in a weightlifting contest, "Huh? Wha…? Rita?" Kale asked confused. Rita slowly stood back up to her feet, "Yes. Wake up honey! You fell asleep on the floor!" Rita said mortified. Her husband sleeping on the bedroom floor was something new. He always had poor sleeping habits, but now he was sleeping on the floor, as if he were some aborigine on an Australian outback, Rita thought. Kale was not wearing The Iowa Tech t-shirt he wore to sleep last night and Rita could see new deep cuts and dark abrasions across his torso that he managed to slip by her before they went to bed. "Damn it Kale!" Rita fussed. Kyle started to cry louder, Rita then walked to her newborns crib and took Kyle out to feed him. "Look, (yawning) I'm sorry fer waken' the baby…" Kale began. "I don't care that you woke the "baby," just look at you!!!" Rita yelled. Kale rubbed across his chest and realized his shirt was off, and knew right then that he was in deep trouble. "You are never gonna' be satisfied, till there's nothing left of you to put in a goddamn box!" Rita screamed. There was not much of anything that could frighten Kale Keegan. In his experiences as a soldier, he had faced many obstacles and beaten countless odds. He routinely faced some of the world's most vile and most hostile extremists that any one man had ever faced in his young years. When engaged in battle, nothing could disturb his cool. But that was in battle, this was Hurricane Rita, Kale knew. One minute, she could be the sweetest thing in the world… until you pissed her off. By then, it would be too late and she would release her crazy Latino side that she loved to hide, "You selfish son of a bitch!!!" Rita cried. Kale stood to his feet with urgency and looked into Rita's frustrated pretty brown eyes and knew he could not find the right words to comfort his mentally exhausted wife. "Rita, babe I'm sorry, but whut do you want me ta' do? Fightin' is all I know how ta' do! It's all I'm really good at!" Kale confessed. Rita stopped pacing the floor with young Kyle and sat down in her favorite rocking chair that once belonged to her grandmother. She bit down on her lip and let out a disgusted huff, "Yes honey, you are "GREAT" at it, and if you weren't great at it, I probably would be still getting raped by those assholes from the Tavern that night!" Rita concluded. Kale frowned at that statement. He never could stand the thought of seeing Rita in any kind of pain, especially after watching his mother wither away, as though she were an autumn leaf trapped in the grip of winter. "But, you're failing to see the bottom line. Every time that you leave this house to go on those….SECRET MISSIONS lately, sometimes, I don't expect you to come back. Did you know that Reesie cries at night when he expects you to be back and then you don't show up like you promise him? Hell, it makes me cry?!? And now, I'm home all alone with Kyle too….Look I never wanted to say anything, but I know you feel obligated to your dad for getting you out of trouble that last time, but Kale…" Rita began, before getting interrupted. "Now that's not fair! It was me who was the one who got drunk with another man's wife, and when he found out, he rushed me and I killed him fer' it, Re!" Kale said emphatically. Rita got out of her grandmother's chair and delicately put their son Kyle back into his crib. She rubbed her soft soothing hands upon her son's tender face very gently to keep him relaxed, "I know it was just an accident, baby, and also a very, very, VERY long time ago….you don't need to keep explaining yourself!" Rita reassured. Kale closed his eyes for a couple of seconds and then looked at Rita, "It wasn't just an accident…." Kale reluctantly admitted. Her husband's words caught her by surprise. She removed her hands from Kyle's face and was looking at him strangely with her head cocked sideways, as if she were inspecting a Picasso illustration. It was as if Rita was gazing at him as if he just landed from outer space and into their bedroom, "What are you saying?" Rita asked confused. Kale reached on the floor for his black t-shirt he spent half the night sweating in and put it back on. "Whut'm I sayin'? No, Whut I'm TELL'N YOU, baby …is that I wanted that man ta' DIE." Kale confessed. Rita's face started to lose coloring and tears began to spew from the corners of her eye sockets like melting ice under a hot and humid sun. She sat down on the edge of the bed, "I don't believe this. I don't fucking believe what I'm hearing right now." Rita said. "Believe it, it's the truth." Kale said coldly. Kale began to undress and pulled out a pair of old blue jeans from the dresser drawer, "I was angry at my dad for a lot of things back then. He was seeing Amy behind my back and invited her over ta' meet me, so when she drove up I took off! I could already see it in my father's eyes that he moved on from my mother, and that he didn't care if I had moved on." Kale said offended. They never talked about the details of what really happened the night that Kale got arrested for killing the alcoholic Andrew Walters. He told her about the incident before he proposed to her, but Rita did not care. Kale Keegan was her shining white knight, the hero who took on five dangerous men for her and won. She knew he would run through a mountain if she asked him too, which was more than enough for her. Rita was no fool, and suspected Kale had to kill people in self defense, as a special ops operative for his country, but to hear the coldness of his voice as he talked about his state of mind "prior" to joining the Army was unnerving at best. "I didn't know his wife before I killed him, but we hit it off well. She jus' left out the detail that she had a husband. I…I saw the ring on her finger…." Kale said shamefully. Rita's mouth dropped open. "And you still…you STILL tried to sleep with her? Kale, how could you!?!" Rita asked disgusted. Kale sat beside her and put on his blue jeans as well as his boots, "I was hurtin' Rita. I was young and drunk and was looking for someone, ANYONE, to take it out on. Before he ever attacked me, I knew that there may have been a chance that he was already waitin' outside. I knew something wasn't right from the way her brother-in-law kep' on starin' at me, like I jus' took a shit in his oatmeal or, sumthin'!" Kale said. "….And the gun?" Rita asked. "What about it?" Kale asked annoyed. "Did it really belong to him, or was it yours?" Rita asked. Her nervous husband stood up off the bed and put his hands on his hips to ponder his response. He looked up at the ceiling and exhaled loudly. Kale dropped his hands and got on his knees in front of Rita. Tears were pouring more and more from Rita's eyes as Kale looked like a man ready to confess his sins. He then delicately grabbed her by the hands, "When ya' lose somebody you love, like the way that I did, a part of you starts to die. Look, I knew I wasn't always the BEST son in tha' world, but there were some things left that I still needed to tell my mother that I was sorry for….I just never got the chance. She was taken' from me, all because of my dad's God damn ego! I thought…I "had" thought, in some small way, that he was giving up on her by allowin' that som' bitch ta' operate on her with his stupid ass so-called miracle cure. He didn't let me set things right, Rita. I was driving FOREVER, until I finally pulled over to the side of a dirt road, right outside of Johnston. I was feeling low, really low and I pulled out my dad's .38. Rita pulled her hands away from her husband in disbelief, "No…!?!" Rita gasped. She was becoming noticeably nauseous and tried to resist him holding her once again. "I didn't, oh God baby, I didn't want to live no more." Kale cried. In the almost seven years of knowing her enigmatic husband, never have Rita once seen him cry, "I didn't plan on shooting him. I saw the bar down the street and just wanted to get some drinks in me to work up the nerve to kill myself! I hid the gun under my waist and it fell out when we fought. I was able to get the gun away from him, but in my mind I thought I was fighting my dad and the gun…just went off." Kale said apologetically. The pounding in her chest and head was so strong and unsteady, that Rita believed she was on the verge of going into shock. Not since Rita Keegan lost her brother Felipe to gang violence some years ago, had she last felt so desperate and confused concerning another loved one. She knew that it was next to impossible for her to imagine the amount of guilt that her proud husband must have been carrying all that time. He clearly regretted his actions, but despite the remorse he had of his past, his state of mind was still being consumed by his grief. Rita drew Kale into her ample bosom as if he were one of her own children, "Oh, Kale…baby, you have GOT to let that go, before it kills you or, before it gets somebody else killed!!!" Rita said fervently. Kale pushed himself away from Rita and stood to his feet. "There's something else babe…." Kale said lowly. Her heart was already beating at the speed of a roadrunner and believed that she could not handle anymore revelations on today, worried Rita, "What is it Kale? You better not tell me you got somebody else pregnant!" Rita said sternly. "I wish…." Kale said. Rita stood up with fire boiling from her eyes and was ready to pounce on him. "No! Whut' I meant was, I wish it were that simple to explain, baby…" Kale carefully reiterated. He sat back down on the bed to compose himself, "Come here. Now, whut I'm going to tell u is…well, it's classified. So you have to promise me that'chu won't repeat it." Kale asked, in his deep Floridian twang. Uneasiness filled Rita's face, as if it were like an empty glass being filled by a picture of ice cold water, but still promised him that she would not tell a soul. "Okay…two days ago, my team and I, were deployed onto Iranian soil at 01:00. Our objective was to neutralize a new Iranian terrorist cell called "The Ahi Zahhak" who was gaining strong military support in Afghanistan. Their leader Malik Kumar Hakim was brainwashing innocent civilians and kidnapping Americans. Our Intel stated that they were operatin' outta' two story refinery building in Kerman, a city south of Afghanistan. We eventually infiltrated their hideout and was immediately met with return fire. I and Sergeant…David, split command. I ordered him to take B squadron upstairs to locate the hostages and to gather what info he could. While me and the A squad were busy finishin' off Zahhakie soldiers on the first level, David had walked right into a trap. As it turned out, there was neva' a Malik Kumar Hakim, he was just some phantom name that was leaked to our government's counter-intelligence agency, to lure and kill traitors who were in Al-Queda. Anyways, they knew we were coming and so they decided to blow up the entire second floor." Kale said. "So, what are you saying? What happened to David, Kale?" Rita asked nervously. Kale swallowed hard and gathered just enough nerve to continue his story, "I ordered the A squadron to evacuate the first floor, while I did recon on what was left of tha' second floor explosion." Kale said. Rita sat up in attention, "You did WHAT!?! Just WHAT the FUCK were you thinking?" Rita asked aggravated. Kale huffed, "Baby, let me finish….I, I barely made it through a small opening near the outer stairwell, and managed to dig through some of the rubble. I could….I could see dismembered body parts of the B team, scattered all along the pavement and blood trails splattered across some of the debris. I finally found David, trapped under the rubble….but alive. Wreckage from the explosion had pinned his arms under even more rubble and steel and I had no possible, or feasible way of savin' him, not without cutting him lose…." Kale said coldly. "Wha….no, baby, tell me you didn't…my God Kale, he's a fucking artist, baby!" Rita cried. Kale needed to clear his throat, "It was his decision, I didn't like it, and I didn't want my best friend to die over some bullshit cover story either. So, I had to do the "ONLY" thing I could do to save his goddamned life!" Kale yelled. His sudden outburst startled their young child, who began to stir in his crib, but not fully wake. The stress created by Kale's incredible tale was so mentally perplexing, that Rita Keegan could not figure out whether to mind her baby or, slap her husband, "His hands. DAVID'S HANDS, Kale!?! Oh my God…you mean to tell me…how could you just chop….that was your best friend's….our children's God father? Our David, who painted Reesie when he was 2 years old? Jesus, this is starting out to be one hell of a morning….I can't take anymore fucking bad news!?" Rita breathlessly stated. In a flash, their eldest son Reese came storming through their bedroom door, "Momma, momma there's no more milk! I can't make any fucking cereal!?" Reese said frantically. Rita was in awe to hear her six year old curse, "Reese!!! You know better than to talk like that! Where'd you pick up that foul word?" Rita protested. Young Reese Keegan innocently pointed towards both his parent's direction, "I got it from you and daddy." Reese said honestly. Kale started to blush despite the anxiety that filled the room behind him and Rita's heated discussion. She let out a huge uncomfortable sigh, "Reese how many times have I asked you, not to go snooping around mommy and daddy's door when we're talking?" Rita asked displeased. With the speed of a set of firecrackers, Rita started cursing in Spanish and was sporting a frown directed towards her smirking husband, "Is this what you want, Kale? Does it make you proud that our son's mouth is as filthy yours?" She asked disgusted. Kale never heard Reese use the F-word; though there was the one time he heard Reese bump his toe on the hallway wall and screamed "shit" by accident, so he was doing his best to wipe the smile off his face by stroking his chin in a thinking fashion, "Kale!?!" Rita yelled. "Okay, okay….Reese, come here lil' fella.'" Kale said softly. The bright eyed child who wore his favorite cartoon pajamas cheerfully did what was asked of him. Kale then wrapped his arm around his eldest boy, "Now partner, that ain't no way ta' talk around a lady!" Kale began to explain. "Ahem!" Rita interrupted. "Uh, what I meant was…that ain't the way to talk, especially for a little tike YOU… eva'!?!" Kale concluded, while searching Rita's reactions for approval. "So, uh, promise your old man, that you won't ever repeat that ugly word again, kay' hoss?" Kale asked. Reese could clearly see his mother's disapproval written on her face like an English subtitle and turned his attention back to his dad and smiled, "Yes sir." Reese confirmed. As Kale stared into his son's glowing and innocent eyes, he was reminded of again of what he admired most about fatherhood, which was offering his reassurance. His only regret was spending too much time away from his young family and missing out on special moments. A part of him yearned for the life of a normal dad, where he could come home from work and spend his evenings and weekends with his kids. But Kale was unlike any of the other father's in his neighborhood. None of the other dads on his son's school PTA had his skill set or, body count to relate too. Kale was a highly trained government killer who was gradually alienating his loved ones. The last thing he ever intended on doing, since having kids, was repeating his father's mistakes and abandoning them. As a loving gesture, Kale took his hand and ruffled the hairs on his son's little head. He also did it to reassure himself that he was fully committed to his family. His son had a strange look on his face, as though he had something on his mind, "Whut is it slugger?" Kale asked. Reese hesitated to respond, as though he were trying to solve a difficult mathematical problem, "Uh, dad? I'm sorry for snooping, but…don't feel sad about what you did to uncle Davey's arms…you had to save him, right? I don't think he will be mad." Reese replied sullenly. His thoughtful son's cryptic words were both profound and unsettling, which caused Rita's eyes to tear up once again, "No Reesie, I suppose not…" Kale said unsure. Regardless, the fun loving and energetic David Lewis meant the world to everyone in their family and no one wanted to see him hurt. The proud gigolo had never married or, ever had children of his own, but it never stopped him from borrowing his best friend's family from time to time. David loved playing video games with Reese and looked forward to babysitting during Kale and Rita's date nights. He was even trying to teach his son how to draw right before they left, which made Kale feel even worse when the thought just crossed his mind. The image of his friend laying up in a gurney was starting to make him antsy. Reese grabbed his father by his face a kissed him on the cheek, "So, can we still get some milk mommy, please?" Reese begged. "Okay, baby. Mommy will go to the store and buy some more milk!" Rita confirmed. Kale refused to get emotional in front of his son and stood to his feet, "No, I'll go!" Kale interrupted. Rita stood up in front of him and put her palm against his stubble face, "Yeah, I think you could use the fresh air." Rita agreed. "I guess we can talk about this some, later!?" Kale suggested. "I suppose so….oh, and Kale?" Rita asked. Kale froze in mid step, just as he was headed out the door. "Yeah Re?" Kale answered, and turned his toward her. Rita let out a deep and exasperated sigh, "Quit." Rita calmly stated. Kale gazed at her awkwardly from the bedroom door, "Quit. Quit before you lose us too." Rita replied.

During his drive to the store, Kale carefully considered his wife's impromptu like ultimatum thoroughly. "Could I honestly surrender my command?" Kale wondered. Killing came so naturally to him. It was if it were second nature, like how the lion who woke up every morning to chase the gazelle. "What would his father think?" He thought. If it was not for him, he may have been doing a life sentence for manslaughter. His dad gave him a second chance at a free life and a way to support his family, how was he going to provide for them, and what about David? Kale worried. How would David appreciate him quitting on the team after he just sacrificed his own livelihood for the sake of his country? Kale pondered. With every mile Kale drove, a new question would take place of the last. Kale intended on driving to the supermarket a few minutes or, so down the road, but ended up on the other side of the state's capitol. He noticed his truck was running low on gas and pulled up at a local gas station. The gas station appeared new and had a loud looking yellow and orange sign with a giant red checkmark on the front that read "Quick Serve." The station did not appear busy, as it only had a beat up yellow Volvo with a large rust stain on the driver's side parked in the front of the store. Kale pulled his truck up to one of the gas pumps, parked, and went inside. Once he was inside the store, Kale was trying to overcome the heavy-handed use of Pine-Sol that someone must have used to clean the entire store with. The interior lighting was as blinding as the beaming spotlights on characters from a Nutcracker production. Kale paid for his gas and nearly forgot about the milk for Reese's cereal. He immediately noticed how odd the store clerk, who was of Afghanistan descent, was trying to size him up. But Kale was not about to allow the clerk's silly apprehensiveness get in the way of pleasing his hungry son, "Excuse me sir, but what isle do ya'll keep the milk?" Kale asked politely. The cashier continued to rudely stare at Kale in an untrusting fashion, and frowned as he attempted to read the tattoos on his arms and neck. Kale felt his right eyebrow rise to the brim of his hat, "Sir, uh (looking at the cashier's nametag) A-MAR-Rik is it? Cat gotcha tongue partner?" Kale asked irritated. The cashier broke his daze, "Uh, yes, the milk. It's in the back… near the sodas." Ahmarik said. He then tipped his hat to him as a salute, "Preciate' cha' much kind sir…." Kale said condescendingly. Lieutenant Keegan was somewhat accustomed to the silent treatment he often received from the Afghanistan people whenever they realized he was in the Armed Forces. It was also no surprise when he walked to the back of the store, where there was yet another Afghanistan clerk, who was suspiciously eyeballing him as well, while mopping the floor. The man seemed to be in his mid to late forty's and was half bald headed and wearing a goatee. Kale opened up the refrigerator door and grabbed a gallon of whole milk. The rude Afghanistan clerk began to slyly mop his way closer toward Kale's direction. His facial expressions had begun to annoy Kale, who was about ready to smash the older man in the face with the milk container, "Ismail!" Ahmarik yelled. The man with the mop looked at the cashier with his eyes squinted, then turned his attention back on Kale and backed away. Kale went back to the front counter and reached for his wallet to pay for the milk. He could still see in the mirror behind the cashier that the Afghan man was lurking his way back towards the cashier's direction once more. His primal instincts were beginning to take over, causing him to reach for his handy Swiss Army blade. What Kale saw in the Afghan man's hand made him back off just in the nick of time. The clerk handed Kale another gallon of milk, "Sorry, my friend, but I'm afraid that milk is no good!" Ismail apologetically said. Kale carefully inspected the milk's label to confirm its expiration date and saw that it was past it. "You see, my friend? (Ismail pointed to the containers sticker) This milk, it's no good for you!" Ismail warned. Kale eased his knife back into its casing, "Kay' hoss….good lookin' out!" Kale said in a casual tone. He paid for the milk and made his way to the door, "Preciate ya'll again." Kale said happily. Just as Kale was heading out the door, the two men's voices caused to him pause, as he could overhear them speaking harshly in their native Afghan tongue. Since he frequented the Middle East so often, he did not have any trouble making out the helpful mop clerk's words perfectly. In the short English translation; the cashier asked, "Why'd YOU care to give that American DOG fresh milk?" The cashier clerk Ahmarik had asked, and to his response "Ismail" replied, "It's better to let a cow rejoice in fresh pasture now, before it is taken out to slaughter! Kale was not in the mood for idle threats, foreign or domestic, and went about his business. After he finished pumping gas into his truck, Kale could still see Ismail in his rearview mirror watching out the store window while he drove away, "Fuckin' Arabs." Kale said irritated. While heading home, Kale thought again about what Rita said about him no longer owing his father anything and about how he may lose his family if he refused to quit the service. Her request was quite clear and an uncomplicated one to argue against, Kale considered. The Army had taught him that dying while serving his country was an honor and after getting promoted to Special Forces, he learned never to surrender. Both were virtues the young Lieutenant took to heart and which made him the best leader for his team. Despite the blood oath he made to protect his country, Kale could not help forget the other oath he made to his troubled wife, "To love and to cherish, till death do us part!" How could he go back on those vows? He wondered. Rita and the boys were his everything, the only thing that kept him tethered to reality in a dark world filled with chaos. Kale stopped at a red light and the view of his children safety seats caught his eye in the review mirror. Suddenly, sadness gripped him tightly as if his chest were being compressed by a steaming iron. Losing Rita was one thing, but losing Reese and Kyle? David always felt he should have named Kyle, Kale Junior, but Kale did not want to jinx his son by sharing the same name that was given to him by his general father. "Jesus, David…that wasn't the right way for a soldier….my best friend, to go out! Why'd you fucking make me do it, huh? Why'd you make me cut off your goddamned hands?" Kale contemplated. Although it had been a while since Kale brought up the death of Andrew Walters, the image of his face, as he shot him, never faded away.

So much had happened in the short time span of Andrew's death, but no matter for all the good he had done, no matter how much he changed, internally Kale was becoming unstable. As soon as the traffic light turned green he slammed his foot hard on the gas pedal. Whenever he got upset, speeding was a cheap way for him to vent out his woes. But unfortunately for him, he would soon have a little company. Like clockwork, one of Kale's ghosts from his past appeared and was sitting comfortable on the side of him. This time it was the ghost of a Chinese warlord named Han Pi Ling. His unit was sent in to take him out, soon after the Pentagon caught wind of six American women hostages were being held against their will and forced to be sex slaves. While his team was directly responsible for taking out his underlings, it was Kale who pulled the trigger on Han. But lo and behold, he was there with him alive, sitting in his truck's cabin brandishing the same large hole in the middle of his forehead. Kale remembered putting the ominous looking hole in his head with his shiny new .50 caliber Desert Eagle pistol. The ghost had not yet spoken a word, and Kale gasped at the streams of blood which covered the dead Asian tyrant's face like a water faucet. His clothing looked as if he had just got out of a Jacuzzi of red ink and his eyes were gaping widely, but even they were devoid of life. Kale was becoming a little frantic with his driving. Even though he lost control of his truck for a second he finally regained his composure. Seeing these types of things was now becoming more and more common place for him. They began as reenactments in his dreams that ultimately bled into his everyday routine, "What the fuck you want?" Kale yelled. The frown that was on the ghost Han turned into a devilish smile, "Soon you will be with me, burning in the hollowed pits of hell, Kale Keegan san! Your blood lusting has cost you dearly and it is time for you pay your debt!" Han said starkly. Kale's heart went numb after hearing the Asian apparition speak aloud. Howbeit in the past, the ghosts never seemed able to speak, but in any event that was not a problem in this case. "Jesus, am I dying from some goddamned brain tumor?" Kale wondered, while rubbing his forehead. Han laughed very loudly, which made Kale jump in surprise, "No Gaijin….no tumor, Kale Keegan san." Han confirmed, while nodding his head. Kale could feel his heart pumping through his shirt and adrenaline began to saturate his mind, "What do you fucking… dead fuckers want! What!?! You mother fuckers got nothing better to do in the afterlife, so you decided to come fuckin' with me? Who the fuck you think you are, anyway? Some fake ass Jacob Marley?" screamed Kale. Up to this point, Kale had been fearless his entire life and always believed that he had control over any odds that were stacked against him. His occupation did not allow him a moment's hesitation when put in the most terrible conditions or, disturbing circumstances. He always got the job done. When it came to choosing between him and his enemies, Kale had no qualms with killing them at the blink of an eye. But this time the situation was different. He was not in control of the situation and felt defenseless against his own active imagination. "I am here to deliver you a message, Kale Keegan san… Only a fool would fight the rain! Do you not have your umbrella?" Han asked, and then grabbed a hold of the truck's steering wheel. Kale lost control of his truck once again, but this time he struck a median in the street. He regained control of his vehicle and slammed on his breaks to avoid someone who was crossing the street. Han was no longer sitting beside him, but was the person crossing the street while his laughter still echoed in his brain. Kale was feeling both dazed and confused. Once he got his bearings, he made his way toward home. One of the first lessons Kale remembered his father teaching (right before he commenced to kicking his ass) suddenly popped into his brain. It was a lesson about how "fear was never being an option" Kale remembered. He also remembered how much pleasure his father seemed to take in bludgeoning him than helping him defend himself. Maybe his sadist father was onto something, Kale figured. Regardless of whatever he may have foresaw, it had finally shown its ugly head and in the first time of his young life, Kale felt a light shiver trickle down his spine.

Upon returning home from the gas station, Kale saw their nosey next door neighbor Mrs. Hines, along with her annoying Shih Tzu Wilma, gossiping with Rita at their front door. Kale did not really care much for butting into other people's business and would love to do the neighborhood a favor by taking the old hag out. He parked his truck and slammed the door in disgust, "Well, hello there…Mrs. Hines. How nice of you to drop by…" Kale said in a patronizing tone. Mrs. Hines had rolled her eyes at his insincere introduction, "Yeah, I'll bet!" said the heavyset Mrs. Hines. Rita looked at Kale and shook her head as to signal peace between the two, "Heard you comin' in late soldier! You on one of those "black op" thingy's again? Who was it this week? Saddam Hussein's niece hijacked a truck full of blow dryers or something? " Mrs. Hines asked sarcastically. Kale could feel the blood rushing over his face like water rapids at a vacation park getaway. Rita already knew Kale's deep-seeded feelings for their red headed and slightly overweight neighbor, but despite his personal feelings, Mrs. Hines always lent her ear when Rita needed to vent when he was not around. "Yes, I was on active duty if that's what you're ask'n? Look, my son's probably dyin' of starvation cause he didn't get to eat his Cheerios, so…" Kale said dismissively. Rita grabbed Kale by his shirt collar and warned him, "Be nice." Rita whispered and gave him a big kiss on the mouth. Mrs. Hines frowned at the young couple as if their long kiss was taking up her time. "Ahem." Mrs. Hines interrupted. Kale gave her one of his famous eye stabbing gazes, “Guess you forgiving me?” Kale asked, “What’s to forgive?” Rita retorted. “So I don’t owe you?” Kale asked. “I didn’t say that!” Rita said in Kale’s arms. Mrs. Hines was becoming noticeably agitated from being ignored, “I said, Ahem!!! I am still standing right here Rita.” She said. “Wait a second, Barbara!” Rita replied, and rolled her eyes back at Mrs. Hines, “Look, there’s something else important we need to discuss later, but first, I need you to do me a favor…” Rita whispered. But before Rita Keegan could make her request known Kale had some news of his own to share, “I’m gonna’ dot it babe.” Kale said gladly. Rita looked shocked, “Do what? I haven’t even asked you…” Rita began before he cut her off. Kale looked his wife straight into her sexy eyes, “I’ll quit.” Kale said firmly. Kale’s news caused her to sob uncontrollably, “Y-You would do that…for me?” She asked. Kale took a deep sigh, “No, Rita, but I would do it for us!” Kale stated confidently. Rita jumped into Kale’s arms and whapped her legs around his waist line. “Rita!” Mrs. Hines protested. “Mrs. Hines, your services will be no longer needed for the day!” Kale punned. He carried Rita back inside the house and slammed the door. Mrs. Hines dog started barking loudly, “Oh pipe down, you little shit.” Mrs. Hines shouted, and drugged the screeching dog back home. Meanwhile, in the Keegan home, Kale and Rita begin kissing each other madly from behind their front door. Kale dropped the bag he was carrying that had the milk in it, as his battle tested lips intertwined furiously with his wife’s soft lusciously warm mouth. Nothing was better than having make-up sex, Rita pondered. She sucked hard on Kale’s hot thick neck and by her doing so, it made Kale’s cock feel harder than a headstone in his pants. Their son Reese was laying on the living room floor with the TV turned up to the max and was too busy enjoying his favorite cartoons notice his parents making out. Kale packed Rita’s hundred twenty-five pound perfectly well built frame up the stairs. Rita was losing control with every kiss she gave her loving husband. It turned her on to be carried up the stairs and to her bedroom. Kale laid her down on the bed and then quickly locked the bedroom door behind him. Rita was still wearing her red silk night gown underneath the pink robe she had on outside. Kale removed his jeans and tore off his shirt, sending the buttons flying across the room. Rita laughed at the sight of it. She exposed her gorgeously golden chiseled thick legs and started sucking on her middle finger. Rita then began to masturbate in front of him. He had never seen her do it before and believed his dick would fall off from over swelling. Watching her play with herself was like watching true poetry in motion, Kale thought. The patient lieutenant was careful to take notes too, as she collected by his count, five to six orgasms. She stopped long enough to use her finger to tell him to come to her. He grabbed her perfectly shaped foot and kissed it very intimately, causing Rita to cum once again. Kale kissed his way up her clean shaven legs to her cunt and buried his mouth deep inside her so, that she snatched off his hat and yanked him by his dark blonde hair, forcing him to taste her even harder. Nothing turned Kale on more than to hear his sexy wife moan in ecstasy, especially when she did it in Spanish. Her accent was on full display when she was being sexually pleased. Rita's clitoris throbbed in euphoria and laughed during each time she came. She let of Kale's hair and sat, then climbed on top of his rugged face, trapping his mouth underneath her. But he loved tasting her every bit as much as she enjoyed being tasted. The more she tried to grind and screw over his long and moist tongue, the more he made her squirm and wiggle from the pleasure of him circling and zigzagging around her clit. Kale could taste her for hours. Rita was shaking uncontrollably and climbed off him and stood to her feet. He did not remember giving her a hint of being exhausted and began to worry about her being satisfied, "Are you okay? You like it, right…" Kale humbly asked. Her husband's audacious inquiry had her looking at him in dismay. Rita smiled and quickly placed a finger over her mouth to hush him. Once she got a hold of her senses, Rita leaned her head in closer and squeezed the base of Kale's penis hard. Kale winced and thought she was trying to rip it off him. It startled him when she deep throated his entire hard on, and only made matters worse when she stopped to tease the head of his cock with her wet hot tongue. When he could not take it anymore Kale flipped her over on her back and rubbed his cock over her starving clitoris and put every inch of manhood deep within her very slowly. She climaxed immediately from both the thickness and anticipation of his throbbing prick. Rita bit down hard on her juicy raspberry lips as Kale increased his pace while he penetrated her overly welcoming vagina. They both moan and groan from the immense sensuality that only a true love was meant to share. The heat made between them caused the room's temperature rise so, that it felt as if the walls might melt like thawed out ice cream. Her legs go from clamping down around his waist to her legs being pinned over his strong tanned shoulders. Kale was well endowed and could always hit her

G-spot, forcing Rita to climax time after time. She began to cry and Kale eventually slowed down his pace, "Why ya' cryin' darlin'? Am I hurting you baby? Do you want me to stop?" Kale kindly asked. Rita stared him directly into his deep steel blue eyes, "I'm pregnant, again." She said. Kale stopped completely. "I found out right after you left. I got sick and realized I missed my period, so I checked myself, and....we're gonna' have another baby." Rita said emphatically. The news startled Kale. First, he conversed with the ghost of a madman he once killed, who in turn tried to kill him on the road, and now this, Kale contemplated. "Well?" Rita asked nervously. It takes Kale a minute to process the information and then became silent for a few moments. Rita was getting worried that the news of having another mouth to feed may have upset her husband, and covered her face and began to cry. In an instant, Kale removed her hands from her beautiful face and gently wiped away her tears, "Is that all?" He asked. Rita cocked her head as if she were both ashamed and bashful at the same time. "You're really okay with that? Guess you're not gonna' still quit now...." She said, and crossed her arms and sobbing. He gently grabbed her by the chin, "Somebody's gotta' be here to help you change all those diapers!" Kale whispered, and kissed her on the mouth softly. Rita had a look of astonishment and yanked Kale by the head and hugged him with the might of an anaconda. "I love you Rita. I wouldn't know what to do with myself if I didn't have you." Kale concluded. Rita began kissing him seductively and turned over onto her stomach. She looked back at him from over her shoulder, "I love you too Kale Keegan. Well, since we got that outta' the way.... I need you to climb up here, and finish what you started." Rita pleaded. It was no secret Kale preferred her anyway he got her, but she realized long ago what made him come the hardest, which was making love to her face down. The gentle and understanding expression rapidly morphed back into the primal one he first began with. He gradually mounted himself on top of her and could feel every ounce of blood flowing back into his midsection. "Let's go cowboy..." Rita commanded. "Yes ma'am!" Kale happily agreed. Kale swallowed hard and resumed making love to his joyful and voluptuous wife.

A few hours later….

After their sex-filled marathon, the young couple's bedroom was left a complete steaming hot mess. The bedroom pillows they used were still strategically placed behind the looming cherry wood head board, as to avoid detection from their ease dropping son and sleeping baby. Their bed sheets were saturated with sweat and carried the aroma of heavenly sex. All their clothing had been flung around the room, as though the bedroom itself had been caught in a whirlwind. On the opposite side of the room little Kyle Keegan slept soundly in his crib. Kyle typically slept harder than most babies and was bigger than your average nine month old. Kale had just stepped out of the shower that he was sharing with his sexy pregnant "again" wife. "Unbelievable..." He thought, as the proud young man watched in appreciation of the gorgeous gentle creature who blessed him not too long ago, with her hand in marriage and now possibly, with his third child. If they were having a boy, he would name their child David, and if she were a girl, he would name her Karen, after his mother, Kale considered. He also considered how difficult it would be for his father to except his decision to quit. But, he loved Rita dearly and he was willing to move heaven and Earth to keep her happy, "Kale?" called Rita, from inside the shower. He smiled as he noticed that the soft tone of his wife's voice made little Kyle squirm in his crib, "Yeah babe?" Kale softly replied, while getting dressed. "About that favor I wanted to ask…." Rita began. Out of suspicion, Kale had his right eyebrow so high that even the Rock would have been impressed, "Yeah…!" He asked suspiciously. Do you mind babysitting for a little while? Barbara asked if the boys and I would accompany her for lunch downtown today to celebrate the pregnancy!" Rita asked. "Sure, I don't mi…hey…..waitaminute? So, how is it I'm babysittin' if all yawl gonna' be chowin' down at some fancy restaurant? Kale asked confused. At first there was silence and Rita shut off the water and got out the shower. She grabbed her bath robe and towel and ran the towel into her glistening dark hair. "Rita….?" Kale asked again. Rita was smiling widely from under her bath towel, "Rita…!?!" Kale asked once more. She began to giggle and kissing him repeatedly, while brandishing the most sinister grin he had ever seen on her precious face, "Now, honey it's only going to be for a few hours…!" She began. "Rita, WHO is it that I gotta bab…….no, O-O-O-O-Oh no." Kale said grudgingly. Kale began to backpedal in his footsteps, but was helpless after Rita subdued him with a sensuous hug around his neck and gazed up at him with pleading eyes. "That mangy barrette wearing flea bag Wilma? Why can't she keep that little crumb fucker locked up like she normally does?" He asked harshly. "Sh-h-h-h, you're gonna' wake Kyle!" Rita cautiously whispered. "Anyway, she can't do it because her niece, Millie, is coming by to trim Wilma's hair and with us going out, we need YOU to be here to give Millie to her. So, can you PLEASE do this ONE favor for me?" begged Rita. His wife was playing dirty and was wearing her irresistible pouty face that she knew her hardball playing husband could never turn down. "Low blow." Kale thought. He could only bear watching her playful act for a few more moments before finally giving in, "Oh…okay." He grudgingly agreed. "That a boy!" Rita said ecstatically, and kissed him on the cheek. "Yeah, but if the first time that dog shit's on the floor, I'm gonna' shove it down the garbage disposal!" Kale promised. Rita slapped him on the arm, "You'll do no such thing! So get on over there right now soldier, she's already expecting on you." Rita ordered. Kale huffed in disgust, and as soon he turned his back to leave Rita slapped him on the butt, "C'mon now git!" She said jokingly. Soon as Rita thought he was gone, Kale quickly returned the favor and scurried down the stairs before she got the chance to lash out. Reese was still where they left him, which was in front of the living room television, only this time he was not alone. His son had been playing with what appeared to be, in Kale's mind, at least a hundred different action figures. Reese was a quiet and soft-spoken child, who seemed to be smarter beyond his childhood years, "What cha' playin' there partner?" Kale asked intrigued. Reese never took his attention away from his toys as he spoke, "War games!" Reese shouted emphatically. Kale chuckled to himself, "So-o-o…who's that fella supposed to be in your hand there? Kale asked, "Grandpa." Reese said. "Oh?" Kale replied surprised. He walked over to his son for a closer inspection. Reese loved playing with his old G.I. Joe action figures he kept since he was a kid, so Kale would by as many as he could afford off Amazon. "And what is grandpa saying to the other guy in your other hand? Whut' he likes on his pizza?" Kale quipped. Reese whipped his head around towards his father direction, as if he were disrespecting some private ritual. Kale took notice that his son did not appreciate his joke, "Kay' then…. (squinting his eyes to show interest) whut' is it that ole' grandpa and that other amigo up to?" Kale asked carefully. Satisfied, Reese turned his attention back to his toy action figures and held up the one in his left hand, "This one is grandpa's best assassin." Reese confirmed. "Really…?" Kale asked curiously. Reese turned his head back to his dad again, "Really." Reese said adamantly. "Anyway, grandpa just was thanking him for taking out all these other bad guys for him!" Reese said proudly. "All these guys? It's at least…sixty to seventy men on the floor…this must be one badass killing machine!" Kale said jokingly. "Yeah, he doesn't care about how many men he kills, just as long as grandpa says so…" Reese implied. Kale stooped down for an even closer look. "KALE…!" Rita yelled, from the top of the stairs. He put his finger over his mouth and cautioned his son not to give it away to his wife that he was still there, "So…this guy kills without question, nor conscience. He mus' be one "lonely" amigo." Kale whispered. "Kale, I know you're still down there!" Rita yelled once again. Kale kissed Reese on the top of his brow and stood to his feet. Every fiber in his joints pop out in conjunction while doing so. Since being home, he had not slept decently and his emotions been taking him on a roller coaster ride all morning with his wife, not to mention their mid morning make up sex session, which left him completely exhausted. "Well, daddy has to run next door, before ya' mom blows another gasket." Kale said displeased. Reese smiled and handed his father one of the figures, "Take this one daddy, I won't need him anymore." Reese said, with finality. Kale slightly hesitated, but went ahead and accepted his son's gift, "Alright…but who's gonna' kill up all these other folk?" Kale asked discreetly. His son looked at the action figure, then back to his father, "I'll leave that up to you dad." Reese said oddly, and smiled. Kale stared at the action figure in his hand and noticed that it had a cowboy hat on its head. "Well…thanks." Kale gratefully said. He glanced back at his prophetic son in disbelief, but decided not to say another word, as he made his way toward the front door. Rita was half way down the stairs, with Kyle in her hands. "I know I know…I'm goin'!" Kale promised. "Kale, wait." Rita said. He just managed to open the front door, but stood frozen in attention, "Yeah babe?" Kale asked tiredly. "I forgot to tell you, Thank you and that I love you." Rita said. Her husband's eyes widen at the sentiment, and then he charged up the stairs with the passion of a Texas bingo winner. Their elongated embrace is seductive and erotic, yet otherworldly somehow to them. "I'll always love you Rita…." Kale insisted, and then kissed his son Kyle on the forehead,

"…and you too little buddy." Kale said. He then placed his hand across her stomach, "…and you three." Kale quipped, and went back down the stairs and happily walked out the front door.

Along came a Stranger

Barbara Hines cared for her pet dog, Wilma, as if it were her who gave the puppy birth. Unfortunately for Mrs. Hines, she was born barren and could not conceive children of her own, so it only seemed appropriate for her to pore what love she had into something that could still love her back. She grew up a big Flintstones fanatic and the character "Wilma Flintstone" was her favorite, so she eventually named her pet after the cartoon. Although Mrs. Hines had not owned many pets as a child, she still felt compelled to adopt Wilma. Her late husband Robert, of 35 years, had been suffering from Alzheimer's disease for the last seven years and had practically become a shell of his former self before he died. The formerly retired newspaper press operator had spent the last several years staring outside their bedroom window before finally succumbing to the deadly brain legions that bore through his deteriorated cerebellum. One rainy day, Mrs. Hines had been beating the pavement in locating her favorite niece a birthday gift. She knew Millie loved pets and was already a practicing veterinarian, and wandered the mall until she stumbled upon a pet store. The thunder was so loud outside that day, that it rattled Barbara, as well as most of the animals in the pet store. She noticed that Wilma appeared extremely shaken inside her cage and immediately felt obligated to protecting her. Mrs. Hines had spent the last couple years spoiling her pet rotten, and it did not surprise Kale after Barbara opened the door, that she over packed for such a short visit to the Keegan's household. Kale stood in awe at the sight of all the dog toys and etc…"Uh, Barbara? You DO plan on this bitch back, don't ya'?" Kale asked sarcastically. Mrs. Hines rolled her eyes at Kale's insensitive remark, "What's the matter hotshot, Wilma too much woman for ya? I already know Rita is, and when did YOU find time to knock Rita up? I was beginning to think you stopped liking pussy, from what she tells me." Mrs. Hines replied. What Rita had not discovered was that he and the wily sixty- something shared a private mutual hatred for each other and whenever Rita was not around, they did not pull punches on each another. Kale snatched the dog toys from her hands, "I suppose so. I guess we DO have something in common after all! I always told her you were an ole' carpet muncher!" Kale responded. Barbara reached for her purse and put her hand inside it, "Careful hillbilly…I got me a brand spank'n new tazer that has ten thousand volts with your scrawny ass name written all over them, oh…..and by the way (sniffing in the air) why does your shirts always look and smell like a monkey borrowed them to wipe it's ass?" Barbara quipped. She pulled her hand from out her purse and picked up the remaining traveling assortments for both her and Wilma, then shut her front door. Mrs. Hines began to leave her porch and confusing Kale in the process, "Uh, ain't you forget'n sumthin,' Barbara?" Kale asked. Mrs. Hines disregarded his question and began to lock her front door, "Yeah, I forgot to ask, if you ever plan on getting a new job, cause' the one you got now fucking sucks for your wife and kids?!" She said sharply. Kale exhaled what sounded like every square inch of breath from his lungs and closed his eyes, then opened them again and smiled, "For your information, you ole' coot, I promised her that I plan on quitting today, that okay wit' you?" Kale asked. Mrs. Hines looked Kale up and down with a suspiciously wry expression over her face, as if she was scanning him for the truth. "Humph." She said unconvinced. Kale cocked his head in protest, "Now what's that supposed ta' mean? You don't believe me? Go ahead and ask her!" Kale erupted. Barbara walked up close to him and gazed into his weak looking eyes, "You look tired Kale…" Barbara said concerned. He exhaled once again, "Seriously, Barb?" Kale pouted. His reaction was enough to satisfy her, "Okay Kale, I believe you. I was wondering how long you planned on being your daddy's little bitch…" She said jokingly. Kale looked surprised at her response. He knew Rita shared SOME information with their nosey neighbor, but had no idea that Rita shared that little detail, "How'd you know about…" Kale began, until cut off mid sentence. "I've known for a while now... about everything. Look Kale, I know we may bullshit each other, whenever your pretty little wife's not looking, but take it from me when I say that no woman wants to live alone! You may have given her, God Bless, three beautiful kids, but what happens to them after you're dead?" Barbara asked quietly. Kale took a second to absorb the elderly woman's advice. "I always knew deep down you couldn't possibly be that big of an asshole you made yourself seemed to be, after all....you didn't let me forget my dog." Barbara said wryly. Kale was staring at his mortal enemy with a new profound respect and satisfaction, "She's in the kitchen, finishing up her afternoon brunch!" said Mrs. Hines, and walked off the porch with her keys still hanging in the lock. Kale's eyes followed her to his front door and called out to her just before she entered. "Hey… preciate' the endorsement....who would've known you'd be still good for sumthin?!" Kale yelled. She looked back at him and smiled, "Go fuck yourself Kale Keegan....oh, and your welcome!" Mrs. Hines thanked.

Kale unlocked Mrs. Hines's door, but just as he was about to enter, he heard the sound of a squealing car passing down the street. Though he only caught a quick glimpse of it, something about it looked oddly familiar to him, but he paid it no mind and went inside. Kale had never been inside his neighbor's house before and could not believe all the fru-fru looking glasses and vases that adorned the strangely private woman's home. He stopped counting all her framed pictures, at a guess of a hundred, and continued his trek to the kitchen for Barbara's dog Wilma. When he entered the kitchen, there the little Shi Tzu stood swallowing down the last of her food and in defiance, began barking and protesting his presence in the home. Kale never liked dogs and definitely did not care for this one especially. He tried to wait her barking out in hopes it would tire, but the frightened little dog refused to go quietly. Kale then decided a more diplomatic approach. He remembered that he had grabbed a small beef jerky packet from his private stash in his nightstand, shortly after getting dressed. He laid down some of the packed doggie toys Barbara gave him earlier and went into his pocket to get it. Wilma started growling at him, as if she expected him to be up to no good. "Cool out bitch." Kale said, and opened the wrapper. The outspoken pup continued its rant, until Kale put the beef jerky into the dog's face and then she began to beg. "Oh, now you want to be my fuckin' friend?" Kale retorted. Wilma stood on her hind legs and begged him louder, "Alright, I'll give it to you, but only under one condition…that you promise not to water my goddamned floor with yer' little puppy pee!" Kale said, and fed her the jerky. Strangely, Kale found himself bonding with the dog for the first time ever, "You know, for such a furry little fucker, you're alright! Now, let's go. Last thing I need is to get caught flirt'n with you!" Kale joked and picked her up. Wilma found herself liking Kale as well, as she began to whine for more of his attention. "Oh, cut it out will ya'?!" He pleaded. Kale made his way for the door and just as he opened it, a voice came from behind him, "Don't go Mr. Kale, only pain awaits you out there." The voice said. Twice in one day was a record for Kale's ghost sightings and he hesitated to turn around to see who today's visitor was, "WHO the fuck is it this time? My long dead bitch of a kindergarten teacher Mrs. Phillips? I never did like you any damn…." Kale said, before his words escaped him. The courageous Lieutenant turned around to face the little person who stood before him. His heart pumped rapidly at the sight of the blood drenched child, whom he did not recognize, standing in his neighbor's living room. It was a small boy who looked of Middle Eastern descent. The pajamas he worn were tattered and saturated in blood splatter patterns all over them, especially from the child's chest area, "Who are y…? Kale attempted to ask, but was cut short, "…to who I am, Kale Keegan, is of no great concern, as it once was, I lived….and was indirectly taken away from this world far too soon." The child said annoyed. Kale looked at the conviction in the child's eyes, "Well then, what do want wit' me?" Kale asked. The child approached Kale sluggishly and seemingly peered into the young Lieutenant's soul, "My business here Mr. Kale, is to save you from your pain...!" He said. Kale whiffed at the boys words, "By doin' what exactly givin' me heart attacks? Don't you ghosts huddle up or whatever, before coming to me? I already HAD a visit from one of you dead guys already!" Kale said irritated. The boy did not appear amused as he continued to intensify his cold gaze, "We care not about the frequency of our duty, as much as you do yours Mr. Kale. But soon, Mr. Kale, soon will your soul be feasted upon in the infernos of hell, where you will be made to endure the endless pleasure of being torn apart again and again!" The child said chillingly. Kale did not appreciate being threatened, by living people or, dead entities, "Look, I don't know whut' fuckin' hell ya bastards crawled out of, but I'm startin' ta get really sick of it! If you fuckers want to do somthin' then why don't you just get it over with and quit wastin' my goddamned time with all your creepy speeches!" Kale said boldly. He opened the door and just as he was closing it behind him, he saw the child rub his stomach and wink his eye at him. Kale swallowed hard and shut the door behind him and locked it. As Kale was leaving Mrs. Hines front porch he noticed a car on the street that was not usually parked at the Anderson's home, which was three houses down, but across from their house. He could not make out who it could have been and felt compelled to further investigate. His arms were beginning to expire from packing the dog and all its junk. With each step closer to the vehicle, Kale noticed that the car was in serious need of a major paint job. Kale remembered Rita telling him that the Andersons were out of town visiting relatives, so Kale figured it was not the pizza man. Since it was a late Saturday afternoon, it could not have possibly been a utility man checking the home on his off day and without a company truck, Kale deduced. If it were a burglary wouldn't the burglar look stupid showing up in such an ugly attention grabbing yellow piece of shi...Kale's thoughts trail off. Then Kale looked back toward the direction of his house, "Oh my God….!" Kale said. He dropped everything in his hands and ran straight for his house.

When Kale arrived to his front door, he had noticed that it had been left wide open. In a wild panic Kale rushed inside and there was Mrs. Hines and his family bunched together in the center of the living room floor. Kale was no stranger to fear and knew all too well what fear looked and smelled like when he had seen it. Across from them, Kale could see the back of a man's head sitting on the sofa, "What a lovely family you have, Lieutenant Keegan. They remind me of the one you had stolen from me…" The man said. Kale did not move a muscle, "Look, friend, jus' what is this all about?" Kale asked, while assessing the room for others who may have been with him. The man stood up from the sofa to reveal himself. Although Kale already figured out his identity from his voice, part of him truly wished that the stranger had been somebody else. His voice belonged to the angry looking attendant at the Quick Serve gas station, Ismail, who had apparently followed him home, Kale surmised. What Kale could not figure out was the "why?" Why would THIS man target him and his family? Kale thought. "What a poor choice of words, Lieutenant. That word "friend" is most assuredly misappropriated." Ismail said. He walked behind Rita, who had Kyle in her arms, and Mrs. Hines, who was hugging Reese. It took everything Kale had to keep his cool. He was a highly decorated soldier who had been trained to kill a man with virtually anything, but that training was only supposed to be reserved for the battlefield and not the middle of his living room. Kale could not take any chances in this situation, especially with his family involved. If it were under different circumstances he would had taken out the bold assailant with one of his many assault rifles or maybe his handy .50 caliber pistol, but the clear choice was to keep the man talking until he could find his chance to make a move, “Ismail, right?” Kale asked. The man had been admiring Rita’s face and looked up, “You are quite correct Lieutenant.” Ismail said. “What exactly did you mean when you said, stole?” Kale asked calmly. Ismail looked at Kale in disgust and put his rugged looking hand gently underneath Rita chin. That move caused Kale to grit his teeth down hard enough to break them from the roots. “Ah-h-, I must say, you DO have splendid taste in women, Lieutenant. Too bad the same cannot be said for her when it comes to choosing her men….such an incredible waste. Kale stayed cool and simply watched Ismail with severe intensity, but also noticed that something other than the man’s mental stability was off about him. The man perspired profusely even though the temperature on the living room’s thermostat read 72 degrees. Was Ismail nervous or just a heavy sweater? Kale wondered. Either way Kale did not like the vibe that his family’s captor was giving off, “Like I asked, what is it that ya’ believe I stolen from ya’?” Kale asked firmly. “Do you believe in God Lieutenant?” Ismail asked. Kale shrugged, “I don’t know. Yeah, I guess…” Kale said. Ismail had appeared both surprised and confused by Kale’s non-committal response, “But isn’t that what you Americans you say you fight for…God and country? Well, Lieutenant, my wife believed, as well as my daughters. I myself, also once believed. You see Lieutenant, in my religion “Allah” is most holy and is the creator of all! Islamic faith teaches us that when we follow his laws “He” will honor us. If we dishonor his laws “HE” punishes us, but not before we take the opportunity to first punish ourselves.” Ismail said. Kale did not like the sound of Ismail’s last statement and sought more clarity, “Is that what this is? My punishment…?” Kale asked surprised. “No!” Ismail yelled. Ismail took a small step forward and it sparked an idea in Kale’s mind. Kale was a knife throwing prodigy and realized he still had his trusty bayonet knife clipped onto his belt. If he could get Ismail to step a little bit further away from his family, Kale knew he could take him out without risking getting anyone hurt or, hitting anyone, Kale concluded. “I am only a facilitator in Allah’s plan! No Lieutenant, your real punishment begins when your putrid soul burns in the great abyss of Jahannam, for all eternity…” Ismail said, and had taken another half step, “That’s it...keep comin’.” Kale said under his breath. "…along with the rest of your miserable Razor Hawks." Ismail said. Kale immediately froze dead in his tracks.

"How do you know that name?" Kale asked in amazement. Razor Hawks is the code name for his special ops unit, so how would this maniac know that? Kale asked himself. "Mommy, I can't hold it any longer!" Reese cried. Ismail took a full step backwards, "Didn't I warn you all what would happen if you spoke?" Ismail said, and reached into his right coat pocket. That's when it hit Kale. Ismail was making veil threats with an unseen weapon. "What could he possibly have used to get in so quickly and quietly?" Kale wondered. If he had a knife or a gun, he would have shown it by now, and judging from everyone's appearance, they had no visual marks, clearly Ismail did not use physical force!? Kale deduced. "But, I gotta go mommy…!" Reese again whined. "Then go where you stand, child." Ismail commanded. Kale was now angered by the humiliation his son was being asked to endure and that was more than enough he could stand, "Please, just…let my kid go to the bathroom, I won't cause no trouble! We can still talk this o…" Kale began before getting his words cut short, "No, he is the son of a dog. He goes where he stands" Ismail screamed. Rita was doing her best to hold back the myriad of tears that were spewing down her checks, "It's alright Reesie…mommy and daddy…mommy and daddy won't be mad." Rita cried. "My God..." Mrs. Hines disgustingly said, but quickly covered her mouth. Rita Keegan spent enough years around her usually quiet husband to know when he was beginning to get angry. She made eye contact with Kale and shook her head "no." "But the carpet will get wet mommy!?" Reese cried, while bent over with his legs crossed. "That's okay…you don't have to be ashamed, buttercup...." Rita said chokingly. Rita often used the knick name to sometimes help her son relax, although Kale would often chuckle at the irony of his child sharing the same name as his favorite chocolate and peanut butter flavored candy. Regardless of his overwhelming shame, the small child could no longer hold back his temptation, and urinated on the living room floor. The cruel act left everyone in shock of how low the maniacal Ismail's depravity could sink. Mrs. Hines was mentally beside herself and no longer cared about the danger she was in and shared her displeasure, "Bastard." Mrs. Hines frustratingly yelled. In a rage and with no regard for the woman's age, Ismail turned toward the elderly woman and brutally slapped her in the mouth. During the altercation, Ismail's coat flung open revealing a square shaped and metallic object concealed inside that did not appear to be a handgun, Kale realized. The young Lieutenant's military mind started to unravel all the clues that should have been so painstakingly obvious. It was over a hundred degrees outside and even if Ismail was concealing a weapon small enough to fit into a coat pocket, why bother burning up in the Iowa heat to hide it? Why not just hide it under a plain tee-shi..." Kale's mind trailed off, until he suddenly came to one very deadly conclusion. What popped inside his head caused his eyes to broaden to the size of two silver dollars, "How could I've been so stupid!?!" Kale internally screamed. This entire time this maniac had been hiding a fucking dirty bomb underneath his coat, and the thing in his pocket had to be the place he was hiding the detonator, Kale realized. Ismail still had a proud look of satisfaction on his face after hitting the defenseless older woman. Seeing Barbara lying helplessly on the floor made Kale feel just as helpless after discovering Ismail's endgame. He knew he had to think of something fast if he was going to change the outcome of their situation, "Tell me Ismail, why is it that cha' want the…Razor Hawks to suffer?" Kale humbly asked. "I don't want them to suffer Lieutenant Keegan….just you!" Ismail said coldly. Ismail opened his coat to reveal the bomb that he had strapped to his torso, "Here, Lieutenant! Here is the vehicle that will take your family to a most unpleasant demise!" Ismail threatened. At that moment, Kale could feel his heart slowing down to a snail's pace. Ismail had to have been affiliated with some form of hidden Al-Qaeda cell his group may have come across, Kale assumed. The biggest mystery that still remained was "why only come after him?" Kale deeply pondered. "You fucking American dog, you still haven't figured it all out yet, have you?" Ismail questioned. Kale only could offer Ismail a perplexing gaze. Ismail then pulled out the bomb's detonator from his coat pocket, "Well then Lieutenant, I suppose I should remind you, then…" Ismail stated. "No!" Kale yelled distraughtly. Ismail chuckled, "No, you say? And where was your empathy, when you destroyed my home…my precious daughters…My beautiful wife, Mayasah?" Ismail cried. Kale's attention was fully on the right hand of the suicidal Ismail, "Look, Ismail…I don't have any idea what this has to do with me or, my team? How can you jus' randomly accuse me of….!" Kale started ask, but is abruptly interrupted, "Two years ago, Lieutenant…just two years ago, you and your men, invaded my native home of

Abbottabad, in search of some American journalist captives!" Ismail accused. It took Kale only a couple seconds to remember that dreary night. It was the one that he would have taken back if he could.

Remembering Operation: "Rogue Mongoose"

It was called Operation: "Rogue Mongoose." Their orders were simple: Infiltrate Middle Eastern soil at 0300 hours, rendezvous and debrief with their inside contact and extract two American journalists, Samuel Wilde and Bonita Worthington, who incidentally wandered off the grid into Al-Qaeda territory and were taken hostage. Government sources claimed the American hostages were being held by a small cell of insurgents in a small abandoned hospital north of Pakistan. The kidnappers circulated video tapings of Samuel Wilde being tortured and warned should their demands were not met they would be beheaded within seventy-two hours. Khalid Al-Sharif Shyadid, who in the past, served as a reliable informant for the U.S., but also unknowingly was working as a double agent for the Al-Qaeda network. Apparently Khalid had been procuring a small fortune misleading American soldiers to their deaths and since he was the most valuable spy in the region, managed to keep away any suspicions. That however did not last very long, after David incidentally discovered a C-4 detonator that was carelessly misplaced inside a mason jar, hidden inside a drinking cooler. It happened sometime after the team dispatched on land, and they rendezvoused with Khalid and then debriefed at one of his various hideouts. While everyone else was busy going over the building schematics of the insurgent's hideout, David, who could never hold his piss, asked Khalid for directions to his restroom. Khalid never bothered looking away from his map, and must have been caught up thinking about all dollars he stood to make from profiting from their deaths. Feeling pestered by David, Khalid finally shouted, "In the back, my friend!" Despite being put off by Khalid's balls to shout at him, David incidentally wandered off towards the wrong room. He saw the odd looking cooler hidden underneath a large table in the dusty room which was full of old antique furniture. David always trusted his instincts and dug the cooler from out of its hiding place and slowly opened the box. It was full of Styrofoam and only the lid to a mason jar could be seen. When David discovered the detonator inside the glass jar, he remembered hearing about a possible stray government informant in the region and decided not to take any chances. He put everything back after his close inspection and returned to the briefing. The group got their gear and was all set to go until Khalid had to go back inside at the last minute for the map. He claimed that he could not afford to leave evidence and did not want to damage any future American missions. After a short ride, the team made the hike to the deserted hospital. It looked as if it had been closed down for years and only had a few guards on the roof. Kale ordered his sharpshooter Specialist Emanuel "Manny" Espinoza to dispatch them and told the rest of his of unit to split up, just as a precaution, while only he, David, and the others proceeded into the building. They took on more insurgent fire, but nothing that Kale and company could not handle. The hostages were supposed to be held up in the rundown buildings cafeteria, located in the center of the facility, but after reaching their destination, the two journalists were already dead, both with their heads decapitated. Their heads still had the faint expression of extreme anguish washed upon their severely beaten faces. The torture they endured on the video tapes could be obviously seen on both the brutally scared faces of Samuel Wilde of New Jersey, who was just thirty-three, while his partner and photographer Bonita Worthington, who hailed from Chicago, who was only twenty-five, stared back at Kale. It was in his experience to never expect the best outcome in these types of missions. Fearing that they may still be under surveillance, Kale ordered them to fan out. Khalid cut them off at the double doors with what looked like a detonator in his hand. David could clearly tell it was the exact same one he had held back in that cooler at Khalid's hideout. The traitorous Khalid demanded everyone to stand down, because the room was rigged to explode. He then ordered Kale to tell the rest of his unit outside to come to the cafeteria. Kale hesitated, but David reassured him with a nod, and Kale distastefully ordered his team to come to the cafeteria. When the rest of the team was rounded up inside the cafeteria, Khalid began to gloat and told them he could not kill them, not until they all knew it was him that pulled the trigger. The frown that covered Kale's rugged face had transformed into a loud burst of mad laughter. Then everyone in the room started laughing with him. Khalid feeling cheated out of his moment, had threatened to push the detonator, "Go ahead Kallie, but you'd just be wastin' your damn time!" Kale said. Khalid slowly backed up and threatened them once more. After becoming displeased with their playful pandering, Khalid began backing up and when he was satisfied that he was far enough, he squeezed the trigger on the detonator. Khalid was struck with shock when nothing happened. David held up the wiring that he previously removed from the detonator, "Kind of hard to work without these, dawg!" David said jokingly. The arrogance that Khalid brandished in the beginning quickly faded to that of complete terror. In a wild panic, Khalid whipped out a small firearm and opened fire on them and ran away. Kale and his group chased after him. They followed him all the way through a poor neighborhood not far from hospital and to the home of a small local family. Khalid forced himself through the front door after firing on the father who answered it. Kale had the home surrounded and figured Khalid had to be out of bullets then, and entered alone. He immediately noticed a wounded man laying face down on the floor and checked his vital signs and could tell he was still barely alive. Khalid was hiding behind a woman with his gun to the back of her head and what appeared to be her two daughters standing beside her in the kitchen. With his weapon drawn, Kale ordered him to surrender and leave the family alone, but Khalid had other ideas. As a backup plan, Khalid himself was strapped with C-4 explosives in case it ever was discovered he was a traitor, and threatened to use them if Kale refused to let him go. Kale did not see Khalid's threat as an option, though. He called the deliriously crazed Khalid's bluff and also pointed out he would need a working detonator to pull off the feat. That was when Khalid brandished an already activated timer on the explosives, which read one minute left to explode. Kale was forced to act quickly and took his shot. Khalid was grazed in the head, but managed to fire his last bullet into the back of the poor woman's skull he was holding. Blood splatter from the front of the woman's cranium shot high across the ceiling leaving insipid patterns, as though it had been painted there like some dark sinister version of the Sistine Chapel. Her body had not completely dropped before the man on the floor, who first Khalid shot, regained enough consciousness to witness his wife's murder. He cried out to the woman and despite his own wounds, managed enough strength to pull himself from the floor. The momentum from Kale's bullet caused Khalid's body to contort, pushing the youngest of the two girls head onto the edge of a table, killing her instantly. Khalid's body landed on top of the eldest daughter and trapping her under him. Kale had merely seconds to escape the bomb's ensuing blast and quickly radioed his unit to evacuate. The wounded man was crying uncontrollably, while holding the woman's head, and lashed out at Khalid when he saw his youngest daughter dead. Kale ran over and pulled him off Khalid and saw the timer on his stomach was already down to six seconds. Kale tried to explain to the hysterically wounded man of the imminent danger they faced, but he grabbed hold of Kale's uniform with a tarantula's grip. Kale used the back of his .45 caliber to knock the raged man unconscious, and grudgingly threw him over his shoulder as the final two seconds ticked off. They made it out the front door just as the explosion went off, sending their body's soaring through the early morning air as if they were birthday balloons filled with helium. David and the team ran over to check on Kale after his rough landing. Kale's hard fall gave him a mild concussion, but it did not distract him from making sure the man he was trying to save survived. His charred and bloodied body was still on the rough pavement. He then turned the man's lifeless body over, but from what Kale had seen was not enough to bother checking vital signs for. Kale detested using deadly force whenever innocent lives were at stake and swore to never make the same mistakes again. The affects of his concussion were getting worse and he started to lose his balance. He then relieved himself of command and proudly gave it over to David. While David was handing out his orders, the civilian man they had believed dead was also paying close attention, "Maddox, you take point, while I carry Lt. Keegan, All right Razor Hawks…move out!" David ordered, and the American soldiers fled to be extracted from their next checkpoint.

The Keegan's home…

….That night seemed more like "twenty years ago" than just the "two" it's been for Kale and being caught in that blast did not do him any favors, he remembered. Then it came to him, "The blast…!" Kale slowly recollected. Kale forced his mind to push beyond his present fears long enough to find the answers that he had sought, and then it finally hit him, "But, it couldn't be…I saw him!" Kale whispered. Ismail's sweaty facade changed slowly from one of anger to that of finality. Kale realized the unthinkable, "But he died, he…YOU, got shot in the chest…. and the blast?" Kale said confused. Seeing Lieutenant Keegan's confusion placed a gleefully evil grin on Ismail's dripping face. "No, Lieutenant…I'm very much alive!" Ismail said and revealed the presently healed gunshot wound on his chest. Little Kyle started crying and Ismail turned his attention to Rita, "Make that bastard be quiet…!" Ismail commanded. Kale took a half step closer just before Ismail whipped his head towards Kale and raised his right eyebrow, "Ah-ah, Lieutenant…!" Ismail said, and flashed the detonator in the air. The young Lieutenant put his hands out and tried again to reason with the delusional Ismail, "Okay…look, I know you're angry, but I did try to save yer' life, remember that? Why do all this? I didn't kill yer' family?" Kale pleaded. Ismail looked at Kale in utter disbelief, "How could you have the audacity to say such a thing? It was YOU, Lieutenant Keegan, who came to my country…and chased that pig into my home. It was YOU Lieutenant Keegan, who shot him and forced him to kill both my wife, and my little Dahlia (he sobbed) and YOU Lieutenant Keegan…YOU, who knocked me out to save yourself and by doing so, left my eldest daughter, Hammasa…inside to die!?!" Ismail cried. Confused, Kale tried to make some sense of the home invader's wild accusations, "Daughter? What are you talking about? I don't remember any other dau…!" Kale's voice trailed off. "Oh, but it was Lieutenant, and as a final insult, you left me alone in the street to die…like a dog!" Ismail yelled angrily. While struggling to quiet down her upset child, Rita Keegan was appalled by the weight of Ismail's terrible claims, "Sh-h-h, baby…Kale, baby….tell me you didn't?" Rita cried. Ismail cut her off, "Oh, but he DID, Mrs. Keegan! But, it was all in Allah's will for me to finally find you and your family! You see Mrs. Keegan…in order for me to catch a mongrel….I had to force myself to become one. I never did believe in the Al-Qaeda cause, but…. it was YOUR husband who brought that savagery onto my doorstep and allowed their hate to consume my very soul." Ismail said regrettably. Kale could not find the words, for he clearly forgot about the other daughter that was trapped underneath Khalid in the heat of the battle. "With so much going on,

Ismail, I…I really didn't mean for things to turn out that way!?" Kale said apologetically. After his concussion, his military doctor warned him of possible memory degeneration, but his family was counting on him to push beyond the mental barriers created from the bomb's blast from the night in question. "No! You clearly disregarded my daughter's safety for the sake of saving your own ass!" Ismail shouted angrily. The memories of that night were slowly flooding back, especially of how much of a raving lunatic Ismail became when he was trying to save him, "That's not fair. Yes, I did do some of those things…but I was try'n ta' save yew' all too! I didn't expect him ta' shoot and wit' yew' actin' so, irrational…. we probably could've had time to save her!" Kale screamed. Ismail stepped a full step forward and Kale went for his knife, at the same time there was a knock at the door, it was Mrs. Hines niece Millie. Cautiously, she walked through the opened front door, "Mr. and Mrs. Keegan? My aunt Barbara's not answering the door and I found Wilma out…" Millie said, and in that same instant Kale reached out to shoo her away, "Enjoy hell Lieutenant!" Ismail said and pushed the detonator button.

Ismail's bomb could be heard all the way down 5th Avenue Rd. Every neighbor at home immediately ran outside to see what caused the loud commotion. What they saw was someone who was once considered to be a simply quiet and helpful neighbor, who also had a very sweet family. The explosion from Ismail's bomb was so powerful that it had thrown Kale through his very front door. Although his body had suffered many superficial cuts and fractures, Kale knew the same could not have been said for anyone else still inside. As Kale Keegan looked upon the roaring flames that were furiously consuming what was once his family home, something inside him began to change. It felt as though some murderous entity was trying to rise to the surface of his psyche to swallow what was left of his tormented soul. His eyes riddled with tears and blood. Somehow, through his mental anguish, Kale had seen his Swiss Army knife on the ground near him. He grabbed the knife with one hand and used it to cut the palm of the other and began to scream hysterically, while squeezing the very blood from out of it and onto his lawn. More and more of his neighbors came storming up the street to get a closer look at his burning kingdom. His dead neighbor's niece also survived the explosion with minor bruises and scrapes and came looking for answers he did not have, "M-M-Mr. Keegan, w-w-what h-h-happened?" Millie asked manically. But, all he could offer her was the look of a lost soul trapped inside a deformed reality. Without the lives of his family tethered to him, he was no longer Kale Keegan, but an uncaring malignant spirit, that after a lifetime gained its own emancipation. It was with this freedom that he could act without care or, conscious with nothing holding him back. Mrs. Hines' niece kept calling out to him, but to no avail will she ever get answer, "Mr. Keegan….Mr. Keegan!?!" Millie asked again and again. Sorry Millie….but Mr. Keegan has just left the building.

Chapter 4:

"The Dissension"

Present day…

Houston, Texas. Many years have passed since the now accomplished Dr. Terry Templeton had last seen or, spoken to his older brother the Reverend Thomas Jr. and his mother Grace Templeton. The last time he remembered seeing them both was over thirty some odd years ago in the family living room, when Senior kicked him out. There was the "one time" he did try to call home. Incidentally, their younger sister Candice had just died and it was his mother Grace who answered the phone. She was extremely upset at the time, and "why not" he then thought. Terry had hoped to come pay them a visit after graduating college, but when his mother told him how hard his father had been taking Candice's death, he felt that the last thing they needed was a bad memory to bring him down even further. So out of respect, Terry decided to stay away completely. Although Terry could barely memorize his baby sister's face, the memory of the receiving the news of her death remained fresh. He also could recall the reporting of Thomas Senior's death on the six o'clock news a while back, and yet again, still believed it would have been in poor taste to show. Unfortunately, it's his mother, sister-in-law Lucinda, and niece Mia who are gone, leaving only Thomas Jr. and his comatose nephew Markus, as the only family he has left. Though he tried to keep his mind fixated on the wet and slippery road in front of him, Terry could not help but glance at his black leather briefcase sitting calm and cozy in the passenger seat of his Lexus. He recollected the despicable horrors that were held inside it, explaining in great gory detail, about the "incident" that happened to his brother and now dead mother, over two years ago. In his heart, Terry knew that turning his back on his only surviving sibling was out of the question, no matter how he came about the information of Thomas Jr. and his family. To clear his head, Terry turned on his car stereo to listen to some music. But the longer he drove, the more depressing it seemed the songs were, which kept him emotionally deflated. The weather had been damp and dreary all morning, while the traffic was just as unbearable, as it usually was during Mondays on his way to work. He took in a deep sigh, as he closely approached the private facility where he worked. After parking in his reserved section, Terry tried to block out the images from last night, as well as the dark messenger who brought the disappointing news to his doorstep. Terry needed to gather himself, so he turned off his car and closed his eyes to meditate for a few moments. Once he was composed, he exhaled and opened his car door and made his way to work.

Long ago, before he ran away as a teenager, could Terry not have fathomed in his wildest, deepest, and darkest dreams of the malice that his family members would have experienced. Though Terry's profession trained him to think objectively on matters of coincidence, part of him still wondered if the Templeton family might had been cursed. He walked briskly through the glass double doors of the Midtown Houston Mental Care building and towards the elevators. When he reached the second floor, he continued the long trek to his office and spotted his always punctual secretary at her desk, "Morning Sheila." Terry said. Sheila Eastland's routine usually consisted of making his coffee and conversing with her husband, "Hold on Jason, morning to you!" Sheila happily replied. She had been his secretary for the last seven years and could tell that something was off with the normally chatty Dr. Templeton, "You doing okay? You have that same look on your face I had when I found out Jodeci was splitting up!" She joked. Terry smiled out of kind courtesy, "Just had a long night…it was, uh…had to deal with a little family emergency, but everything's good!" Terry said nervously. Sheila was not buying his excuse, and was not in the mood to push the issue, "Alrighty then…coffees on the desk, as usual." Sheila confirmed. "Thanks Sheila." Terry said, and opened his office door. "Oh, and Terry…hope it's nothing serious, you know, with the family thing." Sheila said concerned. The odd blank expression on Terry's face sent a shiver down the small of his secretary's back. He hurried into his office and immediately closed the door behind himself.

An hour had passed before Terry Templeton could finally get his thoughts in order to do what he needed to do next. The grieving mechanism in his mind was working in overdrive, which made reaching out to his brother even more difficult. He only learned of their deaths last night, but Thomas Jr. had a head start through the bereavement process two years ago. As his brother, he felt it unfair to call Thomas Jr. under the current circumstances, especially after his brother's terrible ordeal. Terry was always considered the emotional one of the three siblings growing up and never once hesitated to speak his mind, at least until today. The last time he remembered being this afraid to talk to his big brother was after he told him about being gay. Their mother feared for his safety and tried to encourage him live a lie. But despite his mother's behooving to fake his sexuality, it was Thomas Jr. who encouraged him to be real with himself and to be happy with whomever he chose, Terry recollected. "What a shitty way to come out to your parents though," Terry thought grimly, as he took another small sip of his lukewarm coffee. It had taken a long time for the embarrassment of getting caught giving his high school boyfriend a blowjob to wear off. Terry never intended on hurting his father, but he was in love and wanted to express himself to the only boy he knew that could fully understand him. Outside of himself, Terry still believed his family was as close to perfection as any family could possibly get. But for years, Terry proudly wore the badge of black sheep and was going to live his life the way he wanted to, regardless of who his father was. Despite their many clashes, Terry never once hated Thomas Senior, even though Candice and Thomas Jr. received most of his attention than he did growing up. But the Terry "then" was angry at the time, and with him being a homosexual, it constantly kept him in Senior's doghouse, Terry thought back. No matter how much his proud preacher father whooped, threatened, or, berated him in his sermons, Terry could not forsake his nature. After fleeing the state of Georgia, Terry had put everyone he ever loved behind him, which in kind, caused him to go into a deep depression. Terry did not have any money to support himself on the street, so he did what some of the other kids were doing during that time and joined the service. He spent four years hiding his sexuality in the U.S. Navy, where he endured tumultuous amounts of verbal and physical abuse. Things did not start turning around for him until after he met his life partner, former Lieutenant junior grade Lacy Spencer, who was also a fellow Navy man in the closet. They met shortly after they were discharged. Terry was feeling really down after his phone conversation with his mother about losing his sister and felt even worse that he could not share his graduation news. Lacy had been quietly watching Terry from afar, at a sailors bar called The Spindle Bar (The former Lieutenant would later on tell friends, that he had to swim through an ocean of tears just to meet his sweet prince) Terry always favored dark-complected and muscular black men, so when he saw Lacy he was initially sprung. Despite his strict religious upbringing, Terry did not leave much room for God in his life, especially when he was taught that the bible forbade homosexuality. But, the temptations of his heart told him that no woman could ever make him completely happy and that being with men, felt too good to be wrong. Terry knew he was far from perfect, but still believed that God would not have brought Lacy into his life in the first place, if he did not deserve him. Though they never married, Terry still felt an obligation to love and protect his man, even against the demons that had plagued the Templeton family. Lacy never pushed Terry to speak about his past and always respected his reasons for staying away so long, even if he sometimes disagreed with those reasons. He began to wonder if Lacy would have been so quick to honor that policy had he knew about the visitor who dropped by last night, to give him that terrible file on his family members. Probably not, Terry figured, as he sat at his office desk in silence. Terry stared at the "I love you!" text message that appeared across the screen of his iPhone. Lacy typically sent him the message every morning since they began using smart phones. He greatly wanted to come clean to his beloved common-law husband, but the brown folder which contained all that gruesomeness from his brother's brutal home invasion stared back at him like a dirty secret. The more he tried to grapple with the reality of his dead family members the harder it became to find air to breathe. Part of him could only imagine what Thomas Jr. was going through, "Poor Tommie…" He said quietly. Regardless, of the circumstances he came about the disturbing information about his brother and mother, Terry felt more than obligated to call up Thomas Jr. As he struggled to dial each digit, Terry worried more and more about what he was even going to say to his traumatized brother. With all the time having past them and he never so much as sent his only living sibling a single Christmas card, how was he going to explain himself now? Terry contemplated. It had been almost thirty years since he last spoke to his brother and wondered if he would even bother to take his call. "What if he's pissed at me?" He said aloud. Nevertheless, if everything was true in Thomas' file then something had to be done, Terry figured.

Terry had dedicated over fifteen years as one of the leading therapists at the Midtown Houston Mental Care facility. While working there, he had spent countless man hours helping all types of helpless individuals cope with their various social problems and many life issues. The problems he was presently faced with today, unfortunately, started with the man in his own reflection. As a practitioner of medicine, he was told never to self-medicate, or self diagnose, but how WAS he supposed to deal with such a personal dilemma? Terry pondered. The whole idea of going through with the call was beginning to infuriate him, "Dammit!" Terry said angrily, and hung up the phone. He had no plan, and he surely could not just call up and say, "Yo' bro, what you been up too? Oh, really? By the way, how's mom?" He said aloud agitated. Terry was starting to feel a migraine coming over him and remembered barely sleeping about only an hour or two, "mourning would do that," Terry figured. He opened the file once more in hopes of it motivating him to go through with the call this time. His emotions were all over the place and seeing the photo of the gunshot wounds on his mother was not making him any less agitated, "Motherfuckers…she was just an old lady." He mumbled. The more he read through Thomas Jr.' profile, the more he found it both odd and interesting that he fit the same criteria of the latest focus group that was put together weeks ago. Their new outreach program "The C.F.C." (Club for Concerned Father's) are what some in the program are nicknaming themselves, was designed to engage and study father's who could not overcome their psychological breakdowns after child or, family loss under violent and extreme circumstances. From a clinical point of view, Thomas Jr. was the poster child of what the study was designed to investigate. Not only did he suffer the losses of his wife, mother, and children, he too was a rape victim, Terry believed. Terry also never treated anyone that studied in Christian theology before and bringing someone like his brother into his program could possibly prove beneficial to them both and to the rest of the group, Terry contemplated. But how could he think of such a trivial issue? Terry wondered. Yet still, Thomas Jr.' insight from a preacher's standpoint could give just the type of colorful prospective and objective advice on the divine designs of fate his group sorely lacked, Terry hypothesized. "Who knows, maybe he could even talk some sense into that Kale Keegan…" Terry said aloud to himself. But talking to the always distant Kale Keegan was probably asking for a "little too much from anybody!" He retorted. Though the fascination of such a radical idea tantalized his therapeutic nature, his curiosity still worried him. A part of him could not shake the feeling that he bailed out on his family somehow. Terry knew that this was part of the guilty phase he was going through. The thought of never getting to say goodbye to mother was eating away at his primal cerebellum, causing him to fantasize about blood vessels throwing hematoma parties in his brain. Terry hoped to go on remembering his late mother as both the regal and very old fashioned woman she was. Grace never fully understood him, but as a mother she tried not to make him feel alienated as Thomas Senior did. Despite the way she died, he was relieved she did not endure the indignity and indecency that Thomas Jr., his wife and daughter experienced. Terry did not pray often, but what he did hope for was some form of reprieve from his big brother Thomas Jr. He wanted to see him again, hug him again, and most of all, tell him how much he had missed him all these years. Terry picked up his cell and sent Lacy a text back, "I love you too, baby! Have a good day at work!" Terry's message said. He checked the time on his watch and hustled to push the operator button on his office phone, "Sheila?" He said. Terry was unaware that the volume on his speaker was still set on its loudest setting since yesterday's meeting, "Yes sir, Dr. Templeton?" Sheila's said loudly, through the office speaker. "Shit!!!" Terry screamed, and spilled his entire cup of coffee. "Excuse me?" Sheila says. "Sorry, I just...spilled…the coffee…oh, never mind! I need you to clear my 1:00 and also….could you PLEASE bring me another cup of coffee?" Terry asked displeased.

Irwin County, Georgia….

Over the past couple of years, Thomas Jr. had felt as if he had been relegated to living a life of pure unadulterated hell. Each day he relived that horrible night Sonny Korne and the rest of his sadists broke into his family's home, then proceeded to rape and kill almost everyone he ever loved. In the span of one night, his whole world had been tainted by so much unspeakable evil. He spent most of his mornings crying on his knees and begging God for answers to questions that only he could answer. The life he formerly lived felt more like a fairy tale at best, unlike his current state of well being. Thomas Jr. remembered pulling into a private parking space and walking into a well furbished home after a long days work, and to a beautiful family that greeted him like a King. Thomas Jr. could still recollect the euphoric smells of hot spices that filled the air after entering, then seeing Mia and Markus running up to him to give him a great big hug. His beautiful wife, Lucinda, the one who worked part time, but still managed to keep a clean household, greeted him with a reassuring kiss. Her kisses tasted both sweet and pleasantly delightful to him, which often led to them sneaking off for a little "one on one time" alone. Thomas Jr. also remembered how much he relished preaching from his father's pulpit, and could see his proud and dignified mother smiling back at him from the front pew. But now....all of that was nothing but a sweet memory, Thomas Jr. reflected. The man who once stood before his flock at New Mount Greater Faith was nothing more but a mere "shadow" of himself, He believed. These days, he lived alone in a small dingy one-bedroom apartment across town. He had just gotten off his morning bus ride from the hospital, where he visited his son Markus. Thomas Jr. checked his mailbox and just as he assumed, it was it filled to the brim with hospital notices. The buildings elevator was out, so he was forced to walk to his third floor apartment. His legs were wobbling after making the long journey up the three flights of stairs. As soon as he entered into his home Thomas Jr. first reaction was to toss his "mail" to the floor, but decided to file it with the rest on his desk. Because of his massive hospital bills, Thomas Jr. found it virtually impossible to afford to stay in his old north side town home any more. Part of him was relieved, as he could not have fathomed the idea of staying there after everything that had happened anyway. Markus was the last piece of what was left of his once promising family, despite him needing a breathing machine to keep him alive. He had been in a coma every day since that awful night and Thomas Jr. did not have the courage to pull the plug on the only thing left in his life to live for. Their medical bills had been piling up high enough to make God trip over them, yet Thomas Jr. did not care. Thomas Jr. was not preaching very much lately, especially when it took almost a year to regain his strength and get his speaking patterns back on track. Then there was also the colostomy bag issue he was dealing with at the time. His pride would not allow him to go out in public for months, and the last thing he wanted, was people staring at him shitting from a bag.

Although his bullet wounds have healed, Thomas Jr. still carried around the emotional scars left over from his sexual assault. Once word got out about him being sexually abused, people began giving him strange looks at church. His so-called friends treated him as though he had an infectious disease that would harm them, if they came in a breath's distance of him. The church's trusties, as well as the deacon board who were led by "family friend" Deacon Stanley Golightly, even asked him to take what had appeared to be an extended leave of absence. The good reverend was not at all that surprised by their frustrations though. Thomas Jr. had long noticed that after each passing week that they were losing more and more members. His sermons were also very unfocused and radical. Deacon Golightly played back a tape of one of his sermons for him, just before showing him the door and it sounded like he was pretending to be more Tupac Shakur instead of a reverend. He was scaring away the congregation that his father spent his entire life to build. Something else inside of him had also changed. It was the one thing he knew that he did not need anyone's confirmation for. The proud reverend had lost his faith. Thomas Jr. walked into his barren kitchen and took a beer from the small refrigerator and sat quietly on an old sofa that was donated to him by a church member. Every day he had spent his time questioning God about his motives for allowing such pain and anger to fill his once faithful soul. Thomas Jr. knew he was far from perfect, but assumed after getting baptized and following in his father's footsteps, that he would certainly be covered by the blood of Jesus. But on that night, the only thing Thomas Jr. felt like he was being covered by was another man's sperm. After losing so many people dear to him, only hate, confusion, and conceit had consumed his once peaceful heart. On some occasions, he could feel the hatred for those so called "men," boil so deep within his loins that he felt as if he were going to gag on his own tongue. "How long could he possibly last without hope?" Thomas Jr. wondered, and took a big swallow from his beer bottle. That night he had hoped that God would have sent someone to save them, but no one ever came. Thomas Jr. turned on his 19' screen television and an episode of Let's Make a Deal was on. He listened intently, as Host Wayne Brady talked exasperatedly about hope for winning a large prize to a homey looking white woman, who was dressed like the character Raggedy Ann. Seeing her crossing her fingers and praying to herself in hope of changing the outcome of a game made Thomas Jr. cringe. Part of him still believed God was not some genie who granted people's wishes or, some puppeteer who controlled vile creatures like Sonny Korne. Although his respect level for God's power remained intact, undeniable hope on the other hand, was a luxury he apparently could ill afford. With his pride gone and faith reduced the reverend Thomas Jr. had no hope for his soul and no hope for retribution for lives taken from him. Any hope Thomas Jr. may have had left, he was saving for his son Markus. Despite everything his father instilled in Thomas Jr., he still could not shake the feeling that maybe, just maybe…that God really never had his back in the first place…

Terry and Thomas Jr. Re-unite

A few hours later….

Thomas Jr. sat at his kitchen table lighting his fifth cigarette of the day, something he had not done since his college days, and reading an old newspaper. He had not bathed in the previous two days since leaving the Fitzgerald Memorial Hospital, were Markus was being kept. The doctors always warned him of the possibility of Markus never waking up due to all the brain trauma he suffered by Sonny and his "boys." If "wishes" had really existed in this hateful world then he would had wished to see his long suffering son open up his sleepy brown eyes again, Thomas Jr. thought to himself. He felt responsible for his son's critical condition, since it was he who insisted his son too go outside in the first place. With each passing day, the guilt of his actions continued to grow and made it overwhelming to look at his helpless child lying unconscious week after week for two years. "My son didn't deserve this! How could I possibly go on preaching God's gospel, if I lost my boy too? Jesus… If he should wake, how do I explain to him what happened to his sister…his mother…GRANDMOTHER… or, even me?" Thomas Jr. considered. How could he face his son as a man after being raped by one? He often worried. The agitation he was feeling caused him to lose feeling in his throat when he swallowed. Thomas Jr. got up to grab himself another beer from the refrigerator. There was a day when Bud Light was the last thing on his mind, now he could not imagine a day without drinking more than one. He noticed something different about reflection as he passed by his mirror on the wall. When he took a closer look, he noticed a significant drop in his weight over the last few months. His appetite had changed after his surgeries, but even if he did not need those life saving surgeries, he still may have never had much of an appetite anyway, Thomas Jr. concluded. "Oh well…" Thomas Jr. said aloud. After he opened the refrigerator door it became obvious what else contributed to his drastic changes, "Damn. No wonder…" Thomas Jr. whispered to himself. Just as he was reaching for his beverages, the telephone phone rang. In the back of his mind he feared that it may have been his landlord calling to hassle him again about the overdue rent that he owed. While the phone continued to ring, the more skeptical and reluctant he felt about reaching for it. "Then again, maybe it's just the hospital, calling to tell me my baby boy is finally awake!!!" He guessed. It did not take him long to come to the conclusion that it was possibly more bad news, "Naw, Better let the machine do it." He agreed. When the machine answered, the caller's voice on the other end sounded vaguely familiar to him. It was something from the past, but he just could not put his finger on it. The voice on the machine was a man's and he stuttered something awful in trying to explain why he had called in the first place, "Uh, hi? H-h-hi yah doing, uh, I mean…I know this sounds…sounds bad, but…let me try this again…uh,… I don't mean to be weird, but uh, if this is you….REALLY you, Tommie…" The voice on the machine said. "Tommie?" Thomas Jr. thought suspiciously. Thomas Jr. cracked the top off his beer, "Boy, the nerve of these goddamned bill collectors!? I haven't been called that since….since…." Thomas Jr. trailed off. Then the familiar voice on the phone said, "It's me, your little brother, well…your "older" little brother, Terry, ha ha!" the voice uncomfortably said. "T-T-Terry?" Thomas Jr. said aloud, and dropped his beer on the floor. He began tripping over himself as he rushed to reach for the phone before Terry could hang up, "I'm HERE! T-T-Terry I'm HERE lil bro!" Thomas Jr. screamed into the telephone receiver. At first, there was a long pause and Thomas Jr. assumed that he had answered the phone too late, but soon as he was about to hang up the phone, he heard the sound of someone clearing their throat, "Terry? Terry, is it really you!?!" Thomas Jr. asked again. Terry Templeton needed time to regain his composure and when he finally spoke, his voice was both cracked and tearful, "Y-Yeah bro, it's.... it's me...it's really me." Terry said gingerly. Thomas Jr. could not believe the impossible news he was hearing and began hollering in jubilation, "Well praise God, my lil' bro....what happened man, the "rapture" wasn't a long enough wait for you? Unless you just called to tell me it's coming today?!" Thomas Jr. joked. Terry, who had been drenched in his own tears, could not help but laugh at his brother's sarcasm, "Oh-h-h, so that's how it is? Same ole' big Tommie, damn bro, it's really good to hear your voice man!" Terry insisted. "Same hear, but you shole' got a lot of explainin' to do Lucy!" Thomas Jr. quipped, in his Ricky Ricardo voice.

The Templeton brothers were reunited once again for the first time in almost thirty years. Thomas Jr. had, what seemed to be, a gazillion questions for his younger brother and expressed the joy of knowing how great things had been for him all these years. After the jubilance between the two began to wear thin, it became painfully obvious to Thomas Jr. that Terry was avoiding personal questions about his own life, as well as questions about their mother. Instinctively, Thomas Jr. confronted his brother for the truth, "Okay, Terry Fairy, what gives? Thomas Jr. asked frankly. Terry was caught off guard by his big brother's bluntness and was at a loss for words, "Well, what's the matter, cat got your tongue, lil' bro?" Thomas Jr. asked again. Seeing that his brother's demeanor was still despondent, Thomas Jr. had come to the conclusion that Terry calling him out of the blue was "more" than just by chance, "You...you know, don't you?" Thomas Jr. asked assertively. Terry tried his best to hold back his emotions, but guilt and sadness steamrolled over him like a runaway freight train, "Oh...Tommie, I'm so....so, very sorry. Had I...h-had I...known, Thomas...Jesus, man." Terry cried, as he tried to explain. Dr. Terry Templeton had spent so many years trying to straighten out other people's problems that he was starting to feel the rust of trying to solve his own. This time Thomas Jr. was the one who could not find the words or, the strength to comply, "Tommie?" Terry called out. The shame Thomas Jr. was feeling was making his legs weak. He grabbed his chair and sat down and pulled out another cigarette to light. He took a deep drag off the cigarette and exhaled the smoke from his mouth slowly, "...How could you know!?" Thomas Jr. stated flatly. "That's no excuse, Tommie! I should've...I should've been there for you bro." Terry said disgusted. Thomas Jr. took another drag off his cigarette, "Don't beat yourself up, Terr…shit happens, you know bro?!" Thomas Jr. said nonchalantly. Judging from his cold and apathetic response, Terry knew Thomas Jr. was obviously still suffering and spoke nothing like the seasoned reverend he read in the file his brother was. He also could tell that Thomas Jr. had a chain smoking habit, as it sounded as if he had lit a third cigarette, by his count. "Who could blame him?" Terry thought. His brother had been through hell and was left agonizing over a comatose son for two years, not to mention how the rug was yanked from under him at New Mount Greater Faith. Being forced into early retirement from the same church their father built could not have been an easy transition for Thomas Jr., Terry accessed. "Poor Tommie," He thought. Sonny Korne had stolen his pride and his brother's manhood, while leaving his sanity and possibly faith, broken. It amazed Terry to comprehend the amount of hatred it took to force another man to watch his family getting slaughtered right in front of him, like live stock being taken out to pasture. Terry was doing his best to keep himself together when he thought about the prospect of never meeting his nephew alive. The contents of the gruesome file that was given to him was sprawled across his desk with its ghastly images and lengthy pages detailing the last few years of his brother's sad life. Under different circumstances, it would not have bothered him as much reading the gory details of what events took humans over the edge of their own psychosis, but Thomas Jr. was not one of his average patients though, he was family. Terry could feel his intestines tighten on the inside, as if they were being squeezed to death by an enormous elephant. There seemed to be no plausible way for him to tell Thomas Jr. the truth of how he came about his privileged information without causing him alarm, Terry pondered. In order to help his brother achieve some semblance of peace from his thriving torment, Terry had to find the mental fortitude to disassociate his personal feelings and act accordingly. What begun to worry him the most, was the fact that Sam Korne and company, were never caught, and worried about the possibility of them returning to finish the job. And what to make of the stranger's involvement in the case? Terry wondered. When he got a phone call two days ago, that Thomas Jr. was in grave danger, Terry first assumed it was just somebody's sick prank and hung up the phone, but after someone showed up at his front door flashing a H.P.D. detective's badge, that was all the validation he needed. Coincidently, Lacy got an emergency phone call from his mother and had left home, one hour prior before his uninvited guest arrived. The detective was caring a large tanned envelope, which had the dark brown file with the word classified printed in bold black letters going across it. He then told him that what he was about to show him was deemed F.B.I. classified documents, that could land them both in jail if caught with them. To protect his identity he chose to go by the name "Alejandro." Alejandro was too suavely dressed and too good looking to be any ordinary cop Terry was used to seeing and could still remember fawning over his slight Hispanic accent. Terry thought the man could have easily passed for a young Antonio Banderas, because of his slick-backed amber colored hair. Alejandro told him that he was working on a drug trafficking case that may have incidentally involved Sonny Korne and his buddies, but because Korne and the others were under investigation for federal crimes, he was asked to let them be. Terry remembered asking him about what any of that have to do with his brother, and that's when he finally opened the file. Alejandro sat motionless, while Terry screamed at the sight of the black and white photos of his brother's slain family and their dead mother's corpses splattered across them. After waiting several minutes for him to finally calm down, Alejandro then told him that H.P.D. were not allowed to interfere with F.B.I. cases, but if he could lure Korne and his cohorts out of hiding and into his jurisdiction, he could make an arrest possible. Terry automatically read between the lines when he used the term "lure." What Alejandro had in mind could possibly put Thomas Jr. and himself in harm's way. He gave him an emphatic, but courtesy "HELL NO" at first. How could he use his only brother as bait for a sadistic motley crew of killers? Terry thought at the time. After Terry escorted Alejandro to the door he left this on his mind, "I understand you're afraid. You're afraid that you might get your brother, or maybe someone else close to you hurt, but you don't have to be afraid…" Alejandro protested. Terry did not give any consideration to the last part of his sentence at the time. Terry loved Lacy with all his heart and soul, and could not fathom the idea of losing him. But Terry missed his older brother Thomas Jr. badly and felt even worse for his losses. "…You know, try not to think of it as getting someone you love hurt…think of it….as bringing your loved ones killers to justice. Your brother could really use some closure….and oh, you can keep the file." Alejandro said, and walked away into the humid night.

Terry thought long and hard before he finally made up his mind on what to do about Thomas Jr. Does he ignore Alejandro's plan and allow Thomas Jr. to be somewhat safe up in Georgia, or betray the only other man he loved more than life itself? Terry wondered. He spent the entire night weighing his only options, which seemed like baring the weight of a U.S. submarine. Terry tried his best to rationalize why he should not go through with Alejandro's plan, but from a logistical standpoint, he believed that his brother had been through hell, "Thomas…" Terry began. "Uh-Oh." Thomas Jr. said, as he put out his cigarette. "What? I hadn't even told you y…" Terry began to explain. "Negro, the only time you ever call me THAT, is when you either did something, or you want something, so which is it?" Thomas Jr. sternly asked. Terry grinned uncontrollably, "Yep, you definitely my big brother alright…. Look, I was just wondering….about YOU flying out to Houston to come see me?!?" Terry said eagerly. At first there was a long pause on the line, "Man, I wish I could, but things been really….really HARD on me financially, my health isn't what it used to be either, and then there's…there's … (Thomas Jr. begins to cry) my son…Markus." Thomas Jr. cried. Thomas Jr. sobbing caused Terry to pull his phone away from his ear. He believed if he had not then he would be a hot mess himself all over again. When his secretary Sheila knocked on his office door, Terry covered up the receiver with his hand, "Come in Sheila!" He said. As Sheila Eastland walked in, her voice was running at a hundred miles per hour, until she made eye contact with the horrible photos on his work desk. "Thank you Sheila, now shoo!" Terry demanded. She tried to ask him about the pictures, but Terry insisted that she leave. Terry was unaware that Thomas Jr. had been collecting himself while on hold and was waiting patiently for his return, "Uh, so…who's that?" Thomas Jr. asked intrigued. Terry was caught off guard by his brother's sudden directness, "Huh? Oh, her…yeah, sorry about that! That was just my secretary Sheila…" Terry explained. Thomas Jr. began to smirk, "A friend, or girlfriend?" Thomas Jr. sarcastically asked. "A secretary." Terry said abruptly. Thomas Jr. was hardly surprised by Terry's flippant reaction, "Oh, so you still playing for the other team I see…" Thomas Jr. said. Terry rolled his eyes, "Didn't know our dad was on three way, hello Tommie Senior!?!" Terry said sarcastically. They both laughed out loud for a few seconds and then a warm silence came, "You know, Terry, about our pop, he…" Thomas Jr. explains. "You don't have to do that, Tommie. What's in the past…STAYS in the past. I don't want you to feel like you need to…" Terry said before getting interrupted. "No, man I'm not. I know you had your reasons for leaving, as well as your reasons for staying away, but you need to know that, in the end…in the end, our daddy still loved you!" Thomas Jr. said. Terry put the phone down and covered his mouth to conceal his weeping, "You d-d-don't have to say that Tommie…he hated… he hated what...he didn't like, what I am." Terry explained. No Terry, he only hated the choices that you made, and nothing more bro. Every day after you left man, I watched our father change. He hardly left the house, except on Sundays, and people were practically begging him to speak at places, but he'd lost more than his son that day you left man! He lost his passion!" Thomas Jr. said. Terry was in disbelief and was shaking his head still crying at a waterfall's pace, "For real!? I, uh, I-I mean, wow." He said in astonishment. Thomas Jr. lit another cigarette, "Want to know what his last words were?" Thomas Jr. asked smugly. The line on Terry's end was so quiet you could hear a gnat taking a leak on a pillow, "Tell Terry, I never stopped loving you." Thomas Jr. said proudly. Terry fought hard to keep his self together and opened his left drawer and pulled out an old picture. It was a small photo of him and his dad that he had in his wallet the day he ran away. The pressure valve that had been bearing down hard over Terry's guilty conscious had been finally alleviated. Despite enduring all the adversity life had thrown his way, Terry Templeton could now move on with that part of his life. He was free to let go of past grudges he believed he shared with his long dead father, free to move on with the second chapter of the life, he hoped to enjoy with his common-law husband Lacy, and most importantly, free to help bring his brother's assaulters to justice. The point was a mute one, either way Terry needed his brother just as much as he needed him, and he was not going to take "no" for an answer, "Tommie, I got to see you bro. Don't worry about paying for air fare either, I got you!" Terry said gladly. Thomas Jr. was looking at his pile of hospital bills, "Terry, I…" Thomas Jr. interceded. Terry sat up in his chair to help reinforce his point, "Man look…. just come down for a little while and hang out with ya' lit…..OLDER little brother! I know you could use the break." Terry stated. Thomas Jr. thought long and hard about what his younger brother was asking of him. He had not left his son's side after recuperating from his own injuries, and had not made any distant plans too. Thomas Jr. put out his cigarette, and went back to the refrigerator for another beer. Thomas Jr. was taking his time trying to figure out what was best for him to do and took a long gulp from his beer bottle, "Umm. I wanna' come see you too Terr', but Markus isn't…isn't doing…" Thomas Jr. voice trailed off. "…In a coma, yes, I know." Terry said sympathetically. Thomas Jr. almost choked on his beer at Terry's statement, "Damn man, just how the hell you know so goddamn much in the first place?!" Thomas Jr. yelled. "Calm down, preacher man and let me explain!" Terry screamed back. Terry knew he could not possibly tell him the real truth and risk fractioning his already damaged psychosis, so a thought came to mind, "After I left Ben Hill, I tried to move as far away as my fifteen dollars could take me. It was rough! I was penniless for a little while…eating what scraps I could find, doing whatever I could to survive…all that before I got the wild idea to join the Navy. It was there where I got the discipline I really needed at the time. The Navy was cool. I got my degree in psychology and met my companion, Lacy." Terry said happily. Thomas Jr.' eyes bucked, "Lacy? Who's she?" Thomas Jr. said in a condescending tone. "HE's my husband…my common-law husband that is!" Terry said proudly. Thomas Jr. frowned, "Oh, yeah…right." Thomas Jr. said disgusted. "ANYWAY, I been working at a mental clinic for a while…" Terry reiterated. Thomas Jr. started frowning as he turned up his bottle for another big swallow of beer, "So you've already said Terry, just get to the part about how you found out!" Thomas Jr. demanded. Terry had been trying to come up with an excuse the entire time he had been sharing his story, but found himself struggling to do so, "Uh, yeah…sorry, anyway, the other day a trainee from Irwin had asked if I had any relatives in Georgia, and when I told her yeah… that's when she told me the story about…about what happened to you and mom and…your family." Terry said grudgingly. Thomas Jr. leaned all the way back in his kitchen chair and was still unsatisfied with Terry's answer, "Uh-huh. Well, how did you know where to find me? My phone number's not even listed." Thomas Jr. replied. Though Terry despised lying to his big brother, he still felt obligated to help bring him some form of closure, even if it meant he had to create such fiction to pacify Thomas Jr.' idling suspicions. If lying was what it was going to take to get him to Houston "then so be it!" Terry thought. "I simply "Googled" an old acquaintance who still lives there and "He" was the one who tracked you down." Terry conceded. Thomas Jr. slammed his bottle down, "Who tracked me down?" Thomas

Jr. asked suspiciously. Terry had been out of practice when it came to deception and Thomas Jr. was not making things anymore easier with all his questions. He knew it was a long shot, but he called his bluff, “Remember Harvey, from high school?” Terry asked. Thomas Jr. spit out his drink to answer, “Harvey Henry? You mean….the “one” our folks caught you being a “slut puppy” with? Yeah, how could I forget that?” Thomas Jr. confirmed. Terry began to blush and did not know if he should had been offended by his brother’s comment, “Yeah, well HIM…that’s who. We kept in touch after, we…since I left home, dammit!” Terry said irritably. He could feel Thomas Jr.'s unapproved frown through the other side of the telephone, “You sure about that?” He asked inconspicuously. Terry was at his wits end and was beginning to run out of steam. It had been decades since Terry had to be this “deceitful.” Though hiding his sexuality for years to save himself from ridicule and danger was not technically lying, since he had came out the closet, he did not feel the need to be that way anymore. He bit down nervously on his favorite Houston Texans pen, “Yeah, why?” Terry asked. Thomas Jr. took a big gulp from his beer bottle, “Cause,’ …that day when he got home, his momma caught him leaving our house and sneaking through his bedroom window. After politely getting his ass beat, he came clean, no pun intended, to what he’d been up too and paid Senior a visit...” Thomas Jr. said. “Damn.” Terry thought to himself. He was getting so close to finally convincing Thomas Jr. and could ill afford to have everything blow up in his face now, “Yeah, she marched his ass right back over here…right after YOU got put out the house! After she confirmed what happened with Senior, they eventually moved out of town the following week to…to…? Damn, where did they go…?” Thomas asked, “North Carolina. Yes, he told me.” Terry confirmed. That much of his far-fetched story was at least true, Terry reassured himself. Thomas Jr. took his time and contemplated what to say next. When it took him a while to respond, Terry had his fingers crossed, hoping that he had finally convinced Thomas Jr. enough to at least consider a visit, “All right…” Thomas Jr. simply replied. “All right…all right what?” Terry asked warily. Thomas Jr. exhaled deeply, “I’ll come to Houston! Call me later about the details…and oh, you still remember Luke 8: 17?” Thomas Jr. asked. Terry began gathering up the file’s contents on his desk quickly, while he beat his mind to find the answer to an old but familiar question, “Yeah, uh…ah-hem…I’m a little rusty, but I think it went something like…"For nothing is hidden…that it may not manifest…uh, or, something along those lines!?" Terry said distracted. Thomas Jr. put his beer bottle down and swallowed hard before responding, "…Nor is anything secret that would not be known….and come to light!" Thomas Jr. grimly finished. Terry did not need an Associate's degree in Christian divinity to read between the lines of that bible scripture. It was his brother's way of sending him an indirect warning, and Terry Templeton got the message loud and clear, "I will have to keep that one in mind, and hey, Tommie?" He said. "Hmm?" Thomas Jr. responded while gulping down his beer, "I…I love you, bro and…thanks!" Terry said and hung up the phone. Thomas Jr. allowed Terry's words to marinate in his mind a moment or, two and hung up his phone. A long time had passed since Thomas Jr. last heard ANYONE tell him that they "loved" him, let alone mean it. It was as if the idea of hearing those words uttered aloud were like a foreign language. There was a time, he believed, that the people who once flocked to come hear his sermons every Sunday had loved him, but how soon did their hypocritical hearts changed. Most of his church members looked down upon him as if he were tainted goods and unfit to preach the Lord's gospel. Sure some people managed a forced smile or two, or sent condolence letters for a little while, but vicious rumors were being spread that confused Thomas Jr. heart. If there was anything black church's loved more than giving praise, it was gossip, and Lucinda's family members had begun to shut him out after believing a rumor "he" hired Sam Korne to target his family and collect on a huge policy. It was this very thought that caused his eyes to drown in his eye sockets, "How can man be so cruel toward one another Lord? And most of all, how long should I be forced to pray for those who speak such ill will against me, as well as for the sakes of mine enemies?" Thomas Jr. thinks disgustingly. In anger, Thomas Jr. slaps the empty bottles off the kitchen table and into a wall where they smash into a hundred pieces. It was not in his nature to be so angry or, agitated, but Thomas Jr. could not find any possible way to escape the unbearable pain and humiliation he endured. His soul severely lacked peace and the culpability he felt on a daily basis had Thomas Jr. wishing to have done things differently, but wishes he thought, were for children or, people who dreamed about winning the lottery. Either way, Thomas Jr. needed something to believe in since his faith in God had long begun to wane. If there was still anything Thomas Jr. still believed for sure, it was that he needed to believe that his son survived his attack for a reason…not breathing on his own, but alive nevertheless. Terry believed that flying out to Texas will help him escape his problems, though Thomas Jr. suspects that something else may be in store for him once he gets there. His brother, who was once a notorious cheapskate, offered to pay his way, "Whatever happened to Tight Ass Terry?" Thomas Jr. wondered. Thomas Jr. marveled at all the changes in his younger sibling and had admired him for turning things around in his life. "Who knew things would've turned out so badly for the one kid who tried to follow in the footsteps of his great pacifist father? Hmph. No good deed goes unrewarded, I suppose." He thought intently. When Thomas Jr. stood to his feet, he noticed the mess on the wall he made with the beer bottles, "Lord have mercy…maybe I do need a break." He said. What harm could it do? He thought. Thomas Jr. had not visited Houston in what felt like ages ago, back when Senior was still around doing his thing. With his life being turned upside down these past couple years, pain and suffering had not offered him the delectable pleasure of reflecting on his fabled father. To numb what he was feeling internally, Thomas Jr. got himself another beer from out the fridge and goes to his small dingy bedroom. It was the middle of the day and to save money on his electrical bills, he opened the window's blinds to allow the sun to illuminate the room. The sight of the blinding sun caused him to cover his eyes with his hands. "Shit! Keep forgetting how bright that damn sun shines through here." He said aloud. After the focus of his eyes returned, he peered out his bedroom window that overlooked a raggedy playground at a nearby elementary school. The children were apparently at recess until suddenly, the bell rang and off they all went running and screaming enthusiastically, back toward their classes. Thomas Jr. took a big swig from his bottle, but just as he was leaving the window he noticed something odd about the playground. It had appeared as if someone had been looking back at him from afar among the crowd. The thought of someone staring at him so intently would not normally bother Thomas Jr. if it were not for the fact that nobody seemed not to even notice him. It was an old black man and he wore what looked like an oxygen mask covering his mouth. The old man also appeared to be wearing a blue hospital gown that was covered with something deep red. Thomas Jr. almost choked on his beverage as the old man pointed at him, as if to tell him something. When Thomas Jr. turned his head to walk away the old man was standing next to him and pulled off his oxygen mask, "Peace be still, boy…" yelled the old man. Thomas Jr. immediately recognized who the man was and dropped his bottle to the floor. "Have mercy Jesus!!!..." Thomas Jr. yelled. Through the old man's decrepit state, his stature could not be mistaken for non-other than Thomas Senior himself. The only difference was, he had no eyes, his dirty blue hospital gown was riddled with stained blood, and his skin appeared both dark grey and heavily withered. Seeing the sight of his long dead father horrified Thomas Jr. to the point where he felt as if he were going into cardiac arrest. Thomas Jr. had dropped to his knees and was gasping for whatever air he could muster in his small and dank room, "D-d-addy? N-n-no…no, it can't be…!" Thomas Jr. moaned. "Choose blood, boy, you lose blood!" Senior roared. Smoke was coming out of his dead father's mouth as he spoke and as Thomas Jr. looked closely, could see earthworms and other night crawlers crawling about his worn looking skin. Thomas Jr. refused to believe what he was hearing, let alone what he was seeing, so he then closed his eyes tightly in hopes of him going away. When he opened them again Senior was gone. He ran over to the window and looked at the playground area, but no one was there. "D-Daddy…I-I-I'm sorry…please, comeback…" Thomas Jr. said whispered.

How Senior Saved the Day

It had been around the fall of 1966 when Thomas Senior agreed, along with many other top NCAAP members, to spear head some major damage control after the Los Angeles Watts riots were over in 65'. They were constantly flying from city to city and coast to coast, talking on various radio stations, holding press conferences, or at school rallies; whatever they could do to help ease the unrest that had unsettled black America during that awful and violent time. There were grumblings up north of a potentially small militant faction that had formed in the south who was comprised of young frustrated black men calling themselves "The Soul Knights." While the rest of America was trying to heal and understand the violence that plagued California and the like, the idealistic

Soul Knight's leader Jericho "Geronimo" Blackmon had other ideas in mind. He caught wind that the NAACP had plans to have a guest speaker arrive at a local Houston radio station. It was simply by chance that on that day, when the brazen Jericho and his troops stormed the station and armed to the teeth, that that special guest would be the renowned Reverend Thomas Templeton Senior. Senior was in the middle of his interview when the group stormed through the unsuspecting radio station. One of the Soul Knights looked like a familiar former football player, both from his build and also how easily he tossed the studio producers to the ground, Thomas Sr. thought at the time. Thomas Sr. had felt a small sense of irony come over him, as thirty minutes prior to the raid, he had spoke exhaustedly about how blacks were usually the ones who sought peace and equality, and how they never forced aggression upon non-blacks. "Well, so much for that argument," He said to himself quietly.

Meanwhile, Thomas Jr. and his mother Grace, who was pregnant with Terry at the time, were safely listening to the mayhem unfold from the cozy confides of their hotel bedroom, not too far from the radio station. Dangerous situations never seemed to bother his father very much, but it apparently skipped a generation, as Thomas Jr. remembered almost shitting his pants in the wake of the melee. Although his mother would not admit to it then, but even she was unnerved by her husband's unpredictable disposition. Thomas Senior was always like that though, a swashbuckler with ice water circulating through his veins and ultimately turned what was a deadly situation into a positive one. The Soul Knights were originally formed to make a difference in their community and figured if parading around with pistols worked for the Black Panther Party, why not them? They had everything that their rival Panther's practically had in smarts, attitude, and leadership. As a former Prairie View A@M college grad, Jericho was just as educated as both Huey Newton and Bobby Seale combined, and also shared a passionate obligation for standing up for equality of their people. Once word got out over the KHRV radio waves, that the predominately white owned station was being infiltrated by black youths, the Harris county police were immediately dispatched. After they arrived, the police surrounded the loudly yellow colored one story building and begun demanding for the Soul Knights to surrender, but the young men refused and stood their ground. Seasoned radio host Al McDowell, who was a well known public sympathizer and no stranger to the plights of minorities happily invited them to partake in an interview session. "So what brings you here today gentlemen?" Al asked cautiously. Al McDowell was an award winning radio broadcaster and former journalist who served a brief tour in Vietnam, so the fact that the youngsters busted into his booth with guns in tow hardly rattled him. Senior explained later that day, that Jericho was constantly rolling his eyes at Al, and hesitantly took a seat next to him. Jericho put down the intimidating .357 caliber pistol that he was carrying on a table, but never took his eyes off Thomas Senior. "Sir, despite the current circumstances, it's a real honor meeting you!" Jericho said politely. While his father may have thought Jericho Blackmon's words flattering, Thomas Jr. found his statement to be both preposterous and an oxymoron after hearing it live. People did not stick up their heroes, Thomas Jr. thought at the time. Thomas Senior cleared his throat and leaned into the microphone, "I suppose, under different circumstances, the honor may've been mine." Senior said coldly, "Do you have a name, son?" He asked bitterly. The star struck Jericho put his hand out, "It's Jericho, sir… Jericho Blackmon, but my friends call me G…" "Geronimo!" Senior finished, Yes, I thought I recognized you." Senior said. Jericho was surprised that someone of Thomas Senior's pedigree, a man well traveled, would still remember a nobody like him, especially after all the time that had passed, "Unbelievable, after all this time?" He asked proudly. Thomas Senior shook Jericho's hand firmly, "I should remember, after all, I was the person who gave you that nickname in the first place son! You were an excellent debater at Prairie View. I thought you spoke passionately and fiercely in your arguments against Harvard, and compared you to the late great Apache Indian "Geronimo" facing off with Mexico." Senior said pleased. Jericho began to blush and cleared his throat, "T-Thank…thank y-you, sir. My friends have been calling me that ever since then!" He said excitedly. Feeling a little neglected, Al McDowell started ruffling the scripts that were in front of him, "Ahem, well…now all that is out of the way. What is it, may I ask, that you hope to accomplish by intruding on your "idols" interview, especially with a loaded pistol I might add?" Al asked rudely. The smile that occupied Jericho's face vanished abruptly and cut his light green colored eyes sharply at the balding Al, "What I hope, Al, is that you don't ever interrupt me again. I'd hate to split your head open before I get your point of view first." He said coldly. Despite his pride, the usually outspoken and controversial Al McDowell did not speak a word at first, but then a thought occurred to him as he dropped his papers back down on his desk. Al's program The McDowell Show ratings had been leaking like a canoe full of bullet holes the last month or so, now suddenly he found himself dead in the center of a terroristic hostage situation. "Eat your heart out Johnny Carson!" Al thought, as he fought off orgasms to what he felt was ratings gold. "Ahem, (clearing his throat) alright then, Mr. Blackmon from....ahem, Prairie View, the floor's all yours! Speak your mind, son..." Al happily encouraged. Jericho put his hand out to shake his, "Though I'm not a big fan, I still appreciate you having me..."Mr. McDowell," and I also HOPE that the Houston police department and whoever, are patient enough to allow me to be heard, before rushing in and blowing my head off!" Jericho said cryptically. Thomas Senior found the young man interesting, despite his crude methods of getting his point across to the people. He also knew that young Jericho was no stone-faced killer, "I hope you know what you're in for son...but....may God Bless you!" Thomas Sr. stated cautiously.

While the calm and collected Thomas Sr. was busy being courted by young black radicals at the KHRV studio, representatives from the NAACP's southern districts blasted his hotel room telephone with nonstop calls to reassure Grace that they would do all they could to make sure Senior would be fine. Newly appointed Washington D.C. federal judge Jonah Westbourne, a private NAACP supporter, had been notified of the situation and called in a favor to the Houston mayor's office to make sure the police involved handled the situation with utmost care. The last thing that the U.S. government needed, or the citizens of Houston wanted, was another Watts incident on its hands. Though he was very young at the time, Thomas Jr. could still remember the tension he felt in the room that day, as he imagined his great father languishing at the mercy of some armed psychotic Black Panther wannabe. It was the middle of the afternoon and the KHRV radio parking lot was said to have been filled to the brim, with over two-hundred onlookers and enforcement alike. Thomas Jr. remembered Grace telling him to turn on the television set to find out what had been reported on the news. Just as he found a station, it had been reported that F.B.I. agents were also making their way onto the scene. Despair had begun to rattle the normally cast iron minded Grace Templeton, as she was in awe of the agents cutting through the massive crowd that engulfed the backdrop of the news reporter. Hearing the events over the radio was one thing for her, but to see the action unfold live was another one. The gasp she had been holding back sprang from out her mouth before she could cover her lips in time, making the youthful Thomas Jr. nervous. Feeling guilty for her outburst, she rubbed the back of Thomas Jr. head to help ease his mind, "I'm sorry baby….mommy's just a little….emotional…because of the pregnancy." Grace confirmed. Grace's eyes became so watery, that to young Thomas Jr., they appeared as if they were melting glass. He always hated seeing his mother cry and at the time, he tried to offer her some comfort, "It's alright momma…when daddy's through talking on the radio, he gonna' bring you some medicine and make your tummy feel all better!" Thomas Jr. promised. His mother had paused from her frustration long enough to allow her son's words to marinate. Her doe eyed son was trying to be helpful and she began to laugh hysterically at his sweet suggestion. Grace called to him to sit by her on the edge of the bed and gave him a big reassuring hug and kiss on the forehead, "Thank you, Tommie. Mommy really needed that!" Grace said happily.

The present…

Thomas Jr. had struggled mightily to look past his nightmares long enough to resurrect those lost precious moments he once shared of his late mother. Whenever he did try to think about her, his mind refused to allow him to look beyond the night she was murdered at his home. The memory of that warm forgotten moment offered Thomas Jr. enough comfort to overcome the icy reunion he just held with his father's ghost. Seeing his beloved mother alive again, though in his mind, for such a short time caused him to break down into tears of joy for the first time in years. He sat down at the edge of his unmade bed, weeping profusely into the palms of his shaking hands. His shoulders gyrate uncontrollably with each sob and thanking God for at least a fraction of peace that he was being granted. Thomas Jr. had long run out of moral victories to celebrate since last waking up on an operating table, and getting news he was not the only person to survive his family's attack. The company of the symphony of breathing machines that kept his son alive, served as his only comfort. After getting his composer under control, Thomas Jr. walked over to his bedroom closet to find his suitcase, when a thought just occurred to him. When the spirit of his father spoke, it said something that sounded vaguely familiar to him. His father's words clawed at his inner conscious, as he continued to search through the disorganized closet, then suddenly the words began to manifest themselves loudly from the burrowed depths of his weary mind, "Choose blood boy, you lose blood!," those were the words Senior said to Geronimo over the radio, he remembered. Senior was trying to warn Geronimo about using militant tactics to prove a point. But why now, Thomas Jr. was trying to fathom, would his father's spirit wait up until today to spring that parable on him? Certainly there were other things he could have said that might have been of some use to him?! Thomas Jr. thought. Though Thomas Jr. greatly admired his father, he could not help himself from not appreciating his tone when he spoke to him. The more he pondered over it, the more he felt threatened by his dad's unwarranted advice. Thomas Jr. started going through his closet violently, until he finally yanked the clothes pole from its sockets and forcing everything to the floor. Now angry and out of breath from throwing his personal items, he sat back on the edge of his bed. "What the hell did I ever do to deserve such a fate, Lord?" He asked aloud, "Hadn't I been a good shepherd? You have taken EVERTHING from me, and then you take the one person, the ONLY person… I had revered, as much as I do you, to come torment me. Whatever happened to the promise of Isaiah 40:30, "Those that wait on the lord shall renew their strength?" Thomas Jr. protested. Thomas Jr. could feel his frustration swell inside his body like a hot air balloon, "Well lord, I HAVE waited! I have waited MONTHS for my body to heal…MONTHS to speak to my son Markus. Even waited LONGER for the authorities to catch my loved ones murderers, but justice never came. I have no money, I have no food, Jesus I have no life!!! My God, I'm…I…can't get no lower!!!" Thomas Jr. cried. He looked back through his bedroom window for his dad's spirit, "What did you really mean, daddy?" He quietly asked himself.

The McDowell Show…

Almost an hour had passed as host Al McDowell of the local Houston radio broadcast, The McDowell Show, and radical Jericho "Geronimo" Blackmon spent word fencing over their understood, but radically different points of political views. Despite his disposition, Al had grown to respect the man underneath the camouflage army jacket as more than just a black kid trying to play folk hero. Jericho spoke with high intellect, obviously from the degree's he earned in political speaking, and possibly seen more bloodshed than anyone in his twenty years should ever been allowed to see in their lifetime. Anytime Al's tone seemed to rise higher than the young man's, he would not break his composure. Whenever he responded to a given question, he would look directly into Thomas Senior's eyes. It was obvious to Senior that Jericho was waiting on him for something. Jericho talked with his arms folded with his pistol firmly gripped in his right hand and keeping a sharp eye on his fellow "Soul Knights" as they stood guard by entrance of the studio booth. Senior did not understand the young man's true intentions and did not want to risk sounding like a field mouse trying to patronize a king cobra. Either way he felt that something needed to be done and hoped to count on Jericho's admiration for him to work in his favor.

Finally, Thomas Sr. decided to break his silence and leaned closer toward the microphone, "Choose blood, boy, you lose blood…" Thomas Senior calmly stated. After talking at great lengths, Al McDowell was so caught up in the moment that he appeared in shock by the sound of Thomas Sr.' deep baritone voice when he spoke. Meanwhile, Geronimo's young face had a strange look of satisfaction across it. Al had been so distracted by the young man that he had to ask Senior to repeat himself, "I'm sorry, reverend, what was that?" Al confusingly asked, while fondling a lit cigarette. Jericho smiled even wider this time, "The good reverend said, "Choose blood, you lose blood..." Jericho stated with glee. Thomas Senior did not know what to make of Jericho's angle, and had thought he may have stepped over the line with his brash statement. Al had a look of confusion on his face, "What is that Kuroda Kan' ichi?" Al asked intrigued. Senior raised his graying eyebrows in unison, "No, it's what my father taught me." Thomas Sr. said. Al noticed Senior's mind seemed to drift off to some distant place in time for a split second. The usually cool headed radio host began to get a little unnerved by the sudden muteness of the room, "Well, now... don't keep us all in suspense reverend Templeton!" Al said nervously. Senior broke his gaze and stared at Al, then back over to still smiling, but curious Geronimo Blackmon. Thomas Sr. exhaled loudly as if he were trying blow the microphone across the sound booth, "A long time ago, when I was a young boy...younger than Jericho there, my father told me a story about two old pig farmers. One of the pig farmers was more successful than the other and so the other pig farmer grew jealous. So, one night the jealous pig farmer sneaks over to the successful one's land and kills half his stock and ends up being the successful one. When the pig farmer, whose pigs got killed, found out that it was his neighbor that did it, he snuck back over to that man's yard and killed his entire stock. Now, the original pig farmer is back on top again. So the next night, the jealous pig farmer sneaks back over to his land, but this time he goes up into his house. He slices the throat of the man's wife." Senior said stoically. Al was sipping his coffee in utter suspense, while Geronimo sat there soaking up every moment of Thomas Sr.'s tale with a broad grin, "So then what?" Al asked with intrigued. Senior looked over at Geronimo then back at Al McDowell whose expression was that of a child waiting to see what Santa Clause brought him for Christmas, "Well...the pig farmer got angry and went back over to the jealous pig farmer house and killed everybody. Problem was, after the dead pig farmer's brother found out, he had him arrested by the town sheriff. The man was found guilty and was hung to his death at high noon!" Senior said. Al's expression had changed from one of suspense to a look of let down, "Well, that's it? I don't fully understand the moral of the sto..." Al began before being interrupted. "Isn't it already plain enough for you to see, Mr. McDowell? The moral, what you may call it, is that they both lost. Each time they took something away from the other, and each time, the worse it got. Even the last one left standing still ended up with nothing. Not even, his own life. You choose blood...you lose blood, Mr. McDowell. Did I get it right Reverend?" Geronimo asked pleased. Senior was taken aback by his subtleness, "Yes Jericho, that's precisely correct. Jericho gathered himself, "That story never gets old sir." Jericho said. Senior set back in his chair in surprise fashion. "However do you mean?" Al asked bewildered. Jericho leaned forward in Senior's direction, "Because, he already told it to me." Jericho said quietly. Jericho pulled out a folded piece of paper from his coat pocket and tossed it near Al McDowell,

"And what is this, might I ask, Mr. Blackmon?" Al asked puzzled. Jericho leaned back in his chair, "Open it, and see?" Jericho replied. From the tone of Jericho's voice, Thomas Sr. could tell that whatever it was on the folded piece of paper was not only very important to him, but possibly the "primary" reason for the whole elaborate takeover of the radio station. Al slightly hesitated to open the paper and looked at the confident Thomas Senior for reassurance. Thomas Sr. nodded his head in approval, and Al sighed heavily and opened the paper. It was a worn cutout of a newspaper clipping. As Al McDowell started to read the paper, Thomas Sr. was trying to read his facial expressions while the seasoned journalist slowly examined it. The radio booth was so quiet that the only sound that could be heard in the room was that of the heavy breathing of Al McDowell. Jericho was now rubbing the gun along his forehead in anticipation to Al's reaction. Thomas Sr. began to grow more and more concerned as he watched Al take what felt like to him, an eternity to finish one headline. A phone rang loudly from Al's desk and caused Al to jump violently. His face had turned beet red, and he stared at Jericho as he reached for the blaring phone, "May I?' Al asked, "Don't be long…" Jericho ordered. Al seemed relieved by whoever the person was on the other end of the line. He closed his eyes as he responded with a few long "Uh-huh's and "no sir's." After he was finished, he passed the phone over to Jericho. Senior could discern that Jericho was not at all surprised by the phone call and almost snatched it from Al's hand as he passed it to him, "I really don't care to know who you are, so don't waste what little time I have left explaining it to me!" Jericho demanded. It had not bothered him in the beginning, but after seeing Jericho become so agitated that Thomas Senior began to realize the magnitude of the situation, and was now thinking about his son and pregnant wife back at the hotel. He prayed that they were okay and hoped that they were not worried and instead listening to Jackie Wilson on a different station….

That was clearly not the case, as Grace was presently clenching little Thomas Jr.' body to the point his young lungs were begging for air, after hearing Jericho going off on live radio. Thomas Jr. could tell his mother had been afraid for his dad, so much so he tried his best not to complain about her hugging him too tightly. Fortunately for him, a knock at the room door made her ease her kung fu grip on him. He grabbed at his chest as soon as she let him go. She noticed him doing so, "Momma sorry baby!" Grace pleaded.

Thomas Jr. offered his mother a quick smile, "Momma's just get the d…" She trailed off, before the knock came again. "Hold on, dammit!" Grace yelled frustrated. Grace half expected it to be just her security detail doing another routine check on her as she went to answer the door, "We're okay, Wayne! We're doing fine!" Grace said irritably. A booming voice sounding like that of a construction worker rose from the other side of the door, "Excuse me ma'am, but this is the F.B.I. and if you look through your peep hole there, you can see….that I'm not Wayne." The voice said. Grace squinted her pretty brown eyes through the hotel room's peep hole and could see a large white man in a black suit, wearing thick rimmed glasses and a black fedora. He was also accompanied by two other men who also wore the same. Grace had been reluctant at first to open the door, "Uh…just...just what is this all about?" She asked gingerly. She watched the man carefully through the peephole that spoke to her and he looked at his fellow comrades, "Ma'am…you're not in any trouble, we are here to help you and your husband." He confirmed. The large man pulled out his identification and Grace slowly unlocked her door. The agent put his wallet back into his jacket pocket, "We appreciate it if you would allow us to enter ma'am?" The man asked once more. Under normal circumstances, Grace could tell right off if she could trust a person, but with her husband being held hostage caused her to second guess herself, "Come in." She said hesitantly. The man looked at his fellow agents and took off his black hat, "Ma'am." He said, as he entered the doorway. Once the three men came in Grace could see that one of the agents with the large man was carrying a brown folder. She called over to Thomas Jr. and he scurried to his mother in great haste, squeezing her hand and ironically returning the favor. The stoutly built man put his hand out, "Jerrod, ma'am…special agent Jefferson Jerrod!" Jerrod said, and this is agent Whitley and Beauregard." He said. Grace could hardly tell one from the other, and the men both nodded and said "ma'am" almost in unison, "Grace. Grace Templeton. Pleased to meet you…so…how is it that you're gonna' help my husband? Grace asked confused.

The thermostat on the wall of the booth read 72 degrees and yet in still, journalist and radio host Al McDowell was sweating at the speed of a sprinting horses pace. He was clearly disturbed by whatever he read from the newspaper clipping that Jericho handed him, Thomas Sr. could gather. Not wanting to infuriate the young man Thomas Sr. tried to sympathize, "Brother Blackmon, might I ask you…what is worth throwing away such a promising and splendid future by your actions today, son? Certainly your parents wouldn't agree…" Thomas Sr. said before getting cut off. "… My mother killed herself a week ago…sir. She overdosed on painkillers. I'm sure what she would have had to say would fall under the "who really gives a shit column!" Jericho mocked. Al McDowell still did not speak. It was if his tongue had been surgically removed from his usually highly active mouth. Jericho rubbed his pistol along the side of his temple, "I'm sorry reverend Templeton, but I'm having some issues right now, think you can pray for me? You don't have to worry about praying for this piece of shit though (pointing at Al) his fate is sealed!" Jericho said, "He's going on a long trip to hell, you dig? And I got his ticket!" Jericho concluded, while pointing the pistol at Al's frightened head. Thomas Sr. had been confused by all the sudden hostility Jericho had demonstrated toward the elder McDowell, "Son, wait!!!" Thomas Sr. yelled. Jericho shifted his hazel eyes at the speed of a leopard chasing a wild rabbit, "Don't call me that, I'm not your son!!!" Jericho screamed. Still confused Thomas Sr. tried to plead with the young man, "Jericho…look, I'm sorry, so…I mean… I didn't mean any disrespect by it!" Thomas Sr. explained. Senior exhaled frustrated, "Look…Jericho, I'm just trying to understand the question of, why are you so angry? This isn't the bright young man I thought I was inspiring or, the one I seen greatness in! What did this man do to you so bad, that you are so willing to throw both you and your young friends lives away for?!" Senior asked sincerely. Jericho had tears running down his light complected face and dropped his head down for a second as he spoke, "It's not about what you see reverend, but what you didn't see, that you truly don't understand. That "All roads….lead to Rome!" Jericho quoted coldly, and stared at Al McDowell. Al's face seemed to turn white as the light fixtures that occupied the studio walls. He fumbled as he attempted to reach for his cigarettes, but knocked over his coffee cup instead, making a total mess of the neatly typed out interview questions he spent all night reviewing. His suddenness caused Jericho to pull the trigger on his .357 caliber pistol. The echo from his gun sent static feedback across the airwaves…

Back at the hotel, special agent Jerrod had been sorting through his F.B.I. folder and had not spoken one word since introducing himself. Agent Whitley had made himself at home by putting on a pot of coffee and ordering room service, meanwhile agent

Beauregard stood on guard by the hotel door. If anyone was crazy enough to come barging through that door, Grace was more than certain he would not waste two seconds in blowing their ignorant brains out. Agent Jerrod asked for the radio volume to be placed on low, possibly to concentrate or, just to keep her from worrying any further, Grace thought. The silence was beginning to make Grace antsy and just as she was about to speak her mind about how she really felt about their helping her, Agent Jerrod slammed the last of his papers on the coffee table, "Alright!" He exhaled. Grace jumped in surprise, "Oh, my!" She said, while holding her breast. Agent Jerrod took off his thick bifocals, "Sorry Mrs. Templeton..." He said apologetically. He quickly took out a handkerchief and cleaned his glasses and put them back on, "...But, uh...I'm ready!" Agent Jerrod said, as he made a kind gesture for her to sit at the chair across from him. Grace let out a sigh of relief and joined him at the table. She was pleased to see Thomas Jr. had gotten back to his coloring book on the floor and changed the TV station to make him take his mind off his father. Agent Jerrod held up a photo, "Do you know this man, ma'am?" He asked. Grace took the photo for a closer look, "N-no, I don't think so?" She said, and handed it back to him. He pulled out more photos that looked as though they had been taken from afar, "His name as you may or may not have already heard is Jericho a.k.a. "Geronimo" Blackmon. We have been secretly tracking him and his crew, "The Soul Knights," for a little while now. They have been trying to recruit other minorities to join their cause across the southern states, as well as on the east coast." Agent Jerrod stated. Grace began shaking her head and was trying to follow where the agent was going, "Cause? What cause?" She asked. Agent Jerrod cleared his throat, "Well ma'am, what started out as you're above average college kid forming peace rallies, who over night, basically turned into the anti-Christ!" Agent Jerrod concluded. Grace dropped the surveillance photos on the table and stood up, "Now you just wait a minute! Just because these boys are black and ain't afraid to speak their mind, don't make them dangerous!"She yelled. Agent Jerrod looked up at her with sincerity, "No ma'am, they being "black" don't make them dangerous...but, the "guns" sure do!" Agent Jerrod said emphatically. Understanding his point was more than moot, Grace took her seat and looked at the photos some more, "Him and his Soul Knights were thought to be just some harmless upstart radicals, but that all changed after they began attacking whites and assaulting police officers…" Agent Whitley said, in between coffee sips. Though she was skeptical at what she was hearing Grace made him go on, "…then Jericho started preaching hate to his Soul Knights, which we have on tape, and inspired others to follow suit or, be beaten to death themselves." Agent Whitley said. He handed her a copy of an old newspaper clipping and at the top of the article in bold print it read "Prominence is Bliss! Radio Personality Dodges a Major Bullet!" Grace appeared a bit confused while handling the article, "What is this?" She asked puzzled. Special Agent Jerrod leaned forward in his chair, "This is what lit his fuse." He said. Grace began reading the article while agent Jerrod further explained, "A few weeks before you and your family arrived here in Texas ma'am, a man was hit while changing his flat tire on the side of a dark lit freeway. His body had been drug a hundred feet, which made identification hard to do at first…" Agent Jerrod began. Grace had stopped reading the paper and looked up at Jerrod's chubby face, "So who was he?" She asked horrified. Just as he was about to reveal who the mystery of the dead man's identity agent Beauregard opened the door from outside ferociously, "Sir, I just got word that shots were fired inside the KHRV studio and director Hoover just sent orders to go "handle" the problem!" Agent Beauregard said frantically. Agent Jerrod glanced at Grace's face as she covered her mouth in awe, and sprang up from his chair like an agitated rhinoceros, and gathered all his classified information he brought. Just as all three agents were fleeing the hotel room Grace had stopped agent Jerrod one last time, "Agent Jerrod is he…is he alright?" She asked while fighting off her tears. "We don't know that yet, ma'am, but I can assure you, if he is…or isn't… that maniac is still going down!" Agent Jerrod said sternly. Grace still had pondered what the connection was between Al and Jericho. She closed the hotel room door and saw that Thomas Jr. was standing by the coffee table, "Mommy, that big man left his stuff!?" Thomas Jr. said. Grace looked at the paper in his hand with uncertainty at first, but even from where she was standing, Grace could clearly make out the distinction of the paper from the photo of Al McDowell and what she assumed was his lawyer standing next to him. In all the excitement she did not get to really read what the news article was all about, let alone what the connection was to Jericho Blackmon. She wasted no time asking him to give it to her, "Thanks honey!" She said. Grace skimmed over the article and began slowly piecing everything together in her mind. Each paragraph flies by her as if they were like a swooshing bald eagle seeking out its lunch, and in an instant, one name made it all clear. It was the last name of the identified victim, "Oh, my god?!" Grace gasped in dismay.

Al's McDowell's Little Incident

A few weeks ago, radio broadcaster Al McDowell had spent the whole weekend celebrating in New Orleans with other fellow respected writers, former Vietnam comrades, and journalist alike. They all were there for nothing special, just some old friends making last minute plans to spend one last amazing weekend in the Crescent City. The traffic returning to Houston was non-existent and that had boded well for him, since he got a little hammered right before he got on the road. What began as taking a simple nip to knock the chill off an unusually cold Louisiana night, Al McDowell began reminiscing about the horrors he lived through while serving in Vietnam as a private first class in the Army. Before he knew it, he had finished off an entire bottle of ole' Jack Daniels and a pint of Gin. His head was aching something awful and was starting to impair his vision. He managed to make it all the way to the outskirts of the city of Houston before his vision had finally gotten the better of him. Regardless, Al continued to press forward, despite bobbing and weaving in and out of the driving lanes in his newly minted black 63'Coup Deville. The more he continued though, the worse it got for him to stay awake. He realized that he was running too low on gas to make it all the way home and decided to find an exit to the nearest gas station. His eyelids were feeling heavier and heavier by each passing second and the soothing cool air emitting from his car air conditioner was not doing him any extra favors. Al was nodding off at the steering wheel and almost missed his exit. The combination of the long weekend, the even longer six hour drive, and the booze finally took their toll and Al McDowell fell completely to sleep. When Al awoke, it was to the sound of a loud thump and a faint scream. He pressed down hard on the car brake immediately, causing his head to bang violently against the steering wheel. The searing pain he felt, shot all the way down from his bleeding forehead to his neck and grabbed his head in defense, "God dammit!!!!" He yelled. Once the pain subsided, he glanced at his watch and noticed it was four in the morning, "Christ!?" Al yelled in awe. Since he drove nonstop the last four hours, it took an act of congress to pull himself from his front seat, "Jesus, my ass hurts as bad as my fuckin' head!" Al complained. He looked around to assess his surroundings and could see where he first exited the freeway behind him. The gas station he was looking for was half a mile in front of him, leaving nothing but open woods between him and the place. As Al walked toward the front of his car, he realized that he had been driving basically in the middle of the frontage road alongside the 610 freeway. He shook his slightly dizzy head at his error and made his way to his front fender. It was severely bent and had massive amounts of what he assumed was oil along the grill. He rubbed his index finger across the fender and marveled at the realization that the oil really was not oil after all, but in actuality, was blood, "Just what the hell did I hit?" He said aloud.

Both his driving fatigue and the alcoholic effects Al McDowell were feeling were quickly dissipating by the strange new find. Al stood perplexed and rubbed his tired eyes, then surveyed the road once again. For a split second, he thought he had seen a metallic square shape near some trees about a block away near the bottom of the exit ramp. Al was not too drunk to veer very far from his new 63' Coupe, especially since it was still running, and agreed with himself to go half way. With every careful step Al took away from his car and toward the shape, the more concerned he had for himself than for what he had hit. It had just occurred to him that he left his gun in the trunk of his car, but since he walked this far no sense in turning back now, He thought. "If I survived Nam, I can handle this!" He said aloud. There was a trail of blood going in the same direction as the shape, Al deduced. The headache that he had was trying to return with a vengeance. So much so, that he stopped midway to the metallic object to rub his forehead and with his attention on the ground, he saw something burning from the ground. He kneeled down to take a closer look and what it was caused fright to glide down the aging broadcasters back with the same fury as a pack of pachyderms storming down a hill. It was a still lit cigarette. Al looked around but did not see anyone among the woods vastness. A part of him began to feel uneasy and wanted him to make a break to his car, but instead he mustered what little courage he had left to go just a little more forward. What Al saw stopped him dead in his tracks. He looked over his shoulder at his car then back at what he realized what it was he was walking toward. Fear was overwhelming him to the point that he could only walk backwards toward his car. Once he got to the 63' Coupe, Al turned it off, but left on his high beams, and hustled back to his trunk. He pulled out a small black and leather embroidered case and took out of it a shining deep blue steel .357 and loaded it. Then Al heard a noise and the former Army infantry man, cocked the barrel on his gun. Al's breathing went from penetratingly loud, down to a deadly silence. Next, he heard a bump. This time, Al could now determine where the noise was coming from. The sounds were apparently coming from under his 63'Coup Deville. Al let out two quick breaths. then got down on his knees and looked under his car. What he saw caused him to shoot the gun in the air and fall to his back. His adrenaline was running at a record high, "Holy shit!!! Oh God, oh God, oh God, no…" He cried. Al has had some lows in life. He once accidently dropped his puppy from his second floor bedroom window, when he was six years old. When he was in high school, he cheated on his girlfriend with the girl's aunt. Even after joining the Army and getting shipped off to Vietnam, he intentionally jumped in the middle of live enemy fire to get out of staying one more miserable night over there, and received a Silver Star meddle out of it too. Today, Al has hit his all time low. He crawled on his hands and knees toward the car, scraping the gun across the pavement in the process. Al reached into his front pocket and pulled out a lighter. It was the shredded body of a barely breathing black man. Al McDowell began to panic and got back to his feet. His mind was racing in what he felt a hundred different ways. The first thought that had crossed his mind was that he would spend the rest of his life in jail for vehicular manslaughter, especially with the orgy of evidence that they would find. It would be an open and shut case. The man underneath his car let out a deep moan, causing Al to freeze in his tracks. He looked at the gun in his hand and seeing that there was not any more need for it, had put it inside the back of his pants. Al kneeled back down to his knees and looked under his car, "S-s-sir…I'm sooo, so sorry!? Al said apologetically. He could only see the back of the trapped man's head from the driver's side. With each difficult breath Al McDowell took, the more his guilt choked on his conscious. Al stood up and scurried to the passenger's side of the car and fumbled to keep the lighter lit as he moved in for a closer look of the dying man. What Al saw made a man who had seen dead children with their arms and legs missing, the after effects of fellow soldiers who had stepped onto land mines, and who had seen men hung because of their race as a child, simply weep. The only comparison he could make of the poor man's body was that of freshly ground hamburger meat. Al tried his hardest to keep himself together, "S-s-s-sir…I'm going….I-I'm going to have to go get help!" Al said quietly. The man underneath the car was still clutching a tire iron, but still had a free hand. The black man slowly raised his hand to what used to be his lips, and did a hushing noise. Al thought that his heart was about to stop at the man's forgiving jester, "But, s-sir…you're gonna' die if I don't get you some help!?" Al implored. The black man put his hand down, "N—n—n—no—t-t-t-t, g—g-g—on, ma-m—a—a-a-a-kit'!" The man said. Confused at what the man was asking brought Al further internal conflict with every moral fiber he owned, "But, I….I can't just watch you die, sir!" Al cried. Al was scared for the second time in his life, and didn't know what to do next, but part of him wanted to ignore the hurt man's request and leave anyway. But what the black man did next surely caught him way off guard. He pointed toward Al and made another hand jester.

The radio station….

Thomas Sr. did not know if what he was feeling inside his chest was a heart attack or just gas and indigestion from that terrible breakfast he ate earlier from the hotel, either way he was not feeling well. He ducked for cover after Jericho's gun went off, even though he was not his intended target in the first place. Nevertheless, Senior's father did not raise "no fool" and always told him to "duck for cover whenever any "other fool" with a gun was shooting, regardless if it wasn't you they trying to hit!" Senior recollected. Jericho was hovering over Al McDowell like a prowling puma and was breathing profusely while doing so. It sounded as if he was going to suck out all the air from everyone in the room. After seeing how unpredictable Jericho's mind state had become, Thomas Sr. began to worry. Some of Jericho's fellow Soul Knights charged inside the control room to see what had happened, but Jericho ordered them to return to their posts and to await further instructions. Though they were clearly unsure about following his command to leave him, Jericho reassured them that he still had matters under control. The young men left the control room and Jericho grabbed Al McDowell by the arm he apparently shot him in, "Aaagghhhh!!" Al screamed in agony, "Get up you son of a bitch…" Jericho whispered. It had been a while since Al McDowell last received a bullet from someone, and the radio personality did not think the time in between getting shot was long enough. He always knew in the back of his mind that he would die before his time. Al suffered through half a tour in Vietnam, and got shot, then went through two very bad marriages with zero kids to show for it, and now as the ultimate cosmic joke of them all, he gets to be killed live over the radio waves from his own show. Jericho forced Al to get back into his seat by pushing him hard into it, causing Al McDowell to shriek in pain again over his microphone. Jericho cocked the barrel on the .357, but seemed to be taking his time to actually pull the trigger, "Now, before you sign off for the very last time, of your despicable life, you are going to admit the truth to everyone listening!" Jericho yelled into the microphone. Thomas Sr. was growing frustrated from being left out of the loop of things and seen the newspaper clipping out the corner of his eye and slid it close enough to read it in its entirety. Al was feeling defeated at this point, and the guilt he was carrying from not explaining the whole story, the "TRUE" story was still eating at him. It should have been more than obvious to him from the very beginning to whom Jericho really was, but was too caught up in how much of a rating boost his flailing show desperately needed. Besides, It was only weeks ago that Al's famous defense attorney Leon Michael Bigsby Jr. got him off that conspiracy to commit murder and vehicular manslaughter charge. All Leon had to do was prove to the courts that the automobile that he was driving was never the murder weapon, which he made look easy when concerning the facts of the case. Fact 1: That the forensic evidence collected at the scene of the crime, proved the injuries that the victim sustained from the impact of Al McDowell's 63'Coup Deville were not real the cause of death. Fact 2: Police confirmed that the victim was shot at point blank range, and a .357 slug was found embedded in the left temple of the deceased victim after an autopsy was performed, therefore concluding that the victim died of severe head trauma caused by a powerful firearm. Fact 3: No firearm was found at the scene or, on Al McDowell. Fact 4: Al McDowell was the first on the scene and properly notified authorities after reporting he assumed he ran over an already injured animal, possibly a rogue deer. The prosecutor hardly made any fuss, especially since it involved the death of a black man with a criminal record. Robert Blackmon Sr. had been in and out of juvenile hall since he was thirteen years old, and had a laundry list of priors that ranged from burglary, extortion, prostituting and armed robbery that followed him all the way through his established, but shameful adult life. After his former prostitute wife got pregnant, Robert found a new profession on the assembly line at a north Houston industrial plant. They raised their only son, Jericho Jamal Blackmon, to be the "somebody" they always wanted to be, but never could become.

Thomas Sr. did not know what to make of the article at first, should he be disgusted that Al McDowell may have in actuality, killed Robert Blackmon intentionally, or that justice had turned another blind eye on those who didn't fit the status quo? At least, for now, he could make some sense of the extravagant takeover of the KHRV radio station. Jericho must have figured that he could not just simply shoot Al in the dark and make it appear as a mugging gone wrong, he believed he needed an audience. Not just any audience, but one that served as his many peers locally as well as nationally, but the only way he could pull off the national card would be by having a high profile hostage, Thomas Sr. surmised, "It could had easily been Dr. King or even their good friend Jesse…" Senior pondered. He had to give it to Jericho for coordinating a great plan, although he just may fail at executing it, Thomas Senior thought. It disappointed him how the judicial system forces someone so promising and gifted as Jericho Blackmon to seek a low like he was doing today, in order to find justice for his family they justly deserved. Amazing that out of all that concrete that had been the life of a former pimp, hustler, and prostitute was the ability to produce such a brilliant child, "What a crying shame!" Thomas Sr. thought. Al was trying his best to stay conscious, despite his body going in shock from the blast from Jericho's cannon, "W-w-wait…I—I-If you want the t-t-truth, you n—n-need to hear it a-a-all…"Al moaned. The light grey colored vest Al was wearing was now bright red and getting bigger by the second. Jericho erupted at Al's outburst, "You murdered my father mother fucker! That's the only truth! My father may have been just another black ass pimp to you, but to me… he was the reality check, my….reminder, of where I came from and where I wanted to go!" Jericho screamed. Thomas Sr. was looking for a way in and now, he thought he may have found one, "But, it's not too late for you, young Jericho! God has a plan for us all, and sometimes, for whatever reasons we go off script and try to ad lib the rest. You don't have to, just open that big heart of yours, the one "I SAW" take over those debates, and tell this man truly what it is you need of him, so you can move on with your life!" Thomas Sr. carefully instructed. The studio telephone rang again, but Senior immediately took it off the hook and laid the receiver face down on the cherry oak table, "It's just us in here, Jericho…use that amazing brain of yours and search your heart, young man…" He said. Reverend Thomas Sr.'s soothing words weighed heavily on the confused heart of the young man knick-named "Geronimo" Blackmon. Jericho pulled back on the barrel on his .357 magnum, and breathed out a large sigh. At the end of the day, despite how much anger Jericho may have felt towards Al McDowell, he still respected his wise and fearless icon, "Okay, Reverend. I will try it your way…" Jericho said. "Thank you, Jericho!" Thomas Sr. kindly replied. "…But soon as he starts lying…." Jericho threatened. Thomas Senior shook his head in compliance, "Yes, Jericho…We know." Thomas Sr. complied, while looking Al McDowell eye to eye. Jericho put the gun down inside his belt and closed his eyes for a moment to gather his thoughts, then re-opened them, but this time Senior could tell from Jericho's facial expressions that his questions were coming from his heart, "What really happened that night?" Jericho asked sternly. Al had been going in and out of consciousness so, that Thomas Senior had begun to fear he would not have enough strength left to get through Jericho's cross examination, "I-I-I- didn't kill him!" Al moaned. Jericho glanced over at Thomas Sr. in disgust, "It's okay, Jericho…. Just, give him a chance…" Thomas Senior pleaded. Jericho puffed out loud, "Okay, if you didn't kill him, then who did?" Jericho demanded. Al was trying his best to force himself awake, and his eyes blinked repeatedly, as if they were shaking out sand granules to do so, "I…I-I told them…I told them, the truth! But…did, I-I-I did not tell them…h-h-h-he was alive at f-first. I…d-d-d-didn't see...h-him…" Al stuttered. Jericho's blood began to boil and it was showing as Thomas Sr. could see the frustration over the young man's face, as he shook his head anxiously. Thomas Senior once again pleaded to Jericho's vast intellect, “Jericho…a hot tempered man stirs up dissension, but a patient man calms a quarrel….” Thomas Sr. preached. Reluctantly, Jericho fought off the temptation to blow off Al McDowell’s face clean from his shoulders, but instead, swallowed his pride, “Okay, so you saying, you killed my father…but unintentionally?!” Jericho asked. Al nodded yes. “Now we are finally getting somewhere!” Thomas Sr. thought. Jericho grabbed the chair he was sitting in earlier and sat down, “Okay…so were you drinking that night? The toxicology report said your level were high?!” Jericho asked. Al did not hesitate to answer, “Y-Y-Yes.” He responded breathlessly. Thomas Senior was seeing signs of relief starting to form around young Jericho’s light colored-green eyes, and praised God for working on the young man’s heart. Jericho was now fighting back his tears, “How could you be…how could you be so, so selfish, man? Don’t you know my mom…that my mom killed herself, because he’s dead?” Jericho shouted. That explained why he was so cross with him at first when he brought up the mother, Thomas Sr. thought. Both the preacher and the father in him made Thomas Sr. lean over and placed his hand over Jericho’s wounded shoulders. His tears were as allusive as a sail boat caught up in a hectic wind. Even Al McDowell started to weep for the young Jericho. Al McDowell knew that he would have to answer some hard questions one day, but did not expect them to come around so soon. He was not even aware that Robert Blackmon had a family, and now, his spirit is truly broken due to that regrettable revelation.

Now that he convinced Al McDowell, radio personality, slash journalist, slash author, slash American hero of his crime, one thing still remained yet unanswered, “Who shot him?” Jericho pondered. The Soul Knight who was all rocked up came back to the control room window and made his way to the studio sound booth, “Hey man, I ain’t feelin’ what I’m hearin’!” The large man said, “So, what cha’ gonna’ do? That nigga’ just admitted to offin’ yo’ daddy, so whachu’ waitin’ fo’? Be a man for your daddy nigga, and take care of yo’ busi….” The large man yelled, before being interrupted, “Yo Chip, man… I told you, let me handle this!” Jericho said, while wiping his tears away. Chip Harrison was a former team captain and All-American defensive end at Prairie View before he blew out both of his shoulders. He served as Jericho’s number two, but never fully embraced that position, “Man, you got the Soul Knights looking like cryin’ ass bitches all over the mutha’ fuckin’ radio! If you gonna’ settle this, then do this ole’ fool, if not…I'm gonna do it!" Chip shouted, as he cocked the barrel of his gun. Jericho was always two steps ahead of his protégé' and always found the right words to soothe the beast that was used to solving problems with his brawn, "And Chip, how do you believe we sound now that we are arguing with one another over the radio? I'll tell you, like disorganized children who merely seeking attention and not the glory of our former ancestors who died for us in the Civil War, or back in the days of slavery. Right now, you're the one that's making us look like whining bitches!" Jericho stated confidently. Jericho Blackmon was the only person Chip Harrison ever allowed to speak to him in that regard, but had the Prairie View scholar not petitioned his jail release from a false rape charge, things may have been a lot different, "Alright, but you got five minutes…" Chip pouted, and left the room. Thomas Sr. stood to his feet, "Look, Jericho…you got to get a handle on this, and your boys! If I know the federal government, they got this whole place surrounded with agents. You have to consider giving yourselves up, you're young and maybe with the right influence I…" Thomas Senior began, before getting cut short. "I can handle this….and my people. Plus, and no disrespect, don't give a damn sir about the agents. What I do care for though, is to know that since this fool admitted to hitting my dad while drunk at the wheel, how'd he end up shot on top of all that?" Jericho argued. Thomas Senior looked at the face of the fading fast Al McDowell, "Well, Al?" Thomas Senior asked intrigued. Al's eyes were fixated on Senior's eyes, and his breathing appeared to be worsening, "We got to get him to a hospital…" Thomas Senior said. Al McDowell raised his hand in protest, "N-No…n-n-n-not yet…not till, he kn-kn-knows…e-everything." He muttered. Al looked up at Jericho and asked him to sit down. Jericho froze, then looked over at the regal Thomas Senior and he gave him a reassuring nod and he took a seat, "Alright…but be warned." Jericho warned. His breathing was slow and thick, and Thomas Sr. thought they would be lucky just to get him to live let alone speak, "Take your time, Al." Thomas Senior instructed. Al McDowell cleared his dried up throat and asked Jericho to give him a cigarette. Jericho looked back at Thomas Sr. in disbelief, "Yo, is this nigga' serious?" Jericho asked excitedly. Thomas Sr. reached for the cigarette box and passed one to Jericho. He stared at the cigarette before finally putting it in Al's mouth, "Un-be-fuckin'-lievable!" Jericho said underneath his breath. Al reached into his pocket in what looked like more trouble than it should have been, and stared down at the lighter and began to relive that night all over again…

Night of the accident…

Robert Blackmon was trapped beneath Al McDowell's car for over fifteen minutes and yet he refused to allow Al to leave and go get help. The good thing for Al was that Robert was still able to understand him in his mangled state. He decided to wait until Robert passed out to run up the road against his wishes, but the strong willed man never quivered. When Al last communicated with the delirious Robert Blackmon Sr. he was pointing at him with his index finger and thumb in the up position. He assumed at first that he was pointing at the fact that he had a five ton 63' Coupe parked over his head, "But why would the man state something so obvious?" Al wondered. Maybe he's just losing his mind, not that I don't blame him, poor guy, I wished he'd just let me…"Al trailed off into deep thought. The wooded area had been eerily quiet, especially after turning off his car. Having very little light made Al nervous, so he a lit another cigarette to help pass the time …or, at least time to run and get help, soon as the trapped man fell asleep. He could not believe his luck that no other cars had passed him by to ask for help. While Al was busy being distracted by his own thoughts, suddenly the trapped man moaned painfully loud, catching him off guard and causing him to spit out his cigarette, "Holy Shit!!! Warn a guy before you do that again! Christ!!" Al yelled. It sounded as if the trapped man was trying to get Al's attention. Al got back down on the ground and crawled as close as he could. The flame coming off Al's lighter illuminated brightly underneath the massive automobile like a torch blazing confidently underneath the vastness of a dim cave. When he shined the lighter toward the trapped man, he noticed that his hand was making the same jester that he previously made earlier. He had his hand pointing up to the bottom of the car and appeared to mumble. Al thought they could really benefit if the injured man could at least speak, but he did not have that luxury, "I don't understand you! Why don't you just…Christ!" Al yelled. Feeling overcome with frustration, Al crawled from underneath the car and just sat with his back against it, "God damn it. Why me, huh God? Why me? Shit…" Al said angrily. The trapped man began to groan even louder once again. The injured man's grisly sounds forced the tired Al McDowell to put his hands over his ears to keep from losing his mind. The man went on with his muffled sounding screams for a minute before he worn himself out. When the man stopped, Al dropped his hands and winced as he rubbed his back. Thanks to getting shot by a Vietnamese prostitute, Al's back was not what it used to be and the hard pavement and his gun handle was not helping matters. He took the gun from out of his belt and laid it down on the ground. The trapped man shrieked and Al grabbed his gun as a reaction. His heart was beating so hard and fast, that he thought it might push out his chest cavity. Realizing that his friend underneath his car was the culprit, Al pulled his lighter out to give him a piece of his mind. He crawled toward the man, "Look, I can clearly see that you are in a lot of pain, but I'd really appreciate it if you wouldn't DO that! Especially, when you won't even let me help you!" Al said. Holding his gun and the lighter at the same time was getting uncomfortable, so he put the gun down in front of him. Though the injured man was down to one working eye, it had been totally fixated on the deep steel blue .357. Al took notice and picked it back up, "Oh man, I'm sorry if I scarred you, but you don't have to worry, this is only for prote…"Al started, until he saw him make the hand jester once more. Whatever strength the trapped man had saved went into reaching out for the gun, "Hey man, what are you doing?" Al asked surprised. With Al McDowell's hand still firmly attached to it, the man pulled the gun slowly toward his head, "K-K-Ki…." He muttered. It had finally made sense to him, after all the hand signals, the screaming, and the long staring at his gun. The man clearly wanted to be put out of his misery, Al thought. Without even a moment's hesitation Al shook his head "no." The man stated his displeasure to Al's response with a menacing growl. There was no way in hell that he would shoot the same man that he put into this situation, Al thought. He growled at Al once more making him flinch. Al was in disbelief at the man's ridiculous request, "Forget it, no. I won't do it. It was my fault, I hit you! Let me get some help. It's only a little ways to the gas station!" Al begged, but the trapped man continued to disagree, "N-N-N-oh." He moaned. Driving over a defenseless human being in the middle of the night was one thing, but turning around and shooting them after doing so is another, Al concluded. Al McDowell was afraid and wasted no time sharing his displeasure with him, “What the hell are you even doing out here in the fucking first place man, I mean….who does that? It’s after four in the God damn morning!” Al screamed. His emotions were getting the best of him and he was trying not cry in the presence of another man, “I-I-I can’t, no…man…I just c-can’t. In his mind, he knew what he was asking of the stranger was hard, but he lived a whole life of pain and was ready to die. Al could see a tear falling from the corner of the man’s shredded face. Just before Al could convince the injured man not to cry, he grabbed the handle of the gun from Al and pulled down on the trigger. The gunshot was so loud that it popped Al’s right eardrum and the bullet left the poor dead man’s head a complete mess. Smoke was still emitting from his head and Al could smell his charred flesh. Al slowly crawled from under the car and stood to his feet. The morning sky was on its way very quickly and Al McDowell had a new problem to fix before daylight fully came…

At the radio station….

Al McDowell’s public confession of the accounts of the night Robert Blackmon Sr. died sounded like the truth to Thomas Sr. and felt bad for young Jericho. It was obviously not the story that he really wanted to hear, and he could see the young man’s eyes sprinkling tears. Al was not doing very well himself and just before he tried to pass out, Jericho still had other questions that needed answering, “Hold on, Al! I need you…I want you to tell me, why? Why didn’t you just do something from the very beginning?” Jericho demanded. The weary radio personality was holding on by a thread in his chair, “Because…nobody wanted… the…the truth! I tried telling… t-t-the po—hol-ice, but they…they just swept it…hu-under, the rug. I t-t-tried giving them…the gun, they w-w-wouldn’t take it. T-They j-hust said…nobody...w-would c-c-care about another, d-dead…n-nigger. I-I…jus…hid the g-g-gun. It w-w-will have, y-y-your f-father’s prints….s-still o-on it. T-That w-w-will p—prove…I-I-I, didn’t pull t-t-the t-trigger.” Al confessed. Thomas Sr. was shaking his head in disgust at the shame of it all, and had to close his own eyes to pray. Al leaned in closer to Jericho, "I-I-I'm v-v-very sorry, please…p-p-please for…g-give, me…b-b-but, I t-tried…t-tried to help him, but h-h-he didn't want, t-t-to live." Al said apologetically. The anger that had previously spread across the face of the militant minded Jericho was now completely gone. Instead, it was replaced with one filled with guilt, "No, it wasn't just your fault. He would have never been out there in the first place had he not…we argued earlier that night…." Jericho admitted. He could not seem to finish his sentence and Thomas Sr. opened his eyes and placed his hand over the young man's shoulder, "Go ahead, Jericho…" Thomas Sr. insisted. Jericho exhaled and began to open up, "My father wasn't the richest man in the world, and grew up in the gutter, but he was the only dad I ever had, and I loved him regardless! He would have done anything for me if he could…" Jericho cried, but Thomas Sr. encouraged him to go on, "Go on…" Senior encouraged. He exhaled again once more, and continued to bare his soul, "He overheard a personal phone conversation I had with a guy that he knew from back in the day. The brother claimed that white people were giving him a hard time because he was such a successful "black' businessman, and needed the Soul Knight's help. Well, what I didn't know at the time was that his "business was heroin," but all he….he just wanted an army at his disposal. My dad followed me to the brother's hide-out and tried to warn me about how shady that nig…that brother was, but I cursed him. I cursed my father for standing in my way when I was trying to help a brother who I thought was down!" Jericho painfully admitted. Al McDowell put his hand on Jericho's hand, "N-N-Not…y-y-your…f-fault. You…d-d-didn't know. I…got…something…f-f-for you…" Al said, and reached into his pocket for his wallet. Thomas Sr. watched on as Al dug through his unusually thick leather wallet and had passed something to Jericho, "T-T-This, f-f-fell out o-o-of his h-h-hand..." Al said. Whatever the object was, Thomas Sr. could tell from Jericho's weeping reaction that it was of great importance to him, "My dad…he still…he still kept this?" Jericho said to himself aloud. Thomas Sr. could not make out what Jericho had and leaned in for a closer look, "Well, what is it?" asked Thomas Sr. Jericho wiped his teary eyes and held up a tiny old tin horn. The small trumpet was very tarnished, possibly due to its age Thomas Sr. had thought, but he tried to understand its significance to the young man, "Was this yours?" Thomas Sr. asked. Jericho had his eyes glued on the small horn that was barely the size of his finger nail, "Not exactly." He said, and put down his gun. With Jericho's guard down, an open opportunity for Thomas Sr. to get the large .357 presented itself, but instead chose to hear the young distraught Jericho out, "N-N-No…-e-e-exactly? W-W-Well…y-you're going t-t-to have to b-b-be more helpful t-than…that, y-y-young man! I-I took a bullet f-f-for it" Al McDowell chuckled. Al's joke made the brash young man smile, "When I was little, my dad told me how he was in a band once. He was just trying to get his life straight and when he lost his job, he had to sell the horn to be able to buy me diapers…that was his nice way of saying, my mom sold it to buy drugs! I could tell he really missed playing that thing and I despised her for being the addict she always was. Well, one day he brought home a box of Cracker jacks for me and you know what my prize was?" Jericho asked, "T-The toy horn."Al said. Thomas Sr. smiled and could feel the spirit in the room change for the better, "And what did you do then?" Thomas Sr. asked pleased. He could see Jericho's heart trying to open up as he struggled with his emotions, "I t-told him…" Jericho began. Al put his hand over Jericho's, "T-Take your t-time…" Al replied. Thomas Sr. could tell Jericho was now looking at Al McDowell with a different set of eyes and admired him for it, as Jericho was finally letting go of his anger, "I told him…"Here daddy…Since I don't wear diapers anymore, you can have my new horn, and you can take it everywhere and play it anytime!" Jericho said, "That must have been at least ten years ago…I thought…I thought he had lost it!" He cried. Though Al fought to stay awake, his body was losing way too much blood and began to slide from his chair until Jericho and Thomas Sr. caught him in time, "Hang on man, we got you." Jericho said. When Jericho started putting pressure on Al's gunshot wound he winced mightily, "C-C-hrist!!! So-horry, Rev, but t-t-they don't pay me e-enough to do t-t-this s-s-shit!' Al painfully admitted. Due to the prior circumstances, Thomas Sr. was more than lenient to over look his slight of the tongue and nodded in appreciation and understanding. He knew the good Jericho had in him and was more than relieved of what came next, "Its pass time we get you to the hospital…and Al?" Jericho said, holding his arm, "I forgive you." He said proudly. Al put his good hand over Jericho's shoulder, "T-T-Thank you, J-Jericho. T-T-That means…a lot! I...I, w-wish…I wish, I hada'….a son…l-l-like you!" Al cried. Thomas Sr. put his hand over his other shoulder, "Your father would have been proud of what you are doing, Jericho. Let's honor his memory by calling this thing off and going home?" Thomas Sr. suggested. Just as the influential reverend could finish his thoughts, Chip and two other members of the Soul Knights stormed in, "I don't believe this shit!?! Nigga, how you gonna' call this shit off?!? This cracker mother fucker killed yo' pops and lied to keep from going to jail for it, and you just gonna' let that shit slide?!" yelled the hulking Chip. Jericho had spent his entire young life living with a drug addict for a mother, and could tell from Chip's wild behavior that he was not all there in the mind, "It's like I told you bro, I got this operation under control…but since you are here, we need to abort." Jericho said. Chip was beside himself after hearing Jericho's words and started chuckling, "Is this a mother fuckin' joke? Cause I ain't laughin'!" Chip said angrily. He knew Chip had a screw loose and that made it easy to manipulate him in the past, it was only until lately that he grew a mind of his own, "No bro, it's not a joke. I was wrong, you dig? And now, we got to call this off!" Jericho ordered. Looking back at his cohorts, as if he sought affirmation to what he was hearing, Chip burst into laughter once more, "Nigga, you MUST be crazy!" Chip asserted. Little did they realize, that Jericho had begun sliding the .357 closer to himself after they surprised them, and revealed the gun, "It's like I said, I was wrong and missions over. I'm the only one here that actually shot somebody! I'm the one who put you guys up to this in the first place! The worst you guys might get is two years probation!" Jericho pleaded. Chip cocked the rifle that he was carrying, "Bullshit, nigga! That ain't why I came! I came to show these white folks we through playing with they honkey asses! And you sittin' up here, "GERONIMO," suckin' this dude off…" Chip was screaming, before Jericho interrupted. "Yo Chip that's enough! This man here is Reverend Templeton Sr., he works with Dr. King! You can at least show this man some respect!?!" Jericho demanded, while squeezing the broad .357 tightly. Chip sized up Thomas Sr. from head to toe, "Man, I don't give a damn if this nigga was Sam Cooke! What the fuck he gon' do fo' us? Take up a fuckin' collection to get a nigga' outta' jail?" Chip screamed. Having heard enough Jericho cocked his barrel on his pistol, "Go home Chip." Jericho commanded, while pointing his gun at the large former All-American. Chip raised his rifle toward Jericho, "Naw man, I don't think so. But, it is time fo' you to go home…in a pine box, mutha fucka'!" Chip said, as he and the other two Soul Knights raised their guns to fire on Jericho. They were all at a Mexican standoff, "I knew you was just all talk, you lil punk bitch! I'm gonna' blow those big pretty lips off yo' face!" Chip threatened. Suddenly, there were loud noises and then a gunshot coming from the back of the studio. Thomas Sr. could hear a man yelling Federal Bureau of Investigations in the distance and tried to convince Chip to give up, "It's the F.B.I. son, and from the sounds of it, you're short one Soul Knight! Just do what Jericho says and give yourselves up! I may even be able to…" Thomas Sr. said, before getting interrupted, "F.B.I. don't nobody move!" a voice yelled. Chip pointed the rifle at Al McDowell, "Fuck this! I'm still killing this cracker!" Chip shouted, and fired on him. Jericho was already predicting Chip's move and jumped in front of the rifle's target. The agents filled the control room and shot though the glass, killing Chip instantly, "Put your weapons down gentlemen and you won't have to leave here like your friend over there!" Agent Beauregard yelled. The two young men wisely chose to put the rifles down and raised their hands to surrender. Thomas Sr. froze as he saw both Al and Jericho laying face down on the floor, covered with blood. He ran over to Jericho and turned the young man over, only to discover the worst, "My God…" Thomas Sr. said sadly. Jericho had been hit in the chest by the bullet and had only seconds to live. Special Agent Jerrod and Agent Whitley walked into the sound booth, "We need a medic in here!" screamed Agent Whitley, and rushed over to the floor to check on Al. Al McDowell had not been hit by Chip's rifle, but was in shock from the gunshot wound from Jericho's pistol, "Reverend Templeton…Special Agent Jerrod, you okay sir?" Agent Jerrod asked. Thomas Sr. did not bother looking up at the large man, "It's too late for him, isn't it…?" Thomas Sr. asked. Agent Jerrod took his glasses off and wiped the sweat from his eyes, "Yeah, I'm afraid so, sir. You…you may want to say a prayer for him." Agent Jerrod suggested, and put his glasses back on his perspiring face. Thomas Sr. looked at Agent Jerrod from the corner of his eyes, and paused to consider his suggestion until Jericho grabbed his hand, "D-D-Did...I-I, save h-h-him? He asked. The hopeful reverend held the young man's head up, "Yes, Jericho. You did good, son!" Thomas Sr. said. A stunned Agent Jerrod ordered Agent Whitley to check Jericho's vitals. After Agent Whitley checked him out, he only confirmed what they already assumed, and nodded to his superior the news. Agent Jerrod still ordered paramedics to bring a stretcher as a courtesy for the grieving reverend, despite Jericho's waning condition, "Okay let's get this young man moved!" yelled Agent Jerrod. Jericho squeezed Thomas Sr.' hand in protest, "N-No, let…m-me go…wanna' be, w-w-with…m-m-my mom…a-and d-d-dad, p-p-please…" Jericho begged. As a man of God, Thomas Sr. felt that it was his Christian duty to save as many lives as humanly possible, even when those who did not value them cared to be saved or, not. But, this was not just some lost soul seeking a church home. This was someone's dying child asking not to be helped and "also," be allowed to die. When the paramedics appeared with the stretcher, Agent Jerrod held his hand up to stop them. Thomas Sr. looked over to them and looked up at Agent Jerrod, "I…I, don't know what to say." Thomas Senior cried. Agent Jerrod leaned down toward him, "If he does live, he may spend the next thirty to forty years in a maximum facility…if he's lucky." Agent Jerrod confirmed. Jericho continued to plead for his death, "P-P-Please, p-p-please Reverend, l-l-let me g-g-go to my p-parents." Jericho cried. Jericho had endured much psychological pain already in his young life, and now after performing such a brave act, should he survive, faced life in prison, caused conflictions in Thomas Sr.' heart. He hated seeing blacks killing other blacks, especially when they went young. Jericho had the potential to become anybody he wanted to be, Thomas Sr. thought, and the last thing he did not want everyone to remember him for, was the character that came with the nickname he gave him long ago. Thomas Sr. did what he normally would do in times like these, which is to close his eyes and pray. As he prayed, Thomas Sr. could feel the life slip from the young man, but he continued to his prayer, until young Jericho breathed no more. When he completed his prayer Thomas Sr. opened his hand and could see that Jericho slipped the toy trumpet into his palm. Agent Jerrod put his hat back on his head and stared at his hand, "What's that?" He asked. Thomas Sr. laid Jericho's head down on the floor gently and stood to his feet, "Some people might refer to it as just a Cracker Jack prize, but I have another name for it…" He said. Agent Jerrod examined the tiny tarnished horn, "Oh yeah, what's that, sir?" Agent Jerrod asked. Thomas Sr. closed his fist, "Hope!" Thomas Sr. said. Agent Jerrod cleared his throat, "Well, sir I have specific orders by not only my superiors, but your wife as well, to escort you back to your hotel room safely. Thomas Sr. rubbed his head, "Jesus, Grace?! And speaking of "hope," I would have hoped she wouldn't have been listening to all this madness, but knowing her I should probably be holding my breath, right?!"

Thomas Sr. quipped. Looking up from his glasses Agent Jerrod complied smiling, "You can do it in the car, on the way if you want, sir!?!" Agent Jerrod joked.

Interlude:

The thoughts of past events involving his late father Thomas Sr., was a draining process for Thomas Jr., as he could barely find the strength to pack the old green suitcase he found that once belonged to his late wife Lucinda. Thomas Jr. felt a little nervous knowing that within the next twenty-four hours he would be reunited with his long lost younger brother and wondered what the years had done to him physically. On top of all that, what would he think of Terry's husband, partner, or wife, or whatever he refers to him after he meets him? Most of all, what would they think of him? Thomas Jr. worried. Thomas Jr. had let himself go and despite being a preacher, he developed an affinity for swearing, over-indulging in alcohol, and a marijuana habit, the very things his father impressed upon them to never do. Each day his health was deteriorating and his gunshot wounds had not made his life any easier. He was shot over half a dozen times, though most of the bullets went in and out of his body, one of them traveled to his spine and left him with a mild limp. Although leaving his son Markus did not sit well with him, Thomas Jr. still had one friend left in Irwin, a soft spoken nurse named Linda Mae Joseph, who could keep eyes on him. She was someone he believed he could trust should Markus' condition ever changed while he was gone. Linda Mae Joseph (or Mae-Mae) grew up a member of his father's church and had a quiet crush on him, long before Lucinda came into the picture. Thomas Jr. was much older than she was during that time, and had already entered college before she made it to high school. Linda Mae eventually married though, had a child, and moved to Tulsa, Oklahoma. When things soured in her marriage Linda Mae and her son moved back to Georgia. Despite everything that had previously transpired in his life, her feelings for Thomas Jr. remained undeterred. Of course, she would never disclose those feelings out of respect for his son. They would have a cup of coffee together on her break from time to time, but nothing serious. She was surprised by his call and pleased to hear the news about Terry, and also could hear her disappointment that he would not be back for a little while. To put a smile on her face, Thomas Jr. had promised her lunch as soon as he got back, but Linda made him promise to let "her" cook dinner instead. With her smooth caramel skin, tight thickly shaped body, and eyes that only a cat would envy, he thought she could have given Lucinda a run for her money, had he not been already married. Thomas Jr. just was a million miles from thinking about dating anyone and feared that if the opportunity ever arose, would he be able to react to her sexually after him being assaulted, Thomas Jr. wondered. It took Thomas Jr. a very long time just to make eye contact with Linda in the beginning of their friendship. Make no mistake, his preference for being with a woman had not changed, but he found himself struggling internally between replacing the "only woman he ever loved" for twenty-five years and losing his manhood to a homosexually crazed psychopath. No matter how hard he scrubbed himself in the shower, no matter how much he drank or smoked, no matter how hard he prayed; Thomas Jr. could never clean the filth or, free his mind of the hate he repressed for Sonny Korne and his Aryan goons.

Thomas Jr. was walking his luggage to the living room when he heard a faint noise coming from inside his bedroom. The sound was that of a loud hiss, like what steam made when pressurized inside sewer pipes. He immediately dropped the suitcase and clenched his fists. Thomas Jr. slowly eased his way back towards the room, and had hoped he met his quota of supernatural experiences for the day. With every step the hiss grew stronger and louder. All of a sudden the lights went out in the entire apartment. The quietness that occupied the dewy apartment began to smother him, as he anticipated the worst to be seen once he would reach the bedroom. As he approached the foot of the bedroom door, steam filled the air, as if someone had left the shower on too long. Among the blinding smoke, the bathroom lights flickered off and on at random, like a runway at an airport. After Thomas Jr. turned the corner to look inside the bathroom he could hardly see inside it. The light bulbs shuffled one after the other at a hypnotizing speed. As he watched on he saw the shape of two glowing eyes from the mirror. He gasped at the sight of them and tried to take a step backward, but just as he done so, a hand reached out from inside the smoke, "Peace be still, boy!!!" Senior's voice said, and let off a horrific laugh that was not his own. Thomas Jr. screamed for him to let go, but the spirit refused and he could see something being drawn on the mirror. The hand let go of Thomas Jr. just before the smoke cleared inside the bathroom. It smelled to him like someone had burned cider wood or, old rosemary. He looked at what was written over his bathroom mirror and felt his heart drop into his stomach. Something had written a sentence in blood over his bathroom mirror that read, "Have a safe trip to hell, Tommie boy!" Thomas Jr. could hear a laugh echoing behind him and quickly turned around. When he did not see anything, or anyone, he turned his attention back to the mirror and the blood was all gone. He was hoping that he was only suffering from a nervous breakdown and tried to laugh it off. But no matter how hard he tried to discount what his eyes had seen, Thomas Jr. on the other hand could not ignore pain in his arm. The problem was that the wrist that was pulled on, by his father's ghost, was somehow still hurting him. He raised his hands to clear his eyes but, the pain in his wrist was becoming so unbearable that he rolled up his sleeve and to his horror there were large bruises on it. "Why is this happening to me?" Thomas Jr. screamed, "Haven't I suffered enough?!?" Thomas Jr. yelled hysterically. He sat back down on the edge of his bed and put his head into his hands and bawled like child. His frustrations were finally taking their toll on the helpless reverend, "God damn it!" Thomas Jr. cried.

So much had seemingly been taken away from the restless Thomas Templeton Jr. in just over half his lifetime going all the way back to the death of his sweet beloved little sister Candice. He remembered her as someone who was once full of warmth, beauty, and intelligence. Thomas Jr. so badly wanted to be an uncle to her future children but, nevertheless never got the opportunity. After Terry ran away, it was Candice who helped filled the void of his absence all those years until her death. His accomplished father, before becoming the "poltergeist" who now haunted him, was everything he thought he wanted to be as a man. He harked back to his days as a child, when the other kids at school envied him for being his father's son. There was never a need for Thomas Jr. to brag when his dad was always on television helping blacks get established as a permanent social class. When he was not doing his thing on television, his dad managed to save a few souls on Sundays just for kicks. That was just how special his father was to the world, but now, he was gone and probably dead from a broken heart. His extraordinary mother Grace Templeton, who helped keep his father grounded and his children in line, he recollected for her grace and elegance. Whenever she entered a room both men and women would flock to her side to get her opinions on life and would fish for her secrets to her amazing beauty. She was never arrogant or, conceded and always seemingly came off telling people the truth, even when it would hurt. The night of the attack, she was the first to die, right in front of him. Shot down like she was nothing, like she meant nothing. It was as if Sonny Korne thought he was doing HIM a favor for taking out his mother. At that instant Thomas Jr. stopped sobbing. He slowly wiped at the tears in his face. His thought about Marcus getting so badly beaten and how broken he still was. The marvelous take no nonsense wife Lucinda and his fragile virgin daughter Mia, stripped and raped like they were trash, like HE was trash! The overpowering self pity he was feeling was starting to dissipate and replaced it with something brand new. Thomas Jr. stood to his feet. His breathing, no longer erratic and his body stopped trembling in fear. There was an odd calm over him, one that he never experienced before. It was not a feeling of confidence or, compliance exactly, but a small sense of reassurance. A fulfillment towards a possible reckoning was fueling the onetime pacifist. While his teeth gritted rabidly over each other like a mini-trash compactor, one thing was definitely for certain in his mind. So much so, that his teeth unclenched long enough for him to say it out loud, "Man, I seriously need to get the HELL out of here!" Thomas Jr. nervously, and called his brother back.

<u>End of Interlude:</u>

Chapter 5:

"The Curious Case of Jovan Campbell"

Houston, Texas…present day,

Kim Lee had only been a part time club owner for a short while, but knew enough about the club industry to know a good thing when he saw it. On one particular day, he took a different route to his local bank to make a quick deposit, when he drove upon a once popular, but long vacated bookstore. The large bookstore was close by the Houston mid-town district, near the place he co-owned, and instantaneously saw potential in the old two story building. He envisioned the old abandoned bookstore to be converted into his own private mega club. Kim Lee was not known for waiting patiently for many things, but when it came to his "next big thing," he waited the year and half to get it remodeled to his liking. His family was of Korean descent and owned a couple grocery stores and a dry cleaning business on the southwest side, so Kim had firsthand knowledge about what hard work in America got you. Because Kim went to a charter school, he never had to deal with much racism, at least until he was old enough to go clubbing with his other Asian friends. The mid-town Houston club scene tended to profile certain racial groups and often gave anyone of Oriental descent the impression that they were too much trouble to invite them in. It was not that long ago when Kim found out the hard way. One night, he and some friends were invited to a party at the then popular Hazard's Lounge. The door guy was being an asshole and refused to allow them inside, so Kim thought if he could cause a scene at the door, then other people in the line would think twice about going inside. What Kim had not realized was that the doorman was not the regular doorman, but in actuality the owner of the club. The brooding security guy that stood behind the owner was ordered to body slam Kim in front of everyone. Ten stitches, a busted lip, and a few years later, he was able to scrape up enough money to buy a small share of a local pub in mid-town called "The River Pub." The River Pub had the occupancy of barely a couple hundred people, but had a decent clientele of customers. During the weekdays, business was up and down like a child with ADD off their Adderall medicine, but on the weekends they would be totally slammed. Things were changing for the worse as the partners began to party more than they did keeping their books. Money was coming up short and unnecessary firings had to be constantly made to help cover their debt. Kim had been fed up with their sloppy antics and decided to partner up with his cousin, Len, who worked as an accountant for one of his family's grocery stores. Kim loved his cousin and marveled at how well he could transform himself from mild mannered accountant by day, to the new Hawaii Five –O's Daniel Dae Kim at night. After Kim appropriated the old bookstore and had it renovated, he named it "Hi-Prime," after his favorite Transformer character Optimus Prime. The "Hi" in the name was a supposed to be a "hello" and "fuck you" to the doubters that did not believe he could ever buy his own place. The soft opening that Kim gave for Hi-Prime turned out to be a great success, despite Kim's reputation as both a hard ass and a not very likable person in the club industry. Kim did not care much about being liked as much as he loved being respected, and would often call it "staying hungry." He lived by his own credo, "Friends come and go in the club business, but the only thing that stays is the money." Kim fashioned himself to sound profound, though some people just thought he over indulged on too many fortune cookies as a child. Either way, he put in a lot of his time, sweat, and hard earned money into making sure he had a first class grand opening, and did not plan on taking any chances of ruining his big night...until fate chose to step in and decided otherwise.

Kim's Fright Night

Kim Lee spared no expense in the remodeling of the old Diamond Bookstore he bought. Thousands of his hard earned dollars were spent in gutting the place alone, and collected on a favor from an old colleague to furnish and design it. The first floor of the club was at street level, while the uniquely built second floor served as its main dance floor. A place that was once known for its vast catalog of books and magazines was now imbued with posh furniture, giant LCD screens, strobe lights, and many other imaginable assortments that could possibly fill a two story club. Once all the ink dried on the permits and liquor licenses for his new "castle," which capacity held fifteen hundred people, the only thing remained was putting together the perfect staff. Kim sought out some of the industry's most notable DJ's, promoters, bartenders, waitresses, cleaning staff, as well as some of the industry's most heartless doormen. They were brought aboard with promises of larger payouts that far exceeded their previous employers. To get the right talent, he went behind the backs of other owners and made a few enemies in the course of doing so. With that being said, a club is only as strong as its security team and so he hired some of the best bouncers that Houston had to offer. Mike Mann was his first and only choice when it came to finding someone he could trust to put the right guys in place and keep his establishment properly protected. His ex-partners from The River Pub did not appreciate being raided for their number one enforcer. Mike, or "Big Mike," had worked as a bouncer for half a decade and spent the other half hiring and leading security teams. He stood six foot six, two-hundred and sixty pounds, and was a former NFL tight end who loved kickboxing. The transition from professional football player to bodyguard was an easy one, since he spent five years getting paid thousands of dollars hitting players from other teams. Mike quickly built a name for himself as a force to be reckoned with, and soon was sought after by all the top clubs. "Big Mike" also had a "big heart" to go along with his eleven and a half inch hands, and loved nothing more than to help a brother when he was down. Tonight was the big grand opening for Hi-Prime, and Kim and his staff wrapped up one last minute meeting prior to opening its doors to the public. He took great care in inviting everyone who ever rubbed his nose at their establishments, and made sure that his doormen understood to make each of them wait at least thirty minutes in line. The promoting team Len hired "Limelight Productions," put in mad hours in getting important guests booked, including famous rapper Snoop Doggy Dogg, who was in concert across town was even invited to come by. Cash registers were going off in Kim's head after his GM made it aware that every V.I.P. table had been pre-bought and showing him the guest list of at least seventeen hundred people. Kim walked to his brand spanking new office with a clear conscious that everything was going to go his way that night. He plopped down into his new cushy brown one hundred percent leather chair, kicked his legs up, and breathed out a large sign of relief.

Fifteen minutes to opening time, and Kim and his cousin/partner Len were going over bar spreadsheets when the general manager knocked on the office door, "Come it!" Kim yelled. When the general manager did not initially speak, Kim immediately became worried, "What the fuck is it Clifford?" Kim nervously screamed. The well-rounded general manager named Clifford Wallace was not known for panicking under pressure, as he had over eleven years experience in managing nightclubs under his belt. He had seen clubs come and go in Houston and was hired on for his honesty and cool reserve, which unnerved Kim and Len when he stormed into the office like he had just seen a ghost, "I, uh…we, might have a problem…" Clifford said agitated. Kim and Len stared at each other in confusion, "…It's about the front door!" Clifford stated gingerly. Len put the spreadsheets down, "Fuck man, don't tell me the fucking fire marshals here!? We don't need this fucking shit tonight Kim!" Len hollered. Clifford shook his head in protest, "N-No…it's not the fire marshal…" Clifford said eerily. Kim quickly grew impatient, "Then what the FUCK is it then? I got a Goddamn club to run!" Kim said impatiently. Not wanting to further aggravate his bosses, Clifford blurted out the problem with one name, "Jovan." Clifford mumbled. They did not catch the name at first and began wondering why their general manager, who normally spoke with more bass in his voice, decided to be soft spoken tonight, "Ja-what?" Kim asked again. Clifford began biting the corners of his mouth and his fingers were gyrating, as if he was maxing out on the last set of weighted dead-lift exercises, "Jovan, dude! I can't believe you guys picked "tonight" to put "him" at the front door? Are you guy's nuts?" Clifford asked frantically. Kim squinted his eyes in confusion as he came from behind his desk, "Yo dude…what the fuck is a "Jo-van"?" Kim asked bewildered. Len snapped his fingers as if he just came up with a bright idea, "You're not talking about "that" guy, are you? That crazy one…?" Len asked excitedly. A thick frown came over Kim's face as if he smelled putrid flatulence in the room, "Come on man! Why you guys making me feel like the only asshole in the room? Who the "fuck" are you guys talking about?" Kim demanded. Len walked up to his beloved cousin and slapped him on the arm, "Yo! Cliff's talking about that "black guy" dude, remember!?! That crazy "strong" motherfucker that beat up all those guys last year, over at Mason's place!" Len said excitedly. Kim scratched his long thinning hair, "You mean the strip club?" Kim asked vaguely, "Yeah man! Remember when we took you there last year for your birthday?" Len asked. Kim had the look of a lost child in a grocery store, "Nah dude, I got too fucked up to remember that far!" Kim said disappointedly. Len smacked his lips in frustration, "Man, if you don't remember the fight, then you gotta' remember people talking about it!?!" Len asked. Kim went back to his chair and sat down, "Yeah, sure…well, sorta.' Look dude, what the hell does a fight from last year have to do with the front door? We're minutes from opening up man! I don't need this conspiracy shit!" Kim yelled. Clifford was pacing the floor like a hungry lion in a cage, "Yo Cliff, chill man, before you start a fire on the goddamned carpet!" Len said sarcastically. Clifford stopped pacing for a moment, "Look this guy's crazy! I worked with him before! Ever since his little girl died, he…look, the guy hates my guts, okay!" Clifford concluded. The slouching Kim Lee sat in attention, "Wait a minute…did you say dead girl?" Kim asked. Len leaned on Kim's desk, "Man…you really need to come from outta' that fucking rock you been under more often! His name's Jovan Campbell, he used to play college football, and was really good too, but he quit after some fools ran over his daughter, or sister." Len confirmed. Kim rolled his eyes at his favorite cousin, "I never heard of him, and forgive me for not having a fucking life! Somebody had to work to pay off this bitch….and get off my fucking desk would you please!?" Kim yelled. Len stopped leaning on Kim's desk and rolled his eyes, "What the fuck ever. Hey man, why not just get Big Mike to place him somewhere else, some where outta' sight…at least for tonight." Len asked. Clifford started pacing again, "Nah dude, it's not gonna' matter! You never had to work with him, the guy can't be trusted! He's the reason why both Long Fellows Lounge and Club May Day closed down!" Clifford protested. Kim leaned back into his chair, "The fuck he do there? And what the hell does this have to do with a little dead girl?" asked Kim. Clifford looked at his watch and realized that it was time to open the club, "Hey man, I get paid to run your place and try to keep the staff honest…but not be this guy's parole officer! Look, I'll stay on, as long as you promise to keep him far away from me. I gotta' go open up…!" Clifford said, and fled out the office. Len tried to stop Clifford from storming from out of Kim's office, but was too late, "It's alright man, let him go." Kim said. Len was worried for one of the few true friends he made since being in the club industry. He was the one who suggested Clifford to his cousin Kim, and did not want to risk losing one of the city's best bar managers over any bullshit. Kim went back to studying his spreadsheets while Len stood quietly in amazement, "Well!?!" Len asked. Kim did not bother looking up from his paperwork, "Well what?" He responded nonchalantly. Len could not believe that his cousin, his blood, was being so single minded about an important issue, "Dude, Cliff's got a point. The last thing we need tonight is trouble at the front door!" Len pleaded, "I mean, I don't really know the guy, but dude! If you just would have seen what he did to those guys…dude got some major rage issues!!" Len said. Kim decided to put the papers down for the moment to reflect over his worried cousin's words of wisdom. It was plain to see that Len cared enough about their business venture together to not allow any outside conflicts to bring them down and felt like it was time to call Big Mike in for a quick powwow, "Okay, get Big Mike in here. I need to know if we have a walking time bomb on our hands." Kim said concerned.

With the evening just beginning, Big Mike already surmised the reason why he was being summoned over the radio by Len. He gave a brother a chance to make a little extra dough and now it was coming back to bite him hard in the ass, He thought. It was like the old proverb says, "No good deed goes unrewarded," Mike thought. Being head of a security team came with more perks than drawbacks and having the luxury to float, or roam the club was one of them. Mike had posted up by the main entrance to check on Jovan, who was a close friend of the family. Things were not the same for Jovan after losing his daughter Latavia. It was hard for him to keep jobs because he would often become over emotional and flip out on his co-workers, Mike recollected. Either way, he still considered Jovan as family, and when he saw him being in control of himself and the line outside, the better he felt about his decision. With no humidity and 62 degree winds, the evening weather had been ideal for anyone waiting in line, Mike thought. Though the club was officially open Vincent, the doorman, was not allowing any entry inside to customers yet. At the time, Mike was enjoying the view of all the beautiful women who were busy co-signing each other on how good they looked. The ambience outside could not be any more incredible as the sidewalk was lit up with sharply dressed twenty and thirty-some things. Mike shook his head at the mega sparkly marquee near the street. Personally, he believed it was far too extravagant for a nightclub and that it belonged on the Las Vegas strip instead. But it was not his decision to make and was happier doing the job he was being paid handsomely for. He never actually found it enjoyable hanging onto one place for too long and basically jumped at the first chance to leave The River Pub. The place had become a dive for trouble makers who usually could not make it through the doors at other clubs (because of their dress codes). With an owner who was being tight with his money, decided that it would be more affordable to keep extra bartenders than security guys, which often led to frequent brawls. Mike never cared for Kim Lee the person, but respected Kim Lee the businessman, and accepted the sweet pay increase to work for him at Hi-Prime. He also assured Kim that he would bring on an experienced group of bouncers to make sure that the night went smooth as possible, and almost delivered on his promise. Whenever he worked new clubs, Big Mike would always bring on his own people that he trusted to watch his back and later on, after he had built up a rapport with the owners, Mike would trickle in guys new to the business. That process always came in handy during the holidays when his guys needed days off, or when someone might have "torn their drawers" with him and needed replacing. Big Mike had been in the security game long enough to know that every now and then, guys run into problems and cannot make it for various reasons, and tonight was no different. His second in command, Lester Addison, worked as a high school teacher during the day and had messed around and tore up his ankle in a pickup game of basketball. But the seasoned Mike Mann was used to things like that happening and knew that sometimes, things do go wrong. What he did not count on, was his ease dropping wife Teresa over hearing a phone conversation of him having a hard time finding an immediate replacement for Lester. For whatever reason, everyone he called that day had been either busy working someplace else, or they could not do it because they had to get up early for their regular jobs. When Teresa made the suggestion for him to bring her younger sister's ex-boyfriend on, he was very skeptical at first. Jovan had not been in the security business very long and often managed to get into big trouble wherever he worked. Holding his own in a bar fight was never an issue for his herculean friend, but Mike always knew the secret to lasting at any nightclub, a guy had to show restraint most of the time. It was also not that hard to understand why it was so easy to set the dude off, he was there after all, when his little baby girl was run down by drug addicted bank robbers, Mike recollected. He still could remember it like it just happened yesterday, but often tried his best to keep that memory buried deep in the very back of his mind. Mike also had two daughters of his own, Tanya and Sasha, and could not imagine the thought of losing either one of them. It had been at least two years since that happened and the guy was still going through hell, Mike figured.

He knocked on Kim's office door and Len was the one to open it, "Hey Mike!" Len said. Len had a worried look on his face, as if someone accused him of cheating on a science quiz, "What's up Lenny?" Mike asked. Kim was sitting at his desk with a mixed cocktail drink in his hand. Going back to when Kim was still a partner at The River Pub, Mike could count the number of times he had seen his employer with a drink in his hand this early in the night, and knew it could not be a good sign, "Sup' K!?" Mike said. It was also on rare occasions would he be smiling, "What's up "indeed" Big Mike!? Come in and have a seat." Kim suggested. Mike had not been inside Kim's office since the night of the clubs soft opening night and could obviously see it had been refurnished. The room was very immaculate and Mike was impressed by the two new long leather black sofas and chairs, plus the lavish cherry wood book shelves and giant desk that helped fill his room. He compared it to a fancy lawyer's office rather than that of the average club owner. Among the many things on his desk was something that looked like a large black scrapbook. Kim put his drink down on a coaster beside it, "So, Mike…what's new?" Kim asked. The last time someone asked him "what's new" they were about to cut him from their pro football team, and so Mike played along, "Nothing to report yet, other than the extensive line of people at the main door waiting to get in…other than that, things are fine." Mike said tactfully. He caught Kim cutting his eyes at Len and immediately stopped smiling, "Really? Well, I'm not worried about it. The people aren't going anywhere. Anyway, I'm told you brought aboard a new guy for tonight, and working the door too!?!" Kim asked. Mike tried not to react negatively towards Kim's questioning and looked him straight in the eye when he answered, "Yeah, Jovan. He's a good dude." Mike said. Kim grinned and looked over at Len who sat quietly with his legs crossed, "A good dude? That's not what I'm hearing! I heard your man has some really badass testosterone issues, and I'm not looking to get any fucking lawsuits on the first night, Mike!" Kim said. Mike leaned forward in the soft leather chair, "With all due respect, Kim, you did bring me on to make sure shit would be tight around here. I thought that meant you trusting me enough to put a good crew together to do that. If you have a problem with Jovan being there, then just say so! And I'll put him somewhere else!" Mike said defensively. Kim jumped out from his chair like he had been pricked in the behind by thorns, "At the door? Dude, from what I already hear about this guy, I don't know if he should even be at this club!" Kim said excitedly. Len put his hand out to calm his temperamental cousin, "Hang on Kim. Now Mike, it's not that we don't trust you man, but I seen with my own eyes what that guy's capable of. I mean, he got two other clubs shut down for fuck sakes! Can't you just…call somebody else?!" Len asked. Mike quietly sat back down in his chair and stroked his chin. Under different circumstances, Big Mike would usually tell fickle club owners to go fuck themselves if they had issues about the guys he hired, but he respected Kim Lee enough to hear him out, "Okay, look man….I know you guys went through a lot of trouble to get this spot and that you don't want anybody already fucking up your clubs rep, but you don't know that kid's story, or who was really to blame at those other spots he worked. All I know is that that kid out "there," been through hell the last couple years, especially after seeing his little girl run over like road kill in the middle of the street. He needs this, man. He needs an opportunity to get back to working to get his life back together, but…this is "your" club. If you don't want him here, we'll be short handed, but I'll understand." Mike said. The room had gone quiet, as if everyone were waiting to see who would breathe the loudest first. Kim had sat back down into his desk chair and took a big drink from his glass. He put the glass back down on the cup coaster and waited to see if Len had anything to add before he spoke. Len was sitting still as a Greek statue with his hand covering his mouth in deep thought. Kim put his hands on top of the black scrapbook on his desk in front of him, "Do you know what this is Mike?" asked Kim. Mike took a quick glance at the old scrapbook and back at Kim and exhaled, "No." Mike said. His hands sat firmly across the scrapbook as if it contained some hidden treasure only he was aware of, "Well, then I'll tell you." Kim said. He opened the scrapbook and turned it around so Mike could get a better look, "It's a collage of club reviews. Go ahead and look!" Kim said. He could tell from Mike's reaction that he failed to see his point, "Let me explain. I've been in the club scene as both a customer and a part time owner and in my time, I have learned the invaluable truth of Asian discrimination. People claim that we can't hold our liquor, or that we shoot up clubs, so they don't allow too many of us in their place. I want to change that stigma! I want to have a place that's big enough for EVERYONE to party, no matter what your nationality is, and make a decent profit at the same time! If your guy causes any problems tonight, it won't matter if he's black or not, or right or wrong, people will still say, "Hi-Prime's just another bar with out of control Asians." Kim said, and closed the scrapbook, "And so, there it is…" Kim concluded. The last thing that Mike Mann expected to come from the mouth of Kim Lee was a legitimate concern for someone other than himself. He long assumed that the man for a penchant for rubbing people the wrong way actually had a heart after all, "So, what do you want me to do?" Mike asked. Kim leaned back in his chair and clasped his hands together as if he were going to pray to Buddha for advice. His eyes focused on the scrapbook for about a second, then shifted to Len, "What do you think Len?" Kim asked. Len had long been aware of Kim's concerns and shared the same vision, that's why he helped invested in Hi-Prime in the first place. The accountant in him though, could not add up enough reasons to take a chance on Jovan, and if something WAS to go wrong it would crush his cousin's dream night, Len thought. Len knew how important it was for Kim to have the most extravagant night possible and no matter how heartfelt Big Mike might had came across about Jovan's plight, they were going to have to take a gamble on a person that is emotionally unstable. But Len trusted Kim and would respect any decision he would make of the matter, "I don't know…It's whatever you want to do Kim." Len said. His response was not the one Kim was hoping for, but the look on Len's face told him where he really stood on the issue. Though he wanted everything to go smoothly tonight, Kim knew he did not need the safety of the club compromised, or putting his head of security in a bind. Kim picked up his glass and gulped down the rest of its contents and then slowly stood to his feet. He put both hands down on his desk and leaned toward Big Mike, "Can you promise me that you'll keep that crazy fucker in control?" Kim asked. Surprised, Mike looked at Len, who sat quietly with his hands buried in his lap, then back at Kim, "He won't be a problem."

Mike said, "Okay. I'll give him one chance, for tonight only! But take him off the door, and put him in the back by the restrooms…far away from Clifford!" Kim ordered. Len fought hard to contain the grin that was trying to surface on his smooth face and had to turn to look at the wall. Mike stood to his size sixteen feet and put his hand out to shake Kim's hand. Kim took a moment, as if he were trying to examine the hand for an electric buzzer, and shook Big Mike's enormous hand, "Thank you." Big Mike said, and glanced at Len who remained sitting, and walked out of the office. Len let out a big huff and stood to his feet, "I hope you know what you're doing…" Len said cautiously, as he walked toward the door, "…Because if you don't, then this club's dead!" Len said and walked out.

By midnight Hi-Prime was almost filled to capacity. The line at the main entrance was so outrageously immense that it appeared to go on for a mile, which was news that nearly brought Kim Lee to tears. For months Kim had waited for his moment to shine and could not believe the amount of love he received from his detractors that treated him once like an outsider. The music had been both loud and electric as Houston hype man DJ Max Viper played hit after hit, and never allowing the flow of the club to relax long enough to catch it's breath. While Kim was busy collecting all his accolades, Len on the other hand kept a fierce eye on Jovan Campbell. When Mike asked Jovan to switch off with Barry, who usually preferred working at the entrance, from the main door to the back of the club, he hardly even blinked. With Mike being on the move in his floater position, the more sweat he produced under his expensive sports coat he just got out of the cleaners. The thermostat on the wall read 69 degrees, when it felt more like 99 degrees to him. As the line of people continued to pour in by the dozens, Big Mike began constant radio contact with his team. Although it was not his first rodeo working a nightclub of this magnitude, Mike still felt a sense of relief that Len also called in off duty HPD officers to help them out. In his experience having cops around never hurt, especially when being around customers who like to pull out their guns to prove their point, Mike pondered. Mike frequently checked in with Jovan, despite the bathroom area lacking anything to really secure and did not take much patience to manage. Since he felt like shit after moving him, Mike encouraged Jovan to keep any tips he made that night, no matter how much he got paid. For a young man who once used to love to talk, now hardly spoke at all and whenever he did, Mike could still hear the agony of a hurt father. Mike missed those days back when his bereaved friend had an outgoing personality and was also one hell of an athlete. Just like that, Jovan threw away his chance to make a name for himself at the pro level and would have been a force at outside linebacker for somebody's team for a long time, Mike pondered. He also remembered how patient his sister in-law Tasha tried to be with him after Latavia died, and her abrupt decision to move on from him because he could not let her death go. But who could honestly blame him for that? Mike wondered. Latavia's body appeared as if it were minced inside a giant garbage disposal and would be the last image Jovan would ever have of his daughter alive, seeing that was more than enough to have any father committed to a mental hospital.

Later on that night at the club……

So far, with over two hours already in the books, the night was going fine in Big Mike's eyes. The guys working the front door were doing their best job not to allow the wrong element inside the club to put a damper on Kim's wet dream opening. Of course, Big Mike lived in reality and had done security long enough to know that there were plenty of opportunities and time for all the wrong shit to happen. For most of the night, Jovan had kept pretty much to himself, as one possibly could inside a crowded nightclub. Getting moved by the restrooms gave him the opportunity to clear his head of the expected burdens that came with doing his job. In the short while he worked nightclub security, Jovan quickly realized that getting posted by the front door was never in any club's best interest. He hated running into old football fans and former college teammates whenever he would get posted at a club's front entrance. There also was that one time, after a rival player from another team recognized him at a strip club he worked at across town, Jovan recollected. Jovan had only worked there for about a week before that infamous night, but it left a huge impression on the staff and customers alike after he left. Senior Tulane running back T.J. Mackenzie was in town hanging out with some of his old high school classmates and realized who he was. It was Jovan's tackle that broke

T.J.'s leg and ended the best season he ever had as a college player. T.J. still held a huge grudge against him and blamed Jovan for dropping in the NFL draft because of his broken leg. An argument ensued and T.J. and his entourage pushed their way inside the entrance. As a door man, his job was to check his customer's identification and control the front entrance, but because of T.J.'s rude indiscretion, Jovan was forced to do what usually came next. Because he was still fresh as a security guy, Jovan forgot to call for assistance on his radio. Jovan tried the diplomatic route by asking them to leave nicely, until one of T.J.'s homeboy's decided to take a swing at him. The young man missed and three minutes later, Jovan sent seven men to the hospital. Fearing jail time, Jovan left before the authorities showed and never returned back to the strip club for work. Before Latavia's death Jovan lived a peaceful existence and only reserved his rage for the gridiron, but knew something changed in him. Despite her short life, Latavia had been his everything, his inspiration for being the best father, player, and man he could possibly be. After her absence, these last few years, the only thing he felt inspired to do is to tear someone's head off, Jovan thought. It was with those instincts that made him a hot commodity at both the collegiate and pro levels as a linebacker. Jovan waited months before returning to the game and when he did it was painfully obvious he was not the same player he once was. He came back far more aggressive and played with even lesser discipline, all the while causing a critical injury to one of his own teammates. The guilt he felt for severely hurting one of his best friends on the team, pushed him from playing the game forever. These days, he reserved his aggression for the lowlife belligerents and over confident thrill seekers looking to be supremely humbled.

In its final hour, the scene at Hi-Prime was filled to the brim with wall to wall partygoers and industry mainstays alike. Every hotspot in the city was well represented at their prospective V.I.P. tables. The dance floor was so jam packed with people that the light that illuminated from off the floor could barely be seen from above it. Mike had yet to be alerted about any problems and even Kim and Len seemed to forgot all their worries as he spotted them pouring out champagne at their table. All seemed well, until he spotted Vincent, the head door man heading toward a storage closet with a female in his hand. If Vincent was inside the club trying to get his freak on then it left only "Break'em Barry" at the door, Mike assumed. The last thing Kim's club needed was Barry hustling at the door. Barry did not care who he would let come inside a club if the price was right, and this could not have been the worse time, or place for him to start, Mike thought. Without a moment's hesitation, Mike rushed toward the main entrance as if it were on fire. Before he could get to the first floor though, it had already been too late, as Mike could already spot the trouble makers making their way towards the main bar. It would be only a matter of time before the bar manager, or Len and Kim spot the large group wearing their matching baggy clothes and facial tattoos. After berating Barry outside for his misstep, Mike replaced Barry with himself and ordered him to drag Vincent from the second floor storage closet and back to his post. Although Barry respected Big Mike as a leader, he never appreciated him getting in the way of his side money and decided to take his time in doing what he asked. True enough, Barry had been reckless and greedy by allowing the "wrong looking" crowd inside the club, but pretty soon the rough looking group sporting the prison tats will be the least of their worries, as another unknown hidden threat may have already slipped past them.

Entrepreneur Austin Beard was the city's most highly successful club owner and its most notoriously arrogant human being as well. He went from spoiled trust fund brat to the industry's top mogul, seemingly overnight. Kim did not care for Austin, but knew if he could get him through the door it would validate him and his club among the city's elite spots. The proud Austin did not make it easy for him, as he needed his usual laundry list of stipulations in place to do so. What Austin lacked in statue, he more than made up for it with his choices in women. Lately, he had been dating an Italian magazine model named Sophia Hogan, who had a reputation for being highly flirtatious. She loved attention and had a knack for slipping away from him to get it. Sophia dated him out of boredom and not for his money, as the overconfident model believed her beauty alone could get her whatever she wanted. In her profession, her awesome beauty was her biggest asset or, her most lethal weapon, and had never partook in anything that could possibly destroy her God given good looks. The same could not be said for her present boyfriend, as the eccentric Sophia watched Austin in disgust, snorting cocaine line after line. He loved doing a little coke while getting his party on, and in his drug induced state, caused Sophia to feel neglected. Unknowingly, she had been watched all night by a tall dark figure, who managed to ease his way into their private section by supplying the coke. With Austin's attention off Sophia, the well groomed gentleman in the dark blue Armani suit approached her from behind, "You strike me as a woman that doesn't appreciate being ignored." he said, in her ear. Sophia quickly turned around to find out what the rest of that sensual sounding voice looked like. Her pretty eyes widened after making eye contact with the stranger. She was immediately aroused by his good looks and even better taste in clothes, "Well…you strike me as a man (looking him up and down) that may know how to please a real woman!" Sophia said seductively. The stranger in the dark colored suit offered her a quick smirk, "Under different circumstances you would be right, but, I'm not here for myself. You see, it's my friend's birthday, and he was forced to work here tonight." he said. Sophia placed her hand on the man's chest, "Aw, Poor baby!" Sophia said pouting. Suddenly, his face was covered in disappointment and he appeared to struggle for his words, "Yeah. What's worse is…you see, his girlfriend left him a week ago and I can't convince him to even look at another woman…" He said slyly. Sophia was intrigued by the man's tall tale, "Okay, go on." She insisted. The stranger let out a sigh, "Well, to be honest with you, it wasn't just your sparkling beauty that stood out to me. With no disrespect to your boyfriend, you look like someone who could use a good challenge." The stranger said boldly. She could feel her clitoris begin to moisten through her panties over the stranger's over-confident demeanor, "Hmm. This must be "some friend" for you to be coming on this strong!" Sophia said. He reached inside his coat pocket and pulled out an inch thick stack of freshly printed hundred dollar bills and handed it to her, "As a matter of fact, he very much is." The stranger said. Her knees began to buckle when she took the money and held it. If she was not already "cumming" before, she was doing so now, Sophia believed. She felt woozy flipping through the uncountable amount of freshly pressed hundred dollar singles. The well dressed stranger peeped over both his shoulder as if he were a Russian spy trying to avoid detection, "I won't ask you to do anything that you don't feel….comfortable doing….but, my friend could really use a woman's touch. Think you can put a smile on his face?" He asked. Sophia was in a small trance before she could answer him, "Huh? Oh, (looking back at him and the money in her hands) yeah, sure. And I still get to keep the money if I don't fuck him or anything right?" Sophia asked. He fought off the sensation to be coy with her, "No…just…GET him to….FEEL good." The stranger said emphatically. Sophia stuffed the money into her small Louis Vuitton purse, "I can't believe I'm even seriously considering doing this! I don't even know your name...?" Sophia protested. He put his hand out for her to shake it and smiled, "Its Alejandro, and YOU are the stunning Ms. Sophia Hogan, the beautiful swimsuit model. I'm a big fan of your…work." Alejandro said mischievously. Sophia began to blush uncontrollably and reached inside her purse for her compact. She took a last look at herself and put it back inside, "So…where did you say your friend was?" Sophia asked excitedly.

It was almost closing time, and all night, Jovan hardly had to raise his voice towards anyone. For the men that knew him it was all love and business as usual, and for those who had not, still showed him respect. Though he did not have the most glorified position of the night, Jovan really did not give a shit about being isolated. There were two other restroom areas in the entire club and he was designated to the farthest, which meant less traffic. That still did not stop the women from throwing themselves at him on their way to powder their pretty noses. Even through his suit, Jovan could not help standing out with his wide tree trunk arms and shoulders and chiseled face. By refusing their come-ons, most of the women who flirted with him assumed he was playing the hard-to-get role, when in fact it was the complete opposite. Sex was the farthest thing on his mind after losing Latavia and breaking up with Tasha. He had planned on marrying her at one time, but because he could not cope with Latavia's vile murder had drove her away, "Maybe I was meant to be alone," Jovan wondered. Each day after Latavia's funeral his mother Patricia's health had began to worsen. Patricia, who was a health nut, was now on heart and blood pressure medicine while nursing a diabetic problem. His mother was never the same after seeing her grandbaby mauled in the street like a dog. Tasha moved back to her mother's house on the southeast side. It was with Tasha's help that he even got into the whole security field, which ended up being her final favor for him. While Jovan had been distracted by his thoughts, he hardly paid any attention to the very attractive brunette who walked up and wrapped her arms around his neck. He broke his trance and was surprised by her presence, "Huh? Can I help you with somethin'?" Jovan asked despondently. Sophia could barely get her arms high enough to hold him and was very impressed by his muscular physique, "Yes…you…can! Damn, I didn't think you were going to be this Goddamn sexy!?! I may have to change my mind on fucking you after all!" Sophia shouted. Unimpressed by both her bluntness and good looks, Jovan simply disregarded her for being just another drunken woman, "Look here babygirl, the bathroom's that way! Now, I'd appreciate it if you would just…" Jovan said, before being interrupted, "O-o-o-o, you are tough!" She said. Jovan stood there with his hands positioned behind his back and looking at her like a fourth floor ledge does a restless pigeon. Sophia Hogan was not the type of woman who appreciated being ignored, or humbled by lesser men. Not long after starting her modeling career, she was used to men buying her the finest cars and spending loads of money on expensive jewelry just to impress her, but here was this handsome black bouncer (who probably caught the bus to work) giving her shit, Sophia thought frustrated. Despite getting paid handsomely by the mysterious stranger "Alejandro," Sophia always allowed her strongest emotion to get the best of her which was her stubborn pride, but she was not taking "No" from any man. When it came to the male anatomy, Sophia was far from a stranger, and decided to play a little dirty, "Well then…guess mamma's gonna' have to play with big daddy's little cookie dough!" Sophia threatened. Slowly, she ran her soft hands down to the front of his crotch and began to rub it, as though she were rubbing a magical Jeanie lamp. After making hand contact with his barely erected penis, Sophia let out a huge gasp. Things were far from getting out of hand, and Jovan could ill afford to accidently bruise her arms or ego, by grabbing and pushing her away. The only thing he could think to do was try to convince her stop willingly. At the end of the day, he knew he had a job to do, no matter how good her hand might have felt going across his balls, "Look babe, I'm really trying to hold on to this job, and you…y-you're only…" Jovan trailed off. Sophia cocked her head sideways, "Lemme' guess, making things HARDER, "Yeah, I'm beginning to see that!" She said happily, and squeezed his dick tighter than a vise grip. While Jovan had been suffering during Sophia's gratuitous indignities, Big Mike had been trying to contact him over the radio for the last five minutes, "Yo' Joe? Dude, you copy?" Mike yelled, into the radio. Jovan had to force himself to concentrate in order to respond, "Y-Yeah man. C-C-copy that." Jovan faintly replied. Even from the opposite end of the radio Big Mike could tell something was not right, "Yo' man, you taking a dump, or somethin'? Cause if you are, I need you to wrap it up! We got us a situation!" Mike said frantically. Jovan hesitated to speak for a few seconds, "What…ugh…situation is that?"

Jovan asked achingly. Mike paused to adjust his radio, "Hold up…Okay, a missing female….white chick. You can't miss her…real pretty, dark brown auburn hair, about 5'7, 5'9 and wearing six inch high heels!" Mike said. Sophia pulled out Jovan's thick hard-on and shoved him aggressively into the men's restroom, "Man, t-t-tell me she n-not wearing…a short…red dress!?!" Jovan asked, while Sophia continued to have her way with him. Mike was unsure if he was going to be either glad or worried about Jovan's odd query about the missing woman, but he bit the bullet anyway, "Yeeeaah…that's right. Have you seen her?" Mike asked suspiciously. It did not matter to the overly aggressive Sophia Hogan about the men's restroom being pre-occupied, as she pushed the much bigger former linebacker into one of the empty stalls, "Yeah, dude…I-I-I might've!" Jovan moaned. For the life of him, Mike could not figure out why Jovan had been acting so weird. He knew Jovan was not the type of person who played on the job, or let alone drink, "You might ha…dude, you don't sound cool! You want me to come back there and relieve you for a minute?" Mike asked worriedly. Jovan was trying his best to fight off the deceptively strong and hot blooded Italian vixen without touching her, but the more he struggled, the more she wanted him. The beautiful Sophia Hogan did not come from a life of privilege, like her spoiled new boy toy Austin, and before puberty kicked in, learned how to fight tooth and nail to get whatever her heart desired. After taking Alejandro's money though, Sophia first assumed that his friend would turn out to be some giant slob with low self esteem issues. The last thing she had counted on was a well hung chocolate hunk playing hard to get, "G-Good idea, y-you c-come…r-relieve m-me!" Jovan said feverishly. Sophia got down on her well tanned knees and opened her small moist lips as far and wide as she possibly could while masturbating him, "M-m-m-m relax, let me get that baby (turning off the power to his radio on his belt) I'm gonna' make you cum and get all the relief you ever need!" Sophia threatened. While Jovan, who had not had sex of any kind for over a year, could only hold on to the wall for dear life and bear the storm, "Oh, shit…" Jovan whispered overwhelmed.

Jovan Campbell was not a guy that goofed off on the job, or was into taking drugs of any kind either, thought Mike. A little voice inside Mike's head was urging him to get "Break'em Barry" back on the door to relieve him, so he could go check on his friend's status. Once he finally radioed Barry, Mike noticed a young couple among the few people that were leaving. They were all over one another and before he knew it, saw the woman caressing her boyfriend's crotch on the side of their car in the parking lot. He made nothing of the couple doing their thing and even was happy for them, but the more he watched the adventuress couple go at it, suddenly the craziest notion popped in his head, "Joe…tell me that ho wasn't going down on you…" Mike asked, on the radio. When Barry finally came to the door, he appeared overjoyed, "You check on Raz and the others?" Mike asked." Barry was too busy staring at a group of underage teenagers, who were standing on the opposite side of the barrier that Vincent had not allowed entry to yet, "Yeah man, they all cool. Go on Big Mike, I got this!" Barry said, while licking his lips. He stood there rubbing his hands like he was sizing up a large steak, "Yo' man, try and control yourself, and don't think you ain't gonna' come off half of what you already made before you leave here tonight!" Big Mike ordered. Though Barry was wide and muscular like a small tank, Big Mike was still the boss and was by far more imposing, and nodded his head in agreement. By the time Big Mike had gotten to Jovan's restroom post the damage was already being done. There was a large group of people in a circle and Mike could see men being thrown in mid-air like rag dolls by Jovan and the other security guys. As Big Mike forced his way through the excited crowd, he could see at least twelve people already lying on the floor unconscious. Both Kim and Len where screaming at the top of their lungs to get things under control, but their screams had only been in vain as the raucous crowd continued to cheer on the brawl. Mike grabbed the first person he saw that was trying to jump into the melee and gave him a first class trip to the floor. The man's head bounced off the hard pavement, busting his nose and sending him to sleep. It would take both the security and the police nearly twenty minutes to get things under control…

After the dust finally settled, over thirty people were either injured, or hospitalized. A waitress lost an eye, thanks to the anonymous bottle that was flung in her direction for no apparent reason. One of Big Mike's bouncers was stabbed in his shoulder, while another bartender suffered severe lacerations to his head and neck. The bathroom area that Jovan had been paid to secure appeared as if it were a murder scene, with the walls busted open and blood smeared everywhere. Len and the bar manger Clifford could only shake their heads as they surveyed the thousands of dollars worth of damages that was caused. Kim refused to leave his office and could be heard weeping from inside it as well. The police that were already working the club had called for backup and made several arrests, with one still pending. Though there were many witnesses that claimed that Jovan was fighting in self defense, it remained unclear on who or what, started the fight. Big Mike knew that the police who were working for the club would back him up, regardless of Jovan's involvement, but had worried that Austin's clout may interfere with Kim's decision to press charges. Mike had seen Austin curiously hanging around Kim after the lights inside the club came on. What Mike also thought was suspicious was that his model girlfriend, Sophia, was nowhere to be found. When things had gotten under control, Jovan had already explained to Mike about his sexual encounter with her in the men's restroom. They both believed that Austin sent his boys after her and jumped Jovan when they saw them leaving out together. That was not the story that Austin would tell the police, of course. Behind closed doors Kim Lee had been threatened to get his club blacklisted by Austin if he did not have his back. Len approached one of the policemen, who was still taking down witnesses statements, and whispered something to his ear. Jovan could tell by the look on the officer's bearded face when he looked at him that it was not going to be good news. The policeman then approached Big Mike and told him something that caused him to scream and curse so loudly that Barry had to grab him to keep him under control. While it became clear to him where this night was going to end, Jovan ordered himself a double Crown and Coke for the road. He took the drink straight to the head and slammed the glass onto the bar table once he finished it. The officer was making his way toward his direction, but then Mike stood in his way and the officer pulled out a pair of handcuffs and his baton. Once again Barry had to pull his longtime friend aside to allow the pudgy bearded policeman to do his job. Jovan cleared his throat, took off his earpiece and quietly placed it and his radio on the bar. He then put his black sports coat back on, and stood to his feet. The officer walked up behind him, "Jovan Campbell?" the officer asked, "Sir…" Jovan confidently responded, "I need you to turn around, son and face me…" The officer demanded. Jovan turned around and put both his hands out towards the officer. The policeman appeared slightly taken aback by both his statue and his willful gesture and needed a moment to reaffirm himself, "Ahem…Jovan Campbell, you are under arrest, for the crime of aggravated battery and aggravated assault!" The policeman said, as he put the shiny handcuffs over Jovan's thick wrists. He happened to look over the policeman's shoulder and could see the confusion, disappointment, and anger that embroidered both Mike and his co-workers faces. Kim stood with his head hung down, while the gloating Austin patted him on the shoulder and gave Jovan a sinister grin as he watched on. While Jovan was being escorted out through the front door of the club, Mike and some of the staff followed him out, "Yo man, (taking out a cell phone from his coat pocket) I'll let the family know what happened! We'll have you out soon as we can!" Mike yelled. Jovan did not bother to respond, and kept silent during the brief pilgrimage to the officer's patrol car outside. After the police put him in the squad car, Jovan simply stared at them while the car drove away. Big Mike called his sister-in-law Tasha, who was fast asleep at her mother's home, "Hey T, This Mike…yeah, I know what time it is! Listen it's about Jovan, tonight he got arrested and…that was his what? Shit!!!" Mike yelled. Barry and the others were on edge while listening to Big Mike's loud bantering, "Okay, okay. You do that, while I'll see what else I can do, peace!" Mike said, and hung up his cell. Vincent could clearly see something big was wrong, "So, what the fuck was all that about Mike?" Vincent asked concerned. Mike could see that the other staff members were also worried and began surrounding him, like small children anticipating a circus clown's next animal balloon. He put his cell phone back into his coat pocket and let out a large breath, "Its Jovan, man. That was his third strike! If I can't get him a good lawyer soon, he could be gone for a long, long time!" Mike said solemnly, and went back in the club. Barry had chased after him and pulled him on his shoulder, "Yo Mike, wait up! Look, I know you feel like you got to help this kid, because you vouched for him, but he a man! This shit wouldn't have ever happened if he…" Barry said, before getting interrupted, "It wasn't his fault! He lost his only child, when he was barely out of high school, you don't have a clue what this guy been through…I pray none of us eva' do!" Big Mike said, "Excuse me?" A voice behind Mike said. He turned around and there stood a man in an expensive dark colored suit holding out a card, "If you don't mind, I think I can offer you some assistance!" He said, and smiled.

Jovan's Day in Court

Downtown: Harris County Jail……

After being incarcerated the past couple days, Jovan found himself struggling to find any sleep on the hard as granite cot that the county jail provided its visitors. The time away did give him a chance to step back and take a long look at where his life was at the moment. This was his third trip to jail and it hit him that this possibly could be his last time as a free man. The prospect of going away to prison though had not bothered him as much as the emptiness he felt after Latavia's murder. To help pass the time while he was confined, he thought back to some of the few good times he had, as both a child and as a father. It took him over a year to clear his mind of the image of Latavia's scattered body parts that littered Grey Street and another year to talk about it. He remembered how excited he was when Tasha first told him about her being pregnant. Because Jovan was a highly successful football player, Patricia was very protective of her son and did not want him falling into any female's trap to get him for child support. It took time for Tasha to grow on her, especially after finding out about the pregnancy. She was still a little bit skeptical, but after seeing her beautiful granddaughter, whose golden colored skin glistened off the sunlight from the hospital window, all her fears quickly dissipated. He thought about how soft her pudgy light brown fingers were when he would nibble on them and how smart she was after learning how to talk at an early age. Her hair was jet black and wavy and when she smiled, Jovan thought about how incredibly cute she used to look with the two deep dimples deeply implanted in her cheeks. He buried his face into his pillow to weep and to keep the other inmates from mistaking his pain for fear. Jovan never had much to cry over in his life, even when he went to funerals of friends, or other family members. After he lost Latavia though, whatever strength he used for living seemed to have been lost as well.

Growing up in the inner city of Houston afforded him the fortitude of dealing with death since he was child. It seemed like a regular occurrence that somebody was always getting killed that he or someone else in school knew. The neighborhood he was raised in was fairly decent and his home life was a modest one. Patricia worked as a registered nurse at Lakeside Clinic after graduating from TSU and saved enough money to buy a small home in the Macgregor area. She did the best that any single mother could do for her child by always providing stability for Jovan. It did not take a rock to hit her over the head to figure out that her son was special. He remembered all the fantastical stories that his family shared about him on holidays. Even the neighbors had their own accounts about the legend who was Jovan Campbell. One of the earlier stories about him that stood out the most in his mind was the one about his next door neighbor, Mrs. Patterson, who would go grocery shopping every Saturday morning with his mother. Ever since Jovan was able to walk, he was always offering to do things around the house and on one Saturday in particular, gave her the shock of her life. The car was overloaded with groceries and while both Dorothy and Patricia had been distracted by the many bags that engulfed his mother's Chrysler, he decided to give them a hand. Patricia was on her way back to the car and screamed when she saw Jovan as a one year old packing two gallons of water in each hand. Mrs. Patterson would tell anyone who would listen about how she ran out the kitchen to see what was happening to his mom and about the shock she felt at the sight of little Jovan packing four gallons of water. There were many other "tall tales" of various acts of gallantry and everyone seemed to have their own favorite "little Joe" story, but life was no fairytale and sometimes the endings to some stories did not always turn out well, Jovan figured grimly.

It was mid-Monday morning when the time came for his arraignment hearing. As he entered the cold courtroom in his loud colored orange jumpsuit, he could see his ex-girlfriend Tasha, his mother Patricia, Big Mike, as well as many other close friends and relatives who were waiting in the galley to support him. Jovan tried to wave at his mother, but he could tell by both her slow reactions and glazed looking pupils that she was high on her anxiety medication. Tasha clearly had been crying, as her eyes were as bloodshot red as a newly painted stop sign. Big Mike, on the other hand, seemed a lot more at ease than when he saw him last. Everyone else were either praying for him, or pumping their fist in the air to encourage him. He sat quietly as he waited for his docket to be called. He looked over at Tasha again and when their eyes met, he told her he was sorry. Jovan hated what he was putting her and everyone else through. A part of him was looking forward to getting the book thrown at him for being the ultimate asshole towards the only girl who truly loved him for who he was, and not what he could give her. She tried her best to offer him a comforting smile, but found herself helpless to stop the fountain of tears that soon followed. This was Jovan's third assault charge in over a year and his second time breaking his probation. Jovan's football status, at the time, aided him in getting his first arrest knocked down to a misdemeanor. Unfortunately for him, his second arrest came after he quit the team and got put on two year's probation. A third arrest while serving his current probation would equal a felony charge, so the judge in that case promised to put him away for a long time if he ever broke it. To regain his freedom, Jovan knew he would need to get a good lawyer, but he also knew they did not come cheap. His only hope would be in the hands of a useless public defender, which did not amount to very much. Jovan knew enough about the system to know that public defenders did not always have the same resources that the other good law firms had. He also knew that they were usually too over worked, or under staffed to properly handle some their case load. But something was better than nothing and fortunately for him, Tasha had already filed to have one appointed to him. After getting arrested at the Hi-Prime nightclub, he refused the one free call the county granted him, out of fear of disappointing his mother, or anyone else for that matter. He did not have to be a genius to figure out that his former fiancé made the call for him and peeped over his shoulder and told her thank you.

The public defender that represented him looked younger than he was, Jovan thought, but swore to do his very best to represent him. State prosecutor Phillip Lomax on the other hand, was looking to improve on his court conviction record and sought to make an example out him. Lomax was in his late fifties and had grown weary of being a lowly court prosecutor, and who also had big aspirations to make Supreme Court judge one day very soon. He built his reputation off putting away more minorities in jail than the apartheid and desperately needed to put away a few more "bad apples" to solidify his chances of getting voted in. This time, it was Jovan Campbell who was on his radar and did not plan on missing an easy opportunity to improve his credibility for putting away repeat offenders. The judge entered the room, "All rise, for "Judge Louis Winthrop!" said the overly muscular bailiff. Judge Winthrop was no spring chicken and needed a moment to get up the few steps that led to his chair. Jovan could not take his eyes off the elderly looking judge, as he reminded Jovan of the Crypt Keeper from the "Tales from the Crypt TV show." Judge Winthrop was old school and was not used to being eyeballed by young black youths, "Everyone please sit. Is there something wrong with the defendant's eyeballs counselor?" Judge Winthrop asked briskly. The court appointed attorney, Shawn Carmichael, who represented Jovan, had been busy texting on his cell phone, "Huh, what? Uh…no! Your honor!" Shawn said. Judge Winthrop frowned disapprovingly, "Wake up counselor! And put that damn thing away if you want to keep it! Hell, son, I got grass older than you." He ranted. Shawn Carmichael immediately put away his cell phone and began to ruffle through his personal documents to get prepared. The judge shook his head and looked over at Phillip Lomax, "Well, now…who do we have here?" said Judge Winthrop, looking over his tilted thick rimmed glasses, "Why it's future Supreme Court Justice, Phillip Lomax! How kind of you to bless us with your presence!?!" He said graciously. Lomax started blushing brightly like a young school girl being asked out to the prom, "While I greatly appreciate your…gracious endorsement, Your Honor, I must say that the honor is indeed mine! And may I ask how Mrs. Susan's doing? She told my wife Fiona, she had been a bit under the weather!?" Lomax asked considerately. Judge Winthrop smiled broadly exposing his stained yellow teeth as he spoke, "Why, Susan's doing just fine, and thanks for asking! I will definitely let her know you asked about her well being!" He said gleefully. Jovan thought he was going to be sick from all the ego stroking going on between Lomax and the old judge. It was plain to see to him that the two of them were good friends away from work and probably already flipped a quarter about who got to pick the amount of years he gets to spend behind bars, Jovan assumed. His lawyer looked like a man lost, as Jovan watched him perpetrate by thumbing through his vast amount of case files, as if to find something of meaningful importance. The judge pushed his thick rimmed glasses back, "Well, I suppose we should be getting back to business, ahem…Let's see…ah…Yes, Mr. Campbell. You were picked up a few days ago for aggravated assault and aggravated battery…both are felonies…at a nightclub. This also makes it your third arrest and second probationary violation…so bail will not be extended to you. There will also be no need for setting a trial date, due to violating the stipulations of the probation…but, if the defense can produce some sort of proof that says otherwise, we shall proceed with this hearing and possible sentencing!" Judge Winthrop concluded. Things were not starting off well for him and here was this scrawny looking white boy wearing a baggy polyester suit that looked as if it was made to fit his dad that stood in the way of him going back to jail, Jovan contemplated. His inexperienced looking attorney was facing looming odds, so what could he possibly do or say to help him? Jovan thought angrily. Jovan knew that controlling his emotions, while working in a hostile environment, had become somewhat of a recurring problem after Latavia's death. Violence had become the primary answer to dealing with his problems and that was what he knew got him in his current predicament. If there was one good thing that came out of every scuffle he had had of late, it would be the amount of satisfaction his mind felt after pulverizing anyone who reminded him of getaway driver Jacory "Big Cory" Jackson. Big Cory Jackson was still serving his ten to fifteen year sentence for vehicular manslaughter and aggravated robbery, after nearly getting beaten to death by Jovan's hands. For a moment, his mind drifted off to that day when Big Cory and his two drug addicted cronies were evading arrest after robbing a Bank of America and killed his daughter in the process. It was as if there was a switch that Jovan could turn on, that reminded of that painful afternoon, and he would have the strength and the will to overcome anything. But, Phillip Lomax was no Jacory Jackson, or some other overzealous bum whose ass he had to kick out of a nightclub. The outcome of this type of fight will not be determined by the use of his fists, but in the incapable hands of his young attorney Shawn Carmichael. In Shawn Carmichael's eyes, the intimidating Phillip Lomax was the abdominal Prince of Darkness and saw himself as his next sacrificial lamb.

Please, present your case, counselor!" the judge said fondly. Phillip Lomax looked over at the over-matched and ill prepared Shawn Carmichael, "What we clearly have here Your Honor, is a severe case of "poor judgment" by the defendant, Mr. Campbell. Now…Mr. Campbell has been arrested multiple times for repeated assault and battery charges, and despite having current priors he also has broken his probation…twice! While I do not know the defendant, Mr. Campbell here personally, but if I was a betting man? I'd think it's safe to assume that he just doesn't care about his freedom." Lomax said. Jovan did not have to turn around to identify the cries that were spewing from his wounded mother, as the middle aged Phillip Lomax wasted no time dismembering her son's character, "Permission to approach the bench, Your Honor?" Lomax asked. The tired looking judge waved his hand, "Permission Granted..." Judge Winthrop said. Lomax snickered underneath his breathe as he strolled up to the cryptic judge's bench, "This here is a list of key eyewitnesses that can identify Mr. Campbell as the aggressor at a brawl that happened last Friday night at the, uh...how do you pronounce it...Club Hi-Prime?! I also, Your Honor, have video tape and another list of key eye witnesses that can tie Mr. Campbell to other previous open assault cases at two other night club venues. I'd like to admit this evidence as exhibits A, B, and C, Your Honor!?" Lomax said scornfully. Judge Winthrop skimmed over the two lists, and gave Jovan a disappointed frown. The judge then allowed them and the video as admissible evidence. Lomax swiftly turned around and made his way back to his council table, "The state will not only prove that Mr. Campbell (pointing at Jovan) as an immediate danger to the fine people of this city, but also as a threat to himself as well!" Lomax said emphatically. The tension in the courtroom grew thick enough to cut with a chainsaw and the people in the galley began to mutter their displeasure in unison, "All right, alright, order in the court!" Judge Winthrop ordered, "Now, that the court has heard words from the state, how does the defense plead?" The judge asked. Jovan's lawyer was perspiring heavily and dropped his papers onto the floor, "I-In...oops, Innocent. I'm sorry...Your Honor. I-I like to say that the defendant, m-my defendant...uh, Jonah...no, Jovan Campbell, is innocent of these outlandish and ridiculous charges, thank you!" Shawn said. Judge Winthrop shook his head, "Gee golly counselor... that was very moving! But, I do want you to try and relax a bit. You do have someone's future to consider, after all." The judge said sarcastically. Shawn took a deep breath and straightened his papers, "Yes sir, thank you, Your Honor..." Shawn said disappointedly, and sat back down to sulk in his seat. Between his lawyer's inexperience and sluggish pace, and the intense fervor of the prosecution, Jovan figured to be back behind bars before lunchtime.

Public defender Shawn Carmichael had only been sworn in as an attorney for about a month, and did not possess the ammunition to combat someone that was as seasoned in a court of law, as the reputed Phillip Lomax. He watched in despair as Phillip

Lomax argued at great length that his court appointed client, Jovan Campbell, had been some wild, uncontrollable, and overzealous maniac who was abusing his authority instead of providing security. The truth of the matter was that Shawn had no idea what "he" was really being asked to do regarding the case. The case fell into his untested lap early that morning, during a private meeting between him and one of the firm's senior partners Ronald Piper. During that meeting, Piper told him about some confusingly huge filing mishap between the downtown court house, the public defender's office, and Sharp & Associates. Piper also explained that the problem was finally rectified and that Sharp & Associates negotiated to take on a specific case in the public defender's place. In another startling move, Shawn was asked to only enter a plea of "not guilty" and do, or say nothing more on behalf of the defendant, other than stalling the prosecutor. Stall tactics was not a part of his curriculum at Harvard Law though, where Shawn graduated in the top five percent of his class with honors. His present firm, Sharp & Associates, represented twenty-five percent of America's most wealthy and would only perform pro bono work a few times out of the year to gain good publicity. At Sharp& Associates, it was not also unheard of for newly appointed attorneys to acquire experience in smaller courtrooms to help speed up their litigating learning curve. The swap that took place between his firm and the public defender's office was somewhat unprecedented though, but being asked to play games with the prosecution was a whole other matter, Shawn figured. After being hired by one of the most lucrative firms in the nation, Shawn wanted to do whatever he could to make a good impression and did not bother questioning Ronald Piper's highly immoral plan. He weeded through Jovan's rap sheet and could see that he had multiple run-ins with the law in the past. His latest arrest though, may have done enough irreparable harm to keep him locked up behind bars for the next ten years, Shawn presumed. The prosecution had plentiful witness accounts and even a video tape to help complicate matters further for him, Shawn worried. His opening statements had been elementary at best and felt like he might have given cause for suspicion. Over the next ten minutes, Shawn pulled out every court excuse allowed to halt the hearing until finally hitting a brick wall, "Your Honor I would like to take another quick recess to confer with my client!" Shawn nervously asked. Judge Winthrop had grown weary of Shawn's unpreparedness, "And why on God's green Earth would I grant it too you counselor? This is the second time you have requested a conference between you and the defendant and you haven't even given your rebuttal yet! Your request is denied! Now, if you would "PLEASE," make "SOME" sort of objection against the prosecution, or else withdraw yourself as counsel for the defendant's sake!?" The judge demanded angrily. Shawn was caught between a rock and hard place, while running out of ways to bullshit Phillip Lomax, he managed to agitate Judge Winthrop in the process. For his job's sake, Shawn hoped that his objective was achieved and that help from the partners would soon come. During the short time they conversed, Shawn could not tell if the quiet spoken young man beside him deserved a fair hearing or not. What he did know was that something was afoot and that he was caught in the middle of whatever it was. Either way if he did not act fast, the prosecution would be more than happy to expedite a lengthy prison sentence, "I have an objection, Your Honor!!!" yelled an overly confident voice from the back of the galley. State prosecutor Phillip Lomax could not help himself from cringing at the twang at which the familiar voice spoke with, and knew he was about to have a fight on his hands. Shawn whipped his head around and to his surprise was one of the most welcoming sights he had all morning. It was the voice of Sharp& Associates founder and criminal defense attorney Arnie Sharp.

Jovan thought he was hallucinating when the man that represented half the known sports and entertainment world, barged into the middle of his court hearing. To reassure himself that what was happening was for real, Jovan glanced over his shoulder at Big Mike for confirmation. Jovan spotted him through the sea of Sharp supporters and noticed the odd calm expression on Mike's face. When their eyes met, Mike gave him a nod of satisfaction. It was as if Mike had been the only person in the room that was expecting Sharp's visit, Jovan thought. Was it possible that Mike set this all up? Jovan wondered. Big Mike Mann "was" a former professional athlete after all, and could have called a number of his former football buddies to help him out, Jovan figured. Either way, part of him was glad to see the rock star attorney. Judge Winthrop on the other hand, looked mad enough to chew through his brass plated gavel. When Arnie Sharp strutted through the somber courtroom unannounced, it was to the roaring sounds of clapping and cheering. It was due to this disruption that caused Judge Winthrop to lose his cool, "Order in the court, (banging his gavel furiously) now dagnamit! I said order!!! Before, I clear you all out of here!!" The staunch judge ordered. After the courtroom finally quieted down, Judge Winthrop was huffing, "Now just what is the meaning of this counselor? Can't you see the defendant already has representation, and besides, don't you have to be on David Letterman or something!?" The judge asked sarcastically. The eccentric Arnie Sharp was giving Judge Winthrop his famous trademark smile and offered a comforting hand on Jovan's shoulder, "Actually, Your Honor, I don't do Letterman until next week! But thanks for asking!" Sharp said jokingly. The room again filled with laughter after Arnie Sharp's comical remark and caused the fragile looking judge's face to turn blood red, "All right (beating his gavel repeatedly) all right!!! Now, I've had just about enough of that!"Judge Winthrop screamed. The charismatic Arnie Sharp was a well known showman and had a reputation for using both his celebrity and southern drawl to influence and affect his jurors. Both he and the fuming Phillip Lomax had been friendly rivals over the last fifteen years, or so despite Lomax hardly ever beating him in a courtroom. This fact was not lost on him, which was why he was not about to allow Arnie Sharp the pleasure of impeding on what was supposed to have been an open and shut case, "Your Honor, It's obvious that the defense is trying to make a mockery of you "and" this court proceeding, by wasting the court's time and the tax payers of this great state's money, by displaying judicial misconduct and public grandstanding. I advise, Your Honor, that both "young" Mr. Carmichael and his superior, Mr. Sharp, be dismissed from these proceedings on the premises of misrepresenting themselves to the defendant. It's abundantly clear that Mr. Carmichael isn't qualified nor prepared, to adequately speak fairly on Mr. Campbell's behalf. And may I also add how obvious, Your Honor, that his superior Mr. Sharp, felt he needed to correct his mistake of having Mr. Carmichael acting as a counsel at said proceeding, and using stalling tactics and spectacle to undermine the courts precious time!" Lomax said emphatically. Arnie Sharp chuckled to himself and started to applaud Phillip Lomax, "Wow, Phil! That was pretty well thought out and well put I might add, but it's like I said....I object. And I do apologize to you, Your Honor, for my tardiness! If the court can forgive me, I just got back from a Cure for Cancer seminar in San Diego where my wife Laura, who's a cancer survivor, just received an NCRA award for doing outstanding volunteer work. It really meant a lot to her for me to be there, Your Honor, and I didn't want to let Mr. Campbell here down either, so I asked Mr. Carmichael to cover for me until I got back. I hope you don't mind…Your Honor." Sharp kindly implored. While Judge Winthrop was a little apprehensive to accept Arnie Sharp's conveniently vague excuse, but the husband side of him could not ignore his sympathetic plight, due to his own experience with a wife who was a cancer survivor as well. Judge Winthrop also loved the law. As a state appointed judge, he knew his personal feelings towards the attention grabbing Arnie Sharp needed to be put aside to allow due process to do its job, "I won't mind counselor, if the defendant doesn't?" Judge Winthrop finally confirmed. Jovan sat unmoving in deep thought, as he could not believe the luck he was having. This was his only shot at freedom if he wanted it, Jovan thought. But the more Jovan began to salivate at the thought of having his freedom a terrible reality began to appear into his mind. Arnie Sharp was used to getting paid millions of dollars from some of the most world's most influential people, so how was a college dropout going to afford the ballyhooed attorney, Jovan wondered. Jovan started scratching his head nervously and wiggled in his seat, "That depends…" Jovan said, as he looked up into the fiery eyes of the proud attorney. Arnie Sharp stopped smiling and stared at the worried young man, "Depends? Depends on what, son?" Arnie asked puzzled. Jovan glanced over at the irate Phillip Lomax and then at the patient Judge Winthrop. The stern judge seemed to have read his mind and nodded at him in reassurance. Jovan looked back up at Arnie, "…well, it depends on the bill, sir?" Jovan said dishearteningly. Most of the onlookers from the galley concurred with Jovan's blunt honesty, as they were high fiving and passing out amen's to each other. His candid response put a smile back on the seasoned attorney as he let out a low chuckle, "You were represented pro bono son, so technically representation is free." Arnie said gleefully. Jovan took a second to gather himself and then stood to his feet, "Well, in that case…Your Honor, from now on, Mr. Sharp will be my attorney. Phillip Lomax was livid and jumped out his seat, "Certainly you can't be serious, Your Honor? This is highly unethical to even be considering….!" Lomax hollered, before being interrupted, "Are you sure you want to continue going down that slippery slope your putting yourself on…Mr. Lomax?" asked Judge Winthrop. Phillip Lomax rolled his eyes, flopped down into his chair, and threw his hundred dollar ball point pen on the table in disgust, "No, sir…Your Honor!" Lomax said disgustedly. It only took a minute for his arch nemesis to come marching in to monopolize what was supposed to had been a swift sentencing, Lomax angrily thought to himself. Arnie was grinning like a wild piranha at him and winked his eye, "Very charming, you son of a bitch…!" Lomax said underneath his breath. After they took their seats, Jovan reached his nervous hand out to his impressionable lawyer, "Thank you, Mr. Sharp. I don't know how I can make it up to you…" Jovan said. Arnie grabbed the young man's hand firmly, "Don't sweat it kid, you'll get your chance! Just give me about five minutes!" Arnie said wickedly. Jovan turned and gave Tasha a look of comfort and she in turn tried her best to smile back.

It did not take long for defense attorney Arnie Sharp to get into his groove, as he fervently objected throughout Phillip Lomax's tiring account of what Jovan's state of mind as a security guard was. Lomax emphatically read aloud the police reports of each incident that Jovan was allegedly linked to, including what led to his latest arrest. Though the cases varied according to what the actual causes were, or where they happened, one thing remained constant in Phillip Lomax's argument… Jovan Campbell had been at the focal point. When the prosecution tried to bury Jovan under a catalog of eyewitness accounts, Arnie Sharp defiantly contested the evidence and ingeniously proved the lists to be both inconclusive and inadmissible. Since none of the witnesses had been questioned about, or tested for their alcohol consumption, the defense used it as a loophole and had it thrown out. The embattled Phillip Lomax still had one last trick up his tailored sleeve, as he still possessed one of the security tapes from the fight Jovan was involved in at Mason's strip club. In the back of his mind, Jovan knew of the possibility that there would one day be repercussions for his actions, and believed once the film began to roll…it was going to be all she wrote. Inconspicuously, the beginning of the video failed to show who, or what started that particular incident, but the cameras view point showed Jovan unleashing a hellacious right hook to the jaw of another large black man. After laying the young man out, what came next looked like something from out of a Batman video game, as Jovan could be seen plainly wrecking the entire establishment and showing no remorse for the assailant's friends. Jovan's freakish strength and prowess was drawing ooh's and aah's from the galley, as they watched him mangle seven grown men on the forty inch lcd screen, prompting Judge Winthrop to threaten to kick them all out again. Phillip Lomax was describing the violence Jovan displayed in the video as "extreme." He was drawing the conclusion that Jovan sought to challenge any and everyone, no matter the odds he faced, to create anarchy for his own pleasure. But, in the practical mind of Arnie Sharp, it showed a man that was obvious outnumbered, "Objection, Your Honor! I don't know what the court sees, but I just had my eyes checked recently and they both tested at twenty-twenty, and with that being said, I count seven assailants attacking one man. From where I'm standing, Your Honor, the only thing Mr. Campbell appears guilty of is fighting for his basic right to live! Now Your Honor, if the prosecution wants to contend that fending off seven sets of arms and legs as thrill seeking, then maybe he needs his eyes and head examined!" Arnie quipped. Judge Winthrop shook his head in agreement, "Okay Mr. Sharp, you made your point!" Judge Winthrop said. Clearly, Arnie Sharp's cockiness was quickly wearing thin on Phillip Lomax's nerves. After growing weary of playing the cat and mouse game against his rival, he felt it pertinent to cash in on a final verdict, "Your Honor, I honestly feel that we 'd be doing the citizens of Houston and this fine state as a whole, a disservice if we allow young Mr. Campbell…" Lomax said before interrupted, "This isn't city hall, Mr. Lomax, no more speeches. Just stick to the facts, please." Judge Winthrop warned. He had not expected the judge's bluntness and needed a second to loosen his tie and collar, "Of course, my apology Your Honor!" Lomax said apologetically. Arnie turned his head and gave Jovan a light smirk. Both attorneys new that the evidence Lomax held was circumstantial at best and that a decision would be ultimately made by which attorney could sway the judge. Jovan was starting to get the impression that his case was not about him anymore and that Arnie Sharp was using him to prove a point. On one hand, you have the diplomatically inclined Phillip Lomax, whose bottom line was to try and sell him as a menace to society for political gain. Then you have the hotshot superstar lawyer Arnie Sharp, who usually does things like helping baseball and football players beat their steroid cases, Jovan thought. Lomax gained his composure, "What I meant was, Your Honor, that judging by the video and his sketchy track record as a solid citizen…wherever Mr. Campbell here goes, violence is sure to ensue. The law can't allow us to reward repeat violators. The main question here isn't just about if the defendant's guilty of breaking his probation, but how long will it take for the next incident to occur, if the defendant is granted a light sentence. Maybe the next time it happens again, it's your daughter or nephew that gets hurt, or maybe my son and daughter, or maybe…just maybe…they get killed, and the only thing that would save them now, Your Honor, would be for a guilty verdict to be upheld!" Lomax pleaded. It did not take a Stanford law degree for Jovan to understand what Phillip Lomax was driving at. Lomax was seeking to have him locked away for as long as humanly possible. Judge Winthrop looked like a man who was ready for a nap, as he stopped chewing on his glasses to put them back on. Jovan turned his head to look back at his family and friends and tried to give them one last hopeful smile. Again, when he caught Big Mike's eye, he gave him the same blank stare he gave him earlier, causing Jovan to worry about him. Tasha was holding his distraught mother while she wept quietly. Despite his waning supporters, only his former love Tasha Greenwood still held a glimmer of hope upon her preciously light brown complected face. She told Jovan that she loved him, possibly for the last time before he gets shipped off to God knows where, Jovan figured. But either way, whatever the judge was about to decide, he knew he would be at peace with it and shut his eyes. The courtroom was awfully quiet for a full twenty seconds before the unexpected happened, "I indubitably object your honor." Arnie Sharp said, while sitting with his arms firmly folded.

When he opened his dreary eyelids, Jovan could see something was obviously different about Arnie Sharp's usually cool demeanor. The tone in which Arnie spoke caused both Judge Winthrop to slightly flinch in his chair and Phillip Lomax to stop talking in mid-sentence, "Permission to approach the bench, Your Honor?!" Arnie asked. A suddenly energized Arnie Sharp took two identical sheets of paper from out of his briefcase and gave one to the judge and the other one to the prosecutor and returned to his table, "What is this counselor?" asked Judge Winthrop. After Lomax read the mysterious paper his eyes rolled and he slammed the sheet of paper down on his table angrily, as if he were trying to squash a nagging insect, and fell to his seat in disgust. Whatever the two of them were looking at caused Jovan to perk up and pay attention, "What it is, Your Honor, is a name…One name. She is the defense's only witness." Arnie said. Everyone in the courtroom was now at full attention, "Quiet down! Now look here counselor, this isn't a trial and it is highly irregular for…!" Judge Winthrop explained. Arnie Sharp interrupted, "But we have no choice, Your Honor, given the circumstances and the restrictions that you previously put in place at the very beginning of this court hearing. Now, I know Mr. Lomax here has dreams and aspirations and all that, but what the court needs here today is the truth, and not a political witch hunt of my client! And I'm sure once you do hear the truth…" Arnie said before being interrupted, "Objection, Your Honor!" Lomax yelled, standing to his feet, "Sustained…continue Mr. Sharp!" Judge Winthrop commanded. Arnie Sharp rolled his eyes at Lomax, "…Once you hear what she has to say, it will more than satisfy the court and prove my client innocent of all charges." Arnie said confidently. Judge Winthrop rubbed his chin thoughtfully, "If she is here, I will allow her to testify." Judge Winthrop said, "She is, Your Honor." Arnie said happily. Arnie gestured to someone that had been sitting at the very back of the galley. It was a man wearing the cleanest suit Jovan had ever seen, as the young man exited the court to get the witness. When she entered the courtroom, beautiful Sophia Hogan pranced her way up to Arnie Sharp and blew a kiss at Jovan. The tight fitting black dress she wore made her look stunning and seemingly commanded every man in the courtrooms attention. Her flirting with Jovan caused him to blush, but soon felt a rush of regret that engulfed all his primary senses. If Sophia was going to testify on his behalf that meant Tasha would probably never bother speaking to him ever again, Jovan feared. He had unprotected sex with a complete stranger while working at the nightclub his ex-girlfriend got him hired at, and now she will be forced to hear every fucking detail about it, Jovan worried. Politely, Arnie shook the young woman's hand, "Your Honor, I would love to introduce to you and the court, Ms. Sophia Hogan!" Arnie proudly announced. In Jovan's eyes, it appeared as if Judge Winthrop's eyes were going to ram through his thickly rimmed glasses like a pair of crash dummies after seeing Sophia up close. He licked his cracked lips before he spoke, "Ahem. Well, hello there…Miss…Hogan!? Pleased to make your (eyeballing her curves)….acquaintance!" Judge Winthrop said drooling. Phillip Lomax started pouting in disgust, "Your Honor, would you PLEASE explain to me what the court truly has to gain by allowing this witness' testimony? I was not made aware of this witness until a few moments ago and also unprepared to properly cross examine…" Lomax argued, before being cut off. While pointing at the egotistical Phillip Lomax, "Your Honor, in light of Mr. Lomax's tirade, may he need to be reminded that she is speaking to the court as a common courtesy. Especially, when looking at the fact that the prosecution hadn't bothered to even share with the court of her existence, nor that witnesses can place her at the scene and that she was forced to leave before the police arrived!" Arnie protested. He then slammed his hand down harshly on the table, "Your Honor, that's hearsay and you know it, counselor!?" Lomax screamed. Rolling his eyes, "Hearsay!?! I have the head of the security team in the galley, that has a tape of his own, that shows Ms. Hogan being shuffled through the parking lot by her drunken boyfriend, just before the police arrived. Do we need to show it to you? Mr. Mann…?" Arnie said, and turned toward the galley. Big Mike stood to his feet and held up a VHS tape. Lomax started cursing underneath his breath and sat back down, "I didn't think you did…Your Honor? May she take the stand now?" Arnie Sharp politely asked. Judge Winthrop had been in a small trance as he gazed up and down at the body of the exotic looking Sophia Hogan, "Huh? Oh, oh yes, please darling! By ALL means…" Judge Winthrop politely insisted.

The Verdict

When she took the stand, Sophia Hogan told the court her occupation and the reason why she was there at the Hi-Prime nightclub the night of Friday's brawl. She was every bit as beautiful as Jovan last remembered her. Her auburn hair glistened brightly in the dully lit room. Her facial features appeared flawless, as if they were drawn or painted on her. Both Sophia's gorgeously tanned skin and satin black dress could make any man, straight or gay, get a hard on that would bend metal, Jovan thought. She stared directly at him when she spoke, making Jovan feel aroused. It was as if she were trying to undress him or re-live that night in the bathroom, He thought. Arnie saw it too, and as hilarious as it was to him, did his best to ignore her as she was trying to seduce Jovan from the witness stand. Then finally Arnie Sharp began to start asking the hard questions that he would not bare to hear answered in front of his ex-girlfriend, "How well do you know the defendant, Ms. Hogan?" Arnie asked nicely. Sophia raised her freshly manicured eyebrows and gave a devilish grin, "Well, I know him well enough to say…he likes to give a woman one hundred percent on his job!" Sophia said seductively. Jovan turned and looked at Tasha from the corners of his eye and could feel her cold stares on the back of his head. Arnie's eyes bucked, "Just what is it that you mean Ms. Hogan?!" Arnie asked specifically. Sophia gradually ran her tongue across her shiny red lips as if they tasted like candy, "What I meant was…he was the ultimate gentlemen. I was feeling kind of vulnerable that night and had a couple glasses of champagne. I wondered off from my boyfriend that was acting like a dick…oops, sorry Your Honor!" Sophia said apologetically, "It's okay, you can say dick, go on…" Judge Winthrop kindly urged. She looked up at the salivating judge and he winked at her, "Okay, then…. he was being a "dick." (She smiled at the judge) And "I" just needed somebody to talk to." She concluded. Rubbing his chin in deep thought, "So what you're saying is….that you came to club "Hi-prime" with your boyfriend, you left him after you two had words, and ended up meeting Mr. Campbell. Is that correct, Ms. Hogan?" Arnie affirmed. Sophia's eyes were still fixated on Jovan, "That would be a yes." She confirmed, with a broad grin. Jovan watched in anguish as the sexy temptress seemed to take her time dissecting her twisted version of what happened, leaving him on edge, "What would you say his state of mind was when you two first met? Had he been drinking, or displaying any lewd behavior?" Arnie asked. Stroking her eyebrows, "No, he didn't appear drunk at all. When I approached him, it was me that was looking for attention, so when he didn't give me enough, I just ran off into the men's restroom and locked myself inside one of the stalls!" Sophia said disapprovingly. What was her game? Jovan asked himself. Here she was telling one big ass lie after another and making him look good in the same process, not that he was complaining, "Why the men's room? Surely you knew the difference?! Tell us what happened after you locked yourself inside? Did Mr. Campbell try to console you, or convince you to leave the men's room?" Arnie asked. Sophia broke her gaze and looked at the fabled attorney straight in the eye, "I just had a miscarriage and my boyfriend barely blinked when I told him about it, so I wasn't in the best of moods when we got to the club. I was a little tipsy, so I went looking for trouble. When I found Jovan, I couldn't get a rise out of him, so I cracked! All I know is that I just needed someone to care, cause' at that time, my asshole boyfriend sure in the hell didn't….and he, Jovan, seemed like a really, really nice guy to talk to, and maybe…maybe, I came on a little too strong. He tried to convince me to let him in…just to talk." Sophia said. Arnie offered her a sympathetic look and walked toward Jovan, "I see. So, you were highly distraught over your miscarriage and because you were angry, sought comfort from a total stranger?! Now, tell me Ms. Hogan….how did things go from bad to worst so fast?" Arnie asked shrewdly. Sophia put her hands into her lap and looked at the judge as she spoke, "My asshole boyfriend, Austin, came barging in on us! He can be insecure sometimes." She said. Arnie turned around and began to approach her, "I see, and what was his state of mind? Was he "happy" to see you in the men's restroom…with another man?" asked Arnie. She looked back into Judge Winthrop's star struck eyes, "He was irate! Austin previously took a few bumps of coke, which I don't do, and was already full of champagne before I left him!" Sophia said, and began to fixate on Jovan some more. Arnie Sharp folded his arms as he spoke, "So we have your upset boyfriend, who's both inebriated with champagne and high on cocaine, who finds his beautiful model girlfriend pouring her heart out to a club bouncer, in a men's restroom stall…did I miss anything?!" He asked. Sophia cut her eyes at Arnie for a second, "No, that about covers it!" Sophia said hurriedly, and continued her gaze at the uncomfortable defendant. The perceptive attorney could not help himself from asking what had been a burning question, "Ms. Hogan, I'm not sure that you are aware of this, but it seems as if you have taken a liking to the charming Mr. Campbell, would you care to explain why that is?" Arnie asked smiling. Sophia sat frozenly still, as if she were a clothing store mannequin, and hung her head down, "Like I said, Austin gets insecure sometimes and when he found us together, he forced us to open the stall door…" She quietly said. He then leaned against the witness stand in front of her, "Please, go on Ms. Hogan…" Arnie encouraged. Her make-up began to run down her cheeks, causing Judge Winthrop to fumble about to give her some Kleenex tissue, "Thank you, Your Honor! When we opened the door, he started yelling and cursing at me. He pulled me out of the restroom by my hair and punched me in my stomach! That's when…that's when Jovan tried to help me…" Sophia cried. Jovan felt as if he were trapped inside a lost episode of "Tales from the Darkside," while he watched Sophia embellish the truth at will. Besides leaving out the sex, she had been telling a mild version of what really happened, Jovan recollected. Jovan remembered her mocking her boyfriend's smallish penis size, and that's why he punched her in the stomach. Almost everyone in the courtroom seemed moved by her performance, even Phillip Lomax was showing her sympathy, as he shook his head in disgust, "Hell of an actress…" Jovan quietly muttered. Arnie Sharp watched her diligently with his arms crossed, "Ms. Hogan do you mind showing us your wounds, just so we can verify your story?!" Arnie asked gingerly. Sophia took a brief moment to get composed and slowly took off the top portion of her dress, revealing deep dark bruises on her shoulders and stomach. The courtroom started to get into an uproar, until Judge Winthrop ordered them to get themselves under control. She pulled her dress back up and sat back down in disgrace, "I apologize for not holding it together, Your Honor, but for somebody that gets paid to show their body in a magazine for a living, this is the one time I'm ashamed to show it!" Sophia said sobbingly. Judge Winthrop looked at her painfully, as if she had offended his honor as a gentleman, "Nonsense child, what kind of beast do you take me for! You are doing a splendid job so far, and I must commend you for even sharing your story with us. That is very brave of you!" He said modestly. Sophia continued to play on the judge's sympathies, "Thank you, Your Honor." Sophia said. Arnie was primed to drive his last point home, while he had Lomax on the ropes, "As you all can see, Ms. Hogan is not just a witness for the defendant, but is also a victim! How did Mr. Campbell react when he saw you getting physically abused Ms. Hogan? Did he simply walk away as though it wasn't his business, or did he stay and do his job as the club's security guard, and offer you a hand?" Arnie grudgingly asked. The swimsuit model's face began to glow when she told the amazing tale of how Jovan saved her from her abusive boyfriend, while keeping her protected by fending off Austin's friends.

After Sophia Hogan stepped down from the witness stand, Judge Winthrop had grown restless about hearing Jovan's Jekyll and Hyde work routine and was ready to pass a verdict, "I've taken into careful consideration of the previous witness's testimony, as well as the prosecution's compelling case. I'm ready to give a verdict…" Judge Winthrop declared. The overly disgusted Phillip Lomax could clearly see through the old judge as if he was a piece of transparency paper lying on a projector, and feared he was leaning toward the defense, "Your Honor, before you make your decision on the verdict, I need you to also consider one last…!?" Phillip Lomax said, before Judge Winthrop cut him off. Judge Winthrop pointed his finger disapprovingly at Phillip Lomax, "No counselor, I've heard all I needed to know. You will no longer use my court room for some "witch hunt," or "campaign spring board for your political agenda," or even some damn "pissing contest" either! This is a courtroom of justice! Mr. Campbell would you please stand…." Judge Winthrop loudly confirmed. It was nice hearing the elderly judge tongue lashing Phillip Lomax for a change and allowed him to breathe a little easier, Jovan thought. Just as the worn down judge was about to drop the hammer down on his decision, Arnie Sharp took out a pen and pad and scribbled something down on it. When he finished writing on it, he tore out the sheet and walked over to Lomax and handed it to him. Lomax was surprised by the move, but was at least willing to humor the brazen attorney. Jovan did not have a clue what Arnie Sharp had written on the piece of paper, but whatever he wrote was important enough to turn the frown Lomax initially sported into a faint smirk, Jovan figured. Arnie held up his hands in a "make your move" type fashion. Lomax leaned back in his chair and held his hand over his chin contemplating to himself, as if he were trying to figure out food choices on a lunch menu. After needing a few moments to digest a decision, Lomax nodded a "yes," and kept his demeanor inconspicuous, "…and further more "Mr. Sharp," I would greatly appreciate it that in the future, you save your courtroom dramatics for the TV cameras, and not in my courtroom!" Judge Winthrop ordered. Arnie gave the judge his widest million dollar TV smile, "Of course, Your Honor." Arnie said, and glanced over at Lomax. Their eyes met and Phillip Lomax stood to his feet, "Your Honor, the state is willing to drop all charges if the defendant agrees to sign up for counseling at the, uh…"Midtown Houston Mental Care" facility, for four to six weeks of one hour sessions. It's not lost on the state that Mr. Campbell was once a father, who suffered the loss of his two year old daughter, not long a…" Lomax said, until Jovan intervened, "Three! Latavia was three." Jovan stated coldly. Lomax had seen many killers in his lifetime, but never had he been more intimidated by Jovan's ice cold stare, "Ahem, yes, excuse me. As I was saying…we are willing to wave the charges, "if" he signs up for their new parental stress program they started for…"individuals" like Mr. Campbell here. Who knows, maybe the change of scenery will do the young man's rap sheet some good!" Lomax confirmed. Judge Winthrop was skeptical and soaked in the prosecutor's words, "Hmm…interesting. Well, counselor?"

Judge Winthrop asked. Jovan did not know what to make of the offer that was being extended to him by the now remorseful state prosecutor. Arnie wasted no time responding, "The defense accepts the state's terms, Your Honor." Arnie said. Judge Winthrop took a deep breath then picked up his brass plated gavel, "Well….in that case….would you please rise Mr. Campbell. All charges made against the defendant are now dropped and I will waive his probation once he's completed his four week counseling at the Midtown Houston Mental Care facility… case dismissed (banging his gavel down)! You are now free to go…and don't ever let me see your face around here again young man!" Judge Winthrop warned.

Judge Winthrop's decision left Jovan paralyzed in his stance. Arnie Sharp patted him across his back, (which caused him to break his stoic trance) to congratulate him on the victory. He firmly shook Arnie Sharp's hand, "I don't know what the hell just happened, but…I thank you!" Jovan said cheerfully. The fabled attorney gestured in a nonchalant fashion, "Oh…that was nothing. Me and ole' "Lomaxie pad" go WAY back! Besides, you're actually doing me a favor!" Arnie said, and winked his eye at Jovan. Jovan was taken aback by his words, "Huh? What do you mean by that, and why'd you help me out anyway? Did Big Mike put you up to this?" Jovan asked confused. Arnie stopped smiling, put a hand over his shoulder, and leaned closer to his ear before Jovan's family drew nearer, "Big Mike? I don't know who that is. Look son, you just make damn sure you haul ass down to that clinic, or it's my ass! All you need to know is we both have a friend that's in high and low places and expects to see you there. Now, get the fuck out of here...!" Arnie said smiling. Just as he was trying to get a handle on where Arnie Sharp was coming from, Jovan's entourage of family and friends ambushed him with praise. Without drawing attention to himself, Big Mike walked out of the courtroom and into a vacant hallway where Sophia Hogan and a slender built man sporting a nicely dark tailored suit were quietly speaking amongst themselves, "Nice doing business with you again, Alejandro….we must do this again in the future." Sophia said satisfied, while placing a wad of cash into her bustier. Alejandro winked at the persuasive model, "The pleasure was all mine, senorita…oh, and uh, nice touch! You know, with the extra bruises!" Alejandro said jokingly. Sophia displayed her most devilish grin slid on her expensive sunglasses and walked off into the sunset. Big Mike could not help being a man and watched the full figured sultry woman stroll away like a panther seeking its next kill, "Damn man, you sure know how to pick'em….!" Mike said, as he continued to watch the sultry Sophia Hogan strut all the way to her pearl white Porsche convertible. The all business minded Alejandro was not blind and could see the obvious attraction Big Mike had for the gorgeous seductress. But he was no stranger to being in the company of better looking females, "You see one nice looking woman, you've seen them all. Now…I have fulfilled my part of the bargain. It is now up to you, my friend, to fulfill yours! Are you up to the task?" Alejandro curiously asked. Unsure what to say next, Big Mike bit down on his lip and scratched his head as he contemplated an answer, "Well, Mr. Mann?" Alejandro asked again. Big Mike stood at attention, as if he were doing an atten hut in the armed forces, "Yeah man…I'll make sure he goes. I just want to know, what happens now? You people went through a lot of trouble for a complete stranger…how do I know I can trust you with my homie's life?" Big Mike asked concerned. Alejandro slowly approached the abominable Mike Mann and stared him directly in the eye, "You don't. It is my "employer's" business of what HE has in mind for your friend. All we ask of you "Big Mike" is for you to make sure that HE'S there! Remember my friend, what can be done…can be UNDONE! Do we understand each another, hermano?" Alejandro asked sharply. Despite his threat, Mike was not easily intimidated, but decided to play along for the time being, "Hey man, it's like I said…I'm cool! I just wanted to know what my boy was really signing up for." Big Mike concluded, while stroking his chin. Meanwhile, Jovan and his fleet of supporters began flooding the halls loudly in merry concert, causing Mike to take his attention away from the mysterious Alejandro. When he looked back, the smooth stepping Alejandro had been halfway gone out the side door, "Say bruh,' you never answered my damn question!!!" Big Mike yelled fiercely. Alejandro stopped dead in his alligator shoe wearing tracks and spoke without bothering to look back, "War….Mr. Mann. War…." Alejandro said, and raced out the side exit. Mike nervously began breathing heavier as Alejandro's words echoed repeatedly within the crevices of his own psyche, causing him to question his decision. While struggling internally with his decision to help coerce someone he considered a good friend, something on the floor by the exit door caught his eye. He walked up to the folded piece of paper unhurriedly, as though it were a line mine, and kneeled down to pick it up. Big

Mike unfolded the sheet of paper and read it and after he did, his chest went numb. It was the same piece of paper he saw attorney Arnie Sharp pass over to prosecutor Phillip Lomax while they we still in court deliberating. The note had plainly said: Hey Phil, chill the fuck out, or the sniper that's watching your pretty wife at home, through your bedroom window, will squeeze the fucking trigger. Take this generous check as my campaign contribution and call it a day….From your pal, Arnie. The disturbing note left the shocked Mike Mann utterly speechless. Just what the hell was going on that would make someone who lived in the spotlight, like Arnie Sharp, threaten the life of a fellow lawyer's wife and then bribes him as conciliation? Mike wondered. Whatever was going on, his close friend was smack dab in the middle of it, Mike guessed. When Jovan spotted him standing off to himself, Mike quickly refolded the note and tucked it away in his suit pocket. Jovan looked at him awkwardly, but then waved at a frozen Mike Mann to come over and celebrate everyone else. Just before he went, Mike paused and had prayed under his breath that he made the right move, as he was still uncertain of what the immediate future held for his young friend. When he finally joined them, Jovan let go of Tasha's hand and bear-hugged the much bigger Mike Mann and scooped him up off the ground with ease. For the moment everyone was happy, but Mike could not shake the feeling that something much bigger was at play and that Jovan might have been set up for a fall. One thing was obviously clear to him, that somewhere was someone very powerful who was controlling things like a puppeteer commanding his string-puppets on center stage. The funny thing about puppets though….if they get too close together, they can become a tangled mess and if they "were" playing the part of puppet in somebody else's twisted act, then they had better hope whoever's operating the handles knows what the hell he's doing, or they might find themselves trapped in a terrible one themselves, Mike thought.

Chapter 6:

"The Deal"

Three years ago…

The highly turbulent weather that transport entrepreneur Harlan Kruellar was experiencing, from the comfy confines of his private jet at 30,000 feet, would be usually taken as a bad omen. What had made matters worse was the timing his twenty-year old son Haven chose, to share his personal thoughts, on why he deserved a more meaningful promotion. Young Haven Kruellar idolized his father, who was a mogul in the transporting industry. Haven also sought to one day achieve, or surpass his father's successes as an independent businessman. For a man who never attended college, his father still managed to build an incredible empire, Harlan Imperial Express, in a short amount of time. When he turned eighteen, Haven aggressively pursued a place at his father's side, and after two years of hard work, it would become a decision that he would later regret, "I think I'm ready!" Haven said boastfully. Harlan was trying to enjoy both his Cuban cigar and his newspaper, before his son's words rang loud, causing his eyebrows to rise as wide as a rodeo gate, "When we get back to the states, I think we should discuss my position…" Haven said, before his father rudely interrupted, "There's nothing to discuss. You're merely coming along as a courtesy from father to son. Because you hadn't failed at any of the previous tasks I asked of you, I allowed you to accompany me to Mexico. Make no mistake, Haven, you have yet to fully grasp what lines I had to cross to get to where I am today, or what our family had to sacrifice!" Harlan said sternly, and went back to reading his USA Today newspaper. The raven haired Haven huffed in disgust, "Why do you always have to go there? You act like I never heard the stories about how bad you guys had it back then, what does any of that have to do with how good we have it now?" Haven loudly protested. Harlan took a moment to compose himself, then slowly put his newspaper down into his lap and stared despondently at his contemptuous son. It did not take Haven long to discover that he stepped way over the line with his words, as he knew how sensitive his father was about his past, "I-I'm, sorry…dad. I didn't mean any disrespect…but, sometimes, it just feels like…you know…that you think I'm not cut out for what you do, because I didn't have it rough like you did! It's like you think I'm too soft, or…" Haven said, before his father cut in, "What I DO isn't about how soft you are, or how tough you had it, Haven! It's all about understanding and living with the finality of your choices! Now, I went to school just as you did, but I took my education only as far as I was willing to go with it. You don't need to cross the same boundaries I often times do to get ahead in life. You still have the choice to go back to college and become someone important to society, like maybe becoming a doctor, a teacher or, the president…" Harlan humorously said, "…Or like, my once upon a time dirt poor, but now self-made millionaire father? Dad…you're a very brilliant, important, and well respected man that anyone stupid enough not to love you, at least fears you, and besides…if it was good enough for mom, what's so wrong with me wanting that too!?!" Haven asked desperately. His son's thought provoking words stung him deeply and caused him to pause. It was not lost on Harlan that his son held him in high regard. Their relationship had prospered each day since his birth and never once had they argued about any subject since Haven first learned to speak. He loved his son every bit as much as he did him, and it showed as far back as Harlan could possibly remember. When he received high marks in school as a little boy, Haven could not wait to share the good news with his dad or, if his father was present for his prep school games, he would move heaven and Earth to stand out just to receive Harlan's praise. Haven had been everything Harlan could ever want in a son, which is why the eccentric transport businessman had been so reluctant in bringing him along on such a dangerous voyage. They already took a chance by flying through miles of poor rain weather and barely made it through an electrical storm. On most occasions, Harlan would simply cancel or, postpone an invitation, if the weather he traveled through ever became too rough. He was not a superstitious man by nature and was hardly spiritual, but bad weather normally spelled trouble in his history. The man he was meeting with in Acapulco, Mexico was not a person who Harlan took lightly, nor was to be recklessly disregarded. A part of him starts to question his sanity by placing his most prized possession in the whole world in harm's way, while the other sees it as an opportunity to test his son's mantle. Harlan hoped that the experience gained from being in the company of one of the world's most feared men up close, would deter his son's young eager mind in following in his footsteps, and cause him to find other pursuits in life. Deep down though, Harlan knew how stubborn and relentless the Kruellar blood ran in his family, especially more so in the men. If Haven truly believed in his heart that he was ready to do something, then there was nothing that anyone could say or do, to change his mind, "Okay then, son…when we land, you follow my every lead. You do ONLY as I say, and not question my authority whatsoever! Is that understood?" Harlan asked prudently. His son's face lit up as bright as the full moon that could be seen through Haven's window seat, "You can count on me dad, I won't let you down!" Haven said excitedly. Though his tone was very serious, Harlan could not hold back his smile and leaned back into his seat and re-opened his newspaper, "Good, now be quiet and let your old man enjoy his paper!" Harlan said jokingly, Haven laughed at his father's infallibility concerning his age, "Come on dad, you're not that old!" Haven said caringly. Harlan continued to smile while reading his newspaper, "Um-hum…" Harlan said sarcastically. Haven sat back into his seat and peered out his window, as if he lost something among the clouds, "Dad?" Haven asked. Harlan remained fixated on the stock market report in his newspaper, "Um-hum?" Harlan answered irritably, "I love you." Haven said solemnly. Harlan could tell that something else was on his son's heart as he noticed a change in Haven's tone. In Harlan Kruellar's previous experience, when someone told him that they loved him in that same manner of tone they were either going away for a long time or, just before they were about to die. Harlan lowered his newspaper down just enough to see over it and saw Haven staring despondently through the glass. The grave expression on his son's face was making him feel conflicted again, an emotion he could ill afford where they were heading. But, instead of following his first mind to question his son's abbreviated emotions, decided to let it go, "I love you too, son…" Harlan said humbly. His father's warm sentiment broke Haven's piercing gaze outside his window as if it was unexpected. Telling his son "I love you" should have not been anything new to haven's ears, Harlan thought, which did not explain the contrived look on his son's face after smiling at him before giving the luminous sky even more of his personal attention. Harlan believed that their relationship had grown somewhat stronger after his wife passed, but for the last couple years he could sense a slight change in Haven's attitude. He was trying way too hard to become his own man and that made Harlan a little apprehensive in giving him more responsibility. Either way, they were landing very soon, and whatever else that was bothering his son would just have to wait until they returned home, Harlan thought.

Many, many, years ago…

During the early 1940's, just as WWII started, Harlan's immigrant family fled from Germany to America. They eventually settled down in Corona, Queens in New York City, where his mother Agatha mopped floors part time at a glue factory, while his father Hugo was a promising shoemaker, a trade passed down through generations in his father's family. That tradition though, came to an abrupt end after Harlan was born. Harlan had long decided that shoemaking was not what he was meant to do with his life. Even though he grew up poorer than the other kids at school, his parents never allowed him to go without anything. When she was not working, his mother taught him how to play classical music on an old piano his father found by a dumpster. She taught him how to appreciate the beauty of music and other fine arts. Playing the piano was never his passion, but seeing how much his playing the piano pleased his mother, made learning it all the more tolerable. Hugo on the other hand never seemed to have time for anything. To keep food on the table and clothing on their backs, Hugo worked both days and nights at a small shoe shop called McKindle's in Rego Park, Queens. He worked for an old Irishman named Scotty McKindle, who once owned the shop with his brother Johnny. At the time, Johnny McKindle was a gifted craftsman that did all the shoemaking and repairing, while Scotty kept up with the book keeping side of the things. After Johnny died of pneumonia, Scotty had a hard time dealing with the loss of his kid brother and started drinking heavily every day, until fate stepped in and Scotty ran into Hugo, literally. It happened one very snowy Christmas night, when Scotty tried to drive himself home from a local pub in Corona, despite having too much to drink. Coincidentally, Hugo himself was also looking to drown away his own sorrows that night and was crossing the street from the liquor store. Scotty was trying to light his Peterson smoking pipe and accidently dropped the match into his lap. When he took his eyes off the icy road to pick up the lit match, he smacked dead into the unsuspecting Hugo Kruellar. Fortunately for Hugo nothing on him was broken. The stumbling Scotty McKindle dashed from out his dark green Buick Super to offer him some immediate assistance. He felt bad for nearly killing the sluggish Hugo, especially on Christmas Eve, and tried to offer him money for his trouble. Hugo Kruellar was a very proud man and instead asked him for his help to find work. Hugo told Scotty about the trouble he was having trying to find decent work since America declared war against his native Germany. Even in his drunken state, Scotty could tell that Hugo was being completely sincere and asked him his occupation. After Hugo told him that he was a shoemaker, old man Scotty McKindle exploded into tears and fell down to his worn out knees, ignoring the skin piecing snow. What little pain Hugo was feeling began to dissipate, as now it was his turn to feel sorry for the elder Scotty McKindle. It was obvious that he was in much more emotional distress than he was, and asked the old man his reasons for weeping so. The old man cleared his throat before he spoke, "Because God has a funny sense of humor…" Scotty explained. Hugo had a perplexing expression upon his square chinned face that begged for an explanation. Scotty explained to Hugo about how he felt responsible for the death of his brother Johnny, who hid his pneumonia illness up until the day that he died. He told him how he carried the guilt for months and how he could not bring himself to close down the shoe store, despite almost going completely broke. Hugo stood to his feet and knocked the snow from his pants, then offered Scotty his hand to stand. Scotty hesitated at first to take his hand, as he was still in his own feelings, but finally gave it to him. When they got to their feet, Hugo introduced himself, as Scotty did so likewise. It had been a long time coming, but for a mere moment, Hugo Kruellar was able to forget his own circumstance long enough to encourage someone other than himself, "You just made the first step…" He told Scotty. Scotty was starting to believe that the combination of the alcohol and cold weather was making his mind numb, "First step to what?" Scotty asked, "…In getting up, after you fall. The only thing left is to dust yourself off!" Hugo told him. Despite him being emotionally unsure, Scotty took the young man's advice. Impressed by Hugo's resolve and character, Scotty McKindle insisted on hiring him, and he happily accepted. Hugo's presence at McKindle's shoe store did not bode well in the beginning. The Jewish community made up the majority of the McKindle's business in Rego Park. But, because of the Holocaust mass murders that took place in Germany, they wanted no parts of McKindle's business as long as Hugo was there. But the indiscriminate Scotty McKindle was color blind and knew Hugo's heart, and believed he was more a victim than a part of the systematic behavior that went on in his former country. The McKindle's shoe store struggled to stay open for many years, but Scotty did not care what people thought about his friend. It was not until the neighborhood became more culturally diversified that things looked as if they would prosper for the small shoe store. Hugo would go on working for McKindle's for over the next twenty years until both Scotty and Hugo's untimely death…

Harlan's private jet….

Harlan managed to rest his eyes at least a couple minutes prior to his plane's co-pilot Captain Fredrick Hurst alerted him, "Excuse the interruption sir, but you asked me to give you a heads up before we landed. We will be touching down in Guerrero, Mexico in the next ten minutes!" Captain Hurst said. Harlan could feel a slight headache coming on and rubbed the inside of his eyes to circulate the pressure it was causing, "Oh, okay, thanks Fredrick." Harlan said quietly, "No problem sir." Captain Hurst said, and walked back to the plane's cockpit. Harlan's throat was also feeling slightly parched, so he reached out to take a drink from his water bottle and noticed that Haven was sleeping. It had been a long time since he last watched his son resting so peacefully and the scene caused Harlan to feel a little bit nostalgic. He marveled at both how much time had passed and at how much his handsome son had grown. Harlan Kruellar tried his best to find a proper balance between family and business, and wondered if he prioritized too much of his time towards business. Though his father Hugo never made much money, it never stopped him from trying to become the best provider he could be for his family. Harlan could not see it then at the time, because of his own selfish ambitions. Those ambitions almost proved his undoing and what lead to his father's early demise. Hugo Kruellar always envisioned his son taking up the same trade that kept his family fed throughout the generations, but after watching his father struggle financially Harlan's entire life, and suffering through prejudice, made Harlan think otherwise. The makeup of their father and son relationship was very different from the one he shared with his son Haven. Because he rejected going to work at McKindle's after graduating from high school, a void was created between the two. Harlan believed he was destined for greater endeavors, and did not want the stench of a dead end job holding him back. He became fascinated with boats as a young teenager and dreamed of owning his own yacht one day. To be around the thing he loved, Harlan convinced his best friend at the time Emilio Cortez, to get jobs at the U.S. Navy shipyard in Brooklyn. Emilio's family never had much money either, and Harlan would listen to him go on and on about how many millions of dollars that the transporting industry brought in. Working at that shipyard was where Harlan decided what he wanted to do with the rest of his life and eventually made himself into a very wealthy and powerful man.

Harlan's private jet landed at Acapulco International Airport around nine o'clock, which left them with half an hour to get to their next destination. In his mind, Mexico was just too unpredictable and played by its own rules, which made Harlan uneasy. He made sure that there was enough security in place for both him and his son for where they were heading. When they got off the plane there were to two stretch limousines on the ground waiting. After their plane's co-pilot opened the cockpit, Haven could instantly smell the sea. The night sky was incredible as every star in the world could be seen from the ground and the weather was slightly warm with a light 70 degree breeze. Haven had hoped that he and his father would make time after their business is conducted to go enjoy the sights. As they made their way down the boarding stairs, the sound of another car engine could be heard in the background. Haven was confused by the arrival of the third limo, "Three limo's dad?" Haven asked confused. Harlan gave his son a reassuring look, and waved his hand at the people inside to get out, "You're my only son, and I'm not taking any chances!" Harlan said sternly. When the large group of men filed out of the limousines simultaneously, it looked like a small army in Haven's mind. Harlan was paranoid by nature and thought it was more than worth paying the extra two million dollars to hire the twenty former mercenary and secret service men to procure them on this trip. The man waiting for him was every bit as powerful in Mexico as he was in America, and could not be trusted, Harlan thought. Two of the bodyguards escorted them to their limousine and shut the door and got inside the front seat and started the car. Haven was grinning ear to ear and it was beginning to bug his father, "Why do you have that silly grin on your face? You wouldn't be smiling that hard if you really knew who we're about to meet." Harlan said grimly. But, Haven could not help himself, "Look, I know it's bad that I'm doing it, but even you have to admit how badass we look with all these guys!?!" Haven said proudly. Harlan leaned toward his son who was sitting across from him, "If you know it's bad, then stop fucking doing it!" Harlan said coldly. Haven was taken by surprise by his father's demeanor. He was not used to seeing his father out of his own element and immediately stopped smiling, "How many times have I told you to never underestimate anyone or, overestimating yourself? It's that sort of thinking that will get you an early grave Haven, you should know better!" Harlan scolded, and leaned back into his seat. Harlan could see that his harsh words angered his son, which was something he worked hard at trying to avoid. Things were complicated enough before Harlan lost his own father and never wanted to go through those issues with his son, "Haven, I know what it is that you're wanting, but in order to attain it, you must be willing to listen to my every instruction, follow my every lead or, you won't survive. It's a very big world out there and there are rules that even I must follow. Some things can't be taken for granted, not even your family. Promise me you won't make the same mistakes I made son!?!" Harlan pleaded. Haven let out a large breath, "Okay." Haven said dismissively, while showing his car window more attention. Harlan leaned forward again, "Okay?" Harlan asked. Haven turned his head around, "Okay…sir." Haven said, with contempt. Harlan could not figure out what had been going on in Haven's mind and wondered had he made a mistake in letting him off the plane. It was too late either way, as they were already tiptoeing inside the devil's own backyard.

Not very long ago…

Harlan grew up in a modest home in the lower class part of Corona, Queens and quickly found himself constantly at odds with some of the other kids that did not take school as seriously as he was forced to. Both of his parents worked themselves too hard to notice the type of violence their son was going through just to get to school each day. It always felt like a lifetime ago whenever he reflected over his childhood, but it seem that way when reminiscing about Haven's conception. He could remember vividly being on vacation with his late wife Marisa, in the Cayman Islands, as if it just happened yesterday. They owned a quaint 4,000 square foot home on the East End shore. On that morning, Harlan was quietly enjoying his breakfast on the patio when she told him the news. The both of them were ecstatic about the pregnancy after being told Marisa could not have any children. Marisa believed in her heart that the son, she was told she could not have, was going to be someone special one day. She grew up a devout Catholic and wanted to give her son both a strong and spiritual name. After giving it a lot of thought they came up with Haven, which meant "a safe place of refuge." Though Haven, on the other hand, would grow up to accuse his dad of trying to keep the "H" in their names going. During his days as a toddler, Haven had been unusually smart and very independent. Unlike most children his age, he learned how to potty train himself and walk before turning two-years old. Since his son showed so much promise at an early age, Harlan made sure that Haven was enrolled in the finest East Coast private schools his money could buy. Haven excelled in all his courses at every level in school, just as Harlan once did as a child, but Haven was the better athlete of the two. His son was very active and made it his business to never miss one Lacrosse, basketball, football, soccer, etc…game Haven had ever participated in, from his pre-teen years up until his high school graduation. Haven was supposed to be the one who was going to get the things right that Harlan and his father could not. Harlan wanted so badly for Haven to be his own man and not follow in his crooked footsteps. What Haven did not realize was that his father had a dark side as well, and that people had either been killed by his order or by Harlan himself. He believed himself a remorseless monster and could not stomach the idea of his son being likewise. But, Harlan could not stop his impressionistic son from idolizing the ground he walked on. Even though Haven had aspirations to go beyond his father's successful path, he realized that he could not do so from the confines of his overbearing shadow. Haven long suspected his father's involvement with the criminal world, but it was not enough to scare him away from achieving his self-serving quest. The main ingredient that Haven truly believed that was holding him back in his dad's eyes was his lack of street smarts.

When his son was old enough, Harlan tried placing him in managerial type positions at his more legit side businesses, but Haven's hard work and attention to detail was an immediate asset and could not be ignored. The more tasks Harlan put on his intelligent son to complete, the more responsibility he demanded. Haven worked around the clock to prove himself a worthy successor. When he was little, Haven loved to ease drop on his father's personal phone conversations, or when he held his private meetings in his office at home. Nothing made him giggle more than to hear the dad that spoke sweet and encouraging words to him one minute, but then threaten to feed a man his own testicles at the next one. What Haven did not know, was that anytime Harlan Kruellar made a threat against someone's life, one could rest assure it would be carried out. It did not take his father to have an amazing and intimidating body like Terry Crews to instill fear into his enemies or, his allies. It only took what his enormous wealth bought him…incredible power. His German born father had a very slender build and possessed more hair on his goatee than his entire head. To keep from standing out in public, Harlan would dress as meagerly as possible. Taking his lumps in Corona taught him not to stand out, so in public he always dressed down. He would wear khakis with a brown corduroy jacket or, black sports coat to fit in and plaid button down shirts underneath with brown penny loafers. Harlan often discouraged his son to carry himself in a flashy sort of manner, as he believed it put a person at a disadvantage, "When you learn to conceal yourself among strangers on the streets, it allows you to learn their true intentions for you," he would say. He often tried to give his overzealous son useful advice, but because Haven graduated summa cum laude and carried higher testosterone levels than he did, he thought his classroom education and athletic prowess could translate in the streets. Haven pleaded with him for over two weeks to accompany him on his business trip to Mexico.

Despite knowing the potential for danger would be greater there, Harlan gave in nevertheless, as he loved his son's remarkable enthusiasm and him even more. Harlan owned a fleet of freightliners and a few cargo boats that he often used to smuggle everything from illegal drugs, to guns for the military. He was able to amass close to a billion dollars a year and managed to avoid the IRS by paying them off or donating to charity. Marisa believed Harlan made a better politician than crook when she was still alive, but Harlan would always tell her, "Honey, the only difference between me and the politicians, is that they need to hide behind a killer slogan and a podium to fuck you over!" He would say. She never cared for violence and would often plead for him to go back to being a legit businessman. But, Harlan knew that in his line of work that after you cross that line, there was no more "legit." His hands were either too dirty, or knew too much about the wrong thing to give up the only life he ever lived, and they knew that the only way out for him would be death. They lived happily together for ten years before she succumbed unexpectedly to heart failure, a condition they both were unaware she had. Harlan had taken her death very personally and had her body buried on his property in Houston, the city from which she was born. Haven was blessed with his mother's pure athleticism and natural good looks, but also Harlan's keen intellect. Harlan had met, then Marisa Chaney, during her first trek to New York City long ago. She was there playing in a women's tennis tournament at Brooklyn College, while Harlan was there spoiling a colleague that had a daughter playing in the tournament as well. When it was Marisa's turn to play, Harlan was initially floored by her beauty. Harlan watched her intently from his private section as Marisa played her heart out against a formidable opponent, but unfortunately lost her match. He could tell from his future wife's reaction that she was deeply wounded by the loss, especially when she was rated as the highest ranked opponent before going into the match. In the very beginning, before exchanging their wedding vows, that it pained Harlan's soul to see Marisa hurt and seized the opportunity to do something about it. By the time Marisa returned to her hotel room that evening, she opened the door and to her surprise, it was filled to the brim with dozens upon dozens of flower bouquets, along with a small white envelope. Marisa was extremely flattered by the exotic sight and tantalizing smells that engulfed the entire room. She frantically opened the tiny envelope and found a card inside. On the card it read that the flowers were from a huge admirer who wanted to take her out for dinner and would be waiting for her anxiously in the lobby of the Motel 6. Marisa humbly accepted the invitation by getting changed into a sexy satin blue dress she had packed just in case she might need it, and made her way to the lobby. The lobby appeared empty when she first arrived, except for the lone person sitting quietly on the posh grey sofa and reading a Time Life magazine. Marisa did not know what to make of Harlan at first. His moderate attire did not actually scream dinner by candlelight, despite Harlan paying for the room full of expensive flowers, Marisa thought. Though Marisa was not particularly materialistic or, vain by any stretch of the imagination, part of her was at least expecting the author of her mysterious note to look like George Clooney and not a librarian. Harlan could tell that the beautiful tennis phenom was put off by his casual wear and reassured her that he was a gentleman. He introduced himself as a "simple travel investor" that just wanted to treat his favorite athlete to dinner after a hard loss. Marisa could not help but feel intrigued by the mild looking Harlan Kruellar or, his offer. It also did not hurt that he had a massive limo waiting for them by the Motel 6 entrance, she would later disclose jokingly to her future husband. There was also something else about Harlan that stood out when talking to him she noticed. Marisa did not need the psychology training (she minored in at Texas A&M) at school to not only see Harlan's true sincerity, but also signs of a deep emotional pain that he possibly was holding back. Nevertheless, the young blonde needed to vent her frustrations to someone and felt like Harlan could be trusted.

The star struck tourist in her wanted to gaze upon the many vaunted bright lights of Manhattan, since she had never been there before. She was impressed to hear about the Italian restaurant that he owned there, called Sergio's. They talked and drank chilled champagne during their extensive evening drive. Harlan surprised Marisa again, but this time with a small white gift box that had a golden bow on top it, that he pulled from his sports coat. Marisa was floored by the gleaming diamond pearl necklace she found inside after opening it and began to cry. Harlan had been confused by her emotional outburst, and worried if the necklace was too much. He began to apologize and offered to take her back to the Motel 6 immediately, if she was feeling uncomfortable. Marisa took her hands away from her glistening face and started wiping the running mascara that had left two faint lines off her cheeks and eyes. She threatened to hit him with her tennis racket if he tried, then confessed how Harlan turned one of the worst days of her life into one of her best. It was music to Harlan's ears and promised her that it was just the beginning, only if she wanted to continue. Marisa leaned in and placed a soft deep kiss on his lips to signify her feelings. They both would go on to have one of the best nights of their lives in the "city where nobody ever sleeps." They would eventually get married on a beach in Jamaica, and Marisa received her degree from school, despite her never needing it after marrying a multi-millionaire. She later gave birth to her only child, Haven, before her life was prematurely cut short. The couple lived blissfully in their brief amount of time together, and in his mind, Harlan would reflect on those much happier times in order to handle the pressures that come with doing the evil he now does. As far back as Harlan Kruellar could remember all he ever set out to do in the world was to dominate his circumstances and make a family of his own. In his conquest to rid his self of repeating the same destitute existence that his father and father's father lived, Harlan stepped on whomever he had to or, killed if he had to, to achieve his present wealthy status. Mistakes were made along the way that got people he knew and loved killed in the process. Haven was the only thing Harlan had left to live for, and promised Marisa that he would not do anything that would endanger him. Unfortunately, in the real world promises do have a way of getting themselves broken…

Downtown Acapulco…

Haven did not know what to expect when their driver took him and his father through downtown Acapulco. He had visited many places for a man barely in his twenties, but never had he been to Mexico. It was during spring break, and the city's nightlife appeared as if it exploded and left heavenly bodies walking everywhere, Haven thought. Haven watched out the window as they passed every bar and club on the south side strip, and wondered what the music could be like there. Even the restaurants were filled to capacity as they continued through the city and towards an undisclosed destination. The destination was only undisclosed to Haven at least, and it made him believe that his father was holding something back. His father had not spoken one word since they first left Acapulco International, and Haven was beginning to wonder if he was still angry with him. Haven never liked being angry with his father, but he could not help appreciating his situation. Never had he had the pleasure of travelling with so much armed muscle and for a moment, felt invincible. But, his father hated him showing pride in anything that he did, especially when Haven played sports. Because he was always considered the best athlete on every team he participated on, being football, basketball, etc…that overconfidence would most times, rear its ugly head and lead him to not depending on his teammates. It also would lead him to the pleasure of hearing one hour lectures from his coaches, and Harlan. He struggled with being the best at things and being quiet about his successes, which also did not sit well with his father. Haven could not seem to understand his father's reasoning for being so secretive about everything he did. The things he did that were against the law Haven could understand, but not when it came to "being the man." His dad has so much power, so many connects on the street, not to mention financial freedom, and refused to ever enjoy it, Haven contemplated. He also starts to think about some of the lateral moves that he had been making on the side that his father was supposed to be unaware of. Haven was fronting some of the money from his trust fund to buy his way into the transport business, but with the help of one of his father's competitors, his god uncle Emilio Cortez. Emilio was not in the same financial stratosphere as his father, but had enough juice to get him on his feet in the industry without the reliance of his dad. He knew that if his father ever discovered that he went to Uncle Emilio for such a thing, that it would be bad for the both of them. Though he never witnessed Harlan be the man to pull the trigger or, be the one to slice open a person's throat, it did not mean he could not put in the order, Haven grimly thought. Either way, he knew he had to tread carefully concerning the situation, at least until he made enough off his investment to get out from under his father's wing. He was a young man on a mission and refused to stray from the same path that his father once took at his age. Since his father began with nothing when he first started, it gave Haven the impression that his destiny would be far greater, because he grew up under better circumstances. But, with every illusion that life sought to provide, reality oftentimes has a nasty way of disturbing ones dreams, or even keeping a person permanently sleeping.

They were travelling east for the last fifteen minutes and the further they drove through town the less could be seen of the city's fabulous glamour. The car window on Haven's side had been partially cracked open, allowing the aroma of the coastal shore to quickly fill the inside of the limousine. Harlan could almost taste the sea salt in the warm air. It reminded him again about vacationing with Marisa and her fondness for being in the water. Harlan bought them a beach house in Galveston once, where they would sometimes go for short getaways whenever they were in Texas. The sound of the ocean's waves felt orthopedic for her, and also reminded Marisa of how her mother and father used to take her there when she was a child, Harlan remembered. He really enjoyed listening to her share her old childhood memories. Harlan reminisces on the way her face would glow with youthful exuberance whenever she spoke about her parents, causing him to sometimes envy her. As for Harlan, most of his childhood memories only brought back painful thoughts of anguish and death. Judging from the well trimmed landscaping, Harlan could tell that they were close to making their first stop. Acapulco, Guerrero was known for more than its celebratory exclusivity and spectacular ambiance, but also for its gang rivalries. Special previsions had to be made before arriving or, the gangsters would have been lining up to hold them hostage, he figured. To keep Haven safe, Harlan rented an old museum that was close by, giving him the chance of escaping Mexico in case something went wrong.

It was almost 9:30 and Haven wondered how much longer would he have to put up with his father's silent treatment? Finally, the limo pulled into a strange jagged piece of land. He could not make it out, but Haven could see a structure at the top that looked like an old small castle. The limousine parked at the front of the odd looking building and Haven saw a yellow sign with red lettering that said, "Museo Historico de Acapulco." He knew the English translation meant Acapulco Historical Museum, and wondered what they could possibly be doing there. Haven's door swung open from the outside, "Here's your stop." Harlan said, "You're not coming in? I don't under…" Haven began to ask, but was interrupted. "It's for your own good, and no one will ever know that you're here. I won't be long." Harlan instructed. Haven started frowning, "This is so fucked up…" He said. Harlan leaned closer towards Haven, "What the hell did you just say to me?" Harlan asked angrily, "It's not fair! You were supposed to be giving me a chance!" Haven yelled back. Harlan was confused by his son's outburst, "Your chance at what, to possibly die? The man I'm going to meet doesn't play by any rules…he doesn't need to in his own city. If you look around Haven, you can obviously see we are a long ass way from home! I have to keep you protected…" Harlan explained, "Keep me protected, or just trying to hold me back? Well guess what dad? I'm not a little kid anymore, so quit always trying to always protect me!" Haven shouted. Harlan was hurt by his son's lack of respect and did not want to mix his emotions anymore than they already were, "I don't have time for this. I don't know what's gotten into you, Haven, but if you want to be a man, to go out on your own, then I won't stop you. But, until we get back home you will still do as I say. Now, I'm running late to my business meeting, so please, get the fuck out the car!" Harlan demanded. Haven did not speak a word and got out of the limousine and slammed the door. This was a complication that he felt he could seriously do without. Haven was so blinded by his own misguided crusade that there may never be any way to reach him, Harlan thought. A few moments pass and then Haven's door opened up and it was one of Harlan's bodyguards, "Your son is secured Mr.Kruellar." He said. Temptation did not want him to leave his son mad at him, but part of him was already beyond eager to leave Mexico, despite whatever the sinister Alfonso Barrera really wanted. In his experience, when family becomes unbalanced due to "business" affecting it, one could not possibly succeed without the other. The only family Harlan had left in existence was trying his best to not see things eye to eye with him, and trying too hard to be the man he could never be, Harlan contemplated. They live in a "dog eat dog world" and Haven did not have enough "dog" in him to last one day on his own, "Alright…we can go, Mr. Johnson." Harlan solemnly told his bodyguard and took one last glance at the museum entrance where Haven stormed off in. Harlan's limousine pulled off as well as another, while the third team in the last limousine stayed behind to protect his son. Harlan Kruellar had every right to fear the man that the F.B.I. dubbed the Guerrero Butcher. Not many men get invitations to see Alfonso Barrera and live to tell about it, He contemplated. But, Harlan did not scare easily and lived by a code of respecting his enemies at all cost, no matter how much power they did or did not possess. Alfonso's reach stretched all the way to the United States with at least a reported twelve thousand gang members that represented his "Los Locos Confederados" or, "The Crazy

Conferderates" army. With that being said, a man with that amount of men under his control could be either one great ally or one gigantic problem, he thought, so Harlan was very motivated to get a deal done. It was not easy leaving his son in the hands of mostly strangers, but they were paid handsomely to keep him protected and Harlan also promised them a bonus once they completed their security detail. Haven stares off into the evening sky and trying to forgive himself for cursing his proud father. Deep down inside, Haven knew that he truly cared about his wellbeing and only wanted to keep him safe, but that was the one underlining point to the entire problem in his mind. He wanted to be man enough to make his own decisions, to step out and conquer the world like his dad did. No more did he want to have to wait to be a "somebody," when he can be that somebody today. His time was now to make his move, Haven thought. Haven was in his thought so deep that he had not realized it when one of his bodyguards approached him, "Excuse me Mr. Kruellar, but are you okay? Do you need me to get you anything, a beverage perhaps?" The bodyguard asked, "Huh, oh, n-no. I'm good, but thanks!" Haven said, "Are you sure about that, sir? You positive you don't need a coke or, a body bag to keep you cool, perhaps?" The bodyguard politely asked, "No thank you, I'm fine. Wait a minute…" Haven asked. The bodyguard gave Haven a sympathetic look, "What's wrong sir?" He asked. Haven assumed that the water from the ocean nearby must have been affecting his hearing, "Never mind, it's nothing…just keep your eyes open!" Haven said and began to walk away, "Whatever you say Haven." The bodyguard said assuredly. Haven whipped his head around to face the brazen bodyguard, "Haven? Look…uh?" Haven asked. The bodyguard frowned as if hurt, "Santiago." He said. Looking annoyed, "Well, San-ti-ago…Mr. Kruellar will do!" Haven said. The bodyguard turned his lip up at the young man, "You'll never be like your daddy…" He said. Haven froze in his tracks. He could not figure out what exactly where the man who was supposed to be paid to protect and listen to him was coming from. Surely his father would not agree with the man's unprofessionalism, "That will be enough. Now…go do your fucking job already, asshole!" Haven ordered. The bodyguard stood quietly as if he were a parent watching a small toddler throwing a tantrum, but then finally broke his silence, "Okay." The bodyguard said, and then rushed the overmatched Haven. Haven was slammed to the ground and knocked unconscious by the cement. The bodyguard chuckled to himself as if he were reliving a joke he might have once heard. He went into his jacket pocket and pulled out a cell phone and dialed. When the person he called answered, "Yeah it's me, the jobs done! He wants me to do what…you sure? No, it's no problem. Okay." The bodyguard said, and hung up the line. The rogue bodyguard smiled and went into his pocket and pulled out a large jagged blade and kneeled down beside Haven. Not in the deepest darkest corners of his worst nightmares could Haven have imagined himself going through such awful suffering, especially at the hands of someone he was supposed to have trusted with his life. As he bleeds accordingly over the rigid pavement, Haven Kruellar begins to witness firsthand the very real danger he had taken for granted at his father's behest. Very soon, the young and once former outstanding student/athlete Haven Kruellar will be forced to endure the unfortunate experience of becoming father's nightmare come true. Harlan's argumentative son forsaken to stay under the umbrella of protection he tried to provide him. After each cut made to his tender flesh, he cries and screams, and in the recesses of his mind, regretting that decision to forsake his father's wisdom.

Intermission: The birth and the legend of Alfonso Barrera

Reputed Mexican Cartel leader and mass murderer, Alfonso Barrera, is widely acknowledged by most governments today as being one of the most feared men in the entire world. He garnered that dastardly distinction by ordering the deaths of thousands in his country alone. His Crazy Confederate gang is responsible for countless civilian abduction's as well, especially those foreign to his native land of Mexico. He is also one of the United States top cocaine and marijuana distributers, keeping him comfortably at the top of the F.B.I.'s most wanted list. Alfonso Barrera's latest business interests had become human trafficking, and sought to expand on his heinous enterprise. The Crazy Confederate gang had been growing in mass numbers, therefore causing his American politician friends to become even more nervous and greedy, and making it difficult to operate in the states. To avoid detection from the American authorities, he inquired the transporting expertise of one Harlan Kruellar, of Harlan Imperial Express, who came highly recommended for both his discretion and knack for slipping through customs. He also heard about Harlan's penchant for being particular when it came to his services. But, like all men that craved money and power, Alfonso Barrera did not care who he needed to step on to gain or, retain it. Despite his stubborn Mexican pride, Alfonso knew he needed Harlan Kruellar's help to maintain his foothold in the United States criminal underworld. There were no limits, lengths, or any depths that he would not sink to, to get whatever it was he wanted. The word "no" was never received well by the infamous drug lord, which meant an automatic death sentence to all unwilling participants of any of his greedy endeavors. As a self proclaimed businessman, Alfonso Barrera also saw intimidation as a very handy "business" tactic and had no plans of taking no for an answer. He believed a possible business venture between him and the illustrious Harlan Kruellar, was just too great an opportunity to be taken lightly, and would open up doors for his organization that were closed on a global level. Alfonso Barrera "the millionaire" salivated at the idea of becoming Alfonso Barrera "the Billionaire," and would stop at nothing to make his dream a reality. One way or another Harlan Kruellar "was" going to help him…rather he wanted to willingly, or not.

Culiacan, Mexico sometime during the 1970's…

Before he became the internationally feared "Alfonso Barrera," the forty-two year old was born Emmanuel Vasquez, an orphan from the deadly streets of Culiacan, Sinaloa. Life in urban Culiacan was more than rough for Emmanuel, especially at a very young age. Shortly after being born, little Emmanuel was found in a damp shoebox near the dumpster of an old village orphanage. Days had passed before he was finally discovered, by the other children from the orphanage, among the remnants of the other discarded trash and filth that littered the garbage area. His newborn body was uncomfortably stuffed inside the musty box and wrapped in an old potato bag with a note and his name attached. Emmanuel was taken to the owner of the orphanage and it was soon discovered Emmanuel was suffering from pneumonia. Luckily for him, a young American nurse named Amy Whetstone was there visiting the Culiacan village, who happened to be doing some volunteer work to earn extra college credits. She was able to stabilize his fever and Emmanuel eventually got better. Unfortunately, as time moved on, the same could not be said about the rest of his stay there. During the 1970's, the chances of an abandoned child being adopted in Culiacan were slim to none, due to the state's poor economy and left him to become just another stranded statistic. Emmanuel had to learn at an early age how to defend himself from the many tormentors he lived with at the small orphanage. With each passing year, the older kids would constantly chastise and muscle him for any scraps he happened upon. That common courtesy only lasted a short while though, after Emmanuel savagely gouged out the eyes of one of his protagonists with a broken broom handle in the boys shower. After that incident no one in the orphanage would attempt to lay a hand on him, that is until a new cook arrived. Former Sgt. Cesar Alberto Ruiz was an ex-Mexican Federales washout who could not find decent work after he allegedly sexually assaulted another fellow officer's young daughter. He got the cooking job at the orphanage with the help of a cousin who also worked there as a janitor. It didn't take long for Cesar's pedophilic urges to kick in and started molesting some of the orphaned children. Out of fear, none of the children ever spoke against Cesar, as he threatened to end their lives in their sleep. Cesar soon set his sights on the greatly revered and unsuspecting Emmanuel and managed to convince him to stay up late one night to help clean the food pantry. The much older Cesar waited for his opportunity when everyone else was asleep and forced himself on Emmanuel. He had young Emmanuel pinned against the wall by his neck inside the small walk-in food pantry and threatened to break it if he screamed. What Cesar Ruiz did not know, was how cool and calculating Emmanuel Vasquez really was, and allowed the mentally disturbed Cesar to get his quick moment of cheap fills and thrills. Cesar gloated about what he had planned to do to the young man and began rubbing both Emmanuel and himself with his free hand. When he went to stick his hand down inside the front of Emmanuel's pants, something inside them pricked his hand. After Cesar released his neck to check his bleeding hand, Emmanuel dug inside his jeans and pulled out the blade he had stashed inside his underwear and started stabbing him repeatedly, as if he was making holes in a pickle jar for a new found insect to breathe from. Cesar begged for his life, but Emmanuel did not care, and slit the man's throat. Fearing he would no doubt face jail time for Cesar's murder, Emmanuel ran away from the oppressive orphanage and decided to change his name to the alias "Alfonso Barrera" to disguise his true identity. The teenaged Alfonso Barrera, aka Emmanuel Vasquez, grudgingly fled the northern Culiacan village and headed down the southern coast of Sinaloa.

With no money or, home of his own, Alfonso Barrera was forced to find refuge in the city of Mazatlan, and under the wing of a vicious local street gang, who then called themselves "The Bloody Sinaloa Brothers." The gang was comprised of mainly young boys whose ages ranged from ten and up. Like their menacing namesake, they carried out malicious maiming and killings against the other rival gang members or, anyone else who threatened their small, but deadly enterprise. Their founding leader was twenty-three-year old Roberto "The Hatchet man" Del Rico, who allegedly decapitated at least thirty men and women. He ran their base of operations from out of the same mechanic shop he owned. The Bloody Sinaloa Brother's was just in its criminal infancy, while their chief rival gang "The Murder Marauders," had already been previously established across the city. To keep up with the growing inflation of Murder Marauders near his eastern territory, Del Rico had resorted to intimidating non-gang affiliated teenagers to join the Sinaloa Brother's. Alfonso had been shoplifting from one of the tourist gift store's Del Rico routinely shook down, when he offered Alfonso a place in his criminal organization, once he survived his gang's initiation. In order to become a Bloody Sinaloa Brother, one prospect had to be able to survive a knife fight between them and three other current lower level members. If a prospect managed not to bleed to death, he would have earned his "rightful" place within the brotherhood. During his initiation, Alfonso was forced to fight against three older teenaged Sinaloa members, and wound up killing two of them in the process. Roberto Del Rico marveled at Alfonso's will to live, youthful ferocity, and lack of remorse, and made sure that he kept a sharp eye on him. Killing had become second nature to the impressionistic Barrera, who soon gained plenty of respect from his fellow Sinaloa brethren for being so ruthless and unmerciful towards their enemies, and quickly became Roberto Del Rico's most entrusted enforcer. It was with Alfonso's help primarily, that garnered The Bloody Sinaloa Brother's a fierce reputation across all of Sinaloa, as well as the remaining Mexican borrows. When the criminal status of the Bloody Sinaloa Brother's rose, it granted them foreign alliances with both Korean and Columbian drug distributors, who would take Del Rico's street operation to new financial heights. With his gang now using high powered weapons, Del Rico was able to crush The Murder Marauder gang and Mazatlan, as well as the other adjourning states, were soon flooded with heroin, marijuana, and cocaine that were supplied by the Sinaloa Brother's. Del Rico had become a millionaire drug lord before the age of thirty-years-old and accomplished it on the adolescent shoulders of his young apprentice Alfonso Barrera. But, just like any average barrel full of sea crabs, Alfonso was about to learn the hard way what it felt like to be drug down by one of his own.

After a few years, Alfonso's rise within the ranks eventually hit a huge snag along the way. One of Roberto Del Rico's top lieutenants, twenty-year-old Raul Rena, never liked Alfonso, although the feeling was mutual. Raul had a reputation for being too opportunistic to gain favor and two-faced towards his fellow comrades, traits Alfonso despised. Out of animosity, Raul tried to convince impressionistic Del Rico that he was losing face with some of the other members, because he was showing too much favoritism towards the ascending Alfonso. Del Rico was not easily persuaded though, and dismissed Raul's advice as him being too paranoid. His apathetical response did not sit well with the deceitful Raul. In the past, he could easily coax Del Rico into trusting his opinions, but now feared he was losing favor because of Alfonso's presence. Raul figured he only had two choices if he wanted to get rid of him, set Alfonso up to look incompetent or, kill him. Not wanting to complicate matters, Raul decided to do both. As long as he could remember, Roberto Del Rico had been madly in love with his second cousin Norma since they were kids, but found himself at the mercy of both his family's possible disapproval (his mother Rosario especially) and her then husband Jose Lara. Del Rico wanted Norma very badly and ultimately had the husband killed in a drive-by shooting, during their honeymoon in Miami, Florida. Unknowingly to Norma, Del Rico would continue to secretly threaten the life of every man she ever tried to date or, that showed any serious interest in her. Despite his dubious position as the head of a criminal organization, Del Rico still respected his family and his mother's strict Catholic beliefs. It was because of that lone factor he knew he could never have Norma, but saw to it that nobody else would either. Raul long suspected Del Rico's private infatuation with his cousin, due to the ridiculous lengths he took in keeping her single, and devised a plan that would use this knowledge to his advantage. As chance would soon have it, Norma came to pay Del Rico a visit at his new three-story brick home, near Olas Altas Beach during the summer of 93'.

Because Del Rico greatly valued the life of his innocent cousin Norma, it did not take much of an effort for Raul to convince him to make Alfonso her personal bodyguard during her stay. The industrious Barrera, who by that time had grown accustomed to murdering and drug trafficking, loathed the responsibility of babysitting Del Rico's rumored spoiled cousin. That of course would all change after their introduction to one another. Before his promotion in the Sinaloa gang, he had had heard ramblings among the other lieutenants about how attractive the beautiful Norma was, and how attempts at touching her meant certain death. When introduced, Alfonso was stunned by her intoxicating good looks and the obvious amatory expression on her face after shaking his hand. Meanwhile, Raul was getting more than what he was asking for, as he noticed their clear infatuation for one another. Alfonso was put in charge of taking her anywhere in the city she wanted to go and was given a soft warning by Del Rico himself to never touch her. Norma, on the other hand, had other plans and went out of her way to gain the favor of the unsuspecting Alfonso Barrera. With each passing day, Norma tried every way to flaunt her curvy and golden tanned body in either a two piece bikini around the house or, subjecting Alfonso to watching her try on sexy lingerie at the department store. Alfonso was no fool, and could see that Norma was trying her best to get his attention. But, whatever he thought he might have felt for the bodacious young woman, Alfonso respected Del Rico far more than he feared him, and ignored his inner inhibitions. Since the sexual tension between Norma and Alfonso was becoming more and more evident with each passing week, one night Raul grabbed his 35 millimeter camera and followed the two of them out. He followed them to a poplar night club called "Los Pavisa" on the outskirts of downtown Mazatlan. After a few minutes, Raul entered the club after them and stood in the back, where he could have a clear vantage point to spy on them. He had hopes of catching them in the act of doing something he could frame Alfonso with, but from his view point, Alfonso had the pitiful look of a person disgusted. Meanwhile, Norma was partying on the dance floor like a woman possessed with a man in his sixties, who was being respectful and not doing anything incriminating enough for Raul to photograph. An hour and a half had passed, and Raul still did not have nothing juicy to run back to show Del Rico. Just as he was about to give up and leave, Raul saw an attractive young black girl mosey up to Alfonso at the bar. Norma was still busy dancing her woes away to the Banda music that filled the smoke filled air inside the club, but now she was in the company of a younger man. Raul snickered uncontrollably to himself and took a couple pictures just in case. It was evident to Raul that Alfonso was aware of the young man Norma was entertaining, but he clearly chose to ignore his responsibility to keep her away from men. Eventually, Raul was not the only person aware of the skimpily clad black woman Alfonso was presently drinking with. Norma charged the bar and grabbed a beer bottle off a table near them, and smashed the poor woman over the forehead with it. Raul almost dropped his camera in complete surprise because of Norma's reaction to the girl and took even more pictures. Alfonso quickly grabbed Norma and rushed her out of the side exit door before the club security could come. Raul followed them out the side door and could hear him cursing and screaming to Norma's actions in Spanish. They hurried to Alfonso's blue Cadillac and sped off, with Raul not far behind. He followed them to the beach and this time it is Norma that is cursing Alfonso. Raul slithered his way as close to them as he possibly could, but struggled to hear much of anything, due to the sound of the roaring Pacific tide slamming hard against the granite shore rocks. From what he could make out, Norma had been angry with Alfonso because his attention was on the black girl back at the club and not her. Alfonso was angry as well and did not understand why Norma cared at all about what he did, and stormed back to his car. What came next almost gave Raul an orgasm. Norma grabbed the fuming Alfonso and spun him around and kissed him. Raul took shot after shot. Alfonso pushed her off him sending her to the ground, but Norma would not give up so easily and rushed him once more. Before he could wrap his mind about the consequences of their actions Alfonso found himself on top of the luscious Norma in the sand. Raul had more than enough proof to hurt Alfonso, but decided to stay and watch the show. With her high heels spread evenly from east to west, he could hear Norma cum over and over again as the youthful Alfonso at will, pounded and thrust in and out, from between her thick and athletic warm thighs. He then turns her wildly onto her knees and enters her from behind. Alfonso began pulling the sultry brunette by the hair simultaneously while pounding his thin pelvis hard against her soft buttocks, and causing her to scream in uncontrollable ecstasy. He could no longer resist holding back his orgasm and came intensely inside her. Afterwards, he and Norma lay together quietly on the balmy ground staring at the stars in complete exhaustion. Meanwhile, the sneering Raul scurried back to his own car, tripping and falling over himself in the process, in anticipation of revealing Alfonso's trespass.

A few weeks had passed since Alfonso and Norma first made love on the beach that lonesome night, and it had appeared as if they would soon get away with their private affair...for a little while at least. More and more the bold young couple begun sneaking off and going on short excursions to quench their sexual desires upon each other. That was until Del Rico, unexpectedly, needed Alfonso's expertise to carry out a special mission. Del Rico supposedly heard rumors about a possible team-up between two rival gangs and was given the names and whereabouts of a private meeting between the gang's generals. He asked that Alfonso handle the issue personally, which at first glance in Alfonso's eyes, was not much of an odd request. Strangely though, it would be the first time since Norma came to visit, that he would not be in her presence and could not help not worrying about her well-being. Against his better judgment Alfonso grudgingly suggested to Del Rico that Raul should be the best choice to keep his cousin safe. Del Rico surprisingly agreed, but admitted that the present situation was too important for Raul to not be there and was already awaiting him across town with his team. In the Bloody Sinaloa Brother gang, rarely would two high ranking gang lieutenants be ordered to act together in the same hit, unless the hit was actually something else. Despite his suspicions, Alfonso still had orders to follow and made preparations to carry them out. Before he left Del Rico's home, Alfonso warned Norma of the possibility that he was walking into a trap and may never be able to see her ever again. After sharing this notion with her, Norma threatened to confront her older cousin, but Alfonso convinced her to do otherwise, fearing that it would only make a complicated matter much worse. Alfonso was nobody's fool and had not forgotten how much the incestual Roberto Del Rico lusted over his attractive cousin Norma, or how relentless he worked to keep her celibate. It also was not lost on him that Raul hated his guts, and was probably more than willing to be the trigger man that took him out. Nevertheless, one thing always remained consistent before when he went by his legal name "Emmanuel Vasquez," and after he became the Mazatlan scourge "Alfonso Barrera," that he did not fear death or, any man for that matter.

When Alfonso showed up to the address that was given to him, via Del Rico's informant, suddenly he could feel an uncomfortable chill sweep down his narrows of his back. They were at a partially abandoned slaughter house across town. What made matters worse was that the cryptic looking building was located in-between both the Murder Marauders, and another rival gang calling themselves the Machete Kids, territory. Though he arrived with a small contingent of lower level (and his most trusted) Bloody Sinaloa gang members, part of him still could not shake the jitters that were mangling the pit of his stomach. Alfonso's instincts were operating in overdrive as it was already thirty minutes passed nine, and they were supposed to rendezvous with Raul fifteen minutes ago. Just when the temptation to call off the hit entered his restless mind, Alfonso could see headlights blinking from a block away. Del Rico disliked un-organization and had CB radios installed in all of their automobiles to coordinate better. Raul could be heard coming over the system. He spoke in code as he radioed for Alfonso and his people to come in through the side entrance of the building, so they could surprise the two marks they were there to kill. Alfonso did not trust Raul as far as he could throw the young man and advised his boys to keep their eyes open. Not many cars were on the street as they made their way towards the obscure building, causing Alfonso to wonder why two rival gang leaders would bother meeting in such a place without so much as a team to protect them outside. He started thinking about Norma and worried about what would happen to her should anything happen to him that night. When they got to the side door Raul was waiting from the inside and holding his finger over his mouth as if he was shushing a class full of third graders. Alfonso could not stand taking orders from Raul either and just wanted to hurry up and get their business over with. Raul pointed in the direction of the office where the two men they were supposed to kill were conversing. There was barely any light to follow once inside the small murky structure, just the foul stench of dead animals and spoiled fish that occupied the shelves and hooks of the freezer area. As they drew closer to their intended targets, something about Raul's demeanor as he lead them through the dark maze did not sit well with Alfonso. After being initiated into the Bloody Sinaloa gang, Alfonso remembered how "chicken shit" he thought Raul was before he himself became a Lieutenant. He thought about the many drug runs they made together for Del Rico and how afterwards Raul sometimes would order them to pillage and plunder for his own sake, but would never want to do any dirt himself. Never could Alfonso recall anytime "Raul Rena" being the first person going through anyone's door, especially in places where he was supposed to never have been. Raul's demeanor was both comfortable and overtly confident, neither traits that Alfonso ever associated with someone he considered to have "backstabbing weasel" tendencies. But, whatever was really about to go down, Alfonso knew he had to be ready for it. They finally reached the main office where now there was better lighting and visibility for them to strike. Raul stopped in his tracks and turned his attention to Alfonso and his boys and quietly signaled for them to keep pressing forward, so they could now lead the charge. That was the "chicken shit" behavior that Alfonso was accustomed to being around when working with Raul and was expecting to eventually come out. To avoid being seen, he and his men crotched down and duck walked their way underneath a large office window near the closed office door and held their positions and awaited Alfonso's orders. Just as he was about to give the order to attack, something about the view of the window was a little off and caused Alfonso to hesitate. Though the window was rather hazy, he still could make out the silhouette of a person's head through the strangely thick glass, but noticed that it had yet to move. Also, whatever secrets the two men inside were divulging to each other could not have been "so important" that they not dare speak aloud, as it was unusually quiet considering that they were two rival gang leaders. Raul, who was a good distance away, emphatically waved to Alfonso and his group to proceed through the office door. Alfonso found himself in a bit of a conundrum and believed that if he chose to ignore the order, then Raul would have the authority to automatically kill him on sight, if he chose. But, Alfonso also felt that whatever that was in store for him behind the hefty looking rusted door, could not possibly be any better. The condescending Raul began to get annoyed by Alfonso's posturing and irritably gave the command to enter once again. It was the very first time when any of his Sinaloa brethren looked into their youthful lieutenant's eyes and found them drowning in a flood of uncertainty. Grudgingly, Alfonso gave the order to breach the office door and with their automatic weapons they fired at will. The air was thick with clouds of dust, smoke, and asbestos, making it momentarily difficult for anyone to see. Alfonso nodded to one of his young troops to kick in the bullet riddled door and after he did, he sent the rest to follow behind likewise. At first, there was a brief silence, until one of his men yelled for Alfonso to come quickly. When Alfonso came to the foot of the office door, what he saw made both his blood boil hot enough to melt butter and stir his nerves like a blender dicing ice cubes on a high puree cycle. Though his boys brought enough heavy artillery to cut down a herd of rampaging elephants, it had appeared as if someone else beat them to it.

The bodies of the two rival gang leaders they were supposedly there to kill were severely dismembered. Their killers were merciless, as Alfonso and his crew gasped in astonishment to the various body parts and limbs strung up all around the office, with some on meat hooks, as if they were ornaments hanging off a Christmas tree. While Alfonso's men stood around in a befuddlement, it did not take a Mack truck to run him over to understand what was afoot. There was a hit that was supposed to take place alright, but instead of being the one's doing all the killing, it was painfully clear that Alfonso and his boys were obviously the real targets that night. Alfonso managed to snap out of his stunned gaze long enough to realize that Raul was not present. Just as Alfonso gave the order to vacate the office someone from outside the room open fired on them. Everyone inside the room had been killed instantly, except for Alfonso. He suffered gunshot wounds in the chest and leg, but was unable to move. Suddenly, laughter could be heard in the walkway. It was Raul Rena. Raul took a gas container and splashed gasoline everywhere and made a trail that ended inside the office, where Alfonso and his boys were laying. Raul mocked Alfonso as he bled on the frigid and gasoline saturated office floor. He took out his gold-plated cigarette lighter and threw it on top of the putrid smelling gasoline trail, setting the office, as well as the rest of the building on fire. Alfonso was in agony and could feel his life slowly slipping away, as his blood continued to spew onto the dirty office floor. The smoke from the fire was growing immensely and was causing the room to turn black, making it harder for Alfonso to breathe. The flames were also growing closer and closer to his wounded body and the heat inside the room became more and more unbearable by the second. Then, just as he was about to succumb to his current circumstance, a vision of Norma's beautiful smiling face flashed inside his mind. The vision was of her smiling back at him on the sand from that night on the beach after they first made love. That was the best day of his short, misery filled life and now, he was being forced to give her up. Alfonso was born a child of chaos and had never known of actual love before. He began his youth taking life in order to survive and now, for the glory of the same man who was trying to kill him. The pain of his gunshot wounds paled in comparison to that fact and for the first and only time in his life, Alfonso wept. He knew that this was the end for him and despite the immoral sacrifices he made for Del Rico, it clearly never really mattered to the self-centered drug lord.

When the fire started to catch hold of his body, Alfonso initially screamed out in what he first believed was extreme agony. Brilliant flames washed over his young arms and legs like a tidal wave and yet, he was able to ignore the pain. It was as if his adrenaline had taken control and the more his flesh burned, the louder he yelled in delusional ecstasy. His emotional state of mind was now in overdrive, and soon found himself feeding off the fuel of his own rage. The combination of losing Norma and being tossed aside like yesterday's trash at the hands of a parasite like Raul Rena was too much for his proud mind to handle. One other thought began to permeate inside Alfonso's twisted mind state. If he were to die in the fire, it meant everything he had done for the backstabbing Roberto Del Rico would have been for nothing, leaving him the victor. Although the prospect of losing both the woman he had loved and the empire he helped build was a blistering thought, he suddenly realized that something much more was at stake that would burn far deeper than any flame ever could. His choice of "how" he was going to die was also being taken from him. The last thing that Alfonso Barrera ever feared on God's green Earth, was death, and would proudly smile in the face of it just like any other good sacrificial lamb would. But, he always believed it was his choice to make and he was not in the mood for dying. No one was ever going to take his life unless it was going to be on HIS terms. His fatal wounds and fear of the furious inferno became nonexistent, and though his body was racking with pain and engulfed in flames, Alfonso found renewed strength that made it possible for him to scramble to his feet. The building was coming apart around him as he fought to make his way through the burning deathtrap. He could see an exit sign up ahead, but it was getting difficult to breathe, let alone walk with three bullet wounds in him. Alfonso blindly pressed on forward deeper through the unmerciful blaze. Though staggering at a snail's pace he finally made it towards the exit door. Just as Alfonso reached out to open the rusted door, the building exploded and consumed him in a monsoon of violent flares.

Later on that night, Raul Rena was in Roberto Del Rico's private study confirming the executions of the two "rival gang leaders", as well as Alfonso Barrera's untimely demise. To corroborate his story, Raul even played a video tape he made of the slaughterhouse burning down. It was Raul that staged the fake meeting and dressed up two dead Bloody Sinaloa gang members he had killed in their rival's colors. In order to keep their identities a secret, he ordered his cronies to burn their faces and had the bodies hacked to a dozen pieces. Though Del Rico despised Raul's treachery, he hated Alfonso fucking his cousin Norma behind his back even more. Strangely enough, a tiny part of him could not help feel like he had lost a little brother. It was a rarity for the diabolical Roberto Del Rico to be allowed to feel "any kind" of fondness for anyone. For a man in his disposition, it would be considered a show of weakness. Deep within Del Rico's blackened soul he also believed that he owed Alfonso a great deal of gratitude. It was with the young man's "work ethic" that he attained the power that he had garnered over the last couple years. But, Del Rico had to save face and a reputation to uphold. His enterprise was on the rise and he could ill afford room for betrayal of any kind to take place in his organization. Raul also confirmed that Del Rico's cousin Norma's body had been properly disposed of. Del Rico's previous thoughts of what had transpired over an hour ago was almost out of his mind until Raul brought them storming back like lightening to a lightening rod. The news of her current state imbued Del Rico's face with pure unadulterated menace, while at the same time sending shivers down the spineless Raul Rena's back. In his own mind, Roberto Del Rico felt like transgressions were made against him and his Bloody Sinaloa gang family and that both Alfonso and Norma needed to be punished. Since Del Rico's ascension as a crime lord had become greater at the time, he never needed to handle things personally. When it came to handling his treacherous cousin Norma though, it got very personal. He reflected on how he raped and strangled her and how he beat her within every inch of her fledging life. His fists still ached from pounding against her beautiful and warm soft flesh. Norma had hurt him so deeply, he did not care to hear her reasoning for her trespass. After feeling a bit euphoric from his actions, he sent the anxious Raul on his way. Del Rico reached into his humidor on his desk and whipped out a large Cuban cigar and lit it. He placed his hands behind his head and leaned back in his chair. The cigar tasted good to him while he inhaled its rich tobacco flavoring. Raul could be heard closing the door down stairs and giving orders to the two guards watching the front door. The thought of replacing Alfonso was irritating to Del Rico and turned his attention to outside his window. Though it was dark, Del Rico could still see Raul as he scurried quickly to his car. He knew Raul was a rat by nature and would like nothing better than to see himself in his place one day. That was a fact he was never blind of, but knew his cunning ways would always prove useful. He shook his head in disgust and closed his eyes in order to take his mind off his deceptive lieutenant for a moment. Suddenly, a scream could be heard coming from Raul's direction and then the fierce sounds of gunshots. Del Rico immediately broke his trance and could see Raul's body hitting the ground through his office window. In his excitement, his cigar fell completely from his mouth as he stared mystified at Raul's bold attacker. More gun fire could be heard coming from downstairs, then from inside of his three-story home. Del Rico could not seem to move while his assailant was making his way up the stairway. Fear had begun to grip his chest like a starving bear hugging an interloping camper in his cave. Soon, the noises had stopped. From what Roberto Del Rico could gather, either his bodyguards had done their "supposed" job and killed off his attacker or, the footsteps that were drawing closer to his private study were the impeding sound of his imminent doom...

The infamous Roberto Del Rico never put any stock in believing in things like good or, bad karma. He never believed in anything for that matter, other than money and power, after witnessing his father's death at the fragile age of five. His father David was a small time thief that was shot dead in the street by an overweight neighborhood gangster named Pablo Esteban. The grotesquely obese Pablo Esteban was trying to strong-arm his father David into paying him a large percentage to operate, but when David refused, he killed him. Though there were witnesses to his father's murder, many feared suffering the same fate, so no one was willing to step forward. After his father's killer went unprosecuted, the justice system became just another check on his long laundry list of things he did not believe in as well. Growing up in the hardened Mazatlan burrows continued to prove challenging for Del Rico after he also witnessed the raping of his mother Rosario. Del Rico was around nine-years-old when the unfortunate incident occurred. Both he and his mother were leaving the grocery store late one evening, when three much older men approached them while they were waiting at a bus stop. The three assailants were getting drunk at a local cantina next door when they spotted them coming out of the antiquated building. Two of the men forcefully dragged his mother into a dark alley, while the third struck the young Del Rico, deeming him unconscious. When he awoke, the damage had already been done, and his mother would never again be the same.

Rosario Del Rico became devoutly religious after that ordeal and had forced her Catholic ways upon young Roberto. Her heavy handed rules and warped sense of theology became too much for the adolescent Del Rico to handle and caused him to run away from home at the impressionable age of thirteen. Though he hardly went, Del Rico also dropped out of school and found out early on that his street IQ was far better than the one he possessed in the classroom. Like his father before him, Del Rico started out doing petty theft (boosting car radios, shoplifting, pick-pocketing, etc…) that had him landing in and out of juvenile boy's homes all over Sinaloa. It was during one of Del Rico's last boy home "visits", where he would meet the infamous Raul Rena, who himself also had a checkered past. Raul was a shade younger than Del Rico, but seemed to have the respect of the other teenagers on campus. Their initial meeting did not go so well for the conniving Raul Rena, though. He and some of his associates wanted to steal Del Rico's brand new sneakers (that he previously had stolen from someone else) and decided to jump the unsuspecting new kid (Del Rico) in the cafeteria. Del Rico caught wind of the planned attack from a mutual friend, who grew up in his old neighborhood, and made sure he took the proper precautions. Due to the shift change made during the evenings, the incoming personnel were usually more lax, so Raul waited until dinner time to spring his attack on him. Raul made sure that the cafeteria guard was distracted by a fake emergency that one of his associates led him to. With his back to him at the dinner table,

Raul believed they all had the drop on the innocent looking Del Rico, but quickly found themselves at his mercy. Del Rico waited until they grabbed him from behind before spraying them in their faces, rendering them helpless, with a small fire extinguisher he was hiding underneath his t-shirt. He savagely beat the blinded youths to a bloody pulp, sending Raul and his fellow conspirators to the infirmary for an entire week. Word quickly got out that Del Rico was a force to be reckoned with. Soon after the attack, Del Rico would usurp the frail looking Raul Rena as the most feared man on campus. As many months passed, his influence over the other youth offenders in the home became increasingly addictive to his normally standoffish nature. Anyone who opposed or, challenged him during his stay at the boy's home, would suffer deadly consequences at the hands of his young underlings. Though it could never be proven, Del Rico was allegedly behind many of the vicious attacks and mysterious accidental deaths to both staff and youth offenders, at the home. Rosario's youth and health had begun to fade from the taxation of his troublemaking ways. Throughout her son's entire teenage years, Rosario Del Rico would waste a decade of her own life traveling back and forth to the town courthouse (paying fines, making bail, begging judges, etc…) doing whatever she could do to try and save him from the same fate his father suffered. But, no matter how much or, hard his pious mother prayed, no matter how much Rosario begged and pleaded her unflinching son, Roberto Del Rico refused to see the light and proceeded in oppressing his peers. She could only stand by in complete hopelessness while her manic son allowed himself to drown in an intoxicating pool of chaos. Eventually, Rosario had no choice, but to give up on her unruly child and left him at the mercy of the police and Sinaloa authorities. It was at age seventeen when he finally formed "The Bloody Sinaloa Brothers," and out of an act of pity, made Raul his first gang lieutenant. Raul was known for being a fast talker and used his incredible skill for bartering and influencing others to help build their fledging ranks.

After turning eighteen, Roberto Del Rico was considered an adult and were no longer a ward of the state, and was sent back out on the streets to pursue his criminal free-for-all. Although he was released from the youth detention center under his own reconnaissance, Del Rico with the help of his newly formed conglomerate still controlled most of the illegal dealings inside it. Unlike his father before him, Del Rico's transition from "thief" to "the extortionist" was a seamless one. Despite the rousing number of gang affiliates he accrued over time, it would not be until the recruitment of the voracious Alfonso Barrera, that the upstart gang gained respectability and flourished as a major cartel. Sure enough at the time, the Bloody Sinaloa Brother gang had its fare share of natural born killers, but in Alfonso, Roberto Del Rico saw untapped potential that he could use to his advantage. What separated Alfonso from the other members was his uncanny special ability or, "will power" to overcome tremendous odds in any deadly situation. No matter how difficult the task that was being asked of him or however over matched, Alfonso always came out on top. Suffice it to say, Del Rico's other lieutenants were loyal to a fault, but in more ways than one cost him in either losses of man power (unnecessary incarcerations) drugs (confiscated or stolen) and money to replace them all. When the other lieutenants gave second chances…Alfonso did not. If someone owed Del Rico money or tried to skip town, the other lieutenants would do a drive-by shooting at their home…Alfonso would find the person's mother, and personally chop her foot off with a hatchet. Anytime that another crew was foolish enough to invade Del Rico's territory, his lieutenants would willingly die selflessly defending it…Alfonso on the other hand, would endure any onslaught, then seek out and personally destroy his enemies with a bazooka. Del Rico never fully understood the inner demons that drove his savage protégé to excel at such violent extremes, but even he had to learn to respect it. While nurturing Alfonso's "gifts," Del Rico could see the similarities in him that they both shared and could not help the growing attachment that had formed. After making Alfonso a gang lieutenant and also his primary bodyguard, Raul Rena claimed that he feared backlash from the rest of their gang members. But, the pain in Raul's deceitful looking eyes told him that what he really feared the most was losing his only friend. Del Rico knew that Raul hated everyone behind closed doors and marveled at his incredible knack for smiling into the faces of those very people he hated. He did not know very much about Raul's background other than the rumors that were circulated at the boy's home they lived together in. There were many stories going around about why he was sent to the boy's home, but the one story that seemed to be the most consistent was that Raul was there for setting his entire family on fire. Though Del Rico was never compelled to ask Raul Rena the truth, it was plain to see he was not the enemy that he first thought him out to be. It was obvious to him that Raul was still suffering greatly from some childhood event and the only way he coped with it was by causing pain to others. The main reason Del Rico knew this was because most kids from his old neighborhood grew up wearing the very same hurtful look in their eyes.

For Raul Rena though, whatever pain that was haunting him was no longer going to be an issue…as someone else was about to see to that. Del Rico knew he could always count on the confused and misunderstood Raul Rena, which was why he asked him specifically and not the other lieutenants, to devise a plan to dispose of the quisling Alfonso Barrera. During the weeks leading up to springing his trap, Del Rico could not find it in his ice cold heart to forgive Alfonso, or Norma for sleeping with each other behind his back. While Raul was off sealing Alfonso's fate, Roberto Del Rico decided to share his displeasure with his lovely next to kin. Norma implored Del Rico to not kill her as he beat her. Del Rico forced himself on his vulnerable cousin and viciously raped her for hours on end. After Raul returned to his compound, Del Rico then ordered him take his distraught cousin out to the same beach, where Norma and Alfonso first made love, and to put a bullet in her head. Like a good little soldier, Raul did exactly what was asked of him. But before he could ever get to deliver the news of her death, someone decided to show up and unleash hell upon the home of the unenlightened kingpin….

The normally reserved Roberto Del Rico was beginning to worry. Not a sound could be heard and no one could be reached on their walkie-talkies. He tried dialing his house phone, but could not get a dial tone. His two cell phones were both outside in one of his cars outside. A shadowy figure could be seen prominently from the bottom crack of the double door, but the person behind it remained as quiet as a catholic priest listening to a sinner's confession. Del Rico kept a handgun inside a safe that was near his desk in a wall. His fear was almost too much to overcome after the person yelled for him. The man's voice that was coming from behind his study door sounded familiar, but his words were coarse and rough, as if he gargled with soda pop glass. A long time had passed since the last time the usually heavily protected Roberto Del Rico had to act in his own defense. He had taken it for granted that none of his "known" enemies were foolish enough to ever attempt an attack on him at his home, especially knowing full well he had a platoon of loyal goons at his command. Del Rico barely managed getting to his safe in one piece after making a mad scramble to open it to grab his revolver. After drawing out his weapon, the hallway outside his study grew quiet again. With the grace of a cat burglar, Del Rico slowly approached the doorway and noticed that the shadow of the man's silhouette was now gone. His heart was beating at a ridiculously fast cadence and adrenaline was up so high that he feared he would choke on it. Del Rico put his head up against the door to listen for his tormentor, but to no avail, did he hear him or, anything else for that matter. He gingerly got down on the floor and did not see anyone from the crack at the bottom of his door either. Since he was left with no other choice, Del Rico tried opening the door in hopes of sneaking a peek to locate his mystery attacker. Just as he was turning the door knob, then the shadow was suddenly back underneath the doorway and the doors themselves became riddled with bullets. Some of the bullets caught Del Rico in both his chest and arm, causing him to lose his footing and his gun. When the smoke cleared the last thing in the world cartel leader Roberto Del Rico expected to see standing there was a living, breathing, and badly charred Alfonso Barrera. There he stood towering over the frightened Del Rico, huffing loudly like a rampaging giant. In his right hand was an intimidating M16 rifle, while in the other hand, was something big and round. Alfonso was grinning so hard that his saliva dripped profusely from his mouth, and he then rolled the weird circular object on the floor, landing between Del Rico's limp legs. The oblong object had all along been the dismembered head of the former Raul Rena. Growing up under the hardships of an impoverished criminal life, Del Rico had long ago become desensitized to violent acts, but after seeing the horrified expression left on Raul's face, combined with the fact that Alfonso was still alive (despite his Freddy Krueger like condition) confirmed two very chilling facts: One, that the seemingly unstoppable Alfonso Barrera had to have been touched by the devil. Two, judging by the broad smirk on Alfonso's charred face and the intimidating blood drenched knife he was brandishing in his left hand that his short pathetic life was just about over…

<u>End of Intermission:</u>

Alfonso Barrera's promptness for their meeting was a bit refreshing and also well as expected from the enigmatic Harlan Kruellar. His deadly reputation had far preceded him, which made Harlan slightly apprehensive about doing anything with the unpredictable drug lord. He had hoped the five hundred thousand dollar price tag he charged for a mere "sit down" would be enough to dissuade the persistent Barrera, but whatever he needed from Harlan apparently far outweighed any price he could ask of him. The street lights shimmered off Alfonso's pearl white limousine like beams off a disco ball, as it charged up the dark rugged dirt road. Choosing the right place to hold their business discussion was paramount to Harlan, as he believed it could be the determining factor of him and his son making it out alive. It had to be some place open and deserted, and also an area which Alfonso Barrera had no real control, like the United States Embassy. Though he was not THAT bold to conduct such affairs on the actual property, it did not hurt to be near such a well patrolled area, Harlan deduced. Suddenly, as if on cue, Harlan could hear a light tapping from the top of his car, which left him with a puzzled look upon his face. Harlan's driver witnessed his boss' confusion while peering through his rear view mirror, "It's just rain, sir!" He said confidently. Then Harlan could see water droplets starting to dance onto his own tinted window, "Oh, yes! I see." Harlan said intently. He had been too mentally pre-occupied to notice any changes in the weather, "Radio the others…tell them to be on stand-bye!" Harlan ordered. The driver's eyes were no longer full of compassion and morphed into the look of a pissed off Bengal tiger, "Yes sir!" He said. Alfonso's limousine had parked several yards away, but no one had yet to get out of the vehicle. Harlan rubbed his chin in befuddlement while trying to figure out his next move, "The hell's he waiting for?" Harlan said aloud to himself. "If Alfonso Barrera thought international transporting czar Harlan Kruellar condoned business in the elements, he had another thing coming." Harlan humorously thought. Alfonso's limousine headlights flickered three times, which was the signal Alfonso said he would give to reassure Harlan it would be him. Harlan hesitated then gave the order to his own driver to do the same. The rain was getting heavier and heavier, making it almost impossible to look out his window. He could see Alfonso's limousine headlights turn off completely and then the front driver door swung open. Had no one done anything his next order would have been to hit the gas pedal, Harlan thought. He had flown hundreds of miles away from his own comfort zone not to be there in the rain playing these types of games. Harlan was in another man's backyard swimming in his pool, and did not want to take anymore unnecessary chances than he would have had to keep him and his son Haven protected. He gave orders to evacuate his son from the museum and to his private jet thirty minutes after he left. The last thing Harlan ever expected to do was drag his only child into the middle of a dangerous business negotiation in the heart of a madman's city. He should have known better, Harlan contemplated. Either way what was done was done, He figured. Harlan took every possible precaution to assure a safe exit strategy. There was an unmarked cargo ship on standby that was conveniently docked up the block that had at least twelve more bodyguards on board. Had his son Haven known about the extra guns he possibly would have accused him of being paranoid, Harlan assumed. But what his son did not know was that there was another whole layer of darkness he was trying to shed him from. Haven was young and had yet to become a father and could not understand, or fathom the thought of suffering the loss of a child. Anything his son ever desired or believed he needed, Harlan made sure he received it. Never had his son known what it felt like to ever want for anything. It would not be until he would barely become a man before he asked for the one thing Harlan did not want to give him, and that was a chance to prove himself….

Alfonso's looming limousine driver opened up a large darkly colored umbrella and walked to the back their car to open the passenger door. A figure wearing a white suit could be seen getting out of the passenger door slowly, pausing for a moment to run his fingers through his hair, and then the both of them began walking towards Harlan's limousine. Whatever fears Harlan bore for his son's life he had to now hurry and stash them away. Harlan's anticipation to leave Mexico was becoming increasingly greater after every step Alfonso and his large companion made towards his car. By no sense of the word was Harlan a cowardly man. Despite his diminutive statue, he usually stood his ground against any of his adversaries, no matter how big or small a threat they were. He was always a businessman first and knew that it sometimes took making alliances he did not want to make to insure it was a means to an end, even if it sometimes took hurting other's (family or, otherwise) to justify those ends. This time things were sizably different. Alfonso Barrera did not have a heart or soul and had a reputation for eating the hearts of those who denied him with a carving knife. In times past, Harlan would hear the many outlandish horror stories from former investors and F.B.I. officials alike, but just in case would he make sure that their paths never did cross. Unfortunately for Harlan, would he far exceed his celebrity in the transporting industry and became high demand by just about every underworld mastermind, rogue army, and every other criminal upstart alike. Yet, here he was in the snake's pit, and mere seconds from welcoming a mad cobra into his weary lap. The guards inside Harlan's second limousine stepped out from there automobile to be on standby. Two of Harlan's security team quickly and thoroughly frisked Alfonso and his driver, but then only allowed Alfonso to get inside his car. The look on Alfonso's soaked face was an unsettling one to Harlan, and only confirmed what he already knew before he left America, that whatever Alfonso Barrera wanted out of him, he was definitely not interested in hearing it.

Harlan at first did not know what to make of his well dressed rain drenched guest. Certainly, he thought, could this not possibly be the infamous drug czar who was wanted by every government agency south of the U.S. border? Despite a few old artificial scars upon his face and neck, Alfonso Barrera appeared much younger than Harlan was initially led to believe. His choice of clothing surely wasn't helping his cause, Harlan thought, as he stared at his Miami white linen suit and a very open pink button down shirt underneath. A small gold cross was hardly visible due to the heavy amount of chest hair that was burying it. Though his hair was ruined from the heavy rain outside, it was painfully obvious that Alfonso was also either a Don Johnson or, John Travolta fan. Whoever was in charge of the F.B.I.'s sketch artists were either horribly misinformed or, clearly being generous in painting the youthful and rugged looking Barrera as some sinister elder statesman Harlan assumed. Obviously, Alfonso Barrera had to have gone through great lengths to keep himself away from the public's eye to avoid identification, Harlan figured. Out of the sake of appearing rude, Harlan then offered Alfonso a fresh towel to dry himself off. Alfonso was busy rubbing his face erratically, as if it was being overrun by fleas, before taking notice of Harlan's generosity, but then lent him a simple, "Muchas Gracias!" Alfonso said gratefully. Slowly Harlan's discomfort began to dissipate with every passing second. Experience had taught him to never take anything or, anyone for granted, especially those with the same type of influences of an Alfonso Barrera, but part of him could not help contain a small sense of overconfidence in regards to his negotiation power. The overwhelming sensation to leave Mexico was slowly subsiding as Harlan watched the outclassed Barrera fidget in his seat, “Forgive me, Mr. Kruellar, as it is not customary that I meet a “potential” business partner under these…how do you say…conditions!?!” Alfonso said apologetically. Not feeling moved by his forced act of contrition Harlan decided to play along, “But of course. Would you care for a drink…Mr. Barrera is it?” Harlan asked condescendingly. Alfonso’s pause was only for but a brief second, but long enough for Harlan to catch it, “Why, yes. I think I will.” Alfonso said coyly. Harlan reached for a bottle of Louise XIII Cognac inside his portable wet bar and grabbed two glasses. He could see the unnerving grin on Alfonso’s face out of the corners of his eyes as he poured the two of them a drink. It was Harlan’s way of testing the wily looking Barrera, who was apparently all for it, in making sure he was the legit “Alfonso Barrera” and not some stand-in. Part of their agreement was for the two to meet face to face at a place of Harlan’s own choosing. Harlan trusted no one, even if that person paid him half a million dollars just to have a “talk!”

The thunder claps are getting louder by each passing second, and the rain persists to bash the limousine’s windows with a drummer’s enthusiasm. A thunder clap was so enormous that both men had to freeze and stare up, causing them to chuckle, if for a brief moment, “Ahem…as I was saying amigo, it is such an honor to meet a person of your…“statue”…it was unfortunate that we could not meet at my comfortable estate. Where I could’ve had my chefs prepare us a gran fiesta, while sharing the beautiful company of my city’s hottest girls or, whatever you prefer!?!” Alfonso said gleefully. Alfonso could discern from Harlan’s stoic demeanor that he was unimpressed, “But if it is your wish to have us meet inside a hurricane to do business, then I will do it…Aplausos!” Alfonso toasts and swallows down his drink. He was not amused by Alfonso’s macho act and found the slurping down of his vintage wine, as if it were a soda, even less classless, “Ahhhh yes…gracias Senór Kruellar! Truly that was some fine meirda!” Alfonso said in his thick Latino accent. Feeling slightly disgusted, Harlan did not bother to drink from his wine glass, and decided that he was ready to move on to business, "Well then…Mr. Barrera, at the sake of not trying to sound like an impatient man, just how is it that a paltry transporter, such as myself, be of any help to an …"industrious" person such as yourself?" Harlan asked grudgingly. Alfonso peered into Harlan's face as if pigeon shit just landed on it, then slowly put down his wine glass. Harlan could see contentment in his eyes that was not there before, it was as if Alfonso Barrera had the super ability to look into the very depths of his own consciousness. He had the look of a person whose pride had been hurt, "Well, Senór Kruellar, I did not consider the five hundred thousand "American" dollars I gave you for this meeting to as…how did you say, paltry?" Alfonso said bitterly. Harlan could tell it was obvious he crossed a line he was not ready to cross and gave his driver a head nod. It was his way of putting his security guards on standby. Alfonso began flickering at his nose like a person in need of a line of cocaine, "When I sent for you, Senór Kruellar, it was not to waste both our precious time, but to help YOU make us both rich beyond our dreams!" Alfonso chanted. For the first time since the offensive Alfonso Barrera got into his limousine was Harlan Kruellar interested, "I meant no disrespect Mr. Barrera by my earlier comment. But just how is it that I'm going to make US any richer than we already are? I already own a nine figure company and I'm well aware of your "Bloody Sinaloa Brother Cartel" both here and in the states, nets you the same! I ship products, Mr. Barrera, all kinds. I mean this with all due respect, when I say that I'm not looking to ship drugs anymore. It's not really worth my time." Harlan protested. Alfonso started smiling like a man who just won a million dollar scratch off, "I'm not talking about "drugs" amigo." Alfonso said grinningly. The air inside the roomy limousine felt thicker to Harlan, and despite hearing this revelation, part of him was surprisingly curious, "Well then, what is it that you propose we move? Exotic guns, atomic bombs or, is it toxic waste?" Harlan said condescendingly. Alfonso licked his chapped lips, released a faint chuckle, and leaned over closer to Harlan, "No guns amigo…no bombs either." Alfonso whispered. He smiled at Harlan with a fiendish grin then knocked on the window and nodded at his driver who stood diligently in the torrid rain. His imposing looking driver scurried off to Alfonso's car and Harlan could see him open up the back door. Alfonso was ecstatic about the small figure who stepped out from his white stretch limousine. Harlan could hardly make out the person's face, but only that Alfonso's driver had to almost squat down to the ground to keep them protected from the unforgiving rain. When Alfonso's driver opened Harlan's door a small boy in an Iron-Man t-shirt and shorts crawled inside. Confusion and astonishment began to plague Harlan Kruellar's mind, as to what capacity could the presence of the diminutive child serve. The sullen and malnourished looking little boy, who was of Caucasian decent, did not appear to be of any relation to the Latin born and maniacal Barrera, Harlan concluded. Alfonso sat still in his seat staring at Harlan with hand on top of the young boy's dusty blonde hair, "Don't be rude Edgar, say…hello." Alfonso quietly commanded. The child, unmoving, was also gazing into Harlan Kruellar's bewildered face, "…Hello." The boy said stoically. Not since his teenage years had Harlan found himself in any uncomfortable situations, but the demonical tension in Alfonso Barrera's eyes was not sitting well with him, "With all due respect, but who the fuck is this?" Harlan balked. It was not until after he uttered the question to Alfonso that the obvious answer hit him. His father side began to beckon out to him from the back of his mind like a trapped bear inside a hundred foot well. The business man was hoping against hope that his repulsive guess was wrong. But hope was just simply something that was hard to come by for someone like Harlan Kruellar, "Why, isn't it obvious? (patting the small boy's head with his hand) It is our product!" Alfonso said proudly.

A plethora of emotions had surged through Harlan like a current of electricity on a computer's motherboard, with the first being shock. It would take him almost a full minute before he could compose himself and respond to the madman sitting across from him. The next emotion he encountered was one of uneventful disbelief. It was as if, for a split second, that his soul separated from the very atoms that formed his own body hauled off and slapped him, "Product?" Harlan asked befuddled. Alfonso was rubbing his scoundrel hands through little Edgar's head, as if he was feeling through a bowl of uncooked rice, "Why, yes…product. THE product as a matter of fact! You see, I have tapped into a new…how do you say? A new market! Alfonso yelled excitedly, as if he were a math student in class who guessed the correct answer to a complicated equation. It did not really matter who Harlan talked to in his many criminal or, legit circles when the conversation involved Alfonso Barrera. Between hearing all various and disparaging information on him, there was always the one constant to defining Alfonso Barrera…

madness. He had to be a madman, Harlan thought, to be bold enough to even ask "him," a father, to look upon another child as if they were just a thing you can pick up at a local grocery store, "Look, Mr. Barrera, I don't know what all you heard about me, but I'm not a complete bastard. I don't involve children in…" Harlan tried to infer before being cutoff, "Yes, yes, yes I know what you're gonna' say Mr. Kruellar, but please, hear me out!" Alfonso insisted. There was not anything that Alfonso Barrera could possibly say that would change his mind, Harlan surmised. Though Harlan was not completely opposed to human trafficking per se, as he often turned a blind eye to it in the past to launch the empire he has today, but this was "not" new territory he was willing to explore. (Clearing his throat) "Forgive my manners as I have had a long flight…but give me "one" good FUCKING reason I should be listening to anything else you have to say, Mr. Barrera?" Harlan demanded. Alfonso Barrera stopped caressing Edgar's mane and leaned forward, "How about I give you "five hundred thousand reasons," Mr. Kruellar?" Alfonso said irritably. Harlan believed he had every right to feel irrational, but he was always business first and no matter how much Alfonso Barrera's presence repulsed him, he did at "least" have a valid point. After all, he did force him to pay for his time, though outrageously so, but now Harlan regretted taking his money in the first place. Because he had become too distracted, Harlan had not realized he was still clenching onto the full glass of Louis XIII he poured himself, and decided to take a page from the offensive Alfonso Barrera and swallowed the whole glass. Alfonso leaned back in his seat and began fiddling with the child's hair once more, "You see, Mr. Kruellar, I did a little checking…and it was brought to my attention that you don't like me very much!" Alfonso said, in a hurtful and patronizing tone. Seeing Harlan rolling his eyes at the mention of this news only confirmed Alfonso's accusation, "And I know, Mr. Kruellar, through mutual friends and some your competitors, that you also tripled your sit down price…just for "this" meeting, tsk, tsk, tsk." Alfonso said with a smug and disapproving grin. Harlan did not budge as he stared down the fearsome drug kingpin unblinkingly, "The least you can do, Mr. Kruellar… is hear me out!" Alfonso demanded. His blood was trying to overwhelm his face like a giant tick absorbing the essence of its prey, as he tried his best to keep his calm, but Harlan was beginning to lose his patience. In the back of his mind, Harlan could not figure out what disgusted him more about the feral looking

Alfonso Barrera, the fact that he was right about everything he said, or the proposition he was trying to make.

With each passing moment, the rain continued to be both frightful and disrupting as it battered the heavily clouded night sky like an old dusty rug. For one quick moment, Harlan Kruellar wondered if his son Haven might have been still angry with him and thought about the possibility of making amends once they returned home. Maybe they could vacation in the Caymans, like he and his wife often did years ago, Harlan pondered. Lightening illuminated the dark Mexican sky like a New Year's celebration in Times Square, causing Harlan to break his zombie like trance. "No time for that kind of talk!" Harlan thought. He has to give this highly immoral man his chance to finish speaking his mind and then afterwards, only afterwards, could he entertain thoughts of personal business, Harlan concluded. Harlan breathed out a loud and frustrated sigh, "Alright then…" Harlan huffed. Alfonso Barrera sat still as a statue then rapped on the window to signal his diligent driver to open the door, "You may go now, Edgar." Alfonso said distastefully. The small child crawled over him to get out of the library quiet limousine and then Alfonso's driver closed the door. Harlan's mind was a little more at ease without the presence of some strange and withdrawn acting child in the car. Alfonso Barrera's gaze was ice cold as he peered into him, "As I was saying. It had occurred to me, Mr. Kruellar, that in my line of business, in order to make a decent profit, certain…how do you say…"extremes" must be taken!" Alfonso gravely said. Harlan leaned forward to put his empty glass down, "Go on…" Harlan painfully insisted. "You see, Mr. Kruellar, I come from very…humble beginnings. In my country, when you are born an orphan, the drug cartels come looking for you. I did what I had to do to survive! As you may already know, the majority of how I make my money is through distributing and manufacturing drugs here and in the United States, but I also found it more "profitable" helping my people cross your borders or, holding them for ransom. With that being said, Mr. Kruellar, between the increases in border patrol and terror alerts, every day it is getting harder and expensive, to move my drugs and "other" cargo anywhere, especially America. The fucking self righteous politicians in your country are cracking down on my American operations, costing me even more in locking up my products and my soldiers. Don't even get me started with the crystal meth sellers I must compete with…"Alfonso trails off. Harlan feeling confused and perplexed sits back and clears his throat, "Yes, yes, all that is quite unfortunate for YOU, but what does all that have to do with me…and a FIVE-year old?" Harlan asked irritably. While glancing out his window Alfonso took a deep frustrated breath, "Do you know how much money one undocumented child gets you on the black market Mr. Kruellar?" Alfonso asked sinisterly. Harlan looked at his watch impatiently, "I don't know, five to ten life sentences?!? Seriously, Mr. Barrera, I don't have time for…" Harlan implored. Alfonso Barrera turned his attention back to Harlan with a black void in his eyeballs unlike any Harlan had ever seen before from a man, "No, Mr. Kruellar, try two hundred thousand dollars! They are a fucking le mina de oro! A gold mine Mr. Kruellar! I have prostitutas here and in America, making thousands of these little bastards and mucho customers all over the world, ready to get their la rocas off! You see, Mr. Kruellar, in my country I lose a recruit or, some young prospect three times a day, when all I'm trying to do is make a HONEST buck! Why should we continue such a filthy cycle of violence in our streets, when I can offer them so much more someplace else?" Alfonso asked prophetically. Harlan was not moved nor amused by the delusional Alfonso Barrera's self gratified tirade, "By selling them out into possible slavery or, as some psycho's personal sex object?" Harlan vented. Alfonso exhaled and rolled his eyes as if he were trying to explain Chinese instructions on how to build an airplane to a two-year-old, "…or maybe some miserable couple who can't have kids? Look, Mr. Kruellar, don't look at it as us making a fast dollar! We're merely providing a public service by giving somebody's unwanted kid a better shot in life, and not being shot living in a toilet of one. All I need from you, Mr. Kruellar, is legit passage to our el cliente, our customers, and I will cut you in for thirty percent of the profits!" Alfonso said justifiably. Harlan Kruellar spent his entire life mostly doing the wrong thing, but did manage to spare some of the time trying to live right through his son Haven. He loved being a father and that just was not for sale, and neither was his soul. Harlan barely took a second to react, "This meeting is over, Mr. Barrera. My apologies to you, but I don't do business like THAT! Start the car!" Harlan commanded to his driver. Alfonso began to chuckle, "Was it something I said Mr. Kruellar? Okay then, Mr. Kruellar, I'm not a very proud man… how about forty percent!" Alfonso offered. Harlan pulled out his cell phone, "Good bye Mr. Barrera…I might BE a bastard, Mr. Barrera, but

I'm not THAT big of one! Yes (speaking to his cell phone) …Captain Hurst? Is the plane refueled and ready to go? Good! I will be there shortly, is my son on board? Oh? (Harlan looking at a smiling Alfonso Barrera) well give him a moment. He should be there momentarily." Harlan said, and hung up the phone. Alfonso Leaned close to Harlan, "Is there a problem Mr. Kruellar?" Alfonso kindly asked. Harlan was mystified. Certainly, he had thought, that he had done everything he could to keep his son Haven secured. "Was it possible that the team guarding Haven had run into an unforeseeable problem?" Harlan had wondered. Alfonso seemed to be privy to circumstantial rumors (albeit accurate rumors) about Harlan not liking him enough to overcharge for a "talk," but could he possibly have known where Haven may have been this entire time? He began to worry and called Haven's cell phone. The line went straight to voice mail. Alfonso had a look of concern on his face, "Mr. Kruellar…is there a problem? Alfonso asked once more. At this point Harlan was beside himself and could ill afford to let his guard down, even if he felt Alfonso was actually being sincere, "No…Mr. Barrera. There's no problem, no problem at all. Like I said, I'm sorry we could not do business and…" Harlan began before Alfonso's cell phone rang. "Excuse me, do you mind if I take this call, I'm sure it will only take un momento?!" Alfonso asked politely. Harlan was reluctant as he was now in a hurry to meet his son, "Be my guest, but I do have a plane to catch!" Harlan grudgingly said. "Gracias…" Alfonso said. He answered his cell phone in a coarse tone, "Hola…que'? Are you sure? Bien…we're on our way!" Alfonso said assuredly. Time was ticking and Harlan could not wait any longer, "Mr. Barrera, I'm sorry but I really must be going…" Harlan reiterated. The look on Alfonso's disgruntled face troubled Harlan. He seemed to struggle to speak at first, as if he could not find the right words to say, "I believe you are not alone on this trip, Mr. Kruellar?" Alfonso painfully asked. Tension immediately built up inside Harlan's shoulders as if he had become inflated like diesel tire, causing him to feel immobile feel frozen, "Why do you ask?" Harlan uncomfortably asked. Alfonso put his hands together and on his lips, as if he were about to pray, and making Harlan more uneasy, "Because my people just caught someone who claimed to know where he is keeping your son." Alfonso said glumly. Fear consumed Harlan like a violent mudslide suffocating his every breath. The mental anguish Harlan was suffering from could be felt like a forty ton weight, "W-why do you…how d-do you know it's my son?" Harlan asked reluctantly. His eyes met with Harlan's like a sledgehammer striking a rusty nail, "Because, Senor Kruellar, the man my men have captured, said that the person HE abducted was a young American and his name was Haven…Haven Kruellar!" Alfonso said lucidly.

Things were beginning to spiral out of control in Harlan's mind like a wild mustang fighting for traction in the middle of a frozen lake. His tremendous guilt caused him to believe that he had finally failed in his task as a father to protect Haven, and allowed the unimaginable to happen to his only son. Thoughts played in his head over and over again, that Haven should have never come like a song stuck on repeat in an mp3 player. Harlan could not believe that it was only a few minutes ago that he wanted to put as much distance between him and the notorious cartel leader Alfonso Barrera as possible. But things have changed for the worst, as he had to now count on Alfonso Barrera to guarantee his son's survival. Alfonso convinced him to go with him to an undisclosed location near the importing district, close by the museum where he left his son. He imagined his late wife Marisa's disapproval, "Didn't I warn you Harly, to never get us involved in what you do? Now look at us now…" Harlan pictured his wife saying. Apparently Alfonso's cross town rival Francisco El Roga had intercepted a disclosed phone call to the limousine service Harlan rented from, and figured he could send a mercenary, only known as "Santiago", to infiltrate and kidnap Haven for a huge ransom. What Francisco had not anticipated, was running out of gas near one of Alfonso's hidden compounds. Santiago was already on the wrong side of town as it was, but after he went inside the station to pay for his gas, one of Alfonso's henchmen intended to steal his belongings from his car's front seat, and that's when he came across Haven Kruellar's wallet. He immediately notified his fellow constituents who were there and overwhelmed Santiago. Alfonso told Harlan, on their way to his clandestine hideaway, of how well his subordinates beat and tortured the inexplicable "Santiago," until he finally confessed how he came upon the stolen wallet. The news of this brought Harlan little comfort, but he was not going to be completely satisfied until he was totally sure Haven was safe. Part of him wanted to believe that the hideous Barrera was behind the coo. After all, it was rather convenient that his own men apprehended Haven's capturer, Harlan concluded. But that would have been giving the barbaric Alfonso Barrera too much credit, as he personally watched his every move and not once noticed him signal his driver or, use his cell. Harlan simply blamed it on chance, he would have blamed it on karma, but karma was something he did not believe in or could give power too.

After they arrived, Alfonso warned Harlan that it was for his own benefit that his men blindfolded the thrashed abductor. The rain was pouring down nonstop as if it was the great flood of Noah's ark, but Harlan had not cared, and both he and his own security team followed the now determined Alfonso Barrera and his driver inside the disturbingly quiet venue. The dilapidated gas station had a single car garage that appeared to open automatically upon their arrival. At the time, Harlan Kruellar had not bothered to notice the large money green F1-350 parked in the driveway and that it was chained onto something from inside the peculiar garage. Harlan did not have to caution his security team to be on their guard as they all had their guns already drawn and prepared for anything. Though the grimy garage was poorly lit, Harlan could still see his son's alleged kidnapper bleeding profusely on the oleaginous floor. Only a black hood concealed the perpetrator's identity. In a blind rage, Harlan rushed over and began kicking the chained hooded man in the stomach, causing him to release a loud and bellowed groan. Alfonso ordered his men to control Harlan. Alfonso was smiling harder than a Wachovia stockbroker who just received an insider trading tip, "Relax my friend, allow ME to handle this interrogation!?!" Alfonso suggested. Harlan finally came to his senses, but begrudgingly agreed for him to proceed. He commanded one of his underlings to start up the F1-350 truck that was parked in the driveway and told him to drive slowly. This was not the first time Harlan witnessed the torturing of another human being, as he has had his own dealings with ordering a few in the past. The mammoth looking F1-350 sounded like a humungous T-Rex as it roared in the driveway. It pulled out into the street slowly, causing Santiago's body to be suspended in the air like a float in the Macy's parade. A man wearing a dark red apron and a ragged greenish wielders mask handed Alfonso a large chainsaw that sounded as if it could cut through a steel girder. Santiago struggled mightily as his hands were also tied to a gas pipe. Only the sound of violent muffling could be heard as Alfonso persistently threatened to cut Haven's apprehender in half for information. No matter what he yelled or, screamed Santiago refused to respond. At that point, Harlan lost his self control and out of his own confusion and fears ordered Alfonso to cut the man's right arm off. Alfonso kindly obliged and used the frightening chainsaw to slash through Santiago's arm like a hot knife through warm butter. His blood spewed from his shoulder caps like a geyser at Yellowstone Park. His pain tolerance was staggering, Harlan thought, it was almost as if something was holding him back from…then it hit Harlan like a wrecking ball at a demolition site. Could it be possible that the real reason the silently restrained Santiago had not uttered a word might have been because his mouth had been gagged or, taped shut, Harlan fathomed. But why would he do such a…, "Wait a minute!" Harlan screamed too late as Alfonso started cutting the man in half from his waistline, creating a swimming pool of blood across the oil drenched floor. The man Alfonso Barrera's men claimed to be Francisco's second in command assassin Santiago, squirmed like livestock being taken out to pasture, until he was nothing but two pieces of grounded meat. Something stood out from the remains of the man that had been his son's "capture" that he had not previously observed before. After his body had been ripped apart by Alfonso's horror movie chainsaw, something about Santiago's belt buckle looked quite odd, almost…familiar to Harlan. It was shaped like a large silver star, just like the one he bought for his son Haven, before they departed for Mexico. One other thing stood out from the dead Santiago bloody stump that stood out on the putrid surface. His wrist had what looked like a gold Cartier watch on it, like the one Harlan gave Haven on his previous birthday. Had Santiago robbed his helpless son of all his precious belonging before he stored him away like a beast does his meal before the long winter, Harlan feared. Alfonso dropped the insidious looking chainsaw onto the greasy floor like a giant paper weight, "My friend, I will do everything in my power to help you find out where this el muerto asshole did with your son!" Alfonso promised. Meanwhile, Alfonso's men quickly disposed of the deceased Santiago's remains, leaving Harlan Kruellar to forever wonder just who was it that was actually under that black hood. Was it really some assassin sent by a rogue competitor of Alfonso Barrera or, simply some larger twisted scheme for him to be in his debt? Harlan fretted. Either way, someone was going to pay for taking the only thing he had in this world left to love…

Chapter 7:

"The Reckoning"

Houston, Texas….present day,

Though the five thirty traffic was very daunting, Terry could not help but notice how much Thomas Jr. nervously fidgeted with his cigarette lighter in one hand, while simultaneously gnawing on the nails of the other. It was apparent to him that something was clearly troubling his big brother and began to wonder what could have been the cause. He tried his best not to stare at the now full grown man who he once looked up to without causing a traffic accident. The clinician in him expected to see a wounded man who suffered signs of forced traumatic symptoms. But this was not just some ordinary schizoid patient he was dealing with, no, this time it was his own flesh and blood that needed help. "Was there something else plaguing him other than the obvious torment he endured under the slimy hands of Sonny Korne?" Terry pondered. Thomas Jr. had not uttered one single word in the car since they initially left the airport terminal. Seeing each other for the first time in a "very" long while had been both an awkward and nostalgic experience for the on edge Terry Templeton. When he first got off the plane, Terry believed he would have a heart attack at how much Thomas Jr. favored their late father Thomas Senior. Both he and Terry were not big on hugging back in the day, but Terry could not resist the temptation and bear hugged Thomas Jr. anyway. At the time, Thomas Jr. was caught off guard by the move and though he was much taller in stature, had slightly jumped at his pudgy baby faced younger brother. Thomas Jr. was just a child when he first visited Houston and appeared impressed by the city's growth since the last time he was there. At least, that was the impression Terry was hoping to assume from the way he gaped out his car window. The uncomfortable silence was becoming borderline intolerable for the very talkative Terry Templeton. He had a myriad of questions to ask his seemingly tortured brother who sat statue silent as he ignited his forth Marlboro cigarette. It was as if he were trying to set some new world record for nicotine consumption in ten minutes time, Terry joked privately. Terry Templeton was an experienced psycho analyst and could not turn off his clinical instincts, even if Fort Knox offered to pay him to. Just as they were exiting the freeway he caught a glimpse of Thomas Jr. right hand shaking uncontrollably, as if it were an old washing machine missing its leg during its rinse cycle. It only confirmed that what Terry Templeton had already suspected, which was something else had been agitating his big brother. The nervous lighter clicking and chronic chain smoking all were telltale signs of simple coping mechanisms, Terry deduced. Thomas Jr.' appearance, although clean, was another issue that had not gone unnoticed by the observant Terry Templeton. His brother's clothing did not match and clearly was not pressed. Thomas Jr.'s hair did not appear well taken care of and he had a five o'clock shadow that only the musician "Questlove" would love. Other things stood out to him as well, like how unclean and unkempt Thomas Jr.'s nails were, and also judging by the looseness of his shirt collar that he may have missed more than a few meals, Terry figured.

Terry Templeton had a rough start early in life as a runaway, but he eventually found the disciple he needed to survive by enlisting and serving in the United States Navy. In college, he earned his Master's in psychology to help people deal with their emotions, while at the same time, learned to also master his own. When his emotions did manage to get the best of him, he could always rely on Lacy to be his rock to lean on. But with each passing moment, while Terry inconspicuously diagnosed his brother's dire circumstances up close, his emotions begin to betray him once more and the walls built in his mind began to crumble. Terry could feel himself beginning to mentally unravel, as the bloody images taken at the murder scene of Thomas Jr.' home played back again and again, like a slaughterhouse movie inside his head. His pint up anger was making his prescribed Ray-Ban eyeglasses become somewhat of a hindrance, causing him to toss them off his flustered face and crashing into the cars cup holder. The noise made from the eyeglass frames was enough to break Thomas Jr.' deer hunter like trance. He turned his attention to his now panting younger sibling. When their eyes made contact Terry could vividly see the turmoil perched across his brother's weathered face like a bird hibernating in its nest, "You okay bro?" Thomas Jr. asked sincerely. For mere moments as if moving through time and space, Terry could feel his brother's deepest and darkest secrets searching through the closed curtains of his mind. His dismal face that featured layers upon layers of excruciating anguish somehow, for one microsecond, allowed Thomas Jr. a surprising fraction of empathy toward something so inconsequential. "How dare he?" Terry Templeton asked himself internally. Thomas Jr. was the "ONE" who had suffered greatly and been through tremendous HELL, but shouldn't it be HIM asking if things were alright, Terry rationalized. "How could God allow something so vicious and so vile happen to a man of the cloth?" He wondered. Terry thought back to the family photo that was in Alejandro's file that was taken previously before the Sonny Korne home invasion. Thomas Jr. had what appeared to be a beautiful and loving family, and was envious of him having two children to his "none," Terry thought at the time. Being a victim of rape and losing a wife and daughter was more traumatic an experience in its own right, but to witness the death of their mother, despite all of her good deeds. She suffered the greatest of indignities by getting beaten and shot up like some mangy dog in the street. It had to have taken great and unimaginable will for a man to survive such horrific events and still be considered a functional human being, Terry imagined. But here he was, playing the role of big brother all over again and showing genuine concern through some narrow crevice in his damaged psyche. To the untrained eye, a regular person would have disregarded such a pleasantry and taken the act for granted. Terry though, was a student of psychosis and could not ignore the price his brother had to pay, which is why his question "You all right bro?" had torn at his soul like a handsaw cutting through old rotted wood. With his defense system now weakened, the bricks that he used to hold himself together were tumbling, and his life partner Lacy was nowhere in sight to save him...

Ever since he was a child, Terry Templeton was always considered the most sensitive of the three Templeton children and was teased incessantly for it. Over the years, Terry learned to embrace his more sensitive side, which in turn became his greatest strength, but it was not until Lacy came along that he really learned to let his guard down and cry things out. "What would Lacy say to me if he knew I was having all these pent up feelings?" Terry wondered. First of all, Lacy probably would have strangled the fuck out of him for even allowing a stranger into the house to show him anything upsetting, let alone a file on dead relatives, Terry feared. But if it were strictly on the subject of remorse Terry felt or, seeing a tiny reflection of a brother's lost compassion, Lacy would have probably said what he always says, "Go on and get that cry out T-baby…and let's move on!" Terry imagined. Hearing his common-law husband's words play in the back of his head filled his heart with hope and caused his eyes to well up. "You okay bro?!?" again Thomas Jr. asked somberly. Terry tried to fight off the compulsion to breakdown, but found himself chuckling in hysterics, "Me all right? Ha, ha, ha…aw man, are you kidding me? I got my BIG brother back in my life again, (sniffling) sitting right here, next to me! The SAME big brother that always tried to bribe me not to rat on him whenever he would sneak out the house late at night…" Terry said with a gratified smile. Terry tried not to react to the forced smile on Thomas Jr. face when he made it. It probably had been a while since a real smile had last occupied space on his elder brother's somber looking face, Terry gathered. To help lighten the mood inside the car, Terry turned on the radio for inspiration. "My Girl" by The Temptations was already playing on Magic 102 radio station. Their mother loved The Temptations and "My Girl" was her favorite song in the world. She would coerce Thomas Senior to serenade it to her in the kitchen as they danced romantically with one another, they both remembered. Though he diligently preached against singing those secular songs to his congregation every other week, Thomas Sr. was still a human being who was very much madly in love with his wife. Despite his issues with Thomas Sr., Terry always believed in his heart that his father and mother belonged together. As the song continued to play, Thomas Jr. appeared to go deeper into withdrawal, and making Terry debate changing the station. It was obvious he was thinking about their mother. The mother with whom he witnessed being savagely beaten and sexually assaulted. Thoughts of seeing violence done to his family began to infuriate Terry to the point to where his hands tightened around the steering wheel, as if he were strangling Sonny Korne's neck. Thomas Jr. glanced at his little brother and could not help but notice the kung fu grip he had on his steering wheel, "Man, you sure you cool?" Thomas Jr. asked again. Terry looked at his brave big brother with total endearment, "Yeah bro, I'm cool." Terry said while gritting his teeth. Thomas Jr. rolled his eyes, "Boy Terry, you must be pretty good at whatcha' do! This shoal' is one nice ride! It's the new Lexus, right?" Thomas Jr. complimented. Terry was not stupid. He knew Thomas Jr. was just trying to manifest a conversation to avoid what was really on his mind to ask him. It was cool though, Terry thought, eventually his brother would be ready to open up to him, but in the meantime, he had give Thomas Jr. time to adjust to his new surroundings before reconnecting. He only hoped that there would be some time for reconnecting after considering the information that was dropped onto his lap merely days ago, Terry mentally balked, "Hmm? Uh, yeah… right, a Lexus. Appreciate it man, I do alright, I guess. I just try to be a good listener. It's the easiest part of the job!" Terry quipped. After he made that self gratifying comment, Thomas Jr. immediately shut down. Terry was afraid he would, but he could not stop the words from coming out before he said them. They were turning down the street towards his home, so Terry decided to get "The Reverend" Thomas Jr. acclimated to the idea of his preferred "lifestyle." He took a deep breath and peered out the corner of his eye, "So…Reverend. You going to be okay… you know…hanging wit' me and my partner, Lacy?" Terry asked briskly. Thomas was fixated on all the large homes in the area, "I don't know… yeah…I guess. I mean, shit, it is YOUR life. Who the hell am I to judge?" Thomas Jr. regrettably stated. Terry believed he already earned his brother's acceptance or he would not have come in the first place, but after hearing the cold manner in which he answered made Terry feel both trifling and inadequate. "Lord, please just give me the strength to hold on right now…please just let me, just let me make it home." Terry silently prayed underneath his breath. The Thomas Jr. he remembered as a child, was someone who was full of a kindred light and who liked to play and joke around all the time. He would go on and on at bedtime talking about which girl from school let him get the most fills and thrills at a party, Terry recollected. All what was left of his poor brother was a mere soulless preacher, who was just an empty shell of himself, or some old cold carbon copy of his former spiritual being. Terry decided to not ask Thomas Jr. any more personal questions, at least for the time being, or until he could get home fast enough to his lover Lacy. Lacy had a knack for making the tough things in life seem so minute, and always knew the right words to say to brighten up his day, "God, I hope he's home!" Terry said aloud unintentionally. Thomas Jr. broke his street gaze long enough to catch his brother's plea, "He…He who Fairy?" Thomas Jr. prodded. His brother's comment almost caught him by surprise, "Now that's the butthole brother I been waiting to see get off that goddamn plane!" Terry thought gleefully, "It's good to see you're still such an asshole Thomas! Jesus! But now, you're just…more of a reverend asshole…The Reverend "Asshole" Thomas Templeton Jr.!" Terry said jokingly. The both of them fell silent for barely a brief period before erupting simultaneously into uncontrollable laughter. Although it felt good for both Templeton brothers to get that shared laugh out, the tension still felt as thick as a bank vault. Terry felt like he needed it more and marveled at the forgotten sounds of his big brother's thunderous laugh. If any good was not to come from his brother's visit, if only but for a brief moment Thomas Jr. would at least have this small piece of joy, Terry rationalized.

They came to a sudden halt right in front of a tall and luxuriously gated red and white Victorian home. Terry appeared to have been looking for either something or someone behind the large and intimidating looking gate, causing Thomas Jr. to get suspicious, "You here makin' house calls "doc?!" Thomas asked. It was almost evening time and worry began to set in Terry's mind when he did not see his lover's pearl white Range Rover parked in its usual spot. But then Terry remembered Lacy's SUV was getting serviced at the dealer's that day and he was catching a cab ride home. Terry could not have imagined returning home and not having Lacy there to comfort him. Just before he could explain his reasoning for hesitating in front of the aristocratic looking gate with a heart in the middle of the golden initials T and L, "You remember Proverbs 20:17?... "Bread obtained by falsehood is sweet to a man, but afterward his mouth will be filled with gravel?" Thomas Jr. said mockingly. It took everything in him to resist acknowledging his brother's intentionally sarcastic comment. "What does your boyfriend, uh…uh…what's his name again?" Thomas Jr. asked, while snapping his finger. Terry rolled his eyes, "LACY…" Terry answered deftly. Thomas Jr. took a quick puff off his cigarette, "Yeah, Lacy…how HE feel about that doc?" Thomas Jr. asked in a patronizing tone. Terry casually raised his right hand towards his car's sun visor and pressed the button to open the looming gate, "I don't know smart ass…but, why don't you come in, and ask him for yourself?!" Terry beamed. When the illustrious looking gate opened Thomas Jr.' eyes bulged widely, as if he were a cartoon character from the movie Who Framed Roger Rabbit, and began choking uncontrollably on his cigarette,

“Whoa… (Thomas Jr. coughs)…Bruh!?! Who you got on yo’ couch…PRINCE?” Thomas Jr. snapped. “I’m not that kind of a doctor, but I do appreciate the compliment...and if you haven’t, heard Prince is dead!” Terry replied. They unpacked his luggage after parking the car inside the huge three car garage and from there made their way inside Terry’s home. Lacy hollered out for Terry just as he finished dialing in the security code on the keypad, “It’s us babe!!” Terry quickly responded back. Thomas Jr. had been both proud and impressed by his brother and partner’s extravagant home. Despite its vast amount of space, some of the decorum reminded him of his old family home back in Georgia. Part of him had long feared that after Terry ran away as a teenager that destitution, or worse, would have overcome Terry. But then again, the Terry Templeton he remembered as a kid was too stubborn and hot headed to let the streets hold him down, Thomas Jr. contemplated. If only their parents could have lived long enough to see how he turned out, thought Thomas Jr. “Come on Tommy, I want you to meet my big common-law hubby!” Terry said excitedly. His brother’s romantic pandering felt nauseating to the cringing reverend, “Please man, I ain’t even “ate” yet…” Thomas Jr. begged. Terry grabbed his slow prodding brother by the arm, “Quit complaining you homophobe and come on!” Terry ordered. He led Thomas Jr. into their giant living room, where Lacy had been lounging back in a big red leather comforter while watching NBA basketball highlights on a 100 inch HDTV. “Lacy, I like you to meet my oldest brother…Thomas Jr.” Terry introduced. Lacy muted the television and hurried to his feet, “Oh man! It’s an honor to finally meet you!” Lacy said emphatically. He put his giant hand out to shake Thomas Jr.,’ but Thomas Jr. hesitated to return the gesture. Thomas Jr. was amazed at how much great shape Lacy was in at his age and seemed to have lost count of all the muscles in his massive arms. Terry gave Thomas Jr. a slight shove to snap him out of his rude gaze. Thomas Jr. had the scowl of a New York City gargoyle on his face afterwards, but ultimately gave in and shook Lacy's hand. After their hand shake Thomas Jr. thought he would need an ice pack for his knuckles, “Uh, nice to meet you to…damn, so, where do I put these?” Thomas Jr. winced. Though puzzled by Thomas Jr.’ gawking reaction towards him, Lacy reached down and picked up the three suitcases with ease, “Don’t you worry about these. I’ll just run them upstairs to the guest room! Nice meeting you Thomas.” Lacy said politely. He gave Terry a quick peck on the cheek and zipped up the stair case as if he were doing a 100 meter relay. "You never said your husband was Ronnie Coleman. The Negro almost broke my damn hand with them catcher's mitts he has for hands." Thomas Jr. quipped. Terry stood patiently still and found himself unintentionally gazing into his lover's previous direction. So much was happening so fast that Terry almost had forgotten his true purpose for flying his brother out in the first place. He used treacherous means to influence Thomas Jr. to agree to come visit him and will soon have to expose him to the truth, Terry thought. Lying over the phone to his brother was one thing, but to lie right in front of Thomas Jr.' face was going to be an even greater challenge, Terry worried. "Yo Terry…you got that look on your face again." Thomas Jr. said. It was not until that moment that Thomas Jr. gave his little brother a decent look in the face and realized just how much Terry favored his son Markus. He thought about Markus' status the entire flight over to Houston and planned on checking on his son's condition after getting himself settled in. But that call would just have to wait for the time being, as he had to get down to the bottom of whatever it was that Terry may have been trying to conceal, Thomas Jr. suspected. "Huh? What look?" Terry asked confused. "The same face you been making since you were five years old…when you been hiding something. Alright Terr,' spit it out." Thomas Jr. commanded. He turned his attention away from Thomas Jr. and began walking off towards the kitchen, "I need a drink…you want a drink?" Terry yelled. It was made abundantly clear that Terry was trying to avoid his interrogation, but ever since he had seen his father's ghost back home it had left him very much on edge, "Wha…yeah, sure." Thomas Jr. answered inadvertently. "Don't think I'm letting you off that…" Thomas Jr. began to say, until seeing the size of Terry's kitchen area. The kitchen was almost as big as the three car garage they parked the Lexus in, causing Thomas Jr. to be taken aback, "Shit Terry…is this a house or, a damn chapel?" Thomas Jr. quipped. His remark made Terry smile, "What's your poison old man? Or am I too early for communion?" Terry asked. Thomas Jr. sat at one of the half dozen red leather bar stools near a wet bar, "Double Maker's Mark, straight… if you got it?" Thomas Jr. said and whipped out his cigarettes. "You don't mind if I…" Thomas Jr. began to ask. "Sure, if you got any left to smoke..." Terry quipped. He snickered at Terry's cynicism and then marveled at his various assortments of wine and liquor at his spacious black and white marbled wet bar. He and Lacy had an impressive collection of French wine that even Henry VIII would have loved, Thomas Jr. thought. Thomas Jr. decided to put Terry's issue on hold for the moment and decided to change the subject. "You know, Terry…I, uh…I-I really appreciate what you done…for me. You know… by reaching out, and flying me all the way here and all. It's been really… (Thomas Jr. took a long drag from his cigarette) things been real hard on me, especially with my boy Markus in the hospital and everything. I…uh, I-I got…I got nothing left…but him, now." Thomas Jr. confessed. The waxed dipped bottle of Maker's Mark bourbon slightly rattled in Terry's hand as he poured their drinks. He abruptly placed the bottle onto the marbled counter and quickly guzzled down the glass of bourbon, as though he were a thirsty runner swallowing a cool cup of water at a 2k marathon. Both the combined weight of Thomas Jr.' confessed agony and his own hidden deception, draped uncomfortably over Terry Templeton's conscious like a cheap suit. He poured himself another glass of bourbon to calm his nerves, but the alcohol just was not acting fast enough for his liking, "You would've liked him." Thomas Jr. said, and took a sip from his glass. Terry swallowed down his second glass of bourbon faster than he did the previous one and then poured himself another. Part of him was beginning to get a little frustrated at trying to figure out the best viable way to verbally approach and console Thomas Jr. without provoking him. "The last thing in the world he probably needed was his kid brother trying to play doctor…" Terry figured. "Yeah bro, I'm sure I would've. But hey, at least you know you still got me!?" Terry said precariously. Thomas Jr. did not immediately respond and instead took another sip from his glass. Just as Terry started to drink another shot of bourbon, he was startled to see Lacy staring at him from the hallway. "Oh! Baby you scared me…" Terry said. "What are we celebrating?" Lacy asked sternly. Terry noticed his chiseled jaw pulsating in and out like the beating of a human heart, as he stood there gazing at him like a bronze statue. It was more than obvious to Terry that Lacy did not approve of his alcoholic over indulgence and decided to intervene, "Just two brothers letting off some steam is all, care to join us?..." Terry asked. Lacy hesitated for a moment, "…it is Friday after all, babe…" Terry said encouragingly. After taking his comment under careful consideration Lacy began to walk towards the kitchen, but as each step he made towards Terry the more he could see the hurt in his eyes, "Uh-h…you know what…maybe later. I just got back from the gym and could use some rest, so…you guys play catch up." Lacy said. "Don't be too long" Lacy whispered in Terry's ear and walked off. Terry knew that Lacy could read him like a book and relished the thought of laying out his emotions to him privately. "Man, after all these years, I still don't get it...why DUDES Terry Fairy?" Thomas Jr. asked. Terry wiped the tear that almost got away from him before responding, "The heart wants what the heart wants, preacher man." Terry joked. "Whatever man..." Thomas Jr. shuddered. The room had suddenly become eerily quiet for a moment as they drank, until Thomas Jr. broke his silence, "Look Terr,'… I don't know why you REALLY invited me down here, (Thomas Jr. said while twirling the contents of his glass) but, I'm sure whatever the reason is, I suppose it was a very important one…" Thomas Jr. said. The scathing sensation Terry endured during the car ride home was now revisiting him again like an unwanted electricity bill. He tried to convince himself that there was nothing to worry about and that his brother did not have any conclusive proof of being invited under any false pretence, so Terry continued to enjoy his libation in a cumbersome silence. "…at least, important enough that you felt the need to lie to get me here that is!" Thomas Jr. implied. His allegation caused Terry to choke on his bourbon mid drink, "W-w-ha-h?" Terry gargled.

Although Thomas Jr.'s accusation about Terry lying to him was extremely accurate, he still felt the need to hold back some of the truth, "Lie…ha-ha-ha-, what lie? I don't know what you're talking…" Terry protested, before Thomas Jr. intruded. "Cut the shit now, Terry…before you start choking on it." Thomas Jr. instructed. He stared Terry down with the very same scolding and disapproving look his father Thomas Sr. often gave him, way back when they were children. Here it was, many years later, and Terry Templeton still found himself unable to escape his father's piercing gaze, Terry thought. "Harvey..." Thomas Jr. said softly. Terry took a nip from his glass, "Harvey? Harvey what?" Terry asked befuddled. Thomas Jr. rolled his eyes and frowned disappointedly, "That's where you messed up, Terr'…Harvey Henry." Thomas said, while casually sipping his bourbon in an ominous fashion. "He died of AIDS Terry…YEARS before…b-before that night!" Thomas Jr. said, as he stood painstakingly to his feet. When Thomas Jr. rose from his chair Terry believed his big brother was surely about to knock him senseless, but instead Thomas Jr. finished what was left of his drink and left his glass on the counter and walked off. "I take it that the guestroom's upstairs?" Thomas Jr. asked solemnly.

The shame on Terry's face felt heavy as a gorilla sized Halloween mask. He could not bring himself to offer an explanation or let alone, find the strength to apologize. "T-T-Thomas…I-I, I'm…" Terry tried to explain. Thomas Jr. stopped dead in his tracks and turned gradually, "Look man, just save it, okay? I'm getting a little too old for games! Now, I came here because…" Thomas Jr. began before seeing the image of his decayed dead father in his mind, "…because, I missed my little brother." Thomas Jr. said. Despite his guilty conscious Terry was still able to detect that Thomas Jr. himself may have been guilty holding back some "truths" himself. Thomas Jr.' eyes went down and to the left which in his field represented someone creating thoughts, which also meant they were usually lying. "Now, with that being said little brotha,' I've traveled too far away from my son to be here. I don't need you spoiling my trip over any of your crazy bullshit! Is we clear?" Thomas Jr. stringently asked. He nodded his head "yes" and Thomas Jr. began marching towards the guest room upstairs. "Jesus, how could I've been so fuckin' stupid?!?" Terry whispered to himself. Just when he thought they were making some decent headway towards rekindling their lost brotherhood, Terry found himself scraping at the bottom of the oil barrel all over again. What could his brother possibly be hiding from him that was not in the F.B.I. file? Terry wondered. Somehow, he had to regain his brother's trust and make things right between them, so they both can get some closure. But the only way that could possibly happen for them was if he could help Thomas Jr. bring Sonny Korne to justice. Terry swallowed the rest of his bourbon and slammed the empty glass down onto the hard marbled counter top in disgust. On his way to his bedroom Terry spotted Thomas Jr. at the foot of the steps, as if he were anticipating him. He was leaning against the pearl white stair rail gazing down at him with watery eyes, "One other thing Terr'…I did everything I could, to protect my family…to protect…to protect our momma. Sorry I let you down bro." Thomas Jr. said apologetically. He walked away with his head hung low in defeat while leaving Terry in the cold walkway all alone. Terry had had more than enough of the emotional roller coaster for one evening and charged his way through to his bedroom door and lunged into the strong chiseled arms of his partner who had dropped the gym bag he was packing. When he was not busy working as a fulltime bailiff at the county courthouse downtown, Lacy also worked as a part-time fitness trainer at the "2 The Max" health club in the Heights. Lacy was always fascinated by fit men, but could never whip himself into any other shape but round, he believed. Terry never fully understood what Lacy had seen in him in the first place, other than their obvious sexual preferences, they basically were the direct opposite of each other. While Terry was the neat person, Lacy was the slob. When Lacy usually ate on a strict diet, Terry was hoarding ho ho's in his desk at work. He preferred reading a good book while Lacy watched sports all day, etc. Whatever force it was that brought them together, albeit supreme divinity or blind dumb luck Terry was highly appreciative of Lacy being in his life. "Babe, what's wrong?" Lacy asked softly. Terry could not find the words, nor the strength to speak immediately and was squeezing the life out of Lacy' stomach, "Uh, babe…you kinda' squeezin' the hell out of me!" Lacy said winded. But Terry could not help himself and began squeezing harder. "Hmph, I thought I was supposed to be the strong one!" Lacy quipped. His grip was tight as a mouse caught by a Boa constrictor and only loosed it after hearing his common law husband gasping for air. "I'm sorry…" Terry cried. Lacy gently lifted his chin to wipe his tears away, "Hey, it's okay…whatever is the matter you know I'm always here for you!" Lacy assured. His tender words of affection brought a broad smile to his round face, "Why do I even deserve a man like you?" Terry asked. "You know, I been asking that myself that same question every day…" Lacy stated. Terry pulled away from Lacy and then slapped him on the shoulder, "Asshole." Terry professed. "Hey!!! I hope that isn't your medical opinion!?" Lacy protested. Terry turned his back to Lacy and folded his arms in disgust, "I don't need this shit right now Steven!" Terry said vehemently. Lacy's eyebrows stood up in full attention at the mention of his middle name, "O-o-oh…I see. Hmmm…you know it's a dead giveaway whenever you call me that!?! Okay, time to spill the tea!" Lacy said. Terry was afraid to turn around and face his lover. Even though other disparaging issues plagued his mind like a rotten cavity, he could not find the way to overcome his old insecurities, "Look at you Steven…you probably, no CERTAINLY, could have had any man OR woman you ever wanted, but instead…you chose me. And I need to know why? What make me so special?!" Terry asked befuddled. Lacy started shaking his head in amusement and walked up behind the pouting Terry Templeton and held him. “Is this really what THIS is about?” Lacy asked suspiciously. He was weak in Lacy’s large strong arms and tried his best to not allow him to change the subject, “Just answer the damn question!? Terry commanded. Lacy turned Terry around and grabbed his chin, “Because of this…” Lacy said as he kissed him. Terry was dazed by his deep embrace, “Oh yeah…that.” Terry said sedated. “Look, other than my father, I’ve only loved one man and that man is YOU!?!” Lacy confirmed. “Now, are you gonna’ explain to me what this is really…REALLY, all about?” Lacy asked.

Midtown Houston Mental Care Facility: Monday morning…

Harlan Kruellar devoted an entire month quietly studying every last one of the men, up close and inconspicuously, from the other side of a large two-way mirror. Three days out of the week, Harlan relived each excruciating tale of horror, in which they all shared inside the quaintly lit and sky blue colored room. He was never fond of hospitals and clinics and never fully understood how a dully colored wall was supposed to make a person feel at ease. It had been years since Harlan last spent such a significant amount of time near any type of hospital. Harlan spent many painful months watching his wife’s health and will to live fade away, like autumn leaves withering away during a brisk winter. Although Harlan never allowed religion to dictate his way of life, he did believe that his wife indeed had a soul. But, shortly upon her death, he could not shake the feeling that something surely left her body. The light that usually accompanied her brilliant and radiant face whenever she entered a room was gone. At the funeral, her beautiful radiance had been reintegrated with a deep somber calm that seemed to both darken and take all the air in the very room, Harlan recollected. Just as it felt to watch his soulless wife Marisa, Harlan could see the same lifelessness upon the faces of the fathers he secretly gathered. Lots of arm twisting and palm greasing went into securing and “acquiring” these individuals, and here they all were, ten completely different men sharing ten completely different stories, which all had a very tragic ending. Most of them wept as they took their turns sharing each and every cataclysmic detail of the events that led up to their current state of mind. While some of them, like snooty insurance claims adjuster Adrian Atkinson and substance abuser “Skinny Ricky” Wallace, choose to express themselves openly to the group about their grief and despair, others in the room like former super jock Jovan Campbell and the brazen undercover D.E.A. agent Milton Elliot, allowed their anger to do the talking, which oftentimes lead to orderlies breaking them apart. Harlan Kruellar sat patiently through two painstaking hours of suffering and aggravation, while at the same time, not allowing his own demons to interfere with his own private objective. Before the installation of this programs conception, Harlan tried his best to convince himself that he was far different than the rest of the men in the other room. But apart from having a much larger bank account and an incredible ego, eventually realized the similarities they all shared. Like Harlan, each of them lost a child or two, through some horrible circumstance or another, and had worn the agony of their losses like ball room masks. Worst of all, they lacked the will to carry on with their daily lives and often purged on alcohol or, drugs to numb their suffering. His same distresses were their distresses and vise versa. He could easily identify with the pain they felt and the misery of a void that replaced the love lost for their children. Some of the fathers gathered lost their entire families through what some would elude to as “random violence,” but violence was hardly ever really “random,” Harlan believed. Harlan spent most of his life around violence and in most cases, used it like a tool to construct the transporting empire that he created not long ago. He knew it was both an effective, but necessary evil that sometimes bled into other innocent people’s lives. His only regret was that it took the loss of his son’s life to learn the error of his ways. Deep within his troubled heart, Harlan knew he had an obligation not only to himself, but to the some of the men in the room to make amends for “his” past sins. If only his intensions were totally pure, he often contemplated. It was not by coincidence or by chance, that these former fathers were grouped together. The greedy Dr. William G. Becker, who ran the Midtown mental facility, jumped at the $500,000 donation Harlan enticed him with to fund this façade. “What better way for him to seek a proper vengeance than by using Alfonso Barrera’s own money as a ransom for his own demise,” Harlan thought. Harlan knew with his vast resources he could have paid an army of mercenaries to try and exterminate him, but Alfonso Barrera had an army as well, and would make getting close to him much harder on his home turf. He recalled what his father once told him long ago, "The best way to entrap a wild rabbit was by luring him to your garden!" His father's words of wisdom made him smile gleefully in supreme satisfaction as he had JUST the carrot to entrap his malevolent prey. Then and only then, would his mind be at ease and maybe, just maybe, the nightmares that permeated him daily would also fade away. Not a day passed, that the lasting images of his son Haven being savagely ripped apart by his killer's chainsaw did not haunt him. He also remembered the small sense of helplessness that came over him afterward. It also felt as if his soul had been betrayed by his own sensibilities to leave Mexico alive in order to seek proper vengeance. The promise that he made to his late wife Marisa, to always keep their son safe from harm, had been broken. Although her impending death almost destroyed him, it was a mild relief that she had not been alive to witness Haven's fate. Marisa would had never agreed to his crude methods of possibly endangering these men whom he sought in the room, especially since it was "he" who was indirectly responsible for putting them there in the first place. The eclectic Harlan Kruellar had spent an entire year setting a plan in motion that would not only bring about the demise of his foe Alfonso Barrera, but also the hope of bringing some of these men some semblance of peace.

After making the $500,000 donation to the Midtown mental facility, Harlan only had three stipulations to make with the eager Dr. Becker. The first stipulation: was that a focus group for traumatized and distraught fathers to be immediately implemented. His second stipulation: was for Dr. Terry Templeton to serve as the group's "only" attending psychologist. Harlan's final condition: was to be allowed to observe the group in an unofficial capacity. Dr. Becker's decision to comply with those demands did not sit well with Dr. Templeton in the beginning, as he felt it was unethical at best to give anyone other than the patient access to privileged information. Harlan knew he would eventually change his tune once Alejandro gave him the "incentive" to reach out to his brother, Reverend Thomas Templeton Jr. All the final pieces were put into their places and the sight of his own handy work made Harlan feel a high sense of delectable satisfaction. He admired and appreciated Dr. Templeton's ability to surgically flesh out the core aspects of a traumatized person's repressed emotions. Had the circumstances been different, he might have sought his help on a more private level, but that would have been too selfish of him, Harlan thought. Any morals that he still possessed should only be expended on the harnessing and helping of those individual men in the group he hurt, Harlan concluded. In his lifetime, Harlan had seen many violent atrocities brought onto families, which was the main reason why his family fled from Nazi Germany and to America many years ago. The "elephant in the room," Dr. Templeton's older brother the Reverend Thomas Templeton Jr., appeared to be a broken man who was not only uncomfortable because he was among strangers, but because of his past affliction at the hands of a group of them, Harlan suspected. The Reverend's personal file by FAR was the most gruesome to follow, Harlan recollected. Harlan's mind harkens back to some of the darker tales his late father once told him as a young teenager. He remembered the horror stories about how Adolf Hitler used forced tactics to recruit some of the German soldiers to help fight in World War II. If you were of German decent and unwilling to join Hitler's hateful cause, then that person was labeled a traitor and his family members would have been killed or, the man shamed in his own home by Nazi soldiers. His father's allegory of what he and his mother escaped was frightening at best, and seemed impossible to avoid, or imagine, Harlan believed. The much older Thomas Templeton Jr. was only trying to protect his daughter from the very shame he himself endured at the cost of his own faith, He thought. Harlan shook his head in disbelief and began clinching his fists unknowingly. Though Harlan lacked any true religion, he still managed to put faith in Dr. Templeton's aptitude for making the Reverend's presence therapeutic and necessary to the plan.

Terry Templeton was all smiles as he introduced his brother to the group, "Good afternoon everyone! Hope you all have gotten a good night's rest! I would like to introduce to you all someone who is very special and dear to me…" Terry began. Thomas Jr. sat uncomfortably in the metal chair as if he were sitting on a pile of hot coals. He hoped that his presence would not cause any distractions and practically begged Terry for him not to attend in his preaching garb. But Terry still being his always pushy self, talked him into wearing the collar and convinced him that his "Deep Christian views could be of some service!" He recollected. Thomas Jr. scoped out the room, like an astronomer does outer space, and could not shake the disturbing unease in the air, "No offense doc, but I just ate my lunch…ya' mind showing off ya' boyfriend another time?" A thick southern voice said from the back of the room. Harlan's eyebrows stood up in attention like a flag on a flagpole when he heard the slender figure wearing the old Florida University cowboy hat spoke. The coarse raspy voice belonged to none other than Lieutenant Kale Keegan, who usually had to be sedated after waking up from his catnaps. Harlan spent weeks watching him keep to himself and never uttering one word. He often slept during these sessions and would wake up violently from terrible nightmares, which with his training constantly sent many orderlies in the emergency room. Lieutenant Kale Keegan was transferred to the Midtown facility after serving six months in a military psychiatric hospital, in Miami Dade County, for assaulting his commanding officer. The file Harlan read on him said that he was unpredictable and had authority issues, but also talked about his amazing military record as a black ops operative. Men like Kale Keegan, who have a gift for violence do not grow on trees and his vast experience will serve an excellent purpose for his plan, Harlan concurred. Everyone in the room were taken aback by Kale's sudden willingness to speak and stared at him like a group of scientists admiring a new form of tumor, "Well…Lieutenant, so you do speak!" Terry said emphatically. "Jus' Kale…and, I ain't a military man no more, doc!" Kale said drunkenly and took a puff from a cigarette he was hiding. Terry Templeton did not know what to make of the curious Kale Keegan at first. He was the only man in the room who was the most reluctant to speak to anyone openly or privately, Terry pondered. The only thing the Army was willing to disclose about him were his medical records, but judging from his violent outbursts he displayed while napping in group were sure signs of PTSD syndrome. Terry never fully understood his purpose for even BEING in the group in the first place. From what he was told by his superior, Dr. Becker, the focus group was formed for the sole purpose of the study and helping of FATHERS still dealing with violent PTSD, NOT soldiers. It was supposed to be designed for civilian men who lost their kids and not servicemen who been to war. This man obviously needed one on one psych evaluations in the SAFE confines of a veteran's hospital and not a civilian facility, Terry believed. But, here he was, this walking enigma, who decided after many weeks to pick NOW to speak and in dramatic fashion. "Okay, Kale…for your information sir, this is NOT my BOYFRIEND, but my older brother…the Reverend Thomas Templeton Jr." Terry proudly announced. The room that was filled with individual chit chatter had fallen dead silent. Everyone in the group was staring at him with either spite, or contempt in their eyes, "Ahem…Uh, hello…everybody, uh…been hearing great things about you, I mean the group!" Thomas Jr. said uncomfortably. "Thank you for having me!" Thomas Jr. said embarrassed. They all appeared frozen in their chairs, like a collection of Christmas ornaments on a lawn, Thomas Jr. thought.

Thomas Jr. fiddled with his clerical collar, as if he were digging out broken shards of glass on the inside of it, and his forehead began to perspire, as if it was being held too close to a scolding hot press iron. "Looks like you need this drag mo' than me fella'." Kale said coyly, as he held up his cigarette. Thomas Jr. took a hard look at the enticing cigarette butt and could feel his lips begin to chap and slightly began licking them. Kale started snickering in a low tone as if he were like that imaginary devil who sits on a cartoon character's shoulder that tries to convince them to do evil. "Uh…no, thank you!" Thomas Jr. replied and wiped his dry mouth. Terry was getting a little annoyed by Kale's disregard for the rules and the fact he was agitating his big brother, "Do YOU mind putting that away? How many times I have to ask you not to smoke in here anyway?" Terry asked irritably. Kale sat with his legs crossed and put the cigarette out with the bottom of his alligator skinned boots, "Well, all that depends doc?" Kale asked. Terry was reluctant to answer but could not avoid the temptation, "Depends on what?" Terry asked uninterested. Kale's smile became even broader, "…On how high can ya' count?" Kale retorted. His bravado managed to get a couple of chuckles from some of the others in the room, while Harlan from the other side of the two-way mirror stood seemingly mesmerized by Kale's dry candor. A knock came at the door, but Harlan never took his eyes off Kale, "Come in." Harlan said annoyed. It was Terry's assistant Sheila, "Do you need me to get you anything Mr. Kruellar?" Sheila asked. "No thank you…" Harlan said while still peering through the looking glass. Sheila took a quick peek out the mirror and then looked back at Harlan and gave him a disapproving frown, "Okay then, I'll let you get back to…whatever it is, you're doing, sir." Sheila said dryly and walked out. Her sarcasm fell on deaf ears as she closed the door behind herself. He was in deep thought and in those thoughts were a hundred or so, factors concerning Lieutenant Kale Keegan specifically. Before he could set the rest of his plan into motion, he had to make sure that Lieutenant Keegan had at least half a mind to barter with. The NSA file Harlan procured explained just how scattered Kale's psyche was after witnessing his family dying in an explosion in Iowa. The government intelligence contact Harlan has at the Pentagon also shared, that Kale was "already" somewhat of a basket case to begin with, due to his father's (a four star general) willingness to turn him into an animal after his wife died. When his own wife died, Harlan did everything in his power to reassure his son that he was loved and knew in his heart that he could never have treated him cruelly as Kale's father was rumored to have done him. "Who could have fathomed that Kale's future circumstances would have ended in such a drastic travesty?" Harlan thought grimly. Tragedy seemed to always follow those who sought to avoid it the most, Harlan concluded. Unfortunately, in his experience, pain was a foregone conclusion that he knew all too well, and never could afford to get comfortable around it. Regardless of what his hidden agenda may have been, Harlan Kruellar the father, could not help but feel pity for the damaged young man. Both he and his late son were close in age, but Haven sadly was robbed of the future Kale Keegan MIGHT have had, if it were not for the powers that be, "What a shame." Harlan murmured softly.

Terry put on his reading glasses and opened his composition notepad with the zeal of an overeager gourmet chef that is creating a new recipe. He quickly thumbed to an empty page, and just like a knight brandishing a blazing sword, readied his fountain pen to begin his afternoon session, "Alright everyone, you know how this thing goes! Whenever we have someone new to the group we usually open up by introducing who you are, where you're from, and what brought you here." Terry announced. Thomas Jr. had yet to fully relax his mood and was doing his best to put Kale's tempting offer far from out of his mind. He was not sure what type of example Terry expected him to make and surely did not want to make a bad impression on behalf of "Doctor Templeton, Thomas Jr. internally jested." Terry told him earlier that morning, on the way to the Midtown facility, that he wanted him to "just be yourself," but that was asking a lot from a person that was no longer who he once was, Thomas Jr. feared. That person USED to be a proud father who once loved to preach and who loved to get under his wife, Lucinda's, skin at the super market about which snacks to buy for the house. He was no longer allowed be that loving husband or, that cherished father of two and barely the shadow of the well-respected preacher he once was. His whole world had been caved in over the top of his graying head, like a log cabin stuck in a Colorado avalanche, along with his predestined faith, Thomas Jr. thought. In the span of one lifetime, Thomas Jr. felt as though he suffered just about every indignity ever imagined and also felt betrayed by God for his transgressions. "Maybe I do need a smoke, or two, or three…" Thomas Jr. pondered. To gather his thoughts, Thomas Jr. placed his father's weathered bible on the floor beneath him and reached into his pocket for the lighter he often played with when his nerves got the best of him. Kale took notice and grinned as if he hit a million dollar jackpot, "Now wait a minute doc, (snort) what's preacha' man's role posed' ta' be in this little soiree here? Kale asked sarcastically. Judging from both his slightly slurred speech and the color of his eye sclera, it was clear Kale had been drinking prior to their session, Terry hypothesized. "Mr. Keegan, if you're not up to it today you can always go…" Terry began. Kale responded back as if he were a hurt pantomime, "Why, you not tryna' git rid o' me…is ya' doc?" Kale asked innocently. Terry knew how radioactive Kale was when it came to confrontation and was not in the mood for creating one, "You got it all wrong Kale, I DO want you HERE, but if you insist on drinking prior to these sessions, then what good ARE you to the group? It's not being fair to those who actually WANT to be here… (Terry turning his head)…than to those who don't! Ahem!" Terry professed and looked over his shoulder at another young man sitting motionless in the room. It was former college standout Jovan Campbell sitting catty-corner from him. The look on his face was a little unnerving to Thomas Jr. who compared his mean scowl and folding arms to the Martin Luther King memorial statue back in Georgia. Jovan had been daydreaming as he usually did, but broke his spell once former undercover D.E.A. agent Milton Elliot snapped his fingers in his face, "Aye' yo,' Earth to meathead!" Milton shouted. Although he would deny it with a straight face, Terry could tell that deep down Milton liked Jovan, or else he would not harass him so, "Whuh?" Jovan asked obliviously. Terry rolled his eyes and went back to his notes, "Right…" Terry said dryly. Kale leaned forward in his chair and rubbed his dirty hands across his face, "I hear' ya doc…jus' dont' know what holy man's posed' ta' be here for, is all. Sunday was yesterday, and I ain't lookin' fo' no fuckin' sermons… (Kale began to scowl at Thomas Jr.) …especially from someone like him..." Kale said disapprovingly. Out of all the members of the group, Kale seemed to have the most resentment toward him being there, Thomas Jr. assumed. "Was he just another red-necked racist, or did he have another deeper issue altogether, other than his own personal hygiene?" Thomas Jr. wondered. Judging from his dusty appearance, Kale looked like someone who took great pleasure in working on both cars and wet bars…but who was HE to judge? Thomas Jr. thought. Terry Templeton understood all too well the imminent possibility of a backlash coming from some of the members in the group. But the LAST person in the world he expected that backlash to come from was the volatile church mouse of the group Kale Keegan, Terry concluded. Although Kale was beginning to be a headache for Dr. Templeton, his juvenile actions were not enough incentive for Harlan to pull the plug on him. In fact, the resourceful Harlan Kruellar had very much counted on the reverend's presence to agitate a dialogue out of him. Kale had refused to speak in the group since the very first moment he arrived, and Harlan figured that as a former soldier, who killed in the name of both God and country, he would have a BIG problem discussing life and death in front of any preacher. Either way, he trusted Dr. Templeton and his "keen proficiency" at "massaging" the MALE ego, and continued to watch things from afar. Despite being distracted, Terry Templeton only needed a fraction of a second to snap back on his game to try and rationalize with the outspoken Lieutenant Kale Keegan, "Okay Kale, fair enough! But as a man of science and reason, I DO have to keep an open mind, and even I know that there are answers to some questions that just can't possibly be answered with science alone! So, as a favor, I asked my big brother to come all the way down from Atlanta to attend this group…" Terry explained. Kale rolled his eyes at Terry and huffed loudly, "He's not here to patronize you Kale, but with his…EXPERIENCE (Terry looked Thomas Jr. eye to eye) and spiritual advisement, at the very least, you DO get another outlook from an ASTOUNDING man of the cloth who understands…AND knows, as much as you do about pain." Terry said tentatively. Listening to his younger brother speaking about him so sincerely brought a humbling smile to Thomas Jr. face. He figured it was also Terry's way of inconspicuously opening the door for him, whenever he believed he was ready to talk amongst the gathered strangers, Thomas Jr. deduced. One of the "strangers" in particular was one of the newer "additions" to the group, and like his fellow group mates, Noel Brody was no "stranger" when it came to knowing a little something about the anguish of personal loss. Although he could not put a finger on it, Noel thought it odd that he may have either met or, seen

Reverend Templeton some place prior to today's meeting. But that could not have been so, since he never actually visited Atlanta, let alone knew anyone there, Noel pondered. Whatever it was that bugged Noel Brody about the Reverend Thomas Templeton Jr., he knew it could not have been anything good. The room the group conversed in felt a lot colder than usual to him, which reminded him of that long frightful night in the rain when he lost his precious fiancé...

Both he and his pregnant fiancé at the time, Carly, were also victims to "random" violence. Despite their dividing racial lines, the two fell in love after one initial blind date, about four years ago. The twenty-nine year-old African- American Noel was only in his first residence as a Criminal Science professor at the University of Oklahoma after meeting his then twenty-two year-old bride-to-be, through a mutual friend online. Though elementary teacher Carly Skyhorne was born half Cherokee through her father, Samuel, it was her mother Miranda's more voluptuous Caucasian features that stood out the most. The loving pair was heading out of town a few summers back, to visit Carly's parents in Virginia, when they got lost during a very bad thunderstorm that night, somewhere off interstate 64. Out of desperation, Noel pulled over into the parking lot of an old-fashioned diner called Mitch's, to ask for directions, but left Carly in the car while it was running. When he returned from inside the diner, both the car and his fiancé were gone. After several hours passed, the police eventually found the car, as well as his battered fiancé who had also been stabbed, just outside a small town bordering Kentucky. She had been sexually assaulted and barely conscious when the authorities located her bleeding to death along the side of the dark and stormy road. Detectives there at the scene had blamed the assault on some nomadic lunatic hitchhiker and vowed to catch him soon. But their meaningless speculations and empty veiled promises were not enough to console his conscious-stricken heart. Carly had been left with too many substantial physical and mental scars to bear, which caused her to become more and more despondent and increasingly hysterical with each passing day. The grief stricken criminal science collegian could tell Carly was suffering from classic PTSD symptoms, which ultimately led to her jumping to her death off the tenth floor of a hospital bedroom window. Noel's sorrow was far too great to return back to the daily rigors of teaching at the university and so, he resigned. After feeling responsible for both Carly and their unborn child's death, Noel eventually went into a deep depression. When he hit rock bottom, his childhood friend and former university colleague, Cindy Hill, helped him get back on his feet. She convinced him to move to Houston for a change of scenery, where he now worked as a student guidance counselor. He met Dr. Terry Templeton last year at a seminar held at the campus where he was the spokesman. Noel perceived the older and much wiser, Dr. Templeton as a person he could trust and decided to share his grizzly tale over a BAD cup of coffee in the school cafeteria. Though they were never officially close, Noel jumped at the opportunity when Dr. Templeton called him up to join his new program months after they last spoke to one another. Since he joined the group though, things had not been that interesting until today, after the inclusion of Dr. Templeton's brother was made, Noel theorized. He tried to put the idea out of his mind that he already had known the docile preacher from another time and place, but the young Noel Brody was not a man who forgot faces very easily.

It appeared that Terry Templeton's words of encouragement did not fall on deaf ears and to some degree, allowed everyone in the room to relax a bit more. Kale decided to let things go for the time being and chose to play along, "Whatever you say, doc…" Kale said slyly. Terry re-opened his notepad and looked around at the collection of disgruntled faces staring back at him from their chairs, like a group of circus tigers waiting to be led by an overeager tamer. Just as Terry was contemplating making his choice in choosing someone to open the session, he realized that something else was now causing a slight commotion in the room. It was the clicking sound of Thomas Jr.' golden Zippo lighter. Terry remembered how nervously he played with it in the car on their way to his home, "Ahem." Terry interrupted. Thomas Jr. had not realized his forced habit was causing a disturbance, "Huh? Oh, my bad, bro…I'll just, I-I-ll just put, this up…I, uh yeah." Thomas Jr. said squeamishly, and put the light back into his front pocket. Kale was leaning back in his chair with his hands placed behind his head, and was staring the self-conscious Thomas Jr. with a menacing grin. Terry pointed to a heavyset facially scarred Asian man who sat near Kale's side of the circle they sat in, "Hakiro, why don't you go first?" Terry mildly suggested. The man called Hakiro looked around the room and cleared his throat before he spoke, "Yes, why not. Uh, hello everyone, my name is Hakiro Yosami. I am not originally from America, but from Korea…" Hakiro began. "No shit…" Kale remarked under his breath. Terry gave Kale a frosty stare that could cut a hole through glass. In turn, Kale put his hands up in the air to make an innocent jester. Terry rolled his eyes, "Go on Hakiro." Terry asked. "Yes, I-I used to own a small gas station on the other side of town with my brother Cho and…" Hakiro trailed off. Terry looked up from writing in his notepad, "It's okay, Hakiro…please, go on." Terry pleaded. Hakiro was not feeling too sure, but forced himself to continue, "Yes. My family and I, w-we all worked there…sometimes, seven days a week and mostly nights. B-But…late one night, after locking up the store, I was in the back…stocking groceries with my brother Cho, when a woman in a white sports car pulled up to our checkout window. She…s-she appeared to have been b-beaten, and my wife…my wife unlocked the door without informing me. Kym…m-my w-wife, s-she did not know that that the woman was a prostitute and that her pimp had been hiding inside the car. O-Our two sons, Toki and Seri, were playing on the floor with their toy trucks when the man rushed in behind the woman. K-K-Kym did n-not see the pimp coming and tried to make her empty out the register. When my wife refused, he shot her repeatedly, with an automatic weapon. They were both high on drugs and did not realize that…that my sons were playing on the floor, behind the counter. After hearing the gunfire, my brother and I rushed to the front, just as they were running out of the door. When I saw that my wife and my sons had been shot, I grabbed my pistol behind the counter and ran outside. I had never used my weapon before …but my anger did not stop me from shooting at their car as they drove away. Only the prostitute had been wounded, and so her pimp left her at the front of a hospital, to take the blame for the murder of my wife and children. Many months had gone by and I was starting to believe my family's killer may have gotten away. It wasn't until that…that…" Hakiro struggled with his words. "…Mother fucker!?" Kale said despicably. Although Terry did not appreciate Kale's vulgar outburst, part of him would be remiss if he did not find himself in full agreement, he felt, and chose to ignore it. "Yes, thank you." Hakiro said kindly. "…My pleasure." Kale said satisfied. Sharing his story was starting to take a toll on the middle-aged Hakiro, as tears filled his eyes to the point where they looked like two tiny puddles hanging sideways on his face. "…It wasn't until the police pulled him over in a stolen car did they finally c-catch him. The police…they pulled him over and found, oh my God…they f-found t-two young teenage girls, a-a-all bloody, passed out in the backseat. When they searched the trunk, they also found a little red cooler. Inside the cooler were the bodies of two fetuses that he had cut out of them. They said he did this because "they not make him enough money while pregnant!" I mourned for their families as well as my own. My sons Toki and Seri were only five and seven-years-old before they died. Since then, I have sold my store, as I could not bring myself to be there anymore, while my family was not. I had been working part-time at my uncle's TV repair shop, but my misery would not allow me to go free. One morning I was feeling low, so I then decided that I was going to end my life. My brother had been living with me at the time and I did not count on him walking into my room. Just as I was pulling the trigger, my brother Cho grabbed the gun, causing me to shoot myself in the cheek...instead of the back of my mouth." Hakiro shamefully said. Everyone in the room fell dead silent, as they would often do after someone shared their story. The hoarseness from Terry's throat made him sound like it had a V-8 engine after he cleared it to speak, "Ahem! Well Hariko, what have you learned from this near death experience? Do you feel as though you've gained a better appreciation for your own mortality?" Terry painfully asked. Hariko did not take long to think about his answer, "I don't know why this has happened to me and my family, and I don't know why I have NO peace, despite that their killer has been brought to justice. The only thing that I have learned or gained after that experience, Dr. Templeton, is an appreciation for your efforts to console my damaged spirit, and for that I am truly honored. But, since the day I had cheated death, I am still at home all alone. My spirit cannot rest…and for THAT, I'm not very grateful that the bullet had missed!" Hakiro said stringently.

Thomas Jr. was beside himself as he struggled to find some form of understanding for both Hakiro and his situation. After being raised during the Civil Rights days, he had always known the violence that men were capable of, but here it was the 2000's and children are still being killed senselessly, even after trying to show kindness to a stranger. Thomas Jr. could never forget his father preaching about them showing kindness to others, "just like it say's in Ephesians Chapter four (verse 32): "Be kind to one another and tenderhearted as well as forgiving, as God in Christ has forgiven you!" Thomas Jr. could still hear his father say in his head. Hakiro covered his face and wept in his chair like a small child. Harlan Kruellar stood unfazed by the drama and continued to watch the men from behind the two-way mirror. Kale also remained quiet as he watched Thomas Jr.'s curious reaction to the first of many horrors left to be shared. A slightly pudgy Caucasian man wearing a dark blue University of Michigan hoodie was trying to comfort Hakiro by patting him on the shoulder to no avail. "It's okay dude, just go on and let it out bro!" He said in a comforting tone. Terry forced a smile that went away as fast as it came on his face, "Well then, Mason…why don't you go next?" Terry asked. The man named Mason gave Terry a look of terror that only a serial killer could appreciate. He stopped patting Hakiro's thick shoulder and sat up straight in his chair, as if he were a bashful debutant, "Alrighty then…My name is Mason, Mason Lowery and I'm from Lansing, Michigan!" Mason said proudly. "Well go Buckeyes!" Kale chanted from under his tattered Florida University cowboy hat. Mason scratched his forehead uncomfortably, "Uh no, you mean go Wolverines!?" Mason corrected. Kale sat straight in his chair and raised his hat over his eyes, "No man, I mean go Buckeyes! I think the Wolverines suck, I fuckin' hate Michigan." Kale confirmed. Terry was caught off guard by Kale's hostile remarks and sought to put an end to it, "Kale!" Terry yelled impatiently. The progression in Kale's demeanor was fascinating to watch, Harlan thought. Harlan barely could contain his composure at the prospect of meeting him, and slowly traced the outline of Kale's head in the mirror. Terry started frowning at the disruptive Kale Keegan as he again innocently protested by raising his hands. He simply shook his head at Kale, as if he were some disapproving parent, "Go on, Mason." Terry suggested. Mason appeared rocked by Kale's rude comment, but was able to get himself back on track of things, "…So, as I was saying …I had to quit my job at Home Depot five years ago, right after my wife got a substantial raise at her law firm to move down here to Texas. Anyway, we eventually moved into an awesome neighborhood…at least, we thought it was going to be great, until the night "HE" came..." Mason said stoically. Mason's mind seemed to drift into a dark place, forcing Terry to bring Mason's mind back to the present, "Mason?!" Terry called. The morbid memories from his recent past had a vice grip on his attention, causing Mason to become so transfixed that he flinched after Terry called his name, "Huh, oh…sorry. Mason appeared to be around his mid thirties and it was safe to assume that judging from his size, that he did all the cooking in the house, Thomas Jr. assumed. "Anyway…my wife's monthly salary as a lawyer was more than what I could ever bring home in a year working at the Home Depot, so after the move, I became a sorta' "stay-at-home-dad," you know!? I didn't mind doing all the housework and the babysitting of our three kids Beverly, Bobby, and Brian. My oldest daughter Beverly, you know, was just like your average All-American rebellious teenager, who loved the internet and didn't mind sharing her opinion…even when you didn't want to hear it! She wasn't a bad student either. The twins, Bobby and Brian, WHOA…now, those guys are the ones who would keep you up at night with their antics!" Mason said. Mason's mind began to get distracted yet again, but managed to break his starry gaze after noticing Terry waving his hand at him, "Yes, um…so like I was saying! My wife, Betty, was working for a reputable law firm, Barrett and O'Brian, who really made a name for themselves back home. They decided to expand their operation and opened up another firm here. My wife was the firm's newest and hottest defense attorneys…and boy was she HOT! Um-m-m…" Mason joked. Mason's pandering of his wife's virtues got everyone (with the exception of Thomas Jr. and Kale Keegan) to laugh. If there was anyone in the group who was plausibly salvageable, it was the jovial Mason Lowry, Terry believed. Terry found it remarkable how a man who loved his family so much, as Mason clearly did, was still managing to keep his sanity after having it torn apart. His current mental stability, although unique, was not that unheard of and may have been just some acute form of denial, Terry hypothesized. Kale yawned like a man bored out of his mind and when he caught Terry's attention, he blew him a kiss and gave a flirtatious smile. Terry knew that Kale was simply trying to get a rise out of him, and compared his narcissistic act to that of a delinquent child, who "preferred" to be in the principal's office, "Okay Mason, please…continue ." Terry insisted. Mason could hear the urgency in which Terry spoke and continued his tale, "Right, so as I was saying, life "was" pretty good. That was until…until the day she had to represent this seventeen-year-old presumptuous ASSHOLE named Phillip Vasser! Well "Phil," as he liked to be called, was just another rich popular trust fund baby from the Woodlands area. Anyway, he was accused of raping a fellow high student named Sarah Joyner, and it was just my wife's luck that she would be the one who had to defend that blonde headed prick." Mason disappointedly said. "Yeah, I think I remember seeing that case on TV, now. Wasn't he claiming that he was being extorted?" Noel asked. Noel Brody's thought provoking question seemed to both startle and agitate the hefty Mason Lowry simultaneously, causing him to frown with great animosity, "Yeah, that was the first of many lies that piece of shit told the media. He won my wife's sympathy and the public's opinion by playing the role of the victim. You see, Sarah Joyner had transferred from a high school up in Dallas, and already had prior criminal history of underage drinking and misdemeanor shoplifting. Meanwhile, the "innocent Phillip Vasser" had no previous record, excelled at sports, and was his class' valedictorian…not to mention his parents were staples in their "community" with rather deep pockets. Betty was great at her job and eventually got the little turd off. Then one week later, we received an invitation to a going away party for our friend's son who was going overseas, and we decided to give Beverly her first shot at babysitting the twins. Of course, we were against the idea at first, since the twins were barely two-years-old at the time." Mason said. Thomas Jr. could feel a slight chill in the air as Mason's tones and mannerisms began to change as he spoke. Mason always carried a "Go Blue" Michigan Wolverines sweat rag in his pocket that was now being twisted in his hands, as though he was twisting the paltry neck of a farm chicken. The skin on his face had also seemed to take on a metamorphosis of the same shade of his maize Michigan University hoodie. His bubble shaped eyes jittered up and down, as if they were struggling to find just enough moisture to blink, "She convinced us she was ready for the responsibility, so we left to go to our friend's house. What we didn't know, was that Phil Vasser was watching our home as we were leaving out. W-We thought we made it clear to B-B-everly…that under no circumstances, were she to open the door for anyone. The bastard must have "sweet talked" his way inside our home, where he decided to make himself "more comfortable…" Mason said disturbingly. In the two weeks Terry had gotten to know him, this was the first time he believed that Mason Lowry was beginning to show the first signs of finally losing his cool, "Mason, maybe you need a break, or maybe a drink of wat…" Terry began to ask. "No…that…that won't be necessary, thank you." Mason heartbrokenly said, as tears steered down his cheeks. Mason stopped squeezing his defenseless sweat rag and took a deep breath before he picked up where he left off, "…Phillip Vasser blindfolded and attacked my "innocent" thirteen-year old daughter and while he was downstairs…s-stealing her virtue, he didn't realize that she was alone." Mason said sadly. He blew ought a loud sigh before he continued, "And…w-w-when we found her, after we got back home…she couldn't even speak. It was very obvious she had been sexually assaulted, but we just didn't figure out the WHO yet! Betty tried to ask her about the boys, but Beverly was too shaken up to answer her, so I rushed upstairs to find them and….there they were…our two babies just, t-t-they were just there…floating! Floating face down in the tub….. I tried giving them CPR until the EMS people got there but it was too late. Beverly had been giving them a bath when Phillip Vasser knocked on the door and was "too busy" to care about our sons drowning upstairs. They both had suffered severe brain damage and we decided to pull the plug after they had been on machines for months. My wife did everything in her power to get him prosecuted, but Phillip Vasser was too smart and too rich to get caught. Things just weren't the same anymore between my wife and I so, we eventually separated. She took Beverly and moved back upstate to Michigan, but I didn't want to leave. This is where my sons are buried, so this is where I'm gonna stay." Mason said solemnly. The room once again, fell into another awkward inanimate silence.

For the first time, in a very long time, Thomas Jr. did not feel as virtually alone as he initially believed he always was. Thomas Jr. carefully scanned the tearful face of Mason Lowry for any signs of indecencies, indiscretions, or, falsehoods about himself that he had missed, but to no avail he found himself coming up very short. Mason Lowry seemed like a decent enough human being, so to what holy purpose did it serve him to have his family wiped out as well? Thomas Jr. wondered. The only difference between them, as far as he could see, was that he could never find the strength necessary to let go of his son Markus. It may have been selfish on his part to keep his son subjugated to being plugged into breathing machines, Thomas Jr. figured, but Markus was the only thing he had left of value in this world, and he refused to give up on him. Since Thomas Jr. was able to identify so personally with Mason's plight, a sudden urge came over him to offer his condolences, "I'm so sorry, Mr. Lowry. I'm sure…I'm sure your sons are smiling down from heaven on you right now…" Thomas Jr. said apologetically. Mason, who was crying his eyeballs out, was so visibly upset that his sweat rag appeared as if it had been submerged into a kitchen sink, "Th-Th-Thank you, y-you really think so?" Mason sobbingly asked. Thomas Jr. hesitated for a brief moment to ponder the question, but found the courage to answer, "Yes, I…think they are." Thomas Jr. said dubiously.

Terry appreciated his brother's participation and was beginning to feel positive about his decision in bring him, "I think so too Mason…now who else wants to…" Terry began to ask, while looking down at his notepad. "Yur' such a fuckin' hipocrit..." Kale said under his breath. "What was that?" Terry asked. Kale tipped the front of his hat to reveal the five o' clock shadow hovering around his crusted mouth and further exposing his bloodshot eyes, "I said, (quote) that your brother ova' there….is a mother fuckin' hipp-O-crit (end quote) !" Kale repeated. Substance abuser Ricky Elvin Wallace, who sat near Kale, could not stand for any more of his personal attacks against the soft spoken Thomas Jr., "Hey man, why don't you show "Doc Temp" some respect and lay off the old dude?" Ricky passionately pleaded. Insurance claims adjuster Adrian Atkinson, who was also sitting in the same proximity, decided to enter the fray as well, "Yes, please. I too, find your "tone" rather annoying." Adrian squeamishly admitted. Both Ricky's sympathetic plea and Adrian Atkinson's boldness seemed to catch the menacing Kale Keegan off guard, but not enough to keep him from issuing a lewd comeback, "Sure I will, Sticky Ricky… soon as you start lay'n offa' that ole' glass dick of yours. Hell boy, you skinny enough that I could use your arm for a belt!" Kale viciously quipped. This was not the type of dialogue Terry was intending to have out of today's session and it had been past time to put the threatening Kale Keegan to rest, Terry concluded. "That's enough Kale! Your comments today have been anything more than counterproductive and I'm not permitting it to continue." Terry confirmed. Kale put his hand over his heart as to insinuate his feelings being hurt, "Well now, exc-u-u-u-use me suga'! But, I thought we was supposed' ta be sharin' what we been feelin' in here? Well you know sumthin' doc? I guess being a hippo-O-crit muss run in da family…" Kale quipped. Terry Templeton had spent his entire medical tenure trying to help get through to people with all types of challenging personalities, but none have ever drawn his ire as much as Kale Keegan had, especially in such an amazingly short amount time. Although Terry had been "out of the closet for years," he had done his due diligence to carry himself in a reserved and professional manner as much as possible, around those outside his inner circle. But despite everything Terry knew about human psychology, he still allowed Kale's patronizing and homosexual innuendo's to irk him. He already knew Kale was a devout drunk, who was obviously abusing the neurological meds that the army gave him for treating his PTSD. Terry also found it astounding that a person of his slender frame could still function properly, let alone form coherent sentences. It made no sense to him why Kale was choosing to be so aggressive towards people he hardly knew, especially after being so emotionally dormant since the first day he arrived. The only thing Terry Templeton was starting to believe was that his brother's presence was provoking him somehow, and that he could not afford anymore interruptions on his part. Terry did not believe that Kale's issues with Thomas Jr. were racially driven, but if he was going to be of any help to him or, the group, then it meant giving Kale what he apparently wanted….a confrontation. "No Kale, you are correct about one thing….this group IS about expressing one's personal feelings and sharing your past experiences about the role crime has had on all your families. The only thing you have been willing to share with us, Kale, is this fictional disdain for someone you hardly know! If you're an atheist or it's a matter of religion then we can accommodate you, but with all due respect Lieutenant, you don't know ANYTHING about my brother or, what he's (Thomas Jr. nods his head for Terry to stop)…. been through." Terry stated. It did not surprise Terry at all that his big brother took the high road. Even when they were just kids, Terry remembered how often Thomas Jr. allowed some of the white kids from school to spit in his face, when it was their parents who were displeased at THEIR father for speaking at peace rallies. Terry also remembered being the hothead who liked to hit back when challenged as a child, and who often helped out his older brother in any given fight. Thomas Jr. owed Kale nothing, so he did not feel the need to justify himself to one pandering idiot, and he could not blame his big brother, Terry thought. "If you're only here to bring attention to yourself Lieutenant Kale, then I suggest that you seek treatment else w…." Terry began before getting interrupted. "Call me that again…and you'll be the one needing a doctor. Like I already told ya' doc, I ain't a soldier no more. " Kale threatened and stood to his feet. So there it was, the middling thorn that was wedged into the aching lion's paw, Terry surmised. Terry Templeton felt the urge to kick himself after discovering who it actually was that Kale had the clear issue with. He remembered what Kale said just before the group began its session and it did not occur to him until he had become agitated again, after he called him by his rank, Terry concluded. Kale had stated "I ain't a soldier no more" before, so the real question was, what happened to him in his past that had him so angry with the Army? Terry wondered. Like many of the men in his group, Kale's care fell into his lap, but unlike the rest of them, there was nothing to go off on about his past or, private life both in and after his time of service. But whatever his reasons were, hardly justified putting him, his brother, or the group in danger, "Okay, Kale…maybe you should sit back down before…" Terry began to say before immediately getting cutoff. Kale dug into his front pocket for his cigarettes, "Before what hoss? I don't think ya' got anymore of them "order-ladies" left for me….guess ya' gotta do it all by ya' self now, huh doc!?" Kale playfully taunted, and lit another cigarette. Terry knew that Kale was right on the money about his glaring assessment of the clinic's current state concerning their orderly shortages. Word had quickly spread to the other clinics around town about Kale's violent night/day terrors (although they happened mostly during the daytime) that no one was in a hurry to transfer, just so they could get a one way ticket to the hospital, Terry figured. He had heard the trouble the Human Resource Department were having looking for fill-ins, and them resorting to hiring in-experienced orderlies from various temp agencies, just to keep a full staff. Whatever training Kale received while in the Army must have been some type of tactical infantry, or possibly Special Forces judging by the skull tattoo on his arm, Terry assumed. Going all the way back to his Navy days, Terry had seen many fighting exhibitions in his lifetime, but never had he had seen a man move with so much fluidity and speed against more than one unsuspecting opponent. Although his hostile outbursts were brief, the amount of damage he could cause upon waking up from a nightmare was instantaneous and almost second nature. It was as though he was some kind of brutal uncontrollable force packaged inside an ordinary looking man, but Kale Keegan was HIS problem now and not the Army's. Whoever the genius was who placed him at the Midtown clinic apparently did not want him causing problems on their base, and who could blame them? Terry wondered. Either way, he planned on getting to the bottom of the truth before spending another day in Kale's dangerous company, Terry concluded. Terry stood to his feet and pulled out his radio off his belt, "I guess we're just gonna' find out." Terry threatened. Kale simply smiled and lit his cigarette, as though he had not a care in the world. Just as Terry was about to call for backup over his radio, both Adrian Atkinson and the fragile Ricky Wallace stood to their feet, to offer their support once again, "You know what Kale? You ain't nothing but a white trash, self-loathin' drunk ass punk, and you know what else, Lieutenant?" Ricky boldly asked, while pointing at him. Within a few milliseconds Kale snatched Adrian's pen from out his coat pocket and threw it into the back of Ricky's hand, as if it were tossing a throwing knife into a dart board. Ricky cried out as the ball point pen struck his hand at the speed of lightening, while sending him to the floor bleeding. The snobbish Adrian Atkinson quickly found his seat just as everyone else stood up in astonishment of what they just seen. While most of the people were in shock out of reflex D.E.A. agent Milton Elliot decided to finally make it his business to address the maniacal Kale Keagan, "What you just did there was impressive, but it was also assault with a deadly weapon, shit head!" Milton professed. Kale's eyebrow went up and brandished his favorite grin, "What??? Haven't ya'll figured it all out by now? I'm a certified schizoid crazo' Del Loco!" Kale happily jested. That part Terry Templeton did not need any convincing of, as he hurried to Ricky's aid and radioed for help on his walkie talkie. Meanwhile, Harlan Kruellar was breathing so heavily behind the two-way mirror that the glass began to fog up from the heat from his mouth. He knew all too well the insufferable amount of toxic damage Lieutenant Keegan was capable of. It had long been Harlan's hope that Kale would one day break himself from out the mental prison he placed himself in, soon after his family's senseless killing. Although Kale's misery was totally understandable, Harlan could no longer afford to prolong the plans he set into motion. The beast he had been waiting for was now fully awoke and it was time to move on to the next phase of his intricate arrangement, Harlan decided. But just before making his phone call, Harlan was curious to see how the drama was going to unfold between Kale and the brutish and physically imposing agent Elliot, who also was highly trained. The 6'2 and 240 pound former undercover agent clearly had the size advantage to the less intimidating Lieutenant Keegan, who did not appear impressed or afraid. It was only a matter of time before Milton Elliot and Kale would eventually knock heads and Harlan needed to be sure he picked the right men for the job he had in mind.

Sergeant Milton Elliot had been an undercover D.E.A. agent for six years and spent many of those years going up against some of America's worst of the worst criminals. During that six year stint the father of one, needed to make some very difficult decisions in order keep his cover from being blown in the field. Compromises also needed to be made, although "some" compromises could never be taken back, no matter how many of the world's scumbags he could possibly put away. He too was an Army brat like Kale Keegan, and who also joined the Army right after high school in Nebraska, despite getting serious offers from some of the nation's top collegiate programs. After graduating from high school, Milton Elliot was eager to make a difference in the world, so after serving a couple short tours in the Armed Forces, a friend talked him into joining the War on Drugs. It seemed like an easy transition, as most of his more natural instincts for detective work and gifts for causing harm to people were an immediate asset to the agency. Outside of taking some heavy dosages of pain killers while serving in active duty, Milton Elliot had never done any hard narcotics in his entire clean cut life. Long ago, Milton's older sister Evelyn died of substance abuse and he vowed to never partake in any type of drug addiction. Although he was barely in his late thirties, Milton never once had the urge to smoke marijuana, but he was forced to make certain "adjustments" after working in the field as an undercover operative. Unfortunately for him, part of his job requirement was to become a certified drug addict, which eventually bled into his personal life and cut short his marriage. His orders were to infiltrate a vicious biker gang who called themselves "The Road Quakers," and report back any of their illegal activities. While serving undercover, Milton had far exceeded his agency's expectations as an operative and garnered much clout in the surly gang. Since he was quickly ascending the pecking order of the gang's dubious ranks, he was being entrusted with even greater responsibilities than just being a simple getaway driver, or a simple look-out in some warehouse burglary. He eventually earned himself the right to be given his own crew and was entrusted to go on some major drug distribution runs. Ultimately, his reward for all his successfully illegal deeds landed him a chance at a higher seat in the gangs hierarchy, in which all he had to do was carry out a hit on Supreme Court Judge Alice Clair-Walker. The spirited Judge Walker was well known for handing suspected biker gang member's lengthy prison sentences, which did not sit well with The Road Quaker's sector. It was a final move to solidify himself in the gang's circle and to gain their complete trust. Naturally, Milton was opposed to the move and alerted his superiors of the planned hit. A sting operation was set in place to catch Milton and his crew in the act of the crime, which was supposed to lead to the arrest of the Road Quaker's vicious leader, Oswald "Ozzie" Brickwood. After the D.E.A. agency seized Brickwood and his biker lieutenants, they still needed Milton's testimony to make the charges stick. The savvy Brickwood tried to coerce agent Elliot into not testifying at his trial. When he refused a bribe from the notorious gang leader, a contract was put out on Elliot's family that eventually lead to the untimely deaths of both his wife Latasha and daughter Francesca. The agency also failed in prosecuting Oswald Brickwood both on his conspiracy charges for the attempted murder of Supreme Court Judge Alice Walker and the murder of his family. "Ozzie" had escaped incarceration by paying others to take the fall in his stead. Agent Elliot was asked to take a leave of absence after attempting to take the crafty Brickwood's life at the courthouse after winning his case. Harlan was well informed about Brickwood's D.E.A. connections and even remembered doing some business with the Marilyn Manson lookalike long ago. Harlan was trying to move some used M-16's and M-4's that he was asked to import as a favor somewhere in the Middle East, after some forgotten war he did not care to remember. The last thing Harlan ever expected though, after the completion of those deals, were the inexcusable executions of agent Elliot's wife and daughter, who had nothing to do with Brickwood. But that was back in a time when the only thing that mattered to the shrewd Harlan Kruellar was his bottom line, which was making money. Those days were way long behind him now, and his only concern was with what was about to happen in the quant light-colored room adjacent to where he stood behind the large two-way mirror. There they were, two savage warriors staring the other down while waiting for the other to draw first blood. Seemingly without any hesitation, Kale thumped his cigarette into agent Milton's eyes while causing him to be temporarily blinded. He then dropped him with another barrage of non lethal restraining moves that sent him to the ground in seconds. When Milton cried out in helplessness, Kale began to patronize the helpless agent, "Aw-w-w come on now corn bread….you gonna' have ta' do better than that!? You thought it was gonna' be easy didn't yew'? Thought cause ya' all tatted up that ole Kale wuz' supposed ta' just lay on down fo' ya'!" Kale joked. Terry started screaming for help through his walkie talkie and had temporarily distracted the bragging lieutenant. Before he realized it, Jovan Campbell floored Kale with a hellacious hit to the mouth that sounded like a cherry bomb went off in his face and sent him flying across the floor. Kale slowly stood to his feet while chuckling to himself, “Mighty strong punch ya’ got there boy…but it’s gonna’ take more than a lucky punch from some muscle bound spook ta’ take down ole Kale Keegan…” Kale threatened. Despite his asinine comments, Kale had earned Jovan’s respect for taking his best shot. At first glance, the cock strong Jovan thought he would have felt guilty for knocking out some drunk like he usually did as a club bouncer, but he quickly found the undersized Lieutenant Keegan as a force to be reckoned with. “Do us all a favor and crawl back into whatever bottle you came out of!” Jovan quipped. Thomas Jr. had seen more than enough and decided to settle the matter himself, “Alright, that’s enough!!!” Thomas Jr. shouted. Harlan wondered how long it was going to take the soft spoken reverend to grow a pair of balls and smiled shyly behind the giant glass. No one in the room expected the pacifistic Thomas Jr. to holler in such a manner. Even Kale Keegan was caught off guard, and offered pause to look him dead in the eye. Before he attempted to speak again Thomas Jr. tried to swallow his courage, but soon as he did, the back of his dry tongue felt as though it was trapped in cement. Although Kale made it loud and clear that he did not care at all for him, something still needed to be done or, there was just going to be more violence, Thomas Jr. feared. “Don’t move, Ricky.” Terry whispered to skinny Ricky, who was on the floor screaming while holding his bloodied hand. Terry began to slowly make his way toward his brother, but Thomas Jr. halted him before he could come to his aid. The beleaguered Kale Keegan looked like a trapped cougar when everyone in the room appeared to be surrounding him. He stood idly and had been licking the blood off the busted lip Jovan just given him, “Well ain’t ya’ll sweet...Hey Rev, why dontcha’ tell these Jesus Kool-aid drinkers to stand down, before somebody else gits’ hurt!” Kale ordered. Thomas Jr. could see something both in the young man’s eyes and his tone that had not been revealed to him until that very moment. Perhaps it was not “him” whom the mysterious Kale Keegan had an issue with, but may have been with God, Thomas Jr. hypothesized. Unknowingly, to Kale, the orderlies Terry had previously called were quietly waiting by the door way and awaited his instructions. Thomas Jr. held his hands clasped together in a calming manner as he spoke, “He’s right….Everybody back off. This is between him and me.” Thomas Jr. stated. Each of the group members (with the exception of his brother Terry) gradually granted more space between them and the unpredictable Lieutenant. Kale looked around at them all, “See?

Now that wasn't hard." Kale casually admitted. Thomas Jr. offered him a quaint smile, "Your quarrel is with me, not them. We're both grown men, so let's try and talk this thing out like grown men." Thomas Jr. pleaded. Kale re-lit another cigarette and took a deep drag off the butt. The sensation he felt from inhaling Marlboro seemed to calm him, as he needed a moment to close his eyes to take in the sweet essence of it. He then began to fixate his feral looking eyes on the weary preacher, "Sure. I'll go first….when did you start hating God?" Kale asked nonchalantly. Kale's somewhat odd question bothered him, causing Thomas Jr. to rub his hands on his thighs, "Ah-h, I-I don't know what you mean?" Thomas Jr. stumbled. His brother's indecisive response to Kale's question looked highly uncomfortable from Terry's clinical vantage point and began to take a mild interest of his own. Kale gave a light chuckle, "Are yew' kiddin'? Yew' can't hide it from me…..I can see RIGHT through yew preacher…" Kale replied, while covering his eye as though he was peering through a telescope. Harlan continued to watch the two men banter amongst themselves in a comfortable silence and in an eager anticipation for a monumental outcome. Kale adjusted his hat to reveal his face more, which took Thomas Jr. by surprise as he marveled at how young he realized Kale actually was. Although Kale looked not much older than his son Markus, Thomas Jr. could see that whatever trauma that he had previously experienced was slowly killing him inside out and did not care taking anyone else with him, "Really? So what do you think you see, son? You think you know me? I don't believe you even know who YOU are anymore! But what I do see, is a petulant child who respects nothing…not himself or, even God for that matter….my God, what happened to you, son? Thomas Jr. asked defiantly. Thomas Jr.'s words appeared to strike a chord in the raging Kale Keegan, "Oh, like YEW' do? Look at cha', Rev!? Yew' look more like shit, than I do! I can even smell the alcohol running down yo' black neck, daddy-o! Yew up here….talkin' bout respectin' myself and God….when you ain't even practicin' what YEW' preachin'! Now I killed fo' my country, in the name of God, and yew' want ta' know what did he do for ME in return?! I'll fuckin' tell ya what the sum bitch did….he put a fuckin' CRATER where my house used ta' be!!! No mo' wife, no mo' life! So…I know when I started fuckin' hatin' him, but I'm askin' YEW', Mr. fuckin' Know-it-All preacher… why yew' up in here pretendin' that yew' don't?" Kale concluded. Kale's words seemed to echo in the back of his subconscious like dynamite exploding in a cave. Thomas Jr. stood there silently, while struggling to figure out what to say next. Terry could see that his brother was struggling internally from Kale's twisted cynicism and agreed with himself to bring their standoff to an abrupt end. "That's okay Tommie…you don't need to answer that! My brother is an ordained minister, so he couldn't possible have any hate in his heart for God or anyone else for that matter!" Terry confirmed. But Terry knew that last part was an absolute lie. Sonny Korne robbed him of everything he could take in his fit of rage and left his poor big brother helpless and alone. What Kale was suggesting about (himself) hating God made sense to Terry, since it was apparent to him that the young lieutenant was an out of control sociopath, while Thomas Jr. on the hand, had spent many years under their father's holistic tutelage, but still found enough fortitude in prayer to return to the pulpit, despite experiencing a terrible ordeal. "Fuck off doc, this ain't got nothin' ta' do wit'yew'…" Kale threatened, and continued to stare down the befuddled Thomas Jr. Terry saw the orderlies awaiting his ordered by the doorway in the hall and signaled for them to enter the room, "Kale, I need you to calm down and go with these gentlemen." Terry asked calmly. Kale rolled his eyes, "Man, yew jus don't give up do ya' doc, oh well…hope you fellas got good dental…" Kale starkly replied. Terry could only frown in frustration and turned to the orderlies, "Ok guys, hit him!" Terry commanded. What Terry failed in mentioning to him, was that as a favor, Lacy asked one of his weight training client's, who worked as a constable, to start coming by the clinic just in case Kale ever got rowdy again. One of the orderlies hollered for the constable to come into the room as well. The muscular constable's name was Sgt. Paul Wyatt, who Lacy referred to as one "strong ass white boy," Terry remembered. He wore a crew cut and looked like a former UFC fighter, Terry thought. Kale looked a little surprised by the officers sudden appearance through the door and took a step back, "The fucks he doing here?" Kale asked. "He's here to escort you off the premises! Either come back when you're sober or, don't come back at all." Terry instructed. Kale looked back at Thomas Jr. with fierce indignation and spit on the floor, "This conversation ain't over…" Kale said agitated. Tears began to run down Thomas Jr.' face, "Yes…yes it is. I-I'm…I'm g-g-gonna…I'm gonna' pray for you young man." Thomas Jr. grimly replied. Like a match to a flame, Kale started to once again lose his composure and in his frustration, lunged toward Thomas Jr., "Jesus, you just don't fuckin' get it, do ya'!!! What? Yew' think yew' betta' than me? Cause yew' wearin' that white collar and got some "fancy shmancy" lookin' bible? Ha, then the jokes on ye-e-w-w-w, preacher man! I ain't no fool! Me and yew' know the tru…"Kale said, before getting interrupted. "I said let's go, Lieutenant…" Terry reiterated. Kale's face started to scrunch in disbelief, "Tha' fuck yew jus call me?" Kale asked aggravated. Within a blink of an eye was Kale charging after Terry, until the silent no nonsensical Sgt. Wyatt zapped him with 50,000 volts from his yellow and black police taser. Ordinarily, most men twice Kale Keegan's size would be rendered helpless and face down on a floor after the surge, but the officer's taser sent him drooling to one knee. Everyone in the room was both shocked and astonished by Kale's seemingly supernatural pain threshold after getting tased by the officer over again. Kale finally went down to the cold tiled floor after receiving a third jolt. Although he knew the stubborn Lieutenant Keegan could withstand the punishment, Harlan Kruellar feared the horrible truth that still awaited the young man. While Kale's body appeared motionless after being electrocuted, Harlan drew an outline of his body as an act of comfort and wiped away a tear that got away from him. He picked up his cell phone and dialed the number to Terry's supervisor, Dr. Becker. From what his contacts had previously told him, the infamous Dr. Becker was busy vacationing at some lake house out in Lake Livingston. "Probably enjoying his spoils of war no doubt," Harlan surmised. Harlan found spineless Dr. Becker despicable after being so easily bought off with his son's blood money, but glad that men like him were still around to be controlled by their own greed. The phone rings for a short while before someone finally answers, "Dr. William G. Becker, and how might I be at your service, Mr. Kruellar?" Dr. Becker pompously replied. Harlan tried his best to not regurgitate his breakfast at the sound of the conceited doctor's arrogant tone, "Put me in…tomorrow." Harlan demanded. Dr. Becker's ability to speak appeared to elude him for a second, "Is there a problem…?" Harlan asked concerned. Dr. Becker dared not hesitate another minute, "N-No. WHATEVER you want, Mr. Kruellar! After all your….WONDERFUL generosity, it's the LEAST I could do t…" Dr. Becker began, before getting cut off mid sentence. "Good! Then see to it then…and just maybe, I might throw in another $100,000 for Christmas!" Harlan grudgingly promised, and hung up his phone expediently. He noticed that the orderlies were prying Kale's seemingly unconscious carcass off the floor and hoped that the officer's stun gun did not give him any MORE brain damage. It was getting quite difficult to hear any important details over all the mumbling that was going on inside the small room, so Harlan increased the speaker volume inside the private room to get a better listen. Reputed Drug addict Ricky Wallace, who Kale previously impaled in the hand with Adrian Atkinson's pen, was escorted out by a nurse while the rest of the group were trying to get their bearings. Jovan Campbell was in the corner teasing his on again off again buddy Agent Elliot, about getting taken down so easily by a man half his size. In the meantime, Terry Templeton was expressing how embarrassed and disappointed he was with his brother's initial visit to the clinic and vowed to make amends, "I should have seen it coming, I mean…I always knew the potential was there…but I guess…I just didn't think things all the way through, bro! But, I promise you…you won't be seeing anymore of THAT "touched individual" again if I have anything else to say about it! " Terry said apologetically. Thomas Jr. said nothing as he stared dejectedly while the clinic's orderlies dragged Kale towards the door. Just before they exited the room Kale started mumbling uncontrollably. Feeling both concerned and curious, Thomas Jr. followed behind the men into the hallway, "Excuse me, uh….could you gentlemen just hold up a sec?" Thomas Jr. asked humbly. The two stout looking men stopped in their tracks and looked perplexed by the reverend's request. "You a glutton for punishment aye Rev?" asked one of the orderlies, who sported a long brown beard and a bald head. His remark did not jive well with Terry who walked up right behind his big brother, "I didn't catch that?" Terry replied sternly. It was obvious that he clearly stepped out of line with his reckless comment, so the ox of a man kindly digressed, "Nuttin' Doc!" He said. His fellow co-worker smacked his lips and huffed, "Fool…" The large Hispanic orderly whispered sharply. Kale's head felt dizzy and was trying to shake off the effects of his ordeal, but still lacked coherency, "R-R-i-t-t-tah…s-s-so…s-s-o-so-horry, b-b-babe…!" Kale badly stuttered. "Is this totally necessary Terry? You're just gonna' throw the man out? What the hell kind of therapy is that? " Thomas Jr. protested. Thomas Jr.'s sudden interest in helping the troubled lieutenant was beginning to give the younger Templeton a migraine, "You have GOT to BE KIDDIN' ME, Tommie!? Obviously he has more than a couple screws loose and quite frankly, I'm getting fed up with his act. Kale's way too unpredictable and dangerous to be around the rest of the group. He belongs in a military psychiatric ward bro!" Terry concluded. As groggy as he may have been it did not stop Kale Keegan from sharing his displeasure for Terry being so dismissive of him, "F-F-huck yew', d-do-hoc!!" Kale retorted. Terry rolled his eyes and grimaced, "See? I rest my case. Guys please show the Lieu…MR. KEEGAN, to the front doors and make sure that he clearly understands that this will happen if he shows back up here ever again. I don't care who sent him here, he's done." Terry confirmed, and fixed his attention on one of the passing nurses. Although Terry's rash decision did not sit well with him, Thomas Jr. knew it was simply not his call to make, and decided to say a quiet prayer for him, as the two wide built men continued to carry out the staggering lieutenant. After wrapping up a brief prayer, the distant minded reverend could feel an abrupt uneasiness threatening his spirit. His hands began to tremble slightly and in unison, as if he were playing drumsticks on a snare drum. Suddenly, the disturbing conversation he had earlier with Kale started to replay in his head once again, as though it were a cunning thief returning to the scene of a crime. The horrific look on Thomas Jr.'s face was drawing odd stares from the other workers who were passing him in the busy hallway, which in turn caught Terry's attention, "Hey, Tommie…you feeling alright bro? You acting like you've seen a ghost!" Terry asked concerned. Little did his psychologist brother realize, that it was just "what it was" that his palpated brother had seen. It was the return of their deceased father Thomas Senior, who stared at him from down the hall and wearing the same awful putrid looking hospital gown over his decayed flesh. His father was laughing and pointing at him, as though he was just told a humorous joke. But soon after he cleared away his petrified eyes, their father was gone, as fast light traveling from a switch on a wall. "Thomas?" Terry called once more. This time the spell that Thomas Jr. was under brought forth a couple ugly truths he did not believe were pertinent to share after reconnecting with his long lost brother. The first ugly truth was by far the easiest to confess, "Look Ter,' I'm just gonna give it to you straight, cause we both too damn old to be up in here bullshittin' one another. But that boy, you claiming to be a fool, pegged me just right, lil' bro….I don't know how, but HE saw it!!! The young man didn't even know me from Adam, but yet, somehow….he just knew." Thomas Jr. confirmed. Terry discreetly pulled Thomas Jr. into an empty room across the hall to get a more clearer clarification on what it was he was actually admitting, "He? He who? Keegan? Pshaw! Man, don't let his bullshit get to you! You're supposed to be my "spiritual voice of reason" for cryin' out loud, and besides, you have NO idea what he's put this facility through since he started. I've been dealing with his craziness for weeks! He's a damn poster boy for mental illness if I ever SAW one, THAT'S for damn sure!!!" Terry stringently admitted. When it came to psychoanalyzing an individual, he believed his brother had enough credentials on his office wall to be qualified for the job. What Thomas Jr. was feeling deep within his very core was something that could not be simply detected by hypothesis and a sharp intellect, but from one suffering through personal experience. Had Kale suffered a great indignity much like himself? Thomas Jr. wondered. On countless occasions, did he ask God to reveal to him what unforgivable sin had he committed to have earned him the hell he put him in. But, with each unbearable day that sailed by that his prayers went unanswered, Thomas Jr. assumed that God was still punishing him, causing the now hopeless reverend to live life as a faithless invalid. Kale accused him of being a hypocrite and asked him directly, if he "hated" God, and though he could never think it ever possible, or even something safe to consider for that matter, that somewhere in the middle of his confusion, he may have subconsciously began too. "So Doctor Terry, is that your clinical opinion, or is it the geriatrics that's doing the talking? Look bro, I been doing some thinking....and I admit, that I've been repressing a lot of my....feelings. And you may even be right on the money about Kale being a grade- A nut job, but even someone who's considered "insane" had discovered something about myself, that I have been denying on the surface....which was how "actually pissed off" at God I really was, or maybe still am....I'm ashamed to say. Maybe it's because....I just didn't have the damn courage to admit it. I know it may sound bizarre, especially since preachers are often looked at as ambassadors of hope and all, so, how could I possibly have the audacity to hate the same high and mighty lord I swore to serve? Jesus, I'm...I'm so sorry, lil' bro." Thomas Jr. said defeated. The last couple of years had been both highly stressful and extremely turbulent for his psychologically beat down older brother, so Terry was not at all surprised by his brother's heartfelt confession. His brother's facial expression is one of embarrassment and great disappointment, but Terry was not going to no longer allow his only living sibling to revel in anymore self pity. He put his hand on his brother's shoulder to console him, “Sorry for what Tommie? You didn’t do ANYTHING wrong!” Terry protested. Thomas Jr. was feeling like a fraud and was starting to believe that coming to Houston may have been a mistake, “My being here didn’t help anyone, it only ruined your session! Maybe this wasn’t such a good idea Ter’! I mean maybe…maybe I shouldn’t even be h….!” Thomas Jr. began, until getting interrupted. “Stop right there, Tommie! I ASKED you to be HERE for a reason, (albeit for another undisclosed reason Terry didn’t care to share) and despite one minor hiccup, you were….you ARE, of great value to this group! Just in the matter of a day you earned the group’s respect, when it took me weeks to! Hell, you even got that walking hard on Kale Keegan to open up, something that I couldn’t do on my own. In any event, you barely just got here and you’ve flown too damn far, just to be turning yo’ britches back around to head towards home! So, unless you got a switchblade or, something else like that tucked underneath that collar of yours, I’m not letting you leave, bro!” Terry concluded. The meddling uncertainty that overcame Thomas Jr. dissipated from his mind as fast as it came. His brother’s encouraging endorsement seemed to have been doing its job, Thomas Jr. believed, and he gave his younger brother a long reassuring hug. He had become so proud and in awe of the success Terry was able to attain without the benefit of their mom and dad’s support. Who knew that the brother, who stayed under the proper care of two very esteemed and accomplished parents, would be the one in so much dire need? Thomas Jr. wondered. But all that no longer mattered now, he was no longer alone. Although he did not understand God’s reasoning for bringing Terry back into his life now, he at least had someone else to share old stories about what it was like growing up in the same house to look forward too. Despite all the shit life threw into his brother’s pathway, Terry had greatly admired Thomas Jr.’ for the strength he reserved for his son, and for his courage to keep his head high, regardless of his present circumstances, and also for his incredible will to live though terrible adversity. For all the many challenges he had conquered in his own lifetime, the good Dr. Terry Templeton knew that had the shoes been on the other foot, the story would have positively ended far worse for himself, with no one left to tell about it. His only hope was for his brother’s peace of mind and also a speedy recovery very soon for his son. Whatever issues that seemed to be between him and God could also use a break, Terry thought. The only thing Thomas Jr. had left to sacrifice was his life, which was almost taken the first time, but his spirited brother persevered. When the two end their brotherly embrace, Terry laughs hysterically through his tears, again at the shocking resemblance Thomas Jr. shared with their late father, Senior. "Ha-ha-ha, damn bro, if you don't look like our daddy, b-o-o-o-y….! You know what I wish right now, that daddy could see the spitting image of him that you became!" Terry complimented. It was now that time for the other shoe to drop, Thomas Jr. thought. The worst that could happen if he tried to explain his visions to Terry would be for him to have him committed or, start him on some new medication, He suspected. Either way, he knew he had to share them with someone before things start to really get out of hand. Thomas Jr. knew Terry was a man of clinical science and deductive reasoning, but he was truly counting on him in keeping the open mind he was willing to give, when he opened up today's session. If their conversion was to go south Thomas Jr. realized he still had a son to go back home to, "Uh, Terry…about that…" Thomas Jr. slowly began. Terry was jotting down things in his notebook, "Yeah, bout what Tommie?" Terry said with his attention focused heavily on the beat up notepad. Thomas Jr. could not believe that he was really about to tell his brother about seeing their dead father's ghost walking about, OUT LOUD, and feared the worst, "Bout' me…seein'…you know...daddy. "Thomas Jr. hesitated. Terry immediately stopped his mad looking scribbling in his composition book and looked his brother in the face, "Huh, you mean, like…seeing him…like at his grave, you mean?" Terry asked concerned. The perturbed look on his younger brother's face worried Thomas Jr., but he knew it was far too late for him to stop after putting himself out there, "No-o-o…like seeing him. I'm talking like "our daddy" visiting me, or haunting me or, whatever the hell you wanna' call it!!!" Thomas Jr. said agitated. Terry Templeton did not speak a word at first, after his brother shared his unbelievable news with him, and stood motionless with his composition book clenched tightly across his chest. He looked Thomas Jr. straight into his eyes and could see he was being absolutely serious right then. Terry took out a deep breath, "A-h-h, "OKAY"…I think it's time for a damn drink, now….and uh, you're doin' the drivin' reverend!" Terry replied. Thomas Jr. could feel a little of the weight that had been bearing down on him, since first arriving to Texas being slightly lifted, as he further explained himself to Terry on their way to the nearest bar in town. Maybe things were going to end up "somewhat" for the better,

Thomas Jr. pondered. His mind was beginning to finally be at ease with his decision of visiting his sympathetic sibling, despite him trying his best not to pity him, which Thomas Jr. loved and appreciated most about him. Although it did not bother him anymore, that his brother may have still been hiding something from him, Thomas Jr. decided to spend the rest of his visit enjoying the company of someone who could actually speak back…

Outside, in the Midtown Clinic parking lot….

When the lingering effects of constable Wyatt's tazer had finally began to wear off, Kale realized he was being carted off by the clinic's two orderlies and escorted through the front door by the officer who tazed him. They both eagerly dropped him to the pavement of the tranquil looking parking lot. His body fell hard to the unforgiving surface, after the two massive orderlies let go of him and then they high-fived each other and returned inside. Kale was wincing from pain after waking up from his short electrified nap, but soon found himself at strict attention, when Sgt. Wyatt approached him, "Now look here boy….don't you ever come back around here again! I don't give a shit if you gotta' fucking note from the Goddamn president of the United States, so help me if I gotta come back here…" Sgt. Wyatt warned. Kale slowly got to his feet and knocked the dust off from his clothes and grabbed his favorite Florida Gator University cowboy hat from the ground. "Na-a-w-w officer, yew ain't got ta worry bout' ME givin' yew no mo' trouble! From now on…I'm gonna be a good lil' soldier, scouts honor!?!" Kale mockingly said, while making a Boy Scouts hand gesture. Sgt. Wyatt's face seemed to make a giant knot after hearing Kale's obvious sarcasm, "You sassin' me boy?" Sgt. Wyatt asked, while grabbing at his stun gun once again. Kale backed up and held his hand out toward the disturbed constable while reaching for his Swiss Army knife with the other, "That won't be necessary, officer!" a voice said softly from behind the young Lieutenant. Kale was surprised by the quiet presence of the long black stretch limousine that had crept up behind him unknowingly. The high strung Sgt. Wyatt was hardly impressed by the car or, by its unassuming looking passenger who's chauffer was opening his door for, "Just who in the hell are you supposed to be?" Sgt. Wyatt asked perturbed. It was none other than the transport mogul Harlan Kruellar, who patiently waited for an opportunity to privately engage Kale one on one, when the right moment presented itself. Harlan casually walked up to the intimidating officer, "I'm sorry officer, uh…Wyatt? The name's Harlan, Harlan Kruellar." Harlan said humbly, while putting his hand out. "I don't give a damn if your name is….wait a minute, did you say your name was, Harlan Kruellar? As in "Harlan Imperial Express"?" Sgt. Wyatt weakly replied. Harlan glanced over at Kale before responding, which raised the Lieutenant's suspicions about his sudden appearance, "Ah, yes, the one in the same…" Harlan said. Embarrassed by his rude tone, the constable manically shook Harlan's hand, as if he were trying to shake out the last ounce of syrup from an empty container, "Oh man…oh man, oh man… I'm so sorry about that, you know, what I said about…uh, not giving a damn sir! I mean…" Sgt. Wyatt nervously rambled. Although the constable's powerful grip was irritating him, Harlan swallowed his pride and endured the pain, "That's quite alright officer, you were just doing you due diligence." Harlan said nauseously. "Maybe so sir, but it didn't give me the right, especially to such a generous man who donates "yearly" to fallen police men's families. If it's any conciliation sir, the property manager did say that you would be on the premises from time to time….I still should have known better." Sgt. Wyatt concluded. Kale did not know what to make of the meager acting Harlan Kruellar, but whoever he was it was obvious that he had long pockets and possibly had friends in the police department. He also noticed how fixated Harlan's eyes appeared to be on him while he conversed with the constable, as if he had already known him. Whatever may have been going on, if Harlan had not stepped in, he may have carved the trigger happy Sgt. Wyatt into a coat with his trusty Swiss Army blade, Kale pondered. "Well, I won't hold a grudge if you don't, Officer Wyatt…!" Harlan confirmed. Suddenly, Sgt. Wyatt got a call from his dispatcher on his shoulder radio about a 10-19, "Excuse me sir, 10-4 Roger that! I have to report back to my station, but it was an honor meeting you sir! You on the other hand (pointing a finger at Kale) are not allowed back…" Sgt. Wyatt ranted, before getting interrupted. "Yada, yada….yeah, I heard ja' before….anyway, yew' got a light cop? I seemed to….misplaced mine." Kale asked sarcastically, while putting a cigarette into his mouth. “Kiss my ass, freak! Sorry again about the way I spoke, sir!” Sgt. Wyatt said, and quickly made his way to his patrol car. “Don’t suppose you have a light on ya, eh Mr. Moneybags?” Kale quipped, and began to walk away. Kale’s snarky and dismissive comment made Harlan chuckle, “I do in fact have one Lieutenant….” Harlan said, as he reached in to his coat pocket. He then lit Kale’s cigarette, “What is it today with people and their fuckin’ insistence to pissin’ me off?” Kale tensely asked. It did not surprise Harlan that Kale may have been on to the fact that he was not there by mere coincidence, after all, the former Black Ops Lieutenant did have an IQ well above 160. “I’m not here to aggravate, nor insult your intelligence Kale. I suppose, it’s safe to assume that we both know that “I” know who and what you really are!?” Harlan concluded. The cold reminder of his military past did not sit well with the young Lieutenant, and he suspected Harlan may have been there on his father’s behalf, “Did my father send you? It figures. If so, then you can just go fuck yourself!” Kale angrily replied. Harlan again found himself amused by the Lieutenant’s primitive candor, “Now, do I look like I’m from the Army?” Harlan asked humorously. Kale searched the much older Harlan Kruellar for any aspects of a former military background. There were many things that stood out that told kale otherwise, like Harlan’s poor posture. Military men always stood with their chests out, when he clearly did not. Sgt. Wyatt recognized him as a prominent figure who donated tons of cash, another thing that men in the Armed Forces did not make enough of, especially to be driven around in fancy limo’s, Kale figured. “Well, if my dad didn’t send yew,’ which agency did? All yew’ guys always seem to want sumthin’, or somebody dead. Who is it this week, Justin Bieber? Cause if so, I’d be glad to do it!” Kale retorted. Harlan was no longer in a playful mood and looked Kale directly in the eye, “I’m not representing ANYONE Lieutenant, but what I “DO” have is a rare opportunity, and one I’m more than certain, you would not want to pass up!” Harlan confessed. His offer was intriguing, to say the least, Kale thought. But Kale knew that there was not anything left in the world to care for, that the well off Harlan Kruellar had to offer him that would have been of any benefit to him. He did not need money, although he preferred living among the drunken vagrants than he did the apartment that the Army was paying for. Unless Harlan could bring back the dead, there just was not enough motivation for him to be interested, “Sorry Harley, but I’m not interested.” Kale sharply replied, and began to walk away. Harlan anticipated the possibility of the youthful Lieutenant refusing him, which was why he always kept an ace in the hole in every negotiation he had ever been a part of, "What if I was to tell you Lieutenant, that I HAVE worked for your father in the past, at least, in a small capacity!?" Harlan insisted. Kale stopped walking mid step and tossed his cigarette into the grass, "Okay…I'm listening." Kale said grudgingly. Harlan folded his arms and exhaled, "Oh… let's just say, that I may be privy to certain "classified" information concerning your family's killer, that your Army CLEARLY doesn't want you to know about…" Harlan conceded. The enormous carrot Harlan dangled in front of Kale's face was too hard for the heavily grieving soldier to ignore. If there was a possibility of more information regarding his wife Rita and his children's deaths still out there, then he had every right to know. His general father had promised him that he would move heaven and Earth to find the rest of the hidden terrorist cell Ismail had been a part of, who gave him the bomb. But as time went on his father eventually left him with a bunch of empty promises as each of his leads led him from one abandoned place to the next. He ultimately quit marching to his dad's drum and "retired" himself from the Armed Forces, and begun moving from city to city to avoid everyone. The toll of losing his family caused him to have a complete nervous breakdown which led to his eventual court martial and extended stay at a Veteran's Mental Ward. His father did not want to see a soldier of his caliber imprisoned, neither did his superiors, but each time they attempted to lure him back, Kale utterly refused. "Well, Lieutenant?" Harlan asked once again, and pointed to his opened car door. "I see you like to play hardball, but alright, Harlan I'll hear yew' out. But what on Earth could ja' need me for, I can only imagine sumthin' pretty nasty…." Kale regrettably implied, and got into the limousine. "….And THAT, Lieutenant Keegan, is what I intend to carefully explain on the way." Harlan replied, and followed behind him into the long shiny black automobile. The limousine driver wasted no time, when Harlan ordered him to leave and quickly sped away from the Midtown Clinic. Harlan knew that convincing Kale into going along with his plan was crucial, but would not take as much finesse as it was going to take for the others to except the company of the self-destructive Lieutenant. "Who could blame them?" Harlan figured. No one in the group knew anything about Kale's service record or, about the hundreds, if not the thousands of lives he and his team were responsible for saving over the last half decade. Hopefully, what he had to offer them was going to be enough for the grieving fathers to except and also see the fruitions of his devised plot through. Either way, the window of opportunity had finally presented itself the moment Reverend Templeton walked into the room and opened it "just" wide enough for him to stick his head inside of it, Harlan thought. Harlan was going to make the best of the only chance he had at reaching his ultimate goal, which was seeking the total destruction of the rabid animal Alfonso Barrera, who right in front of him, sawed his son in two. Nevertheless, Harlan believed there was a brutal reckoning coming to the savage cartel lord and the rest of those spineless so-called "businessmen" who dared to use him to hurt "their" families. In order for him to seek the vengeance he wanted, Harlan had to form a pact with the "others" he needed and they would then follow Lieutenant Keegan into hell to return peace and balance back into their lives. But most of all, to prevent other fathers from becoming the monsters they had yet to become.

Chapter 8:

"Doubting"

The Midtown Houston Mental Care Facility: Tuesday afternoon…

It had been a long morning and the toll of the exhausting conversation he had at the sports bar Monday afternoon with Thomas Jr., kept Terry up almost half the night. Despite everything his lover Lacy tried to do to take his mind off his brother's distracting woes, his brain just would not shut down long enough for him to find any sleep. Ever since their talk yesterday, Thomas Jr. had spoken very little to him, maybe because he was too embarrassed to or, feared that he did not believe him about seeing their dead father, Terry thought. Whatever the case may have been, Terry found his story both typical and fantastical at the same time. At the end of the day, he was not a believer in ghosts or, the afterlife for that matter, but what he did believe in, was the overpowering feeling of guilt that accompanied most people of persecution and affliction, like his brother Thomas Jr. did. To help further complicate matters was the unexpected and unwarranted visit by the group's primary benefactor, Harlan Kruellar, to whom his presence was forced upon him after an earlier call from his supervisor, and resident pain in the ass, Dr. William G. Becker. Although, he was very well aware of the half million dollars that Mr. Kruellar so generously donated toward the group's inception, Terry felt somewhat pressured into a situation that could have been handled by someone a lot less qualified than himself. But here he was, spear-heading Harlan Kruellar's "pet project" like a good little soldier, with no questions asked, Terry pondered. He did not know much about the observant and enigmatic Harlan Kruellar, other than what he read of him in his online bio, about the independent transporting mogul being filthy rich. Since as long as he could remember, their clinic had been starving for more grant money, so it was not all "that surprising" when Dr. Becker cut short his vacation to be there to introduce his new "meal ticket" to him, Terry figured. When they shook hands, prior to the start of the group's session, Terry could tell that behind all his flattery and the shrewd façade, that Harlan had the eyes of a man who was deeply troubled. He had to have been, for someone of his stature to spend most of his spare time ogling the group from the observation room the way that he had been, Terry concluded. Part of the arrangement Harlan made privately with Dr. Becker, allowed him to survey the group's progress at his leisure. But what did a man, who made a substantial fortune building a vast transporting empire, stand to gain from making such a large investment at a small mental health clinic anyway? And why, after all these weeks, would he decide to finally show his face now? Terry wondered. Was he just another billionaire looking for a quick tax write-off or, was he really attempting to make a difference in other people's lives like he was trying to do? Terry pondered. Terry had been so caught up in his own thoughts that he was unable to hear group member "Skinny" Ricky when he called out to the distracted psychologist, "W-What was that?" Terry asked confused. Ricky "Skinny Ricky" Wallace was fresh out of the emergency room after receiving the pen wound in his hand that Kale was responsible for causing the day before, "You feelin' okay there, doc? If you want, we can wait till the next session to do my…" Ricky humbly began to ask, until Terry interrupted. "No. Ricky…that won't be necessary! You managed to still be here, despite yesterday's….SETBACK….so, by all means…!" Terry confirmed. Ricky took a long look over everyone else inside the room, but stopped when his eyes met Harlan's, who just so happened to be sitting in Kale's old seat, "What about the new guy? It wouldn't be fair of me, you know, taking up the rest of our time…" Ricky began, before getting interrupted once again. Terry turned his attention to the muted and distant-eyed Harlan Kruellar, "Nonsense. Mr. Kruellar is a patient man. I'm sure that….WHATEVER he has to share today, won't take up much of everyone's time. And besides, he's not officially "part" of the group!" Terry said coyly. Harlan could hear the mild disdain and cynicism in Terry Templeton's voice when he addressed him by name and could justifiably understand his possible reasons for having major reservations about his presence there in the room, which was "partly" why he chose him. Although his sexuality had been called into question among some of his peers, Dr. Terry Templeton's glowing reputation as a highly thorough psychologist was undeniable. What Harlan was also looking for was someone with valid credence or, authenticity to show for the money he had spent to have the group formed and the men he needed in one place to recruit. With Dr. Templeton at the helm, no one would ever question the validity of gathering the grieving fathers to field such a study and it would also make his donation appear legit, Harlan figured. In the past, many indignities had been performed "knowingly" to collect on debts owed to him, but none distressed Harlan more than the indignity that had been done to Reverend Thomas Templeton Jr. and his entire family. It proved to be a much harder task to be in the reverend's esteemed company up close, especially after spending much of his time at the clinic inside the private observation room he had been using for so many weeks, Harlan discerned. Terry incidentally caught Harlan staring at his brother for what he believed to have been about the tenth time, but instead of letting it go, Terry cocked his head to get both Harlan's attention and conformation to proceed. After realizing his slight, Harlan quickly nodded his head "yes" and offered Ricky Wallace a humble wave to continue in response to Terry's previous statement. Had he run into Harlan Kruellar on the street, he would have never pegged him as someone of great wealth, Terry assumed. Instead of wearing a sharp looking business suit, Harlan dressed more like a college professor, or librarian, than someone who ran one of the largest fleets of liner cargo ships in the world, Terry thought. Part of him actually preferred the idea of him being back behind the glass two-way mirror, like some silent voyeuristic partner, than the hypnotic distraction he made of himself with his group, Terry contemplated. But Harlan's "donation money" paid for his seat in the room and the clinic's bills, and besides, how he chose to blow off his money was not actually any of his business anyway, Terry reflected. In Terry's mind, the only thing that was supposed to matter was the restoration of the men accumulated in front of him, so he gathered himself and turned to a new page inside his composition notepad, "Ahem, please…. proceed Ricky." Terry politely asked. The malnourished looking Ricky Wallace cleared his throat, which sounded more like someone revving up an old beat up station wagon, Terry thought. "Well, for those of you who don't know me, the name's Ricky, Ricky Wallace, but my friends call me Skinny or, Skinny Ricky! For obvious reasons, ha-ha-ha (ahem) ….anyway…" Ricky nervously said. As Ricky began the tale of his origins, Thomas Jr. felt compelled to open up his bible and turned to the book of John. He remembered the many fond memories of thumbing through his father's old leather bible on Sunday mornings and preaching about all of the awesome miracles of Jesus Christ to the people of New Greater Faith. To him, it seemed like ages ago, when he last broke spiritual bread with his former brethren, and wondered how they were making out without his presence there. After waking up in the hospital room, from his vast amount of surgeries, Thomas Jr. remembered how he once likened himself to Lazarus, to whom Jesus resurrected from the dead after four days. But soon after the euphoria of returning back to the land of the living wore off, the new reality he found himself in only had proven to be an even worse nightmare, Thomas Jr. painfully recalled. The thought provoking recollection of his past caused his mind to drift off, until suddenly, Thomas Jr. heard a slow clawing sound coming from somewhere behind him. When he turned around, Thomas Jr. could see that the disturbing sound was coming from the mirror imbedded in the wall, that apparently only "he" seemed to be hearing, Thomas Jr. realized. Then unexpectedly, the clawing on the glass had become more rapid and violent like an exerted human heart beat, causing him to both wince and brace himself, but the mirror never broke. He eventually worked up the courage to take a closer look. The moment he stood to his feet, all of the gnawing and vibrating from it abruptly stopped. Against his own better judgment, the startled reverend then hesitantly made his way in front of the menacing looking glass, despite his intuition screaming for him not too. After a few quiet moments pass, his curiosity appeared to take control and he decided to give the glass a couple quick taps. Soon as he finished, someone on the other side of it immediately tapped back three times, causing him to flinch uncontrollably. Thomas Jr. found himself under the assumption, that he may have been a victim of a vicious prank being orchestrated by his former trickster of a younger brother Terry, who was known for pulling such stunts as a child. The thought of his brother's playfulness in the past managed to bring him some major comfort, so Thomas Jr. decided to knock three times instead. Before he could finish the third knock, a large pair of degenerated hands broke through the large glass and grabbed a hold of him. It was his father Thomas Senior, who appeared more deteriorated than the last time he remembered seeing him, "Choose blood boy…you lo-o-o-se blood!!! Ha-ha-ha….!" Senior laughed loudly, and commenced to choking the frightened Thomas Jr. by the throat with his decrepit hands. Thomas Jr. pleaded for his father to release him, but instead, he refused his desperate pleas for mercy and forced his son to scream for help from Terry and the other group members, who were casually sitting still, as if nothing were happening at all. His father began to squeeze him tighter and tighter, compelling him to lose his entire state of mind, "L-Let…g-o-o…of m-me…y-y-you crazy….son of a bitch!!!" Thomas Jr. yelled. From out of the blue, he could hear the faint sound of another person hollering his name into his ears, as though they were doing it with a bullhorn. When Thomas Jr. opened his eyes, everything in the whole room had gone completely quiet. There were no signs of his father anywhere and the broken glass from the mirror on the wall was fully restored. The only thing that was different, were the expressions on the faces of the men in the room, who were now staring strangely back at him. Terry appeared worried and placed his notepad into his lap, "That's enough Jovan! I think he's awake now….You okay, Tommie?" Terry asked concerned. Thomas Jr. shook his head, as if he were trying to overcome a vicious hangover. He sat up in his seat and noticed the towering Jovan Campbell standing over him, "Yeah, what happened?" Thomas Jr. asked. Terry looked around the room at everyone's reaction, then back to his light-headed older brother, "Uh…why don't you tell us, bro?" Terry cautiously replied. Jovan Campbell looked every bit the football player Thomas Jr. was told he was, as he watched him slowly take his seat, while still fearing for the excited reverend's condition. "No doubt! Man that must've been one helluva'…uh, no offense…some kind of crazy ass dream, huh Rev!? I can't remember the last time I heard a preacher swear like that before…but, I ain't trippin though, ha-ha-ha!" Jovan quipped. The contemptuous former undercover DEA agent Milton Elliot rolled his eyes in displeasure to Jovan's juvenile candor, "Ps-s-s-sh. Yeah, that's all we need…a cursing exorcist…! Can't believe doc swapped out our old "wackjob" for this new model. …" Agent Elliot joked. The young former football standout wasted no time sharing a little bit of his own disapproval of the rude agents comments, "Yo' Eli, maybe we'll get to see the "Rev" break yo' big country ass down too, like the old one did!" Jovan quipped. Agent Elliot casually placed his hand over the holster of his gun, "That's it….k-e-e-e-p talkin' wise ass…!" Agent Elliot playfully warned. Jovan Campbell did not have the privilege of growing up around many father figures, despite ever yearning for the need of one. But something about the fatigued looking reverend told him that he could be trusted and had the curious desire to protect him. “Okay, enough fellas! Thomas, why don’t you get yourself a drink of water and some fresh air!? I’m sure it will do you some good!” Terry kindly suggested. Terry’s suggestion sounded like music to his ears and he did not hesitate to leave his bible behind, as he made his way toward the door, “That sounds…that sounds like a good idea…my apologies, to you all.” Thomas Jr. wearily said, and quickly hastened away. It was obvious to Terry that Thomas Jr. was experiencing another one of his episodes, but he could ill afford to stop the group to delve into his brother’s private issues, especially with Harlan Kruellar sitting across him, examining his every move. To reassure the possibility of the clinic receiving any future grants, Dr. Becker made it clear that “he” had to put on a good showing for Mr. Kruellar, or risk losing out to another institution, Terry pondered. “Alright, where were we?” Terry asked. “We were at Ricky dropping out of high school back in Vegas to become a professional bi-sexual hooker.” Agent Elliot punned. “Hey fuck you cop! It beats being a fulltime jerk-off policeman any day!” Ricky protested. “My God, is that urban hierarchical substandard really necessary in here today? We do have a guest in the room!” Adrian Atkinson squeamishly asked, while cleaning off the dirt from his glasses. Harlan sat unfazed by Milton and Adrian’s childish bantering and continued to pretend as though he were amused. “Agent, please…!” Terry pleaded. “It’s alright doc, he’s just mad about his dildo not coming in the mail…take a hint tough guy: Steroids make your wee wee tiny, just like your brain. Which I’m not perfectly sure you got….” Ricky retorted. Terry was beyond ready to wrap up his session, not only because he was so beat, but because he wanted to go check on how his brother was doing. With only half his work day gone, he was thinking both long and hard about leaving early to go home and get some rest, which was going to be virtually impossible with the amount of paper work he had left to assess and turn in. He had a mountain of data to pore through and regrettably, was asked to even fax over his findings to Harlan Kruellar’s handlers, something that he truly dreaded after the week he was having, Terry feared. The often quiet Hakiro Yosami was starting to become impatient, “Guys, please?” Hakiro subtly replied. Mason Lowry also raised his hand to lend his own two cents into the conversation, “Yeah guys, I really do have to get back to work in about an hour, s-o-o-o…!” Mason insisted. Somebody get this guy a tampon or, somethin’!”Agent Elliot quipped. Jovan swatted the lewd officer across the arm to get him to calm down, “What?”

Agent Elliot asked innocently. "Cut it out dude. I'm ready to go too." Jovan confirmed. Yes, we all have more important things to do on our schedules…. (Terry staring coldly at Harlan)….than to be here, arguing and tearing one another down. That type of unhealthy attitude will get you nowhere and it certainly will not bring any of your children or, loved ones back! Now if it's your wish, Agent Elliot, you like Lieutenant Keegan, may leave. But, if you want to really get down to the root of your problems and want to help someone else who may be going through what you're going through, then by all means, please stay! Remember your sworn oath as a deputy of the peace? Surely you wouldn't mind trying to find yourself some?" Terry insisted. Terry took Milton Elliot's silence as a sign that he got the message, "Alright Ricky, how about us trying this again….?" Terry asked.

Over the last several minutes, Thomas Jr. had been wondering aimlessly through the Midtown Clinic's hallways, contemplating his return to the stuffy powder blue colored room, where he just dreamt about his father choking the dear life out of him. Wherever his visions were coming from, each one seemed to be getting stronger than the last, which began to worry the drained reverend. Part of him felt embarrassed by his uncharacteristic outburst and was certain that everyone thought he was crazy. "Maybe I am going crazy…" Thomas Jr. thought. He spotted a water fountain near what looked like the clinic's break room. When he pushed the button to take a drink from it the last thing Thomas Jr. expected was to get his eyeball pressure washed by the fountain's spout. The water tasted like it was half made of lead and the other half made of chlorine, but was freezing to his chapped lips. There were a couple vending machines inside the offbeat looking room that also caught his attention and he decided to try his luck. He skipped out on breakfast to avoid another drawn out conversation with his younger brother earlier that morning and now the hunger pains were starting to pound his stomach unmercifully for it. When he entered the empty break room and saw the high prices on both the soda and snack machines Thomas Jr. tried his best to keep from cursing out loud, but could not help himself, "Son…of…a…bitch! Five damn dollars for one damn soda? Four goddamn dollars for a goddamned pack of chips? Lord forgive me…I know I know better." Thomas Jr. confessed, and exhaled deeply. After taking careful consideration in his food choices, Thomas Jr. decided to get himself a Sprite Zero and some Twinkies and dug into his front pockets for any loose change. Instead, he pulled out some Carmex lip bomb, some Tic Tacs, a paper clip, some cigarettes, his lighter and a face cloth. He then scrambled for his wallet and then grimaced in disgust once he opened it. Thomas Jr. almost forgot that he was only in Houston on his brother's dime and that he never actually had a budget for even making the trip, at his brother's urging, in the first place. There was next to nothing in his savings account and in a rush, he forgot to pulse out any money before he left Georgia. As he stared in defeat, at his empty wallet and at the cruelly priced vending machines, Thomas Jr. could hear familiar sounding footsteps casually approaching from behind him. He knew that he had been away from the group for a while and figured that it was only inevitable for Terry to come looking for him, "Was on my way back, bro… just had to clear my head a little. Maybe eating one of these "five dollar" Twinkies might do the trick?" Thomas Jr. playfully said, and put his money into the machine's money slot. When he made his selection, the coil that held the snacks in line got hung up, therefore stealing the humbled reverend's only money, "…Or not. Jesus Terry, you know sometimes, I swear man…!" Thomas began to say, as he finally turned around. To his surprise it was not his brother, but Harlan Kruellar who was standing there quietly, as if he were an innocent angel eavesdropping over his prayers. I thought reverends aren't supposed to swear? I'm more of a Ho Ho's kinda' guy myself…may I?" Harlan gently asked. Thomas Jr. nodded and got out of his way to the snack machine. Harlan gave the machine one hard shove and made his package of Twinkies fall down into the snack dispenser. He reached inside and took them out and held the package up to the speechless reverend. "Thanks. You sure you're a billionaire?" Thomas Jr. asked curiously. Harlan found humor in the suspicious reverend's honest question and smiled accordingly, "Last time I checked." Harlan cheerfully confessed. "Well, you shole' don't act like any I've ever seen!" Thomas Jr. replied. "Hmmm, that's odd. And how many do you know, might I ask?" Harlan gleefully asked. "Humph. Gotta' point there, sorry Mr. u-u-h….!" Thomas Jr. vaguely said. "Kruellar, but please reverend…call me Harlan." Harlan kindly insisted. "What about you?" Harlan replied subtly, as he went up to the soda machine and added money to it. "What about me? Thomas Jr. quickly interjected. He bought two sodas and grinned as he passed a Sprite Zero to the defensive reverend, "I'm just saying, you know, with all the commotion between you and….that other disturbed gentleman, Lieutenant Keegan, and now…. "swearing" in group? I mean, what was all THAT about?" Harlan asked concerned. With the coldness of a barren Antarctic lake did Harlan's cruel reminder strike a chord deep within Thomas Jr.' fragile mind and caused him to feel inappropriate. "What I mean, reverend, is have you lost your way?" Harlan asked. "Y-Y-Yes, I s-suppose s-so…yeah. I've been through a lot! I haven't been able to find any answers for my pain though." Thomas Jr. admitted. "I could tell. You know, to be honest with you reverend, I've been feeling ALOT like that myself lately, no matter how much I prayed for a solution to my own problems." Harlan confessed. "Humph. Most people should be so lucky. God blessed YOU to be a billionaire who's actually trying to help people. Somewhere down the pike, I let him down, and for some reason, I'm still paying for it." Thomas Jr. confirmed. "God….may have "blessed me," reverend, but despite all my efforts, my fortune could not replace what I lost. You see, reverend, I "too" know what it is like to feel constantly frustrated. I too am also familiar with the excruciating pain a father endures after his son is taken away by some goddamned monster." Harlan said angrily. "But my brother, he said that your son died in a plane crash?" Thomas Jr. replied. "That was just a cover story, I'm afraid. No, he didn't die in a plane crash, although he would have been better off just the same. At least, he's with my late wife Marisa, God bless her soul." Harlan said solemnly. "I'm sure if your boy was anything like you then I'm certain your son is in a better place!" Thomas Jr. said. "I'm sure he is…..you know, reverend, I'm holding a private engagement at my home tonight that I'm sure you would definitely find both eye opening and enlightening, if not….interesting. I would also appreciate it if we keep this little conversation to ourselves. We don't really need anyone prying, especially with what I have to offer should you decide to come!" Harlan stipulated. He handed the befuddled Thomas Jr. a business card with something written on the back of it, "What's this?" Thomas Jr. asked inquisitively. "It's my home address." Harlan replied. "Tell me something, Mr. Kruellar…" Thomas Jr. began, before getting interrupted. "Harlan is fine, reverend Templeton. There's no need for formalities." Harlan confirmed. "Well then, "Harlan"…now, I may not be the smartest man in the world, but judging from the way you been eye-bawling me in group and you going through the trouble of "pre-writing" this fine penmanship here, that you WANT something from me. Stop me when I'm wrong!" Thomas Jr. implied. He knew Thomas Templeton Jr. was no dummy, and there was no denying that getting the suspicious reverend to simply "play along" was not going to be a piece of cake either, Harlan assumed. In the past, when it came to conducting business with his more shady "clientele" did he find the truth as anything, but a cancerous crutch holding him back from attaining his primary goals. The only problem was that the embattled Reverend Thomas Jr. was not one of his estranged partners in crime. Far too often, Harlan found deception as his only means to an end, until his wicked ways caught up to him and claimed the life of his son, Haven. His late wife Marisa was the only person in memory to whom he knew how to be himself with, without all the lies and deceit. She meant everything to him, and would probably be ashamed at his willingness to suppress what exactly he had in mind for the reverend, Harlan figured. But since she was not there, he had to try his best to be as forthcoming as possible without the benefit of "exposing" the total truth, "Yes and no, reverend. But most importantly, it's more about what I want FOR you. So please, come tonight…and I'll explain everything. " Harlan whispered. Harlan then placed his hand out toward the apprehensive reverend. He had hit rock bottom a long time ago and did not have anything in his life left to lose, Thomas Jr. thought. In retrospect, his life had already been taken, only to be revived to become the self-loathing and uninspired mess he was today, which made Harlan's invitation much more appealing. Thomas Jr. reached out and shook Harlan's hand, "Alright, Mr. Kru….ahem, Harlan. Give me a couple hours to think on it." Thomas Jr. protested. Harlan had spent many of his years negotiating with all types of people (rather they were poor, wealthy, legit, crooked, etc...) and could always tell when a person's intrigued, "In that case, it was a pleasure finally meeting you Reverend Templeton!" Harlan said pleasantly, and left the clinic break room as quietly as he appeared. "Likewise…" Thomas Jr. said to himself aloud. He placed his snack and the cool bottle of soda on a table near him and clasped his hands over his face, trying to make sense out of what just happened. Was he really considering to just "show up" to some strange man's home, to talk about lord knows what, just because he asked him to? Thomas Jr. wondered. Thomas Jr. exhaled and pulled out a chair and sat himself down. His feet were sore from all the pacing he had been previously doing in the hallways, until his encounter with Harlan Kruellar. He fumbled with the packaging of his Twinkies as if they were wrapped in leather, "Shit, they child proof this damn tha…?" Thomas Jr. began to say, before his mind trailed off. Suddenly, something strange about him and Harlan's conversation hit him like a feather weight sneaking in an unexpected uppercut. He remembered the last thing he told him, just before he left the room. It was something about him "finally" getting to meet him, Thomas Jr. recollected. Could his brother have possibly spoke about him in a prior casual conversation before he ever left home or, was something else afoot here? Thomas Jr. speculated. Harlan asked him not to tell anyone about their meeting for a reason, and whatever that reason was it could not have been anything good, Thomas Jr. figured. While Thomas Jr. was trying to piece things out in his head, his brother Terry came running into the break room, as if he just scored off a fifty yard touchdown, "Man! There you are….I been, schwoo….I been looking everywhere for you! You…huff…you were in here…huff…this whole damn time?" Terry asked exhaustedly. Thomas Jr. grinned and held up his Twinkies, "Yeah, I got hungry for some five dollar Twinkies and decided to come here." Thomas Jr. quipped. Terry rolled his eyes and took his hands off his knees, "Whew…man, I haven't run this much since I punched Barry Mayo in the face..." Terry joked. Thomas Jr. spit out his drink and chuckled hysterically, "Hold up bro….that must have been what….over twenty something odd years ago? Not to mention, that YOU were in the Navy for cryin' out loud!?" Thomas Jr. protested. "Man, why don't you just shut up and pass me one of them damn Twinkies!" Terry insisted and snatched the package from Thomas Jr. "You just mad cause Barry almost whooped yo' ass for pinching his butt…!" Thomas Jr. joked, and began to laugh harder. It did Terry's aching heart much good seeing his typically brooding older brother in a better place mentally for a change. Until now, his brother's visit had been a somewhat frustrating and emotional one, which at one point, made him question if his true intentions were enough to justify lying to Thomas Jr. about why he asked him to come in the first place. At least for the time being, all that did not seem to matter very much to the middle-aged psychologist and he wasted no time joining his brother in some rare, but heartfelt laughter.

David Lewis pays Dr. Templeton a visit

It was two hours past his usual work day and Terry Templeton was in need of some serious rest and relaxation. Since his common-law husband Lacy was already in the neighborhood earlier that afternoon, Terry asked him to swing by and take Thomas Jr. to get a bite to eat on their way home. If it were just any other day, he would have simply taken the rest of the day off, but he promised to deliver his latest dossier on the group's progress by 8:00 pm. He had taken great care in making sure that the files he appropriated for Harlan Kruellar's assistant were as detailed as possible, according to his prior instructions. Most of what he had to share were basically his notes on observations and some medical opinions concerning every group member's mental stability. Terry could imagine seeing a private physician interpreting his findings from the soothing comforts of the eccentric looking transporting mogul's hundred foot yacht. Nevertheless, part of his and Dr. Becker's agreement was to keep him in the loop, which was why he stayed passed his normal 5:00 pm quitting time, Terry contemplated. There was a sudden knock at his office door and he could already tell by the gentle sound it was his secretary, "Come in Sheila, but make it fast!" Terry replied. The sultry acting secretary opened the door and had a troubled look on her face, "What's the matter?" Terry asked worried. Sheila put her freshly manicured hands on her hips, "How much longer am I going to have to keep fielding calls about the one patient you ain't seeing anymore? I mean, I got everyone from the Pentagon to NASA looking everywhere for this fool!" Sheila barked. It only took Terry a fraction of a second to guess who she could have been possibly talking about, "Keegan. So…what did you say to them?" Terry asked humorously. Terry knew that it did not take much to get a rise out of his mouthy secretary, "The hell you thought I told em,' I said we made his crazy narrow ass kick rocks!" Sheila comically inferred. "Now Sheila…?" Terry replied snickering. "What? Even you have to admit his dingy tail had a scrawny looking ass!" Sheila loudly protested. "Girl, what am I gonna' do with you?" Terry asked. Sheila started rubbing her fingers together, "You can start with a raise, and then let me go home to my man!" Sheila staunchly replied, while pointing her thumb over her shoulder. "How about a rain-check on the raise, but hey give

Jason my love!" Terry said cheerfully. Sheila then waved him off and paused just short of leaving Terry's office, "Oh yeah, and some "Army guy" claiming to be an old friend of that muskrat, keeps calling and leaving messages. He keeps saying how important is to talk to you." Sheila said. Terry had been loading his briefcase, but stopped dead in his tracks when he heard the news, "Well!?" Terry asked in suspense. "Well what?" Sheila answered befuddled. Well, did the guy leave his name or, maybe a phone number?" Terry asked emphatically. "He said he didn't want to say over the phone, but would rather call back until he could reach you. Look, I thought the guy was just some weirdo, and since you were so busy, I didn't want to bother you with it!" Sheila said apologetically. Terry appeared to be lost in his thoughts which began to worry the opinionated secretary, "Aw man. I screwed up didn't I?" Sheila replied disappointedly. He had been hoping for any kind of lead that could give him more incite about Lieutenant Keegan's past, but since he was no longer counseling him, the point had been a moot one, "No, Sheila…don't worry about it. Go on home, now. But, if he should call again…" Terry began. "I'm already ahead of you, doc. See you tomorrow!" Sheila said, and then closed the door as she walked out. Terry had lost track of the time and looked down at his trusty Rolex, "SHIT!" Terry yelled. He just remembered that he promised Lacy that he would spend a little quality time with him before he left for the gym that evening, but there was just barely enough time for him to make it home before that could happen, Terry realized. Before he knew it, Terry had shoved everything he could fit inside his briefcase and then grabbed his files and car keys and stormed out his office. Seemingly, he found himself sprinting to his shiny Lexus, as if he were running anchor in a four by one relay. In his rush, Terry accidentally dropped the files he was carrying on the ground while trying to open his car door, "Oh shit! Lacy' gonna' kill me…" Terry said to himself, and squatted down to pick up his belongings. Without warning, a very deep and raspy voice came up from behind him, "You Dr. Terry Templeton?" A man's voice said. Terry immediately dropped everything and felt a large shiver rippling down his back like a loose raccoon caught in his Polo. "What the fu….who the hell are you?" Terry frighteningly asked the strange looking figure, who seemed to be as tall as the Statue of Liberty. "Well sir, all that depends on if you who I'm looking for." The man said firmly. Terry was scarred out of his mind and did not know what to expect from the looming figure that wore a beat up looking Army coat and was in possession of two prosthetic arms, "Alright then. Yes. I'm Dr. Templeton. Now, who the hell are you, and what do you want?" Terry nervously asked. The man smiled and held out one of his prosthetic hands to help Terry off the ground, "The names Sergeant David Lewis sir, but my friends call me Dave…." Dave said politely. For a person who was supposed to be paraplegic, this "David" felt stronger than Terry first assumed after he yanked him to his feet with no trouble. "…speaking of which, I was kinda' hoping that you could help me locate a friend of mine? His name is…." Dave began to say, before getting cut off. "Let me guess…Keegan. You're the message guy who's been harassing my secretary all day." Terry suspiciously asked. The smile that was on the balding skyscraper of a man, quickly evaporated and replaced it with one of selfless desperation, "So he's HERE!? Thank God! Look, I'm sorry for all…THAT. But honestly I didn't….I didn't know what else to do, if you had any idea…" David said regrettably. It was obvious to Terry that both David and Kale shared a possible deep history or, even personal trauma that he had no apparent clue about, which started to irritate the stoutly psychologist, "Then for Christ sakes, why won't somebody just tell me then!?" Terry frustratingly responded. Although he would never admit it to Thomas Jr., but despite all his antics, Terry was still feeling a bit discouraged about cutting Kale from the program. But without having any of the necessary background information how was he ever going to possibly accomplish that? Terry thought. It would have been easier to ask him to try and catch a chicken with both his hands tied behind his back, Terry assumed. In Terry's eyes, David could see real compassion for his long lost friend and could hear the confusion and frustration in the tone of his words. "Look, Dr. Templeton….I can tell "they" left you in the dark, but it would really be better if we just go somewhere and talk in private." David insisted. He found himself doing a lot of crazy things lately, so riding along with some random handicapped stranger will only be another in a long line of knee-jerk reactions made in the vein of correcting an injustice, Terry pondered. Either way, his lover was not going to be pleased and his brother was still at his home waiting on him. But Terry's curiosity was peaked and he knew that in order to fully get Kale Keegan out of his system then he had to learn everything there was he could from the young Sergeant, "Okay, then. I know a place…" Terry confirmed.

Several minutes later, at the Cadillac Grill in the Houston Montrose area,

When he asked Dr. Templeton to go somewhere to talk privately, the last place he expected to congregate with him would be at some gay bar, David thought. He was impressed at how much liquor the middle-aged doctor managed to put away after the first two or three minutes they sat down at the busy bar. David also could tell that Terry was a regular, as the bartender already referred to him by name. It did not bother him that Terry may have been a homosexual, but it was hard to ignore all the "extra attention" he was getting from the rest of the male natives, and part of him believed they were not being mesmerized by his giant sized plastic hands. By his count, Terry slammed down five shots of Patron, as if he were trying to put out a fire on his tongue, and was on his way to ordering more, "Oh…I'm sorry, David. It's been a really long day for me, go ahead pick your poison, it's my treat!" Terry insisted. David seemed to be pre-occupied by all the smiling faces he was getting from the overly friendly customers, "Uh-h-h, I'll just have a soda…" David said anxiously. Terry scrunched his face in disbelief, but flagged down one of the bartenders he recognized, "Alright then suit yourself, Sergeant…"hey Mickey," I need another round….and a club soda, on the rocks." Terry quipped. He could not help but notice how often the young Sergeant kept looking over his wide shoulders, and wondered if it was because David was in trouble or, simply uncomfortable. Regardless, Sergeant Lewis had some humungous explaining to do, "Hey Mick, could you have somebody bring our order to the booth over there, please!? Follow me, Sergeant." Terry asked. The Cadillac Grill was one of Lacy' favorite bar and grill restaurants they would often come to visit every other weekend, especially if it involved a major sporting event, Terry recollected. Lacy was a big sports buff, who trained himself as if he was still on his high school wrestling team. But despite how dominant and strong he thought his body may have been, Terry highly respected his intelligence and adored his giving heart. The last thing he ever wanted was to hurt his common-law husband, especially by placing himself in harm's way for a complete stranger, which was why he picked a familiar place to chat among people who knew him. They moved into a small quaint and secluded booth in proximity to the bar and away from any possible ease-droppers. If he was going to get any of the answers he sought from David, the last thing he needed to make him feel was distressed, “This any better for you Sergeant?” Terry asked concernedly. Despite his disposition, David found the immaculate landscaping somewhat comforting, if not well polished. The table appeared to be made of some type of brilliant cider colored wood, with every possible condiment a person could ever desire at his disposal at the far end of it. The short redheaded waitress who brought them their drinks had the same hair cut as Arnold Schwarzenegger did from the Terminator 2 movie, except with a prettier smile, “Here’s your shots, doc and that, uh…club soda…on the rocks!?” She heckled. “Bless you Marcy!” Terry cheerfully said. Marcy put her hand over Terry’s shoulder in concern, “Tough day at the office, doc!?” Marcy inquired. One by one, Terry downed one shot after the other, “If you only knew….but, this will hold me for now, thanks.” Terry said contently. Although Marcy had been working part-time for her uncle, owner and bartender Mickey Calhoun, at the Cadillac Grill for a short while, it never stopped her from getting to know her customers fairly quickly, which usually equaled out to being on the receiving end of some great tips. With that being said, it did not take her long to realize that the quiet stranger who sat across from Dr. Templeton was not his usual company, “Hey, no prob doc! Oh, and uh…when your “friend” here’s ready for sumthin’ with a little more kick, you jus’ holler!” Marcy replied, and trotted away. Terry’s affinity for getting plastered started to make the grim looking Sergeant Lewis lose a little bit of confidence in the pudgy psychologist, “Hey doc, uh, don’t you think you need to slow down a bit? I mean no disrespect and all, but I ain’t in the mood to be hauling you…” David said, before getting interrupted. “Now hold on, that’s where you’re wrong, son! I’ve been at this game lo-o-o-o-ng since I first joined the Navy, back when you were probably just a tadpole, asking for directions in your papa’s nut-sack!” Terry quipped. David was taken aback to the doctor’s straight forward candor and was surprised to hear that he was also a former serviceman, “Really? I would have never guessed. It makes sense though, you Navy boys are known for putting away your liquor!” David said. Terry took another shot of Patron and slammed his glass hard over the heavily polished table top when he finished it, “Yeah…I suppose you didn’t. There’s a lot about me that you DON’T know son….kind of like our mutual friend, Lieutenant

Keegan. You mind telling me something that I don't know about him?" Terry asked sternly. Terry was through wasting time and was beyond ready in getting to the bottom of the mystery that was Kale Keegan's life story. In Terry's mind it felt like an eternity had passed waiting on David to contemplate his next sentence. He took one long final glance around the restaurant before David decided to open his mouth and then exhaled deeply, "You ever lose anything, doctor?" David whispered. Before he could grant the morbid sounding Sergeant an answer, David placed both of his prosthetic arms on the table. After he did that, it forced the normally assertive doctor to second guess his reply, as if he were changing his mind about going down an unfamiliarly dark road. Terry struggled to see where the calmly man was going with his question, but despite the trepidation of answering incorrectly as a clinician, he settled to lead with heart. "In a way, I have David. As a runaway, I lost my family. But before that, I lost my father's respect. I lied to him about being sick one Sunday morning and he allowed me to stay at home, instead of going to church. Anyway, after forgetting his bible he came back home and caught me fooling around with another boy from school that I liked, so…he politely kicked me out on my ass. So, to answer your question, I would say yes, David. I HAVE lost something." Terry concluded. During his turn to speak, Terry could not help but notice the intensity in the young man's eyes who sat just a few feet across from him. He had Kale's same two thousand-yard stare, of a person who has seen far too much of too many of the wrong things in war. Suddenly, his eyes rolled to the top of his head, as if the irises were playing hide-and seek, and then went back to normal, "Yes. I suppose you have doctor. When I lost my arms in combat, for a second there, I too started to believe that I lost everything. I mean, physically, for a little while at least, I was robbed of my ability to draw and paint, among so many other things "we" as human beings normally take for granted, but after awhile, I learned to adapt. And during my adaptation process doctor, I actually gained more than I could have ever asked for….when I fell in love for the first time of my life with my wife, Jessica. In the beginning, I was never what a person would have called the "marrying type," but when I hit rock bottom emotionally, w-w-when….when I was at the lowest point of my life, doctor….God blessed me with a beautiful angel. Eventually we had twin sons, Donald and Darius and we just recently had a girl, who we named after Kale's late….after Kale's wife, Rita." David said happily. The soothing warmth that enveloped around Terry's heart made him feel slightly good, despite the heart burn that was trying to sneak up on him, due to his over indulgence of alcohol consumption. But much like some of the stories he was accustomed to hearing lately, Terry believed that a dark cloud would not be too far behind in this happy tale. "You have any kids, doctor?" David asked deafly. David's voice had seemed to have dropped a couple octaves, making his voice almost mutable, "I'm sorry?" Terry replied. David leaned forward, with his eyes hardly blinking as he spoke, "Kids. Do you have any?" David casually repeated. His question felt awkward than his last, Terry thought. Regardless of what he assumed was appropriate or, inappropriate Terry still felt compelled to answer him, no, despite what his instincts were screaming, "No…I'm afraid, I don't. My "partner" and I talked about it maybe once or twice, but…I don't know." Terry answered achingly. David leaned back into his seat and closed his eyes while he spoke, "Well then, that's too bad doctor…You know, Kale was a father once. I was with him during both of his wife's pregnancies, even was asked to be the kids godfather until…listen, doctor…Kale and his father, General Patrick Keegan, hardly got along and after his mom died, things really fell to shit. They constantly moved around the country until finally settling down in Iowa. Me and Kale didn't hit it off too well at first, but we got past our differences and have been friends ever since. He wasn't like anyone I ever met before and for a little dude, he really knew how to throw down!" David said excitedly. Terry rolled his eyes, as he was already too familiar with his combat prowess, "Yes, so I've noticed." Terry said displeased. The tone in Terry's voice made David's eyebrows rise and started shaking his head in amusement, "Wow…that boy's never gonna' change. It's not his fault you know?" David confirmed. Terry could not believe his ears and took another shot of Patron, "Please, enlighten me!" Terry pleaded, and slammed the glass back down. David rubbed his prosthetic hand across the brow of his bald head and down to his goatee, "You look like a man I could really trust doctor….I CAN trust you, can't I? Because I'm already putting myself AND the relationship between me and my best friend at risk if I can't!" David protested. Terry reached over and placed his hand over David's, "You can trust me, David. Whatever you tell me will be held in great confidence and since this has to do with someone who I've counseled, no one can force me to disclose any information about that person without that person's consent!" Terry confirmed, and removed his hand. The muscles that were tight around David's thick jaws began to relax and he gave a confirming nod of understanding. David needed a few seconds to gather his thoughts and took several quick sips of his club soda to clear his throat. "Like I was saying before doctor, about you know....Kale and his father, always being at odds with another....well, it was for a good reason. His dad, in all intents and purposes, basically killed his wife Karen by using some experimental miracle cure for Leukemia on her, only....it wasn't really a cure...." David said lowly, as his mind seemed to trail off someplace far away. The news of this caused Terry's eyebrows to fold down to the center of his forehead, "Go on...." Terry carefully instructed. His voice snapped David out of his deep thoughts, "Well...Kale told me that he found out before her operation, that some of the same minerals used in the cure were also being used for his dad's bio-chemical warfare division and that there was a higher chance of her own body attacking itself than of her surviving the procedure. And when she died it...well, it devastated him and Kale." David said, and took another sip of soda. For the first time ever, Terry started to gain some type of clarity on what chain reaction started the volatile Lieutenant Keegan down a spiraling dark path. He (Kale) was obviously closer to the mother, and resented the father for going through with such a dangerous and yet complicated procedure, Terry hypothesized. Although Terry believed as much, that Kale's troubles began at an earlier age, it still was not enough to explain why the Army allowed Kale to be sent to him, of all people, for counseling years later. There were as many holes and gaps in David's story as long as Galveston's sea wall that still needed to be filled in, Terry concluded. "If what you're saying is really true, David, then explain why on Earth did he join the Army? Surely Kale didn't do it to please the one person who was responsible for the death of his mother. That would be one incredibly stupid ass way to show his father some spite!" Terry suggested. He then signaled for Mickey the bartender to send over his next round of drinks. David cocked his head and was examining Terry, "You sure you're okay doctor?" David asked. Terry swallowed his last shot of Patron and slammed his glass hard on the table, "I'm fine. Sorry David....but all I want to know, is how Kale ended up at my clinic? The program he's in...was in...are for troubled fathers who struggle daily with the violent deaths of their children. What I don't understand, is how does a dangerous soldier with severe PTSD symptoms gets dumped..." Terry began, before getting interrupted. "I can't answer THAT Dr.

Templeton, and personally, I would like to know that MYSELF. You said you wanted to know something about my friend that you didn't know, well doctor, that's what I'm trying to do!" David replied, and started to leave the secluded booth. What he said was true and before he spoke, Terry gave David's words time to marinate, "Wait.....you're absolutely right, my apologizes, David. It's just, it's really been a rough couple of days for me and I'm dealing with some…family issues, at the moment. Believe it or not, I still want to help Kale, but in order for me to do that I'm going to need to know "everything!" Terry insisted. Seeing the sincerity in the portly psychiatrist's face was enough to put David's mind at ease, so he decided to stay, "Fair enough, doctor. It's the least I could do, I suppose." David said humbly. The waitress Marcy scampered her way back to their table with Terry's new round of drinks, "Here ya' go doc…and friend!" Marcy said coyly. Terry rolled his eyes, as it was obvious what she was insinuating, that David may have been someone who was anything other, "That'll be all, Marcy! Oh, and put the drinks on my tab will you!?" Terry instructed. What Dr. Templeton chose to do was none of her business, thought the jolly acting waitress, "Whatever you say doc!" Marcy replied and high tailed it away. Terry exhaled exhaustedly, then meditated for a couple split seconds, "Now David, please tell me more about his father and why Kale chose to join the Army." Terry politely inquired. David looked him dead in the eyes as he spoke, like the way a wolf stares down a trapped rabbit in the wild, "You ever see the Manchurian Candidate doctor? Remember how those "doctors" were brainwashing those soldiers into believing everything they thought they were seeing, but wasn't real? Well, what the movie got right, is that there're really people in this world who want to take out the good things that make you who you are inside, just so they can change you into some sock-puppet they think they can control. That's who Kale's father is Dr. Templeton, that's all he ever does. He's someone who has spent an entire career figuring out all kinds of ways he can cause pain to others, as well as manipulating them, including his own son, into doing whatever he wants them to do or, being whatever he wants them to be. Of course, Kale admitted that he didn't realize what his father had been up to in the beginning and just assumed he was actually trying to help him cope with his mom's death in his own sadistic way. You see, the General always wanted his legacy of death to continue, long after his demise, and hoped that Kale would grow up to be that heir to his diplomatic throne. Problem was, well…you've seen him. Kale lacked his father's "ideal" physical make-up and that tormented him for it his whole life. He even said that his father went as far as using subliminal suggestion to alter his mind, and when that didn't work he just beat the living shit out of him. Said it was his way of teaching Kale how to keep himself protected, when in reality, all he was trying to do was create a damn monster. If you ask me, the only thing Kale Keegan ever needed protection from, was his own damn father!" David admitted, and finished his first glass of soda. David's astonishing account of Kale's perverse upbringing was frightening to the imagination, Terry thought. Terry began to recollect all the terrible whippings his own father dished out long ago for him being gay and started to sympathize with Kale's plight. He too was a victim of a harsh and cruel childhood because he was different, which was no better than Kale being victimized by his father for being too small in his eyes. Whoever said physical abuse was only common to the commoner's, had to been a complete idiot, Terry pondered. David grabbed the extra club soda the waitress brought and took a big gulp from the glass, "A-h-h-h…stuff's not bad…thanks doctor." David said. Terry grabbed one of the new shots of Patron, but just as he was ready to drink it down a thought crossed his mind that made him hesitate in doing so, "Amazing. Just…simply amazing…." Terry said stoically, as if he was caught inside a delicate daydream. The psychologist's peculiar demeanor seemed awkward to the young Sergeant, "Uh, what's so amazing? Me thanking you or…." David started to say, until Terry cut him off. Terry leaned forward, "Amazing…that he managed to contain all that rage as a kid, that…. that Kale never killed anyone prior to ever joining the fucking Army! I mean, his father must be some kind of Jedi miracle worker to have kept his mental stability in check…." Terry said astonished, before stopping mid sentence. Seeing the grave look over Sergeant Lewis' heavily burdened face was all the explanation Terry needed to predict what was coming out of his mouth next, "Guess you pretty much answered your own question doctor." David confirmed, and finished what was left in his glass. "You see, Dr. Templeton…long time ago, Kale and his dad got into a huge argument over a woman his dad was seeing, so he stole his daddy's .38 caliber pistol and his car and ended up at some dive bar on the outskirts of town. He….he said he wanted to die, but just couldn't work up the nerve to….to. Anyway, he got drunk and met some woman, who failed to mention she was married, and one thing led to another. What

Kale also didn't know was that the bitch's husband was waiting for them outside when they tried to leave together. Kale didn't want any trouble and tried to leave, but the guy kept pressing and pressing him. Next thing you know, they get into brawl and this grown man is getting mad cause some high school kid is really kicking his ass and so he tried to take the .38 caliber from him. They both struggled for the gun, until it accidently goes off killing the dude, which landed Kale into some deep shit with the cops. He was looking at facing manslaughter charges, but the General made a few calls and got him out of trouble…at least for the time being that is…." David determined. It did not take long for Terry to figure out the rest, "Let me guess….take the red pill and join "my" Army and I'll make all this go away!?" Terry quipped. "…Or more like, "here," take the blue one… it'll scramble your brain, and then your ass is mine!" David finished. Certainly, the guilt must have been great on Kale's conscious at the time, and with his father "generously" sweeping everything under the rug, it had to have made him feel obligated to do what his dad always intended on him doing, which was enlist, Terry concluded. He was positive that Kale's transition to the military was a seamless, albeit an unhealthy one, despite all the heavy handed discipline the Army had to offer. For every enemy he engaged on the battlefield, only created the greater potential for pushing his psychosis to the point of no return and made him an unfeeling killing machine, Terry theorized. Right as he raised his glass to take his next drink, Terry spotted David admiring it for a split second, causing him to lick his lips, as though he were a Rottweiler savoring a taste from his favorite bone. It was clear to him that David was trying desperately to avoid paying the alcohol any attention, which possibly meant that there might have been some bad prior history with him drinking it, Terry figured. Either way, Terry thought he looked like a man who needed a stiff drink just as bad as he did and slid one in front of him. David appeared both guilty and caught off guard by the gesture, "Uh, n-no thanks doctor…but, I promised my wife long ago that I'd stop…" David nervously said. Terry shrugged his shoulders nonchalantly, "No pressure….but earlier, you mentioned something, about Kale being a father once. Did something happen to Kale's family that you're not telling me?" Terry asked agitated. Suddenly, David looked at the drink that was offered to him and snatched it up, as though it were a pair of hot dice on a craps table. His question seemed to rattle the young Sergeant, as he began to look over his wide shoulders once again as if he were trying to avoid detection. He glanced across the table at Terry as if awaiting his disapproval and swallowed it down. The alcohol's flavor and tartness sent a rushing sensation to the back of his bristled jaw line, causing the Sergeant's face to wince unexpectedly, "G-o-o-o-d….damn!!! You know….ahem, you know my wife w-would lose her shit if she saw me with this!?" David confessed. Then David peered into the empty shot glass, as though he were a mystic gypsy searching for answers from a crystal ball, "Kale and I started off at the bottom of the trash heap during basic training together, but we worked our asses off to climb out from under it. Only thing was, the guy never stopped climbing. The boy scored high marks in every combat static that the Army had a test for, and why not? His dad only had been training him in hand to hand combat and Guerilla Warfare since he could walk! It wasn't before long he went out as an infantryman, where he begun earning all kinds of purple hearts and silver star medals for bravery. Even though at that time, I might have been more athletic than he was, but Kale was the one with the gift. We did a tour or two, together overseas. We took down a few hooks, nothing really major. But then, the promotion came…." David said. Terry took off his eyeglasses, "Black Ops!? Terry quietly quoted. David scanned the now very busy restaurant for anything out of the ordinary, like a paranoid Gestapo agent on the lamb. As debilitating as the increasing smell of freshly cooked hamburger meat made him feel, Terry could not ill afford to become distracted at the moment by the hunger, "Are you saying that Kale was Special Black Ops!?!" Terry asked once again. David swallowed hard before he spoke, "What I'm about to say cannot in any way be repeated, but yes…. we both were. It was at the request of his dad, General Keegan. He was putting together a new shadow unit of the Army's best and we called ourselves "Razor Hawks." And let's just say…we had certain kinds of…"freedoms"… that most squads didn't have…" David whispered. Terry grabbed a napkin to clean off his glasses, "A kill squad." Terry said disturbed. David could see contentment in the eyes of the psychologist's round face, "Yeah…so to speak. Sometimes, we went on rescue missions, mostly to the shittiest places you could ever imagine. But, on other occasions, our jobs were to hunt down and take out any major threats to the States. We were the best at what we did, that is until….until someone from our past, showed up at Kale's front door…." David painstakingly alleged. He reached over and took another of Terry's shot glasses and swallowed the sharp tasting drink without a hitch. Terry did not have any issue with him taking another of his shots and merely looked on in consternation. It had been a long time since the young Sergeant went cold turkey and David tried to savor the moment, "A-h-h…. not bad doctor…the guy was a former Afghan citizen, who as an act of revenge for the death of his family joined the Al-Qaeda cause, and somehow managed to slip into America "unnoticed." Anyway, call it dumb luck, karma, or whatever the hell you want to, but he found Kale. The bastard just one day shows up, strapped to a dirty bomb, kills Kale's pregnant wife and two sons; including some neighbor who was simply in the right place at the wrong time. It all happened right in front of him and he's been an emotional train wreck ever since then. General Keegan did everything in his power to find some answers, but the only thing they could find on the guy was a shitty apartment, that he paid cash for and the parts he used to make the bomb. Afterwards, they questioned Kale and they were able to link his family's killer to a hidden, but mobile Al-Qaeda cell that wormed its way up north. Eventually the trail went cold. Meanwhile, by that time I had already been decommissioned due to my injuries and wasn't able to keep a close eye on him. Surprisingly, he was cleared to return to duty, you know, leading missions, even without a proper psyche eval, I was told. It wouldn't be long after receiving his command back before the rumors started to spread about him having "episodes" in the field. From what I heard, Kale had begun to lose control and begun butchering our targets and endangering hostages he was supposed to have been saving. Then finally, during a debriefing, one of our superiors questioned Kale about his "unapologetic" behavior…" David said. Terry leaned in closely in suspense, "So…what did he do?" Terry asked anxiously. The stone-faced Sergeant did not blink, "He shot him. Anyway, the superior survived, and his dad used his influence to keep him out of the stockade, but agreed to have him institutionalized. If you ask me though, he did it because the higher ups knew what an asset Kale was and would do anything to keep him viable for the future. Them putting him away didn't help and it only made matters worse. He would get released and be allowed to go right back to doing what the kid does best, which is killing! Then he would do something else crazier than the last time they'd release him and he'd get sent back to the psyche ward. The last time he was put away, he….he had been saving his meds for over a month and somehow managed to steal a guard's gun. Kale beat up an orderly, took his keys and barricaded himself in a broom closet, where he slit his wrists with a handsaw. He…had the meds with him too and swallowed them, "all forty" or so, tablets that he drank down with water and ammonia. When the M.P.'s finally kicked the door in, Kale had just pulled the trigger on himself. I've been looking for him ever since." David said grimly. Just when he thought that Kale's story could not have possibly gotten any worse, it somehow makes an incredible turn that mirrors a grizzly episode from Tales from the Darkside, Terry thought. His mind seemed to go stagnant and heart numb, causing the middle-aged doctor of psychology to drop a tear down his dark-complected cheek. Over the last decade or so, Terry believed he had heard every unfathomable tragedy any one psychologist could ever stand to listen too, until today. In his heart, had he been privy to the aspects of Kale's previous history then he might have been able to approach him accordingly instead of allowing him to stew with the rest of the fathers in the group. His story was worse, if not just as worse than what happened to his brother Thomas Jr., who ironically Kale had the most in common with, and chose to make an enemy. David seemed to be now salivating at Terry's last shot glass, "Do you mind?" David sincerely asked. By that time, Terry had long lost his appetite for alcohol and was more than willing to pass it along, "Y-Yeah, no uh, David help yourself." Terry catatonically stated. He took the tangy drink back slower this time, permitting his throat to enjoy the sheer piquancy that it had to offer. Wiping off his mouth, "Thanks for hearing me out doctor, and for the drinks too. Also, I'm…sorry, if I…you know, scared you earlier, but I really needed to find my friend. If you see him again, will you please contact me? You can reach me at this number!" David asked hopefully, and casually slid his number to him. David held his prosthetic hand out to him and Terry started to hesitate to receive it. Part of him still had more questions, but Terry knew that they would simply have to wait until next time and graciously shook his hand, "Of course, not a problem." Terry replied. He then climbed out of the booth as if he were trying to get from out of a sardine can, "That Kale…he's one real tough son of a bitch. Any other ordinary man alive would have died from the ammonia poisoning and pills alone doctor, but not him. I don't know what God has in store for him, or have left for him to do, but whatever it is you don't want to be around to see it." David warned, and eased his way toward the restaurants nearest exit. Regardless, the young Sergeant left him with plenty of useful information to chew on, needless to say, that he received it at the cost of pissing off his lover, Terry thought. He looked at his watch and realized it was after 8:00pm and then he saw the three missed calls from Lacy on his cell phone. Whatever he was going to say to him was going to most certainly end with him giving in to anything Lacy desired, Terry groaned. Either way, he believed he got most of what he had been asking for from David and was starting to realize that maybe Kale's insertion into the group was not a mistake after all. Kale's past was deliberately left out in his file at the clinic and certainly someone on the outside was aware of his history and thought it pertinent to include him, Terry figured. The only problem is that the experimental group was supposed to be a simple case study comprised from volunteers, outside of Jovan Campbell, who was court-ordered to be there, Terry pondered. Not wanting to dilly dally any further, Terry gathered his belongings and made his way to the door. "Kale could have just been in the neighborhood and somebody else close to him might have thought it was a good idea that he would join a focus group to solve his problems, or maybe the Army finally got fed up and did not know what else to do with him?" Terry considered. He decided not to make anything more out of the issue than it was, considering the possibility that he would never see Kale ever again. Only thing he knew was that he needed to get home to his brother who may have been wondering where he had been all this time. While rushing with his complete attention on his cell phone, Terry accidently bumped into a passing stranger on the sidewalk, "Oh, excuse me! Sorry, I didn't see you" Terry apologized. The slender clean cut stranger wore dark shades and did not seem bothered by Terry's hasty intrusion, "Hey, it's no problem, I wasn't looking either! You have a good night though!" The stranger said. Something about the stranger seemed vaguely familiar to the usually astute psychologist, but he did not have the time to figure it out, "Okay, good night!" Terry courteously said, and waved him off as he got into his vehicle and drove off. The stranger shook his head contently and chuckled to himself, while he watched him speed off from the dimly lit Cadillac Grill parking lot. He hummed quietly why he reached into his pants for a cell phone. With a pleasing look on his face, the stranger then made a call and when the person on the other end picked up, he removed his glasses from his face, "Yeah, it's me Alejandro. Sergeant Lewis and the doctor just left. You still want me to tail em'? No problem. I'm on my way." Alejandro sneered, and hung up the line.

The Meeting

Across town, on the outskirts of Houston city limits,

It was well after 8:00pm, and the closer his discomforting car ride had gotten to Harlan Kruellar's extravagant home, the more astounded Thomas Jr. was at the sheer size of it. The humungous estate sat on top of a wide hill and was surrounded by well-manicured landscaping, as far as the human eye could see. In the main entrance, was a giant beautiful marble fountain accompanied by three hovering angles in the middle of the huge cul-de-sac. When the elderly looking driver stopped the car, a middle-aged man dressed in a black suit with a salt and pepper goatee opened the back door to let him out. Being over six-foot three, Thomas Jr. repeatedly thanked God, as he labored his way out from the back seat of the cramped blue Volkswagen, that brought him 45 minutes away from Terry's house. Harlan had insisted things be kept on a low profile and was sticking to it, by hiring an inconspicuous and independent taxis service to come to pick him up. Thomas Jr. grudgingly went into his back pocket for his wallet to pay for his fair, "So uh, break it to me gently…how much I owe you for the long…." Thomas Jr. began to ask, until the driver interrupted. "Don't worry about it, son. You're already taken care of!" The driver kindly stated. "Of course it was..." Thomas Jr. thought to himself. Although it was considerate of Harlan to pay for his ride round trip, on the other hand, Thomas Jr. still had his pride to consider, "Are you sure? I mean, c-cause, I HAVE the money if you know…if you…." Thomas Jr. insisted, before getting cutoff. "No need. I'll be right here, waiting on you." The driver strenuously concluded. He did not know what to make of the strange circumstances that lead him to such a marvelous looking place and felt somewhat transfixed by its gaudy, but tranquil ambience, "Okay then. Thanks for the lift!" Thomas Jr. agreed relieved. In the back of his mind, Thomas Jr. knew he could not afford the unplanned trip he made to Harlan's version of "Never-land Ranch, but was trying to save what little dignity he had left in meantime. He stared intently at his greeter, who stood a few inches shorter than he was and about half a decade younger, "…And thank you too! You know, for opening the door and all." Thomas Jr. told the silently stiff figure. Before he uttered a single word, Thomas Jr. could see through the obvious forced smile on the man's clearly annoyed face, "Good evening sir, Mr. Kruellar has been…expecting you." The man painfully said, and closed the car door. He then directed his hand out to guide Thomas Jr. toward the front door of the lavish home, "Right this way, sir…" The man courteously suggested. Despite his tentativeness, Thomas Jr. began to follow his cautious looking escort. During their brisk walk through the Harlan's gargantuan abode, Thomas Jr. could not shake the fact that his presence there meant the same as lying to both Terry and Lacy. Regardless, of the "oath of silence" he took earlier in the Midtown clinic break room, Harlan was not family and Thomas Jr. knew that he did not owe him anything. Not to mention, it was on his brother's dime that he was even in Texas in the first place, Thomas Jr. recollected. But here he was, allowing himself to be escorted through some stranger's wondrous palace, as if "he" were something of importance again, Thomas Jr. thought. On their way to Harlan's private study, Thomas Jr. noticed what seemed to be a huge family portrait on a distant wall. The tall frame of it was brilliantly trimmed in a metallic gold and on the stylish painting itself, was a much younger looking Harlan, who was standing behind his wife, and one who appeared to be their son in her lap while she sat smiling in a chair. Thomas Jr. went over to take a closer look at the craftsmanship of the impressionistic painting. One of the details that stood out to him in the picture first, was how happy and proud both Harlan and his young wife looked. His handler in the suit had not realized that the curious reverend had stopped to steal a glance from the old painting, whose delicate strokes long ago were used to preserve a precious moment that was once filled with awe and treasure. But to his employer, the only purpose it seemed to serve lately was just another ugly harsh reminder that happiness is sometimes a fleeting thing and was not always promised to the dark and disenchanted, the suited man thought. The art critic in him could not blame Thomas Jr. for wanting to stare at the beautiful painting and decided to join him for a moment, "Amazing isn't it? It was the happiest day of their lives!" The suited man said. Thomas Jr. did not take his attention off the picture, "Yes, it is SOMETHING….but, look I don't mean to pry…" Thomas Jr. began to ask, until the suited man intervened. "Then don't." The suited man concluded. Appalled by the man's arrogance and his apparent disdain for his company, the passionate reverend sized up his well dressed middle-aged chaperone up and down, "Hey, your BOSS was the one who invited ME here! The least you could do Mr. Belvidere, is lend me the common courtesy of answering a few simple questions. Or, do I need to go cram my black ass back inside that blue go-kart I came in and head back home!? I'm guessing MR. KRUELLAR, wouldn't be too happy with YOU if I did that, so-o-o…." Thomas Jr. warned. Although agitated, the man considered Thomas Jr. painful request and looked at his watch and winced like a college basketball coach stuck in overtime, "Alright. But first, I must caution YOU about having some…discretion, Reverend Templeton. Mr. Kruellar doesn't like people asking questions, but….if it will make you fill any more comfortable….what is it that you wish to know?" He grudgingly asked. Thomas Jr. bit hard on his lip and pointed at Harlan's smiling wife, "Let's start with her! Now, Harlan told me himself that she died, so….what happened to her?" Thomas Jr. dubiously inquired. The answers that Thomas Jr. sought caused the gentleman to become highly fidgety. He reached inside his Saks Fifth Avenue Black coat pocket and pulled out a scarlet red handkerchief to wipe his mouth, "Mrs. Kruellar, she was such a vigorous and vibrant woman….I can't remember EVER meeting anyone who enjoyed being alive more than she did. She was taken away far too soon, and it all happened right here, in this house, where her life expired. It left everyone devastated." The suited man remorsefully stated. Thomas Jr. was unaware of the timing of the death of Harlan's wife, but still wondered about the circumstances surrounding it, "You said "it" happened in this house….you not trying to tell me that he was the one…" Thomas Jr. began to say, before getting interrupted. "For heaven's sake reverend, no!" The man angrily whiffed. He stuffed his handkerchief back into his jacket pocket, "He would NEVER lay a finger on Mrs. Kruellar! He loved her, more than life itself." The suited man shamelessly justified. His egregious insinuation that Harlan possibly murdered his own wife at home was a bit of a reach, if not a cruel and insensitive accusation, Thomas Jr. figured. Despite his willingness to be open, to some degree, the suited man had yet to be forthcoming about one single detail, "My mistake. But, if he didn't do it, what did?" Thomas Jr. replied. Suddenly, a mild-mannered voice came in from behind them, "It was her heart, reverend! She, my wife Marisa, had died from a rare and deadly heart condition." Harlan said wounded. The sudden and surprising presence of his employer startled the brazen man in the suit, "Oh! I'm terribly sorry, Mr.Krueller…I…he said, he would leave and…" The suited man stuttered. Harlan nonchalantly walked over and placed a reassuring hand on his assistant's shoulder, "No, it's quite alright Oscar, you have always been loyal. But, thank you, I can take things from here." Harlan confirmed confidently. The man in the suit who Harlan referred to as "Oscar" acted as if frightened by a ghost, making the insecure reverend wonder if Terry saw the same look on his face after seeing their dead father. Without hesitation, Oscar excused himself, leaving Harlan and the humbled reverend alone. Harlan reached out to shake Thomas Jr.'s hand, "Hello again reverend, I was beginning to wonder if you might have changed your mind about joining us this evening!" Harlan said gladly. Thomas Jr. likewise shook his host's freshly moisturized hand, "What can I say, Harlan? I'd be a liar if I said I wasn't at the least interested. But what's with "Alfred" and all this other cloak and dagger stuff? I ain't here to do an exorcism am I? " Thomas Jr. jokingly asked. Harlan had found the reverend's charismatic personality to be very favorable and had a pretty good feeling about tonight's gathering. He put his hand across the back of Thomas Jr.' shoulder and began to lead him toward his intended destination, "My assistant, Oscar, I'm afraid, is NOT my butler, but he IS my most trusted personal assistant. As far as to the other "cloak and dagger stuff" you were referring to reverend, you'll have to excuse me. My other guests and I would not appreciate it if anyone else was made privy to this "private meeting." It would make things rather, how would you say, "counterproductive," for any future endeavors we have planned." Harlan calmly explained. Thomas Jr. to listened intently, despite the distraction of all the expensive artifacts they were walking passed that filled his expansive hallways, "Okay. But, who is this "we" and what do you all have in mind that's so important, that I have to lie to just to even be here?" Thomas Jr. asked baffled. Harlan responded first with a large Machiavellian grin, as if he had just been asked if he loved being rich, "What I…excuse me, what "we" have in mind, reverend, is one commonly unique perspective about the way things are in this world when they happen and what we are prepared to do when they DO happen! Ah, here we are…" Harlan cheerfully said. They stopped in front of a gorgeously multi-patterned hand carved wooden door, which familiar voices could be heard coming from behind it. Harlan grabbed the door handle, "Tell you what reverend, how about you just come in and "we'll" explain things further…" Harlan insisted, and opened the door. When he opened the elaborately designed door, Thomas Jr.' was immediately surprised to see half of Terry's group standing around having a very animated discussion. After he and Harlan entered the room, everyone in the entire room became disturbingly quiet, while staring peculiarly at the confounded reverend. One individual sat with his back toward the door, but had yet to turn his head. Harlan was doing his best to have some class and contain the overwhelming amount of glee he was feeling during the moment, but ultimately could not help himself and chuckled uncontrollably. He held his hand out to both welcome and usher Thomas Jr. into the spacious room that served as his private office, "I'm guessing no introductions are needed, eh reverend? Please, do come in!" Harlan cheerfully replied. As Thomas Jr. slowly stepped through the regal looking office, still no one said a single word. The ceiling appeared higher inside the Venetian decorated room and the walls were adorned with built-in shelves filled with a plethora of books of every size, shape, and color, Thomas Jr. thought. There was a gorgeously polished all black Steinway piano on the far side of the room, across from Harlan's cherry wood desk and another tall painting near his massive window, Thomas Jr. noticed. It was a painting of a young man, who looked an awful lot like Harlan's wife did in the other picture, Thomas Jr. contemplated. Thomas Jr. was in awe of Harlan's impressively decorated office and had not realized that he was standing right behind the individual that had yet to turn around. His concentration was immediately broken up by the heavy stench of cigarette smoke that he indirectly walked himself into. He got a closer look at everyone's faces that were in attendance for this special meeting: The jock Jovan Campbell, DEA agent Milton Elliot, the meth-head Ricky "Skinny Ricky" Wallace, former store owner Hakiro Yosami, and one other as yet to be identified person who sat patiently muted. Thomas Jr. could see the top of the person's dirty blonde hair and figured him to be the only non group member who was invited, "How's it going, gentlemen, I didn't expect to see you guys here!?" Thomas Jr. said. With his face turned away, the person sitting down quietly in front of Thomas Jr. had unexpectedly slapped on an old beat up straw cowboy hat, "I guess ya' can also say the same bout' me too, Tommie boy!" A man's voice said. The seated man's thick southern drawl sounded vaguely familiar to the now panicking reverend and caused him to step back. When he stood and faced him, it was none other than Lieutenant Kale Keegan smirking back at him in the flesh, "Howdy reverend! I believe we got us sum' unfinished business ta' take care of…." Kale said grinning.

The Proposal

The mere sight of the roguish Lieutenant caused the confused reverend to gasp in horror. Without a second moment's hesitation, an irate Thomas Jr. demanded an explanation, "Just what the HELL is going on here? I didn't come out all this way for this!?" Thomas Jr. barked. Harlan seemed unfazed by Thomas Jr.' imagined plight, "Relax, reverend…everything is fine!" Harlan insisted. Unconvinced, the staggering preacher began to backpedal his way back toward the office's entrance, "Everything's fine? Look, I don't know if you up on current events or not, but the man's dangerous!" Thomas Jr. warned. Amused, the young Lieutenant began cracking his rugged neck and smirking mischievously at the frightened reverend, "Why thank yew,' preacha' Tommie!" Kale quipped in his thick southern drawl. In disgust, Thomas Jr. whipped his head around to clarify his statement, "That wasn't meant to be a compliment…" Thomas Jr. snapped irritated. It was clear to Harlan that his brazen approach may have been a tad bit ambitious, even by his standards. After all, the last time Reverend Templeton Jr. had last seen the frosty Lieutenant, he was being packed out of his brother's counseling session for trying to attack him, Harlan recollected. But, at the end of the day, Harlan was a shrewd businessman, who believed in his ability of power over persuasion and remained poised. With the stealth of a fierce scorpion, Harlan went up to Thomas Jr. to offer him some reassurances face to face, "Please reverend, I can assure you that "NO" harm will come to you! I only ask that you hear me, and the rest of us, out before you leave!" Harlan pleaded. It made plenty sense to him why Harlan asked to keep their meeting a private one, as Terry would have shit a thousand page textbook if he found out that his group was meeting behind his back, especially at Harlan's estate, Thomas Jr.

figured. Not to mention the fact, that he would also be in the same presence of the lunatic who acted like he wanted to tear him a new hole just for the fun of it, Thomas Jr. remembered. The wealthy and enigmatic Harlan Kruellar was asking a lot out of the beleaguered reverend, who noticed a serious lack of security inside the massive room, "I don't know about this…" Thomas Jr. said tensely, while carefully watching Kale. As if his chair were filled with germs, Kale started sweeping off his seat with his hand and turned it around to face the leery reverend, "Here….yew' could even take MY seat, Rev!" Kale playfully insisted. Every fiber inside him urged the middle-aged preacher to cut and run, but because of the sincerity in which Harlan had spoken with and brandished upon his enervated face, it was just enough to dissuade him from leaving, "Alright….but, only if he promises to behave himself…" Thomas Jr. concluded. For a brief second, Harlan took his eyes off the troubled reverend to look at Kale. Although Harlan was sporting a harmless looking grin, through it somehow, Thomas Jr. could faintly see the hidden ire of a man who was not to be trifled with. He seemed "overly" confident in fact, it was as if he were in possession of some kind of kill-switch in his back pocket that could incapacitate the slovenly dressed Lieutenant, Thomas Jr. noticed. Thomas Jr. went ahead and sat down in his chair and could smell alcohol coming through the flannel tee-shirt Kale was wearing. Unexpectedly, there was a sudden knock at the door, "Yes?" Harlan called out. It was his formally dressed assistant, Oscar, who was carrying a varied assortment of colored folders. He entered the room discreetly, "Here are the dossiers that you, "requested," sir." Oscar stated. While Thomas Jr. continued to watch the eccentric Harlan Kruellar from afar, it was obvious to him, that whatever was inside the colored folders had to contain the primary reasons for their invitations, Thomas Jr. guessed. For someone who was supposed to be an invited guest, Kale appeared a little "too comfortable" for his taste at the marvelously crafted wet bar inside Harlan's private office, "How yew' take yah' poison, preacher….Clean or dirty?" Kale asked cordially. Despite his tempting offer, Thomas Jr. hesitated to answer, as part of him felt the desire to keep up appearances for his brother's sake, "Ah-h-….thanks, but I really shouldn't…" Thomas Jr. painfully replied. "Oh, come now, Tommie boy…whut's wrong wit' sharing a lil' drink among friends? Whut? Yew' think we gon' "run tell" yo lil' brother on yew'? I mean (starts to laugh) we all friends now….ain't we?! Tell yew' whut'….We won't tell, if yew' won't!" Kale wisecracked. Thomas Jr. scanned everyone's faces carefully and did not find any objections, "Alright then....make the bitch dry and dirty." Thomas Jr. happily replied. The former football jock Jovan snickered at the reverend's seedy reply, prompting Milton to tap him across the arm to focus on the task at hand. Kale laughed uncontrollably while pouring him the tall drink, "Ah man after my own heart! Yew' know what preacher, there just might be help for yah' after all...." Kale said optimistically, and brought him the glass. His eyebrows stood up in immediate attention when Kale sat down comfortably with an entire bottle of Jack Daniels in his lap. "Thanks, but I wish I could say the same." Thomas Jr. quipped. Thomas Jr. waited to see how Harlan would react to Kale's inappropriateness, but instead the laid-back transporting mogul appeared oddly pleased. Harlan began passing out the folders his assistant brought him moments ago, and like everyone else who received one, Thomas Jr. could not help but notice that it was sealed with red tape. The only person left out though was Kale, who seemed peculiarly more interested with getting wasted than with participating, Thomas Jr. assumed. After passing out the last folder, Harlan leaned his back up against his ample sized cherry-wood desk, "I want to first "thank" everyone again for coming and for your patience. I know you must all have other "pressing engagements" that might need attending, but I can certainly promise you....what I have to share with you, I feel, will be well worth any inconvenience." Harlan announced. The human broomstick Ricky Wallace raised his folder in the air, "Uh...What are these supposed ta' be? I didn't come way out here to take some damn SAT's test!" Ricky stated. His snarky comment did not amuse the often tolerant magnate, who rolled his eyes in disdain, "No, Richard. This isn't a test. But, what you "do" have in your little mummified hand there is an opportunity!" Harlan said sharply. Both the mountainous Agent Elliot and the former collegiate standout Jovan Campbell were looking each other in profound befuddlement, "An opportunity...for who, exactly?" Agent Elliot asked suspiciously. Harlan was squinting his eyelids, as if he were peering at an alien organism through an unfocused microscope, "THAT, Agent Milton Elliot, is completely up to you!" Harlan concluded, and folded his arms in grand satisfaction. Agent Elliot glanced at his on again off again comrade Jovan to see if he had any qualms of his own, but the young man was non committal and simply responded back with shrugged shoulders. As if on cue, Ricky began to fidget in his seat, "Can't we just… like, "skip" through the whole "Rod Serling" act? My pain meds are starting to wear off!" Ricky complained, while waving his heavily wrapped hand. In sly fashion, Harlan gestured to Kale with his eyes. Kale, who was trying to make mince meat out of the entire liter of Jack Daniels he was inhaling and leaned toward the struggling drug addict, "Why don't cha' just chill out Teenie Weenie, and let tha' man speak… fore' I bust this Goddamn bottle over yer' fucking head and stick yew' in the "other fucking hand" with it …" Kale threatened, and went back to gulping down more alcohol. Thomas Jr. was beginning to wonder how long it was going to take the unstable Lieutenant to mentally unravel and start terrorizing someone. Just as clear as he could read a restaurant menu Harlan was starting to see anxiety forming over Thomas Jr.' face. Fearing the possibility that the rattled reverend might be getting second thoughts about staying Harlan interjected, "Please, gentlemen… Trust me when I say, that "this" is the time when we must all pull together and gather our strengths. Now….what I'm about to tell you will certainly be "incredibly unnerving" at best, so I'm just going to come out and say it…..I've been watching you all very closely, which I'm sure some of you already may be aware of, but…..what all of you are "not aware of," is that I have researched each and every last one of your individual cases and have tracked down every person responsible for the deaths of your children and loved ones. I have each of the locales they all operate, any possible known affiliates, where they sleep…hell….I can even tell you what they had for breakfast, if you're interested." Harlan said boastfully. Each of the men's faces went down in unison and staring at the folders, as if they were holding onto the Holy Grail itself. Former store owner Hakiro Yosomi and Ricky Wallace cried almost instantaneously, while both alpha males Agent Elliot and Jovan Campbell simply gazed intensely at their multi-colored classified folders, as if they were stuck in some type of hypnotic state. The good reverend Thomas Jr. on the other hand, overreacted, "Y-You….d-did what?!!" Thomas Jr. asked nervously. Everyone (with the exception of Lieutenant Keegan) had just come to the realization that he too was also in possession of a folder, suggesting a horrible past they were clearly unaware of. Harlan reached into his sports coat and pulled out an engraved sterling silver cigarette holder, "What I said, my dear reverend…Is that I "know" where your killers sleep." Harlan whispered stoically. The weight of Harlan's news hit the breathless reverend with the impact of a runaway school bus. Instantly, Thomas Jr. became nauseated and dropped his folder onto the lavishly maroon carpeted floor, "I…I-I think I'm gonna' be sick…..Why Harlan? W-What on Earth, would "possess" you to do such a dreadful and deceitfully misguided thing?" Thomas Jr. asked exasperated. A furious Milton Elliot jumped out of his seat, "Yeah, and just what in the hell do you expect us to do about it? Cause, if it's what I think it is then, I suggest you stop talking right this Goddamn minute!" Agent Elliot warned. Ricky angrily tossed his file across Harlan's desk, "Jesus, Harlan, you got all the goddamned money in the world and you still can't buy a fucking clue! I mean, look at me, Harlan. I'm just a goddamned junkie from Las Vegas, in case you weren't paying attention earlier. My story's pretty much cut and dry….me and my girl did dirt and pissed off the wrong androgynous bitch who forced me into prostitution and her into doin' porn! Then made me watch her overdose, and oh yeah, not to mention, the cunt sold our goddamned son to God knows who! So, I pretty much already know the "who's, the what's, and god-damned where's," Harlan! What I want to know is jus' what the fuck lil' ole' "ME" supposed to do about it?" Ricky yelled desperately. Harlan's unexpected broadcast struck a major nerve with almost everyone in the room, with the exception of former college football standout Jovan Campbell, who was shaking his head in confusion, while trying to find clarity of the news he just heard, "I don't get it? I mean….the asshole that ran over my baby girl is still locked away! He's already doing a fifteen to twenty year sentence up in Leavenworth! So…I don't know what chu' tryin' to say, man!?" Jovan hollered mystified. Harlan had always been very fond of the old credo that "seeing is very much believing" and often times incorporated the practice in the past, by maybe having a person's arms and legs removed or, their life taken after attempting to steal a client's cargo off one of his vessels. He found the expression to be the most thorough and best viable of ways of getting a point across and knew the same had to be done to motivate the muscle-bound youngster, "Go ahead and open it. Then, you tell me." Harlan replied confidently. The former football star /turned club bouncer ripped into the sealed file, as if he were a bear digging out a piece of spam from inside a small tin can. Jovan began reading the many surprising and disturbing contents, which gradually caused the features on his youthful face to contort into a vicious frown. Unknowingly, Harlan previously played out every possible scenario, facet, and contingency a year in advance before ever meeting the grief-stricken fathers, and counted on them to lash out at him. Regardless, of the profane way in which they addressed his admission, Harlan still remained both calm and collected. He opened his personal sterling silver cigarette holder and pulled out a single for himself. Kale took notice and quickly stashed the towering bottle of Jack Daniels in-between his legs and began clearing his throat to get Harlan's attention. Harlan disregarded his forced callow act and started scouring both over his desk and pockets for a light. Kale stood up and lit Harlan's cigarette with an engraved Lotus Terminator IV torch lighter that looked all too familiar to the transporting mogul. "Thank you, Lieutenant. Care for one?" Harlan offered politely. The young Lieutenant took off his hat and placed it across his heart, "…Why, that's awful nice of yew'!" Kale jested, and took one out and sat back down. Kale threw his weathered Florida University hat back on and used the stolen lighter to fire up his cigarette, "I trust you will be putting "that" back on my desk before leaving out tonight?!" Harlan quipped. Nonchalantly, he leaned back into the plush chair and took a long drag off his single, and then grinned, "Maybe….if yew' ask me nicely!" Kale teased. Thomas Jr.'s mind was frantically racing like a Formula 1 race car, and had begun to feel every bit as violated as he once did on the night of his home invasion. Before he ever agreed to speak to the group, Terry promised to keep his past off limits and was to only be divulged when HE deemed it necessary, Thomas Jr. remembered. But Harlan's interference threatened to "out him" as a rape victim, which was the last thing he wanted the prying billionaire to do, "You….you had "NO" right to do what you did, Harlan! I guess it serves me right thinking I could trust somebody like you!" Thomas Jr. hollered angrily. Just before Harlan could respond to the agitated reverend's accusations, Jovan Campbell's blood also was starting to boil over, after discovering what he had found in the file, "Is all this shit true?" Jovan asked furiously. Unflappably, Harlan took a drag of his cigarette, "Every damn bit, I'm afraid." Harlan calmly confirmed. "What's the matter with y…?" Agent Elliot began to ask, just before Jovan threw his chair clear across Harlan's office. The one-time college phenom was quivering with rage, "You son of bitch!!!" Jovan screamed. Agent Elliot had never seen his on again off again young friend so upset and immediately scrambled to the floor to gather all the contents from Jovan's folder to figure out what might have set the young man off. As a former football player who thrived off uncanny aggression, Jovan Campbell would be the easiest among the other fathers to eventually persuade, Harlan deduced. Little did the rest of them know was that there was something unique in all of their case files, which were waiting to yet be realized, Harlan contemplated. Thomas Jr. stood up from his seat, "What did you do, Harlan?" Thomas Jr. accused. Milton Elliot walked in between Thomas Jr. and Harlan, "No, rev…it wasn't him. I'm looking at affidavits from the Attorney General's office. It says, that due to over-crowding, that sum-bitch who killed Joes' kid, got a goddamned get out of jail free card. On his chart, his parole officer even states, "That he's been a solid citizen" and is also a fucking CEO of a record label, if you can believe that shit!?" Agent Elliot replied. Jovan was becoming increasingly more frustrated by each passing second and started swinging punches at the air, "I knew I should've killed that motha'fucka when I had the chance…"Jovan yelled savagely. Standing silently and smoking his cigarette Harlan's eyes began to light up, "It's funny you should say that. But please, reverend…do have a seat and at least allow me the benefit to fully explain my real…"intensions." Harlan pleaded. Although Thomas Jr. had half a mind to smash him in the face, part of him was moderately curious to know exactly what the prying billionaire dug up on Sonny Korne, especially if he really knew his possible whereabouts. Thomas Jr. was slow to move, so Harlan extended his hand out toward Thomas Jr.' chair, "Please." Harlan insisted. The fuming reverend was doing his best to remain humble, "Alright. But know this, "Whoever trusts in his own mind is a fool…" Thomas Jr. said intensely. Harlan took a second or two, to chew on the reverend's heeding words, "…Yes, but "he who walks in wisdom, reverend, will also be delivered." Proverbs 28:26…..I'm also familiar with that one, as well." Harlan replied sharply. Thomas Jr. was taken aback by his knowledge of the bible, but took his seat nevertheless. When he sat down, Thomas Jr. noticed the oddly crooked smile on Kale's ruggedly young face and wondered if there ever was a time when the scowling Lieutenant ever bathed. Outside of the old beat up black army tee-shirt he worn, he basically was dressed in the same exact clothes he last saw him in, Thomas Jr. considered. He found himself amazed at how well someone with Kale's slight frame managed to keep his balance, after consuming over a liter of "straight" alcohol in one setting. Despite his incredible talent for over-indulgence, suddenly something about the wily Lieutenant stuck out like a missing limb to the perceptive preacher. If it had not been for Harlan's confession, he might have missed the fact everyone from the group were given concealed folders, with the exception of Kale, Thomas Jr. realized. "What made him so special?" Thomas Jr. wondered.

After he was done smoking, Harlan disposed of his cigarette into a pretty crystal ashtray that his wife Marisa once gave him on his desk and took his seat. The look on his face was one of menacing assertion and was poised to unload more unexpected bombs on the rest of the unsuspecting fathers, "I need you all to "please" open the seals on your dossiers." Harlan kindly requested. Fear of the unknown started to overcome each one of the fathers, as they all took their precious time peeling off seal after seal, as if they were dissecting a pack of hydrogen bombs inside their living rooms. One by one, they all read line after difficult line, forcing them to relive the most horrible moments of their miserable lives, which had to have felt like ripping the duct tape off a swollen canker sore, Harlan thought. In his file, Agent Elliot discovered valuable, yet disheartening things about his case, against the "Road Quaker" leader Oswald "Ozzie" Brickwood, facts that were not allowed to be disclosed during his trial. Due to some shady bureaucratic nonsense behind the judge's chamber, he was able to cut a side deal and turn in state's evidence on other open federal cases, to beat his attempted murder rap on Supreme Court Judge Alice Walker. But, by the time Brickwood made his deal with the federal prosecutor, Milton learned that his testimony would not have mattered either way and that his family was slaughtered for mere sport, while "Ozzie" received a slap on the wrist for doing it. Much like gazing at the final seconds of a setting sun, Harlan patiently and painfully watched the remaining light in their eyes become extinguished by his crushing reports.

He looked into the defeated face of Agent Milton Elliot and saw the reflection of a betrayed patriot who fought valiantly in the name of justice. All the while, squandering the lives of his precious family in the process, under a system he vowed to uphold, but who allowed their killer to go free. Hakiro Yosomi, former store owner whose family was shot up during an attempted armed robbery, wept like nobody else's business, and who could blame him? Harlan thought. Murderer, pimp, and reputed sleaze-ball Romelle "Hot Pocket" Hatchette, never served one night in jail for his dastardly deeds at the Yosami store. Hatchette had a stable of tricks that varied in ethnicity and ages that ranged from fourteen and up, and because of it, had connections in some of the right places, Harlan recollected. However, Romelle Hatchette did serve a light sentence for the two dead fetuses found inside the stolen car he was pulled over in. At the time, the state's prosecutor did his damndest to get a case built against Hatchette for the Yosomi murders, but since the authorities never found the murder weapon and no witnesses, "Hot Pocket" was eventually allowed back on the streets. The face that concerned him the most was of the frozen visage of Reverend Thomas Templeton Jr., whose tear drops were smearing the ink on the paper in his file. Kale watched Thomas Jr. with a curious eye, while he drank and smoked and wondered what was in the file that made the soft-spoken preacher weep so. Although Harlan gave him the rundown of what type of threats he wanted "handled," Reverend Templeton's information was specifically on a need to know basis, Kale remembered. Thomas Jr. gasped out loud when he stopped at a page in the half quarter inch thick document that stated Sonny Korne's last known whereabouts. The confused reverend's raised his head, "H-He's…he's h-here…in Texas?" Thomas Jr. stuttered. Harlan confirmed his affirmation with a head nod. Thomas Jr. did not know what to make of the disconcerting news at first and was biting his tongue not to speak. For months his nemesis has been able to dodge the authorities seemingly at will, but in the span of one outing with a total stranger, he learned that the malicious Sonny Korne would be hiding in the very same state as his long lost brother, Thomas Jr. pondered. He began to wonder why Harlan never shared that valuable piece of information with his brother, considering the fact that they were related and that Terry was running his program, Thomas Jr. wondered. It would have only taken a phone call and justice would have been served, Thomas Jr. speculated. Harlan sat unmoving with his hand clasped on his desk, "I take it that everyone is "somewhat" up to speed about the current situation of your various offenders? Despicable isn't it? All of them…murders…killers…predators…even rapists, all just walking the streets free as dandelions floating down a windy sidewalk. When I pitched my program to the board of the Midtown clinic it wasn't just because I wasn't looking for a media grab, it was because "I too" knew what it felt like to have vermin rob you of your children!" Harlan announced. Most of them were surprised by Harlan's candid admission, which prompted an immediate response from the disgusted reverend, "Then if you already knew this,

Harlan, then why not use "your" resources to get them prosecuted? I mean, you had to have known about Korne's whereabouts long before you even met my brother!? Why didn't you just come clean?" Thomas Jr. demanded. Harlan appeared to have been wounded by Thomas Jr.' seemingly obvious suggestion and stroked his mouth with his hand to contemplate, "Yes, reverend. You do make a strong point…" Harlan agreed. Jovan Campbell decided to add his own tidbits to Thomas Jr.' argument, "Got' damn right he got a point!" Jovan shouted angrily. Agent Elliot put his hand on the young man's chest to help calm the angered former college standout, "Hey now, take it easy…before you pop a testicle or sumthin!' I'm sure Harly's got one HELL of an explanation for sitting on these…" Agent Elliot insisted. Harlan was surprised by Milton's willingness to defend him, "Very astute of you Agent." Harlan agreed. "Just whatever the hell it is, it better be fucking good or I'm gonna' let this fucker tear you a new asshole!" Agent Elliot warned. His threat made the transporting mogul blush and tried not to expose the grin he was fighting off, "Um-hum. Well then I'll do my best to be clear…" Harlan said coyly. It amused Harlan that everyone was so clueless to the origins of his vast dynasty. Once upon a time, he knew it would not have taken much, but one simple phone call, to have someone put a bullet in the head of the stocky DEA agent and have his body parts served to a wild hog. But, he was no longer "that man" anymore and overlooked the lewd agent's slight. Either way, he admired their spirit, which made him become even more drawn to them. Harlan felt totally responsible for each of the bloody paths their lives were taken, costing them a shot at true happiness. It saddened him every time he would stare into the eyes of the painting of his son on his office wall, making him recollect the living nightmare he wrought on himself and had almost driven him to the brink of madness. No longer was there any one left for him to love, regardless of his immense wealth. He knew no amount of blood money could ever fill the void created from the death of his wife and son. Although he believed it was too late to save his own soul, in some small way, Harlan still wanted to atone for his wrongs and give the troubled fathers what they had not yet realized that their hearts truly desired: the complete annihilation of the people who wronged them. "The reasons in which I have suppressed my findings are two-fold gentlemen, although you Agent Elliot might be hard-pressed to believe the truth, I will gladly share the first….The fact is, I couldn't possibly turn in

Sonny Korne, even if I wanted too, because quite frankly, reverend, the law simply doesn't want to help people like you!" Harlan said coldly. In a matter of seconds, Harlan's thought-provoking statement caused the entire room to fall Pet Cemetery silent. Milton Elliot was momentarily in awe and dropped the folders in offense, "Now just what in the hell is that supposed to mean? If you talkin' bout the law, asshole then know, you're also talkin' bout me!?" Milton warned. Harlan leaned back into his leather desk chair in dismay and peered into the former DEA agent's scorned eyes, as if he were staring at something stuck underneath his shoes, "Ah….still playing cop, I see. Well, let me remind you, that it was people in your OWN department who betrayed you, and you want to know what's the real kicker here, agent? Oswald "Ozzie" Brickwood isn't just some average punk biker, but actually was born "undercover officer" Eric Christopher Braxton. Yes, that's correct. I said UNDERCOVER. Don't believe me…check out the NSA file in the back of your dossier. You claim I'm the asshole, hymph! I can't speak for your own ankles agent, but at some point, even a whore gets tired of getting fucked and quite frankly, Agent Elliot, you should be too!" Harlan said emphatically. The rawness of Harlan's words shocked Kale, forcing him to spit out his alcohol, "Goddamn Harlan! Spoken like a true poet!" Kale wisecracked. Confused, Agent Elliot retrieved the folder from off the carpet floor and immediately flipped to the file Harlan mentioned and was floored by what he read. Thomas Jr. was still searching for more than just some affirmative action rhetoric for Harlan to justify not going to Terry, or the authorities with what he had on Sonny Korne. Thomas Jr. stood up out of his chair, "Enough with the posturing Harlan, why didn't you fork over Korne's location to my brother? And don't give me some bullshit about us against them, cause honestly, Harlan….you don't "financially qualify!" Thomas Jr. protested. The preacher's unsettling words stung like a group of hornets against his chest and slowly he stood to his feet, "In all earnestness, reverend, I know my financial circumstances doesn't quite fit into your "box of the ill-deprived," but despite all my wealth, I am not completely as immune to this world as my money would lead you to believe."Harlan said hurtfully. He gazed into the painting of his son Haven that was on the wall and could still remember the day it was created. Although it was made posthumously, it served as his daily reminder of the love he once shared and the love that was now lost. He walked back toward the front of his desk and leaned against it with his arms folded and exhaled, "It's like I told you before reverend, I too lost a son…and because of my own arrogance, Haven was the one who paid the price for it. The reason I didn't turn "him" into the police, reverend, is because there were police involved in your….the ATTACK…. and it's the police who are fighting to keep him hidden." Harlan concluded. Thomas Jr. had the look of a person who had been blindsided by a broom handle, "W-What? T-There's n-no way….I…w-w-why? H-H-How…? Thomas Jr. stuttered, while stumbling backward.

Harlan's account of possible police involvement in his family's attack nearly mentally destroyed him, and caused the reverend to lose his balance, until Kale caught him, "Whoa there preacher man." Kale said, and helped him back into his chair. Thomas Jr. did not know what to make of this new revelation and could not find the strength to properly respond. Jovan Campbell had begun pacing the floor, but stopped abruptly after hearing Harlan's news, "Just when I thought MY shit was all fucked up….so what he saying rev? That the "poe poe" took your family out?" Jovan asked dismayed. In disbelief, struggling drug addict Ricky Wallace was bent over in his seat and shaking his head, "Shit….no wonder Doctor T. had you there with us, man….you just as FUCKED UP as the rest of us!" Ricky said obtrusively. Harlan cut his eyes at the frail looking youngster in baggy street clothes, "Easy, Richard…!" Harlan softly warned. After catching his breath, Thomas Jr. barely managed to find the strength to respond to Ricky's statement, "Y-You have NO idea….H-Harlan, you said… (ahem)…you said, the police are hiding him?!" Thomas Jr. asked bewildered. Harlan turned his attention back to the breathless reverend, "That's correct." Harlan confirmed. Feeling overcome with frustration, Thomas Jr. could only rub his hands across his weathered face in disgust, "Goddamn it!? Jesus, how could they….wait a minute, let me guess….the cops involved.....they Aryans too?" Thomas Jr. asked. Standing unmovable as the Titanic, Harlan answered, "Yes." Despite what Harlan confirmed to be truth, the harder Thomas Jr. still found the truth to be believable to his ears. Either way, it made perfect sense that the slimy Sonny Korne would be protected by other asshole racists like himself, especially this far down south, where some law enforcement was questionable to say the least, Thomas Jr. assumed. Ricky anxiously dug into his pants for the painkillers he received from the urgent care, earlier that morning, and shoved them in his mouth and began crunching on them, as if they were pieces of peanut brittle, "You know, ALL this sharing is "fine and dandy," Harlan….but, where does this shit leave us now?" Ricky asked agitated. Unflappably, Harlan went back into his sports coat for his fancy silver compact, and noticed Kale looking innocently back at him with puppy dog eyes and offered him another. Kale leaned in and took another single and grinned, "Mutch' O' bliged!" Kale replied, and winked at him. His fixation with the young Lieutenant Keegan began as a fascination for his deadly and immoral capabilities, but the more time he spent around the feral soldier the more likable he found him personally and tried to play off the soft chuckle he let out by casually looking away. "Well, like I said before, Richard, that depends on what you "all" are prepared to do!" Harlan replied. He walked over to his impressive wet bar and poured himself a tall glass of Johnny Walker Black on the rocks and took a giant sip. The taste sent a well needed shockwave to the back of his throat, causing his taste buds to explode, "Ah-h-h." Harlan said satisfied, and paused a moment to reflect on the liquor's coarse flavor. He made another drink and brought it to the muted Hakiro Yosami, who had been disturbingly distant ever since reading the personal file Harlan had given him. His scarred face was heavily flushed and his flabby cheeks were glistening from all the weeping he had been doing, Harlan noticed. Despite hesitating at first, the stoutly built South Korean -American still accepted Harlan's thoughtful gesture, and took a sip from the glass in hopes of finding an escape. For a moment, Harlan stood silently under the elaborate portrait of his son, as though he was reminiscing on a stolen moment, "I think it's about time that I be honest with you. I began funding Dr. Templeton's "experimental program" with the good conscious that it could actually benefit other desperate and conflicted fathers like me. Fathers who would put aside their selfish pride and their egos long enough to share with others like themselves, their faults, their demons and worst nightmares. All of them, sharing the same vision, the same hope of scraping off the mentally oppressive lesions around their saturated hearts and souls. Providing these men with the best and the most sophisticated psychological resources that my wealth could ever possibly provide them….since I've already done that, I believe it's time for me to introduce a better solution, or "proposal" if you will…" Harlan said. He walked back to the front of his desk and stood with his arms folded, "Every monster that you all have encountered continues to wreck havoc on other innocent children, on other families….creating even more twisted versions of the fathers who are left to mourn them all! And I, gentlemen, wish to no longer stand idly by, while vermin like that is allowed to roam freely through neighborhoods like yours." Harlan said emphatically. "What do you "propose?" Hakiro asked, in a hushed tone. The former store owner's strained and hurt-filled voice caught everyone by surprise when he spoke and briefly quieted the room. Smart-mouthed and nervous-acting drug addict Ricky Wallace began scratching at his throat, like a feline clawing at a piece of timber, "Yeah, Harlan, what DO you propose? Shit, with all the bread you got, you can afford to pay somebody to just off 'em, either that or "buy" world peace!" Ricky joked. Ricky's sarcastic retort made the drunken and unusually well-behaved Lieutenant Kale Keegan chuckle. Harlan exhaled loudly like an irritated parent who grew tired of an over petulant child, "Yes. Yes, Richard, I guess could just "do" that!" Harlan said vexed. Harlan leaned back against his desk and placed his hands into his pants pockets, "But if I did that, Richard, then you would be robbed of the very thing that has continuously escaped you…." Harlan replied. The former linebacker star shrugged his wide shoulders, "Yeah, and what's that?" Jovan asked intrigued. Harlan slowly leaned in toward his direction, "Closure!" Harlan happily responded. The transporting mogul went behind his desk and pulled out another file and dropped it on top of the grand cherry-wood escritoire, "I've…"acquired"….a surplus of unregistered weapons….firearms, explosives, unmarked vehicles, etc….you name it! Anyone can see an army coming from a mile away, and just like with any group of rats, like Sonny Korne, or Ozzie Brickwood, they just find another hole to go crawl inside. Well, gentlemen….I want to be the one who goes and drops a grenade "into" that little rat-hole! So, tell me, Richard….why spend a fortune on an army, when I can just simply give it all to you?" Harlan asked offhandedly.

For half a minute, no one uttered a single word. Each one of the fathers stared back at Harlan with the same staggered expression, as he stood smiling back at them. Only the impaired Lieutenant Keegan seemed to be the only person in the room not bothered at all by Harlan's wild suggestion, Thomas Jr. noticed. He simply sat there patiently in his chair swallowing down Harlan's bottle of Jack Daniels, while also enjoying a cigarette, as if he were all by himself awaiting a Metro bus at a transit station. Their silence was finally broken by Ricky Wallace's nervous chuckling, "Awe man, you just fuckin' wit' us, right? I mean (laughing) you can't POSSIBLY be for real?" Ricky stated. Harlan sat down in his genuine leather Geffen office chair and covered his face as if he were about to pray, "What do YOU think?" Harlan boldly replied. Thomas Jr. could see the intense seriousness in the middle-aged billionaire's face and began shaking his head incredulity. Jovan Campbell wiped his eyes as if he was trying to shake off a mirage, "Yo' man you can't be serious….I mean, who we look like, The A-Team? Come on, man…tell him….he's crazy, right?" Jovan asked, while awaiting a response from a silent Agent Elliot. Agent Elliot's blank expression lasted for a brief second, until finally turning towards Kale, "You sharing that thing tonight, cowboy?" Agent Elliot asked nonchalantly. The young Lieutenant was surprised by the former DEA agent's tall request, but wasted no time handing over the large bottle to him, "Naw bro….help yur' self!" Kale cheerfully responded. He then turned up the entire bottle, as if he were trying to drown himself with it, while at the same time unintentionally impressing the young Lieutenant in the process. Kale offered a quaint grin of satisfaction to the highly observant Harlan Kruellar, who also replied back with unsuspectingly raised eyebrows. "Why should WE take such a dangerous risk, Mr.Kruellar? Surely you could…" Hakiro said, before getting interrupted. Ricky angrily jumped out of his seat, "It really doesn't fucking matter Hakie! No offense Harlan, but excluding this maniac's present company, if you haven't noticed…..we ain't Goddamn soldiers! I don't even know the first "thing" about killing somebody!?" Ricky shouted, and began to walk off. Flabbergasted by his comment, the transporting mogul flopped back into his chair, as if his feelings were slightly hurt, "Oh? Come now, Richard….you're among friends here. Surely, you remember killing your Jamaican dealer, back in Vegas? What was his name again? Oh, YES….Felix. Felix Juan Hotcho. But, you only knew him on the streets as, uh, what was it again…oh yes, "Hot-boy!?" Harlan eerily replied. His more than accurate accusation froze the fidgety and terrified Ricky Wallace dead in his tracks. Ricky instantly made an about face, "W-W-Who told you th….?! Look, t-that was an accident, I-I can explain!" Ricky pleaded. Harlan shook his head in disapproval, "The point is, Richard, "YOU" don't have to! You were deep in debt and the man threatened your son's life, I get it. It was either going to be you, or him, so I'm not going to judge you for doing what you believed you had no choice to do. What I "am" offering, Richard, is a shot at your only chance at getting YOUR son back! But, it's totally up to you if you believe he's worth it! That goes for ALL of you. Now's the time gentlemen, that you need to ask yourselves, "Isn't the cost of the lives you've lost, already worth setting the wrong things right? And if so, what am I really prepared to do about it? I know what "I'm" prepared to do. I'm not looking for vengeance. All I'm asking is for "you" to allow "me" to help you get the justice you richly deserve and the peace that the law failed to grant you." Harlan concluded. Harlan's words weighed heavily on the men's hearts like a five hundred ton boulder.

Although Harlan spoke of instituting vigilante justice, all but one did not seem to have a problem with the prospect of actually considering it. In a state of confusion, Thomas Jr. decided to interject into the conversation, "You HAVE clearly lost your mind, Harlan. I'm a man of God…what makes you think I would even "dare" to be a part of such wicked blasphemy?" Thomas Jr. asked, and stood to his feet. Harlan sat erect in his chair, "How could "YOU" not reverend? Out of everyone in this room, it was "you" who lost the most! Look at you. I mean, REALLY take a good look at you. Ever since your "attack," you've been forced out of your own father's church. Your son, Markus, is still in a coma. Every day you're "scrambling" to get hospital bills you cannot afford paid. You have no money, no home, no family, and most importantly, no more self respect! While you're wallowing away in self-pity inside some shoebox apartment, Sonny Korne and his Aryan disciples are just, "traveling the globe," celebrating what they've done to your wife….your daughter….your son….your mother…..and to you. Right now, "they" are the ones who are winning, reverend. "They" get to move on with their lives, while you're left "stuck" standing over what's left of your son's." Harlan concluded. Everything he had just mentioned was completely true in the mind of the seasoned reverend, but found Harlan's invasion of his private life a little unnerving, "You've got some Goddamn nerve…sitting there, trying to play devil's advocate to a bunch of emotional and irrational men. You should be ashamed of yourself. How DARE you pry into my past, like it's some kind of loose documentary on a Wikipedia page for you to skim through? I may not have a home, no money or whatever, Harlan, but I still have God!" Thomas Jr. loudly boasted. Harlan slowly stood to his feet and had a sad expression on his middle-aged face, "Yes, I suppose you do. But, tell me, reverend….why "did" God choose "YOU" to be assaulted? Were you not a good little preacher? Or were you stealing money from your congregation, or maybe you were sleeping around with another married man's wife? I mean, you "must" have been doing SOMETHING wrong to deserve such terrible wrath?" Harlan replied. Thomas Jr. was stunned by Harlan's observations and heard more than enough for him to stand for one night, "To tell you the honest truth, Harlan, I don't know "why" God chose me. But, all I do know is that he did! Who am I to question God's work? I'm not saying that I fully agree with him allowing my family to be taken from me, but I've got to trust him!" Thomas Jr. said earnestly, and handed his empty glass to Kale. Thomas Jr. stood to his feet, "Thank you for inviting me out to your lovely home, Mr. Kruellar. But I'm afraid that I must be going, now….good evening gentlemen…" Thomas Jr. said, and made his way toward the door. Harlan had long ago prepared and predicted Thomas Jr.'s probable exodus, and for the man who made a fortune off negotiating million dollar deals, he always kept an ace, or two up his three thousand dollar sleeve to curve the good reverend's enthusiasm, "Before you go, reverend, I just wanted you to know that I paid off ALL current and future hospital debts you owed….including flying a world class medical specialist to oversee your son's current condition." Harlan said casually. The fuming reverend stopped abruptly at the foot of the massive door. He exhaled loudly, but refused to turn and look at the intruding billionaire, "Y-You did what? Why…y-you didn't…you didn't have to DO that!? It wasn't your problem…" Thomas Jr. insisted. Everyone (with the exception of Kale Keegan) had glad looks in their eyes and gave praises to the more than generous tycoon. Regardless of how grateful he may have been, part of him felt violated once again by Harlan's intrusion into his God-awful past, "I'm truly grateful for what you've done Harlan, but you still had no right to intrude into my personal life! I'm not one…I-I mean…I'm not a part…" Thomas Jr. stuttered. Harlan began to ease his way up toward the conflicted preacher, "What? Not a PART of your brother's group? Take a good look around reverend! You have ALWAYS been a part of THIS group, whether you like it or not! What? Just because you're supposed to be "a man of God," doesn't mean you don't have feelings, or even that you're better than the rest of us?! If that were the case, my dear reverend, then you and your family might not have been attacked at all!" Harlan protested. It was hard for him to argue with Harlan's cold and twisted logic and yet his pride would not allow him to turn and face the younger middle-aged man, despite his contempt for him. The dreadful toll his emotions put on him caused the drained reverend to sob. As an act of kindness, Harlan placed his hand on top of Thomas Jr.' shoulder, "Look at me, Thomas…!" Harlan kindly instructed. After wiping the tears away from his frustrated eyes, Thomas Jr. worked up the courage to face him, "What do you want from me? I mean, really? Cause if there's anything I do know, Harlan, it's people. In all the years I've been living, no one just….just….DOES anything like "THAT" for a complete stranger. Not without having to repay a heavy price." Thomas Jr. insinuated. Harlan appeared wounded by the reverend's suggestion and folded his arms in disapproval, "I thought you believed in miracles, reverend?" Harlan coyly replied. Likewise, Thomas Jr. casually folded his arms as well as to show him some disapproval of his own, "I guess it's kind of like what you said…I got feelings too. And they're telling me, that there's MORE to what you're telling us." Thomas Jr. accused. Of course, what Thomas Jr. suspected of him was absolutely true, but in no way was he stupid enough to ever own up to the complete truth, at least not yet, Harlan thought. He held back "plenty more" from all of them, but the timing was not right to disclose any intricate details of his underlying agenda, despite whatever good intensions he may have. But, he knew if any of them ever discovered the truth about how his indirect involvement led to the deaths of their children, they would had "literally" ripped him into a hundred pieces, Harlan imagined. In order to successfully pull off his coo, he could not ever allow them the luxury to become privy to the very sins he was so desperately trying to atone for. Finally, after many long hours and days of scheming, his plan was coming full circle, but sorely lacked the final piece he needed to complete his monumentally complicated puzzle. Much like the good Reverend Templeton Jr., Harlan was also a student of people and their patterns of behavior. A small fortune was spent to attain whatever information, incriminating or otherwise, that could possibly be gathered on each of them, henceforth granting him a clear bargaining advantage over them. Harlan huffed and walked back to his desk and sat down and began staring at his son's portrait from his chair, "Yes. I suppose I am….I 'm dying. It really doesn't matter from what, but the only thing of importance here is what I'm willing to do for each of you, before my….untimely demise. I'm well aware of the hardships that you all are facing, take you for instance, Mr.

Campbell here. Both you and your ex-girlfriend, Tasha Greenwood (but mostly you) are chest deep in student loans and legal debts, without a good leg to stand on to pay any of it off!" Harlan said disappointingly. The harsh reminder made the hulking former college standout fall back down to his seat in disgust. Harlan quickly glanced over to the face of the inaudible Hakiro Yosami, who was busy peering at his glass of whiskey, as if it were some strange ancient artifact he just discovered, "You Mr. Yosami, are a former South Korean army deserter who moved here to America….illegally." Harlan began, before getting interrupted. "How in Buddha's name could you…" Hakiro replied astonished. Although the answer to Hakiro's question was more than obvious, the priceless "what's my name" look on Harlan's face was more than enough confirmation for the pudgy former store owner to hold his tongue. "Now, we both know how South Korean deserters are treated now don't we, so going back home is definitely out of the question. And since you didn't make good on the loan you got from the bank to buy your store, your creditors are calling for your head….not to mention, what you still owe the people for even bringing you here illegally." Harlan concluded. Both Lieutenant Kale and Agent Elliot were still busy getting hammered like nobody's business, "And you Agent Elliot…" Harlan began. Agent Elliot exhaled harshly, "Yeah, whatabout' me? That fucking mind job won't work on me, Professor X! Cause' I don't owe nobody jack shit!" Agent Elliot yelled, and took a big gulp from Kale's Jack Daniels bottle. Harlan cocked his head in a queer fashion, "No…I suppose you don't owe anyone….at least financially, that is. But, there's still the small matter of that EVER growing price on your head and the last I heard, it went up a mill. You don't strike me as the "relocating program type," cause' the quiet life….just doesn't seem to fit you. And judging from your "co-worker's" history, it's only a matter of time before one of them decides to sell you out and cashes in. So, if you expect to survive another week, Agent, you're going to need enough money to leave the country and start your life over. And you, Richard…." Harlan began, before getting cutoff. The lanky Ricky Wallace wobbled to his feet, "Wait, wait, wait, let me guess….unpaid senior dues? Oh, Oh, or maybe it's some old truancy tickets my folks never got around to paying and are on the hook for not getting around to it? I mean, c'mon…. gimme' a break, dude!" Ricky said disinterested, and waved Harlan off. Despite his fragile disposition, he found the ballsy and malnourished appearing Ricky

Wallace to be quite unique. Although, he would never admit it to him personally, Harlan likened the spirited and shifty-eyed Ricky Wallace a lot to himself. Unlike Ricky, he was never at the mercy of an oppressive and abusive father, nor endured the humility of performing sexual acts to survive on the streets, but Harlan could see underneath all of Ricky's bravado one primal constant: That they were both willing to go to extreme lengths for the preservation of their families. Before he was going to drop the final and the biggest bombshell of the night, Harlan took a long sip of the neglected and sweaty glass of Johnny Walker Black that adorned his glistening cherry woodened desk. Seeing each of the fragile minded men up close was beginning to take a toll on him and when Ricky Wallace's eyes met his, Harlan could see both the shame and the pain Ricky fought so greatly to conceal with his heavy drug dependency and constant wisecracking. But all the drugs and the jokes in the world could never relieve the depressive drug addict of the agony of what he was going through, Harlan thought. It pained him immensely to recollect the role he unknowingly played in the young man's life, despite never meeting him. In a selfish quest for power, his arrogance blinded him and allowed his status in the underworld to set off a nuclear chain of events that would ripple through each of these men's lives, Harlan contemplated. Ricky was the closest to his son Haven's age, but had seen more downs than ups for two lifetimes, Harlan thought, as he took another sip from his glass. "I know where Liova is keeping your son…" Harlan said.

Chapter 9:

<u>"Making Right, Right"</u>

Harlan Kruellar's home office,

It was hard for Harlan to imagine Ricky's abusive father, who was twice his size, bludgeoning him over and over each day for whatever his sick reasons may have been for doing so. Ricky eventually got tired of being his father's punching bag and both he and his African-American girlfriend Sandra ran away from home. They thought they were in love and immediately got married and tried to start a family. The thought of such a noble assumption put a quant smile on Harlan's face and, almost for a micro second, forgot about how quickly life can turn a corner when a person's not wearing their seatbelt. After failing at finding decent work and with the added stress of taking care of a newborn, both Ricky and his newfound family were back out on the streets, where Ricky tried his hand at drug dealing. Things began to turn around financially for the young couple, until his wife ultimately caught the eye of a dangerous lesbian photographer by the name of Liova Rourke-Shelton. Liova had connections with the local police and got Ricky incarcerated by dealing methamphetamine to an undercover cop. With an unsuspecting Ricky Wallace locked away, there was no one left standing in Liova's way to get at his wife, who was left with a child she could not afford to keep fed. When she gives Sandra a gig as a model, Liova convinced Ricky's naive wife to move in with her, where she soon found herself addicted to crack cocaine. In the long run, Sandra goes from doing photo shoots at car shows and event fliers to filming porn. "The horror he must have felt to find out what his young cute little wife had been up too while he was put away?" Harlan pondered. After serving a month in jail, Ricky eventually tracks Sandra down and runs into a Jamaican street hustler and enforcer for Liova by the name of Felix Juan Hotcho, or

"Hot-boy" which he was known by on the streets. He convinced Hot-boy to arrange a meeting to negotiate the release of both his wife and son, but in a desperate attempt to save them, he only made matters worse, Harlan recollected. Liova shipped his son off to be raised on a private Nevada ranch with a half Indian slave trader named Calvin Rusher, and in exchange for his son's safety, Ricky was required to help out with some "other" services the part-time photographer offered. Liova was more than a simple photographer by day, but also a powerful madam by night that began blackmailing Ricky into being a male companion for both her male and female clientele. Six months go by and Ricky Wallace has yet to see his son. He becomes impatient with the situation and storms into the middle of one of Liova's porn sets to confront her. What came next did not come as a total surprise to Harlan, who read the file on Ricky a hundred times over. Sandra goes into cardiac arrest after Liova's urging. In a panic, Ricky threatens to go to the cops and gets into a fight with Hot-boy outside of Liova's Las Vegas studio. They begin to struggle and Hot-boy eventually overpowers him. Hot-boy threatens to personally decapitate Ricky Wallace's son, which in kind incites him. Ricky lashes out and charges the "armed" Hot-boy. During their struggle, his gun goes off and the next minute, the "cold blooded" Hot-boy was just another cold body left on the sidewalk. Afterwards, Ricky made himself disappear, despite the fact that no one was looking for him in the first place. Hot-boy had been skimming money off the top in Liova's drug business and she was looking to have him killed eventually anyway, and saw the opportunity as someone doing her a big favor. Ricky hitch-hiked his way to Houston where he had been homeless until a shelter took him in. He developed an on again off again relationship with his crack and meth addiction to offset the fact that he left his son to die in order to save his own life. He found living life on the streets a tumultuous one and with some small "nudging" he volunteered for the group which leads him up to today. Without any hesitation Harlan decides to drop the final kicker of the evening, "….and I'm readying a plane for Vegas as we speak, and I'm prepared to pay you ten million dollars to follow "this man"…..to go and retrieve him." Harlan said with a straight face, while pointing his finger. Harlan was directing his finger at a grinning Kale Keegan who was still laying waste to the giant bottle of Jack Daniels with Agent Milton Elliot. The room went sea diving quiet for a long moment, and then all at once everyone (with the exception of Kale and Harlan) burst out into roaring laughter. Their laughter began to become contagious to Kale as well and joined them, until he snatched the bottle of Jack Daniels from Agent Elliot's hand and finished its contents and threw it high over his shoulder into the air. In what appeared to take but half a second, Kale jumped out of his seat, spun around and shot the bottle with a .357 Magnum before it ever hit the floor. While everyone else was in awe both of the young Lieutenant's drunken marksmanship, Harlan and Kale were the only ones who were still laughing. Harlan cleared his throat, "Ahem….well, as you can clearly see, I'm deadly serious. Now, I know what you're thinking, that Mr. Keegan here appears "too" young…too inebriated lead a room of fifth graders to the cafeteria lunch line…" Harlan began until interrupted. "Hey, fuck you, Harlan!" Kale snarled. Harlan rolled his eyes at the lewd Lieutenant, "Bear with me for just a minute, would you please?" Harlan asked irritated. Realizing that Harlan was only trying to make an honest point and not trying to intentionally ridicule him in front of everybody, Kale quickly changed his tune, "I mean…sorry, Mr. Kruellar. By all means, please continue…!" Kale politely said. Just as he was about to Ricky began to sob, "Y-You really know where lil' S-Stevie is?" Ricky stuttered. Harlan put his drink down on top of his desk, "Yes, Richard. And I'm going to help you get him back. But, we can't do it alone. Now, I'm VERY willing to make it worth "everyone's" while, all I ask, is that you follow one simple plan….and not only will I solidify your financial futures, but also grant you the type of "closure" that you truly seek!" Harlan said. Jovan Campbell was trying to wrap his mind around Harlan's multimillion dollar offer, "Wait-a-minute…you sayin' you'll just GIVE us ten million dollars to go all Rambo on the people who stole Rick's son?" Jovan asked befuddled. Harlan stood to his feet and grinned widely, "No Mr. Campbell, I'm not giving ALL of you ten million to do that….I'm giving "EACH" of you ten million dollars to perform a public service! My vision is to see that every last person responsible for your present well-being to pay dearly with their very lives and what a better way to see that they do, by becoming the harbingers of their untimely demise. I want you all to take a close look at our Mr. Keegan here. Despite what you all may think, or believe he is way more than what meets the eye! You saw what he did with my very expensive bottle of Jack Daniels. In just a short amount of time this young man had climbed the ranks to "Lieutenant Commander" of a Special Black Ops Unit, whose primary jobs were to be dropped into the toilets of the world and take out the threats that never live long enough to make the nightly news. He is not only a three time Medal of Honor and Silver Star recipient, but a proficient leader, expert marksman, and specialist at Guerilla warfare tactics. No one will ever see you guys coming. Some of you know firsthand what he can do…. Now, imagine how nasty he would be to someone he cared nothing about!" Harlan concluded, and sat back down. While each of the beleaguered fathers thought heavily about considering Harlan's unbelievable offer, Thomas Jr. on the other hand, was trying to rationalize Harlan's "irrational" decision to include not only a policeman, but an ordained reverend to commit crimes of murder, "Why US Harlan, and what happened to the rest of the group? Or don't they count too?" Thomas Jr. asked confused. Despite covering his mouth when he leaned back into his seat, Thomas Jr. could still see a partial smile on Harlan's face, "Why am I not surprised that YOU would be the one to ask….well reverend, each of you are quite unique in your own way! Take you for instance….as a former Olympic swimmer you were once a fine-tuned perennial gold medalist in one of the world's most grueling of sports…." Harlan began, until getting interrupted. "So?" Thomas Jr. hollered mystified. His ineptness caused Harlan to frown at the elder reverend, "SO, it was that fact alone that helped you survive being shot multiple times, and not just bad aiming! Although you stopped competing years ago reverend, you never stopped your swimming regimen."Harlan said nonchalantly. Thomas Jr. contorted his head in confusion, "Now just how the hell…oh, never mind." Thomas Jr. replied and waved him off. Jovan suddenly jumped out of his seat in amazement, "Yo Rev, you really get blasted!?" Jovan asked ecstatically. The enthusiasm in his tone was causing him an instant migraine, and he stroked the temples alongside his forehead vigorously, "Yeah, but don't sound so beat up about it…" Thomas Jr. said dryly. Harlan smiled and came from around his large desk and leaned against the front of it once more, "Yes, it was four times, I believe…" Harlan guessed despondently. Thomas Jr. looked up from his hands, "Try six." Thomas Jr. stated coldly, causing everyone including a shocked Kale Keegan to stare in astonishment. Harlan folded his arms, "Yes and you're still here! That takes will and dexterity, something that the other fathers like house husband Mason Lowry, or that flippant insurance adjuster, Adrian Atkinson truthfully lacked. Look at them, reverend, both the brave Agent Elliot and the powerful Mr.

Campbell are but mere flip sides of the same coin. While they both were exceptional athletes once upon a time, they took their gifts into very different, but somewhat similar directions. One wanted to protect and serve the people of the public, while the other....wanted to serve and protect the people, but at night clubs. But together, reverend, no one can match their physicality...and despite his "stature," Mr. Yosami here is an exquisite Taekwondo master, who for several years, trained soldiers while serving in the South Korean Army, before defecting to America." Harlan confirmed. A humbled Ricky Wallace felt inadequate among his peers, "I was once my school's mascot, but I guess that don't count?" Ricky quipped sobbingly. Suddenly, the entire room lit up with laughter, even garnering a snicker from the grimacing Thomas Jr. and fanatical Harlan Kruellar. Kale got out of his seat and rubbed his hair around his head, as if he were mangling a little brother, "Yew know toothpick, yew alright with me!" Kale said proudly. Harlan was more than glad to see how quickly everyone began to finally bond with one another, after spending so many weeks pouring out their hearts on a daily basis. Ricky's infectious personality and son gave them the push they needed to go in the direction Harlan needed them to go. Clearing his throat to regain his composure, Harlan wasted no time promoting that fact, "No son. You're more important than that! Out of everyone sitting in this room, Richard, you're the only one left who still has a shot at a second chance to be with your kid! And I'm sure that you all agree that that's a dream worth fighting for! And with Lieutenant Keegan leading you, the justice that had eluded you these past couple of years, will finally be in your grasp in mere days!" Harlan said emphatically, pounding his fist on his desk. Thomas Jr. could see it in everyone's eyes that their minds were made up to take Harlan's offer to go on his ten million dollar killing spree. What frightened the leery reverend the most was that part of him actually "agreed" with Harlan, and if he were in Ricky's shoes, he might have jumped at the chance to join his foolhardy crusade. But how could he possibly endorse taking lives when he had sworn to protect them? Thomas Jr. thought. And what to make of his incredible generosity, was Harlan going insane and doing this whole "Brewster's Million's" act to get his rocks off by actually trying to help them, or was it something much deeper at play going on here? Thomas Jr. wondered. The only thing that Thomas Jr. "was" sure of was that the evening was getting way too long and that Terry would be worried if his recent house guest did not return home soon. Although his right mind was telling him it was time to go, a small part of him yearned to join them on Harlan's plane to attain the retribution he promised. But he was supposed to be better, a man of God and even if he could see the face of that bastard Sonny Korne, did he have enough hate in his heart to murder another human being, in spite of the evil he wrought onto his family? Thomas Jr. wondered. Harlan noticed the worried look on the reverend's flustered face, "Something the matter, Thomas?" Harlan asked concerned. Thomas Jr.'s eyebrows stood up in full attention to the sound of Harlan saying his actual name aloud, "Uh, yeah…I was just thinking, about a story my dad used to read to me when I was just a young boy. The story was about a city called Hamelin being infested with rats…" Thomas Jr. said. It only took Harlan a fraction of a second to respond snapping his fingers, "Ah, yes! Rattenfanger von Hameln, the dreary story of the disenchanted Pied Piper! Yes, my father read it to me as well, as a boy, all three versions in fact!" Harlan heartily replied. Slowly, the beleaguered reverend stood to his feet, "Good. Then maybe you can explain what happened to the rats in the end!?" Thomas Jr. stated. Puzzled by Thomas Jr.' nonsensical line of questioning, Harlan responded cautiously, "They all drowned….where're you going with this, reverend?" Harlan demanded. Thomas Jr. turned around and looked into everyone's faces and then back to Harlan, "You told us how…"great"… this "young man" supposed to be…!" Thomas Jr. said, pointing his finger into Lieutenant Keegan's face. Kale immediately rose to his feet and extinguished his lit cigarette gradually onto his own neck, "I am. And try ta' keep yo' hands…..outta' my face, T.D. Jakes." Kale said coldly. Thomas Jr. swallowed hard as he watched the highly volatile young Lieutenant casually burn himself, as though his neck was a separate and inanimate ashtray. He just could not seem to win around the young man, but either way, he was through trying to avoid a conflict and was going to speak his mind even if it might had cost him to get punched out in the process, "Look, all I'm saying here is that you're expecting us to just simply "follow" his lead unconditionally. Well, if that's the case Harlan, isn't this just like the story? Only in this case, you're the Pied Piper and Kale's the flute. But what I'm most afraid of, other than going to jail with the rest of you, is I can't tell if we supposed to be the rats falling or, the water that they drown in?" Thomas Jr. casually implied. Harlan was pleased to see the reverend stand his ground with Kale and even more impressed with his analogy, "Your argument is a sound one, reverend, but you have things way off base…" Harlan began to explain, before getting cutoff. "I'm the one "off base!?" Thomas Jr. shouted. Seeing that he may have incidentally spoken out of context, Harlan tried to no avail to clean up his statement, "I'm sorry reverend. What I meant, was that you're simply misjudging my intent! I only want what's best…" Harlan started to say, until getting interrupted. "It doesn't matter, Harlan! You want to know why? Because, I'm leaving….As a man, I honestly can't blame any of you for wanting to go along with him, but as an "active" preacher, I can't condone it. But, you're all grown ass men and you're going to have to be the ones, who are going to have to deal with the consequences of your actions, not me! Oh, and since I was never here, "none" of you have anything to worry about, I'm not telling Terry anything. We'll simply consider this a "confidential" confessional. You gentlemen have a good evening…you too Kale." Thomas Jr. graciously concluded and made his way to the office door. Harlan grinned widely and reached into his coat pocket and pulled out a thin black cell phone, "In case you change your mind, please, take this with you. If you don't, then throw it away. No pressure!" Harlan confirmed. Thomas Jr. looked into Harlan's eyes and could see the face of a man still unconvinced, "Right. Don't hold your breath…oh, and Harlan?" Thomas Jr. asked. "Yes?" Harlan replied nonchalantly. "My father once told me, "that an eye for an eye doesn't just leave everybody blind, but unable to see the truth hidden in their mistakes," probably like the one you ALL are about to make! I know you're a bible reader….. "Vengeance is mine; I will repay," so says the Lord!?" Thomas Jr. quoted. Rubbing his chin while he pondered Thomas Jr.'s bible verse, Harlan needed only a few seconds to recollect the answer, "Romans…12th chapter, verse 19." Harlan said confidently. His knowledge of the bible never ceased to amaze him, "Yes, Harlan and in reality, I believe it's salvation that you're truly seeking…but it won't come to you, or them. Not like this." Thomas Jr. warned. For what it was worth, Harlan did respect and appreciated the reverend's word of wisdom, but the last thing he needed was him to cast doubt into the minds of any of the remaining fathers, "Go home and think things over, we have a couple days until we go looking for your family's murderer. I was wondering reverend, had it ever occurred to you that maybe….just maybe, "God" has called on YOU "now" to BE his wrath? Only, you're just "too afraid" to follow the plan?" Harlan suggested. He found

Harlan's audacious statement ridiculous at best, but did not want to stick around any longer to tell him so, "Good night, Harlan." Thomas Jr. replied, and walked out the door. Harlan went to his desk phone and pressed the speed dial. A man suddenly answered the line, "Hola?" The man's voice said from the loud speaker on his desk. "Ready the helicopter, please." Harlan stated, and hung up the line. He leaned on his desk with his knuckles, "If any of you want to back out, now's the time!" Harlan said. A knock came at the door and it was his well dressed assistant Oscar standing in the doorway. Everyone looked around to see which of them were going to be the first to back-out next. Suddenly, Ricky Wallace sprung to his feet and faced the remaining fathers, "Look guys…..I don't really give a shit about the money. I just want to do right by my kid, but I can't do it on my own!" Ricky said. Wasting no time, the sculpted Jovan Campbell along with his on again off again mountainous companion Agent Elliot stood up out of their seats, "Don't worry toothpick, you won't be….besides, I hear Hawaii's the shit this time of year!" Agent Elliot stated. "And I'm sure that pasty white ass of yours could use it, but yeah dude, we gotcha' back one hundred." Jovan confirmed. A seemingly rejuvenated Hakiro Yosami stood to his feet as well, "Your son is in great peril and needs his father. I could not imagine a more honorable reason to help you." Hakiro said emphatically, and put his hand out. Without hesitation, Ricky Wallace shook the former store owner's pudgy hand and was awestruck by the overwhelming amount of support everyone was giving him. His eyes began to fill up with both tears of joy and fright, as he anticipated the journey into madness they were about to embark on.

They were ready, Harlan believed. He gestured to his assistant who stood quietly at the doorway, "Although, it saddens me that Reverend Thomas won't be there to assist you, I still believe that what we're doing here is the right thing. Just stick to the plan. In the meantime, I'll be opening individual offshore accounts in your names of ten million dollars each. As far as our strategy is concerned we have to move fast, my contact inside tells me that Liova's slave handler, Mr. Rusher, has plans to move Richard's son sometime tomorrow. But, don't you worry, Richard, we already have a plan! Oscar will escort you and the Lieutenant to my…." Harlan began, before getting cutoff. "I think we need to talk, Harley." Kale said. Judging from his tone, whatever it is that was on the young soldier's mind sounded urgent, "Of course. Oscar? Please take the others to the helicopter." Harlan asked. "Yes sir. Would you all please, follow me?" Oscar said stoically. After the room cleared out Harlan went into his sports coat and took out another cigarette from his fancy silver holder. He felt around for his lighter once again until remembering that Kale was still in possession of it, "Would you mind?" Harlan asked with the cigarette hanging from his mouth. Kale walked up and reached across Harlan's desk to light his cigarette, "Here ya' go. Now…yew' wanna tell me what the hell am I missin'?" Kale asked. Harlan took a long drag from his cigarette and sat down in his chair. He closed his eyes briefly as he slowly exhaled the smoke, "I beg your pardon?" Harlan replied innocently. "Cut the shit, Harlan. You know who I'm talkin' about. What's his story? And tell me the truth, or so help me…" Kale said agitated, before Harlan intervened. Harlan stood to his feet, "Or you'll do what exactly Lieutenant? Kill me? Am I "not" compensating you to do that already? Besides, why do you give a shit?" Harlan yelled. Kale chuckled and took his hat off in frustration, "Why do you? I mean, asking these other guys to kill is understandable but, a southern Baptist preacher, Harlan? And everyone calls "me" the fuckin' crazy one….Yew' either come clean now, Harlan or, the deals off." Kale said cynically. He could look into Kale's cold bloodshot eyes and tell that he was deadly serious about keeping his promise. At this juncture, he did not see any harm in sharing the reverend's dark past, considering it was a long shot that he would even come back to join them, Harlan assumed. Harlan took one more last puff from his cigarette and then beat it out in his ashtray, "Alright. No more games. But, what I have to share mustn't be disclosed with the others! There will be ample time for that possibility, but at this point, I don't need their minds compromised beyond this mission." Harlan requested. Kale wiped the sweat from his forehead with a rag and put back on his favorite Florida Gator cowboy hat, "All right.' I'm listenin….'" Kale replied unfazed. Harlan cocked his head, "Thought you didn't like him?" Harlan asked. Kale stared silently at the stalling billionaire. He picked up his glass of Johnny Walker and took a sip, "Hmph. Well, you might have a slight change of heart after you hear this though…!" Harlan replied.

An hour later, blocks away from Terry Templeton's home....

For all the wrong reasons, the drive over from Harlan's giant palace out in the boondocks, felt a bit longer on the way back to Terry's house, Thomas Jr. believed. Part of him wanted to stay with them, not out of obligation for repaying Harlan or, what he was offering, but mainly as a voice of reason. But what was really the point of doing that? Thomas Jr. asked himself. Surely, he could have run through a few scriptures from the Bible and beat a dead horse about God's wrath or, about the trials of Cain and Able, but what good would any of that might have been? Thomas Jr. pondered. Clearly, there was not a sermon in the world he could have given the troubled fathers that would have brought any of their loved ones back from the grave. The charismatic Harlan Kruellar had something a lot more "tangible" to offer them instead, something buried beneath the frail surface of their very souls and also craved in their hearts darkest desires, Thomas Jr. thought. How was he supposed to compete with that when he barely had enough faith to believe one day God would restore some amount of order in his own life, let alone bring his son back to him? Thomas Jr. wondered. He thought hard about Harlan's wild suggestion that he may have been standing in the way of God's plan by "not" choosing to act on his carnal human nature, but what did he know? Thomas Jr. pondered. Thomas Jr. knew full well that Harlan was a bona fide atheist with a broken sense of ideology, and also a competent businessman who was trying desperately to peddle snake oil to a Boa constrictor. Despite Harlan's obvious knowledge of the Bible, he still lacked the fundamentals of respecting the theology behind how true salvation is attained, but the weary reverend could not blame the cunning billionaire for a lack of trying. The same as the last time, the elderly Uber driver had not uttered a single word during the entire ride. He parked the small blue Volkswagen in front of Terry's house and turned around and offered a faint smile to the brooding reverend, "Well son, we're here. How was your visit?" the elderly man asked. His question felt somewhat misplaced and caused Thomas Jr. to grimace. He tried to brace himself as he began to climb out of the cramped vehicle, "Educating. Jesus, couldn't you have gotten something bigger than this clown car?" Thomas Jr. asked displeased. It took all of a split second for the old man to lose his smile and his composure, "What she lacks in size, she more than makes up for in dependability.

It's probably more than what you got boyo…." The elderly man snapped. His tone caught the unsuspecting reverend by surprise. Seeing how his insensitive comment affected the older gentleman, Thomas Jr. then tried to make things right with him, "Hey look, I'm sorry. I'm just tired. It's been a really long day." Thomas Jr. confirmed, while speaking through the front passenger window. The elderly man took off his driving glasses and wiped them clean with a rag, "A word of advice, reverend….whenever trouble knocks you down, never take a "shit" on the hand of the person who's trying to help you off the floor! Good night to you." The elderly man stated, and sped off down the street. "Shit!" Thomas Jr. screamed, and jumped back out of the car's way. He simply shook his head at the elderly driver's hasty exit, "Hmph…Texas drivers." Thomas Jr. replied, and walked tiredly toward the keypad near Terry's gate. No matter how stupendous Harlan's mega mansion may have been, the proud reverend was still highly impressed with the type of life his runaway brother from little Ben Hill carved out for himself. After typing the code to the home's front gate it opened wide and invitingly. Thomas Jr. was glad that Terry's "spouse" was considerate enough to give it to him before he left the house for his evening workout. He took his time making his way toward the front door of the large home. Although his mind should have been more focused on how psyched out his brother sounded over the line during the ride back, Thomas Jr. found it difficult to shake off the sullen imagery of Ricky Wallace' discolored and crusted looking face when Harlan told him the location of his son. It was amazing to him that it was not until now, that he actually wondered how God rewarded soldiers who went off to fight wars, especially against individuals who chose tyranny over freedom. All of a sudden, the story of Sampson popped into his mind from the Book of Judges in the Bible. God did once empower the mighty Sampson to kill 1,000 Philistines, with the jawbone of a donkey of all things, in order to free the very same Israelites he was punishing, Thomas Jr. contemplated. Then there was Moses from the Book of Exodus, who also led two different armies and was directly responsible for drowning thousands of his enemies to save his people from Egypt, Thomas Jr. remembered. He went up to Terry's front door and grudgingly rang the very loud and harmonious door bell repeatedly. While he patiently waited for his brother to answer the door, one last thought occurred to him before his brother answered it. If Harlan, along with his merry band of concerned fathers were going to go shooting up bad guys at night, how were they going to explain ending up in a morgue instead of their morning group sessions? Thomas Jr. thought nervously. Thomas Jr. could hear his brother frantically snatching back one lock after another, until finally opening up the heavily varnished door. At first glance, the look on Terry's face reminded Thomas Jr. of the scornful look Senior used to give him after catching him sneaking back into the house really late. Judging from the shot glass Terry was toting, he had been up drinking, Thomas Jr. figured. Initially, his obviously perturbed little brother did not say one discouraging word, and simply gazed at his big brother up and down to make sure he was unharmed. After giving Thomas Jr. the once over Terry's expression immediately changed to one of relief and exhaled, as though he was trying to be the first runner across a finish line, "Jesus Tommie! Couldn't you've tried to had at least called a brotha' sooner! Where the hell have you been anyway, Negro?" Terry said relieved. For the time being, Thomas Jr. knew he had to postpone his previous thoughts of Harlan and the others from the group until a more convenient time. Right now, was all about him clearing the air between him and his younger sibling who forgot he was the youngest, "Sight-seeing…just like I already told you on the phone!" Thomas Jr. uncomfortably protested. Terry almost choked on his drink, "Wha…*cough*…Sight-seeing, huh?" Terry asked confused. "Yep. Uh….you plan on letting me in, or are you gonna bring a nigga a pillow? " Thomas Jr. said. Despite being slightly infuriated with his brother, Terry Templeton could not keep from laughing, "Man, get yo'old ass in here….you wanna' know something else? You cuss too "good" for a damn preacher!" Terry joked, and closed the door behind his brother. The last thing Thomas Jr. wanted was a petty argument with a brother he had not seen in decades. To settle his thoughts he decided to join his younger brother for a short nightcap next to wet-bar near the kitchen, "You mind I make one of those?"Thomas Jr. asked, while pointing at Terry's shot glass. Terry looked at his glass as if he forgot that it was even in his hand, "Uh, yeah…man, make yourself at home!" Terry said, as he followed Thomas Jr. to his impressive collection of booze. "Appreciate it Ter." Thomas Jr. said gratefully. He put down the cell phone he was carrying that Harlan lent him and cracked open the bottle of Maker's Mark he had been already working on and poured himself a drink. His big brother's first glass of liquor went down so fast, that he could have missed it had he blinked, Terry thought.

Without taking a moment's hesitation, the antsy reverend quickly poured two more shots, while Terry watched in awe as each one disappeared faster than the previous one. Obviously, Thomas Jr. was having the same kind of rough night he was having, but he was willing to drop the issue, until he realized his brother, who could not afford a cell phone bill, was now mysteriously in possession of one, "So….see you found yourself a new phone!?" Terry said suspiciously, while pointing to the cell phone on the counter. Thomas Jr. felt like kicking himself after forgetting he was supposed to have been keeping his whereabouts low key, "Oh. Oh that…Uh, yeah… picked it up at uh, Verizon!?" Thomas Jr. said disenchanted. Terry almost spit out his drink in protest, "What, nobody at Verizon had an extra phone for you to borrow why you were busy buying that one?" Terry said agitated, and took the bottle of Maker's away from him to pour himself another round. Thomas Jr. rolled his eyes at his younger sibling, "Who's supposed to be the big brother here? (Thomas Jr. looking around) Where's Romeo?" Thomas Jr. asked, and swallowed back another shot. Terry slammed his glass hard onto his counter, "The same S.O.B. who's supposed to be MY house guest! Anyway, Lacy's asleep….look bro, I'm not your keeper (no pun intended) but, if you gonna' be out "sight-seeing," you should at least give me a heads up and let me know you're okay! That's all." Terry pleaded. From the frantic expression on his face, it was pretty clear to Thomas Jr. that his brother Terry was more than just a "little" worried about him being out late in his city and not calling. Terry poured himself another drink and quietly sat back down on his bar stool. Then it hit the bewildered reverend. He looked at things from his brother's perspective for a moment and immediately understood where he was actually coming from, "You thought I went back didn't you, back to Georgia. Now Ter, you actually think I would just up and leave…. (He exhaled)….man. I deserve more credit than that bro." Thomas Jr. stated. Looking down at his glass, "Man, I didn't know what to think! I mean, I know "things" aren't what you're "used" to, plus the fact, that I've been dragging you back and forth to work with me and having you listening to other peoples pro…" Terry began, before he was cutoff. "Let's get one thing straight here baby bro….you're my "brother" man. I'm not your priest! This whole…"thing" between you and Lacy is "completely" your business! And besides, it ain't like I just "woke up" and "found out" you're gay, cause I always thought "that" since we were little!" Thomas Jr.

insisted. His last comment drew dirty looks from his highly buzzed younger brother, which prompted Thomas Jr. to quickly get to his point, "When it's all said and done, Ter, I'm not really much different from the other guys you're helping at your job and don't forget, it was "me" who agreed to go with you. Wanna' know something else? Thanks to you and Lacy, this is the most "comfortable" I've been in years. And secondly, what I look like skipping out on the brother who flew me all the way to Texas first class? I'll tell you what, a damn fool!" Thomas Jr. confirmed. It relieved Terry to hear that. He both appreciated and applauded his brother's fairness concerning his true feelings about him and Lacy' relationship, and especially for his own involvement with the group. Terry put down his shot glass and reached across the counter to shake his brother's hand. In the middle of pouring his next drink, Thomas Jr. saw him extend his hand from the corner of his eye and paused for a brief moment, and then put everything down and shook Terry's hand firmly. He could see a sense of gladness inside his brother's eyes, "Good to know, bro and I can't thank you enough." Terry said peacefully. Thomas Jr. waved off his kind gesture, "No need to thank ME bro, you're family!" Thomas Jr. concluded. Although it pained him greatly to ruin such a tender moment, the psychoanalytic side of him was curious to know whether another family member was still reaching out, "Yeah, uh, speaking of that. Are you, ah…still seeing dad?" Terry asked grudgingly. Surprisingly, the thought of it had not occurred to him that he did at the Midtown clinic, prior to going to visit Harlan and the others, "As a matter of fact, Ter….I did. Earlier today….why you asking man?" Thomas Jr. asked startled. An exhausted and slightly inebriated Terry Templeton started rubbing his eyes roughly, as if he were trying to erase them from the sockets of his face, "Call it a possible theory, or a hunch…hell, call it crazy, I dunno. But, I'd be lying to you if I didn't say that I saw a pattern between the two of you…" Terry admitted peculiarly. Thomas Jr. paused once again mid sip, "You two, who?" Thomas Jr. asked befuddled. Terry thought long and hard before answering his brother's inquiry. If he were to ask him to put things off until the morning, then Thomas Jr. would demand to be told now, but if he told him now, there was also the slight possibility of an argument ensuing and then neither of them would never get any decent sleep, Terry pondered. Either way, if they were going to get down to the bottom of his brother's violent visions of their father, then Terry knew had to start from the beginning. Terry went to his refrigerator and pulled out a whole 5' inch thick lemon meringue pie and grabbed two plates from the cabinet, along with a knife from the drawer. He then grabbed two silver folks and sat down back in his stool. Whatever it was that Terry was ready to drop on him, had to have been bad enough for him to start pulling out one of his favorite deserts, Thomas Jr. figured. It was an old dead giveaway, recollected the middle-aged Georgian reverend. In the past, it was always his brother's way of breaking things gently to him after he had done something behind his back, or had bad news to break to him. He got it honestly from their mother Grace, who was the master and queen of the massive letdowns in his life. Terry cut them both a big slice of the pie and tore into his, as if he had been starved and shipwrecked on some barren island for the last thirty years, Thomas Jr. thought. "Plan on chewing any of that? Jesus Ter…" Thomas Jr. quipped. Terry paid his big brother no mind and went back to enjoying the enticing sweet lemony taste that the pie had to offer, even if it was only but for a brief distraction, "I was talking about Kale…" Terry replied. Thomas Jr. spit his alcohol back into his shot glass, "Kale?! (Thomas Jr. began choking) What about him?" Thomas Jr. asked disturbingly. Terry slid the other plate he made for his brother to him slowly, "Here bro, have some pie….and then I'll tell ya'!" Terry promised. Thomas Jr. reluctantly put down his glass of Maker's and was giving him the types of looks one would give a person if they came walking in from a smelly sewer, Terry thought. He quickly cut himself another big piece before Thomas Jr. could even take his first bite from his first slice, "You know… it's not against the law to breathe in between bites?" Thomas Jr. quipped. "Whatever happened to not judging me?" Terry replied. "That was BEFORE I watched you eat this Goddamned pie…now what's Kale have to do with me?" Thomas Jr. demanded. Terry belched loudly from instant indigestion and needed a minute to compose himself, "I have to tell you something but, you have to promise me that it stays right here!" Terry insisted, pointing down at the counter. Unfazed, Thomas Jr. nodded yes. Terry took in a deep breath, "Okay. I met someone today…" Terry began, until interrupted. Thomas Jr. started shaking his hands into the air, "Hey man, I'm not EVEN trying to hear your dirty laundry!" Thomas Jr. replied. Terry slammed his fork down in disgust, "Hey fuck you bro! Now, try to pay attention would you, please…today I met a guy. His name was David Lewis and he came looking for Kale over at the clinic today. Anyway, he explained to me how they were best friends and…" Terry said, before getting cutoff. Rolling his eyes in repulsion, "A friend of Kale's, huh? Well, isn't that just marvelous. Now we got ourselves "two psychopaths" to worry about, instead of the one." Thomas Jr. said. Terry was shaking his head, "Are you finished? Good. Like I was saying, he was telling me about how Kale was experiencing the same thing that you're experiencing, only difference is, instead of seeing a dead father, Kale is being haunted by the ghosts of the people he's killed in combat…" Terry replied. Thomas Jr. was trying to do the math in his head, but some things were still not adding up, "Okay, wait. So-o-o-o, what you're saying is…that I'm seeing dad, because I feel like "I'm" the one who killed him? I don't get it?" Thomas Jr. guessed. Terry stood up and walked over to his misunderstood big brother and placed a hand on his shoulder, "No! That's not what I'm saying Tommie. What I'm saying is….for some inexplicable reason, "you" feel directly responsible for what happened to you, your family, and for our mother. Your mind created a false interpretation of who our father really was and your guilt did the rest. It's the same with PTSD. When the human mind becomes exposed to severe traumatic experiences, things sometimes get very confusing. Sometimes, we even see things that may seem real, but are in fact just in our own heads!" Terry reassured. Is there a cure? Or, am I going to have to stay crazy for the rest of my damned life? Just…I just don't want to scare Markus is all." Thomas Jr. asked. Terry brandished the widest smile he could muster, "Well, I can't speak for you being crazy, but the "visions" will go away, probably once you figure out a way to start forgiving yourself. It's either doing that, or finding it in your heart to forgive their murderers face to face…which is probably out of the fucking question!" Terry quipped. Thomas Jr. took into account everything that his younger, more experienced brother had to share and trusted his knowledge. One thing began to bother him though, after taking considerable time thinking about it, "You said that this…David…was looking for Kale. Did he ever say why?" Thomas Jr. asked. Terry cleared his throat and immediately took his seat and started munching away at the half-eaten pie. His silence only frustrated the exhausted reverend, "Aw-w-w, don't bitch up on me now, bro! What else did he tell you? Thomas Jr. asked infuriated. Terry, who was busy with his head down into his plate, jumped at the sound of his brother's agitated tone, "Alright, calm down! Shit man you almost gave me a fucking heart attack!" Terry pleaded. "Look, I was planning on telling you later… (Thomas Jr. began to scowl) but, I guess there's no better time like the present, I suppose. A warning though, his past is every bit as ugly as yours, so…" Terry said, as his mind seemed to trail off elsewhere. Thomas Jr. was snapping his fingers in his brother's pudgy face, "Yeah, so? Spit it out!" Thomas Jr. asked confused. The sound of his brother's fingers broke him out of the short trance he seemed to been in, "Well, let's just say….he has a few "very good reasons" for being "every bit" as crazy as we all "think" he is…" Terry said.

Interlude:

6:49 AM Friday, At the Sleepy Inn Hotel near Downtown…

Honorably discharged former Sergeant David Lewis had been spending the last twenty-two minutes of his morning trying to explain his current whereabouts to a flustered and paranoid wife over the phone. His stomach grumbled and croaked loudly, as if it were a bloated toad crooning from its lily pad. Although he missed his wife's good ole' home style cooking, part of him could not get off the phone fast enough to check out the hotels breakfast buffet. He had been spending the last few days wondering about every dive in town trying to find his best friend and hardly anytime at the dinner table. If his wife, Jessica, was aware of the terrible eating and sleeping habits he picked up since being out on the road, she would have cut his trip short a long time ago, but he was not fool enough to divulge such information. The room's air conditioner was still something to get used to, as it consistently blew freezing air despite lowering the settings. Civilian life came with an adjustment period and soft beds have always been a problem for most infantry men like himself. Between the usual subtle nightmares and an aching back, rest was in short supply and the thinly cold carpeted floor did him no favors after spending the last few nights on it. But he knew he had been through worse, as he looked down at both prosthetic hands. Fearing a long conversation, he stood up from the edge of the bed and walked into the miniature kitchen area to make him a quick pot of coffee. David was highly displeased after discovering too late a strategically misplaced white card showing the price of the expensive coffee. After he was done making his coffee, David took a seat at a small black wooden table near the hotel room window and subconsciously picked up the TV remote. Despite skating on thin ice with his significant other, David nervously turned on the television and started flipping through all the available cable channels.

Jessica, who from the beginning, was totally against him leaving home to pursue a friend who was obviously not interested in being found. And who could blame her? David thought. She fought tooth and nail to help him get back on his feet, after he lost both his limbs during his last mission in Afghanistan two years ago. There were times where part of him just wished Kale would have left his arms entrapped inside that massive rubble, but leaving him to die would have probably been too much to ask of any friend, David imagined. He often thought about what he would have done if the roles were reversed. David tried to convince himself that he would have had enough nerve to have done what Kale did, but in retrospect, knew he did not possess the heart to dismember someone he cared about, even to save their life. It must have been hell on his best friend to go through such a painfully brave act, David believed. When he tried to apologize to him for his actions, David would not hear of it. Kale was their Lieutenant Commander for a good reason and in the heat of battle was forced to make a crucial and judgmental call, "despite" his urging to abandon him, David recollected. But David knew he should have known better. He and Kale were more than just best friends, they were brothers. And like any other brotherhood, there was nothing that one was not willing to do for the sake of the other. After Rita and the kids died in the explosion, he stopped seeing his friend though, and hearing from him over the phone even less, until finally, not at all. Not even Kale's father "the General" was excepting his phone calls anymore, which did not come as much of a big surprise. In his experience, the only thing that ever seemed to concern the bloodthirsty General Patrick Keegan was giving his next kill order. Another close friend from their Black Ops unit, Specialist Emanuel "Manny" Espinoza was doing his best to keep him in the loop of things, until he himself was killed in the line of duty. It was through Manny that he found out about Kale falling off the rails during missions and his attempted suicide. But part of him could not blame his friend for losing his mind, as Rita was someone who was widely considered very special and seemed to bring out the best in everyone she ever came in contact with, David remembered. He would often reminisce on how mesmerized he was by not only her incredible outer beauty, but her genuinely down-to-Earth fun loving soul. Their eldest child, Reese, was very much like Rita in that regard, David recollected. Much like his vigorous mother, little Reese was full of energy and spunk, and was also very inquisitive for a child. To lose them, his baby Kyle, plus an unborn child the way he did was more than justifiable enough to drive any good man insane, David figured. It hurt him deeply that Kale decided to shut him out during the roughest time of their lives, even if it were for good reason. When he lost his own mother to liver disease, it was up to him to look out for his little "big" brother Daniel, who went off to play football in Oregon, and ultimately, left him all alone. Lucky for him, he met Jessica Goodman, who was his physical therapist at the time. His year-long rehabilitation was a grueling one, considering how much time he spent dedicating his young life to playing sports, fighting, killing, and painting. On top of all that, Jessica also had to help him overcome a life threatening drug and alcohol dependency that was trying to destroy the man she felt deep down he really was. Whatever she had seen in him though, made him feel very fortunate during a time when he was close to giving up on living life. She always had a knack for telling him the right things whenever he was at his lowest and pulled no punches when he would begin a pity party. That was one of the many attributes he respected most about her, other than her cute face and even more incredible bedside manner. But, unfortunately for him, now was not one of those moments where his spirited wife was in any comforting mood to soothe his aching psyche' or, easing conflicted minds. "It's been twenty minutes and I've heard nothing but empty apologies and possible leads about your buddy, when are you bringing your big grumpy ass home David? Donald and Darius are both driving me crazy and now little Re Re's sick! I have a career, David, and I can't keep doing this shit ALL BY MY SELF!" Jessica screamed. His wife comes from a highly diverse cultural background with her musician father being a bi-racial black man from Harlem and a full blooded Lebanon born mother. He could always tell which ethnic parts were coming out whenever she was upset, "You have every right to be upset Jess, but I'm telling you babe I'm closer than I've ever been! I just need a little more time…" David said, before getting interrupted. "You've been on the road for weeks, hell almost months! You have a family now, David! And if your "friend" was everything you claimed him to be, then he would at least understand and respect you enough if you came back to be with your family?" Jessica pleaded. She sounded overwhelmed and frustrated, but most of all scared, David thought. While his generously patient wife was steadily building up a mountain of reasons for his return home, he was coming up short of excuses not to. This was the closest he has been to catching up to his long lost brother, but was regaining a brother truly worth him losing the only person who stood by his side during his darkest days? David wondered. All David knew, was that he loved them both dearly and if it was not for Kale saving him, then he would not have ever met his future wife in the first fucking place, David thought. He finally settled on leaving the television on a local news station, while he and Jessica continued to work through their personal issues, or at least until the bleeding stopped, David?!" Jessica hollered. Caught off guard, David jumped in his seat and had not realized that he had become so fixated by what was happening on the 32 inch flat screen, "Huh?!" David sputtered frantically. Jessica huffed loudly into her phone's receiver, "Either you quit watching that FUCKING television and talk to me or, by God…!" Jessica demanded. The louder she became, the more of her father's agitated side began to be on full display, "Hey, hey, hey! Calm down, now! You know how I feel about you cussin' in front of those babies….look, Jess, all I'm asking for is just a couple more weeks, and I promise you baby, I'm gonna' come…" David began, until getting cut off. "What?! A few wee….tell you what soldier boy, you have one…..and if you're not here by then, I'm boxing up your shit!" Jessica casually threatened. David shook his head in defeat, "Fine. I'll give it another week, and then you'll see!" David protested. The last time he remembered his wife pressing him so, was during his early rehabilitation days after first getting acquainted with his prosthetic arms. Only this time around, she was not pushing him to re-learn how to open a door, or to pick up and hold a glass of water, but pressuring him to choose between finding his best friend and losing his family, David thought. As unmercifully taxing as he and Jessica's discussion had been, the now distracted Sergeant Lewis could not take his eyes off two particularly odd headlines that were splashed across the TV screen. Both headlines were Las Vegas related. The first was a report about the apparent drug overdose of thirty-eight year old photographer Linda Rourke-Shelton, ex-wife of the former late actor Erick Shelton, and the other, a seemingly unrelated attack on what was being reported to be an underground youth slave farm. Even though the LVPD had yet to discover any possible suspects behind the murders, they did disclose to the media that they believed it did not appear to be a random robbery, but a possible hit on the slavers themselves. The camera man at the scene did manage to provide a few glimpses from the massively violent carnage to the viewers at home. Although David was no stranger to seeing violence, he could not remember the last time he had seen so much blood, except in those days when he and Kale served together. Just before the segment ended, it was reported that the owner of the property was civil rights activist Calvin Rusher, who not only had had tons of cocaine found in a barn at his farm, but thirty to forty-five children waiting to be sold. It pleased David greatly to see scumbags like Calvin Rusher get theirs in the end and David had a pleasing sinister looking grin on his face, until his wife broke his concentration, "Dammit David, I mean it!!!" Jessica barked. He had almost forgotten that she was still on the phone and on the brink of losing the best thing that ever happened to him, "Jesus Jess, okay! Just one more week and "then" I'll come home, alright? Shit man, I wish you'd quit worrying about nothing…!" David said drained. As soon as he completed that statement, David Lewis already realized he fucked up, "You selfish bastard. You left me….left us, to go "trotting the globe" to find the same sick, crazy motherfucker, who's responsible for putting you in the physical condition you're in! Just how in the hell do you expect me to deal with all that? Knowing that every time you been around this guy….nothing "good" EVER comes out of it for YOU, David!" Jessica pleaded. Her misappropriation of his best friend's character stings him like a fallen hornet's nest landing on top of his head, "You got him ALL wrong Jess! Kale's not some boogey man. He's my brother! And I got to try to do whatever I can to help him remember that. He would do the same for me….not to mention, that it WAS "Kale" who saved my life. I thought YOU of all people would at least understand that!" David contested. In the back of his mind, David knew that no matter how many times he would bring that point up, that his wife would become less and less moved by it. Either way, bringing it to her attention always seemed to be enough to calm her down, if not just for a little while, "Okay, okay… I just want you to take care of yourself, David. I don't want our kids growing up without their father! So promise me, in a week…..you'll give up?" Jessica pleaded. David took a second to ponder his response and bit down hard on his bottom lip and then exhaled exhaustedly, "That's funny. I thought your job was to encourage guys like me not to do that sort of thing?" David quipped. His playful response managed to get her to laugh, albeit nervously, "Oh, NOW you got jokes?" Jessica said tensely. David picked up his steaming black glass cup, "It's not ALL I got for you...." David chuckled sneakily. He could hear his wife licking her sweet lips through his cell phone, "Oh really? Well, the sooner you can wrap up that "business," the faster mommy can play on daddy's little brown pogo stick...." Jessica taunted seductively. Jessica had a way with words and always knew the right things to say to get under his skin. David swallowed hard, and tried to take his mind off the numbing erection he was getting inside his heavily starched blue jeans, "Not fair babe. You playing dirty...I ain't even had my coffee yet!" David begged, while staring into the inviting cup of Joe.

Just as David readied his watering lips for his first sip of coffee, another breaking story flashed across the TV screen. This time, the story took place on Houston's Northwest side of town and concerned a vicious home invasion at the home of an alleged street pimp by the name Romelle Hatchette, aka "Hot Pocket." It was being reported that Romelle Hatchette, and others at the home who are believed to have been his bodyguards, were ambushed late last night by a group of unknown assailants who used (per the reporter at the scene) military styled weaponry to gain entry into the house. Thirty two-year Romelle Hatchette was found dead in his panic room with his head cleanly severed from his body the news reporter also stated. Much like the previous Las Vegas story, the attack did not appear to be a robbery, and even though the police did not have much to go on, they did however, discover a small group of malnourished under-aged girls chained against a wall and pounds of illegal drugs stashed in his basement. As curious as he found both Romelle Hatchette and Calvin Rusher's murders were David figured that their deaths were meaningless when compared to what he was missing back home, "So, are my favorite set of terrible twins up yet, I don't hear them?" David asked concerned. The next second after the former Sergeant asked about his son's welfare, scenes from the Hatchette murder were replayed on the news, only this time something in the background stood out that he missed from the earlier telecast. He put back down his cup of coffee and grabbed the cable remote and used the cable's DVR settings to replay the segment over again.

When what he was looking for reappeared on the screen, David clicked on the pause button to better examine the intriguing image that at first glance, seemed splattered across a far wall. Despite the camera man's poorly taken angle of that particular scene, the confused Sergeant Lewis was still able to make out the bloody drawing on the wall. His wife called out to him repeatedly, but the former Special Black Ops soldier's mind seemed to blank out and was unresponsive. Regardless, of what his eyes were seeing on the television screen, a shocked David Lewis was still in disbelief. What he saw was a discarded commemoration from his past, during a simpler time when he was supposed to have been fighting for a greater cause. It was the same drawing that the leader of his former unit, The Razor Hawks, often left as their calling card during their missions. David rolled up his sleeve to compare the disturbing image from the television to the tattoo on his right bicep that he and the rest of the Razor Hawks team received together. And there it was to his ultimate horror. Etched into the wall of some miserable asshole's house was that same red capitol letter "R" with an outline of a bird's beak sticking out in the front of it, along with an eye inserted inside the letter itself. His trance is finally broken by the sound of his wife screaming his name into the receiver, "David! David! David! What the hell's the matter with you? David, please say something…" Jessica begged. Another scary thought popped inside his head and he clicked the rewind button on the remote control back to the Calvin Rusher murder video. He peered into the high definition screen with the attention any world class sleuth would be proud of, until finally discovering what it was that he was so desperate to find. Although the image was brief, David was still able to catch enough of the cutaway scene to make out a distinctive picture. He clicked on the pause button once more and there it was, standing out like some proud flag, both bold and brightly red as the last drawing from the Romelle Hatchette incident. David dropped the TV remote control onto the floor in dismay, "My God…." David said terrified. And in the back ground poor Jessica Lewis continued to scream for what she may have felt have been an eternity.

C.E.O of Death

10:00 pm, at Da' Mose Dope Record headquarters in Sugarland, Texas….

"Do you know WHY I called ya' out here Brian?" asked a perturbed Jacory Jackson, from behind a wide marble topped desk. Stunned by his employer's odd question, the young man who sat across from him nodded, "Nah, Big Co….but, I guessed it HAD to be important for you to call me out here at the last minute, though. So…what up?" Brian asked cautiously. Jacory was leaning far back into his chair, with his hands clasped behind his head as he spoke, "Yeah, sorry bout' that. I know you and ya' girl Kala over there had plans tonight, but I promise you…this won't take long to straighten out….that is, if ya honest." Jacory said, with a wide grin, and sat upright in his chair. Unsure where his peculiar acting employer was going with his point, the dressed up young man decided to humor him anyway, "Uh…yeah, cool. Just lay it on me. The club ain't going no-where, right." Brian said nonchalantly. His smile evaporated as fast as it came, "Cool. Well then…(standing up and walking over to his office window) I heard it through the grapevine that you no longer satisfied with being with Mose Dope….that you even thinking about taking DJ Tony Switcher with you back to Philly, to start up ya'll own" thang? That true?" Jacory asked, while watching his warehouse workers through his window. Rapper/Singer Brian Dillon never cared much for the state of Texas and because he was obligated contractually with Mose Dope, via Backdough Records, had no choice but to stay with his new label. But with only a few months left under his old contract remaining, the twenty-two year old Dillon was going to be free to sign with whoever he pleased. As part of a shady package deal, Brian Dillon never fully trusted the crooked ex-con CEO of the Houston based "Da Mose Dope Records" label and wanted out. So, he and best friend DJ Tony Switcher, decided to take some of Mose Dope's artist's (those formerly of Backdough) and form their own independent company back in their hometown in Philadelphia. Their ambitious plans however, were supposed to have been shared between just the two of them, in order to have kept them both safe, but instead, he was summoned for an emergency late night meeting to confess to his alleged scheme, "What!? Man, where all this coming from, Co?" Brian demanded. Jacory snickered and turned around to look Brian directly in his hazel-colored eyes, "For now, let's just say a little birdie told me....speaking of which, you like stories nigga?" Jacory asked. Brian looked to his bodyguard, who stood observantly by the door and then at his stunning dark complected girlfriend Kala, who sat quietly next to Jacory's slimy cousin EJ on a black leather loveseat. Jacory's facility was littered with armed security guards and even had three personal bodyguards upstairs in his office (in the meeting) with him. Dillon knew that if things were to go south all of a sudden, that there was no way possible for any one of them to make it out alive, "Sure man. Hip me on..." Brian said warily. After his prison release, it was not long before Jacory Jackson was trading in his brightly colored red-orange jumpsuits for silk and linen suits, in order to look the part of a successful and certified CEO. Since he had been traveling in new circles these days (as an upcoming Rap and R@B mogul) Jacory eventually acquired new tastes in cuisine and fine wines, but nothing pleasured him more than the tantalizing taste and smell of a fine Cuban cigar. He even had a seven-foot wide humidor installed in the wall next to his desk. Jacory opened the humidor and grabbed a cigar and took a giant whiff from it, "Ah-h-h. Cool...." Jacory said, and clipped his cigar and lit it. He made his way to the front of his desk and sat on the corner edge of the four inch thick marble slab, "The story goes a little something like this (puffing smoke from his cigar) ....One day, a man goes out for a walk down a quiet sidewalk....spots a lonely frail baby bird on the ground. Now, it's obvious that the bird fell from its nest, but it wasn't dead just yet. Seeing how much pain the bird was in, after falling from so high to the ground, the man was left with two choices: leave the bird to die from its injuries, or put the little fucker out of its misery. There also was an unlikely third choice; he could possible try and climb the tree in search of the nest, but that would have put his life in danger if he fell. Anyway, instead of "trusting" the struggling bird to "maybe" eventually fly away, or risk leaving it to get ate up by some hungry cat, the man finally decided to take the bird's life by stepping on him. Wanna' know the moral of that story?" Jacory asked, while blowing smoke into Brian's nervous face. Brian swallowed hard and looked back to his bodyguard for reassurance, "Uh...look before you leap?" Brian quipped uneasily. Jacory smiled when he saw his cousin EJ giggling and stood to his feet slowly, "Naw man...that' a good try....but the real moral of it all is this: Never leave the nest, cause you never know when someone with "higher power" gonna' come and take everything away from you!" Jacory said and waved his hand to his bodyguards. Eddie quickly grabbed Brian's girlfriend by the throat, pulled her from the loveseat and pinned her to his hulking cousin's desk. Brian stood to his feet in protest, but was immediately hit over the head with a gun by one of Jacory's bodyguards. Just as that happened, Brian's personal bodyguard who lunged into action from the office door, reached into his coat pocket for his gun, but was not fast enough and instead was made to drop it on the floor by another of Jacory's other bodyguards in the room. At that point, Brian was sure they were all going to die, "Look Big Co, I don't know what you're talking about dawg! You don't have to do this!?" Brian pleaded. Despite the proof he already possessed, Jacory grew up around enough liars to spot one when he seen one, "Brian, Brian, Brian…." Jacory said, and went into his desk drawer. The young rapper/singer was on his knees and rubbing the back of his bleeding head, "Yo man, I don't know what the fuck this all about, but I'm telling you the…" Brian began, but then paused after Jacory hit the play button on a little gray tape recorder on his desk. It was a steaming recording of DJ Tony Switcher promising some random chick stardom on his future Philadelphia record label during sex. Brian stood up in awe, "Yo nigga, w-what that got to d-do wit' me?" Brian yelled. Stoically, Jacory stopped the recording and went in to his drawer. He then pulled out and tossed two bloodied fingers across his desk, one of which had a vaguely familiar looking golden ring on it. It was a high school class graduation ring, just like the one he had back in Philly, "What the fu…naw man…tell me you didn't?!" Brian begged. Jacory was grinning ear to ear while enjoying his stogie, "What this got to do wit' you? (Laughing) Nigga', this WHOLE situation got something to fuckin' do wit' you. Of course, I had to fuck up ya homeboy a little bit, before I could find out what the fuck he meant, until he finally threw yo' sorry ass under the damn bus. So, since you chose to go behind my back to take my artists and lie to my face about it, somebody going to have to pay for it…" Jacory said, while looking down at Brian's flailing girl friend Kala bent over his desk. The smiling Eddie Jones gradually let go of her throat, but then walked over to the opposite side of the desk and snatched her hands, causing Kala to scream. Jacory chuckled to himself, as if he remembered a funny joke he might have heard prior to what was happening, and then unzipped his fly, "Aw man, please…don't do that shit! I'll pay you…I'll give you whatever you want…" Brian pleaded. Suddenly, Jacory's eyebrows stood up on his forehead in attention, as if he just had an epiphany, "Alright then. How bout' you come over here instead." Jacory ordered. Brian could not believe his ears, "Nigga' you trippin'....you can't be serious...." Brian protested. He looked around the room and into everyone's faces and could see just how serious he was, "Anything but that man, anything but that..." Brian cried. Jacory passed his cigar to one of his henchmen, "Okay then. Hold this shit." Jacory commanded, and then lifted up Kala's skirt. He then forcefully stuck his penis as deep and as far as he could inside her vagina, causing her knees to buckle from the strain of its incredible size. No matter how much Kala yelled and screamed Jacory refused to stop and just kept pounding her harder and harder from behind, causing everything on his desk to fall and vibrate. When he was done, Kala's exhausted and petite body fell to the floor and she crawled her way back to the loveseat. Jacory ordered two of his bodyguards to grab Brian and pinned him over his desk in front of him, "You next butter cup....this will teach you not to run out on me or to fuck wit' my money!" Jacory said, and pulled down Brian's already sagging jeans. The undersized singer/rapper from Philly was being easily manhandled by both of Jacory's two gorilla sized thugs, no matter how much the young man tried to struggle, "Hold that bitch still..." Jacory ordered. He took one last big drag from his expensive six-inch-in a half long cigar, spread open his butt cheeks and shoved it inside of Brian Dillon's asshole, burning and searing his delicate sphincter. Jacory and his goons laughed uncontrollably while young Brian writhed in pain on the floor. He noticed Kala holding her purse tightly, "Yo Ed, get the bitch's driver's license. And if you do try to go to the police, Imma' send a hit squad over to yo' momma house and do the same shit to you and that bitch! You got me, hoe?" Jacory concluded. Kala nodded distraughtly. Jacory then stood over the defenseless young man, "I guess this meeting's adjured! Now, if ya'll both would be so kindly as to get the fuck out of my goddamned office....I got a company to run." Jacory jested, and picked up his phone to make a call.

<u>Interlude:</u>

Not many cats from the hood often get a second reprieve at life after hitting rock bottom like "all world felon" Jacory "Big Cory" Jackson did. A thief and a crook since birth, the new C.E.O. of "Da' Mose Dope Records" conglomerate made his early living off the pain and suffering of others, but yet still managed to be running one of the south's hottest upcoming Rap and R and B record labels. Of course, none of this would have came to fruition, if he would have still been serving his original ten to fifteen year sentence for aiding and abetting, along with vehicular manslaughter to a little child almost three years ago. Much like a cat with nine lives, Jacory Jackson went unscathed crime after crime. It was not until his last incarceration that he would become influenced to build himself a Rap empire. His cellmate at the time Ronald Threat, who went by "Rogah-that" was a small built cat from Philadelphia, who was better at spitting fiery rhymes than protecting his own ass. Jacory ran with a gang in Leavenworth who called themselves the "Real Black Ballaz'" and offered the diminutive rapper protection, so long as he could afford money for commissary benefits. After a while, Ronald became a somewhat positive influence on the much older Jackson, and Jackson could plainly see the young man's potential as a rap artist. He often made promises to the hefty future C.E.O. that if they ever got out of prison, he wanted the goliath of a man to represent him. Because he was facing so many years, Jacory never made much of the young man's delusions of grandeur and disregarded the notion of becoming the next Russell Simmons. Soon after Roger-that was released from prison, he eventually went on to record his first album with a small independent label called "Backdough Records," back in his native home in Philadelphia. Despite his jail release, Ronald still kept in touch with and often wrote to his former cellmate and bodyguard Jacory, who was still incarcerated at the time. Despite his album going platinum, "Rogah-that" became displeased with his contract situation with Backdough Records, after hardly getting any financial returns for his increasing record sales. Meanwhile, in a major turn of events, the Leavenworth prison had the nefarious Jacory Jackson transferred to a minimal security facility in Ohio, where he eventually spent most of his time earning a bachelor's degree in business management. It was partly through the encouragement of the anti-political Ronald Threat, who loved rapping about fighting the system, that Jacory further educated himself. On the flipside though, Jacory was also aware that having a degree on his file would look good come parole time as well. All the while "Jacory Jackson" was busy trying to better himself, his "Big Cory" persona unfortunately had yet to turn over a new leaf. Even though he transferred to another prison, Jacory's previous gang affiliations still afforded him some influence between him and the other inmates. While his ex-cellmate Ronald was on the outside struggling to get paid for his rhymes, Big Cory was quietly educating himself and acquiring a private army of hardheads behind bars. In just two months time after his transfer to minimal security, Big Cory had gained much influence with the prison guards, and as well with his newly formed "Real Black Ballaz'" gang. Regardless, of the other rival gangs involved, there was hardly an illegal deal going down in the entire building that Jacory's faction was not being a part of. For those who tried to resist his involvement, often either ended up a human-sized piñata, or a glorified pincushion. It was not long before "Real Black Ballaz'" began to show up in towns like Whitehall and Cleveland, allowing Jacory to extend his foul and sadistic reach. But, as Big Cory was flourishing, "Rogah-that" was growing more and more frustrated with his record label. After the label refused to renegotiate his contract, Ronald began to purposely miss board meetings and skip out on his mandatory interviews to get the owner's attention. When that did not work, he then stopped appearing at local showcases and concerts in hopes of getting a sit down with him. Backdough's primary owner though, Sidney "Kid Sid" Copeland, had been in the music industry since working as a house deejay as a teenager back in the 80's, but now the almost fifty-year old was making records and was well known for screwing his artists out of their publishing rights. Ronald finally got his meeting after taking his contract issues to social media and accused Copeland of financially raping his artists, which did not sit well with the shrewd owner. Instead of opening his books to him, Copeland offered "Roger-that" a forty city-wide tour, a house, and a seventy-five thousand dollar bonus, if he was willing to record another two albums and extend his contract. The egocentric minded Copeland figured that his incentive laden deal was more than generous enough to satiate the appetite of his easily excitable artist. But as somewhat enticing as it initially sounded to him, Ronald was still wondering about the missing money Copeland was not already paying him for the success of his first album. Copeland then went into an unmercifully long tangent into explaining the recipe for paying his artists after an album had been sold. Once he finished breaking down how everyone from the graphic artist to the studio engineer got paid, Ronald still could not understand why he was living in a tiny apartment on a small month to month cash stipend from the company.

Seeing that he could not persuade the inquisitive rapper to accept his deal, Copeland accused "Rogah-that" of already being in breach of his contract and threatened to sue should he try to quit the small, but burgeoning label. With Ronald being under Copeland's crooked thumb, he quickly found himself up against a mountain of a wall and decided to handle things in a different way. Meanwhile, as Ronald was licking his wounds, Big Cory was getting the news of a lifetime after receiving an unprecedented parole visit from the state of Ohio. Due to an increasing prison over-crowding situation, the state decided to try-out a new special second chance program. The program involved fast forwarding parole to both first time felons and prisoners already eligible for parole in the coming seven years, provided they previously completed twenty-eight percent of their current sentences and had exemplary behavior. Before he could share the news of his upcoming release, Ronald paid Big Cory a visit to the prison and explained to him his impossible situation with Backdough Records. In exchange for a solution to his contract problems, Ronald had to agree to keep his word and allow Big Cory to manage his career. Three weeks later, after Ronald's visit, Jacory was released from prison and immediately set his plan to emancipate his future client into motion. Over that three week time period, before Big Cory's release, Ronald's job was to act normally and also gather up as much private information about his boss as he possible could and pass it on. Soon after Ronald completed his part of the plan, Jacory then took with him a couple "friends" out to Pennsylvania to get an up-close view of the dubious Mr. Copeland. Jacory was impressed by the amount of detail Ronald wrote down and was easily able to track him down in mere minutes, which led him to a day spa called "Spot-On" in downtown Philadelphia. Copeland never traveled alone and usually had three to four armed bodyguards with him at any given time. Unfazed and hardly impressed by the slightly overweight Sidney Copeland and his play-set of goons, Jacory went with the next phase of his plan: An introduction. Since he had his routines in front of him, Big Cory was able to get a head start on the Backdough Records owner's next visit, which was a Sicilian restaurant on the eastside called "Uncle Benny's Place." His (Jacory) intentions were not to carry-out an all out frontal assault against the older Copeland, but to size him up in order to know where to go next with his twisted strategy. It cost Jacory two hundred dollars just to get a seat close enough to approach the anal retentive owner, but Big Cory did not care, as the planned payoff was going to outweigh his meager loss. The air was full of ripe garlic and spicy tomato herbs and also freshly cooked bread, which made it understandable why Copeland often ate there, Jacory thought at the time. After Copeland entered the busy restaurant and took his seat toward the back, Jacory waited until he received his meal before finally approaching him. His bodyguards were not too thrilled when he did, but the arrogant Copeland did not fear anyone, as long as he had hired help to take care of his dirty work for him. Figuring Jacory may have been just another aspiring artist he allowed him to have a two minute sit down. He introduced himself as a personal friend to Ronald Threat and just wanted to give him a fair warning, should he not agree to release him from his contract. Feeling shocked and disrespected, Copeland spewed the much bigger Jacory Jackson a streamline of expletives right before he demanded that he leave the entire restaurant. After his sit down with the unscrupulous record owner, Jacory learned everything he needed to know about his prey and knew just how he needed to proceed with the final phase of his crucial scheme. Five days later, after the meeting at Uncle Benny's Place, just like clockwork, Sidney Copeland returned for his weekly visit to his favorite spa at "Spot-On." While he was in the middle of partaking in his usual steam bath session, a tall beautiful slender black woman sashayed her way inside the heavily clouded room and sat right beside him. Despite being already married, the over-eager and highly pretentious record owner could not resist the temptation to flirt with the much younger fellow bather. To his surprise the woman was just as enthusiastic to make her acquaintance. It was not for long that he had locked the steam room doors and had the dark brown skinned female down on her knees in front of him, and giving him the blowjob of his life. He then fucked the long haired woman lasciviously from behind, causing her to shout vehemently, until he finally came. When they were finished, the young lady introduced herself as "Stevie," which Copeland found attractive for a woman's name. He asked her to come by his office whenever she was in the mood for another hook-up, which she happily agreed to do. Two days later, Big Cory came to pay

Mr. Copeland a special visit at his Backdough Records office on the Westside of Philly. Not in the mood for another half-baked shake-down, Copeland refused to see the husky one-time felon. When he told his secretary he was there to talk about their mutual friend "Stevie," the apprehensive record owner dallied no further and ultimately invited him in. Jacory then confidently moseyed into Copeland's large icy office and threw down a long brown envelope on top of his wide double-pane glass desk. At Jacory's behest he slowly opened the dirty brown envelope and removed a set of pictures that featured both him and the woman named "Stevie" having sex inside the spa's steam room. The bold record owner balked at the photos and was unafraid of Jacory's initial threat to show them off on social media if he did not release Rogah-that from his label. It was not until Big Cory's confession that the woman who they both knew as "Stevie" was not in fact an actual woman, but was a transgender man. That got Copeland's complete attention. Jacory had another photo in his back pocket that he took out and tossed next to the brown envelope on his desk. On the picture was Stevie's before photo, which caused the grimacing record owner to viciously whelp up. Fearing that he had everything to lose outside of his marriage and reputation, Sidney Copeland agreed to release him from his record label a.s.a.p. But to his surprise "that" deal was no longer on the table. Jacory not only wanted just Rogah-that, but "all" of Backdough's top artists and 2 million dollars to start his own company. Of course, he begged him stringently not to go through with blackballing him, but the heartless Jacory Jackson did not give two shits about what Copeland stood to lose, but only about what "he" stood to gain.

A month or so later, Jacory had used the money from the Backdough deal to set up shop back in Houston, along with tent pole artist "Rogah-that" and half of Copeland's former Rap and R @ B roster at his disposal. With them as building blocks to push his brand new label "Da Mose Dope Records, "Big Cory" Jackson had a solid foundation of fearsome talent to be reckoned with. But unlike his melodic artists, Jacory's primary "talent" was for instilling fear in to others and often used medieval methods to intimidate and maintain his control over them and his street goons, who helped operate his side criminal enterprise.

End of Interlude:

Midnight, at the front gate of Big Cory's record compound….

As usual, it was just another typical gravy train of a work night for security gate guards, Micah Peterson and Jason Reeds, who normally passed their time in the security booth discussing every topic they could think of to keep each other awake. Rarely, had the two ever worked a post without the other, and were experienced enough to select posts that came with the least amount of trouble. So, not long after their company AddBar security received the account for "Da Mose Dope Records" company, they immediately jumped at the opportunity for a transfer. Despite both thirty-something's being from different sides of the train tracks, Micah Peterson an African-American who grew up in middle class home from La Marque Texas, and the Caucasian Jason Reeds, who grew up poor in a trailer park in Mississippi, they had a mutual affinity for Rap Music. And with that shared affection, they were not lost on the record label's violent reputation and knew someone would have to be completely insane to ever come there looking for trouble….that is, until tonight. "Look man, I'm tellin' you…with "D-Howard" coming back more focused the Rocket's going ALL the way this year!" Micah proudly proclaimed. Micah's basketball prediction caused the cynical Jason Reeds to smack his lips in disagreement, "Yeah, the Rockets going ALL the way alright….ALL the way "down" to the bottom of a shot glass at the strip club….man, you said THAT shit about the Texans last year and look what happened?" Jason retorted. His snarky reply made the much bigger Peterson snicker, "Yeah, I did…but, how'n the fuck was I supposed to know, that our quarterback was gonna' get brain damage and throw fifteen Goddamn interceptions by halftime?" Micah quipped. He then passed him a clipboard to initial, "Here….D.A.R. (Daily Activity Report) time. Maybe, he was taking too many painkillers and could've just been high that night?" Jason replied sympathetically. Reminders of the performance that night made Micah roll his eyes, "He was high alright….high off being stupid! Hey…is…is that somebody coming this way? And wearing a fuckin' cowboy hat!?" Micah asked surprised. Jason quickly stood to his feet and walked outside the booth for a closer look, and lo and behold, it was someone actually walking down the quiet and secluded strip of road, drinking and singing loudly. Their post at Da Mose Dope Records building was not far from the 59 interstate and was, in reason, close enough to walk from some of the surrounding private neighborhoods. As the stranger drew closer and closer to them, Micah could vaguely make out the figure to be a white male, as he passed under the few street lamps on the road. In the approaching singing man's hands was a big gas can and a bottle of alcohol, which the two security officers did not find that out of the ordinary for a person possibly stranded. Jason grabbed his walkie talkie from the booth just in case, "Think we should call it in?" Jason asked. Micah was a wrestling champ back in high school and was probably a foot taller and seventy pounds heavier than their unexpected guest, "Nah, don't waste your time. Dude might fall over if you sneezed too hard on him…." Micah joked. Jason recognized the song the stranger was terribly singing, "This dude's drunk out his mind…but, at least he got good taste in music!" Jason confirmed, while smiling. Micah shook his head in disapproval and frowned, "The fuck you say! The nigga' sounds like a raggedy chainsaw "cutting into" another raggedy ass chainsaw!" Micah quipped. Jason tapped Micah on his chest, "Come on man, that's Phil Collins! You know….Miami Vice, "I can feel it…comin' in the air tonight, Oh lord" that was the shit back in the 80's!" Jason said emphatically. His co-worker's enthusiasm was starting to become unbearable, "Okay man, I get it! Get off the nigga' dick already…maybe you can ask him for his autograph or somthin'…..YO man…you lost or what?" Micah shouted. The man in the hat stopped singing instantly, as if he was surprised to see him, "W-Whu? L-Loss? Me? Nah, hoss….jus' out of gas is all. My truck jus' "clunked out" on me….about a few miles back. I thought I saw a gas station this way, so I jus' thought I'de…." The man said, before getting cutoff. "Wait, you said you "thought" you saw a gas station?" Micah asked bewildered, while rubbing his tired eyelids. The stranger was finally face to face with them both and he could see exactly what Micah meant when he told him, "the dude could fall over if he sneezed too hard on him," Jason recollected. After getting a good look at him under proper lighting the young man's eyes appeared bloodshot red underneath the filthy Florida Gators cowboy hat he worn, as if he just been on an all night bender at some fifty cent dive bar, Micah thought. His skin was smudged with dust and he wore highly scuffed snake-skinned boots, with tight fitting dirty blue jeans, and no shirt underneath the opened brown Scully suede vest he wore. "Yeah, I thought I seen ah "Git and Go Mart" down here…" The stranger said, and took a big drink from a whiskey bottle. Micah rolled his eyes in frustration, "Sorry to be the bearer of bad news sir, but the "Git and Go Mart" you're referring to, is about five miles back the other way! You know, it may not be my business sir, but I really think you might need to call yourself a…" Micah began before getting cut off. The stranger raised both his arms in defiance, "Whut? Drinking or passing gas?" The man said and farted loudly. Jason thought if the smell of his breath did not kill them, then the smell from his ass might have, "Dude!!! Fuck this Micah! I'm calling this fool a ride…you got I.D. sir?" Jason asked perturbed. The stranger grinned widely, "I…I-I Dee? S-Sure!? S-Sure I do….H-Hold...hold that, please…" The man said, and handed the bottle of whiskey to Jason and passed the full tank of gas to Micah, while he reached into his back pocket for his wallet. When Micah felt the full weight of the gas can, he held it up to his nose, "Say blood…thought you said you needed gas?" Micah asked suspiciously. Without a moment's hesitation, the stranger threw his Driver's license into Micah's eyeball with pinpoint accuracy, blinding him. And then with the same motion and lightening speed, chopped Jason Reeds in his throat and kicked him in the stomach sending him to the ground on his knees. With blurring speed, he kicked Micah hard in the balls and then knocked him clean out with a severe right hook to the jaw. Finally, he finished Jason off with a side-kick to his face, knocking him unconscious as well. A second later, the stranger's cell phone rang, "Whut?" The stranger shouted agitated. He then finished off the bottle of whiskey and threw it, "Hey Kale, you done fucking around?" A voice said jokingly, over the receiver. Kale turned around and flipped off Agent Elliot who was watching him from far away, through a set of high powered binoculars in a hidden vehicle, "Yeah, yeah…I love you too tough guy, we about to pull up to the back gate…" Agent Elliot said. Kale began pouring gas all over the security booth, "Good fer you, meathead! Now get the fuck off the line and get ready for my Goddamn signal!" Kale ordered, and hung up the phone. "Geez, dude what an asshole…" Ricky said and started the truck they were in. He then pulled out a cigarette and started smoking casually. In the meantime, Agent Elliot and Skinny Ricky drove to the shipping and receiving area in the back of the building, in a makeshift delivery truck. They pulled up to the security gate and the security guard there was not an actual Addbar security guard, but one of Jacory's goons from the Black Ballaz' prison gang, and he was all business, "The fuck ya'll doing here? (checking his clipboard) I don't see any scheduled deliveries being made for tonight…you motherfuckas' in the wrong place!" The hotheaded security man said firmly, and picked up his landline receiver. As a reflex, Agent Elliot squeezed on the handle of his Tech 9, but when saw his reaction, Ricky quickly reassured him, "Relax big dawg, I got this…" Ricky whispered. "Uh, yeah dude, that' was actually MY bad! This was actually a special delivery I forgot to make here earlier, but between you and me, the boss' wife got a mad crush on ya' boy, so when he busted in on me to make the call, I was in the restroom. But what playa didn't know, was while the fool was talkin,' his wife was standing in the stall with ya boy, taking me to slob town, know what I'm say'n?" Ricky jested. The security man smiled and put back down the phone receiver, "Slob town? That's good….but, let's jus' say for a second I believe yo' silly ass …who the fuck is "Nowhere Electronics Boutique?" He said pointing at the makeshift sign on the side of the truck. Ricky turned and smiled at the still unconvinced Agent Elliot, "My man….I thought you'd never ask!" Ricky said happily, and got out the truck to escort the jumpy guard to the backdoor of it. Ricky unlocked the door and raised it and the cabin was stacked with everything from video game consoles to stereo equipment and etc…Impressed by all the elaborate trinkets, the guard still needed more information, "Let me get this shit straight…my boss-man bought all this shit? And waited to bring all this shit out here, till now?" He asked warily. Ricky put his arm over the man's shoulder, as though he were trying to keep what he was going to say a secret, "See, it goes like this….what I told you about the blowjob thing was real. What I didn't tell you was that a month ago, YOUR boss man was at MY boss man's store and what YOUR boss man didn't know, was that MY boss man was getting extorted by some Mexican gang. Well, once they realized that YOUR boss man shopped at MY boss man's store, as a favor to YOUR boss man, the Mexican gang stopped coming around. So, as a favor to YOUR boss man, MY boss man asked me to bring all this shit to YOUR boss man! You got me?" Ricky asked. The security man was quiet for a full twenty seconds before he finally spoke, "Alright. I'll let ya'll through. But I get to have an Xbox and some of them games." He said. Ricky's face lit up like a Christmas tree, "Hey man, fosho!" Ricky said and climbed in and passed him the electronics he wanted. When he got back in the cabin of the truck Agent Elliot was shaking his head, "Dude, just what the fuck was all that shit about?" Agent Elliot asked confused. He started up the truck and waved to the security man as they passed under the red and white striped barrier, "It's a black thing…you wouldn't understand." Ricky quipped. The sound of Ricky's bravado was getting on Agent Elliot's nerves, "Get the fuck otta here! Yo pasty white ass is as black as this white truck we drivin'!" He yelled. Jovan who was hiding strategically in-between some pallets in the back could hear them pestering each other, "Why don't the both of you nigga's shut the fuck up! We should be almost to the shipping and receiving dock by now! So quit trippin and get ready to put yo' game faces on!" Jovan demanded. After he finally parked the delivery truck, both Ricky and Agent Elliot calmly got out of the delivery truck. They were immediately greeted by a small group of heavily armed dock workers, who were highly eager to see what goodies were inside. Agent Elliot unlocked the back door to the delivery truck to unveil the pallets of electronic goodies they were told was coming their way, via the security gate. While the guards were busy ransacking the delivery truck, Agent Elliot inconspicuously slipped through the open bay door to meet up with Hakiro Yosami. The unassuming looking Hakiro disguised himself as a humble janitor and had already infiltrated the building, prior to their planned assault. With Hakiro doing recon all day from the inside, it gave their team the advantage of knowing what to expect from Jacory and his group of heavy hitters, Agent Elliot thought, as he maneuvered through the cluttered warehouse building. Meanwhile, as Kale and his team positioned themselves throughout Mose Dope's headquarters, Big Cory Jackson was still in his office, sharing a bottle Cristal with his second in command Eddie Jones. When his office phone rang he grudgingly answered, "This shit better be important….!" Big Cory warned. The voice on the other end belonged to one of his camera monitors who were overseeing the property, "Sorry to bother you boss, but some little white boy just whooped up on Reeds and Peterson in the front and then set the damn boot on fire! You want me to call the cops?" The camera monitor asked excitedly. Angrily, Jacory threw his champagne glass down on the floor, "Why the fuck would I want the Goddamn cops here, when I'm already paying ya'll? Hell naw. Send some guys to the front, and keep yo' damn eyes open….this might be a setup!" Big Cory commanded, and hung up the line. Needing a moment to think, Jacory took at seat at his desk. Puzzled by his big cousin's drastic change in mood, Eddie went to Jacory's wine cabinet to pour him another glass of the highly expensive champagne. "No cuz, we got problems….but, what I do need….is for you to grab some heat and take Herbert and Sean with you down to the basement to secure the product….make sure everything's all copasetic. "Big Al" can stay up here, just in case…" Jacory ordered. Despite not having any inkling of what was happening his loyal cousin wasted no time to argue, "Alright bet!" Eddie confirmed. Without delay, Eddie went into Big Cory's gun closet in his office and handed out automatic weapons to the two massive bodyguards and grabbed two more for his self. Just before he went out the door, Eddie pushed one of his guns into the chest and hands of the remaining bodyguard, "Yo Al….take care of my cuz!" Eddie commanded, and slammed the door behind him. Jacory then took a seat at his desk and went into his drawer and pulled out a giant chrome 50' caliber pistol and cocked it. Clearly, someone was trying to send him a message, but his mind raced rapidly trying to piece together who the organization may have been that was doing it. On a street level he had many enemies, but with his criminal connections and affiliations, he knew no one from the state of Texas who was foolish enough to take him head on, or was bold enough to make such a threatening move. Jacory grabbed the sweaty bottle of Cristal he and his cousin EJ were sharing and took a big swig from it to help gather his thoughts. In his mind, the only local group brazen enough to have pulled such a stunt might have been the police, but even that idea sounded farfetched to him, after already paying them a small fortune every month to prevent these sort of unwelcomed surprises. No, whoever was responsible, it had to have been on a personal level, Big Cory assumed. But the only person who came to mind that may have been holding a grudge against him might have been his company's disgruntled benefactor, Sidney Copeland. After all, it was with Copland's blackmail money that he was able to launch his "Da Mose Dope" record label and thanks to that two-million dollar contribution, Jacory was also able to turn a quarter of that money into a lucrative drug business. For as much as he enjoyed the fanfare that came with being a popular CEO by day, nothing pleased Jacory Jackson more than shunning that spotlight at night by keeping his crooked hands in the putrid grime of the city streets. By doing so, he purchased and renovated an old multi-foods distribution building in Sugarland and turned it into Mose Dope's headquarters, which gave him a place to both run his record company and afforded him a front to manufacture his drugs. It was considered the perfect camouflage, under the opinions of his fellow criminal constituents at the time, as he was able to produce and sell massive amounts of ecstasy and cocaine under the very noses of his other "higher standard living" rural neighbors. Suddenly, he heard a blast that sounded as if it came from the front of his building, "What the fu….?" Big Cory yelled. From where his office set, Big Cory was at a disadvantage to see anything, but the top of the smoke was coming from the security gate in the front. He rushed to pick up his office phone and called the camera monitors for a status report, "Yo…what the fuck was that? I thought I told you fools to put that damn fire out? I don't wanna' draw any more Goddamn attention to this place!" Jacory ordered. There was a brief pause on the line, "Well, yeah…we sent some of the security there, but no one is responding back, boss! I could get some of the fellas' in the back to stop unloading the truck to…" The camera monitor on the phone said, before getting interrupted. Jacory immediately sprung up from his seat, 'Hole'up….whatchu' jus' say?" Big Cory asked surprised. There was another pause on the line, "Uh…the delivery truck, boss!? Most of the guys are out back helpin' out unloading all your stuff!" The camera monitor replied puzzled. The bewildered two-hundred and ninety pound CEO started scrambling through a small stack of paper work on his desk, "What fucking delivery truck? Big Cory asked confused, as he scanned sheet after sheet. Once again, came another long pause, "The "Nowhere Electronics" truck boss!? Yeah, they just brought you a ton of shit, boss man! At least six pallets," The camera monitor concluded. Jacory slammed down a fistful of invoices in disgust, "Dudley…..is the fucking driver still there?" Big Cory asked lowly, while grinding hard on his gold plated teeth. The country minded camera monitor wasted no time to reply, "Yes sir, boss….why you askin' fo'?" The camera monitor swiftly replied. Big Cory's jaws began to pulsate in and out, like headers vibrating on a V-8 engine, "Cause Dudley…I'm not expecting any damn deliveries till next week! I want you to radio the fellas' in the back and tell'em to put a bullet in his fucking head!" Big Cory commanded, and slammed down the receiver. Just as he pulled out his cell phone to check on Eddie, his bodyguard at the door peeked his head inside, "I heard you yelling, boss…everything cool?" Big Al asked concerned. Jacory stared at him coldly, "Does everything sound fucking cool? Just shut the fucking door and be on the look out!" Big Cory screamed. While dialing his cell number, Big Cory was beginning to regret not listening to his cousin when he suggested that they increased their security staff, "Yo Ed!? Forget about the product. Man instead…I need ya'll to come ba…hello…hello? Ed? Yo Ed, can you hear me? Fuck!" Big Cory yelled, and hung up the line. Just as he was beginning to worry about his cousin, Jacory remembered how hard it was to keep a phone signal in the basement, due to the thick concrete. The more he thought about their present situation, the more he hoped it was only a signal that was lost.

At the shipping and receiving dock,

With most of Big Cory's gang/security team busy raiding the back of the delivery truck for electronics, Ricky Wallace discreetly excused himself toward the cab of the vehicle, upon hearing Kale's booming signal. As soon as he opened the driver door, he heard someone cocking a gun from behind him, "Where you headin' off too Shaggy? You just got here…" The voice said. Ricky casually turned around with both his hands up in the air, "Yo' relax MY man…just went to go grab my pack of "smokes" is all! You want me to light one up for ya,' big homie?" Ricky asked nicely. The man who was holding the intimidating looking automatic weapon on him stopped pointing it at him when he saw the cigarettes and lighter in his hand. Ricky pulled out a single and lit it, "Yo' blood…I really think you need to switch to decaf!" Ricky quipped. On the man's belt was a walkie talkie that was turned up loud enough for Ricky to clearly hear the dispatcher's orders to shoot him. Before the much larger security man could respond, Ricky swiftly stabbed the security man in the eye with his cigarette, causing him to scream and fire his weapon. Shooting in a wild panic, the wounded gunman incidentally shot Ricky in the leg, causing him to fall to one knee. Hastily, Ricky mustered all the will he could to get back up and limped to the cab and dove into the truck to avoid anymore gunfire. He grabbed a small red and white aerosol horn off the floor and squeezed the trigger on it and banged on the wall behind the seat of the cab, "YO JOVAN! Time to wake that bitch up, bro…!" Ricky screamed. Suddenly, before any of the men could react, bottles of tear gas flew from the back of the truck disorienting them and then came sounds of rapid gunfire. Jovan Campbell, along with the massive Dillon M134D Gatlin gun he was carrying, tore through the remainder of his disguise, as a tall unassuming pallet of gift-wrapped electronics, cut down everyone in sight. Ricky could see some of the men running his direction through his side view mirrors and without hesitating, stuck his custom full automatic 100 round 9 mm out the window and dropped all three men in mere seconds. To no avail, a few more security men/Black Ballaz' came running out the open bay door and again Jovan open fired, killing some while holding off others until they finally closed the bay door. In amazement, Jovan looked around at all the dead bodies that were littered all over the ground and the truck like a bunch of old soda cans, "Shit!?" Jovan muttered, to himself. He could hear the injured Ricky Wallace moaning in pain from the cab of the delivery truck and wasted no time to go check on him, "Yo' Rick!? Yo Rick!? You cool!?" Jovan yelled, as he tossed off his gas mask and came running toward the driver door and opened it. Not realizing it was his partner who was yanking on the driver door, the high strung Ricky Wallace drew his gun on Jovan, "Hold up motherfucker! It's just me!" Jovan hollered. Ricky put down his gun and exhaled loudly, "Shwew…thank God. Cause, I wasn't really in the mood to kill anybody else, dude…." Ricky joked nervously, and grabbed his bleeding left leg. Jovan saw that Ricky's leg was bleeding uncontrollably and looked around for something to tie around it and spotted a red bandana hanging inside the passenger door panel. He hurried over to the passenger side of the truck, threw his gun down, and pulled open the door. As soon as he did Ricky open fired at Jovan, "Yo' man….the FUCKS WRONG WIT YOU….!?" Jovan shouted angrily, and began feeling all over his chest. Ricky had a frightened look on his face, "Look behind you." Ricky said, breathing heavily. It was another one of Big Cory's armed security men laying flat on his back and who was trying to sneak up behind him, before Ricky killed him. A relieved Jovan Campbell picked up his Gatlin gun off the ground, "Guess I'll hold onto this…good lookin' out bro!" Jovan said gratefully. The sweating Ricky Wallace dug into his pockets for his painkillers, "No problem….now wrap me up before I pass out!" Ricky quipped, while crunching on them. Jovan climbed inside the truck and wrapped the red bandana around Ricky's wounded leg, "Oh, did I forget to mention…that that was supposed to have been Milton's lucky bandana?" Ricky replied sarcastically. Jovan chuckled, "Serves his ass right….well, I don't believe in luck." Jovan said sorrowfully. Wincing in pain, Ricky closed his eyes for a brief moment and surveyed his comrade for his soul, "Well then, what do you believe in?" Ricky asked. Jovan looked around the perimeter for anymore signs of trouble before he answered, "That either good things are gonna' happen for you or they won't. Look Rick, life's already too damn hard and too fucking complicated for anyone to put all their faith into any one object, let alone some god. Trust me I know. My mom made sure I got my daughter baptized after she was born, and my baby…she still ended up…. this world we living in….for ALL the GOOD that's in it, is pretty fucked up! I mean, it's like some giant ass…rotting garden! And just like anything planted with nobody doing any pruning then the threat of disease just continues to spread and create monsters like you and me." Jovan cryptically concluded. Just before he could reply, Kale Keegan called them on the trucks CB radio, "Wasp to FLY do yew' copy? Kale asked casually. Ricky grudgingly picked up the CB radio, "10-4 Wasp…" Ricky groaned. Kale immediately responded, "Copy that! The fucks wrong wit' yew" Fly?!" Kale asked anxiously. Jovan snatched the radio from Ricky's hand, "Yo this Prospect-1, RW's down. He took one in the leg! You copy that!" Jovan replied smartly. There was a brief pause, "10-4 Prospect 1. Can he move?" Kale asked. Jovan stared at Ricky's blood soaked blue jeans, "Not without help. What's your 20?" Jovan asked curiously. There was another brief pause, "Takin' care of tha' cameras….I don't know about you, but I ain't lookin' fo' my mug ta' be plastered all over Facebook, or TMZ. So here's whuts' goin' down…yew' get back to the bay door and Boss Hog will work his way back ta' yew' ta' let you in…" Kale began, before he was interrupted. "Hold up a second, what about RW? We're not just gonna LEAVE him out here alone are we?" Jovan asked flustered. He could hear Kale snickering from his end of the radio, "Yew' said he got clipped in the leg, right? And yew' took care of his wound didn't you?" Kale asked condescendingly. Jovan was still checking his surroundings from right to left, "Yeah man! I did it just like you showed me! What's your God damn point?" Jovan impatiently replied. "…then he's safer in the truck! Besides…all he needs is one working trigger finger! But it's probably fo' tha' best yew' skipping out on whut' I'm about ta' go dew ta' yo' daughter's killa' and all…." Kale said nonchalantly. Although he had long crossed over the line, when he picked up a gun to play both judge and executioner along with Harlan's merry band of misfits, Jovan still felt compelled to do what he thought was right in his heart. But in the case of his daughter Latavia and the unforeseen event that led up to her untimely death, there was no room for forgiveness, or despair. In his last three outings, he had become adept at taking life from those they deemed undeserving. While all the religious prognosticators were out there whining about all the violence and the bloodshed in the streets, they were actually doing something about ridding the world of a few of its tyrannical oppressors, Jovan believed. The ill-reputed Jacory Jackson may have been one of the low men on Kale's totem pole of infamy, but his death, much like the late Liova-Rouke Sheldon and Calvin Rusher's, would be considered another glorious offering in their ultimate quest for justice. And in no way was he going to pass up the chance to see things all the way through, "No….no one touches him. Let Boss Hog know I'm on my way, Prospect-1 out!" Jovan confirmed and tossed the CB on the floor. Right before Jovan climbed out of the cab, Ricky grabbed his arm, "Wait Joe. I just want you to be the first to know, that when we get back….I'm out. I thought I could bring my fiancé some peace by helping you guys, but I forgot the fact that she's already at peace…in the ground." Ricky said. Jovan paused and turned to look Ricky in the eye, "What are you tryin' to say Rick?" Jovan asked agitated. Ricky let go of Jovan's arm and exhaled, "What I'm sayin' is Joe…is that I'm no monster and you don't have to be one either! Now, you can go in there and blow this guys brains out, but believe me when I tell ya' that it won't make you feel any better." Ricky concluded. After contemplating his advice Jovan cocked the barrel on his Gatlin gun, "Yeah, that's easy for you to say…you know, I appreciate the heads up, but at least you get to go home and be with your kid. Some of us don't have that luxury. You watch yo' ass till we get back dude!" Jovan said, and jumped out of the truck.

When he arrived at the bay door, Agent Elliot opened another regular exit door adjacent to it, to avoid any suspicion of their presence. As Jovan and Agent Elliot were readying themselves over the next phase of Kale's planned strategy, Hakiro Yosami was gradually carrying out his part deep within the shadowy basement. While still disguised as a humble janitor, Hakiro painstakingly followed the weasel-like Eddie Jones and several of his cronies down to a large room where Big Cory's ecstasy drugs were being processed. The room was stacked to the brim with drug making paraphernalia, where at individual tables naked men and women were hard at work appropriating each and every vial and accounting for every pill. There were also large wooden crates along the wall that Hakiro suspected were filled with hundreds of cocaine bricks. He quietly and patiently observed them from afar, all while not breaking character, until he was given the signal to make his next move. Meanwhile, in another part of the wide building, Kale had finally dragged out the last of the five dead camera/security men who previously attacked him and then generously tossed two live grenades into the expensive looking surveillance room. After hearing the massive explosion, from afar Eddie fired his automatic weapon into the air and ordered all the drug workers to leave. Eddie was quite surprised to still see the lone remaining Asian custodian, hard at work on their battered basement floor, "Say man....the fuck you still doing down here? And who told yo' Kim Sun eatin' ass it was okay to be down here in the first place? Yo' we can't take any chances....Herb, Sean...ya'll take his wing dinner makin' ass out!" Eddie commanded. Big Cory's two extra-large bodyguards, plus the two extra security men Eddie grabbed along the way, blindly charged after the overmatched Hakiro Yosami. Unknowingly, to the angry group of men, Hakiro was hiding two Japanese sickles in his mop bucket. It only took a matter of seconds for Hakiro's deadly blades to dice through the four men, like a hot knife carving through warm butter, into numerous pieces with a surgeon's precision. In an insane panic, Eddie Jones began screaming and shooting at the stoutly built Korean, eventually pinning him behind a table. On the upper level, both Agent Elliot and Jovan Campbell heard the loud commotion that came from the building over and started to make their way toward Big Cory's office, where they were promptly met in kind with aggressive gunfire. With the few remaining Black Ballaz' scattered throughout the spacious warehouse side of the building it gave them a mild tactical advantage, but what Jovan and Agent Elliot lacked in subtlety , they more than made up for with brute force. Once everyone ran out of bullets, Jovan and Agent Elliot took the advantage by choosing to engage with hand to hand combat. After serving his time on the force under cover, Agent Elliot often found himself in extreme circumstances, which more times than not, led to putting lesser men in the intensive care ward of the hospital. His extensive training in both Aikido and Judo allowed him to easily outmatch the dimwitted and disorganized group of gangbangers who were trying to attack him. What Jovan lacked in field training and fighting disciplines he more than made up for with sheer power and athletic prowess. Jovan used Mike Tyson level punching power along with speed and stamina to pound each of the remaining foes who were dumb enough to rush him. Both of them, young and virile, proudly stood back to back as they ferociously pulverized their inferior competition without even breaking a sweat. They gave each other celebratory high fives and just when they went to pick up their weapons they heard the sound of breaking glass. It was Jacory Jackson, madly shooting from his office window and was aiming at Jovan. Without taking a second to think about it, Agent Elliot immediately ran over to push the oblivious Jovan Campbell out of the way of Big Cory's raging onslaught. Jacory managed to graze Agent Elliot in his side with his 50'caliber and then reloaded. Jovan dragged Agent Elliot from out his of line of fire. What Jacory did not count on, was Kale crawling through a nearby ceiling window and when he got close enough, Kale threw his knife as if it were a Nerf football and it landed directly through Jacory's hand, causing him to drop the gun from out of his office window, "Betcha' didn't see that cumin'….hell, I should win a prize!" Kale joked. When he got stabbed in the hand with Kale's knife, Jacory's last remaining body guard (Big Al) made his way inside the office and started shooting at Kale through the office window, but was too late, as he already had made his way downstairs. While Kale and company were getting a handle on things upstairs, Hakiro Yosami was dodging for dear life from the crazed and trigger-happy Eddie Jones. As he was chasing him, Eddie would pick up another gun from one of the already dead security men on the floor and start shooting at him all over again, "Come out you yella' bitch! You can't hide that fat ass of yours forever!" Eddie wisecracked. It felt like he was running for days, but the patient Hakiro Yosami was too disciplined to crack under pressure, "I may be fat, but your mouth is fatter, Chris WR-ock!" Hakiro quipped. Eddie was surprised by the mysterious Asian's heckling, "You fat sour motherfucker!!!" Eddie yelled and unloaded his entire clip of ammunition. When he realized that Eddie's clip was empty, Hakiro came out from behind his hiding place among the drug equipment, "Now, are you willing to make this a fair fight?" Hakiro asked. Eddie looked at him stoically as if he were offended by the notion, "Fair fight? Okay, yeah.....but first, drop them goddamn knives, bitch....so, I can whip the whip-cream off yo' stankin' ass!" Eddie demanded. Hakiro smirked and threw his knives into the wall behind Eddie, "You stupid motherfucka'..." Eddie said and drew out a pistol that was hidden underneath his suit coat behind him. As soon as Eddie began firing, Hakiro instantly rolled onto the ground and picked up a gun and threw it at Eddie hitting him square in the mouth. Before he could recover Hakiro was already standing directly in front of him with his sparkling set of shiny sickles in his chubby hands, "What? You gonna' kiss me now punk?" Eddie asked. Hakiro simply smiled and turned away. Just as he did Eddie pointed his gun to the back of Hakiro's head. But before he could even aim the gun to pull the trigger, Hakiro had turned back around with the speed of a copperhead and sliced him in three places. When Hakiro walked off Eddie Jones Skinny body fell into pieces. On his way out something on the boxes stood out that he had not noticed since seeing them earlier. It was a strange looking marking, yet somewhat familiar, but he disregarded the notion and quickly left to rejoin the others upstairs.

Kale had made his way over to the injured Agent Elliot and Jovan Campbell to assess the damage, "Turn'em over....it's just a scratch. He'll live....I wish I could say the same fer' that asshole shooting up there though." Kale growled. Jovan leaned Agent Elliot up against a wall, "Yo' man, what you did was stupid! You could have gotten yourself killed!" Jovan yelled. While wincing from putting pressure on his side, "W-We all could die h-here. By the way, I-I didn't think....you c-cared...Heisman!?" Agent Elliot said. Kale looked over his shoulder at them, and could not shake the feeling of how much the younger Jovan Campbell reminded him so much of his own best-friend Sergeant David Lewis, back in Des Moines. When one of Big Al's bullets hit too close, Kale instantly broke his trance and saw blood in his eyes, "Here take this. As soon as I leave, yew' draw that sum' bitches fire, yew' copy that?!" Kale commanded, as he handed over his .357 magnum. Kale made a wild break toward the stairwell that led to Big Cory's office and Jovan quickly began firing at the window with reckless abandon. When he got close enough, Kale tossed his last grenade threw a broken window, "Say cheese motherfucker!" Kale screamed chuckling. The grenade landed right in front of Big Cory's desk and Big Cory immediately picked it up and unintentionally launched it in front of his bodyguard, blowing him into chunks of flesh. Out of fear, Jacory knocked over his own desk to get away from the next grenade he thought may have been coming, "Yo man! I give up! I give up! Fuck man….?!" Jacory pleaded, while holding his bloodied hand with Kale's knife still hanging out of it. Suddenly, Jacory's office door slowly cracked open and a tall muscular figure wearing army pants and a tight black tee-shirt quietly entered the room. It only takes Big Cory but a half second to recognize the man who almost beat him to death in real life and in his dreams at night. It was the father of the little girl he ran over with his getaway car a few short years ago, "Sup Big Co….looks like you've been doing REAL good for yourself…you remember me don't you?" Jovan asked politely, while looking around at his fancy office. Jacory timidly came from behind his turned over desk to get a closer look at his nightly tormentor and searched his eyes for the demon who had no mercy, "What's the matter Co? Look like you seeing a ghost or sumthin? I…I mean, you HAD to know that THIS day was coming?! You took someone from me. Someone who meant everything to me…and here I see you, able to walk around the city….living like some kind'a God damn king!" Jovan roared. The more he looked into the young father's hurtful eyes, the lesser he felt afraid of him. He had just come to the realization that Jovan Campbell was no beast, but in actuality just a man and a younger one at that. After crashing his getaway car he was not in his right mind and half concussed and would normally make short work of even guys twice his size, Jacory thought. What he needed was the right opportunity to strike when his guard was down and he came up with the perfect way to do it, "I'm sorry Jovan. I mean…I know that I really, really, fucked up and did a terrible…TERRIBLE thing to you!" Jacory pleaded. Jacory's sudden apologetic outburst made him resist the urge he had to strangle him, but still remained cautious, "Oh yeah? Well, what do you propose we do about it Jacory?" Jovan asked, in a patronizing tone. He shrugged his shoulders daintily and tried to put on the best non-threatening looking face Big Cory could muster, "I don't know man. All I know, is what we did was unforgivable and so, so, stupid. My cousin's friend Taleek was the one who actually snatched the wheel from me, right before…the accident." Big Cory said hurtfully. Jovan was beside himself and could not help but smirk, "You can't be serious? You must think I'm a fool or somethin'? Cats like you don't feel remorse or even pity. The only thing that affect guys like you is losing money!" Jovan protested. Big Cory continued to gradually ease even more closely to the bewildered former collegiate standout, "Naw man! You got me all the way wrong! I mean look at me…look at my hand! I'm a human being, and I bleed just like you! Look, I had my one chance and I blew it by doing the wrong shit, then I get out with another chance and I guess I blew that one now too. If you want me too, I will walk right over there and call the cops on my God damn self, if that's what you REALLY want me to do. Surly, they won't let me back out after everything they might find here so, it's really on you and what it's gonna' take to satisfy you, cause I give up!?" Jacory humbly confirmed. Jovan could not believe that he was seriously considering Jacory Jackson's gentle surrender. When he first arrived, all Jovan Campbell could see was Jacory's blood plastered all over his giant fists. He had never came any closer than where he was today at achieving that one time life goal of killing him, since finding out about his prison release. But at the end of the day, Jacory WAS right about one thing, the cops would have more than enough reasons to keep him locked away behind bars. Although he would be still alive, jail might be the best place for the sinister Big Cory Jackson after all, Jovan figured. Jovan folded his arms and called Jacory on his bluff, "Alright. Make the call. But this better not be any bullshit…" Jovan warned. Jacory grinned widely showing off his golden grill, "Cool! But first, you think you can help me take this damn thing out my hand first?" Jacory kindly asked, and put his hand forward. When Kale came to the door and distracted him, Jacory pulled the knife out himself and sliced Jovan across his chest with it, "Damn man, I really had yo' stupid ass goin' didn't I? Well, sorry bout' that dude…but I had to see for myself what you had in you. And you wanna know what I saw….I saw a lil' bitch!" Jacory hollered, as he swung at Jovan wildly with the knife. Big Cory had the look of a man possessed by pure evil, "And you want to know somethin' else motherfucka? When I saw that little bitch of yours crossin' the street, I instantly stepped on the gas…hoping I was gonna get 50 points! But I guess I gotta settle for three, huh?!" Jacory quipped nastily, and swiped at Jovan once more. In Jovan Campbell's short time span alive he had to overcome an insurmountable amount of life's difficulties. He endured growing up without a father, whose sketchy past draped over him like a cheap suit since birth. Not to mention, that as an athlete his body was constantly being pushed to their limits, regardless of what those limits were to command greatness. Then there was his breakup with his ex-girlfriend Tasha Greenwood, whose heart he constantly broke over and over, after losing the one thing that he never thought he could possibly get over. But the one straw that repeatedly broke his back were always the constant reminders. A total stranger or someone who may have been a former fan would come up to him and ask about what happened to his daughter and every time he chose to share what happened, he had to relive that woeful moment over and over again. What Jacory Jackson was doing and saying was downright despicable and evil, and despite how cut up he may get trying to get a hold of him, once he did, he was going to kill him. He swung too high at Jovan's face which allowed Jovan enough time to duck and lock Jacory's thick arm behind him until he finally dropped the knife. Jovan kicked the knife away with his boot and let Jacory free. He was giving him every opportunity to make his last stand, before he would send him off to oblivion. Big Cory landed a few lucky haymakers, but soon ran out of gas, and afterward, Jovan indiscriminately tore into his head with thunder shot after thunder shot. His punches were so loud, that even the injured Agent Elliot got to his feet to come see the fireworks. When he could not stand anymore, Jovan climbed on top of the larger CEO and began to choke him with his bare hands. Just as Jacory was passing out, Jovan began to sob uncontrollably, as he could see a faint image in the back of his head of his daughter Latavia. Maybe "Skinny" Ricky had a point about them not being monsters. Or just maybe, the true pain of losing her had finally surfaced for the first time, after trying to repress his feelings around everyone by trying not to show weakness. Agent Elliot knew all too well what the wounded father was going through, as he could see so much of himself in the younger man, "Jovan you don't have too…we'll understand." Agent Elliot said softly. Jovan looked at his friend from out of the corner of his eye, "I don't want to, but I can't let go either…" Jovan cried. Without hesitating one moment, the hulking Agent Elliot went over and kneeled down and pulled slightly on the young man's wrists, "Come on brother….come with me. Me and you will go and just "get some air." Agent Elliot confirmed. As he was passing by him, Agent Elliot gave Kale a nod and took Jovan downstairs and out the door. Kale smiled and picked up his knife, "I guess yew won't be needin' this anymore pard-ner….besides, she's already spoken for!" Kale said, while putting it back in its holster. He caught a glimpse of something else on the floor that glistened brightly off the lights in the room. It was a heavily smudged business card for Sharp and Associates. Kale studied the card intently, "Huh…now where have I heard that name from…? Tell yew what? I'll jus' hold o ta' this fo' ya…besides firecracker, cause where yur' headin'…. I doubt yuwl' need it…!" Kale menacingly said, and pulled out his long .357 magnum. He stood right over Big Cory's barely breathing body and aimed it at his face, shooting him straight in the forehead, killing him instantly. Kale blew out the smoke from the barrel of his gun and began singing, "And another one bites tha' dust, hey!" Kale sung happily. He blew off the nozzle of his pistol and moon-walked his way out the door.

David and Kale's Reunion

Saturday morning at St. Morgan's café, near Third Ward…

Much like any other average day of the week, Lieutenant Keegan could not find any rest at the sleaze bag motel he was staying at part-time. It was barely a few minutes past 10AM and already he was working on his third pack of Marlboro's and his fourth bottle of Jack Daniel's, before even setting one foot into the local dive he was currently drinking at. While sitting alone at the empty bar, Kale stared intently at the tattered business card he found on Jacory Jackson's office floor last night, but for the life of him could not place the name on it. Whoever "Sharp and Associates" was must have been of some minor relevance to him, or it would not have plagued him so, Kale wondered. With his full attention on both the worn card and the shot glass he was picking up, a tall wet figure had crept up right beside him, "Is this seat taken, Mon Ami?" The voice asked eerily. Kale quickly swallowed down his drink and then poured himself another, "Why not? Still a fuckin' free country ain't it?" Kale said unflappably, without even bothering to look. The tall and dripping figure pulled out a stool next to Kale, "Merci Beaucoup! I suppose it is, monsieur….considering, you can just "KILL" whomever you'd like?" He said disdainfully. Appalled by the stranger's daring words, Kale finally glanced over at him from the corner of his eyes. Who he had seen, caused him to spontaneously choke on his drink, "The fucks wrong with you?" The bartender asked, while cleaning out a beer glass from behind the bar. Apparently, he was suffering from another one of his many mental breakdowns and was the only person who could see the blood entrenched stranger, wearing an all black Givenchy suit, smiling beside him, "Yes, Lieutenant…what the fuck IS wrong with you, eh? You act as if you have seen a ghost? Clearly, this could not be the case, no?" The man said pretentiously. Kale waved off the much older cranky bartender, "I'm good. Just swallowed a fly is all…" Kale said, while staring nauseously at the grisly looking man. Despite Kale's peculiar behavior, the bartender went back to restocking his glasses, "Fuckin' grunts…." The bartender said, as he stormed off. It had only taken a second for Kale to recognize the ghastly looking thirty-something-year old (who had a hole the size of a baseball through his chest and part of his shaggy auburn head gone) as former kidnapper and terrorist, Martin Napoleon Le'Geaux. Mr. Le'Geaux and his network of underground Euro thugs, who called themselves the "Chamberlain Syndicate," loved playing with explosives to get their points across, Kale remembered. The Chamberlain Syndicate was too well-organized for the local authorities to flesh out, so his group of specialists was tasked with neutralizing the fanatical group after they orchestrated a cowardly attack on a crowd of people during a televised professional soccer game between France and the United States. His industrious father General Patrick Keegan wasted no time negotiating with France's reluctant prime minister for powers to act on their soil, especially after they picked the Embassy of the United States in Paris as their next target, Kale recollected. As usual, his father went through his customary back channels to gather hard to find intel on the Syndicate and discovered their whereabouts just in time to threw a massive monkey wrench into their plans. Meanwhile, as Kale was in the middle of reminiscing about the past, the presently deceased Le'Geaux began snapping his fingers loudly in his face to get his attention, "Excusez-moi, monsieur Kale?! But, you and I have already been down that road…I just came to deliver you a message!" Le'Geaux said stoically. Kale took off his Florida Gator's cowboy hat and scratched his head wildly as if he had fleas, "Yew' know…yew motherfuckers ain't got nothin' else better ta dew' than come fuckin' wit me? Why don't cha try gettin' wit tha' times and send me a goddamn text sometime, instead of poppin' up while I'm taking a shit or eatin' my Cheerios?!" Kale quipped, and took another shot of whiskey. The blood that was pouring from the decrepit Le'Geaux's head and chest sounded like nonstop tropical rainwater and leaned in closer toward the aloof Lieutenant, "Oui! Laugh all you want, you arrogant little asshole…cause very soon, your tender flesh will be ablaze! Burning, so hotly and so vividly, that you're going to fucking wish for the demons of hell to get tired, but they will not, no. They will be barely warming up for the sins that YOU have yet to atone for, my devilish and diminutive looking friend and I will be there to lay witness to the blistering glory of your putrid soul as it swelters throughout eternity…." Le'Geaux said pleasingly. Kale took a drag from his cigarette, "Yew' fuckers need new material…Well, if yur' finished, there's just one thing I got to say ta' yew, before I put that big ole' hole threw yo' head, hoss….Lego My Ego!" Kale jokingly replied, and began to laugh uncontrollably. Infuriated, Le'Geaux seized Kale by the throat and began to choke the air from him, "This is not a fucking game you American cocksucker!" Le'Geaux screamed. But as soon as he grabbed him, Martin Napoleon Le'Geaux disappeared as if he were never there. No matter how many visions Kale had of the people he was ordered to kill did their visit end quietly, "Bar keep? Anotha' round, please…!" Kale asked distracted, and put the card back into his vest pocket. Suddenly, a familiar voice came in from the front door behind him, "Yeah, better make that "two" bartender…!" David said smiling. The blood rushed to his neck and to the sides of his cheekbones, "Well, well, well….wouldja' looky here? How's bout a ten hut Sergeant Lewis?" Kale quipped. The last this Kale expected to see was an actual salute from the man whose hands he removed. Seeing the prosthetic hand did not do him any favors as it caused the hard-nosed Lieutenant's eyes to water, and forced him to get up. He paid for his drinks and tried to walk past his friend of almost ten years, "Please Davey, I thought I could do this….just let me go." Kale replied sadly. But before he could react, David hugged his best friend tighter than he ever had before. Kale wept in his arms and tried to beg for forgiveness, "You stop that kind of talk now. Like I tried telling you before, there ain't nothing for me to forgive! Look at me, Kale….I'm ALIVE! I'm ALIVE, man….because of you! It's time to let that go bro. You have to…because it's eating you alive. Please, now I'm begging YOU. For my sake…for your family's sake and for my family's sake, please bro….forgive YOURSELF!" David pleaded. Kale looked him in the eye, "Alright bro, but only cause ya' askin' me too!" Kale cried. The bartender held up their drinks, "I take it that you two ladies are gonna be hangin' round for awhile…here these are on the house. Look like ya'll need'em!" The old woman said dryly. David and Kale got a much needed laugh at the expense of her sarcastic candor. They wiped their faces and took a seat at the closest booth.

An hour or so later,

"So this is…" Kale asked, while holding up pictures of David's son's. David was pointing at his boys, "Over here that's Donald and the other is Darius. But when they together, I call them the "Wreckin' Crew! And it ain't because they great at rapping either! The little monsters…" David insisted. Kale snickered at his joke, "Yeah, I'm sure those apples don't fall far from the tree!" Kale retorted. David took a sip from his drink, "You probably right about the falling part, cause they be acting like they crazy man!" David quipped. Kale laughed and shook his head, "Hey don't go talkin' bout my nephews! Oh, and who's this? Is this the woman who tamed the beast that refused to ever get married? Not "Mr. Lexington Steel," himself!?" Kale teased. David popped Kale on the arm with his prosthetic hand, "Hey man, watch that thang!" Kale said jokingly. He popped him again, "Okay, Okay. She seems kinda nice. So, whut's her name man?" Kale asked. As soon as he asked, Kale could already see his face light up with joy, "Yeah, bro…its Jessica. When everyone went M.I.A. in my life, she was what kept me going bro. I had a tough time with substance abuse and alcoholism…" David said, before getting cutoff. Kale grabbed David's mixed drink and poured it out, "Alcoholism? The fuck yew drinkin' this here shit for? I have the right mind ta' call her up and have her come out here and kick you in the nutz!" Kale shouted. David shook his head, "Same crazy ass…look, like I was saying, she put me back where I needed to be. Oh…and there's one more pic you still hadn't seen yet!" David teased. Slowly, Kale pulled out the last picture from the bottom of the stack. It was a picture of his youngest child, "Wow! She's gorgeous bro!? What name you give her, let me guess you named her after you mom…" Kale said, before getting interrupted. David spoke with a straight face, "Naw, man. Her name's Rita. Rita Marie Lewis!" David said stoically. It was if everything in the entire bar became eerily quiet, as Kale tried to soak in what his best-friend had just shared with him. He shut his eyes to remember her sweet beautiful face again, to recollect the times they spent hanging at the beach when they would go visit her parents or how she often liked flying in a helicopter. David broke him out of his short trance, "Yo K, you alright bro?" David asked concerned. Kale instantly opened his eyes and remembered what sent his imagination flying off, "Seriously? You named her, after Rita? After MY Rita..?" Kale said tearfully. David put his hand over his shoulder, "Yeah, I mean…If it's okay with you? I don't want you to be mad at me or…." David said before getting cutoff. Kale held up his hand in a stop gesture, "Nonsense. She would be happy. I'm happy that yew' did. Thanks bro. This really…this really means a lot ta' me." Kale replied gratefully. David started stroking his head nervously, "Naw, man…it's the least I could do. I'm just glad that I was able to finally track your ass down to let you know…" David said humorlessly. Kale hurriedly took a shot of whisky that he almost forgot about, "…That reminds me…how the hell yew' find me anyway?" Kale said intensely, and poured himself another whisky shot. David's lips began to water from watching Kale guzzle down shot after shot as if it were ice cold Kool-Aid, "I'll admit, in the beginning it was rough. Sometimes I had to revisit the same city just in case you might have decided to double back, or if I might have misinterpreted one of my tips. But trust me…you didn't make it easy on me, or my wife, who probably has everything I own in public storage as I speak. Honestly, it wasn't until I started seeing your artwork on the morning news that things got easier. Jesus, Kale…just what the hell are you doing? You're going way off the reservation here and how long before you think your dad, "The General," figures out everything you and whoever you're working with, been up too? Oh…and did I say "The General?" David said excitedly. Kale rolled his eyes and swallowed down another fireball whisky shot, "I got everything under control. And to be honest…I'm counting on that senile fucker to catch me." Kale cryptically admitted. David didn't know what surprised him the most, the fact that Kale was so quick to confess, or that he WAS trying to go out of his way to antagonize his four star general father, "Okay. So what is it that you…and whoever…think, you're doing? I mean it's obvious that you're going after the same type of scumbags we used to, but on a more local scale…" David began, before getting interrupted. Kale slammed down another shot, "We have room fer one more guy, if you're interested. We had ta' let go of one of em'…Hell, consider yew as an upgrade!" Kale asked sportingly. David stared him in the face to see if his best friend was being serious but when his expression did not change David became a little worried, "I don't know, man….I promised my wife I wouldn't let you kill me!" David quipped. Without warning Kale spit out his drink and burst into laughter, "Yew' did what? Come on now Davey, yew' think I'm gonna' jus let yew' get killed after all tha' trouble yew' went thru' jus ta' find me? And don't be mad, but fo' the record I knew yew' were followin' me fo' a little while now…" Kale confessed, as he swallowed yet another glass of whisky. David stood up in disagreement, "Bullshit you did!? And if you are telling the truth…that's pretty fucked up, you leading me around in fucking circles!" David said agitated. Kale winked his eye at him, "Come on now…how many black friends do you think I got, with TWO prosthetic arms? I did receive "some" of your messages, but honestly, I just wasn't ready for a face to face….so don't judge me Davey!" Kale concluded. David snatched the bottle of whisky off the table, "I won't…but I do feel like kickin' yo' ass…" David said angrily. Kale smiled broadly, "Yew' could try….but didn't we do that dance already?" Kale wisecracked, and held out his hand for him to give back his bottle of whisky. Grudgingly, he handed it back to him, "Fuck you Kale. Alright…I'll come along, but only if you promise to come back to Iowa with me…other than that then the deals off!" David instructed. Kale paused before he took his last shot, "…Okay…" Kale replied noncommittally. When David reached for his bottle again, Kale beat him to the punch and snatched it first, "Alright…I'll come back." Kale grudgingly complied. David was grinning from ear to ear, "Good! So now let's get the fuck out of here go and get something good to eat, a nigga starving!" David said. Kale stood to his feet and left a tip on the table, "Yew' know I hate it when yew' use that damn word! But whatever, I'm ready to leave anyway, I got some toys I think you might be interested in checkin' out!" Kale said pleased. David put his hand on his shoulder, "Sorry about that man, I forgot. But you know how "ignant" I "GETS" when I "GETS" hungry! So let's roll the fuck out and yeah, I'm buying!" David said anxiously, as they both made their way out of the bar.

Chapter 10:

"Exodus"

Saturday afternoon, at the Sugarland Police Department…

The vast amount of bloodshed left over from the chilling murders at "Da Mos Def" Records headquarters was unprecedented, even to a veteran police detective like Preston Cartwright who served on the SPD force for the past 20 years, after starting out with the busier HPD. By transferring to the SPD long ago, the sixty-one-year-old believed he was doing himself a large favor by shedding the weight of the inner city's brutality in favor of a quieter existence there in Fort Bend County. Although his current countrified oasis had its fair share of malfeasance, the elder detective felt it had beaten the seemingly ritualistic mayhem he dealt with on a daily basis on the unforgivable and gritty city streets of Houston. Detective Cartwright could still remember the proud gaping smile across his father's chiseled face when he first began as a twenty-one-year old cadet on the force, just as he could still recollect the manufactured one at his funeral. His father, Carl, was considered a former HPD legend and was widely respected through-out the black community, especially on Houston's south side. The dedicated officer rigorously volunteered for blood drives, passed out food to the homeless, gave second chances to first and second offenders, spoke hope to the masses at church, and donated money to men's shelters across the city, the detective recalled of his father. As a man, Carl Cartwright was everything the then young Preston ever wanted to be, even up until the very day he was killed. Despite his father's many prestigious commemorations and sparkling collection of Medal of Valor medallions, it still was not enough to prevent a stray bullet from entering his neck during a routine traffic stop that ended his short life at forty-four-years old. The emotional detective recalled how hard he took his father's loss and how eager he was to jump into any fray his job description allowed him to at the time. By catapulting head first into his police work, Preston was able to garner many of the same distinctions his late father was awarded and by his mid thirties, managed to get himself promoted to detective. After becoming a highly decorated officer and a fairly good detective at that, Detective Cartwright finally eased the brakes on his assiduous lifestyle and settled down with a pretty lady fireman named Monica Miller. The fiery Monica Miller was a 5'8 one hundred and thirty five pound former collegiate softball player from Sealy, Texas who refused to quit the job she loved to appease her eventual policeman husband. They were very much in love and were able to enjoy "some" good years together, but ultimately as most occupational hazards went, she succumbed to third degree burns after getting trapped on the thirtieth floor of the Chevron towers building downtown. When she passed on, his willingness for delving into thoughtless acts of intrepidness began to wane, causing the distraught detective to seek peace of mind elsewhere. At least, that is what he believed he was getting after trading in the HPD for the SPD long ago. For the most part, his decision to leave the more hostile inner city Houston area for greener pastures turned out to be a sound one. He had neighbors who he actually liked, that the usually leery detective greeted every morning before leaving for work. His current case load is less than half as it once was back when he last lived across town and could actually leave work early on some days. In his spare time, he played basketball at the YMCA near Stafford to keep his wind up and even began to learn the game of chess. When he was not busy gasping for breath on the basketball court, or getting his ass handed to him on his neighbor's chess board, he often shot pool with his roguish partner Detective Michelson once every weekend. The seventeen-years-younger Detective Daniel "Danny" Michelson had been twice divorced and no kids, who also was a balding Caucasian hound dog that hit on anything that wore a miniskirt. It was Danny that invented their weekly pool night getaways. Although he originally did so to encourage him to get back into the dating scene, Daniel also was looking for anyone who did not mind being an impromptu wing man. But the lonesome detective was not interested in replacing his long past love and only agreed to go to help take his mind off being at home alone. Much of how learning to play chess did for the meticulous minded detective, and shooting pool allowed him a chance to unwind while evaluating the things that were happening in his life, which were predominately work. On most occasions, he looked forward to playing his pool games, as it also offered him the opportunity to unleash any unnecessary sexual tension or, frustration brought on by his much younger co-worker, Sasha Scottsdale, who loved hitting on him in the forensics lab. Sasha loved dating experienced men and found him to be a tough nut to crack. But no matter how much the attractive lab worker pined for the affections of the grieving detective, part of him could not see past the unforgettable charred face of his late wife. Daniel called him "crazy" for passing up the chance to fuck a "fine piece of young ass," but the proud detective was desperately trying hard to be faithful to his wife's memory. Though his promiscuous partner did not fully understand his rationale for being unwilling to move on, he did at least, respect it. Despite his lack of couth or code of ethics, Danny never stopped having his back since first partnering up with him 10 years ago, Detective Cartwright concurred. Their approach to the job on the other hand, could not be any more night and day. While he was the more intuitive and cerebral of the two, the instinctive and former cage fighter, Daniel "Mad Man" Michelson, was more of the "hands-on type" who preferred going "door to door" to getting his police work done. He often employed his ardent temperament for getting the most hardened suspects to talk and often followed his own gut when it came to solving crimes. Regardless, of his limited intellect as a polished sleuth and patience for piecing together clues on some occasions, in Detective Cartwright's personal experience, no one on the SPD force had as much heart as his courageous partner. A South Boston bred native, the highly spirited Daniel Michelson, much like himself, was also raised in a family of dedicated and decorated policemen. Unfortunately, after his second seedy marriage to a much younger former nightclub stripper dissolved, the usually cold blooded Detective Michelson needed a change of scenery and decided to move down south, under the blister of the Texas heat. After overcoming a rocky start to their subsequent companionship (one that led to him getting grazed in the arm by a fleeing suspect in a wheelchair) both he and Daniel overcame their differences and grew to make one great tandem.

With a ninety-five percent arrest record, the duo earned a great deal of respect from their department, which is why by default they were assigned to the "Da Mose Def" Records case. But something about their latest murder case really bothered the grim detective. Slowly, Detective Cartwright carefully examined every item on the looming six by six foot bulletin board that stood in front of him. He stroked his bristled salt and pepper colored chin restlessly, while shaking his head in confusion and astonishment. The only thing he began to discover, as he stared intently across the wide array of bloody photographs, was that "Pool Night" might have to be put on an extended hold. Since his transfer to the Sugarland Police Department, he could count the Saturday's he had spent at work and being there felt odd to him for some reason with only half the staff present. His overzealous partner on the other hand, was taking the news of the new case far better than he had expected him too, "Wouldja' believe this fuckin' shit? I mean look at this! Look at that shit!" Detective Michelson yelled from his desk. With his back to him, Detective Cartwright slightly smirked, "Believe what Danny?" Detective Cartwright replied diverted. Without a moment's hesitation, the two-hundred and twenty-five pound Michelson balled up a wad of paper and threw it at the bulletin board, "I'm talkin' about THAT fuckin' shit! Boy did the captain shiv us up the ass with this one…!" Detective Michelson angrily protested. Surprised by his partner's seeming misplaced outburst, the elder detective looked over his shoulder, "Really? How you figure that?" Detective Cartwright asked intrigued. While sitting down in his chair, Detective Michelson hastily scooted up closer to his bewildered looking partner and pointed at the pictures, "Look at ya' fuckin' bill board, Cartwright! What do ya' see? I know what the fuck I see! I see us "wasting time" on a beautiful fuckin' Saturday afternoon on bunch of dead degenerate mafia wannabes!" Detective Michelson said disgusted. Detective Cartwright could not believe what he was hearing, as his eyes were agape as he spoke, "And that makes ALL this shit okay? The hells wrong with you Danny?" Detective Cartwright yelled. He knew his partner long enough to know, that deep down, he did not really mean his nonsensical comment. But it was quite obvious that Danny was not at all happy about the assignment and continued to show his displeasure, "Look, all I'm sayin' is that Young and Mitchell were MORE than capable of handling this piece of shit case! As far as I'm concerned, there ain't nuttin' special about what happened to those assholes! I mean, JESUS Cartwright you read the report….they found enough Ecstasy pills in Jacory Jackson's basement to have gotten me off for the next fifty-years!" Detective Michelson claimed. The senior detective was trying his utmost to fight off the oncoming migraine brought on by his cynical behaving partner, “And your point is, Daniel?” Detective Cartwright asked nauseously, while rubbing his eyes. Detective Michelson sprang up from his chair like an excited life-sized jack in a box, “My point is “detective,” is that Young and Mitchell work “narcotics,” WE (pointing at them both) are “robbery and homicide” and from what we can already tell, there was NO robbery…just tons of fucking drugs! It was their collar to make, so why in the fuck did our “cap” kick this shit down to us?” Detective Michelson protested. His colleague of 10 years was not making much sense and began to slightly irritate him, “Uh hello? Behold…all these fucking dead guys! They ain’t up here posing for playgirl in these pictures, Hence the “blood” and all!” Detective Cartwright snapped. A fuming Detective Michelson threw up his hands in frustration and fell back into his seat like a pouting teenager getting his car privileges revoked, “Jesus Cartwright, I’m not fuckin’ blind. And to your point, yeah, I can SEE that there were a shitload of bodies left at the scene. But you worked in this business long enough to know, that whenever large quantities of drugs are found at a scene, it automatically becomes a “narcotics issue” not an “our” issue…and look, Pres, I get it…none of this fuckin’ shit makes “any” sense. On one hand, you gotta’ crooked and untouchable CEO, along with the rest of his jailbird buddies, looking like they just been cut-down in a cheesy Dolph Lundgren B movie. Then, there’s the weird military style precision of the kills and not to mention, that in the coroner’s report, it claimed that not one dead body was accounted for that didn’t already fuckin’ belong there. So, whoever it was that attacked Big Cory’s “Wonderland” were either bullet proof, or were too damn paranoid to leave any of their own dead guys lying around…and what the fuck they afraid of anyway? It’s not like we can serve the dead guys any warrants!? Either way, the cap should’ve left this bullshit with narcotics!” Detective Michelson concluded, and slammed the drawer in his desk. The seasoned detective worked too many years with his Irish companion to not spot something off with him, “Now just what the hell is this really about, Danny? I mean, on any other day you would have been all over a case like this.” Detective Cartwright curiously asked. Guessing by the thick bags under his eyes, whatever was really bothering his agitated partner was causing him to lose sleep at night, Detective Cartwright hypothesized. He also remembered noticing him pouring liquor into his coffee earlier that same morning, a ritual he rarely partook in, but who was he to judge?

Detective Cartwright thought. Daniel was the closest thing he had to a good friend and he was not going to be satisfied by him dodging his question, "Well, spit it out!" Detective Cartwright demanded. Grudgingly, Detective Michelson closed the manila folder he was writing in and exhaled loudly, dropping his black ballpoint pen on top of it, "Alright…It's about my ex." Detective Michelson replied lowly. Detective Cartwright cut his eyes at him and grinned, "Which ex…the first, or the second one?" Detective Cartwright quipped. His wise-ass remark got the young uptight detective to smirk, "The first one, Brenda…she's getting' remarried…..and to my old partner, if you can believe that shit!? Anyway, she just wanted to be the one to tell me before anybody else from home did and the shit's been eatin' me up ever since! You know, part of me…wanted to jump on a plane to Massachusetts last night and find the both of em' and shove my Beretta down their throats and pull the fuckin' trigger…but then I thought about all the perp's I helped lock away who would've had fun playing pass the bread basket with my delicate little keister! I already got two alimony checks comin' outta' my ass and last thing I need is somebody else's giant ass cock going back in it!" Detective Michelson joked. The generally serious minded Preston Cartwright tried with all his might to prevent himself from blurting out with laughter, "Yeah, I suppose you would have been in a "tight spot." But hey man, didn't you always say you wanted to be in a threesome?" Detective Cartwright joked, and laughed even harder. He watched in disbelief while his partner poked fun at his expense, "Hey fuck you Cartwright! That wasn't the kind of fantasy I had in mind you asshole! Geez, I thought you were supposed to be my fuckin' friend…?" Detective Michelson laughingly replied. "Hey man, I'm with you! Believe me, the "last thing" I want to see is you in lock up wearing plats and barrettes! But seriously, Danny….shouldn't you be considering Brenda's second chance at happiness? I mean…she didn't go all Steven Segal after "you" left "her" for wife number two now, did she? No, she didn't….and yes, I know it's fucked up who she chose to marry, but you really need to ask yourself, after all the shit you done put her through, is it fair to stand in her way? So, as your "friend" I'm telling you, (placing his hand on Daniel's shoulder) to follow your OWN damn advice and move on." Detective Cartwright suggested, and walked over to his desk. As much as he disliked the notion, part of him knew that his partner was speaking the truth, which was one of many virtues the younger detective admired the most about his older wiser comrade.

Although Detective Michelson respected his partner's grand prudence, his pride on the other hand, was reluctant in heeding the message. Maybe he "was" being a little somewhat selfish, Detective Michelson thought. Unfortunately, he realized much too late that Brenda was the best thing that ever happened to him and he knew it was going to be one hell of a hard pill to swallow to finally let her go. Imagining him doing so made the doleful detective become choked up, causing him to clear his throat, "Yeah, ahem…you're probably right. But enough about "my" Goddamn love life, Cartwright…for now, how about we just get back to this lousy case! Besides, I know the way that egghead of yours works and I know you're already working on some kind of angle!?" Detective Michelson playfully assumed. Despite his cheerful facial expression, it was evident that Daniel was having a hard time excepting his loss, but for someone all too familiar on the subject, Detective Cartwright knew the only cure to numb his sorrow would be the magnanimous embrace of time. In his experience, work was also a great distraction for soothing the humbled soul, "As a matter of fact, I'm glad you asked…." Detective Cartwright began, just as his desk phone rang. When he answered the phone, Detective Michelson could tell by his companion's flushing cheekbones and extra cool demeanor, exactly who it was on the opposite side of the phone line, "Ah-h…I see ya,' playa playa!" Detective Michelson quipped. Detective Cartwright frowned and threw a paperclip to quiet him, "Hey! A real man would throw their tongue between her legs! I'm jus' sayin' Pres'…!" Detective Michelson joked once more. The humiliated detective covered the receiver with his hand, "Would you knock it off?!" Detective Cartwright whispered, and went back to his private conversation. A minute later, he hung up the telephone, but had a worried look on his face, "What the fucks wrong with you? You look like somebody just took a big shit in your Fruit Loops." Detective Michelson quipped. His partner's unwelcomed crudeness broke the glazed look in his eyes, "Goddamn Danny, can't you stop acting like a fucking third-grader for five minutes? That was important!" Detective Cartwright yelled. It was more than obvious, to the meandering younger detective, that the sultry Sasha Scottsdale was the primary reason behind his partner's sudden hostile change in attitude, "Let me guess, Sasha just asked you out…again…for like what, the two-hundredth time? Jesus, when is that broad gonna' buy a clue for Christ's sake?" Detective Michelson tiredly replied. Again, Detective Cartwright was starring at Detective Michelson as though he had seen a ghost, "She made us dinner reservations for eight o'clock tonight at some fancy place in midtown, called the Reef?" Detective Cartwright said despondently. He put his pen down and leaned back into his chair and whistled, "Yeah, I know the place….the foods not bad! Broad's got taste. Boy, I guess she wasn't taught to take rejection much as a kid, oh well…what're you going to do?" Detective Michelson asked concerned, and picked up his Boston Celtics coffee mug. The stoic looking detective shook his head befuddled, "I don't know…I told her, I'd try and make it...but…I don't know if I'm ready…for that….ready for her?! Dammit Danny, she's just a kid!" Detective Cartwright protested worriedly. His co-worker's audacious statement caused the younger detective to spit out his coffee, "Some fuckin' kid!? That woman's ass sticks out far enough to sit my coffee mug on, for cryin' out loud! You know…I don't know what constitutes as a "kid" in that highly educated brain of yours, but out here in the real world, "thirty-years-old" ain't exactly robbing the fuckin' cradle! So, you can chill out with your odd "geo-semantics" about which age group can date who…cause technically, that's bullshit! She's a grown ass woman that knows who and what she wants and likes, Pres! You said I should be fair to Brenda, by giving her a second chance at happiness….but what about you? Why don't you deserve one? I know you really like her, so the least you could do is not stand her up tonight." Detective Michelson pleaded. For the first time, over the last ten years he had known his good friend, did he seriously consider his suggestion, "Okay, I'll go…but, only dinner… nothing else." Detective Cartwright replied. Detective Michelson thought he was about to fall out of his chair when he heard the words, "Seriously? You're not fuckin' with me, are you?" Detective Michelson asked excitedly. The senior detective politely smiled and shook his head, "No…I'll do it." Detective Cartwright concluded. An excited Detective Michelson put his coffee mug down and stood up and reached across their adjourning desks and shook his partner's hand, as if he just won a sweepstakes with Publisher' Clearing House, "Well, alright Carty!" Detective Michelson shouted. But before any celebration could begin, there was another piece of valuable information that the elder detective had yet to discuss with his gleeful confidant, "There's something else that she said, concerning the case, Daniel..." Detective Cartwright said grimly. His anomalous tone did not sit well with the younger detective, "Okay then…spit it out!" Detective Michelson said brazenly. Just as Detective Cartwright was about to disclose with him what he and Sasha discovered, their department's captain, Victor Valladores, was making his way from his private office to check on their progress, "So, guys where are you with the Jackson case? You have any solid leads yet?" Captain Valladores asked frantically. It was odd hearing their usually calm and collected minded captain sound so uncharacteristically dire, Detective Cartwright thought. Detective Michelson closed the file on his desk and leaned back in his chair, "Nothing "Earth-shattering," boss. But, from what we can tell, this looks and smells like a highly organized hit of some kind…." Detective Michelson said. On key, his partner followed him up, "At first, we assumed it may have been a drug deal gone south, but since none of the drugs found at the facility "don't appear" stolen, we can obviously rule that one out..." Detective Cartwright interjected. "…plus, Jacory Jackson was shot in the head at close range…which my gut's telling me cap, that whatever happened there last night…might have been about something personal." Detective Michelson concluded. The five-foot-eleven Captain Valladores stood quietly as he crossed his arms contemplating his detective's findings, "Okay…are there any actual witnesses from the scene who can verify that? How about the attackers themselves, did they leave anyone behind that we can possibly identify through our criminal data base? What about a motive?" Captain Valladores asked. Detective Michelson lounged out of his seat as if it were full of hot needles, "See that's the fuckin' thing cap, these guys didn't leave diddly-squat! Ballistics is still running a check on the electronics found at the shipping and receiving dock, but we're sure they'll come back negative for prints. Whoever these guys are though, were well-organized enough to launch an all-out assault, not five miles from a gated community, without so much as one phone call for disturbing the peace!" Detective Michelson confirmed. Detective Cartwright looked up from some case reports he was reading and snickered, "Yeah, turns out it wasn't that uncommon for the neighbors to hear "fireworks," even late at night during the month of October….go figure." Detective Cartwright groaned. Although it was not the news that he hoped to hear, the tense Captain Valladores still believed in their investigative prowess, "Either way, you guys keep digging…I don't care if Jacory Jackson "was" a piece of shit, "nobody" pulls that crap in our city! Boogie men or not, I want some answers!" Captain Valladores demanded. Detective Cartwright's eyes bulged in their sockets and stood to his feet and flashing the report he was reading earlier, "Bingo! I think we just found our first lead! Approximately two days ago, around the same time, the same thing happened across town to a pimp/drug pusher named Romelle Hatchette and before him again in Las Vegas, to some jive-ass activist named Calvin Rusher, who was secretly running a slave farm full of kids. It's all right here, the same M.O. and everything, even right down to their gun preferences!" Detective Cartwright said excitedly. But before the dazed Detective Michelson could get it in his hands decently, Captain Valladores immediately snatched the report from him, (ignoring what just happened) "Cartwright you son of bitch! I KNEW you were fuckin' holdin' out on me!" Detective Michelson yelled happily, while pointing at him. Captain Valladores was both surprised and relieved, "Jesus, Cartwright where did you find this?" Captain Valladores asked shocked. Detective Cartwright had eased back over to the giant bulletin board with the crime scene photographs, "I called in a favor this morning and asked a friend from HPD to send me anything out of the ordinary they had concerning any current mass killings. Come to find out, they were just as confounded as we were, that is until they found out about the Calvin Rusher case. The uh…"guys" in the crime lab, also confirmed that the ammunition used in the previous two mass killings were a "complete match" with most of the ammunition used on the victims from last night's onslaught!" Detective Cartwright said bleakly. Surprised by his partner's impressive discoveries, a livid Detective Michelson was taken aback by him sitting on the information, "So when the fuck were you planning on sharin' all of this shit with me, Sherlock? Here I've been watching you staring at that fucking thing all day, as if you're putting together some high school scrapbook, or sumthin…!" Detective Michelson angrily shouted. Captain Valladores closed the report and handed it back to the agitated detective, "It really doesn't matter, detective." Captain Valladores replied. He glanced over the papers in his hands for a moment, "Oh yeah, well it fuckin' matters to me…." Detective Michelson shouted, and threw the report across his desk. His subordinate's undermining tone did not sit well with the already vexed official, "You watch yourself detective…" Captain Valladores warned. But before the passionate detective could fire back another response,

"Would you two knock it off! Now....I had to be sure, which I wasn't, at least not until five minutes ago "after" getting confirmation from the crime lab. But here "is' what I'm able to gather: What we are dealing with here, Captain, "isn't" about some randomized hit, or a retaliation tactic." Detective Cartwright cryptically explained, while stroking his chin. The puzzled Captain Valladores felt an unnerving sensation trickling down the base of his neck and struggled to clear his throat after swallowing. Confused by his partner's outrageously sounding claim, the intrigued younger detective challenged his theory, "So what're you saying, Cartwright? I mean...how in the hell could it not be?" Detective Michelson asked befuddled, while leaning on his desk with his fists. He turned around to face them with his arms folded tightly, "How about we start with the fact that everybody who's already "dead" were considered highly regarded "career" criminals..." Detective Cartwright began before interrupted. Detective Michelson giggled to himself, "Well, ain't "that" clearly stating the fuckin' obvious!?" Detective Michelson interjected jokingly. His outburst perturbed the fifty-five-year old captain, "Alright, that's ENOUGH out of you, Michelson...but, in all honesty Cartwright, I have to agree!?" Captain Valladores replied mystified. Hardly surprised by his co-workers penchant for moments of ineptitude, the anxious Detective Cartwright could only frown disappointedly, as he went to retrieve the report his partner threw a second ago, "Look...EXCUSE me, (staring face to face to the belligerent acting Detective Michelson, who was unknowingly leaning on the report) ...it's all right here in the report! (Michelson throwing up his hands without protest, while moving out of his way) In all the cases, after all these..."attacks," the only thing that was "allowed" to be left unblemished was what the so-called "victims" were hiding. (Flipping a page) Take Calvin Rusher for instance, after his place was raided, the police found at least "40" missing children who were on the F.B.I.'s top missing person's list. Then Romelle Hachette, who was hoarding a group of drugged up under-aged prostitutes, before getting decapitated in the privacy of his own damn panic room, and now....Jacory Jackson. The bad news, Captain, is that there may be "others" we still haven't found out about yet, but one thing remains consistent in "all" these cases.... that it seems that the killers "wanted" the police to find out what "they" already knew." Detective Cartwright confirmed, dropping the report back on top of Michelson's desk. The severity in the seasoned detective's tone bothered the beleaguered captain, "Which is?" Captain Valladores asked. Without fail, the younger detective finished his older associate's sentence, "That they were "all" guilty." Detective Michelson replied solemnly. "Holy SHIT....vigilantes? HERE? Jesus Christ, Cartwright!!! Are you sure?!" Captain Valladores asked worriedly. Detective Cartwright casually walked back toward his bulletin board, "As sure as I am that the day is long, as they used to say." Detective Cartwright concluded. Suddenly, it was as if the very room itself had gone deftly quiet.

When he got up out bed this morning, after a peaceful night's sleep, "vigilante" was the last word Captain Valladores expected to hear come out of his mouth when he came in to work today. It was not like things were not already bad enough on the streets with people committing ordinary crimes, but with the possibility of a group of sociopaths loose on his city, meant some heads were going to role in their department, Captain Valldores suspected. (Rubbing his face) "Okay...okay, okay, okay." Captain Valladores said nervously. Both detectives turned and looked at their odd behaving superior as he ran his hand threw his hair uneasily, "Good job...the both of you. But, we're gonna' have to sit on this thing... that is, at least until we can get some more confirmation. The Chief's already nipping at my ass-crack as it is behind all this shit and the last thing I want to do is start sounding off any false alarms! So, you guys do what you have to do and find me some suspects!" Captain Valladores replied. Their captain quickly bolted off to his office and slammed the door behind him. Both detectives had worked together long enough to already know what the other was thinking when they stared at each other. Detective Michelson giggled and shook his head and sat down at his desk, "Boy, the cap really needs to get those hemorrhoids under control, before he fucks around and gives birth to a ten pound ulcer!" Detective Michelson quipped. A smiling Detective Cartwright resumed his mental chronicling of the gruesome crime scene photos, only this time much more slowly. Due to his new discovery, Detective Cartwright knew none of them could afford to leave one stone unturned, "Hey Cartwright, why don't cha give your friggin' eyes a break will ya? I'm sure your cataracts would appreciate it!" Detective Michelson playfully remarked. But the diligent senior detective would not hear of it, "Don't worry about me, Danny-boy, I can do this all ni...." Detective Cartwright said, before going catatonic mid sentence. When the articulate detective's voice stopped abruptly, a mystified Detective Michelson looked up from his paperwork, "Carty? You alright bro….?" Detective Michelson asked concerned. But when his partner failed to acknowledge him, he instantly got up from his desk and approached him, "Hey Press…hey Press man, you alright in there?" Detective Michelson asked stealthily. The motionless detective finally broke his spell and had a look of dread in his eyes when he turned to face his partner, "Confusion now hath made his masterpiece…." Detective Cartwright quoted. His puzzling behavior was beginning to worry the brazen detective, "The fucks wrong wit' you today?" Detective Michelson asked agitated. Without saying a word, the stoic detective casually walked over to Michelson's desk and grabbed the report and handed him it to him, "Its William Shakespeare…" Detective Cartwright explained. Although he was merely stating a quote, his unrefined comrade mistook his suggestion literally, "You saying Shakespeare's responsible for doin' all of this?" Detective Michelson asked annoyed. Exhausted by his colleague's limited cultural knowledge, the veteran detective dared to explain his point, "No, what I'm saying is tha…oh never mind that, just turn to the last damn page!" Detective Cartwright instructed, and took down two crime scene photos off the busy bulletin board. When Detective Michelson turned to the final page, it was of a copy of one of the crime scene photos taken from the Romelle Hatchette murder case, "Alright, so what am I looking for in this dead dirt-bag's "not-so-safe" room…other than him doing a Headless Horseman impression?" Detective Michelson quipped. Look, in the background…over on the far wall…" Detective Cartwright insisted. Despite the roll his clever partner had been on, part of him was beginning to believe he may have been overextending himself, "Come on Carty, there's nothing here, just a bunch of this wrack job's blood splatter…" Detective Michelson began nonchalantly, before his partner merged the two photographs in his hands together. To further convince his skeptic companion, he then held the two photographs next to the picture in Detective Michelson's hands, "I don't know about that….cause the last time I checked…blood splatter doesn't "draw" patterns, my friend." Detective Cartwright concluded. What was mistaken for common blood splatter on Jacory Jackson's office wall was in fact a spray painted drawing of the letter "R," much like the one he found in the Romelle Hatchette crime scene photo. His findings elated the staggered detective, (Bumping him on the arm with his elbow) "Holy SHIT, Press! How the fuck did you catch that?" Detective Michelson asked excitedly. "Jesus Daniel, It's not like I “haven't been” spending the whole damn day looking for it!? And besides, “this” only confirms what we already knew!” Detective Cartwright said warily. He went and had a seat back at his desk leaving the confused Michelson standing at the bulletin board scratching his head, “Which is…Mr. Encyclopedia Brown?” Detective Michelson asked jokingly. A very weary Detective Cartwright composed himself then looked his friend of 10 years directly in his eyes, “That there's somebody hurting out there and they're highly pissed off at the way we're doing our job. And whoever he is, hates criminals “more” than the police do.” Detective Cartwright said. He contemplated his statement for a moment, but the analytical side of him knew there was a little more to his claim, “And…” Detective Michelson asked, while winding his hand in the air. Detective Cartwright exhaled deeply, “And…who, probably has the resources to hire highly trained killers, possibly mercenaries, to conduct this war…” Detective Cartwright surmised. In his mind, use of the term “war” to loosely describe what was happening on their city streets sounded a bit contrived, even for someone as intelligent as his partner, “War, Carty?” Detective Michelson asked laxly, sitting down at his desk. He clasped his hands together on top of his desk and slowly leaned in, “Make no mistake, Danny…all this shit we been finding, here, in Houston…Las Vegas? All this is just the opening act. Yeah, give it some time. These so-called “vigilantes,” they've been meticulously working their way up the criminal food chain for God knows how long and probably won't stop until they reach their final end game!” Detective Cartwright warned. It took a lot to rattle the Boston native, but his partner's candid remark was enough to bring him slight pause, causing him to lose taste for his spiked coffee, “So, what do ya' think that is? You know…their end game?” Detective Michelson asked tensely. Without needing to take a moment's hesitation, the seasoned detective offered a simple synopsis, “…Carnage....” Detective Cartwright grimly concluded, and then quietly excused himself to confer with their captain in his office.

Later on that same evening, at St. La' Croix's Seafood Bar and Grill Restaurant…

The minute Thomas Jr.'s tattered shoes hit the pavement outside of Lacy's lavish SUV, his nose was instantaneously entrenched with immense and familiar aromas that reminded him of his late wife Lucinda's cooking. Lacy gave the young valet attendant in the front a generous tip and they made their way inside. Since their table was reserved, it did not take long before they were promptly seated on the patio of the extremely busy restaurant. The atmosphere was quaint on the seven hundred square foot patio, unlike the loud and dimly lit inside portion of the burgeoning restaurant. Without further ado, Lacy ordered an expensive bottle of Moet, which was champagne he had not enjoyed since his days working as a Hampton University's AD. It was at his brother's constant urging that he agreed to a private dinner between just him and Terry's significant other, Lacy Spencer, who appeared more nervous than his herculean frame would seem to indicate, the quiet spoken reverend noticed. He also could not help but notice the amount of attention his well groomed escort was drawing from the crowd of people. Despite his jet black sports coat, blue jeans, and snake-skinned boots, Lacy's incredible muscles were still on full display for the ladies in attendance. Thomas Jr. snickered to himself at the thought of their chances with his brother's "undercover" stallion. They had not talked much since his arrival in Houston, so Terry thought a nice intimate dinner between the two would be just the "ice-breaker" for them to get to know one another. Before the main course arrived, they mostly passed the time with basic small talk about how he and Terry met and the many struggles they had endured to conceal their "complicated" affections, while serving in a non-openly diverse Navy, many years ago. Regardless of what his own religious beliefs may have been, Thomas Jr. could not help but smile proudly for hearing how far his once aggressively minded little brother had come, despite being on his own. Thomas Jr. knew in his heart, that had their father been still around (and not the asshole phantom version of him) he too would have been very impressed, if not pleased with how well Terry's life turned out….at least, with the parts that did not involve Terry being with a man twice his size. He learned that Lacy received his hulking frame from competing as an amateur body builder while in the service and eventually, became a personal trainer afterwards. When asked how someone who was so well in-tuned with physical fitness could fall for such a nervous eater like his rotund brother, Lacy eagerly directed the blame at Terry's heart as the cause. Lacy emphatically explained to him that despite his brother's outer flaws, the man he fell in love with had a priceless soul of an angel that meant more to him than how many pushups he could do. As a reverend, Thomas Jr. was not allowed to condone what he and his brother did behind closed doors, but as Terry's older brother, Thomas Jr. could not imagine a better soul-mate for his fortunate sibling. After their waitress finally arrived with the main course, both men put their chit chat on hold to savor and appreciate the brilliantly cooked gourmet feast that adorned the table in front of them.

It had been ages since the much maligned reverend from Ben Hill enjoyed such an incredible meal, much less had the appetite to finish one. Since his ordeal with the vicious Sonny Korne, any type of food was almost next to impossible for him to keep down, but for whatever reason, his mind was actually starting to feel at ease being around his new surroundings. Their waitress was a young slender red headed Caucasian woman named Janet, who had been on point with her service, and soon had brought out an entire double-layered strawberry topped cheesecake for them to devour. Due to his strict diet constraints, Lacy often avoided eating sweets like the black plague, but he decided to make the generous sacrifice just this once to celebrate their (Thomas Jr. and Terry's) reunion. When she was done cutting their individual slices of the mouth watering appearing cheesecake, the ambitious minded waitress stood at attention for Lacy' next instruction, "Will that be all Mr. Spencer?" Janet asked politely. Lacy thought hard for a fraction of a second before he answered, "Uh-h-h…no, I believe we're good!" Lacy said. She grinned widely and clasped her hands together jovially, "Awesome! Well, I hope you gentlemen have enjoyed your meal and your service!? I will be back in a moment with your check!" Janet happily replied. Lacy smiled back at the enthusiastic waitress, "That would be great! And yes, the food was off the chain! Don't you agree, Thomas?" Lacy intrigued. Thomas Jr. had a mouth full of cheesecake and had not been aware of their conversation, "Huh? Y-Yeah…yes, yes the food was damn good. Thank you!" Thomas Jr. muttered. Lacy chuckled lowly, "Ahem, well…there you have it! The service was top notch as well, as usual!" Lacy confirmed. Instantly the young waitress's cheeks filled with blood, "Why thank you, Mr. Spencer! I'll be right back with your total!" Janet replied gleefully, and quickly withdrew herself from the patio area. Soon after the waitress left, Lacy began quietly observing the famished Thomas Jr. who was already on his second piece of the towering cheesecake. He thought about the long conversation both he and Terry had that first night after Thomas. Jr. first arrived and could not even imagine the ordeal he had gone through. Even had he not known Terry and had heard Thomas Jr.'s story from someone else, part of him would have still felt sorry for the downtrodden reverend. Instead of him poking the sleeping bear, Lacy decided to let his and Terry's intensions be known, "Uh, Thomas…I just want you to know…how much I "appreciate" you…you know, flying all the way down here at the last minute and all. It really…it really took some courage on Terry's part to make that call and quite honestly, I can't remember the last time I've seen my man this happy!" Lacy said excitedly. Thomas Jr. continued to slowly chomp away at his cheesecake in silence, while curiously trying to figure out where Lacy' conversation was going, "Right. So…uh, me and Terry have been thinking, you know…since you're family and all…thinking that maybe….maybe you should move in with us…you know, down here!?" Lacy gingerly concluded. Thomas Jr. could hardly swallow his desert anymore and put his fork down. His eyes became fixated on Lacy,' as if he were trying to psychically burrow through his mind for something that might have told him otherwise, "Just like that, huh?" Thomas Jr. asked unconvinced. When he and Terry spoke on the subject earlier that day, Lacy anticipated some resistance, especially after being previously warned about his brother's stubborn ways. But as a fulltime court appointed bailiff, dealing with obstinate behavior was a part of his everyday job, "Just like that! And we're not taking "no" for an answer!" Lacy insisted, and proceeded to cut himself a thin slice of the delicious looking desert. Initially, Thomas Jr. was overwhelmed by the gesture, but part of him still had his share of doubts, "And what about my son? I got responsibilities…the both of you can't really expect me to just "up" and…" Thomas Jr. began, before getting interrupted. "Of course we don't! Markus, when he does recover, is ALSO welcome. (Putting his fork down) Look, Thomas…I'm not going to sit up here and pretend like I don't know what you've gone through, but I can sure as HELL tell you, that you don't have to go through it ALONE anymore! Let us HELP you, I mean…when your son does finally wake up, you're gonna' need all the support you can get and we just want to be there for you both! So please, Thomas, at least for Markus' sake….allow us this chance. I promise that you won't regret it!" Lacy pleaded. In the back of his thought provoking mind, Thomas Jr. knew that Lacy had a good point. While he was more hopeful of the prospect of Markus waking from his lengthy sleep, his doctors on the other hand, were not too reassuring of that possibility, Thomas Jr. recollected. There were no changes in his condition since the last time he called his nurse friend Linda and checked in on him. For a brief moment, he began to second-guess turning down the deal Harlan propositioned him at his home a mere days ago. But how was he going to live with himself knowing he accepted blood money just to save his son's life? Thomas Jr. pondered. It still was bothering him that Harlan pried into his personal life and also went behind his back to settle his hospital debts. Since it was virtually impossible for the hospital to refund him Harlan's money, Thomas Jr. banned all "new" incoming coma specialists from operating on his son without his consent. Harlan's so-called "generosity" came at a great moral price, in which he tried to leverage his son's health in exchange for playing a part in exacting out his twisted schemes, Thomas Jr. hypothesized. For all intents and purposes, he staunchly believed Harlan was completely insane, but the wary reverend was in full agreement with the eccentric entrepreneur when he said that justice had "failed" them all. In the eyesight of the Lord, none of them had the right to actually take someone else's life, no matter how dastardly the person's deeds were, at least, that was what he was trying to convince himself to believe. Regardless of his Christianity, Thomas Jr. knew he would only be lying to no one but himself, had he said Sonny Korne did not deserve to be put down. Nothing would please him more than to cock back the barrel of Kale's massive .357 Magnum and slowly blow the racist bastard's head clean off his shoulders, but he…the "preacher" was "supposed" to have been ABOVE all that type of thinking, Thomas Jr. contemplated. Although he did his best to follow the doctrine of the Holy Bible and preached the gospel of Jesus Christ, Thomas Jr. realized the hard way that at the end of the day, he was merely just a man. But as a man, didn't his feeling ever account for anything? Thomas Jr. pondered. When Harlan was busy playing devil's advocate, he brought up a lot of the same things that he was either feeling, or questioning about his place with God and worried if Harlan may have been right all along, Thomas Jr. feared. Whatever the future may have held for him and his son, part of him could not shake the feeling that they were somehow caught in the middle of something else…some kind of spiritual warfare and the ultimate prize were their immortal souls, "Yo' Thomas? You cool man? You look like something else's on your mind." Lacy asked concerned. Thomas Jr. waved him off, "Naw-w-w, man…I'm good. Just taking my time…you know, processing everything. After all, you did give a brother a lot to chew on….literally and figuratively! But you and Terry been real good to me, thank you….and I suppose, maybe we 'could" you know….work something out." Thomas Jr. said happily. Without warning, Lacy slammed his hand down on top of the dinner table so hard and fast, that he startled Thomas Jr. enough to drop his fork, "That's what I'm talking about! So you're really down? Lacy asked excitedly. Thomas Jr. was holding his heart, "Only if you promise NOT to slap that damn heavy ass hand of yours down again, as if we in the middle of some damn domino game…but yes, I'LL "consider" it! This place ain't exactly (sticking his finger into his clerical collar) collar friendly, but for Markus and Terry….I'm willing to overlook it." Thomas Jr. confidently replied. The rugged Lacy Spencer smiled as brightly as a Yankee Stadium light bulb, "Well alright!!!" Lacy replied elatedly. Lacy put his hand out across the table to shake Thomas Jr.'s and without waste an instant, the humbled reverend eagerly obliged him. There was an overwhelming glimpse of sincerity in his eyes that was not there during their initial meeting when they shook hands, which caused Thomas Jr. to wonder what "all" did Terry disclose about him. Suddenly, Lacy's cell phone began to ring. When he looked at the name of the caller, he appeared genuinely surprised to the intrigued reverend, "Hum-m-m…I wonder what's this is about? Excuse me, Thomas…this should only take me a minute….hello?" Lacy said confidently, into the phone's receiver. His eye-brows stood up in the middle of his shiny forehead, as if they were black curtains being drawn at the beginning of a stage play, Thomas Jr. noticed. The conversation was brief, but whatever it was that Lacy and the person on the opposite end of the phone line were discussing sounded bleak. Lacy hung up the line and shook his head in amazement, "Everything alright?" Thomas Jr. tentatively asked, as he continued to enjoy his desert. Lacy had been so distracted by the person's news he almost forgot where he was, "Huh? Oh, sorry Thomas, that was just work! It's no big deal, really!" Lacy confirmed, and picked up his fork. Unfortunately, that was not the impression the wise reverend got judging from his tone, "You sure about that? Cause it sounded like a big deal to me…what happened? The gym not revoking your membership, are they?" Thomas Jr. quipped. Thomas Jr.'s wise-cracking remark made Lacy laugh, "You know what…your brother did warn me that you were a smart-ass! But anyway, that wasn't the gym calling. That was my "co-worker" calling from the courthouse. Look, I don't know what all YOU know about "rap music," but he told me that Jacory Jackson, you know…the C.E.O of "Da Mose Dope Records," was found murdered in his office sometime late last night…" Lacy said astonished. Despite not having a clue about what record label Lacy was referring too, something about the name he mentioned did sound vaguely familiar for some odd reason, "Jacory Jackson?" Thomas Jr. replied confounded. Thomas Jr. was at the most, a decade older than he was, so it did not surprise him when the out of touch reverend had a stoical reaction to his news, "Yeah, Jacory Jackson! Everyone in hip hop and Rand B called him "Big Cory" for short. He used to be one "crazy ass" dude…but off the record, I'm glad he's gone. And I know what you're probably thinking, being a preacher and all, but trust me when I say, the world is "better off" with THAT "street trash" gone!" Lacy concluded. Judging from Lacy' harsh tone, the somewhat recognizable man he spoke of was obviously not a very pleasant person, Thomas Jr. figured. But like an unexpected kick to the head, the whereabouts from which he frightfully remembered first hearing the name "Jacory Jackson" popped into his brain like a needle through a busted balloon. It was back in Harlan's office when the young football player, Jovan Campbell, was shouting and Agent Elliot was reading his profile. He remembered it was "Jacory Jackson" who was the man that ran over Jovan's little girl and was also one of Harlan's primary targets. Thomas Jr. The memory of it all upset his stomach so, that it caused him to wince in pain loudly, "Hey Thomas you alright bro?" Lacy asked as he sprang up from his chair. Out of fear, Thomas Jr. tried to compose himself as quickly as he could, (holding his hand out) "N-No, I-I'm f-fine…just ate… j-just ate too m-much damn cheesecake…is all! Y-You know what they s-say…too much dairy…w-will kill ya'!" Thomas Jr. replied frantically. Unsure, Lacy caught the attention of their waitress and called her over to bring him the check. Despite worrying about Thomas Jr. having any more spasms Lacy took his seat, "Okay, but I'm not taking the blame for bringing you back sick! Desert "is" done." Lacy insisted, and slid Thomas Jr.'s plate away from him. He then closed out his tab and they went to the valet area to give the attendant Lacy' ticket to get his SUV.

During the long drive home, Thomas Jr. could not have been more pleased that they were spending their time talking about sports and not the Jacory Jackson shooting. Although he was not present for Jackson's murder, Thomas Jr. still had prior knowledge to a crime in which he did nothing to stop, a fact that was not sitting well with the nervous preacher. Lacy's surprising, if not extensive knowledge of all things sports related, was refreshing to the beleaguered reverend who had almost forgotten he was gay man who was living with his brother. The car ride was running smoothly, until Lacy suddenly turned up the volume on his car radio. Unfortunately, one of the hosts of a sports radio station was making an important announcement about the death of C.E.O. Jacory "Big Cory" Jackson of "Da' Mose Def" Records. Disgusted, Thomas Jr. cursed underneath his breath and stared out his passenger window in disdain, as the lady host continued her broadcast, "Although, details on "why" the feared music mogul (along with well-over a dozen of his own personal bodyguards) were found murdered are still sketchy…police did say: they discovered over several hundred pounds of Ecstasy and other drug paraphernalia, hidden in a massive storage basement of the notorious C.E.O.'s Sugarland headquarters…." The host said. Lacy turned the radio volume back down and celebrated with a fist pump in the air, as if his favorite basketball team just scored on a last minute basket. While in the mist of him reveling in Jacory Jackson's murder, Lacy did not notice the fright that was splashed across Thomas Jr.' face as he watched him. It was already painfully obvious how he felt when Lacy uttered the words "better off" and "street trash" back at the restaurant, but seeing him rejoicing so fervently over Jackson's death, caused Thomas Jr. to wonder if something deeper may have been going on, "Wow, Lace, you must really do hate that man...care to share what he did to you?" Thomas Jr. asked. Lacy stopped smiling and looked at Thomas Jr. with a puzzled look on his face, as if he had forgotten that someone else was even in the car, "W-Wha…me? Nah…I "did" hate him, yes, but he didn't do "anything" to me!" Lacy replied confidently. Thomas Jr. took a second to close his eyes and exhaled, "Okay, then…who'd HE do "it" too? And don't try to tell me no one, or you wouldn't be in here acting like you just won money on a bet!" Thomas Jr. said. Lacy snickered to himself and rolled his eyes at Thomas Jr., as if he were fascinated by a rancid looking abstract painting, "You ARE a stubborn S.O.B.! Look, I meant what I said, when I told you it wasn't "me" he did something to…it was my best friend's little brother, Ronald Threat. That phone call I got from work, back at the restaurant, well that was from Ronald's big brother Rodney. Anyway, Ronald was what you would call a "small-time" Philly hustler, that is, until he got locked up. In jail is where he met his soon to be boss, Big Cory, who was so-called "protecting him" on the inside. But, soon after Ronald got paroled, he went back to his first love, which was rap and went by the name of "Rogah-that." Eventually, Ronald got himself a record deal with a rap and Rand B label, called "Backdough" Records. But while his first album was busy breaking records and his concerts being sold out, Ronald's managers at "Backdough" were cheating him out of his royalties. Rodney told me that his brother kind of "looked up" to "Big Cory" and knew he had the right "connects" to help him get out of his contract problems. Well, next thing you know, Jacory Jackson goes from running gangs in prison, to running his own recording label….but, with most of "Backdough" Records own artists. At the time, things looked like they were going great for Ronald. He had the number one rap album in the country, big house in the suburbs, pretty girls, and more cars than any "one" person could ever need, until he realized he just simply traded one slave master in for another…" Lacy confirmed. For a brief moment, it seemed as if his mind had drifted off to another place in time. Thomas Jr. was starting to get a good sense from where all the animosity concerning the late C.E.O. began, but had yet to completely understand the "why." Clearly, Jacory Jackson was no saint, especially considering he once went to jail for killing a three year old child and judging from all the drugs the police found at his headquarters, Big Cory was apparently producing more than just "albums" for the streets, Thomas Jr. figured. With all that being said, the curious reverend figured there had been more to the Lacy's story than mere hatred for Big Cory's underhanded business practices, "So-o-o…what you're telling me is, Big Cory deserved to die…because he was a drug pushing cheapskate?" Thomas Jr. asked confused. Lacy immediately pulled over on the side of the road and whipped his wide body around to face Thomas Jr., "What I'm saying, Thomas, is that that piece of shit Jacory Jackson is not only responsible for the murder of my best friend's brother Ronald, but also my niece Angela, who was just at the wrong place at the wrong damn time!" Lacy confessed. And there it was finally, the truth, sprawled out in front of them, like some hefty-sized comforter blanketing the thickness that was now filling the air between them. Lacy had been bottling up his guilt very much like he did, after what happened to him and his family back in Georgia, Thomas Jr. thought. He grabbed hold of the steering wheel, as if he were imagining twisting the neck off a Thanksgiving turkey, "I let my little niece talk me into it. She…she really wanted to meet Ronald, and I told her…I told her that I worked with his big brother down at the courthouse. Angela was so excited. So, I convinced Rodney to set everything up, so he could meet her and maybe get his autograph, you know…but….I didn't know! I didn't know about Ronald's financial issues with Big Cory, who he had been avoiding for weeks out of spite. Anyway, I brought my niece to his studio to eventually meet him, but as soon as I left to go to the bathroom, three hooded men….they kidnapped Ronald AND Angela. My sister, she was a hollering mess after I called and told her. They both went missing for weeks, until one day a stranger, who was innocently out looking for buried treasure with his metal detector, stumbled across two decomposed bodies out in the middle of the woods….it was them. The "coroner's report" said that Ronald had been both bludgeoned and stabbed to death with what may have been a gun handle and a hunting knife. His…"penis" had been sawed off and placed into his own mouth. They…they basically tortured him for days before they finally got tired of playing with him, and then slit his throat. My poor Angela…she…they…they tore her to shreds. She had been beaten and raped repeatedly. Those…those evil motherfuckers…they removed her tongue and even cut off one of her breasts. Angela used to have the prettiest, if not the longest hair, I ever seen on a black girl her age...but when they found her body…her head was completely shaven, possibly to shame her. The cops questioned "Big Cory" first about his involvement, since it was rumored he and Rogah-that were having problems. But he claimed he was out of town on a business trip to Puerto Rico. That bold bastard had the nerve to say he was "breaking in new talent" and considering opening up a "meat market" there in San Juan! His alibi checked out of course…but everybody knew. So, if you ask me if I'm glad that those guys finally "popped" that piece of shit, then yeah…I'm HIGHLY satisfied!" Lacy concluded emphatically and started up his SUV. He quickly sped off from the shoulder of the busy road, but was eerily silent while he drove. Part of him wanted to kick himself for prying so into Lacy's personal life, but what kind of friend would he have been had he not at least tried to get him to open up? Thomas Jr. wondered. But the last thing the apologetic reverend wanted to do was upset him after the great evening they had hanging out together, "My apologies…I didn't…I had no idea. I'm so very sorry, for your loss." Thomas Jr. replied humbly. Lacy looked at Thomas Jr. oddly, "How could you know? Hell, you didn't even know I even existed then. Either way bro, I'm cool! Anyway, that's what family supposed to do for each other, right?" Lacy confirmed and stuck his fist out for Thomas Jr. to hit it. Though still somewhat unsure, Thomas Jr. slightly hesitated, but ultimately did likewise and they bumped them together in unison, "Now that's what I'm talking about…" Lacy said happily.

They were but a few minutes away from their subdivision, when Thomas Jr. was replaying Lacy' words back from their previous discussion and it got him wondering if the police knew more than what they were letting on. Lacy was back in a good mood and the last thing the inquisitive reverend wanted to do was possibly spoil it, "I don't want to beat a dead horse, but earlier you said something about how glad you were "those guys" popped Big Cory…who was it that you think did it?"Thomas Jr. asked warily. Lacy looked at him and frowned for a brief second, "Does it really matter, Thomas? I mean….somebody's already out there solving the problem." Lacy said unapologetically. When they pulled through the gate, Lacy could easily see the concern all over Thomas Jr.' weary face, "Alright…now what I'm about to tell you don't even leave the car. I mean not even Terry can know..." Lacy insisted. After parking the freshly washed SUV in the spacious three car garage, Lacy waited for confirmation of autonomy from the anxious reverend, "Okay?" Lacy asked stringently. Thomas Jr. immediately shook his head in compliance, "Well…this may turn out to be just all "bullshit," but a friend of a friend who works out of the Sugarland Police Department, overheard the lead detectives on the case….and they believe that a group of vigilantes might have did it…In fact, they think they're responsible for taking out quite a few major lowlife's like Jacory Jackson!" Lacy said excitedly. Suddenly, it felt like all the blood in his body shot up past his neck and to up to the middle of his forehead all at once, causing the worried reverend to grimace in pain once again, only this time Thomas Jr. turned his face toward the passenger window to conceal his discomfort. In the back of his mind, he knew it would only be a matter of time before someone would have caught on to the eccentric Harlan Kruellar's antics. Thomas Jr. could not help but wonder how much longer before the authorities managed to gather them all up. Nevertheless, whatever shame or insecurities Lacy may have had before when broaching the subject of murder in front of him, appeared to be all but gone now, Thomas Jr. felt. It was also surprising to him that Lacy, who was a courtroom appointed bailiff, almost sounded "relieved" that Harlan's group was illegally taking the law into their own hands, "And you're good with that?" Thomas Jr. implied bewildered. Lacy exhaled loudly, as if he were catching his breath after making a long sprint on an Olympic track, "I'm not saying that I'm "condoning murder," but do I honestly feel SORRY about what happened to "Jacory Jackson?" He-e-e-ell naw! And why should I? ....Because the church said so? (Lacy pointed his hand at Thomas Jr.) I might not have been to as much church as you and your brother, but even "I" know God never said I HAD to! Look, I'm going to level with you Thomas....you know, just as well as I do, about the monsters out there who know how to beat the system…and with all due respect to the law, it never seems to be enough. Yeah, I know that it may sound crazy, coming from a cop, but when I start to think about all those missing children that were saved back in Las Vegas…" Lacy said before getting interrupted. "Missing children?" Thomas Jr. asked confused. Lacy smacked his lips displeasingly and gave him a sideways stare, "Man, don't you watch the news? Yeah, it's like I said before, our "connect" across town believes the guys who popped Jackson, were the same ones who just freed a bunch of kids who were being sold into slave labor and also saved a group of underage prostitutes after that! So, if there are people out there, who're "trying" to make a difference, the LAST damn thing I'm going to do is stand in their way!" Lacy said, and took his keys out of the ignition. He then got out of the car and closed the garage door behind them, "Come on T, we can talk about this shit later. Besides…Terry's gonna' be "extra nice" to me tonight after he sees what we brought him!" Lacy said emphatically. Thomas Jr. rolled his eyes in complete disgust at the thought, "Unless you'd "prefer" to have a gorgeous pink puddle of vomit on the floor of your precious ride, you bet not make them kinds of comments in my presence!" Thomas Jr. warned. The heavily muscular Lacy Spencer froze mid-step before entering the door that led into the house inside the enormous garage, "You wouldn't d….?" Lacy asked. Thomas Jr.'s eyes did not blink once, telling the proud two-hundred and fifty pound Olympian more than what he needed to know, "Fair enough. See you inside Thomas!"

Lacy said happily, as he went through the door. He grinned and gathered his leftovers off the floorboard. It was hard to imagine living there with Lacy and his brother full-time, but at this venture of his life and everything he been through, it was past time for a well needed change. Without warning, a strange thought occurred to him as he slowly climbed out of the pearl white SUV. When Thomas Jr. first remembered seeing the apparition of his father he told him, "Choose blood boy, lose blood." After all that time past, it was not until that very frightful moment, that the tormented reverend finally understood exactly what he actually meant. He was trying to tell him, although in a highly cryptic way, that he was going to have to make a "choice" that would affect his own life, Thomas Jr. hypothesized. Just as Thomas Jr. turned his back to shut the passenger door he heard a low growl from over his shoulder. His spine tingled from anticipation from what would come next, as he knew full well to whom that very growl belonged to without even bothering to turn around. He swallowed hard and slowly turned and faced his long dead father. His body was far more decomposed than it was from the last time he seen him, yet still managed to have enough mangled teeth inside his decrepit mouth to form a disgusting looking grin, "Hello boy." Thomas Senior said, and pushed Thomas Jr. into the SUV. Thomas Jr. was caught off guard by his ghastly father's strength and needed a moment for his head to recover. He shook off the pain and stood to his feet, "I know…I-I know w-why you're REALLY here?" Thomas Jr. said. His father's ghostly self grinned malevolently and pushed him even harder once more, "Then choose, boy… …or are you still…afraid?" Thomas Senior asked smiling widely. Before he knew it, Thomas Jr. was back on his feet, only this time he had a different look on his face. No longer did he have any more fear of the poltergeist that was standing before him in the stolen form of his once beloved father, "You know what…I think I've had about enough out of you. As a matter of fact…I'm fucking tired of living my life on Goddamn eggshells!!!" Thomas Jr. screamed. Surprised by his son's sudden burst of courage, he tried to reach out and push him once more, but Thomas Jr. grabbed him by the shoulders and threw him into the garage door with everything he had, causing a large bang. A shocked Thomas Senior stared at him in awe and immediately sprang to his feet and laughed. From out of nowhere, Thomas Senior was in possession of a crowbar and charged after him while laughing madly. The bold reverend stood his ground unafraid as the maddening phantom charged after him, until suddenly the door opened, "Man, what the HELL is going on out here?" Lacy asked agitatedly. When Thomas Jr. looked over his shoulder both Lacy and Terry were staring at him as if "he" were the ghost, Thomas Jr. thought. He turned around and just as he figured, his father's dilapidated body and was gone. Terry walked over to him while holding a big plate of cheesecake, "Jesus Tommie, you got a WWE audition we don't know about?" Terry asked concerned. Even Lacy decided to join in on the fun, "Shit, I thought "dude" was in here getting jumped by a gang of wild possums!" Lacy quipped. Breathing heavily, Thomas Jr. asserted himself and then quietly went near the garage door to pick up his bag of leftovers and noticed the cast iron crowbar lying on the cold floor, "Huh….Oh, yeah...I-I thought I saw…s-saw a rat. But whatever it was though, I think I finally…I think scared it off!" Thomas Jr. confirmed. Terry listened carefully to his brother's tall tale through squinted and unconvinced eyes, "Really? Wow…. (Terry staring at the crowbar)…that must've been so-o-o-o-me RAT! Please tell me he wasn't using "that" to break into one of the cars!?" Terry joked. Although Thomas Jr.'s mind had drifted off for a second, he still managed to catch his brother's last comment, "Wait wha…? Hey Screw you "Fairy! It wasn't like I had time to set up a rattrap and find a block of cheese to catch the som' bitch!" Thomas protested. Terry and Lacy laughed and escorted him into the house. As soon as he sat down at the mini bar near the kitchen, Terry slid him a glass of Maker's Mark, "Here…looks like you need this more than I do!" Terry said, while still in possession of the big plate of cheesecake. Thomas Jr. scowled as he watched his pudgy brother sadistically gorging out on the delicious looking desert, "Don't hate me, bro bro…"hate" the chef!" Terry said spitefully. He chuckled underneath his breath, as he recollected how bratty his younger brother used to act when they were kids and how much he loved rubbing things in his face when he had them, "Anyway, I heard you said yes! That's awesome!" Terry said excitedly. Thomas Jr. took a big sip from his drink, "Hmm? Oh, yeah…I did….sort of. I told Lacy I'd consider it!" Thomas Jr. said. Worried, Terry put down his plate, "Considering wh…?" Terry began to ask, before already seeing the reason in his big brother's aching eyes. Terry cursed himself underneath his breath, "S-Sorry bro... I-I don't know where my head was at. I didn't mean to be so inconsiderate…I just…I just…" Terry began before getting interrupted. "Hey, don't do that, Ter. I "know" what you meant. I'm just…I'm just in a weird place right now and the idea of NOT being there when and "if" Markus wakes up, just kinda' scares me. You understand, don't you?" Thomas Jr. asked apologetically. Without taking a moment's hesitation Terry complied, "You know that I do Tommie. Just, whatever you "do" decide…just know we'll be right there to back you!" Terry said with an eye full of glad tears, and stuck his round hand out to shake his. Thomas Jr. looked at his hand awkwardly and instead yanked his little brother toward him and squeezed him tightly, "I love you Ter. Even when I didn't get to see your face everyday after all those years…I never stopped man!" Thomas Jr. confirmed, and gave him a peck on the side of his head. Terry bit hard on his lip as he wept on his brother's shoulder. Despite the fact he was there hugging on him, in some small way, Terry felt as though Thomas Jr. was telling him goodbye for the last time, which was something he was not ready do.

If that meant he had to continue to conceal the truth about his strange encounter with the detective who showed up at his doorstep, and prompted him to reach out to his troubled brother, then he was ready to take that secret to the grave, Terry contemplated. That the handsome Detective Alejandro, the police or, "whoever" was going to have to find another way to get what they wanted without his help, Terry thought. At the end of the day, he basically cared too much for his brother's well being to drop that big of a bombshell on him, and depriving him of the least bit of joy he seemed to have found during his visit there, "Hey man, you not going anywhere! I ain't letting you! We "all" just have gotta' grow older and grumpier together…and Markus? After he wakes up….we're gonna' hook him up with a fine looking nurse to marry! Lacy and I will even build them a room over the garage to live in together…it's going to be great! You'll see!" Terry concluded sincerely. Thomas Jr. reassured him by patting Terry on the shoulder, "Of course it is." Thomas Jr. confessed. Terry wiped off his streaming eyes and giggled for no apparent reason, "What's funny?" Thomas Jr. asked and picked up his glass of liquor as he took his seat. Terry slightly hesitated, but then grudgingly put the plate back down, "Well…I was just thinking…about how we used to fight when we were little, but then mom would force us to sit down together and watch movies until we got along…." Terry said shyly. Wondering where his conversation was heading, the intrigued reverend peered into the bottom of his wine glass objectively, "Uh huh…but I don't remember us fighting just now, were we doc?" Thomas Jr. asked jokingly. Terry rolled his eyes at the notion, "Yeah, I know. I'm just saying…I had a thought and I guess what I'm trying to say is, is I would like for us to just, you know…hang out like we used to and watch some old movies. Lacy makes some of the best damn popcorn you'll ever taste and it even gives him an excuse to break out his "new" popcorn maker!" Terry suggested. Kicking back and relaxing with his little brother and watching movies on the big screen did sound tempting to the amused preacher, "I see. Well, I don't know Ter. You NEVER had any good taste in movies…" Thomas Jr. quipped. The smile on Terry's face immediately morphed into a vile and hostile scowl, "Least I'm not choosing to allow my family's KILLER to roam free!!!" Terry sinisterly replied in Thomas Senior' crackled voice. Thomas Jr. jumped back in shock, "What the HELL did you just say to me, Terry?" Thomas Jr. asked angrily. Only this time, the scowl that was previously occupying his face was completely gone, "The part about you choosing a movie on Netflix? Or, about the free movie coupons I collected from my cable company?" Terry replied confused. He knew what he had heard and clearly, there were other "issues" at play that still needed his immediate attention that had been ignored long enough, Thomas Jr. believed. Terry warned him before, that as long as he was not completely free of his guilt the more prone he was to psychological attacks by his deepest and darkest demons, "Tell you what….let me give the hospital a call and check on Markus' status…you know, make sure everything's ok. Then, "maybe" we can watch some TV!" Thomas Jr. said. This was music to Terry's ears, as the huge smile that accompanied his portly face was beaming like a comet in the sky, "Really? I mean, cool…cool! Hey bro, make your call, here take my phone if you…" Terry began before getting cutoff. "That's okay, I have one now." Thomas Jr. pulled out the cell phone Harlan gave him from his coat pocket. Terry peered at the phone with a perplexed affection, "You got a what? When did you find time to…look, it doesn't matter! Just "call" and check on my nephew, while I go give Lacy the good news!" Terry said and scurried off to his bedroom. When he was sure no one else was in hearing distance Thomas Jr. looked up the only number that was locked into the untraceable phone and hit the call button. The phone rang three times until someone on the other line finally picked up the receiver. Although it had been a while since they last spoke to one another, it was not difficult for the now confidant reverend to discern who the raspy voice on other end of the line belonged to, "You had me worried for a moment, reverend. But I had, "hoped"… you'd come through." Harlan said starkly. Thomas Jr. was taken aback by his self-serving statement, "Oh? Well that's funny…cause' I was "really hoping" you'd call off all this "madness," after I left that palace you mistake for a house…" Thomas Jr. said, while anxiously looking down the hallway for any unwarranted eavesdropping. Harlan paused for a brief moment, but then chuckled lightly, "Yes…and here we are. Is this call an "intervention," reverend?" Harlan said dully. His eyebrows stood on top of his forehead when they raised, "And if it were?" Thomas Jr. asked suspiciously. Harlan let out a loud and tired breath, "Then you'd be wasting your time. Now, is that all I can help you with or, was there another reason you called?" Harlan replied sternly. Thomas Jr. was manically gripping his cell phone as tight as a Norwegian polar bear does a lost cub, "You know damn right there is. While I'm not condemning, nor am I condoning the manner in which your "side business" is being handled, Harlan, I can't argue the result...." Thomas Jr. declared. An intrigued Harlan was sitting in quiet anticipation, "Yes…?" Harlan replied eagerly. He looked over his shoulder one last time, "I'm in. I'll do whatever you want, but I won't kill. Besides, at the rate everyone's going, you all could stand to use a little extra prayer." Thomas Jr. declared. Harlan wasted no time making his decision, "All right, reverend, you have a deal. But for the record, reverend, I never fully intended on you actually "killing" anyone…only your blessing." Harlan said pleased. Suddenly, Thomas Jr. could hear Terry and Lacy voices approaching, "Alright, well now you got it! What else do you need me to do?" Thomas Jr. asked.

Taking on the Devil Sonny Korne

11 p.m. at Baylor St. Luke's Medical Center…

In making final preparations for Kale and company's next planned assault, Harlan wasted no expense in securing a private wing of the gargantuan hospital's fifth floor. They had been using an old operating room that had been "officially" closed off to the hospital's staff, due to asbestos poisoning, which in reality was a ruse that allowed them to have a base of operation. Tension inside the chilly room was thick enough to cut with a high powered Briggs and Stratton lawnmower. No one in the room spoke a word, as each of them knew the stakes were going to be a lot higher going into the type of hostile environment they were about to enter that night. But no one else was more on edge about their prospects of survival than Agent Milton Elliot, and for good reason. He had worked undercover inside the "Road Quakers" gang for many months and could just as easily recollect how nasty they loved to play. It had not been until now, that a part of him was beginning to feel a bit of uncertainty that having the depraved and maniacal Lieutenant Keegan on their side was going to be enough to go up against such a savage and ferocious force. Unlike the currently deceased Jacory Jackson's Black Ballaz affiliation,' The Road Quakers were going to be a lot more to handle than some above average street gang, Agent Elliot thought unpleasantly. What was even more unsettling to the rugged and hulking Nebraskan was the crooked grin on the young Lieutenant's face, when he offered to give a little background information on their intended target. At the time, he kept silent while reloading his favorite 357 magnum revolver, as his cobra-like eyes gleamed back at him dementedly, as if he could care less who "Ozzie Brickwood" might have been, or what the Road Quakers were all about, Agent Elliot recollected. He first assumed Kale's callous dismissal as his usual bravado, but after being around the former Special Black Ops Army Lieutenant up close for many weeks, instead believed he was a man on the verge of insanity. After hearing what happened to his wife and kids though, how could he possibly not be? Agent Elliot figured. Agent Elliot recalled their trip back from Las Vegas after they took down Calvin Rusher and his crew. Jovan had somehow managed to convince Kale to open up enough tell them about the suicide bomber who killed his family. Although that was all he was willing to "share" about his past, it was more than enough to validate his presence among them, Agent Elliot concluded. Much like the younger Lieutenant Keegan, he knew what personal loss felt like, but unlike him tried to allow the system he fought to uphold to do its job. But nothing broke his spirit greater than discovering how much more the law cared about what it stood to profit, than what it did for bringing a cold hearted killer to justice, let alone, the steep price he had to pay to apprehend him. Coming into the realization that his wife Latasha and daughter Francesca were murdered senselessly may have been enough motivation to have helped fuel his rage up to this point, but the reality of losing the friendships he garnered over the last few weeks within the group, only created doubt in his mind. For as impressive as Kale's tactical and combative skills were, they were not enough to protect them psychologically if and when someone from the group died, Agent Elliot hypothesized. Although the former undercover D.E.A. agent cared little for his own well being, he had grown somewhat attached to the people from inside his own ensemble, especially Jovan Campbell, to whom he was against bringing. But the bullheaded youngster insisted on being there to have his back the same way he was for his, which made the thought of losing someone else he cared about that much harder to live with, Agent Elliot agonized.

To further add insult to injury, the idea of Kale adding a paraplegic to their team without giving them a heads up did not sit well with the distrustful agent. Kale had a long metal briefcase that was hand delivered by Harlan's assistant/helicopter pilot Alejandro in his hand that he sat on top of tall a box, "Hey Dave come here and check this out…" Kale asked proudly. The towering David Lewis was enjoying a 2 liter of diet Coke from the bottle when he walked up to his best friend, "What cha' got Key?" David asked suspiciously. Kale took a drag from his cigarette and smiled at him with his patented crooked grin, "Well, that all depends, hoss… (Kale clicking the buttons on the metal briefcase) If yur' on the wrong end, then I'de say "ass is grass," but (Kale opens the top to the briefcase) in yur' hand's…and no pun intended…then you'd be one BAD motherfucker!" Kale said sinisterly. Harlan did not bat an eye when Kale asked him to purchase the two pricey and powerful weapons that were customized and fashioned overnight just to David's specifications. David almost choked on his soda when he saw the futuristic arm/guns, "What the fu…? Dude is this shit for real?" David screamed excitedly. Kale chuckled, "I could pinch you in the butt if yew'd like?" Kale quipped. He hit Kale in the arm, "Come on, stop playing!" David said sternly. Kale threw his hands up in the air, "Alright, alright, don't git yo' panties all twisted up…but, I could still do it if yew' still want me too, big fella'!?" Kale joked. Both Hakiro and Jovan heard Kale's remark and started laughing, but stopped immediately once David stared at them with his 1,000 yard gaze. Kale took out one of the weapons, "Alright, this one here's the automatic...good for suppressive fire, while this baby's (Kale pointed at the other arm/gun still in the briefcase) great for making…" Kale said before getting interrupted. "Yo what the fuck is this? We filming a Quentin Tarantino film, or what man? We ain't got time for this Wizard of Oz shit, we need to load the truck if we gonna' stick with the plan!" Agent Elliot yelled. Kale was not stupid and could easily see the fear in the agent's eyes as he spoke, "This "IS" part of the plan, Eli. So try to relax yo' self a bit why don't cha'?" Kale insisted. It was no secret to the rest of them the "real" reasons why the agitated Agent Elliot was so worked up. He let his opinions be known prior to them meeting up at the hospital, when they dropped Jovan off at home after leaving Mose Dope's headquarters. But Kale had reminded him once more that he was not either of the men's keepers and would not stop Jovan from coming if it were his wish to continue. The young lieutenant also could tell that the former undercover agent may have thought they were slightly overmatched, which did not bruise the Floridian's ego in the least. He had spent his entire life being underestimated and relished proving people wrong who that they had the advantage because they were either stronger or bigger than he was. Kale always knew he was special and that his purpose was to be born a warrior and although he would not admit it, his father knew it too, Kale believed. Agent Elliot grabbed his gear and started to make his way toward the service elevator they normally use, "Fuck it, do what you want, I'll be down in the van…" Agent Elliot said. At the same time the service elevator doors were opening and who he saw caused him to drop all his belongings onto the floor, "Tha' fuck you doin' here?" Agent Elliot asked bewildered. Smiling, Kale walked up behind the thick necked Nebraskan and leant up against his wide shoulder, "Cause Cornhusker, we invited him ….howdee there, reverend?!" Kale said pleased. Thomas Jr. discreetly waved to both him and the stunned agent, "Good evening…I'm sorry if I'm running a little late, had to wait until my brother fell asleep." Thomas Jr. said exhausted. Kale grinned widely at the paranoid Agent Elliot who looked back at him in awe, "Na-a-a-aw, yew right on time! Come on, reverend…lemme' show yew' 'round!" Kale said excitedly.

It did not come that much as a surprise to the oddly impressed reverend, seeing what lengths Harlan was willing to go to help masquerade his somewhat macabre-like enterprise. It seemed like such a morbid, if not, oxymoron of an idea to build a hideout for taking lives into a building that was used for saving them, Thomas Jr. thought. Most of the recovery rooms were either filled with exotic weapons or crates full of gun ammunition. He also noticed a small area where they had a group of laptop computers and what appeared to be radio equipment. Once their quick tour of the command center was over with, Thomas Jr. asked to speak with him privately, so Kale escorted him to a secluded examining room to talk. Unknowing to the young Lieutenant, Terry broke the doctor patient privilege he had between them by sharing the second hand information he received from David Lewis about his past. But by doing so, he was looking at Kale with new eyes, "I uh, I just…I'm not here to question, if what I think you're doing is right or wrong (not that I think it would even matter) but I'd be lying, if I said that I didn't care about what happens to your souls. I'll go with you…only in the capacity of offering some semblance of moral support. So, please, try not to hold įt against me when I say that I still won't kill." Thomas Jr. confirmed. Kale was inspecting the confident looking reverend up and down as though he were a doctor admiring the health of a patient. His weird glaring began to unnerve the conscientious reverend, "What?" Thomas Jr. asked agitated. Kale tilted his old Florida University cowboy hat up, "Oh nuthin' …. jus' that yew' look a hell of a lot better without that "monkey" on yo' back is all…" Kale said satisfied. For all the riches that the vaunted Harlan Kruellar possessed, it was virtually impossible for either him or Kale to have known about the spirit of his father haunting him and tried to disregard his comment as pure conjecture, "I don't know what you mean or what you may have heard but I…" Thomas Jr. began before getting interrupted. Kale put his hand over Thomas Jr.' left shoulder almost startling the shocked reverend, "I know "all" about what happened to you…to yo' family…and I ain't gonna' "judge" YOU neither!" Kale firmly replied. Thomas Jr. bit his bottom lip and dropped his head in shame, "Did you t-tell…do the o-others know?" Thomas Jr. asked lowly. The young Lieutenant cocked his head down to look the embarrassed reverend in the face, "No sir…and "they" ain't gotta' know. Look, I know a thing or two about whut' it feels like to have "ghosts" at yo' back! But yur' one of the lucky ones reverend, cause yew' was able to beat yur's! Me on the other hand…well, I'm still in my "prime!" But yew' can rest assure of one thing, reverend…. Sonny and "all" the rest of them son's of fuckers gonna bleed sumthin' really awful for what they did…and I ain't gonna' let NUTHIN' get in my way..." Kale vehemently promised. At first, the flattered Thomas Jr. was at a loss for words. The last thing on Earth he pictured happening when he arrived was having Kale standing up for him. It was not until this moment that he could see a hint of a soul behind the rough exterior of the young Lieutenant and believed there may have still been some hope left for him. This was the first time they had been so close without Kale wanting to rip his throat out and could see just how much older he was compared to him. Who would have known that behind all his wild drunkenness, serial killer stares, and Mel Gibson Kung fu moves, was actually a normal half decent looking young man, Thomas Jr. thought. Despite Kale's heartfelt threat, as a clergyman, he knew it would be un-Christian-like to encourage the death of anyone, including someone who may have richly deserved it as much as the vile and despicable Sonny Korne. But he did not have to stop him either, "Then I'll be praying for him too…God speed!" Thomas Jr. said and put his hand over Kale's shoulder. Kale chuckled and dug out a pack of cigarettes from the front of his jean pocket. He went into his back pocket and pulled out the stolen lighter he took off Harlan back at his mansion, "Yew' know…. back when I…when I had my old unit, we used to…we used to have this sort of chaplain. He used ta' read verses from the bible "every time" we went out to do what we had to do. I could never really remember them all (laughing) …but the one thing that he always said ta' us that always stuck…." Kale said distantly. A captivated Thomas Jr. quietly and patiently awaited his reply. He took a long drag from his cigarette and exhaled the smoke slowly, "…He said: "Evil has not met the real me who is yet been delivered…but remember until then, we are all but God's unholy instruments!" Kale said cryptically, and handed Thomas Jr. his cigarette. Thomas Jr. pondered his chaplain's vague, if not Edgar Allan Poe-like advice and grabbed the cigarette and took a few puffs from it and gave it back. Kale looked at his watch, which looked more like a clock on his smallish arms, Thomas Jr. thought, "Alright reverend, we gotta' scoot! I got one mo' surprise fo' the fellas before we ride!" Kale said excitedly while rubbing his hands together. When they got back to their primary meeting place in the operating room, Kale picked up a gift bag that was on the floor near the corner of the spacious room. Jovan immediately came up to Thomas Jr. and put his fist out, "Man, I thought Eli was just fuc… ah, was just "messing" with your boy, when he said you showed up! I'm kinda' glad you'd changed your mind though, from what I hear….things gonna' get hella' crazy pretty fast and we could use the backup!" Jovan said encouragingly. He fist-bumped the young former collegian, "That wasn't the kind of backup I had in mind when I decided to come back, Joe." Thomas Jr. reiterated. Although the reverend's steely response caught him off guard, the powerfully built ex-linebacker was still to some extent relieved by his presence, "Well, hey man…I understand. It's all good Rev!" Jovan replied and put his hand out to shake his hand. Thomas Jr. contemplated his reaction, but then reassured the young man by excepting his gentlemanly gesture and shook hands. Kale signaled for everyone to gather around him at the operating table in the center of the room. He opened the oddly designed black gift bag and pulled out a set of plastic masks that he laid out on the table. A vexed Agent Elliot walked up next to the unsuspecting reverend, "Good, then maybe you can talk some sense into that thick head of his, before he gets it…" Agent Elliot stopped mid sentence after the bulky Jovan Campbell came and stood beside him scowling. Thomas Jr. saw the awkward expressions on their faces and could tell there was more friction than usual between the two off again/on again associates, "Before what agent?" Thomas Jr. whispered. Jovan's unmovable frown was still frozen on his dark-complected face when the former D.E.A. agent looked at him, "Just forget it." Agent Elliot angrily replied. Kale began handing out masks to Hakiro and the others in the room. Thomas Jr. was a little taken aback when the mysterious Sergeant Lewis came lurking in from the bathroom, "Hey man, don't forget about your boy?" David said emphatically. He was everything his brother Terry described him to be; tall, dark, mean looking, and paraplegic in both arms. David nodded at Thomas Jr. after he caught him staring at him as if he were some sort of Frankenstein monster. The livid Agent Elliot chuckled at the warped looking Porky Pig mask that was given to him, "Yo cuz, just what the fuck is this? I mean, it was cool giving us code names for the sake of the assholes who might be listening over the radios, but masks…seriously?" Agent Elliot said perturbed. "Halloween's at midnight, Eli, jus' make'n sure we "keepin' wit' the spirit" of it all, besides…if there's one thing I learned in the military, it's that cowards flee from the responsibility of understanding. We need'em ta' believe we're crazier than they are so, when they see us comin'...they won't know what the fuck ta' think!" Kale snarled. Agent Elliot contemplated his rationale for a second and smiled, "You know what, Keegan? By far, you're the most....smartest..."twisted-ist" fucks I ever met!" Agent Elliot passionately concluded. Kale winked his eye at the impressed husky agent, "Flattery won't git' ya' nowhere here, hoss!" Kale quipped. Jovan traded masks with the always deadly silent Hakiro, who had an O.J. Simpson mask in his possession and gave him his mask, which was an awfully made up one of Woody Wood Pecker. Kale reached into the once more bag and pulled out a small wooden box and handed it to his eager best friend, "Now don't let the appearance of these fool yew,' they're fully functional high-tech night spectrum specs, which have onboard "ultra violet" N.A.V. gear, with grid...pretty "basic" ta' use!" Kale confirmed. David twisted his mouth sideways, "Why is it, whenever you say that shit, it ain't ever true?" David replied starkly. Kale snickered as the towering David Lewis opened up the wooden box and revealed a wide pair of dark colored shades, which appeared to the wincing Thomas Jr. as if the sunglasses were still stuck in the 1980's. Kale looked at his watch once more and raised his hand, "Alright fellas, yew' know the drill. We hit'em hard, we hit'em fast! Leave no stones unturned or it jus' might mean somebody's ass!" Kale instructed. An awestruck and anxious Thomas Jr. felt a little out of place, after realizing he was the only man in the room who was not picking up and brandishing some kind of dangerous looking firearm and began gripping his bible across his chest, as if it were an uncovered newborn. It had also just occurred to him, that one of the gathered fathers who were invited out to Harlan's estate was not present and started to fear the worst. While each of the men filed into their hazmat disguises the worried reverend went up to the adrenaline pumped Agent Elliot, "Uh, excuse me, but what happened to Ricky? He isn't, uh....?" Thomas Jr. started to ask before getting cutoff mid-sentence. "What, dead?" (Agent Elliot laughs) nah Rev, Rick's fine, the lucky bastard. I'll tell ya' all about it along the way...!" Agent Elliot said and grabbed his gear. Kale had two noticeably large Army satchels in his hand that appeared bigger than he was when he walked up to the reverend. He placed them on a dolly and Jovan took them to the service elevator, "A-a-a-h, so.....what's the plan?" Thomas Jr. asked excitedly. His grin was so wide it looked like a half moon across his rugged face, "Yew' know whut, reverend....I'm kinda' glad yew' asked that!?" Kale said and threw his arm around his shoulder, as they made their way to join the others on the service elevator.

12:15 a.m. outside the Monolithic Church of Modern and Philosophical Beliefs in Pasadena, Texas...

The forgotten origin of the enormous stretch of land, which now encompassed the famous mega church, was that it once long ago belonged to a scandalous slave owner by the name of Donald Trevor Manning. During the American Civil War, the entrepreneurial Donald Manning made a fortune off supplying the Confederate Army with coats, scarves, and other weather prohibitive apparel in their cause to defeat their Northern rival statesmen. From 1861 through 1863, Donald Manning accumulated a rather large number of slaves to meet the high demands for his booming enterprise. But by 1865, there were no more battles left to fight, as the South had surrendered and he was forced to close his factory doors. What made matters more complicated for the thriving businessman was the abolishment of slavery that soon followed. Although they were technically free because of the Thirteenth Amendment, the stubborn slave owner refused to release his slaves and either shot or boiled them in a huge vat of tar, if they were caught trying to escape. Despite amassing a vast amount of wealth, the bored and unfulfilled Donald Trevor Manning had begun over indulging himself with dangerous opioids and alcohol, which led to him engaging in wild sexual orgies with a lot of his female and male African slaves. Eventually, the idiosyncratic Manning would meet and wed the vivaciously alluring half Spanish/Italian Monica Florentia Belladonna, who worked as a server at a pub in town. It was rumored that she once worked as a nurse/doctor for the Confederate Army, until it was speculated that the disturbed Belladonna may have been killing wounded soldiers instead of rendering them aid. All that did not matter to the madly in love Manning who wasted no time moving the seductive waitress into his spacious plantation home. No one knew exactly what caused the deranged Donald Manning to lose his mind first, his overindulging opioid abuse, or the sinister persuasion of the demented

Monica Belladonna, who herself often loved playing strange games with the slaves. Unfortunately, many years would pass before the public discovered that Donald Manning and his bride were practicing witch craft and devil worshipping at his estate and that they were also sacrificing the lives of their slaves to appease the Assyrian demon goddess Lilith. What began as games of debauchery and carnal pleasures had quickly manifested into the ritualistic and violent defilement of over a two-hundred innocent African-American lives. One by one, the Manning's slaves were lined up and butchered over a pentagon of blood and those who were not maimed or castrated, suffered a far worse immoral death. It was even claimed, that hearts of slave children were removed as an act to sustain the vile seductress's outer beauty. Fed up after enduring years of various cruel indignities at the hands of the disturbed couple, a revolt was finally led against them, which led to their mysterious disappearance. The Mannings were never seen or heard from again, but rumor has it, that after being torn apart by their own slaves, their remains were scattered and buried throughout the old cottons fields behind their then plantation home.

But since those old dark days, the former slave plantation had long been excavated and in its place presently stood the self-proclaimed beacon of hope, which is known by most who watched church on television, as the "Monolithic Church of Modern and Philosophical Beliefs." The current owner and pastor of the concert hall-like religious institution is none other than Reverend Casey P. Gregory III (who according to Harlan Kruellar's classified intel) was allegedly accepting donations under the table from the Road Quakers biker gang and was also offering asylum to the fugitive Sonny Korne and his other three loathsome underlings. Much like his crooked Louisianan grandfather and father before him, the high profile Reverend Gregory III often preached to a massively large non-denominated congregation, while primarily catering to many of his upper class members. Even some of the country's most highly recognizable celebrities could be seen frequenting the popular church on his locally televised Sunday morning program. But despite the white, clean-cut, and evangelistic image he was selling to the rest of the American public, the slick talking and slender-framed Casey Gregory III was in fact guilty of committing several felonious crimes. He had been either linked to or culpable in everything from wire fraud, to embezzlement, tax evasion, and bribery. Upon hearing the extensively long laundry list of Reverend Gregory's heinous acts, from the impressively informative Agent Elliot, it caused the disgusted Thomas Jr.'s stomach to quiver inside the driver's seat of the "borrowed" vehicle he was driving. Was there "no end" to the levels of depravity men would sink to to keep themselves rich in a dying world? Thomas Jr. wondered, while puffing on a cigarette and rolling down the car window. For someone who was supposed to have been "of the cloth," did the misguided Reverend Gregory accidently "glaze over" the part in the bible, about a man profiting the world only to lose their immortal soul? Thomas Jr. thought shaking his head disappointedly. When he pulled up to the main security gate of the monstrous campus, Thomas Jr. was mesmerized by the flourishing prosperity the opportunistic Reverend Gregory afforded himself, all in the name of God. Before letting him out to take his position, Agent Elliot also told him the entire layout of the area (which featured outside of the church building itself) two Olympic-sized pools, an indoor full court basketball facility, theatre, five-story parking garage, a warehouse and plenty of land to spare. Cosmetically, the Monolithic Church of Modern and Philosophical Beliefs was everything he always envisioned his father's church to be before God said otherwise, Thomas Jr. figured. Maybe his own selfish ambition was what brought down God's wrath upon him and his family and now as penance, has to atone by helping the others, Thomas Jr. pondered, while tossing his cigarette out the car window. Either way, their presence there only reinforced his belief of two things in particular: That one way or the other, Casey Gregory, Sonny Korne, and the others, were soon to reap for the sins they had sowed and the second, that maybe it was always meant for him to be there to bear witness of it. A proverb came to the reverend's mind, as he watched one of the three "no-nonsense" appearing security guards, who worked inside the roomy security booth, opened the glass sliding door. It was one of his favorites, Proverbs 22:4, "Humility is the fear of the Lord; its wages are the riches and honor and life." Thomas Jr. thought. What the security team was unaware of was that prior to the raid on Jacory Jackson's "Wonderland," Skinny "Ricky" Wallace paid the church a small visit during a bible study that was open to the public, Thomas Jr. recollected being told. As a former drug user, he was able to use his testimonial and guile to infiltrate and make his way around parts of the building, where he left customized frequency jammer tech (bought directly from the

U.S. secret service by Harlan) inside the bathroom toilets disguised as cleaning pellets, Agent Elliot had said. In real time, the tech is designed to temporarily form an invisible radius around the building, while scrambling all camera images and also disrupt any outside cell phone usage. When the thought of Harlan "knowing his shit" crossed his mind, Thomas Jr. chuckled to himself, immediately drawing the ire of the "all business" security guard, "Are you lost, sir?" The security guard asked sternly. Meanwhile, hiding in the heavily wooded far left side of the humongous property, Hakiro Yosami turned on the jamming remote, which would need a full minute for its signal to reach across from where he was. The remote had two red blinking LED lights on the front that turned green after sixty seconds, "Shadow-U to Holy-One, the jammer is now activated!" Hakiro whispered into his headset. Back in his college days as an elite swimmer, Thomas Jr. was used to being given nicknames for his marvelous prowess in the pools, but after hearing his code name spoken aloud for the first time (from his discreetly hidden earpiece) seemed to stimulate the sixty-something, "Uh, no actually…my name is Reverend Run, and I was told a "Black Lives Matter" rally was being held here, so I jumped at the chance to come…" Thomas Jr. began before getting interrupted. "Excuse me, sir…did you say, "Black Lives Matter" rally…here!?" The guard asked confusingly. With no time to spare and with all the cameras momentarily scrambled, Thomas Jr. hastily put on a pair of unsuspecting reading glasses and handed the guard a flyer, "Yes sir, here…I even have a flyer…" Thomas Jr. said. Unconvinced, the guard took the pink flyer, but still kept his eyesight on the curious looking preacher, "A fucking Black Lives Matter rally this late at night?" The guard said shaking his head. When the guard looked closely at the odd looking flyer, it had one small sentence written in the middle of the page. It read "Hello and Fuck You! Love, Kale!" and a second later the paper caught fire, causing the guard to become partially blinded. The special combustible flyer was made from the same flash paper type material most magicians used on stage to perform their routines, and much like a magician, Kale too was a student of the art of misdirection and jumped at the chance to use the trick to the reverend's advantage. Thomas Jr. then hit the guard with the car door sending him flailing to his knees. But before his fellow co-workers could alert anyone, a masked Agent Elliot tossed a flash grenade through the office window, causing the two men to become severely disoriented. Agent Elliot quickly ran inside the spacious security booth and pulverized both guards, until they were both rendered unconscious. The staggering guard who Thomas Jr. knocked to the ground got to his feet and reached for his side arm, but before he could fire Agent Elliot clocked him in the head from behind with his gun. "Thanks." Thomas Jr. said relieved. He kneeled down and picked up the guards gun and tossed it away, "My pleasure, Rev." Agent Elliot said. It was highly unnerving for him to talk to the massively built DEA agent, while he stood there smoking a cigar through the oddly intimidating Porky Pig mask, "So…is it really necessary for you guys to wear all that crazy shit?" Thomas Jr. quipped. He slightly shivered listening to Agent Elliot's muffled snicker underneath his gruesome mask, "It's Halloween Rev, get into the spirit! Boss Hog to Wasp, front gate's been neutralized…we're going in!" Agent Elliot said through his earpiece. "Roger that, Boss Hog!" Kale said over their private radio. After tying up all three guards, Agent Elliot and Thomas Jr. disconnected the phone lines and took the guards cell phones. They then jumped into the stolen Silver Lincoln and proceeded slowly through the mile-wide and twelve-foot tall bricked barrier. At the same time Thomas Jr. and Agent Elliot were discreetly approaching the sanctuary half the campus's security team was busy being distracted with getting their cameras back online, while the other half was scrambling to put out fires set off all around the large structure. Obviously, cleverly hidden jamming paraphernalia was not the only thing left during the currently estranged Ricky Wallace' social call to the Machiavellian tabernacle, Thomas Jr. assumed. Agent Elliot referred to them as "other parting gifts" when the reverend asked him about it. Thomas Jr. learned that before the bible service ended, Ricky simply dropped (what appeared to the casual eye) regular looking dollars and quarters inside a collection plate, that were in reality, experimental and far ranging low impact explosives being detonated from the woods by the stealthy Hakiro Yosami. Though the intent was not to cause physical harm to the parishioners, the same could not be said for Reverend Gregory's treasury room, which received the most explosive charges. Once he and Thomas Jr. chained the front doors of the church shut, Agent Elliot radioed ahead to both Kale and Hakiro, who was in the process of doing the same to the backdoors, "Boss Hog to Wasp, Main doors are secured! What's your status, Shadow-U?" Agent Elliot asked. After dismantling two unsuspecting security guards who were taking a quick smoke-break, the portly Hakiro chained the back doors and finally radioed back, “Had some last minute “pruning” to do, Boss Hog…but, the back doors are “now” secured.” Hakiro confirmed inconspicuously. Although Harlan’s sources put both Sonny Korne and the Road Quakers on the premises Kale and the others still had to figure out their exact whereabouts, with only the twenty-two minute window provided by the carefully placed jamming equipment. Kale figured if they isolated most of the security team inside the main building, then his team could split up and freely check the four remaining places on the massive lot they could possibly hide. Without hesitation he radioed in the next wave, who so happened to be the athletic Jovan Campbell, “Wasp to Propect-1, yur’ up…” Kale said through his headset. On the east end of the property was a ten-foot tall electrical fence, which was deactivated before the former college all-star cut a hole through it and made his way to the guard’s gate. Inside the security booth was a Nigerian guard who was sleeping heavenly underneath a thin golden quilt, while the other was a brawny white man who was enjoying a hot cup of coffee and reading a news paper. Jovan smiled and tossed a rock against the window. Initially, the guard ignored the sound and went back to enjoying his paper, before finally getting up after a second stone hit the glass. Irritated, the guardsman left the booth to inspect the area and when he saw that everything seemed in place, he hurried back to his newspaper and noticed his co-worker was still sleeping soundly underneath his blanket. Not wanting to disturb his Nigerian companion, who went to college during the day, the brawny man quietly took his seat. But when he put his back to him Jovan Campbell, who had been disguising himself as the sleeping Nigerian, threw off the blanket and security hat and choked the brawny guard from behind, until he finally passed out. After he zip tied both guards together, Jovan opened the electrical gate and quickly made his way toward his next position, which was the indoor basketball facility, “Prospect-1 to Wasp, delivery entrance is null and void!” Jovan said emphatically. Despite having some reservations of his own about having the uncharacteristically eager Jovan Campbell in attendance, Kale still believed he was an asset, “Roger that, Prospect-1. Wasp ta’ Armadillo…yur’ on standby to backup Prospect-1! Everyone else, you know what to do. The minute yew’ spot Quakers or Sonny Korne, give the signal and then take’ um out!” Kale ordered. One by one they took out any straggling security guards who walked the desolate property aimlessly, while they each made their way to their designated buildings. Hakiro was the first to encounter several Road Quaker members who were hanging out and drinking beers near the pool. But before either of them could get a decent hand on him the South Korean martial artist diced each and every last one of them into pieces with his two razor sharp sickles. Suddenly, before he could radio Kale, he heard the sounds of someone screaming for their life from one of the locker rooms. Hakiro followed the screams to the women's locker room, where three more Road Quakers were raping a heavily tattooed and brunette white woman. Enraged, Hakiro Yosami quickly took on the three men, beating them senselessly with his expertise in vast hand to hand combat and sword prowess with his savage sickles, even cutting off one of the men's penis in the process. When the debacle was over, Hakiro immediately helped the woman off the cold floor, "Are you alright, ma'am?" Hakiro asked politely. The woman screamed and stabbed Hakiro into his chest, then reached for a gun off one of the dead Road Quakers, "You fucking bastard! I was enjoying that!" The tattooed woman yelled. With his puma like reflexes, Hakiro threw one of his sickles into her face before the woman could get her shot off, sending her hard to the floor into a pool of her own blood. Exhausted, Hakiro fell to the floor, "Shadow-U to Wasp…" Hakiro said over his radio.

In the parking garage,

Thomas Jr. still could not believe he was smack dab in the middle of what was sure to become an all-out warzone. He tried not to allow his nervousness to show as he quietly drove up each garage level, but failed miserably in doing so in front of the seasoned D.E.A. officer, "Relax Rev, I gotcha'! Besides, the chances are… nobody's probably even in here!" Agent Elliot said, while smoking his cigar through his disturbing Porky Pig mask. If only he could be so lucky, thought the worried preacher. What Agent Elliot saw when they reached the edge of the ramp that led to the fifth and final floor of the garage, caused him to urgently cock the barrel of his gun, "Hold up a sec, Rev…you see that? It's Road Quakers up ahead…." Agent Elliot said wide-eyed. Thomas Jr.'s eyesight was not very good at night like they used to be, but he could still make out the motorcycles from his point of view, "Okay, so there's Road Quakers. Call "Keegan" and have the rest of them come back y…" Thomas Jr. began before getting interrupted. "Fuck that! Pardon my French Rev, but we need to go up there and get those bastards now and hit'em hard while we still have the drop on em'!" Agent Elliot insisted. Confused, Thomas Jr. looked at the odd behaving former D.E.A. agent, "What the hell happened to sticking to the plan, Milton…you know…the whole "element of surprise" thing? What if Sonny or Brickwood's not up there? If I go driving up there and YOU start shooting…won't that just scare them off from wherever the hell they may be actually hiding?" Thomas Jr. asked agitated. Infuriated, Agent Elliot reached over and grabbed Thomas Jr. by the front of his coat, "Let's get something straight here, Rev….the Road Quakers hide from no one. They don't have to. Secondly, if there's a chance I can end this now, before something happens to Joe, then I'm taking it! To hell with what Keegan says!" Agent Elliot said angrily. Obviously, during his time away, there must have been some personal issues between Agent Elliot and Kale about Jovan coming along on their misadventures, Thomas Jr. surmised. Either way, they had worked too hard and come too far to allow pettiness to now cloud their judgment during a critical moment, "Look, Milton…I get it. You care about Joe, and so do I. As a matter of fact, I care about all of you, including that sawed-off sociopath who's leading us! But if we go up there half cocked like a bull in a China shop, we might get the others hurt as well!" Thomas Jr. said sincerely. Agent Elliot deeply exhaled and pondered the skeptical preacher's words for a brief moment, "You know…maybe your right!" Agent Elliot said and got out of the car. He began charging up the ramp, "maybe "I" should just be the one to "run up here instead!" Agent Elliot said excitedly.

The indoor basketball/gym facility, fifty yards away from the secondary entrance…

Just as the fleet footed Jovan Campbell went to pull on the gym doors, someone else was already coming out and without hesitation, the powerful All-America linebacker punched the man out cold. He then dragged the unconscious bald headed man he cold-cocked back inside the chilly weight room. After zip tying his arms and feet together, he covered the two-hundred thirty pound stranger with the same blanket he had taken off the Nigerian security guard he stashed away. When Jovan stood to his feet, he realized that there were also three other much larger white men standing near a water fountain, on the far side of the expansive weight room that began to approach him. All three men looked like they could play offensive line for the Houston Texans to the sturdy Jovan Campbell, who himself was no slouch in the weight lifting department, (Pulling out his assault rifle) "That's right assholes…you got the idea. Just come on over here quietly…and lay ALL ya'll giant asses face down on the floor!" Jovan commanded, holding them at gun point. Although they were outfitted in sweaty workout apparel, it did not take a master's degree in Language Arts for the former All-American to decipher their various gang tattoos. As the three Road Quakers drew closer to him they did not appear fazed that the young one-time college phenom was brandishing a powerful CZ-805 assault rifle and slowly prepared to rush him. One of them had long curly black hair and beard and favored the late great Lyle Alzado, "The fuck you supposed to be wearin' that fuckin thing…Obama-Man?" The man quipped. Jovan had all but forgotten that he was still wearing his mask during all the excitement, "What? Oh, this? Nah man…this O.J. bitches! So don't ANY of you "thick motherfucka's" try anything stupid or you just gonna get hurt…" Jovan threatened. It was beginning to make sense why Agent Elliot warned him about the infamous Road Quakers, as it was very apparent that death seemed to be the least of their worries, "Why? Cause you got a gun boy? (He snickers) Only thing getting hurt tonight nigger…is your sorry punk black ass!" The curly headed man said and lunged at Jovan. Jovan instantly shot the man in the shoulder sending his body flailing into a piece of machinery, but then lost the gun after getting tackled by the other two bulky men. To no avail, they each tried to overpower the adrenaline fueled Jovan Campbell (who was easily out classing them one on one) tossing them left and right over and into the weightlifting equipment, until the wounded curly headed man snuck up behind Jovan and clocked him over the head with the butt of his rifle. With the Jovan dazed, they quickly pounced on the young man, pulverizing him over and over with dumbbell handles and Olympic plates, until finally falling helplessly to the ground.

In a field not far from the church,

Nearly twelve minutes had passed since anyone last checked back in with the disgruntled Lieutenant Keegan, who was busy passing time drinking Jack Daniels straight out of the bottle, while leaning back on the back end of a rather long Semi-truck trailer. Part of him was starting to wonder if the twenty-two minute window to find Sonny Korne (as well as the Road Quakers) was going to be enough to operate, considering the large amount of landscaping they had to cover. Had it been his old Special Black Ops unit, the Razor Hawks, then it would not have been any cause for concern, Kale believed. But even in the short while he had gotten to know his new team, Kale could not deny the special bond or link he seemed to share between them. Unlike his self absorbed Razor Hawks, who mainly enlisted into the service to earn a decent paycheck or to earn a free education, (or shoot badass guns) it was these fathers tragedies that were bringing them all together for a single purpose, while their loved ones were beckoning them from beyond the grave for justice. For all of the former Lieutenant's formidable rage and all the excruciating heartache he endured after losing his promising young family, he found it both incredible, if not troublesome, of rediscovering his capability to still care. He chuckled at the thought and believed the moment caused the need for a serious cigarette break. After lighting up his sixth Marlboro, Kale checked his watch once more. Sensing something was wrong, Kale signaled Alejandro who was on his cell phone in the semi. It was odd for him to see the usually sharply dressed Alejandro draped in all black tactical gear, "Change O' plans, Pretty-boy…" Kale said. His surprising move drew a bit of concern from Harlan's young assistant, "What's wrong? What happened?" Alejandro asked alarmed. Kale took off his hat and ran his hand threw his scruffy long locks, "Don't know…could be sumthin…could be nuttin…Either way, we still got a job to…." Kale said reluctantly. Incidentally, Hakiro Yosami was the first to finally respond through Kale's headset, "Shadow-U to Wasp, come in Wasp…." Hakiro said urgently. Kale put his hand up to silence Alejandro, who climbed up next to him onto the covered trailer,

"This is Wasp, Shadow-U…whut's yo' 20!?" Kale replied relieved. The portly built South Korean sounded winded as he spoke through his micro radio, "I'm in the cafeteria…" Hakiro said weakly. Hakiro's reply caused the confused Southern Floridian to shake his head, "We ain't got time fo' snack breaks Shadow-U! Is Prospect-1 there too?" Kale asked ecstatically. At first there was a slight pause, "Negative. But I ran into more trouble after I left the Pool area, while searching for first aid..." Hakiro said achingly. Kale snapped his fingers and pointed to the chains that were supporting the huge covered object they had been transporting, "How bad yew' hurt?" Kale asked. Hakiro was panting exhaustedly, "I'll survive, but if I was a betting man…I'd say...our targets…are either hiding out in the theatre or the storage house…" Hakiro confidently confirmed. Pleased by the news from his always resourceful and Oriental scout, Kale was ready to move to the next phase of his plan, "That's good, Shadow-U! I want yew' ta' hop in wit' Boss Hog and Rev and go see whut's takin' Prospect-1 so long…" Kale began before getting cutoff. There was another long pause on Kale's headset, "Boss Hog and Rev are not here either…" Hakiro confirmed. The young Lieutenant stopped dead in his tracks as he went to help Alejandro with his load, "Say whut'?" Kale asked flabbergasted. Uh, yeah…Wasp, I don't think they ever left the garage…" Hakiro said. But before he could respond back to ask, sounds of rapid gunfire could be heard coming from the direction of the Monolithic church. Without needing three guesses, Kale already knew the man responsible for blowing their cover too early, "Milton…" Kale muttered angrily. Just like a leaping cougar, Kale jumped back onto the trailer and snatched off the cover that was concealing the large hidden object, which was revealed to be a powerful MD 540A compact assault helicopter. The gunfire was getting worse after every passing second, "K' Shadow-U, hold yur' position! Wasp to Armadillo…yur' closest to Prospect-1, I need ja' ta go fetch'um! Me and Pretty Boy will go offer Boss Hog and Rev some needed assistance!" Kale ordered.

Back in the garage,

When Agent Milton Elliot played high school football back in his hometown in Nebraska, he was not really known for having what some would call “elite speed.” His coaches though, often commended him for his considerable skill and effort on and off the practice field and lauded his ability of having a “high motor” during games, the agent remembered. Yep, those were the good old days, Agent Elliot thought. He recollected how hard it was to please his tyrannical position coach who often rode his ass like a rodeo bull back then, whenever he was “not” giving his all. But boy, if his position coach could see how fast his ass was moving while dodging machine gun bullets he would be “highly impressed,” Agent Elliot assumed, while swiftly jumping into the car with Thomas Jr. “Punch the Goddamned gas Rev!!!” Agent Elliot screamed, and returned fire on the chasing Road Quakers. Thomas Jr. did not need to be told twice and hit the gas pedal on the lavish Lincoln, despite driving backwards. It did not take long before the crazed bikers from the roof of the garage to catch up with the tandem and continued to express their feelings with hoards of gunfire, causing the manic driving Thomas Jr. to crash into one car after another while trying to escape, “The fuck taught you how to drive, Stevie Wonder? We ain’t in no fucking bumper car, Rev!” Agent Elliot shouted and returned fire, causing the Road Quaker’s high-powered motocylces to topple over one another and explode. Meanwhile, Hakiro Yosami had to take cover, as a myriad of bikers began to spew out from the storage facility, “I don’t know if you assholes are still alive in there, but if you are…you have lots of company coming your way!” Hakiro warned over the radio. When they finally reached the bottom garage level, Agent Elliot could hear the sounds of what felt like a hundred angry Harleys, “Fuck!!! Look, I know you don’t want to die Rev, you still have your kid…so I won’t blame you if you want to get out…” Agent Elliot said. Thomas Jr. took one second to respond, “I’m not leaving you. We came here together…we leave here together.” Thomas Jr. said sternly. The husky agent stared at the reverend wide-eyed and pulled up his mask, “I don’t care what nobody says… you’re one beautiful fucking man, Rev!” Agent Elliot confirmed. His remark made the contented reverend smile, “I think I liked you “better” with that thing on…” Thomas Jr. jokingly replied. Agent Elliot laughed and pulled his mask back down over his face and reloaded his assault rifle. But just as the bikers started to ascend on them, blasts could be heard hitting the ground as well as rapid gunfire from the top of the five story garage. They looked at each other and both assumed what the other was all ready thinking, as they spoke the same thing out load, "Kale."

In the basketball/gym facility,

When he awoke, Jovan was zip tied on the floor to a piece of workout equipment and surrounded by the man he punched out and his three friends. The man with the curly dark hair that he initially shot was holding his own weapon on him. His body felt extremely sore all over, including his teeth, and could hardly breathe out his bloodied nose. Although he knew he was about to die, the only thing he could think about was the possibility of seeing his daughter Latavia again. But if he was going to die it was going to be on his terms, "So, what chu' bitches waitin' for? I thought you gun runners knew how to shoot…" Jovan muttered. The bald headed muscle-head he punched out kicked him in the stomach and stomped on his face. Barely moving, Jovan spit blood onto the floor, "That all you got…bitch?" Jovan said. But just before the bald headed man could go to work on him again, the curly headed man stopped him, "Naw…he's had enough...for now. Besides, we need'um alive long enough to find out why the fuck he's really here and who the hell he brought wit'um…" He said. Just as he finished his statement, David Lewis came through the door, "Well that's easy, he's with me!" David said, while pointing a customized prosthetic gun at the small group. After realizing too late that another uninvited guest was in the room, David quickly cut them all down with modified gun/arm before anyone could react. He then hurried over to check on Jovan who was giggling on the floor, "Anymore questions?" Jovan quipped. David kneeled down next to him and cut the zip ties off him, "Armadillo to Wasp, I got Prospect-1, he's down…" David said into his earpiece. Jovan rubbed his sore wrists and stumbled to his feet and, "…But not out the game." Jovan replied. His bravery and toughness impressed the hardnosed Sergeant, "Well, you heard the man, Wasp." David stated proudly. Kale could be heard chuckling through his radio, "That's super! But now I need ja' ta' haul ass back to the Antenna and pick up Shadow-U, before he gets too bored. Then head over to the storage area and try and locate our targets. Meanwhile, me and Pretty Boy will provide cover for Boss Hog and Rev till they can get to the theatre! But we gotta' move fast! Our window of opportunity's closin' and then it'll be a matter of minutes, befo' the cops come O' runnin!" Kale said emphatically. David and Jovan made a fast break for the specially modified ambulance they used to come and go undetected with from the hospital, which was parked in the back of the gym. But unlike any other typical hospital vehicle, the bullet proof van was fully weaponized with heavy duty artillery and other sophisticated tech. Driving like a bat out of hell, Thomas Jr. and Agent Elliot came zigzagging away from the garage just in time as the ferocious looking helicopter Alejandro and Kale were piloting came roaring down on top of the fifty, or so impeding Road Quakers. The militarized helicopter came with an arsenal of its own, firing Apache missiles and twelve hundred rounds of ammunition unmercifully. Despite the rising amount of casualties and vast discrepancy of firepower, the Road Quaker gang members refused to go down quietly. After picking up Hakiro Yosami from the church's cafeteria, David and Jovan also joined the fray. With their numbers dwindling fast, the remaining Road Quakers stood their ground near the church's storage and theatre hall, causing them to become difficult to penetrate. Realizing the helicopter was out of ammunition and missiles Kale had to quickly go to plan B, "Armadillo I need yew' ta' take out that God damned storage dock!" Kale instructed. David then pulled over and gave the wheel to Jovan, who he ordered to make a donut right in front of the dock where most of what was left of the Road Quakers was shooting. He detached his prosthetic arm and attached the custom made rocket launcher to himself and opened the ambulances double doors, "Fire in the hole!!" David yelled and fired a rocket into the storage's main door. The violent blast left many of the traumatized gang affiliates either dead or withering on the ground in severe pain, allowing Jovan to virtually drive through the debris freely. Seeing the paraplegic's handy work up close caused the young All-American to turn green with envy, "Damn man, how come you get to shoot all the cool shit?" Jovan asked perturbed. David casually took off his rocket projectile prosthetic and gave him a cold stare, "Maybe I can get Kale to cut your arms off too so you can..." David chillingly replied. Jovan's mouth dropped instantly, "Hold up, are you saying that Kale…but I thought he…ain't that nigga yo best….now "that's" just plain fucked up!" Jovan replied stutteringly. The former Army Sergeant snickered to himself, "Hmph…thought so. Now, since you're hurt, I need you to stick close to the Antenna until me and Shadow get back! Anybody swings back behind us you waste their Harley Davidson riding asses! Copy that?!" David ordered intensely. Since he was in no place to argue with a man with a machine gun for an arm, Jovan gave the intimidating Sergeant Lewis two thumbs up. He looked at the silent and steady minded Hakiro Yosami and gave him a reassuring nod and they both fled the armored ambulance.

Outside the theatre,

The sixty-something-year old reverend from Ben Hill had never seen a real-life pissed off biker gang up close before and was quite frankly, amazed at their malevolent tenacity to do him bodily harm. In the back of his mind he was sort of relieved that he was next to someone who was just as much of a malignant force as they were. Just as Agent Elliot had the few strangling Road Quaker members on the run, his M-16 ran out of ammo. He then quickly retreated to the trunk of the bullet riddled Lincoln to get more clips for his assault rifle, but then noticed how Thomas Jr. was frozen still, as though he had seen a ghost. It was the loathsome Sonny Korne and his bunch staring back at him through the glass doors, but only it was "them" who were feeling as if "they" were the ones staring at a ghost. His mouth dropped when he realized that Sonny was also still wearing his son's favorite baseball cap he had stolen from him the night they ambushed his family. But seeing that hurtful reminder suddenly snapped the stoic preacher out of his apparent trance, "You dirty motherfucka…." Thomas Jr. said aloud and instantly gave chase. In shock, the quartet themselves took off as well when they saw the highly agitated reverend coming for them, "Hey Rev! Rev, wait up!!! Fuck…Yo Wasp, I need you to ditch the chop, looks like Rev spotted Korne and he's flyin' in solo!" Agent Elliot said on his radio. He began chasing after the hell bent preacher (that was surprisingly quick for his age) and who was also acting as if he were bullet proof, "Yo Rev!! You ain't got no GUN, man! Shit!" Agent Elliot screamed and followed him through the glass double doors. Fortunately for the former undercover agent, the darkly lit theatre had but one floor available for Sonny Korne and his flunkies to hide, making it less painless to find them or, the flustered reverend, Agent Elliot calculated. After silently making his way around dimly lit corridor after corridor, the seasoned officer faintly heard the shouting preacher, who sounded as if he were nearby the theatre's mammoth-sized auditorium. In his policeman's gut, he knew Sonny Korne and his friends were leading Thomas Jr. into an obvious trap, as the Agent Elliot could also hear them taunting the angry reverend as well. But just as the former D.E.A. agent opened the red auditorium doors, a loud communication filled with static in his earpiece distracted him and one of Sonny Korne's smallest Lieutenant's Pete hit Agent Elliot over the head with a baseball bat, rendering him unconscious. Pete commenced to kicking the defenseless agent repeatedly until blood began to leak out from the mouth of his dank Porky Pig mask. After beating and mocking him ad nauseam, the gloating Pete threw down the baseball bat and slithered his way back through the doors amongst the shadows of the closed concert hall. Thomas Jr. slightly flinched as he heard the doors slam behind him, as he wondered aimlessly throughout the darkly lit aisles. Though the immovable preacher was too angry to be unafraid of his tormentors, he could tell that they were trying hard to rattle him in the darkness with their constant ranting and laughing from all directions, "Aren't you God dammed cowards sick of running? Why don't ya'll just come on out…you don't have anything to worry about, Sonny, I'm not armed." Thomas Jr. shouted. As he cautiously edged closer toward the front of the long stage, Thomas Jr. could make out the shapes of two tall figures that were flanked on both sides of it. When he was close enough to recognize who the two men were Thomas Jr. stopped mid-step. It was the beastly and evil grinning brothers Revis and Clevis. All of a sudden, a spotlight appeared onto the stage and then the curtains drew and a third person walked out into the middle of the platform and took a bow, "You wanted me nigger preacher, well….her I am. Only problem is, in order to get to me you gonna have to go through my boys…I betcha' you remember ole' Clevis fo' sho'….yeah. I remember back when ya'll two got re-e-e-a-a-a-l close!" Sonny Korne quipped menacingly. There he was in the flesh…the devil himself, the man who took everything that was so good and wholesome in his life, all in the span of one night, Thomas Jr. thought. A sick demon, who felt the urge to purge his family from this precious thing we call existence, only to satiate a fiery blood lust, all in the namesake of his dead and dreadful son, Samuel. For all the strength he had been praying for up till this moment: to live through his personal wounds (both mental and physical), strength for his son to overcome his coma and one day wake up, and most of all, strength to speak his peace had he lived long enough to see this day. But since that day has finally arrived, the only thing he was hoping for was the fortitude to not be compelled to kill the one man who he knew full well deserved it. Had he been physically the same man he was thirty years ago, then the fuming reverend would have liked his chances, but since he was not, Thomas Jr. knew it was going to be a one way trip. Growing impatient, the sadistic Sonny Korne began to goad the hesitant preacher, "Awe, what's the matter preacher man? Cat gotcha' tongue? Hmm…oh, wait…now I get it. Now that your family's all gone…you ain't got a reason to beg no more! But man, (bending over and putting his hands on his knees) I tell you what, between me and you that ole' wife of yours, Lucy…pussy s-u-u-u-re w-a-a-a-s good! And not all "tight" like that whore of a daughter. What was that bitch's name again? Mildred, Mya, Mariah…" Sonny joked. Clevis turned around, "Na Son, I think it was more like "Malisa" or "Marrisa" or maybe it was "Malcolm." Clevis playfully interjected, before getting interrupted. (Putting his hand out) "Nah, Cleve…you getting her mixed up with her brother, what's his name, Mason?" Revis kiddingly said. (Tapping his self over the forehead) "A-h-h-h, shit man…I forgot. Shit, sure hate I didn't get to fuck him…" Clevis quipped mockingly. Infuriated by both their flagrant disregard and disrespect for his deceased loved ones, Thomas Jr. started clenching his fists, "Mia and Markus…" Thomas Jr. said through gritting teeth. All three men stopped talking simultaneously. After a couple awkward seconds pass, a smiling Sonny Korne put his left hand above his eyes as if he were a captain at sea searching for land, "You say sumthin' there, Tommie?" Sonny asked sarcastically. Disgusted and fueled with rage, Thomas Jr. began to storm the stage, "My children's names are Mia and Markus you soulless son's a bitches!!!" Thomas Jr. screamed. Both Clevis and Revis quickly and aggressively tackled the maddened reverend to the ground. The middling weasel Pete, who was working the stage lights, followed Sonny down the middle of the steps as if he were the star of a Broadway play, "I tell you what, for a nigger…you sure are tough! I shot you…like what, six times? Shit. And here you are…like a piece of shit stuck on a pair of new boots!" Sonny said cynically. Thomas Jr. continued to struggle while the dastardly twins held him down by his arms. He then pulled out a pistol from behind his waist, "A damn shame we out of time preacher boy…I'm sure Clevis here would've liked catchin' up with ya (Clevis blows a kiss at Thomas Jr.) for ole' time's sake! But we gotta run… (aims his gun at Thomas Jr.' face) hope you mind not getting shot in the face this time?" Sonny quipped. Suddenly, there was a thunderous roaring sound coming from above them and something came crashing through the ceiling's skylight, "What the fuck?" Sonny yelled surprised. Pete quickly shined the spotlight on the object, which turned out to be a shooting Lieutenant Keegan, who had jumped from the helicopter he was attached to. In one swoop, Kale managed to shoot out the spotlight and get off a head shot on Revis, while also clipping Clevis in the shoulder. Just as Sonny began to open fire on Kale, Thomas Jr. hit him across the jaw with a thunderous uppercut causing him to lose the gun he had. Kale instantly detached himself from the wire he was hanging from and noticed him running away, "Son of bitch…" Kale said and started shooting at the scruffy looking twenty-something. But as he was trying to flee through the red theatre doors, Agent Elliot smashed him in the forehead with the bat he used on him. He then proceeded to stomp the young man, until finally stepping on his neck and killing him. When he finished, he gave the Lieutenant (whose face was painted like Paul Stanley from the rock n' roll group Kiss) a thumbs up. Kale had almost forgotten that Thomas Jr. was still pounding on the face of Sonny Korne and could hear the preacher cursing him after every blow. Although the riled reverend was bludgeoning Sonny unmercifully, the sweet satisfaction of pulverizing him out of existence felt intoxicating, so much so, that it caused him to weep maddeningly. Kale finally reached down and pulled the tired and emotional Thomas Jr. off the motionless Sonny Korne, "He's not worth it Rev…be better than him." Kale said, but then pulled out his 357 magnum and shot him twice in the head. Thomas Jr. barely flinched, "What happened to being better than him?" Thomas Jr. asked. The young Lieutenant looked down at the reverend's former tormentor in disgust, "Well…guess yew' gotta' do it fo' the both of us." Kale replied starkly. Thomas Jr. did not know to reply, but smiled when Kale tapped him on the chest, "Come on….we still got us one last problem to solve…" Kale insisted. A dazed Thomas Jr. rubbed his aching head, "Oh yeah, and who's that?" Thomas Jr. asked looking at Sonny. Agent Elliot came hustling down the theatre aisle, "Brickwood. They didn't find the son of a bitch!" Agent Elliot said. Just as they began to walk away Thomas Jr. almost forgot to get one last thing himself, "Wait a sec…" Thomas Jr. said and went to Sonny's lifeless body. When he kneeled down to take the ball cap off Sonny's head, nobody realized that Clevis was still alive and was pointing a gun at the backs of Kale and Agent Elliot. Then suddenly, a single shot was fired hitting Clevis in the back of the throat, killing him instantly. Both of the shocked men stopped mid-conversation and looked at one another in confusion and then behind them at Thomas Jr., who had shot Clevis with Sonny Korne's lost gun. Kale went to the reverend and took the gun out of his hands, "Alright now, let me have that….yew' know what Rev? If I wasn't already crazy…I'de think yew'startin' ta' like me." Kale quipped.

Next door at the church's storage facility,

An infuriated Agent Elliot was punching the storage walls in repulsion, "Son of a bitch!" Agent Elliot hollered. To calm him, Jovan placed his hand over his friend's shoulder and after he did, the angered former undercover agent immediately stopped. Road Quaker leader Ozzie Brickwood was still missing and they had only moments before the security guards (that were still trapped in the sanctuary) would have the capability to call the police. Lieutenant Keegan (who was pacing back and forth like a leopard with his gun resting on his shoulder) was in denial as well, "Now, are yew' guys SURE yew' looked everywhere?" Kale asked irritated. David walked up to his best friend looking him straight in the eye, "We've searched everywhere! Look around K…there ain't nothing else here, but "dead bodies" man. Are you sure that intel's clean? I mean…couldn't there've been a chance they might have gotten things wrong on this one?" David asked emphatically. Considering the fact that their filthy rich benefactor had never been wrong, the thought never crossed the young Lieutenant's mind. Despite feeling somewhat hesitant, he went ahead and reassured him, "Yeah, usually…till now. Fuck! We get (karate kicking a box) one asshole away from completin' the last objective and we lose'um, like a fuckin' fart in the wind!" Kale said frustrated. The last part of Kale's intriguing statement caught Agent Elliot's attention and caused him to do an about-face, "Last objective? I thought "this" was supposed to have been the last fuckin' objective!" Agent Elliot stated. He gave the beaten Jovan Campbell a worried look and then charged the young Lieutenant, "What else do you and Harlan have going on, bro?" Agent Elliot asked suspiciously. David too quickly joined in on the discussion, "Yeah, I'd like to hear that shit too." David replied displeased. Frustrated, Kale slammed his assault rifle on a large crate, "Okay!!! But…we REALLY don't have fuckin' time ta' talk about this shit right now, yew' know….wit' the cops comin' an all!? But yeah, me and Harlan got other plans…plans that don't "involve" any of yew'!" Kale confirmed. As the three men argued back and forth, Hakiro who had been quietly studying a large number of familiar looking crates finally reached a conclusion, "Okay guys…?" Hakiro said, with his back turned to the group of yelling men. When he tried to get their attention again they ignored the soft spoken South Korean. But then without warning Hakiro threw one of his sword sickles into the wall next to the men, "Guys…I've seen these crates before…well, (pointing at a logo on the crate) at least I've seen this symbol before." Hakiro said. Kale and the others swiftly assembled around the portly former store owner. Everyone began to carefully examine the strange looking symbol, but without needing to take a second look, both Kale and David knew the insignia's origin, "Where else did yew' say yew' saw this?" Kale asked sharply. His sudden change in tone grabbed the group's attention, which made Hakiro slightly apprehensive to respond, "Yes, uh…the first time I saw this… was when I and my family fled South Korea. It was on many of the cargo in the vessel that brought us…" Hakiro confirmed. The intimidating Kiss make-up on Kale's face made the South Korean a bit unsure if he should continue the conversation, but continued at the young Lieutenant's calm urging, "Go on, Ro.'" Kale insisted. Then, I saw it again…when I was fighting in the basement…lots more crates were stored there." Hakiro began before getting cutoff. "Are you talking about Big Cory's warehouse?" Jovan asked, holding his ribs. When Hakiro nodded yes, Kale became even more irritated, "The "fuck" why yew' didn't say nuthin' Ro? We suppose ta' be a fuckin' team aren't we? Kale asked, while throwing up his hands in disgust. Confused, the former store owner tried to explain himself, "How was I supposed to know that "it" was of any importance?" Hakiro pleaded. Walking off in a fit of perplexity, the young Lieutenant picked up his assault rifle and cocked it, "Yur' right Ro, but in any case we gotta' move!" Kale ordered. David ran up to him with a look of astonishment on his face, "Bro, if what we just saw means what WE "think" it means…" David began, before getting cutoff by the eavesdropping Agent Elliot. (Standing in his way) "Hold up Keegan, what so special about a "sword" going through a "star" that you're keepin' from us, huh? What's it mean?" Agent Elliot demanded. In the little while he had gotten to know the wily ex-soldier, this was the first time he appeared actually worried, "For you guys? Nothin.' For me, (looking at David) maybe…I dunno'….could be somethin,' could mean nuthin.' Either way, we gotta pack up and go before ole' Johnny law gits' here." Kale insisted. Moments later, just as the group grabbed their gear headed outside to join Thomas Jr. in the makeshift ambulance, someone on the roof began shooting at them with an automatic weapon. Hakiro was the first to receive the worst of the onslaught and was quickly cut down by a barrage of bullets. Jovan Campbell took a bullet to the back, just as he is thrown to the ground and shielded by Agent Elliot. By instinct, both Lieutenant Keegan and Sergeant Lewis managed to avoid the shooters attack by dropping and rolling onto the ground. The duo immediately returned fire on their attacker, striking him simultaneously and caused his bullet riddled body to fall hard to the pavement. Kale sprung to his feet as fast as a jack rabbit and rushed over to the dead man's unmovable carcass. Kale leaned down next to the tattooed-faced shooter and grinned widely, "Well, well, well…guess ole' Oswald "was" here after all. We appreciate yew' droppin' by, but don't yew' worry bout' us Ozzie…we'll show ourselves out!" Kale snickered and fired up a cigarette to celebrate. When the gushing Lieutenant went to rejoin the others by the ambulance, he saw that three of his friends were still on the ground, "Whut'?! Whut the fu…" Kale said and fell helplessly to his knees between a dead Hakiro Yosami and a gurgling Agent Elliot, who was shot through the chest. Although he was able to save him, Jovan Campbell could not move, "Yo Eli, get yo heavy ass up off of me…you making my legs feel numb, man!" Jovan quipped. David helped Kale remove the heavily bleeding agent off of Jovan, who was still having issues getting to his feet, "Uh, fellas….I think my legs done fell asleep or sumthin'…you think one of ya'll can help a nig back up? And Eli, man…quit playing around…we ain't got time for you to do impressions man." Jovan joked, while lying on his back. Fearing the worst, David Lewis kneeled down next to the former super athlete, "Hey Joe, I wanna….I-I'm gonna roll you over, just for a quick sec." David said calmly. Bewildered by the strange request Jovan at first resisted, "Yo D, I'm good! My main dude managed to do something right for once and saved his boy, I'm straight. I just need a little h…" Jovan began before getting interrupted. "I still need to you to do it! Please Joe." David asked politely. No matter how hard he fought the temptation, but seeing the frightening look in Jovan's eyes made the proud steel-hearted Sergeant Lewis's eyes fill with moisture, "This'll only take one second. I promise." David insisted. While David was busy tending to Jovan, Kale was applying pressure to Agent Elliot's chest, but even he had been in enough battle situations to know a dead man when he saw one. Despite his urging him not to speak, the stubborn former D.E.A. agent still wanted to speak his mind, "I-I-Is…Joe…i-i-his…is he ok?" Agent Elliot asked. Kale shook his head yes. Although he was bleeding profusely through his mouth, Agent Elliot smiled brightly, "G-G-Go-hood. D-hid… (coughing up more blood) D-D-id y-y-y…?" Agent Elliot struggled to say before getting interrupted. (Kale wiped a tear from his eye) "Yeah bro…we…we popped that sumbitch' good." Kale chokingly confirmed. The news of Oswald Brickwood's death made him smile once more and suddenly, he reached out for Kale's hand, "T-T-hell J-J-hoe…s-sta-hay o-out of…tru-ball…I-I got to go s-se-e my f-f-am-lee n-now!" Agent Elliot said and then died holding Kale's hand. When David finished inspecting the young collegian it was just as he feared, as young Jovan was struck in the spine during Ozzie Brickwood's ambush. After their eyes met, the look on David's face was more than enough to explain to Kale what happened to the young man. Jovan immediately became worried by the awkward silence, "So what's up doc? You lettin' me back in the game or what? Yo' Eli! Time to get up off yo' ass man and… Eli? Hey…h-how come…how come you not sayin' nuthin man?" Jovan asked sobbingly. Slowly, Thomas Jr. got out the ambulance and walked over to Hakiro's body and kneeled down next to him and silently prayed.

Interlude:

Sunday morning in Madrid, Spain.....

Cartel leader Alfonso Barrera had been partaking in a private meeting at the beach home of business partner and crooked politician Andre`s Araya, with whom he had been very displeased with after their latest business venture. Before the obese Araya could even greet the manic Barrera with a "hello," he shot two of his personal assistants and a bodyguard in the face and slammed his head though a glass table. He then pinned his sweaty forehead face down on his wooden wet bar and was threatening to remove his entire ear with a pair of gardening pruners. Petrified with fear, the short and plump Araya tried to rationalize and understand the reasons behind his usually cool-headed partner's violent outburst, (panting loudly) "Clearly, by your actions Mr. Barrera, you are very upset ..." Andreas stated. Araya's presumptive remark only further infuriated the tyrannical cartel leader, prompting him to slice his earlobe off. Screaming in excruciating pain, the crooked Araya began pleading for his life, "Please, Alfonso...I beg of you, don't do this!! Tell me...my friend, what is it that I have done to deserve such hostility?" Andre`s said from his marbled deck floor. The sinister Alfonso Barrera picked up his business partner's earlobe off the table and cornered him up against a sofa. Smiling, he kneeled down and handed the portly man his earlobe back, stood to his feet and pulled out his gun, "You're no different from any other fat pig, Andreas...I provide you protection, I even kill off your competitors every once and a while. I see to it, that everyone who knows you respects you! But then, I give you MY money and then in return, you send me a container full of dead whores! So like the fucking pig you are and if you want to breathe in the next five seconds ....you're going to have to swallow that fucking thing!" Alfonso threatened, while holding a gun to Araya's face. The frightened Andreas had known the psychotic Alfonso Barrera long enough to know he always meant what he said and grudgingly shoved his earlobe into his mouth and choked trying to swallow it down. Pleased, Alfonso helped him off the ground and then put his gun back into his suit coat, "Now, my friend…we're going to further discuss, how EXACTLY you're going to make this back up to me…" Alfonso concluded.

Thirty minutes later, on his way back to the airport….

Feeling gratified by the end results of his latest business dealings, Alfonso Barrera received an unexpected phone call on his cell from an old associate from his past. The number belonged to longtime friend and the current governor of Mexico, Francisco El Roga, who was about twenty years his senior. Although unknown to most of the republic, it had been with El Roga's blessing that Alfonso had been able to operate within certain Mexican territories without receiving much resistance from the government. Every now and then, as a show of good faith, Alfonso would roll over on one of his local connects to make the shady governor look good in order to conduct his business worry free. It also did not hurt that at one time they both had love for the same woman, "Hola, Governor El Roga! How good it is to hear from you as always…" Alfonso began to say before getting interrupted. "Sorry my good friend, but what I have to say will be VERY "hard" for you to hear and even "harder" to except. But I don't want to explain ANYTHING until you see what I have to show you. Are you near a computer?" Governor El Roga asked tensely. Alfonso could sense the tension in his long time associate's voice and reached for his silver laptop, "Yes, I have it. But what is the meaning of th….?" Alfonso started to ask, before getting cutoff mid sentence. "It is better that I show you, my friend. When you are finished with the file, call me back immediately." Governor El Rogo instructed, and hung up the phone. The clueless cartel leader could not explain Francisco's irrational behavior, but instead decided to humor him. Within seconds, the file Governor El Roga sent popped up in his mailbox. Despite being a little apprehensive, Alfonso clicked on the file and opened the attachments. There were multiple pictures of a familiar looking woman and a child playing at a park that he did not recognize. When he came across one of the photos that were of a full frontal view of the woman and child, Alfonso maximized the picture. What he saw next caused him to drop his laptop on the limo floor,

"Impossible!!! T-That's not her! T-There's…it's just not possible!!! Jesus Christ!!!" Alfonso yelled, while gasping for air to breathe. His bodyguard who was in the passenger seat overheard the commotion and instantly opened the window panel on the cabin wall, "Hey boss, you okay? I thought I heard a noise." The body guard asked concerned. Stunned by the image on the photo, Alfonso Barrera could not find the strength to speak and waived off the husky man. While the perspiring gangster stared at the shiny laptop down on the limo floor, he was suddenly overcome by an emotion not felt in a very long time, not since he was a small child. It was a poignant sense of fear that ran borderline to the unimaginable in his mind. Surely the woman in the photo could not have been the love he believed was once lost? Alfonso rationalized. After working up the courage, the distraught cartel leader grabbed the laptop and placed it back onto his lap, took a deep breath and reopened it. When he saw her picture again, the man who was notorious for cutting off the limbs of his enemies began to sob. He ran his fingers gently around the outline of the woman's beautiful face, but then something on the little boy's shirt caught his attention. Alfonso wiped away his tears in order to see the image more clearly and after he did, his stomach felt as if someone had just drove a car over it. The words on the boys dark colored suspenders had a picture of the Cookie Monster from the Sesame Street TV show that had a bubble that read: "Mommy's little monster!" on the front. Nothing about the mysterious photos was making any kind of sense to the frantic cartel leader, so after composing himself, he immediately called back Governor El Roga. When El Roga answered the phone, he knew the questions before Alfonso could think to get them out, "Yes, my friend…it's really her. Apparently, my half-sister did not die as we both assumed and had been living in America with her son…your son." Governor El Roga confirmed. Alfonso could not believe his ears and almost choked the words out, "M-My…s-s-on?!?" Alfonso asked bewildered. Governor El Roga deeply exhaled, "Yes, Alfonso. We have much to discuss…" Governor El Roga concluded.

<u>End of Interlude</u>

Letting Bygones be Bygones

Sunday late afternoon, Harlan Kruellar's estate…

Harlan had been in his office staring at his son's portrait as he often had ever since his death when his confidant and assistant entered the room, "Mr. Lara is here, as you expected." Oscar announced, and left the room. Alejandro often wondered what went through the mogul's mind when he would walk in on him gazing into the painting for long periods of time. If there was one thing he knew that was real about Harlan it would be the love he had for his son Haven. Why else would the man devise such an intricate plan and pour vast amounts of his own resources into catching his son's murderer? Alejandro thought. When he explained to him how Haven died, Harlan primarily took responsibility for placing his son in harm's way, but part of him could not forget the large role Alfonso Barrera played in his death. What also made his death so unbearable was unknowingly cheering Haven being torn apart by a chainsaw and having the will power not to react after realizing it was him. Harlan decided to play the "long game" to repay the venomous Alfonso Barrera back the favor and with his help, will finally have the chance, "As I have already told you, Mr.Kruellar, Hakiro Yosami and Agent Elliot are both dead. The football player Jovan though, is now out of surgery and it's just as we feared...he will never walk again. You're down to only three men, Mr. Kruellar. One who refuses to fight, one who's handicapped and the other….unstable, I should say the least. We may be a bit in over our heads considering our lack of m…." Alejandro said before getting interrupted. (Standing with his back to him) "Have you spoken to your uncle yet, Alex?" Harlan asked briskly. His curtness while changing the subject caused the sharply-dressed twenty-something to roll his eyes in exasperation, "Of course, I did." Alejandro confirmed nonchalantly. The doubtful entrepreneur glanced over his shoulder at the young man, "And you're certain he'll pass along the message…without alerting that "jackal?" After all….if what you say is true, Governor El Roga stands to lose a very valuable asset." Harlan asked sharply. Alejandro took a seat near Harlan's desk and crossed his legs, "It's a shame….that after all we've been through…you still don't trust me." Alejandro said disappointedly. Perturbed, Harlan exhaled loudly and approached the young man quietly until he was up in his face, "That's only because we're too deep in the game to allow not even "one" mishap, Alex. This is my only shot at getting that paranoid bastard into the country and I don't want to fuck it all up!" Harlan shouted, while standing over him. The harshness in Harlan's tone struck a huge cord in the young man, (sitting up on the edge of his seat) "Hey, I know how much this means to you…means to us! That's why I came to you remember? This crazy plan of yours wouldn't have worked without my help!" Alejandro protested. In the back of his mind, Harlan knew full well that Alejandro's statements were far from mere hyperbole, but part of him wished that it was just dumb luck that brought him to his doorstep. Rather their meeting been predetermined by divine will or catastrophic misfortune, the ripple effect that altered the state of their lives had finally settled and eventually merged them on the same path together, had they wanted to be or not, Harlan believed. For the foreboding circumstances that led Alejandro to his proud estate began many years ago, after his pregnant mother Norma, in fear for her life, fled Mexico for America. He told him how his mother struggled for years working many odd jobs and how they had to move from place to place, until eventually meeting and marrying tour helicopter pilot Anthony Flores. Upon moving to California, Alejandro admitted to being very rebellious as a much younger youth and often got into trouble, but all that was before finding his passion in life, which were video games. Years later, after getting his degree from UCLA, Alejandro quickly made a name for himself as a software engineer in the technological world and became extremely successful as a video game creator. But, if there was one thing as a successful business tycoon that Harlan Kruellar already knew, was that "successful" did not always exactly translate to "safe." With his newly acquired wealth, Alejandro was able to relocate both his mother and stepdad to an even more extravagant home near Beverly Hills, where his mother often jogged. Unfortunately, on one fateful morning, Alejandro said that a small gang of punk teenagers abducted Norma and had taken her to an abandoned home, where they savagely beaten and raped her for hours on end. After the group left her for dead, a passing neighbor spotted his bloodied mother, who had managed to crawl out of the home until passing out on the sidewalk and called for help. Alejandro explained to him that when she came too in the hospital, (that after many years of keeping their lineage a secret) Norma finally explained to him their true origins and how it all correlated to her attackers. She divulged only to Alejandro, that the young men who brutalized her bore the same gang tattoo that the members of her cousin's old Bloody Sinaloa Brother's gang once wore. Norma ultimately succumbed to her wounds, which sent his stepfather Anthony spiraling into a major depression and an alcohol dependency that later caused him to die during a fatal helicopter crash. A year or so passed and yet, the police still did not have a single suspect in custody and therefore, prompting Alejandro to use his own resources to investigate his mother's murder.

He would spend the coming months chasing after any clues that could have helped the police catch his mother's killers, only to come to the realization that the police neither wanted nor needed his help in the endeavor. When Alejandro's private investigation pointed to the possible involvement of the Crazy Confederate's and Alfonso Barrera's cartel, without any key eyewitnesses or any concrete proof, the police dragged their feet, allowing his mother's case to go cold. On the verge of almost giving up, Alejandro told him that it was not until he had heard the news report of Haven's accidental death in Mexico that piqued his curiosity into Harlan Industries. After doing some rather expensive prying, Alejandro heard from Harlan Industry competitors that there were some rumors and speculation about his questionable clientele, including possible dealings with corrupt government officials. Though what he ascertained was no more than circumstantial innuendo, the young man became even more suspicious when he found out that there was never an autopsy report filed after Haven's death. The software engineer smartly hypothesized that he was concealing his son's murder and believed that the only person in Mexico powerful enough to get to him would be cartel leader Alfonso Barrera. Despite Alejandro's inability to prove that allegation when he came to him, still he could not have been more impressed by well groom engineer's intellect. It was not until he shared his mother's story though that his jaw to hit the floor. Since he had exhausted every plausible idea and attempts at plotting Alfonso Barrera's demise, with Alejandro at his side, he finally had the perfect Trojan horse to bring his son's killer down once and for all. Once again, remembering what an invaluable asset he was fortunate to have, Harlan casually took a seat right across from him, "Yes, Alex (smiling)…I remember. And you're absolutely right, there's no way in hell I could have gotten this far without your assistance, and for that young man, I'm eternally grateful. I don't apologize very often but…" Harlan began before getting interrupted. Alejandro put his hand up, "And there's no need for you to start now, old man. Besides, it's like I was saying… although Barrera doesn't know it, but my uncle really hates him and promised to convince him to come. He says, that with him gone, not only would it finally give his half-sister some justice, but would also level the playing field…whatever the fuck that means." Alejandro stated. Despite being in deep thought, Harlan chuckled, "What?" Alejandro asked. Harlan had a slight grin on his bristled face, "Basically, with Alfonso out of the way…your uncle gets controlling interest on the rest of the cartels, as well as putting him in the driver's seat for a possible shot at the Mexican presidency. Hmph….that's a smart move. Your uncle's as shrewd a business man as me. His statement makes Alejandro laugh, "I suppose so….but uh, you know Harlan, I've been wondering. If a mass murderer, like Barrera, is so paranoid to even show his face in public, why risk coming to America for a child he never knew existed? I mean, what does he expect? He's a sadistic murderer, does he really think we're supposed to "hug it out" and live happily ever after?" Alejandro asked. The answer to his question was no different from the last few times the young twenty-something presented it to him. And likewise, Harlan stood to his feet and strolled over to his mini-bar and poured them two glasses of Johnny Walker Black. He then returned to his seat, while also handing a glass to Alejandro and sipped slowly. He took his time both contemplating his answer, as well as savoring the dark amber-like flavoring that often bombarded his eager taste buds. With their night to host their despicable guest so close on the horizon, the transporting mogul had somewhat of an epiphany of sorts, which made the moment feel that much more enlightening, "You know, when I think about the culmination of events that brought you here…they only make me miss my son that much more. When I look at you, you remind me so much of him. Like you, he was very confidant, intelligent….quite pleasing on the eyes (a trait which he no doubt got from his mother, rest her beautiful soul)" Harlan quipped. His levity was a refreshing change of pace compared to the brooding and haunted soul he usually was, Alejandro thought. For as flattering Harlan was of him at the moment, Alejandro could suddenly feel the weight of his guilt bearing down on him, as if it was trying to compact his chest cavity. To deflect the attention off himself (and his son Haven) Alejandro tried to down play his compliments by getting him to focus more on the point at hand, "I get that and I appreciate the compliment, but that's not really answering my question Harlan…" Alejandro insisted. Harlan began staring intently at the drink in his lap, "My point is this…even "without" the help of your connected uncle Francisco, Alfonso Barrera still "considers" himself a father at the end of the day and even to a madman like him that still means something. Rather we like it or not, most fathers want to see the best parts of themselves in their sons, just as much they hope they don't inherit the bad ones. And despite the "strict stipulations" that's in place to see him, Alfonso still feels comfortable that his Crazy Confederate gang will be enough to protect him and he will be SORELY mistaken! He's betting on a loyalty…Hmph…but I'm putting "my" money on a sure thing, I'm betting on Kale Keegan. So…when you ask me, do "I" think he'll show….then the answer is yes, I know he'll show…He'll come, Alex, because most times even "monsters" care for their son's." Harlan concluded and finished his drink.

Tuesday 1AM at the Houston Ship Channel….

Despite what small reverence he may have held for his longtime friend and ally, Governor El Roga, cartel leader Alfonso Barrera was unwilling to take any chances when he chose to meet his estranged son in the middle of a barren American shipyard. Upon entering the enclosed expanse, which was surrounded by thousands of shipping containers, he posted a couple of his most trusted lookouts at one of the only two entrances that lead into the meeting spot. Although he agreed to come to the heavily secluded meeting with but only a few of his personal bodyguards, the schizophrenic kingpin made sure that the area was discreetly surrounded by a committee of at least two-hundred of his "Crazy Confederate" gang members. With so many of them at his disposal, he could make a clear break for the boat that had brought him, just in case he was walking into a trap, Alfonso believed. Regardless, he sat impatiently inside the glossy black and bullet proofed limousine, awaiting the child he never knew existed from the only person on Earth he could have ever possibly loved. It wounded him greatly discovering that Norma had actually survived that horrible night long ago and had been living carefree with a son in the "one country" he refused to ever enter. He convinced himself that had he known she was still alive and well, he would have been made the desperate trek to America years ago, despite his present circumstances. The pressure of meeting his fully grown son was taking a humongous toll on the eager Barrera, who had since developed a severely bad cocaine habit over the last couple days. But despite what may have been in his best interest to not show, the anxious cartel leader felt ready for anything, "There he is." Alfonso said, while snorting a line of coke off the back of his thumb. Brightly lit headlights could be seen slowly approaching from the opposite entrance to the enclosed area, until finally coming to a complete stop about seventy yards or so away. Suddenly, the driver of the parked vehicle flashed their headlights three times to signal the skeptical cartel leader. Taking a moment to contemplate his next move, the doped up Barrera then instructed his driver to do the same. After a couple seconds pass, the driver from the other vehicle got out of the car and went to open the backdoor. One lone figure came out of the vehicle and began to walk in Alfonso Barrera's direction, until stopping half way. The fidgety cartel leader snorted another line of cocaine off the back of his thumb, "Alright, amigos...let's go have a look at papa's little mijo!" Alfonso said fiendishly. He then ordered his driver to pull up closer to the lone stranger, who appeared unfazed by his shadowy guests. When he was close enough Alfonso ordered the driver to stop the limousine and he, along with his three other bodyguards, got out to greet their host. As they all walked toward the well dressed young man with the smooth face and thinly cut moustache, the more emotionally unraveled the sinister crime lord became. Though known by most F.B.I agencies for being directly responsible for countless mass murders at home and abroad, Alfonso Barrera began to weep, as he could clearly recognize the very same smile that once belonged to his former lover on the face of his long lost son. Gradually, Alfonso went up to Alejandro and gave him a long hug, but the young man did not return the favor. When Alfonso got a hold of himself, looked into his son's cold eyes he could see the reflection of a tormented soul staring right through him, "My son…I-I know…I-I wasn't always there for you, but…papa's here now! Let me take you home…" Alfonso said sincerely. The more the cartel boss spoke, the more disgusted Alejandro became and pushed Alfonso off of him, "There's someone here who may have a problem with that, "dad." Alejandro said chillingly. His son's cold and callous demeanor was not that big of a shock to him, as he was once an orphan himself, but the news of some "other person" on the other hand baffled him. But, before he could even ask who that person was the backdoor to the other side of the limousine Alejandro was in swung open. When the Mexican crime lord could make out the mysterious stranger's face, suddenly a chill scurried down the nape of his spine, "H-Harlan? Harlan Kruellar? Harlan…my "friend," is THAT really you!?!" Alfonso gingerly said. Immediately, Alfonso's three big body guards started to draw their weapons, until he waved them off, "Wait…Harlan's a friend. How long has it been now, amigo? You are looking well!" Alfonso asked. Harlan came and stood next to Alejandro and nonchalantly wiped the dust from his shoulder, "Hello, Alfonso…I don't know….but it's definitely been "too" long…." Harlan said dryly and put his hands into his coat pocket. The scathing Barrera knew something was obviously amiss with Harlan's unforeseen presence, but decided to play along, "And what do I owe you for the pleasure of this visit my friend? I suppose, I have YOU to thank for this…special reunion?" Alfonso said and put his hands behind his back. Harlan caught him signaling his men and simply smiled, "Yes…yes, I suppose you do…NOW Kale!" Harlan screamed. Lieutenant Kale sprang out from a hole that he had been hiding in (covered up by a three by three foot piece of flat metal and dirt) and began killing Alfonso Barrera's personal bodyguards with an automatic rifle. Alfonso's two lookouts who stood near the entrance behind him, heard the loud gun fire and tried to come to his aid, but both men were swiftly dealt with from afar by Sergeant David Lewis' deadly accurate sniper's rifle. Just as the nefarious cartel leader drew his pistol on Harlan, Lieutenant Keegan (whose face was now painted like a member of the Baseball Furies from "the Warriors" movie) threw his knife into Barrera's hand, causing the wretched crime lord to drop the weapon in painful agony. Feeling betrayed, the cartel leader dropped to his knees for both mercy and understanding, "W -

Why Harlan? Why are you doing all this, my friend? Wasn't I…wasn't I a "good friend" to you? Given you money? Even brought to you one of your son's kidnappers, "Santiago," on a platter! And now… you spit in my face, by killing my men!" Alfonso pleaded. Harlan casually took off the belt he had been wearing for the last three years and tossed it in front of the drug kingpin, "You mean the one who wore this? Yes, I've been meaning to explain that to you, "friend" …..(Harlan ran up to Alfonso and punched him in the face with all his might) …that "kidnapper" you butchered three years ago was my "son" Haven, you sadistic motherfucker! But of course, YOU already knew that! You retaliated against me for turning down your twisted fucking scheme to sell kids, admit it motherfucker!!" Harlan yelled angrily, while kicking him repeatedly on the ground. Alejandro grabbed the overly excitable middle-aged transporting mogul, before he could catch a heart attack, "Get a hold of yourself for Christ's sake Harlan!" Alejandro insisted. While grinning widely, Alfonso started howling at the moon, "Don't worry about your papa, mijo…It takes a lot more than some old "puta" to hurt your old papa. Just so you know, Harlan, I got a few friends coming! And then, I will take my mijo out of here…away from this fucking joke of a country! And with him at my side, NOTHING will ever fucking stop us!" Alfonso threatened. Harlan began to laugh uncontrollably, causing the fiendish Barrera to become severely annoyed, "What the hell is so funny you fucking puta!" Alfonso asked irritated. After composing himself, Harlan stood over the cartel leader and leaned as if he were talking to a five year old throwing a temper tantrum, "Well, you see the thing is Al…."no one" else is coming…" Harlan replied cryptically, with his hands perched on his knees. Alfonso Barrera balked at Harlan's ridiculous insinuation, "I'm the fucking "commander" of one of the world's most dangerous cartels and besides, I promised my Confederates two million dollars for my safe return!" Alfonso confirmed. Harlan chuckled while running his hand through his thinning hair, "Well, I just "gave" them twenty-five million more reasons to leave! So, you need to go ahead and face facts asshole…because YOUR ass, "now" belongs to me." Harlan concluded. Figuring he could play to his sympathies, the foolish Barrera tried the desperately misguided father card on the young man, "Surely, you do not wish this dreadful person to do your papa any harm now, do you mijo? I mean, I know I'm not perfect (I may have killed a lot of people who may have deserved it) but with your help mijo, I know we can make things right…" Alfonso began before getting interrupted. (Pointing at Alfonso) "You're not my fucking dad. And you want to know something else? I'm not you're God damned son, either." Alejandro admitted. Though Alejandro's words deeply disturbed him, the stubborn cartel leader refused to believe him, "You, can fucking say what you want mijo but, there's just no other way that you can't be! Your mother was pregnant BEFORE leaving Mexico. She was in love with me!" Alfonso yelled. Alejandro shook his head and squatted down next to the feeble minded drug lord, "Yes, she did mention that before she died. But she also knew that you would never give up the gangs to be with her, so when my real father, Raul Rena, promised to bring her here to America, she felt she owed him something, since it would ultimately cost him his life for him to do so!" Alejandro confessed. The growling crime lord stood to his feet and peered into the young man's face once more, to see if he could find one last ghost from his past, on a face he briefly believed may have belonged to his. Infuriated by their treachery, pried Kale's knife from his hand and charged after the young man. But before he could lay one finger on him, Alejandro reached into his suit pocket for the pistol he was concealing and shot Alfonso Barrera several times in the torso. A joyful tear of satisfaction streamed down the side of Harlan Kruellar's face as he watched his flailing body drop to the ground. He went and stood over Alfonso's dying body, "See you in hell, Al. Harlan turned his attention toward the still panting young man, "Thank you Alex…for helping bring us "both" some peace. And now, Lieutenant Keegan…would you please be so kind, as to remove this piece of shit." Harlan asked. Without uttering a single word, Kale casually dragged the bloodied Alfonso Barrera and dropped him into the same hole that he used to hide in and covered it up. Just as Kale finished disposing of Alfonso Barrera's body, another pair of ominous looking headlights pulled in and parked near the entrance behind them. Whoever the shadowy person was, could not have been with the police since there were no flashing, or some wandering shipyard worker, as he made certain that his port had been closed off to anyone, Harlan assumed. Kale stood silently beside him and watched intently while the tall stranger began marching towards them, "You don't seem surprised, Lieutenant. Were you expecting company?" Harlan asked puzzled. Though the intense expression on Kale's face said otherwise when he looked at him, "Don't know just yet…it's really dependin' on which "version" of him that decided ta' show up..." Kale said bitterly. As the unknown visitor approached, Harlan could begin to make out the polished military uniform he was wearing, as he passed under the refracting lights of the dewy shipyard. Kale put his assault rifle over his shoulder and reached into his back pocket for his flask, took a quick swig and tried to share it with Harlan, who was too entrenched into knowing the person's identity and waved him off. When Harlan realized who the person actually was he turned to Kale, "I've changed my mind, I think I'd like that drink now…" Harlan requested. He grinned and handed the shiny sterling silver flask over to the startled transporting mogul.

Their mystery guest was none other than Kale's father, the distinguished General Patrick Keegan, who did not seem too thrilled about seeing Harlan either, "Well…this is awkward." Harlan said and handed back the flask to the young Lieutenant. After stopping five yards from in front of them, the four-star general stood eerily silent. General Keegan took off his hat and rolled his eyes at Harlan and had a perturbed look on his face as he spoke, "At least NOW I know "how" you did it...Do you mind explaining yourself, soldier?" General Keegan asked irritably. Kale took another drink and screwed the top back on his flask and tucked it into his pant's back pocket, "Ya' know…that's kinda' funny, cause I was bout' ta' ask "YEW'" that same thang…." Kale replied nonchalantly. He took a few steps forward and stared intensely at Kale with his bulging and piercing eyes, "Just what the hell did you expect to happen, when you go around killing civilians and leaving your fucking calling card at the scene of the crimes? Not to mention, the fact that you tried to use back channels to gather sensitive and classified information about me…So, son…. (Stepping closer to Kale) why don't you just tell me what the hell were you looking for?" General Keegan asked intrigued. Kale took off his old Florida Gator's cowboy hat and ran his hands back through his long dark blonde locks and snickered, "So…yew' "were" followin' me…" Kale said distastefully. His father took another step closer toward him, "I made you, Lieutenant or have you forgotten? I'll always know where you are. But, the real question here is "why" YOU'RE teamed up with some "spineless billionaire," whose been snooping TOO much around into official government business?" General Keegan barked. Despite his inauspicious past, the offended Harlan Kruellar always considered himself a man of utmost honor and carried himself with dignity and integrity. So the last thing the transporting mogul was going to stand for was to be belligerently misrepresented, "Dear Kale, if you don't mind....I no longer "wish" to partake in this discussion with this arrogant buffoon. You have performed your duty and I have "obviously" fulfilled my end of the agreement....now, when you're ready...." Harlan said and straightened his collar. Without a moment's hesitation, he pulled out his 357 magnum, "Goodbye Harlan." Kale said and shot him point blank. An awestruck Thomas Jr., who had been sitting in the limousine the entire time, jumped out of the car and began running in their direction. Unsurprised, Alejandro kneeled down next to Harlan's lifeless body and closed his eyelids and completed several Hail Mary's. Harlan had long disclosed to him the cryptic side deal he made with Kale to have him killed once everything was revealed, despite his protest. But he knew he had to respect his wishes, as he truly wanted to be anywhere else than with his son. Outraged by his son's mindless act, General Keegan grabbed Kale by the front of his vest, "Just what the hell is wrong with you? Don't you know what the fuck you've just done?" General Keegan yelled. In defiance, Kale yanked himself away from his father, "yeah, daddy...I know what the "fuck" I just did....I just killed one of the other men responsible for Rita and my kid's death!" Kale protested. Out of breath, Thomas Jr. ran up next to General Keegan and saw Harlan lying on the ground motionless, "My God...Kale." Thomas Jr. muttered. Although the sudden appearance of the black preacher was somewhat head-scratching to the general, he did not allow his presence to become a distraction, "Who in the... never mind. What does killing Harlan Kruellar have to do with that? He never sent that terrorist to your house!?" General Keegan insisted. Kale pointed his gun at his father and cocked the hammer, "No, "he" didn't....but yew' did." Kale confirmed. Both Thomas Jr. and Alejandro stood to their feet in unison, while gazing at the guilty looking four-star general. For a brief moment, General Keegan dropped his eyes to the ground in shame, but then out of nowhere, appeared an unemotional and expressionless face of someone the young Lieutenant hardly recognized, "It wasn't supposed to happen that way. But in the heat of battle, Kale you already know that sometimes...things don't always go according to plan. How did you figure it out?" General Keegan asked stoically. The shaking young Lieutenant bit down hard on his lip and could fill his chest cavity getting bludgeoned by his pounding heart, as he steadily pulled the trigger of his large firearm and shot his father in the arm, "Oh, it wasn't so hard...as to say as....shootin' yew' in the arm?! But I'm goin' to let yew' in on a little secret, "dad".... imagine "my" surprise, when I found out Harlan's business was a subsidiary for the Army, namely yew'! Them little "mission's" yew' so often "loved" ta' send me and my team on? Well, I recognized the branding on the confiscated cargo was an "exact" match ta' the crates found in possession of the same degenerates we've been taking out...so whut's tha' matter, huh? Yew' runnin' out of international scum ta' fight?" Kale asked, while pointing his gun at his father's head. The wincing and bleeding general glanced at Thomas Jr. and Alejandro before looking his son directly in the eye, "Yes...and no..." General Keegan said. Suddenly, the wily general reached for the Desert Eagle pistol he had concealed in his waist and shot both Alejandro and Thomas Jr. and then pointed the gun at his mortified son's head, "Now...that's enough of this bullshit...Drop the gun son! You're coming back with me." General Keegan ordered. From his vantage point, Kale could assert that the wounds suffered by both Alejandro and Thomas Jr. did not appear fatal, as they were still moving on the ground, "Yew' shoot a priest and a kid? Why am I not surprised...Yew' ALWAYS been a heartless mutherfucker. Yew'....yew' killed everythang' I EVER loved...includin' my momma...Rita....even yo' grandbabies...and for what? Huh daddy? Why yew' feel the need ta' destroy my life?" Kale asked sobbingly. Unfazed by his son's plight, the cold-hearted general cocked his gun, "Everything isn't all about you and what you aren't able to have, soldier. There're many threats in this world and it's up to men like "us" to help protect our way of life. You knew that the minute you swore an oath to uphold that promise. Although it wasn't my intent to unleash Ismail on your family, I had to do something to keep you motivated and focused on that mission...on THE mission! Look around son, our society is slowly deteriorating! Pretty soon, there won't be any need for any borders because all our threats are already here! There HAS to be order." General Keegan shouted. Frustrated, Kale stopped aiming his 357 Magnum at the general, "So yew' let a few of yur' own terrorists through to do your dirty work for yew'? Just so yew' can what? Stage a war right here!? Yew' out ta' look in tha' mirror mo' often old man...Cause the only threat I see here, is yew'! I'm through killin' for yew,' daddy." Kale replied and threw his gun on the ground. He then walked over to check on the ailing reverend and the young Alejandro. His defiance started to infuriate the four star general, "Just what in the hell do you think you're doing soldier?" General Keegan asked offended. The young Lieutenant continued to ignore his father and helped both Alejandro and Thomas Jr. get to their feet. Alejandro was grazed in the upper shoulder, while Thomas Jr. took a bullet in the leg and was barely able to stand, "You're not going anywhere but with me, are you listening to me Lieutenant!?" General Keegan screamed. When Kale refused to answer to his delusional father, in a rage General Keegan opened fired on Thomas Jr. striking him in the chest, while incidentally hitting Kale in the neck. In a panic, General Keegan ran over to his gargling son to evaluate him, "Now look what you've gone and made me do…" General Keegan yelled, while trying to apply pressure to his hemorrhaging throat. But the more he pressed, the more blood spewed from his son's lacerated neck. Fearing the worst, the war mongering general decided to cut his losses and to help put his son out of his misery. He re-cocked his pistol and pointed it directly at his head as he was saluting him, "You've served your country well soldier, you deserve better." General Keegan said and closed his eyes. Kale whispered something that made him reopen his eyes at the last second, "What is it? What are trying to say, son?" General Keegan asked grudgingly. He bent down beside his flailing son, "D-Da…" Kale struggled to say. General Keegan frowned and assumed Kale was losing his mind and started to disregard his ranting, "I can't understand you, son. I'm sorry Kale, but I'm going to have to do this…" General Keegan warned and began to pull the trigger. But Kale finally mustered out just enough air to speak two simple words, "David help." And just as he said them, there was a single gunshot that seemed to echo for miles and then everything went dark.

Three weeks later, at Memorial Herman Hospital…

When Thomas Jr. awoke in the hospital for the second time in his sixty-some odd years, it was to the tunes of the R@B group H-town, who were on an old Soul Train rerun on the television. His mouth tasted like a disposable paper plate when he swallowed and his eyelids felt glued together when he tried to open them wider. Thomas Jr. was startled by the IV connected to his hand after he tried to wipe his face, "What the hell???"

Thomas Jr. said shocked. The sound of his voice caused his brother Terry, who had been sleeping soundly in a chair next to him, to stir in his seat. He was curled up tightly inside a brown and thinly wool hospital blanket, when he noticed him in the room, "Terry?" Thomas Jr. called softly. Assuming it was his partner Lacy calling out to him, Terry kept his eyes closed and head down as he tried to hush him, "Hey, keep it down, Lace! Before you guys wake him!" Terry instructed. Thomas Jr. grinned and then folded his arms, "Uh, it's a little too late for that, Fairy…" Thomas Jr. quipped. At first, Terry thought he was dreaming, but when he heard his big brother call out to him once again, he finally opened his eyes, "Tommie?" Terry replied surprised. When he turned around and saw his big brother sitting up with his arms folded like some old stone Apache statue, Terry immediately jumped out of his chair in grand elation, "Jesus Tommie! You're awake!" Terry yelled and hugged Thomas Jr. tightly. As much as he appreciated the kind gesture, Thomas Jr.' wounds were still not completely healed and Terry's grip was taking the wind out of the sluggish reverend, "Please Ter, I did just get shot you know!" Thomas Jr. said, with a slight grimace on his face. Although he completely understood his point, Terry could not help himself. After being in surgery for nine hours three weeks ago, Terry thought he was about to lose his brother for the second time in his life. Things only became even more complicated after Thomas Jr. slipped into a mild coma, which was something the doctor's had not expected to happen. But now, here he is, the same smart-mouthed preacher he was before taking his almost month long nap, "You're just gonna' have to get over it, cause I ain't never letting you go bro!" Terry said. Just before he could plead for mercy Lacy entered the room, "Let the man breathe, babe! Yo T, it's good to see you up man! You had a brother worried for a minute." Lacy yelled joyfully, while holding a cup holder filled with coffee cups. Slowly, Terry had finally released him, "Yeah, (clearing his throat) I can see that!" Thomas Jr. said. Lacy sat the cup holder down onto a cart next to Thomas Jr.'s bed and reached out to shake his hand, "Ah man, you know how mushy your little bro gets!" Lacy joked. Thomas Jr. shook his hand and winced as Lacy gripped him like a man holding onto for dear life off the side of a cliff, "Outside of that "blender" you got for a hand …I'm kind of glad to see that nothing's changed." Thomas Jr. replied relieved. Suddenly, a voice that sounded authoritative could be heard entering the room from behind Lacy's wide shoulders, "Oh, I don't know reverend…. Maybe your boy "Markus" here could change your mind!" The voice said. Immediately, Thomas Jr. shoved Lacy from his view to see what was going on behind him and who he saw took the breath out of him. It was his son Markus, who was obviously out of his coma, standing next to a much older black man (around his age) who was decked out in a dark colored suit and had a badge dangling from his waste. His son had seemed to have filled out some and appeared taller than he last remembered and had facial hair which caught Thomas Jr. off guard, "You have a goatee?" Thomas Jr. asked with tears in his eyes. Markus who also had tears in his eyes walked up to his father very slowly, as if he were a tabby cat sneaking up on a house mouse. He stood over his father who was trembling in his hospital bed, "Well? You just gonna' stand there and look at your old m…" Thomas Jr. began, before getting interrupted by his son hugging him. Both father and son embrace one another, as though they were clutching a light post bracing for impact of an impending tornado. The weeping reverend began to repeatedly thank God for bringing back his son. In the back of his mind, he figured in some way Harlan too played a part in Markus' return, despite him telling him not too. While his brother Terry was already brought to tears, his prideful partner Lacy was fighting valiantly not to be, but instead found himself overwhelmed and powerless by the love that radiated off the father and son reunification. Markus' suit wearing escort started clearing his throat before he spoke, "Ahem. Well, I know this may seem like not the best time to ask, but do you remember how you got here Reverend Templeton?" The man asked concerned. Thomas Jr. finally let go of his now grown up son, "What? Uh, no…excuse me but who are you again?" Thomas Jr. asked bewildered. He smiled and pulled out his identification as he came forward, "I'm sorry, reverend. My name is Detective Preston Cartwright…I'm with the Sugarland Police Department." Detective Cartwright said. An intrigued Thomas Jr. swallowed hard, as thoughts of his reunion with his son appeared to have been prematurely short-lived, "Yeah dad, he's been coming by checking on you almost every day." Markus said. Detective Cartwright placed his hand on Markus' shoulder, "Your boy has been great company. To be honest with you reverend, I been stopping by in hopes that maybe you could help me." Detective Cartwright confirmed. Despite his suspicions, the apprehensive reverend decided to indulge the well-spoken detective, "Sugarland? Hmph, aren't you a little out of your …uh…" Thomas Jr. began, before getting cutoff. (A smiling Detective Cartwright but his ID back into his coat pocket) "…Jurisdiction? Yeah, well…that all depends on if what happened to "you" is in "anyway" connected to a case I've been working on. I know I may be fishing here, but do you know of a man by the name of Jacory Jackson, who went by the name Big Cory?" Detective Cartwright asked carefully. Everyone's eyes were now fixated on the hesitant reverend, who was taking his time to locate an answer to Detective Cartwright's question, "Jacory Jackson? Jacory Jackson…Jackson…. "Big Cory" you say?" Thomas Jr. asked confused. The curious Detective Cartwright's eyes began to squint as he watched the plodding reverend struggle to answer his simple question, "Yes, reverend. Big Cory Jackson, he was the CEO of Da'MosDef Records?" Detective Cartwright said stoically. Thomas Jr. scratched his head and picked up one of the coffees that Lacy brought and took a sip, "Ahem…Big Cory of Mos Def Records did you say?" Thomas Jr. asked befuddled. Just before he could answer him, a group of men wearing three-piece suits and carrying briefcases walked through the door, "Don't answer that Mr. Templeton! My client isn't well, detective and we would appreciate it if you would wait for me to confer with him before we can answer ANY questions that you may have at a time convenient for him!" A balding man wearing glasses said. A team of lawyers who filed one by one into the room was not only impressive, but worrisome to the intimidated detective, "You're his lawyer? But…how?" Detective Cartwright asked stunned. Smirking, the balding man walked up to the detective and put his hand out to shake his hand, "No…Detective Cartwright, "WE'RE" his lawyers. What? Did you think you were the only one coming by? WE'LL be in touch!" The man concluded. He gave both the reeling detective and Thomas Jr. a business card, but when Thomas Jr. flipped his over there was something written on the back that said, "Don't worry Rev, my guys will take care of you! Will soon be in touch! –Alex" When he turned his head and saw the surprised expression on Thomas Jr.' face, it was enough confirmation that his hunch was right to come to the hospital and also that the humble Reverend Templeton obviously had friends with VERY deep pockets, Detective Cartwright assumed. Though his gut feeling told him that he knew more than what he was letting on, the detective took something out from his pocket and handed it to Thomas Jr., "This is what the nurses found in your hand when they found you…it looks very expensive…..figured you would at least want it back. It was the Terminator VI lighter Kale had stolen from Harlan. For the life of him, could he explain or understand how in the world he could have possibly ended up with it. The last thing he remembered was Kale's crazy dad standing over him (Kale) with a pistol and threatening to put him out of his misery. Thomas Jr.'s mind seemed to trail off some place before the detective broke his train of thought, "Oh, uh…one last thing before I go, if you don't mind answering Reverend Templeton, off the record…..is it over?" Detective Cartwright asked. Thomas Jr. simply looked up at the concerned detective's eyes and then back into the sparkling lighter in his palm and causally grinned.

<u>The End</u>